OBSIDIAN'S
COMMAND
ASH BORN
BOOK TWO

Written by: Konn Lavery
Edited by: Cara Flannery

reveal
BOOKS

eBook ISBN-13: 978-1-990542-09-1
Paperback ISBN-13: 978-1-990542-10-7
Published in Canada by Reveal Books.
Photo credit: Nadia Dzyakava.
Cover illustration by Lee Nielsen.
Book interior artwork and design by Konn Lavery of Reveal Design.
First Edition 2024

THE
MACROCOSM
STORIES

AUTHOR MESSAGE

MIDWAY VISIONS

The Ash Born novels are an intense ride, blending multiple genres together. Why? Well, this novel fits within *The Macrocosm*, an ongoing universe housing all my writing. It spans from the fantasy past to modern horrors and the dreadful cosmic future.

The series is a pivotal point in *The Macrocosm*'s timeline. It is a story I've been wanting to share with you, the readers, for as long as I can remember. Numerous cameos appear in this novel. For the mega-fans of my work, you'll love it. If you're new to the writing, no problem, it doesn't interfere with the tale. Continuity is key, and foundational rules cannot be broken. Any superverse must set the same boundaries to avoid a convoluted plot. Plus, a book should be enjoyable for the reader and not alienating. It makes the whole idea of a shared universe a rewarding, delicate, operation.

This isn't the end of the Ash Born series either. The story of Lola Cabello is not over yet. The old world is rising. Long and forgotten powers threaten the fabrics of reality. What does this mean for our hero? We'll find out.

THANK YOU

Thanks to my continual support from family, friends, and readers. Writing is a lifelong journey and you're all a part of it.

An extended gratitude to my mother, Brenda Lavery, for the endless love and enthusiasm. Thanks to my dear partner Lindsey Molyneaux for reviewing my work in various stages and riffing with me on creative ideas. We come up with the funniest and coolest concepts.

Thank you, Sarah Hein, Kit, Mikayla G, and those mentioned above for beta reading this novel. Thanks to my editor, Cara Flannery, for polishing this story. Thanks to my friends Nastassja Brinker for the excellent photography and Lee Nielsen for the fantastic cover illustration in this book.

The Macrocosm continues to grow and expand. Let's see where it will take us.

TABLE OF CONTENTS

CHAPTER 1
FOR THE ENEMY

Life in Canada's prisons isn't too harsh if you've had a life like Lola Cabello's. Anyone with half a brain takes federal centres over provincial because there's no need for the ridiculous jumpsuits. Regardless, being behind bars wears the psyche down. Even the most wilful crumble.

Sorry Mom, is the thought that loops Lola's mind day after day in her cell.

Correction, jail is rough, and Lola isn't managing. She reminds herself she isn't in the orange suit. If she had money like some of the other gals in the Women's Correctional Centre, she could bring in her own TV. Canada prisons differ from their southern neighbours. It doesn't match the United States in a lot of ways.

Goddamn ash, is the second phrase that enters Lola's mind while rising from her bed. Her arm begs for a scratch even after two years.

A guard unlocks her cell. She waves at Lola with crusted fingers and guides her down the white hall, passing the other deep blue cell doors under each fluorescent light. Like a wise inmate, she doesn't dare look into any of the open doors. It's rude. You will start a fight. Keep your eyes forward. Spend enough time here and the unwritten rules become ingrained in your mind. Beyond the bars, freedom is a limitless expanse. In Lola's view, no one is exempt from being restrained by covert systems and concealed intentions. Sinister motives run the system.

The guard escorts her into a spacious room flooded with sunlight that illuminates the flint plastic chairs and tables. It's been ages since she last laid eyes on this place. Good little inmates have close interactions with people in the open visitation department, under the watchful eye of supervision. Most civilians have closed visits, separated from their dearests by a barrier of glass. Others must use the wretched video screen centres converting loved ones into digital ghosts. Why? Hell if Lola knows. That was a wise move, Canada.

The space has seven other inmates sitting at tables. One woman holds her wife's hands with a grip that says, "We'll be okay." Another young girl has her frowning parents. A middle-aged lady and a moustached man face each other. Tears and frowns leave their relation undetermined.

The guard stops by the door and closes it with a clang, chewing her gum with a loud smack. Lola walks into the area, spotting her guest. At the far corner of the room is a man in a deep blue suit. His cupped hands cover a folder. Brown eyes watch her through circular glasses.

"There's my gal," says the man with a thick Polish brogue. "You're a minimal risk offender, keeping that inmate score nice and low." He smiles, emphasizing the wrinkles across his aging face.

Lola raises her palms while sitting down. "Look at me." *It took rotting for two goddamn years*, she thinks. Lola would love to relapse on the simmering anger that lives below her behaviour. Hate is the fuel that keeps her fire burning inside. She can control it.

"Oscar, why are you here?" Lola asks. "I haven't seen you in what, over a year? The last time you tried to get me out was pointless."

"No. Your case is closed nice and tight. The evidence points to you. We could plead temporary insanity, if you'd prefer."

Lola's hands clench, the fingernails digging into her palms. "No way. I've told you, I didn't do it."

"Stay calm. We're not here to go over the past. I don't care. The chances of getting you out of here any time soon are next to none."

"Which is why I'm keeping low. Maybe I can get a parole officer, be put in a community. I don't know."

"Unlikely. The public wants your head for Ashley Amber," Oscar says. "Imagine if Canada had a death penalty? Wowzers."

Right, Lola thinks, recalling the precious goddess that she, apparently, stripped from this world. Her wrath consumes her mind as she rests her chin on her palm, losing interest in her lawyer. If she stays in her cell, she can finish her sentence. She'll walk free. Oscar is wasting her time. "We lost a genuine hero," she says. Her kind words don't reflect her cynical flat tone, reflecting on the late pop star Ashley Amber's rise to fame. Music, movies, and gossip kept people hooked. Then, Lola took that away.

Oscar squints. "No need for sarcasm. I brought you a far more interesting gift." He slides the file folder to Lola. "Go on, take a look."

Lola flips the binder open and sees a mug shot of a young girl, early twenties, a good five years younger than Lola. The gal has short, spiked hair with buzzed sides and defined cheekbones. She hasn't seen an official police document of a criminal profile. This validates what she'd presume. To the right of the photo is a two-column format: age, birth date, address, offence, and name. Sierra Palacio.

"You see her before?" Oscar asks.

"Yes, she showed up here a month ago. What of her?"

Oscar leans in closer, his voice lowering into a whisper with coffee breath pushing from under his moustache. "She has flown too close to the light, scathing her wings."

Lola's hands turn to ice. Her throat closes thinking the word, *Moth*. She speaks through her teeth. "I knew you fucking worked for them."

A grin spreads from cheekbone to cheekbone on Oscar's face. His top teeth extend by a half a centimetre into pointed fangs. "Oh no, sweetheart. Oscar was a solid lawyer for you. Yes? Played by the rules with a few bends here and there." The man's brown eyes swirl, saturating the colours. The sclera dye's black fading the irises with a glimmer of deep rubies.

"God damnit," is what Lola can say, leaning on her palm. She hasn't seen an old world being since confinement. It's why prison isn't so bad. That tormented Alice in Wonderland part of her existence was severed, along with the rest of her life, when those cuffs went on. The isolation was another nice perk of Canadian prison. It felt like a vacation. This Moth's words are encoded and clear to her: murder.

Oscar pushes Sierra's documents closer to Lola. "We need you to do what you do best." His eyes and teeth blip to normal in a single blink and he leans back. "In return, we will reward you."

"A shapeshifter?" Lola asks. Curiosity is getting the better of her and she jumps to the conclusion.

"That's stating the obvious," the alleged Oscar says. "Ever meet one on your adventures?"

"No. What does a Crystal Moth shapeshifter want?"

"Ah, the prize will be of great interest. Yes."

Lola leans back, folding her arms. "What did you do with the real Oscar?"

"There's no need for that. Unlike Sierra Palacio here, he was innocent." His sausage ring finger taps the document.

"What is that?" Lola asks.

"It's amazing that you don't recognize her," Oscar says.

"You know these open visitation hours are limited?"

"She was there the day you discovered ash and an original street dealer who distributed the first shipment."

The fateful day was long ago. Another memory eroded into the sand in her mind. Her world spun around, twice, ever since she chased that damn drug. Lola stares at the man, or whatever he is, knowing what he is going to request.

Oscar continues, "Remember Chen, that original ash dealer? We need you to do what you do best."

"I didn't kill Chen," Lola hisses as her face scrunches.

"Indirectly killed him?" Oscar raises a bushy brow.

"All I did was turn him in to the police. You people have corrupted the law."

"You knew that. Therefore, an accomplice."

"I gave solid evidence to real cops. They're out there."

"I'm familiar with your history, Lola Cabello. The law is evil. The Crystal Moths are the big baddies who ruined your cute life of being a reporter. The media is in on the game too. It's one big conspiracy that is working against the poor little goth girl who's too foolish to realize that she is solely responsible for destroying herself. Yes? Murdering celebrities, innocent workers, and even guilty Moths won't give you saviour status."

Lola will get nowhere with this thing. Her best interest is to stay calm, not argue, and learn what it wants.

Oscar says, "Don't forget there's a clever cryptic key tattooed on your hip."

Lola straightens her posture.

"These real cops, as you say, would love to have that evidence." He taps the table. "Besides the point, Sierra must go. She has shared too much with the do-gooders in the law and the people. The Crystal Moths have deemed her a target to silence."

"Permanently?" Lola asks.

"Bingo." Oscar takes the open folder from Lola and turns the page. "In return, we'll give you one of these." He points to a photograph of a charcoal diamond-shaped scale.

Lola snorts. "Really?" Under the table, her leg bounces. Seeing the photo of an ash diamond is enough to rattle the brewing addiction that rumbles below the simmering flame of vengeance.

Oscar presses his lips together and nods. He lifts the page's corner, showcasing a small transparent bag containing charcoal powder taped to the back of the folder.

Take it, take it, take it, dumb bitch, are the words slithering through Lola's mind. They are not her own. She recognizes it as the drug. With each passing moment, the ice bites harder at her fingers, causing her face to flush red and her heart rate to skyrocket. It's right there, within arm's reach. The power.

Oscar closes the folder and places it on his lap. "You're an interesting specimen, Lola. You're tuned into the old world. How? We'd like to know, yes? Before, the Crystal Moths wrote you off as a fly. Now here we are, working together."

"Took you idiots long enough," Lola says.

"No other ash-dasher can withstand the continual temptation of that poison. Hell, they would have jumped at first sight of it. Not you though. You discovered the old world. This intrigues Mastema."

The name makes Lola shiver. She hasn't met the drug lord or seen his face. Words have a potent effect on the mind. "No,"

Lola says. *Do it*, Lola presumes she thinks. It's hard to tell as the addiction distorts her consciousness.

"Let's make it easier for you," Oscar leans on the table, whispering. "How about we take care of your brother and father the way we did your mother?"

Lola's nostrils flare, getting nose-to-nose with him. "Touch them and I'll break you."

"I'd love to see you try. You know that's not possible. Work for us, and we will reward you. Your relatives stay safe."

"I need to get out of here," Lola says.

"We could squeeze that into the arrangement. You can become an official family member of the Moths."

"I'd rather rot in prison."

Oscar shrugs. "Suit yourself. Yes? You must perform this task for us." A pointed object pokes Lola's leg. It isn't visible unless Lola makes a scene. It's far too sharp to be the tip of a shoe, more like a needle or a knife.

It jabs her.

Oscar's eyes point to the motion.

Lola slides in her chair, careful so the guard doesn't see. Her hands explore under the table, grazing against a warm and smooth tentacle shaped object akin to skin. Another poke tells her she reached too far. Her hand moves back, reaching the end of this appendage to a metal handle. This is not a limb. It's a tail.

Great, Lola thinks. Her hand follows the coiled tip to a sharp, thin, cool item. Oscar is offering her a knife.

"Lift," Oscar mutters.

Lola gets the message. She lifts her tank top with one hand, below the table, for the shapeshifter to slide the knife under.

The tail tucks the blade nice and close against the elastic of her sweats. The cold metal tingles against her skin. Lola doesn't dare look down, keeping her eyes on Oscar to avoid suspicion. The tail slides from her torso and she drops the fabric. Oscar buttons his blazer while standing and cupping the folder, no tail in sight. He nods at the guard at the far end of the room.

"Ponder it, and act quickly. Yes?" He taps the table with four fingers and leaves Lola and her simmering anger. The guard's keys jingle from behind her.

Lola cannot escape the Moths. She opened Pandora's Box, ignoring warnings. The Crystal Moths are persistent and unforgiving. She has limited choices. The last thing she wants to do is become their assassin slave. Then again, she can work with the enemy and strike from within.

That ash would be a perk to get her brain firing.

She squeezes her arms. It's not the stress of living behind bars, or the threat to family that makes her want to kill Sierra. Her hungering vengeance ties Sierra, a Crystal Moth, to her. Each gangster needs to pay. Lola's scheming is masterful. Or, the drug addiction is talking, whispering sinister ideas into the doomed ash-dasher's soul.

CHAPTER 2
BETWEEN THE LINES

Lola didn't intend on killing. Manslaughters occurred prior to imprisonment. Death is a constant presence within the domain of gangsters. To her, those situations were in self-defence. Intentional murder is a whole new ballgame.

Throughout the night Lola ponders the Crystal Moth mission. Oscar, or whatever it was, presents a challenging proposition. Lola is no assassin, not yet. If she gets caught, that strong inmate score she has will flush down the tube. She'll get the "administrative segregation" treatment, fancy lingo for solitary confinement. Murdering a convict won't go unnoticed. Parole for first-degree murder in Canada is twenty-five years, minimum.

If she doesn't complete the task, her brother and father will pay the price. Moths are merciless. Lola has lost too much already. They can't suffer more. Not once have they come to visit. Twenty-one months since the cuffs and not a single word or message from her own blood.

The past is irrelevant. At this moment, she faces a decision. The shapeshifter issued a deadline-free ultimatum. Knowing how barbarous the Moths are, it's best to get the job done fast.

There is the enticing part of Oscar's offer: ash.

She has abstained from drugs since her incarceration. Dealing with the withdrawals has been a challenging and grueling process. Quitting an addiction cold turkey is no picnic—it's like being thrust into a whirlwind of withdrawal symptoms and cravings. The mind becomes a chaotic battleground. The constant night sweats, shivering body, gut rot, and lack of energy are a handful of the physical side effects. Lola would be a fool to take ash again.

Her addiction was not about chasing bliss. Ash was a tool. It created the better Lola. She is aware of the irony that the drug comes from the mobsters. With ash coursing through her veins, her neurons fired at an accelerated rate. If she got the drug, she could devise an elaborate scheme to break free from jail. Her sober mind cannot. Yes, it could help her work with the gangsters, gain their trust, allowing her to infiltrate their ranks from the inside. Crystal Moths like to believe they can absorb people. Lola needs to comply with the shapeshifter.

Committing a murder in a public space is ill-advised. An audience of prisoners will send the wrong message. Guards overcrowd common areas, posing a hindrance to completing the task. Security cameras are in each hall and shared rooms, not in prisoner cells. Jail teaches you to be cunning.

The typical technique to off a target in Canadian prison is to take some frozen tuna cans, stuff them in a sock, and bam—smash their face in. That's if you must improvise and have no other tools. Luck is on Lola's side. She doesn't have to resort to barbaric acts because Oscar provided her with an effective mechanism. Lola inspects the weapon once she returns to her jail cell, keeping it tucked under the mattress. The instrument is a small surgical blade: bona fide sharp.

The next day, Lola plots the deed. Sierra is new. Lola is required to familiarize herself with her routine. Most prisoners sit in their cell throughout the day, while others take on jobs to get a better inmate score and a chance to earn parole. Lola will find the cell and strike when the target is relaxed. She is unfamiliar with Sierra's roommate. Perhaps Lola needs to commit two murders.

Doubling in a cell is new to the Women's Correctional Centre. Federal prison is supposed to provide personal cells. This spiralling nation's economy is falling with record profits for the suits, meaning crime is not far behind. Civilians face arrest and imprisonment, becoming roommates with strangers. An individual living space is out of the question. Despite not having a TV, Lola hears conversations. The entire nation gives off an atmosphere reminiscent of a penal establishment.

The centre contains minimum, medium, and maximum security detainees, meaning it's obvious which wings to go to. Based on the profile document, Sierra was a street dealer, distributing ash. She is new too, and should have an inmate score no different from Lola's.

The prisoners have recreational time outside. After, they return to their cells. Sierra is easy to spot with her short hair with buzzed sides and a tall narrow frame. She presides over the sea of t-shirts and tank tops through the hall. She walks into a wing adjacent to Lola's, accompanied by an older stout lady who has a wobble in her walk. The two enter a cell, nine from the turn. That's her roommate. Lola knows the scope, the location, and can strike at an opportune moment.

In the evening, inmates have a second downtime. Lola's mind runs in circles, pondering her devious actions. What would her mother think? Becky or Michael? The Trinity of Souls is why she is here. Their deaths beg for redemption. Is assassination doing their name right?

A gentle hand glides against her jawline, transporting Lola to the present with the soft, lean figure resting on her chest.

"Where did you go?" asks the green-eyed girl wrapped under her arm. Her voice leaves a tingle against her ear.

"Not important," Lola says. Right, Kendra, the prison comfort device. The girl can't be any older than nineteen and pissed her life away with manslaughter. Not that it matters. Their physical bond is a mutual benefit.

"You sure?" Kendra asks, tone tender. Her buzzed head bristles against Lola's bare arm.

It's obvious Kendra doesn't share the same views of their connection. The gentle waft of her natural lilac scent provides a refreshing contrast to life prior to confinement. Lola's previous ways had too many men. Change is healthy. This is shifting a gear for self-gain. It's Kendra's fault for thinking otherwise.

We don't have a relationship, Lola recalls saying countless times, despite Kendra's affectionate persistence. Actions count in this world. Lola takes her arm off of her and rolls over. "Our time is almost over," she says. It isn't a reference to the recreational time.

Day two since the assignment: Lola attends to the humble task of laundry duty in the light grey room. She's come accustomed to the flickering light source. She's seen as suitable for performing the delicate obligation of cleaning the clothes for the other inmates. It's not much. The job keeps her sane and clear of trouble. Monotonous movement is far better for the psyche than sitting in a cell. That modest role will change today. Under her outfit, Lola keeps the knife in her pants.

While folding towels, she ponders the old world lawyer. What is a shapeshifter? Oscar could be a demon. One demon had crossed paths with Lola, and a reptilian ended their life. Correction: vazelead. She's learned reptilian is a derogatory term. A vazelead killed a succubus. It makes Lola wonder, *If a demon dies on Earth, do they go into Hell?* Poor Lola, being dragged into the old world with more mystery than directness.

She finishes her shift and takes the long way to her cell, circling to Sierra's. A few prisoners watch her from their beds, others leaning against the deep blue bars of the open doors. They're curious who the newcomer is. One middle-aged woman with cannons for arms gives her a wink. It's free time for a lot of these prisoners. In the minimum security section, they can roam during the afternoon. The usual guards won't be concerned. The cameras are the time-stamped eyes, watching her take a new route. It's fine. Nine cells down, the cell door is open. This is the opportune moment for assassination.

Four cells away, Lola takes one glance around the fluorescent hall, the buzz of the overhead lights filling the air. A few heads turn away. Two prisoners keep their gaze. Two cells away, her heart pounds against her chest, a rhythmic reminder of her anticipation. Her ears ring, detecting the mumbling conversations of nearby inmates. One door away, a strong odour wafts towards her. A prisoner, or prisoners, neglected to wear deodorant. The taste of stress lingers in her mouth, leaving a metallic and dry flavour.

At the cell, she steps inside. Sierra reads a romance book in the lower bunker, one leg up. Her roommate is above, watching an old soap opera on television from the mounted screen on the opposite wall. It's muted with subtitles on.

Luxurious. Must be nice.

Sierra spots Lola at the corner of her eye and closes the novel. She sits upright. "Who the fuck are ye?" she asks. "Get'da fuck out here."

"We need to talk," Lola says. *Keep it cool*, she thinks. Her nerves must be in check.

Sierra eyes Lola from head to toe, starting with the signature three diagonal scars across her eyebrows that end at her cheek. Moving down, there's the bullet scar on her left clavicle. It matches a smaller one on the other side. They're a handful of countless noticeable scars on her body. The particular bullet and face markings are Lola's signature identifiers.

Sierra smirks and says, "Nah, shit. You're the vigilante."

Lola raises her arms. "Wasn't my title."

Sierra stands, chucking her book onto the bed. Her gaze does not leave Lola while stepping closer. She keeps her head high, sizing herself. The cocky prick has no clue of the danger she is in.

"Ye comin' for me too? The way ya did for Chen?" Sierra asks.

"What makes you say that?" Lola says. "I have questions." That's a partial truth.

"The kind questions ye had for Chen?"

"How do you know Chen?" Lola asks. "The police locked that up."

"Please. We've been goin' missin' since you started sniffing around. Those cops found him zap strapped to a chair at dat abandoned warehouse. There's only one psycho bitch that would do that. You, Lola Cabello. He vanished. Poof! Eh? Magically found again on the beach, decapitated. It was on the news. Ain't that right, Myra?"

The roommate speaks in a hoarse voice. "Mmhmmm."

Lola says, "Right. I didn't kill him, dipshit."

Sierra shrugs. "They went missin' and later found dead. Prissy boss Kye Pung walks away clean. Guess she got those good knee pads or somethin'."

"Right," Lola says. *Do it*, comes a voice inside.

Working on it. The skin on her body is ice. Lola questions if she can even go through with killing a person. This is another human life.

"The Crystal Moths were messy with that first run, eh? Sure. We heard a sound that day in the sewers while ye were creepin' around. Chen saw it. I'm guessin' that's why you went after him?"

Vazelead. "He got lucky. Why are you here? Squealed on your employers?"

"Nah. Guess you've been in here for a bit, huh? Moths changed their strategy. Ash is more scarce, in higher demand. Those rumours sprouted where ash comes from. One by one, after Chen, my bros vanished. The Crystal Moths are sealing their leaks. I ain't no fool and knew what was happening. The streets are not safe. Nah. Prison was my best choice. I mean, look at you."

"Me?" Lola asks. Her heart is hitting against her chest.

Sierra smirks, shaking her head. "The infamous Lola Cabello. The vigilante from Edmonton who thinks she can crush the world's most sophisticated crime organization. You are the talk of the country and did a helluva job of runnin' from the Moths and cops. Your bitch-ass ways caught up with you, didn't they?"

"Or transformed me."

"Pff! Transformed? Into what?" Sierra asks, taking a step closer, inches away.

Kill her now, comes a voice in her mind. It's the primal animal that drives her desires. Revenge for her family. Anger to protect her brother and father. The addiction to ash. Sierra is a Crystal Moth. They all die.

"Into what I need to be to rid of scum like you," Lola says.

Sierra laughs. "You wanna go? Okay. You're going to rough up some Crystal Moths, climb your way to the top? Mastema will devour you. Shit, I'll beat the fuck outta you before he does, ya goof."

Bingo. Sierra said the magic word. Any inmate without a brain knows you don't call a Canadian a goof. Lola didn't catch the abbreviation or reason for it. She heard it, saw it, and is aware: goof means fight to keep the respect of the inmates. Even a guard would be a buffoon to intervene. It's what Lola came here to do. Except she is bringing a knife to a fistfight. Dirty. A part of her hoped Sierra had new Crystal Moth information to share, such as why they want her. Too late; Lola is a goof.

Act fast, the presumed Oscar's voice echoes in Lola's mind.

Sierra takes another step closer, an inch from toe to toe. She looms over Lola by a head and a half. She doesn't blink as her head tilts. "So what's it gonna be, vigilante? You gonna fuck off, or should I make you my bitch?"

Sorry Mom, is the last thought Lola has. In a quick and calculated move, she raises her fist, causing Sierra to lose focus, enabling her to snatch the blade hidden beneath her pant elastic. She shoves the knife in. Her foe slams her forehead against Lola's nose, creating a sickening crunch. She staggers backward, feeling the impact of the blow, yet refusing to let go of the weapon. It slides sideways, leaving a slick trail behind as it disengages from her opponent. The ravaged flesh spews pink tubular innards out of Sierra and into her hands.

"Oh my God!" comes the croaky cry from above. Lola forgot the roommate was here. "Help!" Myra shouts, blue eyes wide in shock.

With a swift and forceful motion, Lola plunges the knife deep into Sierra's chest, eliciting a sharp gasp of pain. She delivers a series of relentless stabs, puncturing the lungs and heart with precision. Each hole in Sierra's shirt oozes moist red, contrasting against its once white fabric. She topples onto the ground: assassinated.

"Hey," the roommate says, her gaze is as wide as her mouth.

Lola hurries to the jail door and swings it shut with her non-bloody hand. She raises the cherry coated knife to her lips. Myra is quick to obey, understanding the danger. Lola must think fast to resolve the situation. The cameras saw her go into the cell. There is a witness. Lola can't climb and kill Myra fast enough. She can alter the narrative, like the good old media.

"You won't say a single word, understand?" Lola says, stepping away from the bars.

The roommate is stone, caught in pure terror.

"Do you understand?" Lola says. "Or do you want to end up like her?"

The roommate shakes her head several times.

"Good." Lola takes a deep breath, mustering her strength, and slashes the knife down her own chest.

Distant steps reverberate from outside in the hall.

"What the fuck?" the roommate says.

Lola hacks herself again for an extra precaution and plunges the blade into her shoulder. She groans, biting her lip, trying to keep herself muted. She doesn't have much time before the guards arrive.

"You know what happened here, right?" Lola asks while leaning to Sierra's body.

"I don't understand," Myra says. Such a sweet lady in minimal security.

"I came here asking about Crystal Moths. Sierra attacked me. She had the knife on her, and I disarmed her. Things got ugly."

Lola wraps the weapon around Sierra's fingers, getting the fingerprints over the chrome handle.

Myra bites her lip.

Lola stands, chucking the knife on the ground. "Do you know what happened here?" Lola asks again.

"I do."

"Say it," Lola says. "Then I'll open the door."

"Sierra attacked you."

"The complete story. Why did I come in here?"

"You were asking about the Crystal Moths. Sierra attacked you and you took a knife."

"You were watching TV, not listening to our conversation. Got it?" Lola asks, reaching for the bars.

"I didn't hear nothin'."

Lola pulls the entrance as her face masks into a frown, eyes squinting, eyebrows scrunched in pain, staging fear. She leaves the roommate to muster over the events and stumbles into the hall. She cries for help, exaggerating the discomfort she is in. The smashed cartilage of her nose is real. The slashes and shiv to her arm are familiar sensations. Lola's been through far worse. Crafting improvised assassination plans is what's different. For Lola's sake, let's hope they buy it.

CHAPTER 3
AN UNLIKELY ALLY

Manipulating the narrative is a cunning skill. The media gobbles facts and shifts them for favourable views. Governments use these tactics to suppress and control. Lola capitalizes on this method to cover up her vicious deeds. She crawls on concrete, smearing her own blood. With a dash of luck, Myra won't rat on her. Snitches don't do well behind bars. She will remain quiet. The story is credible: Sierra referred to Lola as a goof. Fighting words and prison weapons go hand in hand. It's that simple.

It doesn't take long for the security to arrive at the scene. Other prisoners cheer and bang their cell bars. Others shout and chant, making a ruckus of excitement. Who doesn't love a fight? People can't divert their attention from blood and murder. The convicts are aware of Lola's vicious background. She's the star in her own live-action television show. The directors? Crystal Moths. The writers? In this scene: Lola.

Two officers restrain Lola, snagging her by the arms, cuffing her, and take her away from the boisterous halls: whoops, clanging, and stomping of feet. More guards rush in to control the situation. To Lola's left, in her peripheral view, are green eyes belonging to a young buzz-cut girl with a sharp jawline. Kendra. The sight of Lola's red-drenched body leaves her lips parted.

Bye, Lola thinks. She wants to mouth the words. What would be the point? Her next phase in life starts. In truth, a goodbye would serve as a small compensation for Lola's emotional neglect.

We are nothing, Lola finishes her thought. Kendra doesn't matter. The Moths do.

Lola's feet drag on the ground, playing the wounded victim. Once they tend her injuries, they will grill her on the details of the attack. They'll ask her the usual inquiries she's familiar with from years of dealing with the law. The questions are:

Why were you in Sierra's cell?

What made it escalate?

What time did you go to her cell?

Who made the first move?

How did you get the knife?

Can you tell us again?

The list goes on to evaluate if she will adjust her answer, a clear sign of lying. Lola won't change the story, the same one she had Myra repeat. Stories have to be tight when playing cover-up. Neither can slip. It's easier to maintain the fake narrative after the moment. Time erodes memories of illusions. They will reveal the truth. Lola prays, to any entity listening, that Sierra's roommate doesn't rat.

The doctor patches Lola in the medical bay. Her wounds need stitches, for the slashes run deep. The last one is a light cut, patched with bandages to prevent bleeding. As for her nose, it's broken. Sierra got a nice bang on her. Lola remains silent during the encounter with the doctor. Her complexion appears younger than Lola's. Her slow movements and refusal of eye contact speak fear. Lola's reputation grows beyond her immediate world. Their interaction is brief and Doc deems her okay.

She's taken to an interrogation room, and the template questions roll in. The law enforcement officer sits with her thick legs close together and gut flopping over her belt. The single radiant fluorescent light casts sharp shadows, thanks to the barred window to their left providing additional sun.

This officer asks, "Who made the first move?" Years of cigarettes leave her voice deep and raspy.

Lola says, "Sierra attacked me."

She wipes her chin. "Why?"

"Because I asked about the Crystal Moths."

"You walked into Sierra's cell and she attacked you?" she asks.

Lola says, "Sierra attacked me. I was asking about the Crystal Moths. She was one, wasn't she?"

"Yeah." The officer scratches her short bowl cut scalp, looking at her notebook, pondering new ways to question her.

The screening goes on for an hour while Lola sticks to her guns, not slipping. Sierra attacked Lola. Lola shouldn't have asked questions. The interrogator deems her investigation done. Security takes her to a maximum restraining room. No windows and the small square footage are her punishment. The one bulb in the corner by the door offers a white, cold light. She waits. The Moths or the law will come.

She fidgets with her fingers, nervous about the conclusion. Dried blood cakes her nostrils and the sidewall hangnails of her fingers. There's deep red stains splattered on her shirt and pants. Thanks to bullet shots, broken bones, and stabbings, this doesn't faze her. It's why she has the iconic scars. As if her "natural beauty" cupid's bow wasn't signature enough, the past wounds on her skin either entice people or strike fear.

Memory of her horrendous deed replays in her thoughts. The aggression was fierce and unrelenting. A vivid flash of a gentle smile on a wrinkled face follows. Dark, frizzy hair grazes her mind. It brings unconditional love. The cupid's bow and nose match her own. Lola feels warm scarlet liquid spraying onto her hand. She didn't stop. Next, a sly grin emerges from behind swaying red dreadlocks: friendship. *Lola Love*, she would say to her. The sensation of human innards sliding between her fingers made her recoil in disgust, or so she likes to tell herself. Killing the Moth felt invigorating. The broad jawline of a man reassures Lola's safety. A smug smirk rises on his stubbled jaw, above his lip are shrouded due to the shadow of his hoodie. He approves. Sierra collapses; her body hits the ground with a wet thud.

Shit, Lola thinks. She rubs her cheeks, dismissing these mangled visions of killing an inmate and the Trinity of Souls. Mom, Becky, and Michael deserve better than what Lola has become. Michael justified his killing sprees, as Lola does. She had to. The rest of her family is in danger. Becky would agree. Her mother? Not a chance.

An indefinite amount of time passes with Lola judging her own actions. It's the nature of prison. To her best estimate, she's been waiting for twenty-four hours. At some point, the door to the small cell opens. Two security guards, both with short buzz-cut sides and muscles beyond Lola's comprehension of physical limits, enter. One tosses her a fresh shirt and new sweatpants. The other unlocks the shackles around her ankles, wrists. The first keeps her hand near the gun at her hip.

"Change into these," the second guard says.

The carbon copy guards step out and close the thick metal door with a clang. They poke their head through the small window to watcher. Lola obeys their dagger eyes. Changing strikes a hot pain that blooms throughout her body from her wounds. She winces to suppresses the agony.

After, the security personnel open the entrance and cuff her. They escort her from the room as another prisoner with a rolling hamper enters the cell, taking the clothes like a convict with a low inmate score would. The guards and Lola march through the corridors where prisoners' eyes glue to them. The old, young, scared, and the tough rubbernecked. It's considered rude in prison culture, but, this is Lola Cabello with

OBSIDIAN'S COMMAND BY KONN LAVERY

an impressive past, well-behaved for two years, then has a spontaneous outbreak of murder.

She's taken through the winding ice lit halls. The guards' utility belts jingle with each step on the polished, coated concrete. They pass several gates divided by locks. Lola hasn't seen this section of the centre since her arrival. The hall windows don't have bars on them. The guards keep leading Lola until they reach a set of doors to the outside.

Transfer, Lola thinks. She could ask the clones. Silence is in her best interest. They will manipulate her words, tell their higher ups, and she doesn't need more trouble. Sierra is dead. Lola's family is safe. The shapeshifter will give her ash.

They walk under the scorching summer sun. A chain-link fence awaits them down the dirt road. It hums once unlocked by remote control, thanks to the two watchtowers on each side. There's a second enclosure on the opposite end. In between is a police unit and one officer shaped like an upside-down triangle leaning against the car. His hands tug on his belt. The large aviator shades on his eyes conceal most of his emotions. A smug smile rests above his long chin as his teeth grind on gum with exaggerated chews. This guy will be a case.

"Beauty," the man says in a natural booming voice. Some people are born loud.

"She's yours, Officer Clarkson," the first guard says.

The new cop, Clarkson, opens the rear door to let the guards put Lola onto the leather seat. This is abnormal. Lola isn't familiar with the finer details of the prison system. A white bus moves prisoners to and from locations. If this was a transfer, they would have taken Lola's belongings, too. Wouldn't there be a second officer? And both women? She has no court dates. Her first instinct tells her this is a Crystal Moth scheme.

The door slams and the two carbon copy guards leave. The new cop settles behind the security grid in the driver's seat. He starts the engine, shifts into gear, and drives to the second set of gates. They unlock via remote and the police unit exits the facility. The event dumbfounds Lola with a hollow pang in her chest. Silence served its purpose.

"And you are?" Lola says.

Officer Clarkson chuckles in a slow, *huh, huh, huh*, as if each one is a finger jabbing at her. His left hand grips the wheel at twelve o'clock, the usual power move. Officer Clarkson is in control.

"Is that funny?" Lola asks and leans forward.

"I admire your attitude, Lola Cabello," the man says. He chews the gum, ending the sentence in a moist smack.

"I'm a humble servant. What's this police unit, and just you, about?"

"You know, for a chick who's done so much in the past, what, four years? 2014? Shit. You are stupid."

Lola smirks at the insult. She's tired, in pain, and must keep her guard. Sarcasm lightens her mood, even in grave situations. "I have my theories."

"That so?" Officer Clarkson raises a brow that Lola catches through the car's rear mirror.

"Four years made me wiser, and I don't spill my intel at once."

"If only you could have told yourself that back then. Maybe your loved ones would be alive."

There's no reason to mention the Trinity of Souls that haunt her psyche. This man must be a Moth. Unless he's some cocky prick who has a personal vendetta. Regardless, his comment ignites fire within her belly.

"Well? Are they safe?" Lola's nostrils flare.

"Who?" Officer Clarkson says.

"My family," Lola says.

"How the fuck should I know that?" Officer Clarkson's voice goes up a notch. "If you hadn't meddled with the law, your family would have avoided unwanted attention from the start."

"Okay, are we going to keep playing games, or are you going to tell me why am I here?" Lola presses her lips.

"My job is to drive you. You stirred quite the trouble."

"That's why you're attempting to belittle me?" Lola asks.

He shrugs. "I gotta have a bit of fun. Driving troubled girls like you around gets kind of old."

"So you're some ordinary cop doing his job?" Lola cocks her head.

"You got it," Officer Clarkson says.

"Uh huh, with a major ego problem," Lola says.

"Think what you like." He twirls an index finger by his face. "You've always been a little screwed in the head."

"Seems odd." Lola pauses. "Don't prisoners get moved on a bus? Female officers?"

"You're a special gal," he says with a low tone.

"With a single officer?" Lola's brows furrow.

"Budgets are tight." He keeps his gaze on the road, voice monotone.

Lola sits back and gazes through the window, watching them drive from the prison and along the highway. The man's lack of answers nips her with concern. Some Crystal Moths are well-behaved. There's plenty of crooked cops who work for them for an easy buck. Other times they're threatened into submission like Lola. It doesn't help the leader of this country is in cahoots with the gang.

Officer Clarkson speaks with an elevated volume. "Yep. I watched your case when you were on the news. A unique Canadian icon, for better or worse. Some vigilante girl, protégé of an ex-cop with an anger problem. Revenge is kind of hot."

Lola bites her lip because his last sentence makes her feel as if she were stripped down to nothing. Creeps are everywhere. The grunge of society blends in with crooks, robbers, gangsters, and the law.

He continues, "When I found out I was moving you, I looked into your case a little further. You were right there, involved, during that shootout at the slaughterhouse in British Columbia. That terrible incident with the Crystal Moths, a lot of good officers died."

Officer Clarkson steers the car off the freeway and onto a side road. Bumps and potholes fill the gravel path that rock Lola side to side. She gazes out the window to see farmland that stretches on forever. He puts the automobile in park beside a battered old shed. The engine's constant rumble runs up her bones. She swallows as he steps out of the driver's seat.

Damn it, Lola thinks.

The man walks around the vehicle. With a sudden jolt, the passenger door flings open. He yanks on her ankle chains, dragging her from the back seat and into the hot open air.

"Fuck off!" she shouts.

"I knew those officers," Officer Clarkson sneers.

He forces her onto her feet and slams the car door shut with his boot. The man pulls her towards his coiled fist, slamming it into her face. Her nose cracks, more than it already has, and she stumbles against the car's trunk with a bang.

"I worked with those people while stationed in BC." He throws another punch into Lola's gut, which expunges the air right out of her lungs. The third one lands on her ribs. She winces as a gnawing anguish explodes from her bones. "I'm just getting started, cop-killing bitch."

He grabs her by the hair which pulls on her scalp. He drags her towards the slanted shed off the road. It's evident where this is going. Crystal Moths or not, Lola needs to think fast. Officer Clarkson brings her into the structure and out of view from the flat plains of Manitoba.

Inside, Lola grunts due to his tight grip on her hair, feeling as if the strands will rip from her head at any moment. She scans the room with heavy breaths escaping her nostrils. A couple of rusty metal shelves and a table are in the far corner. Sawdust and dirt blanket the wooden crates on the ground. Officer Clarkson leads her to the splintered table. Lola slams her right foot down, resisting his persistence. The man growls and forces her face onto the table's surface with a shove, raising dust.

"Get the fuck off me!" Lola shouts, kicking at him with her chained feet. The restraints give her little room.

"You're going to keep quiet, understand?" he whispers through grinding teeth. His forearm pins her onto the table as he leans into her ear. "Out of all the gals, you're the one I've wanted. Waiting for a slipup, you waste of breath. Not even worth a fuck."

Lola squirms, using her might to lift him off of her. Her arms burn and shake which sparks a sear of pain in the wounds across her chest. It's no use.

Her ears twitch at the rustling of his holster as he chuckles. *Huh-huh-huh.* "Time to pay." The gun cocks and the tip of the cool firearm presses against the warm skin on the back of her head.

He grunts. His body stiffens. The gun slides against her neck. Hot droplets of a liquid fall onto Lola's back. The pressure of his body against her eases and she rolls over, ready to fight for her life. Officer Clarkson stands in front of her with his mouth hanging open. The gun falls to the ground. His other arm goes limp. A black spike pokes through his forehead, blood drizzling from the bridge of his nose.

Standing at the entrance of the shed is, at first glance, a naked woman. As Lola takes a deep inhale, she can see that the chalk skin, lack of nipples, hairless form, no ears, or nose tell her otherwise. A porcelain tail pokes from behind this newcomer and ends pegged into the back of Officer Clarkson's skull. A shimmer of rubies sparkles from her pitch-black eyes boring into Lola's brown irises, sending a cold nip onto her skin.

A C T I

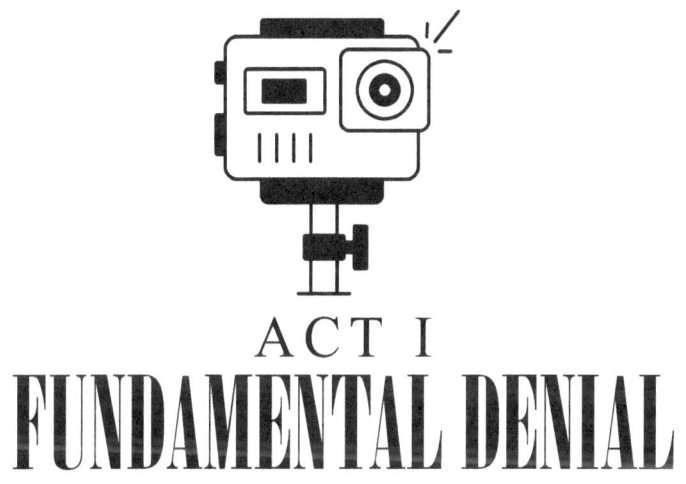

ACT I
FUNDAMENTAL DENIAL

[Lola Cabello Documentary: CAMB Originals]

[Take 1: Raw]

[2018, November 22]

[Aaron Cabello: Brother]

[RECORDING:

Should I start? Okay, yeah, well, like she was my little sister, you know? Into more boy toys than dolls. I didn't think she had this in her . . . oh . . . Talk about her personality, then onto . . . gotcha.

I'm Aaron Cabello, Lola Cabello is, or was my little sister. Hard to say. We grew up in a pretty standard lower-middle class family. Mom had a part-time job while taking care of the house. Dad worked his ass off with his cleaning business. I've got a good six years on Lola. So she was off doing her own thing with her friends while we were in school. Other times, she was helping Dad with his bike. It was the only thing they did together.

As a toddler, she was a typical kid. Curious, explored, her favourite question was, "Why?" Man, she'd ask why about everything to the point you'd have to tell her, "That's the way it is, Lola." She wasn't fond of that answer. Who is?

She and her friend Becky, Becky Murphy, were tight. I think they influenced each other. Dad and me are also responsible for her love of alternative music. It was his hobby, and I played in a few grunge bands in high school. Becky and her went all in. They loved that underground stuff when they hit their teens. That's where her angst began and it fed her interest into messed up crime stories on the TV. She aspired to be a reporter because of it. It's that "why?" she loved to ask.

Mom, Dad, and I wanted her to stay in Toronto after high school. She didn't want to leave her friend Becky, who was going to Grant MacEwan university out west in Edmonton, Alberta. I think Lola feared losing touch with Becky. Fair enough. We were mad at her. Considering what happened since 2014, moving isn't what upsets us now.

I mean, in her defence, she didn't think it would lead to this. Again, it's that endless questioning in her. If she didn't go snooping around where she wasn't supposed to, she wouldn't have gotten into the wrong crowds. Becky was also to blame for that. You know how it goes: underground music scenes lead to drugs, which lead to dangerous people.

Lola stood her ground. I get it. She was obsessed with that Edmonton vigilante, hashtag YEGman. One viral video of a crazy guy beating thieves into a pulp was what it took to tempt her into danger . . . yeah? . . . Yeah.

YEG is the airport code for Edmonton. YEGman is catchier than Edmontonman.

Her being involved with YEGman led to the Crystal Moths, which led to the corrupt police, dead Becky, and dead YEGman, and the kicker: Mom's death.

It hurts. Mom. Whatever, we weren't in touch with Lola during her university days. Dad was working. Mom got a full-time job at the supermarket to pay for the mortgage before the police raid and the heart attack. I went to a trades school to become an electrician and stayed in Toronto. I've got a family to take care of. Dad is old, and our parents taught us family came first. He's private, you know? It's why my dad didn't want to come on this show sensationalizing what Lola did. I think it's important people hear the truth about her, the police, and those gangsters. Lola wasn't all bad. You could say they made her. Curiosity was there long before.

Lola . . . something else was, is, in her. Something none of us thought was possible. We thought the silent treatment would teach her a thing or two. Instead, it severed her lifeline from any chance of normalcy.

END]

CHAPTER 4
LIFE'S GIFT

A solid way to kill addiction is cold turkey. It's rough. Not everyone can handle the harsh transition, stripping themselves of the thing they desire most. Ash shares properties with workaholism in this example. Ricardo Iglesias once dove deep into his job, believing you possess the power to make a difference in the law with a few personal sacrifices. A little bit more. That's how addictions start.

He does not differ from the deranged vigilante Lola Cabello that once roamed the Canadian roads. Two years since, his life is different: glued to this black fabric office chair, handling paperwork. Without the streets, the adrenaline simmers, and the hype of finishing a case withers. The workaholic demon is dead.

Iglesias lets out a long, exasperated sigh. The clock at the bottom right of his monitor states it's mid-afternoon, and he is working through files provided by the other RCMP Major Crimes officers regarding ash. He wishes to go home and be a father.

His existence used to be similar to the law enforcement personnel out there. He'd find the street dealers and uncover the Crystal Moths. It's dumbfounding that two years on, scientists don't understand what ash is. A lot of details that happened baffle him.

That was another life, and a different version of Iglesias. He is a desk man. His prime purpose is being a father and catching up on lost moments with his son. If the kid wanted him, that is.

Iglesias goes to take a drink from his coffee cup. It's out. Time for more fuel. The workaholic mutated his kick into speed. Caffeine. That's an acceptable drug. You need consumptions to power through the mundane, monotonous tasks of paperwork. On the plus side, he no longer uses cream, helping the tire around his gut.

He takes his mug and marches past the rows of desks in the grey hall to the break room. The tables are plastic and the chairs are of equal cheap quality. A brunette woman with straight hair is getting a cup of joe. Her blue plaid button-up shirt, devoid of any wrinkles, complements the flawless smile that reveals her too perfect white teeth.

"Archer," Iglesias says, leaning on the counter. "I thought you were out dealing with that Moth yahoo they brought in?"

"Done and done, boss." She finishes filling up her cup.

"You don't have to say that anymore. You're a phase two detective," Iglesias says. Her words are nice to hear.

"Hey, you're still the boss. The detective title says so, and I say so."

A closed smile rises across Iglesias's face. He says, "Yeah. There is such a thing as a muted demotion."

"At least we're working on the ash case."

"If you can call it that." Iglesias takes the pot and fills his coffee.

"We'll get them. We're in this together."

"Try sitting on the sidelines," Iglesias says. He marches for the door.

"Iglesias."

He stops, turning to the young gal. Her bold stance and attitude don't fail to surprise him. Considering how pencil thin she is, she casts dominance well.

"Drink after work?"

Iglesias chuckles. "Stop hanging out with grizzly old men. You gotta find a person your age."

"So that's a yes?" She blinks twice, giving him a crooked grin.

Iglesias can't resist. The girl is a literal mirror reflection of himself at her age. Cunning, smart, and doesn't take no for an answer. He says, "Okay, usual spot?"

"You got it."

Iglesias slaps the door frame and returns to his desk. With his hot coffee in hand, it's time to truck-on through the rest of the day. In a previous incarnation, he wouldn't want to grab a drink, being riddled with guilt for what his son's mother became. The birth of ash changed his stance. That drug transformed the country and his life. Iglesias's late work hours increased. Hours turned into days, into weeks, and months. He failed to catch the prime years with his son. No young adult wants to spend their time with their father. Iglesias missed the boat. José listening to his old man ramble about how things used to be isn't cool. Iglesias tried many times to stay hip. He comes across as a sad shadow of what he once was. A refreshment will do well.

The mundane tasks of white sheets of paper consume his view. Once in a while, he gets to peer into the computer screen and log in entries. How exciting! The clock hangs closer and closer until his shift finishes. Drink time.

He snags his coat off the office chair and heads down to the elevator. A wave of relief washes over him, leaving him lighter. There is weight in his heart. Corruption lingers in the department like a dark cloud. Moths are everywhere. That's another haunting of a past life that he suppresses.

Iglesias exits the station into the Ontario summer scene. The sky is clear, the glass towers reach for the heavens. It's beautiful. The entire country is with its range of landscape. Sharp and high mountains, endless grass fields, dense wilderness, crystal clear lakes, and coastal regions. The breadth of geography makes this country worth defending.

He gets into his SUV and drives to the usual watering hole. He's gone there for years. Correction: gone for decades. Lubrication of the mind is required for a job like this. Hell, he doesn't blame folks taking weed to unwind. Anyone who can do it straight edge isn't human. There's humour to such a statement.

Not human, Iglesias smiles to himself. He squeezes the twelve-o-clock mark on the charcoal steering wheel. "*It was real, a fucked-up whack reptilian humanoid thing.*" Chen, the deceased Moth, once told him. José does not need his father going off the deep end.

He parks the car by the old brick pub. It used to be a fire hall a century ago. *Ashley's* is the name of the place, presented with a lit white sign complete with red and forest green outlines closer to the centre of each letter above the door. This whole thing reeks of the eighties. It's the type of place that attracts old men like Iglesias.

A moth to the light, he thinks. It shouldn't attract promising gals like Archer, though.

Iglesias enters the bar, walking across the emerald carpet as seventies rock plays. The after-work crowd comprises other officers. Office employees who labour in the neighbouring skyscrapers and government workers drink too. This is the working class. Most of them are unfazed by the disturbing evil that is pulling the strings of their society. It haunts Iglesias. It haunted Cabello.

Iglesias got a taste when talking to Chen and Lola Cabello. A darkness lingers underneath the smoke and screens of civilization. These are deep thoughts that he shouldn't concern himself with, and yet he can't stop fixating on it. *Reptilian people*, he thinks. Those two words unleash a blast of thoughts firing one after the other: the ash drug is from reptiles, eyewitnesses have seen humanoid scaled creatures with the Moths. Iglesias almost bought into the rumours.

Archer beat him here, sitting at the bar on the gunmetal stool complete with red pleather. She has a whiskey on the rocks, sipping, while watching the news that faces the bar mounted on the opposite wall. The Canadian All Media Broadcasting (CAMB). The reporter icon Hucker Dime is on. He yammers about the Prime Minister, using his trademark bewildered appearance that the consumers adore. The media is another troubling entity run by demons. A reality check reminds him they are the metaphorical ones.

"Hey boss," Archer says.

"Yo," Iglesias says. Little enthusiasm leaves his cool wording as he sits. The stool creaks. A bartender, another young chick, pours him a whiskey. He watches her blank face, fixated on a thick ring pierced into her right nostril. It's new. One of eight stamped over her face.

Hucker Dime catches Iglesias's eye, and he looks over his shoulder. With the audio muted, the subtext provides the context:

. . . *And jobs are at the lowest in the past decade across the country. It's tied provincial budgets, preventing premiers from supporting their people, thanks to the federal government. Poverty is on the rise. Tension leaves people concerned.*

Prime Minister Stephen Trudell has promised prosperous roads ahead. This is thanks to a forthcoming merger. Alberta-founded energy and transport giant Allen Oil Site Solutions and American-based tech and bio lab Manageficient Enterprises are looking to grow together. The

Prime Minister is directly involved, claiming this will provide jobs in all sectors.

Hucker Dime's jaw drops and his eyes narrow in his signature expression.

For who? The Americans? If you ask me, these suits are pushing the common man around . . .

That's enough of that dip shit. Iglesias turns to Archer and speaks. "Anything exciting on the street today?"

Archer laughs, tucking her hair being her ear. "You like to mention that. Only that one street dealer we busted. He had a small pack of ash on him."

"Yeah, I figured. I'm just curious. The damn military sealed our progress and we're stuck doing the grunt work." Iglesias folds his arms.

"I am. Consulting for you."

"Sure," Iglesias says.

"It was two years ago, boss. We did what we could with the resources we had. It wasn't good enough."

"The covert operation branch isn't doing better than us with their supposed 'limitless budget'. Imagine if we had that?" Iglesias raises a brow.

"Fair point." Archer lowers her voice. "We could get into dangerous territory talking shit about these guys. They're big."

"Consultant my ass." He takes a swig of his drink, drowning the jaded spirit attempting to escape his mouth.

"Look at the bright side. You got your life back when those guys came in. You spend time with José."

"A horny kid with a girlfriend? Please. He's eighteen and with those friends of his. I sit at home and worry. That's it."

Iglesias runs his tongue along his inner lower lip to suppress his frustration with his son's friends.

"If you'd like, I can screen Tanner again." Archer scans Iglesias's face, hoping he says yes.

"Thanks. No need. It hasn't shown value. I swear, that kid is involved with the Moths. I can't get proof." Iglesias finishes the rest of his whiskey.

The bartender catches it from the corner of her eye. Round two is on its way. Archer downs hers. She likes to pretend she is one of the old boys. It's not doing her favours of cynicism. "Like I said, you got your life back."

"What life?" he says. "You're doing what we did before. Busting drugs, grow-ops, chasing real winners and knowing damn well that the Crystal Moths are the ones who are puppeteering it. That gets fed to the fucking covert operations who say they have the public's safety in their best interest, thanks to the DND. As if we didn't. They've done fuck all."

Archer glances around, for Iglesias raised his voice. The music is too loud and people are engaged in their own conversation. There are a few other officers here from the station that would make a mental note of Iglesias's harsh words. He doesn't care. The weeping workaholic is reborn as an undead desk monkey.

"Seriously, Ricardo." Archer speaks in a quiet voice. She doesn't use his first name like this. "There's nothing we can do. We were getting dangerously close to the Moths, to Cabello. A lot of people died."

"I'm aware," Iglesias says.

"Why do you think Beckman got out? The Crystal Moths aren't messing around."

"I know, I know," Iglesias repeats. He reflects on his old partner Beckman and the sweat they put into the case. Wise Beckman called it a day and retired earlier. He spends time with his wife and kids, the important things in life. Iglesias says, "I don't enjoy losing. I've lost enough."

He swirls the ice surrounding his drink. The rotten skeletons of his past resurrect thanks to the phantoms of today. He wants to blame Archer for mentioning it when he is aware he did. Iglesias can't pretend to enjoy his position. José is too close to his job and on the wrong side. Iglesias is a desk clown. Dig further and he is resentful of his old marriage. His wife did little for their son. Peel another layer and Iglesias was once like Archer, hotheaded. Go deeper and he was a street dealer himself who used and abused the goods. Go full circle and the youthful habits live through a fixation of work and drinking.

He blinks several times, realizing his spiral, and takes a deep breath, smothering the brewing past. Those corpses will stay where they belong. "I could go on forever."

"You usually do," Archer says. Her smug smile rises as she takes a sip of her drink.

"Thanks," Iglesias says. "I don't have a lot of people to vent to anymore."

"Neither do I," Archer says. "We're two peas in a misery pod. You think I can relate to people my age? See these officers around here? They're naïve enough to think that they're helping."

"Who's talking like an old man?"

"You know it's true. I was lucky to work with you and Beckman. Give these guys and gals enough time and they'll unravel the bitter truth. That ash case fucked things up for me. We're putting out fires and not getting to the source."

"Not looking to settle?" the other asks.

"That again? Please."

"You don't want to be alone forever."

"Guys in their thirties talking about babies and marriage. Forties? I don't aspire to be the other wife of a resentful man. Fifties, that's a lost cause. No offence, boss."

Iglesias shrugs. "None taken."

"Don't get me going on dating girls. Bunch of stuck-up prudes validating themselves on dating apps. They don't care. Then there are ones that do want a kid. I'm sick of the endless wave of fake ones who are looking to experiment. Where are the real people? Life has so much to give. Settling kills that. I want a partner to live life with. Travel, explore. Not get a house, kids, and rot."

Iglesias takes a drink. "At some point when you've been alone for so long, you realize this is how life is going to be, and you are okay with that."

"Wise words of self-reflection?" she asks.

"Yeah. Hey, by the way, did that latte drinking hipster get in touch with you?"

Archer snorts. "You need to be more specific."

"About the documentary, them filming a mini-series on Lola Cabello and the Crystal Moths?"

"Oh, right. Yeah. They did. I'm unsure. You?"

Iglesias shakes his head no.

"It's easy money."

"They'll skew whatever we say to fit the story they want to tell. Documentaries aren't about facts."

Archer's eyes widen, which isn't the reaction he expected. Her gaze pierces past him and smacks onto the television. Iglesias turns to see a real-time feed of a reporter on the CAMB channel. She's standing outside the Women's Correctional Centre in Manitoba.

The subtitles aren't of interest. What's fascinating is the mugshot to the right of the live feed: a young gal with hazelnut eyes and short, messy black hair. Three long scars run along her eyebrow, past her iconic sharp angled nose and signature cupid's bow to her jawline. Lola Cabello.

Appearing behind the moving subtitles is the headline message in capitals on a red background stating: HIGH-RISK OFFENDER ESCAPES FROM PRISON — LIVE

"No shit," Archer says. Her mouth hangs open.

Iglesias squints, giving a dumbfounded expression that could rival Hucker Dime. This reeks of Crystal Moths. Another mind-blowing layer plasters onto the mystery. It took a couple of years, and they delivered.

CHAPTER 5
LOCALIZED ANGER

Smoke billows from the charcoal ground, creating a saturated atmosphere around the leather-clad figure on her knees. Her sombre claws hold a warm chunk of lava rock, illuminating red glowing etchings of an ancient language. Half of the object is on the ground beside her, for it exploded moments ago.

Pockets of flame surround her. Two broken pillars are on each side of where the explosion took place. It's amazing the shards missed her face.

A cool wind blows against the tan map in her other hand. Speckles of dirt and blood cover it. She looks at the illustration. Black ink forms mountains, notes, and ritual circles surrounded by the same crude glyphs carved in the lava rocks. These symbols match those of her wretched childhood in Hell.

Useless, she thinks and crumples the document in her claws. This gate didn't work, and the instructions proved futile. The demon either lied or was unaware of the damaged gate. She leans to the former. Demons enjoy toying with mortals, regardless of their kind: human, nymph, or vazelead. Now, Lerief Scalebane has no leverage against that damn balancer Synarion.

This isn't her fault, for the map isn't hers. The succubus's red fluids staining the paper prove it. Besting a demon in hand-to-hand combat means zero when the one person you love most is beyond reach.

A croaking voice pierces into her psyche, breaking the two-year flashback of her failed scheming. "Vazeleads," says a thin man. He shakes his head, rubbing his toxic green goatee, matching the brows and eyes. "I can't understand your kind's hate for the unusual."

His sound sparks a repulsive rage, humming deep inside her. It makes her tap the leather handle of her chrome sai. In fact, his very essence detests her. Halfbreeds are a revolting concept. Abolishing them is a must when they're conceived. His existence proves his parents did otherwise.

Abominations, she thinks.

The two stand on a walkway overlooking a warehouse floor below. Men in white tank tops, T-shirts, and even dress shirts pack charcoal scale diamonds in black vacuum sealed bags on portable tables. They work with haste, aware that their superiors are watching.

"And your parents elude my reasoning," the vazelead says. The leather mask muffles her dry voice underneath the metal muzzle, complete with a frown and long canine fangs. The soulless goggles hide her gaze.

The halfbreed presses his elongated fingers together, ending in pointed fingernails that graze his skin. Jekos is his name. It's one she had to learn whether she prefers it or not.

"I accept the abnormal, unlike you. How a human and an imp met is not of my interest. From what I gather, it was unintentional or unwanted. It doesn't matter because here I am."

"Here you are." Scalebane grips the sheathed sai, resting along the belt below her leather-bound armour. Both sai's three blades per handle shimmer in the warehouse's bright lighting. Her claws fiddle with the winged edges on the shaft. Her tail coils around her leg, wrapped in leather, concealed under the black hooded cloak. The humans below are clueless to who she is, or what she is. Considering the discreet nature of the ash drug, she prefers to keep it that way.

Jekos speaks. "None of us asked to be born, Scalebane. None of us asked to be in this situation. There are bigger pieces at play, and we do our part."

Not again, she thinks.

"I'm no fool. I know you continually request that King and Mastema sever our ties. Why do you hate me so much?"

"The same answer as before, halfbreed. You come from my home; I detest that forlorn place and its demons. Then to watch humans and others freely infect the world by creating mutations is disgusting."

"I see," Jekos says.

Scalebane inhales through her black-scaled rimmed nostrils. Even through the mask, she can distinguish the aroma of her companion. His fruity cologne with hints of birch doesn't hide the lingering burning plastic of his natural odour. She has become accustomed to his smell, like she is used to the agonizing shit-stench that comes from the soft skins below.

"We'll be able to get these across both countries?" Scalebane asks, preferring they stick to business.

"Without a doubt. Allen Shipping Solutions will send these to the United States. Canada is simple as we have done. Once we're in the states, Mexico is no problem. We have a few contacts in the UK. You think it is wise to go into the rest of the continent with a heavy hand?" Jekos asks.

"It doesn't matter what I think. I execute King's and Mastema's wishes."

"As we do." Jekos clears his throat. "Scalebane, I sure hope you take my warning seriously."

"Which one?" Scalebane asks. "The repercussions of refusing to join your secretive club, or of Mastema?"

Jekos chuckles. "The latter. I'm not worried about the previous. You'll make your way to me." A toothy grin spreads across his face. Inside, the thin pointed teeth are too far from each other, creating one of the ugliest smiles Scalebane has laid eyes upon.

"You sound so sure of yourself," Scalebane says.

"You will need allies. Mastema doesn't care about your people, or any of us. It's why I came to you. We cannot be enemies."

"We aren't. Our work arrangement is mutual, isn't it?" Scalebane asks.

"It is. I can tell without a moment's hesitation you would end it. You people cannot counter Mastema alone."

"King and I shall deal with the fallen angel when the time comes. For now, I am their command. We will send ash to the other side of the world, into Europe, Asia, the Middle East, and trickle into Africa."

"We don't have the distribution means for that. The limits of your people's scales are being tested. You would have to breed more vazeleads, meaning you and—"

Scalebane cuts him off by saying, "I am aware of what King wishes of me. I will not."

"Well, your sister fails to return, and if you aspire to be as aggressive as King commands, I don't see how you're going to do it."

My sister, Scalebane thinks. She hasn't seen her sister since the slaughterhouse with Cabello. It aches her heart, shrivelling it into a small raisin. Synarion will pay for what he has done. Not today. Someday.

Scalebane tightens her tail's restriction around her ankle, suppressing the growing emotion. Humans. Halfbreed imps. The pressure from King and Mastema. Jekos mentioning her sister. It will make her snap. Her squeezing flares a burning sensation running up her leg, reminding her of a too recent injury. She frees the limb.

She speaks. "We'll distribute strategically, treating it as a designer drug, not like before. Place it in the right hands, as we have, and they'll pay top dollar. Rumours of it will spread and people of influence will come to us, forging powerful allegiances for the Crystal Moths."

Jekos says, "Uh-huh. That is phase one." His eyes skim to the opposite end of the steel walkway where a second vazelead comes from the exiting door. He, too, wears a long dark cloak with the hood and mask concealing his identity. Jekos sighs and slaps the railing. "I'll leave you to it."

He strides down the path, his dress shoes clicking as he passes the newcomer, limbs springing in a wide spasmodic arch. He nods at the vazelead, who growls. Vazeleads dislike the halfbreed. Their people value purity because of the critical decline in numbers.

Rithu Blacktooth, the heir to the vazelead throne. He stops a metre from her, leaning against the railing. He overlooks the humans below through his mask that matches Scalebane's, created with leather and metal. The polished steel of the front shapes a masquerade human visage. Etchings of his family's crest, intricate linework, run along the goggles bolted to the eye sockets and the edges of the steel to form flames and bat wings.

At the moment, the young vazelead is the same height as Scalebane. Give him a few hundred years and he will grow taller with full muscles. The boyish frame detests Scalebane, squishing her bodily functions deep inside. His natural odour is a perfect reflection of his age, too sweet and desperate. The youthfulness is the opposite of what any sane female vazelead would mate with.

She's not a breeding factory. She is a hunter hellbent on a few things that matter in her life: Namsruc, her dear sister. Years have gone by and she hasn't returned. She stays with the damn nymph. Why? Scalebane does not wish to say a word to Rithu; he is a child. Their circumstances force them to work together, like Jekos.

"Mastema is going to be displeased with our ash production," Rithu says.

"He tries to squeeze more ash. It's physically impossible to generate ash at the speed he wants. He refuses to accept it."

Rithu's gaze lands on Scalebane. His movement is slow and his shoulders slouch a pinch. The unconfident boy isn't stupid and is aware of what his father wishes for him to do with Scalebane. Considering he is the youngest, and only other male, he hasn't bedded. Nervousness beacons from his posture, laying eyes on the opposite sex; fearful and longing.

He says, "I hope so. I don't know what else we can do."

"It's not for you to concern yourself with, Rithu." Scalebane folds her arms, adjusting her stance because of the one leg's sudden weakness. The heat lessens thanks to the tail's release. "Why do you approach me?"

"Apologies," Rithu says, straightening his posture. "I wanted to inform you that the soft skin, Sierra, is dead. The original three humans who saw your sister are no more."

"Excellent. The shaper was convincing?"

"Without a doubt. Cabello completed the task the next day with a disembowelment."

She's a beast, Scalebane thinks. It's admirable.

Rithu continues, "We're fortunate the Moths accumulated a shaper."

"They are rare."

"I have ordered Kye Pung to meet with you and Jekos in Toronto. Once she perishes, no human will know of the vazeleads. Of course, except for Lola Cabello."

Lola and the painter, Scalebane thinks. A hidden detail that her comrade does not need to know. She says, "We will obey the orders of King and Mastema. Cabello is to live."

Rithu speaks. "More than anything, I would prefer to kill her myself. Her knowledge is vast."

"The threat to her family will keep her silenced. Don't ponder over what should happen. You've completed your task and are proving useful."

Rithu's chest puffs. "I do what I must do for our people, whatever that entices. Like you do."

His words make Scalebane squirm. It's a subtle twitch of her head that Rithu notices. His shoulders sulk again, feeling ashamed of his gentle forwardness. It was a clever move, as he's done in the past.

Rithu clears his throat. "As we must do for the good of our people."

The child keeps digging himself deeper into embarrassment. She'd best save him from further awkwardness. "In fact, I'm gaining confidence in your abilities."

Rithu stands straight again.

"I would like you to oversee operations with the halfbreed, as I need to step away for several days after dealing with Kye Pung."

"I don't understand. I should only work with Jekos?"

"That's what I said."

"What about your strategy? And managing my father's and Mastema's expectations? The workers will have questions for you, which city to distribute to."

"As I've stated, I'm gaining confidence in your abilities. You and Jekos will manage."

Rithu is making it far more complicated than it is. Playing foreman for the ash operation is a dull and uninteresting task since they have taken care of Lola Cabello. No challenger stands in their way. Synarion, the nymph, is gone with her sister. The law is compliant. Human media has no information. Politicians are in their pockets. Old world beings stay clear of them.

Rithu nods several times, convincing himself that he can do the job. "Of course I will do this for you, Scalebane."

"You seize control immediately. If you need me, use the soulstone to reach King and he'll contact me." Scalebane takes a step away, leaving Rithu to ponder his new responsibilities. Her stride swings her left leg in a long arc, thanks to its lack of movement. Her boot hits the ground with a stiff thud. A strange spike of pins-and-needles run along the limb, with sections remaining numb. The limping motion is too new. Two years is too soon.

Rithu calls to her, "Where will you go?"

She does not answer, heading for the door. She hobbles from the hallway and down the stairs, leaving the warehouse under the night sky. The boy shall do fine with Jekos. They're worms who listen to the fear that enters their mind. Unlike Scalebane, Rithu needs an authoritative figure to respond to because he lacks life experience.

Jekos is another creature, with his own schemes, playing the role of an obedient worker, no different from Scalebane. Matching Jekos, she has her own agenda. The current task at hand requires her to meet more souls that she detests.

The painter. He excites her. Like hate, excitement is an emotion that she must suppress to remain in control.

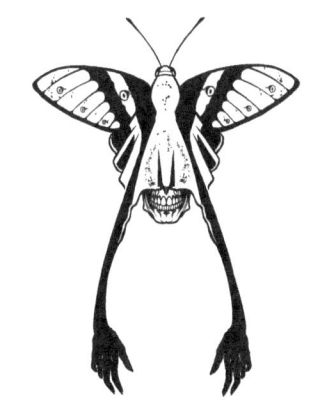

CHAPTER 6
THROUGH DEATH, NEW BEGINNINGS

There's no doubt that Rithu lacks spirit regarding his new task. Despite Scalebane's distaste for him, she has assurance in his skills. She acts keen on executing the utopia King and Mastema have planned. Oh, has she blinded them. This is where the painter comes in. First, she must finish one note of business with Jekos. Unlike the other assassinations, Kye Pung is intriguing because Mastema is involved. He's flown to Toronto to deal with the matter.

Unaware of the dangers ahead, Kye Pung sits across from Jekos and Scalebane in the limousine in eastern Canada, Toronto. She's tapping away on her phone, operating under the assumption that she is the top dog of Toronto's ash wing. Jekos and Scalebane will deliver her. If they sent her on her own, it would raise suspicion.

Kye Pung's foot swings, shoulders relaxed. Scalebane can smell the stench of human mixed with Jekos's. A chemical perfume of vanilla rests on the top layer of Kye Pung. Below that, her natural scent is sweeter than a male soft skin. It reeks of excrement. Goddamn apes, worthless. Below her pores, past the muscle, are her blood veins. Stress, fear, and nervousness raise the temperature of the human body, creating heat and releasing more sweat. At the moment, there's no indication of these properties in Kye Pung. She is at ease. Their plan is working.

The limousine drives through the bustling Toronto downtown at night. They veer off into an alleyway by the loading dock of a glass skyscraper. A blue neon sign above the garage says: Allen Sky Tower. The discreet location keeps Jekos and Scalebane in the shadows as they exit the vehicle. Kye Pung's high heels click with each step.

She speaks. "I've ordered my men to distribute the last batch of ash to our colleagues in Hollywood. The elite can't get enough of it."

Jekos says, "Excellent."

Two Crystal Moths in white blazers and black pants open the docking station door as the three approach. One is bald with a protruding, long jawline. The spiky-haired one stands tall, exuding an air of authority. His extended angled nose gives a signature look. The shade-covered eyes of each contribute to an aura of mystery.

The spikey-haired one speaks, showcasing his extended fangs, voice flat. "This way."

The group step inside as the old world moths close the door, locking it. They take them through a large open warehouse loading dock and through another entrance, along the hallway, and to the lobby. White marble floor shines under golden chandelier lighting. To the right is a front desk with a security guard, watching the locked door. The tower is empty at night. He nods at them and flicks a switch under the table, activating the elevator to his left.

They enter the shaft and Jekos uses a key card to unlock the top floor at level eighty-five. Slow tempo jazz music plays on loop in the background, attempting to create a relaxing atmosphere in the all-glass, gold-tinted encasement. The two vampires stare at the door. Scalebane stands beside the spiky-hair one. The fangs, and pale skin, and the odour are blaring lights, telling her what they are.

Vampires, Scalebane thinks. Their cheap, tangy cologne doesn't hide the blood of countless dead running through their veins. She's seen these goons before. They join Mastema everywhere.

In the current civilization, no human could tell the difference. They look like soft skins. To the untrained nostril, you would think so. Scalebane smells the slight corpse stench on the outer layer, blending with the foulness below. Thousands of mixed fluids from decades of stolen life flows through their system. The living's blood prevents their flesh from rotting. These old world beings aren't too different from Scalebane. For example, both of them are deathly allergic to the sun. It's why the meeting is at night. Vampires also have a prominent smell. They sniff Scalebane, deciding if her essence is of value. Scalebane wonders what is going through each of their minds. A halfbreed imp and vazelead must be a tasty treat compared to the usual feasting of human blood.

Kye Pung asks, "Think Mastema will finally share more of his plan?"

Jekos shrugs. "It's impossible to say."

The bald vampire scratches his head. Both are aware of Kye Pung's fate.

Kye Pung continues, "I feel we've been operating in the dark. Cash is endless with ash, the red market, and Allen Oil Site Solutions. Our connections are better with each passing week. We can't sit in this country forever. We're slow moving into the states. Mastema is more sophisticated than that."

"Moths to the light," Jekos says.

They reach the top floor and the elevator dings, sliding open to showcase black flooring. Glass windows cover the entire circular space, presenting a three-hundred-and-sixty-degree view of Toronto. Lake Ontario is on the southeast below the moon. Endless lights dance in the distance on the northwest metropolis. A panorama blessed to the upper class.

The five exit the elevator. Those vampires stay by the closing doors as Scalebane, Jekos, and Kye Pung walk to the centre of the room. A circular matte blue bar fills the core space with a gold pillar inside. This column supports the skyscraper's foundation.

Behind the counter is a lady dressed in a white vest and black dress shirt, polishing several glasses. A soft skin would wonder why such a beautiful specimen such as this woman would settle on bartending. Her silky, lush hair dangles in a messy bun. The balanced features complement the smooth complexion of her face. A touch from her would tremble weak willed men. Upon closer inspection, one can see pointed ears tucked under the long locks. Strings tie them behind her skull. Her violet eyes watch the three newcomers as they walk towards her. The bartender pours four drinks. This woman is a nymph, like that damn Synarion.

He isn't the last, she thinks, reflecting on the old fool's claims.

Dress shoes click from the opposite end of the vast space, echoing as they come closer to the group. From behind the pillar, a man cups his white shirt. They match the pearl pants. He extends his hands, the gold rings glimmering under the chandeliers above the bar, projecting a soft amber light over the room.

"Welcome, my fellow Crystal Moths, my family," says the man. His voice is too smooth and cold. He brushes his long, bone white hair. The gold cuffs on his wrist jingle. The hair is as pale as his skin, matching the pure whiteness of his clothing. He reaches the bar and leans against it as the bartender slides him a dark amber drink.

"I hope bourbon is okay," he says.

Jekos takes a bow, as does Kye Pung. "Master Mastema," he says.

Scalebane does not lower. She has not spoken a word during their interaction leading here. She has no need for them. Her comrades will say what needs to be said and act according to Mastema's and King's demands. Scalebane's goals are undisclosed.

Mastema raises his drink. "Please, don't be shy."

The three listen to his invitation and take one glass. Mastema walks from the bar and to the other side of the room whence he came. The three follow, playing along with his theatricals.

"You three have been so busy," Mastema says. "I must say, I'm quite impressed."

"Thank you Master Mastema," Jekos says.

They stop as Mastema reaches the window. Jekos is on one side, Scalebane on the other, with Kye Pung in the middle. He overlooks the city below, swirling his bourbon, rattling the ice cubes. The tower sits five storeys higher than the next tallest. Scalebane extends her drink to Jekos, shoving it in his burgundy velvet vest. She doesn't drink, and there's no way in hell she's going to take her mask off in front of a soft skin.

"Since we have revamped our operations, we've made progress on phase one. It's slow, and worth a cheer." Mastema turns and walks to the three, focused on Jekos.

The half-imp expresses a toothy smile, holding both drinks.

Mastema observes the human.

Kye Pung takes a swig of her drink.

He looks at Scalebane.

She is unfazed, aware of his intimidation tactics. Her stance shifts, giving her left leg a break from its growing burn.

Mastema smiles at her with perfect teeth. It fades as fast as it had risen. He circles the group. "Ever since Scalebane kindly removed Erol Terzi, we haven't had a lick of problems. Secret production plans of ash no longer exist. With Scalebane and Rithu working alongside Jekos, we have kept King and his people pleased."

He will get to his point. The crime lord thrives in painting the broad picture as a visionary does. Scalebane wishes he would remove Kye Pung now. He likes to punish, let the sinful understand their wrong ways. As the flatterer of the Creator would.

Mastema continues, "To think that rumours of vazeleads spread among the human civilization was concerning. The sloppy operations Erol Terzi enforced showed his egotistical pride in his ability to control the media. Being the CEO of the Canadian All Media Broadcasting company doesn't stop people from whispering ideas. The digital age changes informational exchange."

He stops behind the group. None of them dares to turn around.

The moment holds.

He walks again. "Two years on, thanks to Scalebane's brilliant innovations once more, the rumours are fizzling out. She's a born leader, and it's an honour to work with her."

Kye Pung takes another drink. Scalebane can detect her blood running hot. The sweet smell of her sweat pushes the vanilla away. Jealousy, fear, and anticipation linger in the soft skin's mind expressed in her flesh.

Mastema makes a full circle, facing them, a metre apart. He stops in front of Kye Pung, raising the glass. "Cheers to us."

Jekos and Kye Pung clink their glasses together and drink the bourbon. It's Mastema's first sip. He holds it. Then spit flies from his mouth, projecting towards Kye Pung's face. The liquor and saliva splatter onto her skin and hair, with little droplets smearing her white suit. Kye Pung blinks several times, mouth closed. Makeup runs down her cheeks.

Mastema wipes his chin. "How I wish I could consume the lavishness of the human experience. Yet, the thing I feed off of is far more delicious." He closes his eyes and takes a deep breath through his nose and exhales. "The pride that lingers from the three of you is distinctive." He gazes at Jekos and says, "You, not so much." He looks at Scalebane and a wide smile spread across his face. "You are exquisite."

Scalebane coils her tail around her left ankle, her classic suppression method to handle anger. Damn fallen angel, complete emotional leeches.

Mastema turns to Kye Pung. "Yours is interesting. You wish to rise amongst the ranks of the Crystal Moths. Is that right, Kye Pung?"

"I do," Kye Pung says. Trickles of saliva and bourbon drip from her chin.

"You're willing to do anything, correct?"

"I do. This is my life. This is my purpose."

Mastema's face twists into a knot, raising his nostrils. His eyes widen as his brows slant. His sneering lips expose teeth as he slams his bourbon onto the stone flooring. The glass shatters on impact with little shards bouncing away.

"Then why in the name of the Creator would you listen to the foolishness of Erol Terzi?"

Kye Pung shakes her head sideways, communicating *no, no, no*. Words fail to leave her mouth.

Mastema brushes the dangling hair from his face and his cool smoothness returns. "Answer me."

"We knew the importance of distributing ash. The supplies were low, and you wanted to increase the creation of it. We are taking initiative. We thought—"

Mastema interrupts her. "You thought wrong." He circles the group, putting his hands behind his back. His dress shoes crunch fragments of glass. "I would have let this slide, because you are a valuable asset overlooking this city's drug distribution. You were useful. You've done well, and I have no criticism."

Kye Pung lowers her head, biting her lip.

He stops behind her. "Except we have changed gears. I must respect my partners. The vazelead people wish to remain hidden. You and Erol Terzi let other humans see their people. You two spread the rumours that ash comes from sentient reptilians."

"It wasn't the intent. They are rumours, sir," Kye Pung says.

"Taking initiative once again?" Mastema asks.

"No, sir," Kye Pung says.

Mastema cackles a low laugh that even causes Scalebane's stomach to twist. She releases her leg with her tail, remembering the endless nerve damage. The fallen angel circles around once more, stopping in front of them.

"Scalebane has assigned King's protégé, Rithu, on a side project. Do you understand what that project is?" Mastema asks.

"No, sir."

"She's put a hit on each human that laid eyes upon an exposed vazelead."

Kye Pung swallows a thick ball of saliva, understanding the seriousness.

"One by one, she and Rithu have strategically removed those that spread the rumours." He jabs his index finger into Kye Pung's chest and says, "Except for you."

"I've never said a word. Never," she says.

"I understand. Each of us in this room does. You're the last human."

"What of Lola Cabello? The vigilante who—"

Mastema waves his hand, dismissing her words. "We're not done with her. She has value."

"So do I," Kye Pung says.

Mastema raises his eyebrow. "You're dangling your pride for me to feast."

Kye Pung regains her composure. "Sir, you said so yourself."

"Yes, you will be difficult to replace. It's not impossible. Some will climb the ranks and oversee the drug distribution in this fine city."

Kye Pung points at Scalebane. "Because she decides she doesn't want me around, you want me dead?" Her voice rises. "Yet you and Scalebane let that scum vigilante live? She's far more dangerous than me. She knows too much. I've been loyal from day one!"

"You have, my dear." Mastema takes a step towards her as she moves away. He keeps walking forward, passing the other two. His shoulders graze against theirs. It makes Jekos clear his throat and Scalebane's tail to coil. He keeps pursuing Kye Pung.

"Please, sir. Please, my Lord." Kye Pung says far quicker than she should.

"Lord?" Mastema smiles. "We're getting desperate."

"I'll do anything you ask!"

"Anything? I ask of your death," Mastema says.

Kye Pung halts walking backwards. Her legs shake. She laughs in several nervous exhales. "No way you'd do this. It's a test, isn't it?"

Mastema pauses, putting his hands behind his back.

Kye Pung nods to herself as if she's uncovered the monumental secret of this meeting. "Yes. That's exactly what this is. It's one of your screening tests."

Mastema takes a breath in, feeding.

"You do this to each recruit, interviewing them. You test their worth." She laughs with tension leaving her jaw. "You want to test my loyalty?"

"Are you loyal?" Mastema asks. He sidesteps to face the pane.

"I am, sir, Lord."

"Prove it."

Kye Pung takes a deep breath through her nose and exhales through her mouth in loud breaths. Her gaze focuses on the window. "This shit is crazy," she mumbles to herself.

"Have I ever steered you wrong?"

"No, sir," Kye Pung says.

"Are you aware of what we're building?"

"No, sir."

Jekos looks at Scalebane, and she glances at him from the corner of her eye.

Mastema says, "A better tomorrow, under the Creator. We need the bravest. It's why I test my family. Are you family?"

Kye Pung takes another step. "I am."

"Are you?"

"This is a test," she says.

"Prove it."

"You'll save me?"

"Devoted Moths grow wings."

"I'm loyal."

"Fly to the light," he says.

"I can fly to you."

"Fly to the light!" Mastema shouts, raising his hands towards the glass.

"To the light!" Kye Pung roars and darts from her position. Her high heels click, running at full speed in those awkward shoes. She accelerates, ten meters from the window.

Eight meters.

Three meters.

One meter, and zero!

She leaps, shielding her face with her shoulders colliding with the glass. It shatters. She flies through the frame and into the vast expanse, followed by hundreds of shards descending to the concrete streets below. Cool wind floods into the space with the sound of traffic and honking cars beyond. A faint scream comes from Kye Pung falling from view. Several seconds pass and a subtle crash onto metal follows. A car alarm blares. They're so high that it's surprising that they can hear it.

Mastema turns to face Jekos and Scalebane. He raises his arms. "How's that for true power?"

Jekos says, "Impressive sir."

"Influence, my dear half-imp. Influence is why we're moving at the pace we are to take this world. The trick to controlling humans is to not lay a finger on them. Make them think it's their idea and the next thing you know, they will believe and do anything in your name."

Jekos speaks. "There's no soft skin that is aware of what we are."

"Lola Cabello," Scalebane says.

"Not a concern, yet," Mastema says. "Besides her, it's only us from the old world, the way you like it, Lerief Scalebane."

Jekos nods.

Scalebane says, "We are distributing the latest growth of ash. We should have a package personally for you within the next few days."

Mastema nods. "Excellent. In time for my meeting with a few key members from the United States. Their Vice President will open the doors to their president whom the Canadian Prime Minister endorses as well. Not that his opinion matters. The more politicians we get into our hands, the sooner we can tilt the tide of Western politics before spreading further east."

"It will be a few days," Scalebane repeats.

"Good," Mastema says. "Oh, and don't think I've dismissed synthesizing ash."

Scalebane's tail perks with interest.

"Some of the ash you'll deliver me is for testing in this tower's lab. I will find an alternative if you vazeleads can't resolve your breeding issue."

"There's no issue," Scalebane says. *Not this again*, she thinks.

"Oh, there is an elephant in the room, my friend. The nine corrupt are great for creating ash. They served us well to this point. Those poor souls are weak, peeling the scales off their skin time and time again. They can't produce at the speed we need. Zoefani Blacktooth and King are infertile. Your sister has abandoned the cause. That leaves you, Scalebane. The last female of your people."

Jekos takes hold of his wrist, squeezing. This is not his battle.

Mastema continues, "If I had to perform such an honourable task for my people, sex isn't such a terrible performance."

"The First has no people," Scalebane says. "How can you relate?"

Mastema raises his eyebrows and nods in agreement. "That I cannot. Like I fail to understand the basic brilliance of primal needs. The sins that you mortals devour. I wish I could taste. Food, liquor, lust, uncontrolled anger, anything. This is the curse of being the First."

"Sir," Jekos says. "You are blessed with infinite knowledge and wisdom, guiding us to the Creator."

"Thank you, Jekos. You're too kind." Mastema looks at the ground, his face frowning. It springs into a smile. "See? We can have these discussions without humans around. You two are special, being linked to the afterlife. No other mortal can feel the way we do. The nymph back there, or those bloodsucking vampires we have for guards, it's in one ear and out the other with them."

"I'm glad you understand," Scalebane says. "You won't be able to synthesize ash."

"Give me time. There are private enterprises within the Allen Shipping Solutions's sphere of influence that can prove useful. A Dr. Lang, who will be here shortly with the Prime Minister and the CEO of Allen Oil Site Solutions, will shed light on the topic. We'll keep the old world hidden as best as we can. It won't last forever once we pass phase one."

"How so?" Jekos asks.

"Well, the Prime Minister has had his hands involved before I met him. He had an affair with a succubus who fed him ash. Mr. Patterson is one to dive into conspiracies, true or false. Dr. Lang is wise enough to comprehend ash is not in modern human textbooks. He asks the right questions."

This is the last thing Scalebane wants to hear.

Mastema says, "This is where Lola Cabello comes into play."

"Her apparent ties to the old world won't prove fruitful," Scalebane says. "Work with me. I will find my sister. She agreed to King's arrangement with his son. I didn't."

"Yes. You get your sister and produce little vazelead hatchlings. King is far more persistent than me. Remember, I'm on your side. You're family, as far as I'm concerned."

"Thank you, Mastema." Scalebane would love to spit at his words. It's better to remain diplomatic. A painter awaits her arrival.

"If you'll excuse me," Mastema says. "I have a meeting I must attend."

"Of course, Master," Jekos says. He takes a bow.

"I will walk you to the elevator," Mastema says. He speaks as the three move. "I do miss our meetings. We should do these more often."

Jekos says, "Yes. We enjoy your presence."

"Yet we're so preoccupied. I thought I had a sense of character with Erol Terzi. It was his position as CEO of CAMB that made him enticing. A charming man, wasn't he?"

The three reach the lift, and Mastema extends his hand to it. The bald vampire presses the button with his fob's edge.

"Until next time." Mastema takes a slight bow as the doors slide open.

Three men in business suits exit the lift, led by another suited Crystal Moth. With a quick sniff, Scalebane confirms they are human. The largest's face is flushed pink. The shortest is at least five feet with a feeble body. Mastema's last guest is broad shouldered and of average size.

"Ah yes," Mastema says. "Prime Minister Stéphane Trudell." He shakes the hand of the blush-faced man wearing a deep blue suit and tie.

"It's a pleasure to see you again," Prime Minister Trudell says in a thick French Quebecois accent. His cheeks shake as he nods his head in sync with the motion.

"Likewise." Mastema extends a hand to the other two men. "Mr. Patterson. Dr. Lang."

"A bit brisk," Mr. Patterson, the average man, says.

"We had a fall." A wide grin stretches across Mastema's face.

Jekos and Scalebane enter the elevator. They ride the shaft down with the two vampires. The familiar jazz plays until the lift reaches the main floor. The Moths lead them beyond the lobby. Outside are flashing ambulance lights, police tape, and bystanders watching the aftermath of Kye Pung's fall. Her body indeed crashed onto the roof of a silver car parked in front. They go through the hallway to the loading dock and outside. The vampires slam the door and lock it once Jekos and Scalebane step into the nipping night.

Jekos sighs. "That went well."

"Quite," Scalebane says.

"I hope you feel more at ease. The rumour should stop spreading," Jekos says.

"Have the media relations monitor it."

"That's been the goal. At least, Mastema's and King's goal." Jekos straightens his posture. "Scalebane, have you given any thought to my offer?"

"I'm not joining your club," Scalebane says. "We'll work together as long as our goals align."

"They'll align, Scalebane. Why do you think we continue to wrangle members? That nymph bartender at the top, she is one of us."

"If what you say is true regarding Mastema—"

Jekos cuts in. "It is true."

"Mastema is as ancient as life itself. He is the First. Do you think your band of misfits will have any power to stop him if he wishes to unleash hell?"

"You forget too easily that the world is different. You refuse to reflect on the unknowns beyond the afterlife realms. Heaven is dormant. Dega'Mostikas is as passive as the Creator. Demons run rampant and angels serve no gods. Relics of power and beings of exceptional knowledge scatter throughout the domains. Many of them are here in the mortal realm." Jekos takes a step forward, lowering his voice. "We are walking on eggshells with our operation. Souls dabble in arts punishable before Heaven's vacancy. We are blind to what lies ahead of us and we could awake forces greater than our control. That's why Mastema focuses on influence and not the brute force methods you're fond of."

Scalebane awaits his next words. She forgets how forward Jekos can be when he chooses to.

"Power has dispersed and is accessible by orders like mine," Jekos says. "We have an urgent procedure underway. If it goes as intended, you would be wise to be a part of the movement."

"You won't give me a hint of what it is?" Scalebane asks.

"It will ease the pressure of King's breeding. In fact, it will wipe your concerns away."

A rattle comes from the depths of her throat. "Do as you wish, halfbreed. Betrayal cannot entice me with vague promises."

Jekos looks to the ground, tapping his foot. He sighs and locks gazes. "Hunting for your sister?"

"Speak, halfbreed."

"You get what I am and where I come from, as a . . . halfbreed. There is insight there."

Scalebane's throat rumbles, a low frequency, detectable by Jekos.

"In due time, you will see the other side." Jekos walks to the limousine.

Scalebane proceeds until they arrive at the alleyway at a slower pace. Her left leg's weakness isn't her reason.

Jekos opens the vehicle and turns to face her. "Are you coming?"

"I have other matters to attend to and will be gone for a few days. I've informed Rithu. He has a soulstone and can reach me if needed."

He puts on a closed smile and gets in, closing the door. His limo zooms from the alley, allowing Scalebane to focus on the important task of finding her sister. Her tension regarding soft skins lessens from this meeting. Mastema will take care of Lola Cabello when needed. The vazeleads can stay in the shadows as they have for thousands of years.

CHAPTER 7
FULL CIRCLE

If your enemy comes to your rescue in your darkest hour, are they a hero? It's the question Lola asks herself, fixing her clothes as best as she can while cuffed. Exhausted breaths push floating dust from her face. Blood runs past her lip. The porcelain old world being lowers its tail.

That's no vazelead. Lola reflects on her first encounter with this type of appendage. Based on the eyes, this is the former Oscar. The shapeshifter.

"Normally a thank you would be in order," the being speaks, its voice devoid of any trace of a Polish accent. The tone is lethargic and monotonous, lacking wakefulness.

Lola swallows some saliva, wrapping her head around the scenario. To her side, in the soil, is the officer who attempted to kill her. The shapeshifter is a saviour at the moment. They also blackmailed her into murdering a prisoner.

"Are they safe?" Lola asks.

"They? Your remaining family?" The shapeshifter takes a step forward; the sharp claws on her two toed feet press into the dirt. The eyes don't blink. "Yes. We had a deal, and you did well, didn't you?"

The feminine figure becomes less discernible in the absence of light. Her bald head, fangs, and lack of a pointed nose are distinct characteristics next to the tail and claws. Defined muscles sit on the thin frame without an ounce of fat. The legs and arms are longer than a human's. The uncanny fisheyes are enough to make anyone shiver in fear.

The shapeshifter leans over the deceased police officer's remains and pulls a key ring from his belt. They step towards Lola and raise one key, showing which one to use. A sharp sting radiates from the shapeshifter's form as if they were a swarm of insects over a rotting corpse. Lola lifts her arms, and the Moth unlocks her wrists, followed by her ankles. At last, sweet freedom. This is presuming the shapeshifter doesn't have more sinister plans.

"Your release is a bonus," they say.

"Why?" Lola asks. "After all these years, why the sudden interest in me?"

"The reasons for your life are beyond my own pay grade. I simply follow the order. Yes?"

"Right, like most of you people do. Because of Mastema?" Lola asks.

"Partially."

"Partially?" Lola asks.

"In good time," the other says.

"Were your orders to threaten my family?"

"They don't care about my methods. They wanted Sierra dead and you alive."

"The ash?" Lola is pushing her luck. She's been clean for years and the urge doesn't die.

The shapeshifter's hand slides into its stomach and a slab of skin lifts. They take a small vacuum sealed black bag from within. The long-awaited ash. "I promised you this. An addict can't get away from what they want, yes?" They extend their palm to Lola and she snags the ash.

My family was enough, Lola thinks. She puts the drug in her pocket and says, "Great, so we're done, or are you going to pester me again?"

"I don't ask the questions when I'm given orders."

"Really?" Lola asks. The idea of seizing the officer's gun and questioning the shapeshifter crosses her mind. This Moth threatened her family. It is an unwise move. She is clueless to what the old world being is and is capable of.

She says, "You wait around until Mastema sends you orders?"

The shapeshifter shakes her head. "He's far too occupied to meet. You unravelled a bit in your time, Lola Cabello, yet your knowledge lacks. The Moths' wings span wide as they soar far."

"Moths prefer influencing humans to do the dirty work."

"Best to remain in the shadows when your numbers are few."

Why is she here? Lola thinks. "Partially take orders from Mastema, hey?" Lola asks. She looks through the officer's jacket, belt, and belongings. Cash, paper, anything of value will do. That Glock is suitable. She takes the gun and tucks it into her sweatpants. He has a stack of money in his wallet too.

Lola uses the man's shirt to wipe off some of the blood from her face, making her look less discreet. Her evidence taints this crime scene. Him being deceased with her DNA on him doesn't make a difference.

The shapeshifter ignores her question and speaks. "You would be best to not stay here for too long. Officer Clarkson was transferring you to a new facility. They'll be expecting you soon, I am sure."

"I want answers. It's not every day a shapeshifter rescues you from prison before you're beaten into a pulp."

"I detest dishonest action and cruelty."

Lola wonders if the shapeshifter can grasp the irony in her words. Her unmasked personality is a flip compared to the cheeky Oscar. "If what you say is true, you understand why I am doing what I am."

"I have knowledge of your background and would do the same in your position."

Lola skims the rest of the shed for helpful items. A jacket would be nice. The place is barren, even with the table and broken crates of wood.

The shapeshifter adds, "I look forward to seeing you again, Lola Cabello. You pique my interest."

Before Lola can reply, they pry their jaws apart beside the deceased Officer Clarkson. A snap comes from the middle of the bone, breaking their mouth apart and showcasing a legion of small sharp teeth. Drool oozes into the splitting skin running down their neck. The chest cavity splits apart with more teeth inside, transforming their torso into a giant vertical mouth. The shapeshifter lunges onto the corpse's head, using their sharp fangs and muscles to push the body within.

Hopefully it is later rather than sooner, Lola thinks.

Officer Clarkson is no more. The bone and flesh fuse to their normal place while the shapeshifter stands. Not an ounce of blood trickles their body. More bones snap while her tail shrinks. The skin mutates into a pink tone. Their limbs reconfigure and the skeletal frame expands until the old world being is gone. Officer Clarkson resurrected, naked.

The shapeshifter exits the shed in their new form and Lola joins. The shapeshifter looks at the police cruiser as Lola examines the sunny summer Manitoba afternoon. One glance around at the open, flat landscape makes it evident Lola is in the middle of nowhere. The Women's Correctional Centre is near Winnipeg; the direction remains unclear. The sun is her best bet for guidance.

Crunching of bones rises with the slight breeze.

Lola says, "Are you going to give me a ride? The Crystal Moths have free expenses. If I'm going to be working for you—" Lola turns to face the shapeshifter and stops talking. They're gone. Above her is a cawing crow. The bird flaps its wings, elevating into the atmosphere.

Right, a shapeshifter. Lola thinks. *Animals too.*

Lola hugs her arms, shivering at the fact that the Crystal Moths are watching her. They want her to do more for them.

That's why she is alive. They'll strong-arm her by threatening loved ones again and again. The Moths will use her as their personal pawn. Lola pondered before if they'd pull this card. Those pricks know her family is the reason she is doing this.

The Trinity of Souls, Becky, Michael, and Mom, keep her burning soul aflame. They remind her of her failures to apprehend those responsible for the terrors they've caused. That's why Lola has more than a Plan A. Her clever tattoo is her failsafe if the scheme goes south. The Moths have no control over it as long as Lola can get access to a phone's camera.

At this exact moment, the Crystal Moths are her saviour. She needs to stay clear from prison. Media outlets will plaster her name. Based on her international fame, the rest of the world will watch her with a close eye too.

She walks on the dirt road, using the sun as a guide. She's careful not to retrace the steps of the officer's vehicle. It is near the prison. With her amateur geographical navigating skills, she travels on the side of the dirt road, circling around the prison's general location. Step after step, she moves under the beating star until tall buildings appear as small specks. It must be Winnipeg. There's no other city that size in this area of the country.

The hike along the parking lane is long and tiresome, with sweat running along her spine. Lucky for her, the self-inflicted wounds and the few beatings she took don't slow her down, and she keeps a steady pace into the city. She has double luck today. There is one person who lives in Winnipeg she can use. They had a single interaction and haven't spoken in a while.

The perspiration benefits her under the cloudless sky. She uses it to wipe the blood from her face. Vehicles buzz by on the highway. Thanks to her filth-ridden appearance, she looks like a cliche hitchhiker, and not a gal who escaped prison.

That's the third streak of luck: Lola was in federal confinement and didn't have to wear the classic jumpsuit. For once, life is on Lola's side. She'll take it while she can. If things don't work out, she has that delicious treat in a sealed bag and a gun.

Hours pass and Lola walks into the first corner store she finds, keeping her head lowered. Her stomach growls. She could quench her thirst, too. She has not had authentic food in years. Plus, she isn't an expert on the city and needs a map. Inside, the air conditioning blasts against her hot skin. She marches to the back and snags a water bottle, one of those "hot 'n' ready" hotdogs, a baseball cap to hide her scars, and a map of the town. She drops the goods onto the counter for the clerk.

"That is sixteen-ninety-eight," the middle-aged man says.

Lola slaps a twenty and snags the belongings. "Keep the change." She takes her things and leaves, putting on the white cap with an embroidered maple leaf on it. Ah yes, that patriotism. She inhales the hotdog on the move. The stale bun and processed mystery meat is the best thing she has ever tasted: warm food with a hint of hickory. The water, in the name of God, it's exquisite, hydrating, and washes the blood in her mouth.

The hotdog is gone in seconds. She unfolds the map. Based on the streets, she can worm her way through main drags, highways, and neighbourhoods to get to her destination. Winnipeg isn't a large city, and it is feasible to drive from one to the other in fifty minutes. Walking is another story.

Her feet are sore, and she could use rest. There's no time. The hours push the day away, raising the night. She keeps travelling, ignoring her body's request. The aching system weighs on her from the moment of freedom to the ultimate point where she stands in front of the old banged-up wartime stucco home. The lawn is dead and covered with weeds, like the other homes in the neighbourhood.

You better be here, she thinks, walking up the concrete sidewalk. The lights are off this late at night. She's trekked so far, to her best guess, it's three in the morning. She taps on the white chipping paint.

No answers.

Her knuckles hit the wood with more force, and no answer. She steps from the front door and around the side. There was another entrance, if her memory serves right. There is indeed a second door. She pulls the screen aside and knocks twice.

She glances both directions to make sure they're not being watched at this hour.

A chain rattles, fumbling of a lock, and the entrance swings free. There stands a dirty blond-haired man whose messy hair says he was fast asleep. He scratches his scruffy beard. His grey sweatpants are just as soiled as Lola's. Jack Harris is as lackadaisical as Lola remembers.

CHAPTER 8
ORACLE PAINTER

The Crystal Moths provide Scalebane with a blank cheque and endless resources. Whether she is on the West Coast with Rithu orchestrating ash, or east in Toronto meeting Mastema, she has what she needs. For personal agendas, Scalebane prefers to be on her feet, despite the limp. The Moths wouldn't understand what she is doing.

Scalebane stands on a concrete rooftop across the brick building containing Dasco's condo home. The upper class enjoys expensive lofts made from repurposed historical buildings, like this former bank. Their character gives them an attractive appeal to those desiring material goods rich in history. The alleyway works to reach the black fire escape ladder. An ineffective leg doesn't weaken her other three limbs. She slides down to the back street under the radiant moonlight and leaps onto the ladder and up to Dasco's corner unit on the highest floor. The limited range of motion in her left lower limb makes the acrobatic feat a challenge. She's no better than a human.

The painter's window is unlocked, allowing her to hop from the railings to the accessible frame. Scalebane snags onto the brick ledge with a thump. She pulls herself into the loft. Her boots land on the spacious flooring of the open space, which her left toe feels nothing of, under unfinished fixtures.

Twenty-five feet away on the other side of the room is the man himself. He's sitting on a stool, brush in hand, mid stroke on a canvas paper. He freezes, brown eyes fixated on Scalebane. The cloak, hood, and mask conceal her entire figure, including the tail.

Dasco drops the tool's handle. Pigment splatters sky blue paint onto the ground. He combs his curly black hair with his paint-coated fingers. His knuckles rub the bags under his eyes. A five o'clock shadow surrounds his open mouth. In disbelief, he stands to get a better look. The man's green button-up shirt remains undone. He wipes his hands on the dark splatters coating the black cargoes and takes a step closer.

"I don't believe my eyes," Dasco says. "It's you."

Scalebane speaks in her usual rasped tone, muffled because of the fanged muzzle. "I see you keep your window open as I requested."

"Each day for two years. Every day I wait." Dasco stops a meter away, shaking his head. "It truly is you. So much time has passed. I believed you a dream, a mirage of the muse. Yet, you, the shadow, the Anima, are the one thing that keeps me going, the dark beacon beyond the visions of blood and whispers of violence."

The poetic expressions resemble a madman to an untrained ear. The encrypted words are the truth from what Scalebane has experienced. It's why she is here. Dasco, a mere soft skin, has images of Hell.

"My Anima, why did you visit me now?" Dasco asks.

To a human, two years is a long duration. For vazeleads, a couple of years is a few months. She forgot this minor detail. Dasco has had time to stew in his own thoughts for an extended period.

"Shadow, why now?" Dasco repeats.

Scalebane keeps her identity hidden from the painter. He does not know that she is a vazelead, nor that she is flesh and bone. She enthralls him, for they share the mutual knowledge of Hell that few do.

She walks across the floor, her boots echoing against the empty walls in a rhythmic motion thanks to her condition. *Click ...click, click ...click.* For having such wealth, the painter doesn't embrace his riches. His studio occupies one half of the area. The other has an attempted living room with a small loveseat, rug, matte black table, and bookshelf opposite of the kitchen near the open window. There is no dining room. The bed exists on the second level, accessible by the staircase beside the washroom. There's no electrical glass encased in plastic: the machines humans are obsessed with. Scalebane respects his dedication to the craft without digital distractions.

She says, "You have had two years to let your mind simmer regarding Dega'Mostikas's Triangle."

"What you have told me of Hell, the afterlife, has not left my thoughts. I did not believe you were real at first." Dasco taps his chest where a long scar runs to his rib. "I feared your attack and pondered it. I understand. I wouldn't have believed you otherwise, thinking you were another trick of the muse. But no, the Anima must act as a shadow does. Unknown. You are actual proof while the muse remains evasive."

"I assure you, Dasco, the muse is real, and concerning to me. It's why I speak to you after years of silence," Scalebane says. "This entity is showing you continual visions of Hell."

"For my whole life," Dasco says. His brows furrow and he blinks once.

"I've been following your work. You haven't released a new series since your last opening in 2016."

Dasco looks away, one hand on his scar. "That dreadful day. The bloodshed and terror. I wonder if the muse orchestrated it. The muse doesn't reply, only tells."

"The muse wasn't involved that night." Scalebane stops several metres from the man. "What occurred at that gallery was a massacre by flesh and blood. The muse is having you paint their visions of the past, present or future."

"Do you think so?" Dasco asks.

"That is what we are to find out, Dasco. What has the muse shown you in our time away?"

"Many things, my Anima."

Anima, I am not, Scalebane thinks. The soft skin's belief that she is a fabrication of his inner soul carries no harm. If it convinces him to be dedicated to her, she will humour his nonsense.

Dasco extends his arm, revealing the portion of the loft filled with stacks of paintings against the brick wall. Next to the paintings, shelves hold tools and supplies for the painter: rolling paper, canvases, paint, and brushes.

"You can look at them. Please. I have so many questions for you. Stay as long as you wish. I desire to speak to a soul, for I am going mad in the studio since I lost my dear husband Erol."

"Erol Terzi," Scalebane says.

"Have you spoken to him?" the other asks.

Such a naïve man, she thinks, recalling the hateful sneer Erol had on his face as her claws crushed his esophagus. Yes, Scalebane once knew Erol Terzi. This is the same Erol Terzi that Mastema mentioned. These are details Dasco fails to know, and never will.

She answers, "No. I have not. As I said, I knew Erol while he was alive."

"But you are from the afterlife!" Dasco shouts. "The inner self piercing past physical space. How have you not seen him?"

"You must control your temper. There are more realms than the single Hell you painted, Dasco. Billions of souls reside outside the mortal realm. Your people's history showcases various versions of eternity, with many names." She swings her one arm out, reaching for the stars. "Few hold a sliver of truth. Your kind abandon your previous ways, far beyond the last war before the old world's collapse. The days of shining knights in armour, catapults, and horses are long gone. Glass towers replaced castles. Archers with gunmen. Metal shielding is camouflage gear and suits. Transportation is gas and electricity, retiring the hooved beast. Soft skins have mastered the oceans, the land, and gone airborne with advanced technology stemming from the industrial age. You are the one species who has flourished since the collapse and were so willing to forget the rich world you came from."

She takes a deep breath, gathering her composure. Dasco clears his throat and stands straight.

He speaks, "I haven't forgotten your teachings, Shadow. Nor the muse's visions of a lost past. Yet I cannot deny that this realm, or the one Hell I paint, exists. To think there are two more? I pray Erol is not in any of them and instead is thriving in some form of nirvana that I have not seen. You know I didn't take his last name? I had too much pride, protecting my precious art career. I couldn't change names. I should have. But I couldn't."

"I cannot answer what happens to us once we die," Scalebane says. *There's one truth for you*, she thinks. She doesn't grasp her own soul, birthing from the land of the damned and returning to the living. She continues, "We can learn this together, find Erol and the afterlife. We must understand the nature of the muse. It has its own agenda and chooses to use you. How much longer can you control it?"

Dasco folds his arms. "I can't."

"Come again?" Scalebane takes a step toward him. "Has the muse taken over?"

"Many times. Why do you think I lock myself in here? Sometimes I wonder if I should shackle myself to the radiator and give you the key."

"Elaborate on the muse's nature," Scalebane says.

Dasco squeezes his bicep, tapping his foot. "I fear it, Anima."

"As you should. The afterlife does not speak to mere mortals. Those days have long gone."

"Before the collapse?"

"Yet it speaks to you." Scalebane walks to the first stacks of paintings.

Dasco's work is world-renowned for revolutionizing artistic expression. His post-religionism style moved the industry forward from the days of pop art and postmodernism. The painting in front of Scalebane is a perfect example. It showcases a grizzly man clutching his head in a medical illustrative design: detailed, precise, and accurate to the human form. The man's skull explodes into an array of flesh forming sacred geometry above. If one understands a sliver of visual literacy, they would see that the shapes expand according to the golden ratio, being related to mathematics. Further up, as the spiral expands, are religious iconography of shimmering gates and a dirty blonde woman looking down at the man from atop a scarlet mountain.

Finishing details of the painting contain gold foils and a glossy varnish. The transparent substance creates countless mosaics of triangles, squares, rectangles, and lines. While the gold forms an ancient language. It's one that is unrelated to human civilization. For Scalebane, it's another thing she recognizes: the symbols of her home Hell, Dreadweave Pass, and the same shapes on the lava rocks from the demon's map.

This is one masterpiece of nearing a hundred varying in completion scattered throughout the studio. Scalebane could spend hours comprehending each piece to decipher the encrypted messaging that the muse provided. Few people understand that art is the single historical record that has survived the test of time. They speak about the civilization of an area, what they believed in, their culture, their sciences, and their state of the consciousness. Artists encode these details into each creation they make. That is visual literacy.

Dasco's education is a technical feat, though abused as a vessel for the outerlimits. The soft skin can transcribe messages into visual representations and tell stories of realms older than what the modern mortal realm contains. This perks Scalebane's interest. The muse is a mystery; she wants to understand her own past, and to learn about her people's partner, Mastema. Why is the First in the mortal realm?

Scalebane steps to Dasco, so close that she can smell his natural stinging stench seeping from his pits. The man hasn't showered in days, and his odour slithers into the breathing holes of her mask, nibbling her nostrils. She is immune to such smells, working with the Crystal Moths. She places her claws on his shoulder, misjudging her own strength, and the weight pushes his bony form. Humans are feeble.

The touch makes him jump. His eyes are wide, a fearful prey. "You are too real," Dasco says.

"That I am, Dasco. I am the shadow of a long-forgotten time birthing from the realm you paint for the muse. I am your Anima, guiding you to your greater truth. You must tell me of your work and what this muse is channelling through you."

CHAPTER 9
SEASONED LIPS

Déjà vu summarizes Lola's moment. Standing outside of Jack Harris's house in the middle of the night brings eerie memories of the first and single time they met. A couple years ago Lola was so young and naïve, and fearful of this man. He appears smaller, Lola's height, and thinner.

"Jamie?" Jack asks. Hearing the name gives her the warmth of nostalgia. It was her alias she used on her fake ID before prison. Jack rubs his eyes and blinks, unsure if he is dreaming. "No way. You are her."

"In the flesh. In the news. Whatever." Lola squeezes her arms. It irritates her wounds. "You gonna let a girl in?"

Jack steps to the side, shaking his head. "Uh, Yeah. Sorry. Christ, it's so early."

Lola enters, and Jack locks the door. Relief floods her, no longer on edge, wondering if a cop car will pull up and drag her to the prison. She says, "I sure do. I wouldn't have come here if I had other options."

"Yeah, I figured. It's not like I know who you are. I mean, I see on the news."

"People do. At least the version of me on their fabricated story."

He rubs his face again. "I went to your site. Man, watching that video of you in Edmonton with your friends being killed. Fucked."

"Yep, fucked." Lola has discussed her actions countless times since 2014, running from the cops and chasing the Moths for clues, leading to the arrest in 2016, and two years in prison. Unlocking the true history of the past, the old world, with the help of the damn balancer Synarion is her secret to keep, for now. She's tired of talking about it and thinking of it. The Trinity of Souls blazes her existence.

Jack steps from the dirt-covered mudroom to the blue-and-white tiled kitchen, flicking the light on. "Looks like you got the shit kicked out of you."

Another flash of the past brings Lola to this kitchen. It's as she remembers: a dirty sink piled to the top with dishes. Black blotches, likely mould, run along the white running boards. Filth covers the tile flooring and random splatters of cooking oil speckle the stove. God knows what else is on the baby blue walls. The fluorescent light above has a nice hum to it that used to cast fear. Today, it shines as a symbol of hope.

Concerning Jack's statement, it is a classic moment to utter a foolish statement like "you should see the other guy" because it applies to both Sierra and Officer Clarkson. Instead, Lola says, "You have anything to drink?"

Jack shakes his head. "I don't drink. Smoke?"

"Please," Lola says.

Jack pulls a box of smokes and lighter from the countertop and passes a dart to her and one for himself. He lights his and Lola's before sitting at the small kitchen table tucked in the room's corner beside the fridge.

Lola joins him and inhales the cancer stick. The delicious nicotine swirls into her mouth, running along her gums, tongue, and down her throat. The warmth is soothing. She exhales, face relaxing while watching the smoke rise to the speckled ceiling.

"I needed this," Lola says. "Thanks."

"Don't mention it." Jack takes a puff. "You sure aren't the same girl I remember."

"A lot can happen in a couple of years."

Jack stares at the scars on her body. Her signature bullet scar on her clavicle was visible when they first met. The rest are new, adding to her iconic characteristics. He breaks the silence. "How can you show up randomly at three AM on my doorstep? I figured last time I scared the shit out of you. You vanished in the morning without a trace."

"Yeah, you also had a Crystal Moth hanging out. Any around?" Lola asks.

"Nah. My roommate downstairs is asleep. Separate unit. Deals weed. Other than that, it's you and me."

"Why did you have a Moth here?"

Jack shrugs. "They have the drug supply in a choke hold. Ramon and I chilled on occasion. I didn't know he was stalking you. Jesus."

"How sweet. You followed my case." Lola takes another puff.

"How couldn't I? I have to say, you wanting that tattoo raised red flags. This time? Those flags grew ten times. They say you killed Ramon."

"I didn't," Lola says.

"You killed Ashley Amber and Timothy Shepherd at Dasco Amoss's art opening in North Vancouver."

"Didn't kill them either."

"The slaughterhouse? Those cops and workers?"

"Moths and law enforcement shootout. Not me." *Sort of.* "Didn't you say your place was a revolving door for the underground?"

Jack snorts. "You remember that."

"I recall that day vividly."

"Ash will do that."

She scratches her neck.

"You take it?" Jack asks.

"When I can. Not recently, obviously. You?" *I will though,* she thinks and caresses her pocket containing the bag.

Jack shakes his head. "Can't say that I do. That stuff became so difficult to get hold of. Too expensive. Once in a while some fake synthetic version makes its way to me. It's bullshit. You can't recreate ash."

There's no way in hell Lola is going to tell Jack Harris that she has a full diamond in her pocket. That's hers to use as a tool, not to get high. She also doesn't plan to stay here long. The guy has a soft spot for her and she'll exploit it.

"So why are you here?" Jack asks.

"Should be pretty obvious. I was in jail?" Lola says.

"Oh, yeah. That jail outside of town." Jack takes a puff of his smoke, eyeing Lola from her feet to her facial scars. "I barely recognize you. Prison transformed you into a badass. Pretty cool."

"I wish it was only prison," Lola says. She presses the butt into the ashtray on the table. "What I actually want is to be the same girl I was five years ago, going to school thinking I could get into journalism." *With Becky,* Lola thinks. Poor Becky Bubs: dead. "You wouldn't have recognized me."

Jack raises an eyebrow. "A nice Christian girl?"

Lola smirks. "No. Some Goth with a nose way too high in the air."

"I get it. I was a punk kid. I focused on my tattoo apprenticeship after jail time, stayed mostly clean since."

"I remember," Lola says. "You tattooing?"

"Sure am. People like you and many others who need to be on the down low come here. I gotta pay rent and there's no way in hell I'm getting some regular job. Be a matrix robot. Plus, shops are too formal. It's best to stay here and watch my expenses."

Lola raises an eyebrow. "So responsible. Especially considering what you have here." She twirls her index finger at the filth.

"I do a damn good tattoo. That QR code of yours looks identical to the print off. Just because the OG is botched isn't my fault."

The paper, Lola thinks, recalling the first time they met. Lola exited in such a rush that she left the design with Jack. The man identified the QR code from the heart-shaped square-mosaic collage. It's no surprise he scanned it.

What Jack doesn't know is with the right smartphone app, the tattoo acts as an encrypted key, unlocking a hidden intranet cloud storage. One scan and the digital files propagate across the Internet. Her sleeper social media accounts, dormant blogging sites, and her journalism website would mass distribute the proof she has on the Crystal Moths and the old world. It's Lola's nuke and a last resort if her plan goes south. The facts will be available for the public one way or another.

The collection of evidence she has is immense and disorganized. Her emotions want her to unleash the data as is. It needs to be tailored into a message viewers can understand. People like Jack, the common individual, need to be lowered with ease into the rabbit hole. The way Lola was so long ago. Thus, Jack will remain in the shadows.

She clears her throat and says, "Hey, you have that paper of the design?"

Jack shakes his head. "Chucked it. Why?"

"Curious." *Good*. There's no other copy of the key. It exists on Lola's skin. She says, "It means a lot to me."

"A memorial tattoo or something?"

"Something."

Jack finishes his cigarette, placing the butt in the ashtray. "That's a better answer than the constant lies you fed me."

"There's a lot you shouldn't concern yourself with, Jack. It's better for you that way."

Jack folds his arms. "Yeah, I gather that. You're in some deep shit with the law and the Crystal Moths. When Ramon saw you, he left the next day and never returned."

"I'm popular."

"Hence, you need a place to hide."

"I've come to the revolving door," Lola says.

Jack's moving eyes analyze who the hell she is. He met a mirage of her in the past. Today, he's clever enough to understand that the version of her here is not the same as the one in the media. Therefore, Lola can trust him.

Lola says, "Please. One night. I'm not sticking around in Winnipeg. The law will look for me."

"Yeah, that's fine. I'm curious, where are you going to go?"

"You worry about me?" Lola smiles.

"Nah." His cheeks flush. This is a side Lola hasn't seen of Jack. He cast a cool, tough guy so well last time. He even hit on her. She caught him off guard. Three AM will do that.

He says, "It's dangerous on the streets. The Moths aren't in the news as much. That's not the reality. Stay here for the night. Or longer, if you have to. Not too long though, okay? I'm staying low."

"I totally get it. I gotta get my shit together," Lola says.

She is clueless of what comes next. *Synarion*, Lola thinks. Her first thought is to find the nymph and continue where they left off. She also doubts if she can trust him. Lola has no other places to go on this side of the country, and is starting from square one for supplies.

She has her hidden cloud storage and her journalism site should be online. Her emails too. The first step is getting a new computer and rebuilding what she had in security layers so she can access the Internet. Yes, Lola can start where she left off before Synarion's betrayal.

The thought of her family crosses her mind. She would love to see her older brother's smile filled with crooked teeth. He has that electrician job, so likely got them fixed. She longs to relive his magnetic laugh. That will not happen if she visits him. He'd loathe her presence. Their aging father would ignore her. As far as they're concerned, Lola killed her mother.

There is one other she could find, her only living friend. Correction, former friend. He severed her long ago and is an unlikely choice. Plus, considering Lola escaped, the police will go to him and her family. She's best to leave Donnie Morris and Aaron Cabello alone.

Lola's main goal is to reach Mastema and break him. Her clues pointed her west to the furthest province, British Columbia. Port cities work to import drugs. None of the data she has to date says where Mastema is.

The Crystal Moths shroud their key players in darkness and misguide people via media and law. She needs to find another Moth and do what she did before: interrogate them for information. There are no depths she won't descend to feed her revenge. Murdering Sierra brought her a level lower. The more evidence she gets, the better her case will be when she detonates that bomb. She'll hit the Moths and the old world where it hurts.

Jack's revolving door is her haven. The sense of déjà vu washes away. Transformed Lola is experiencing the space anew. She's not the naïve, scared girl running from the law. She is on a mission, and no one will get in her way.

CHAPTER 10
MIDWAY VISIONS

Scalebane flips through Dasco's collection representing mathematical rules of the Fibonacci Sequence with spiralling ghosts. Another piece showcases sacred geometric circles, ranging in size, forming the famous Pi, creating landscapes. The next has a fifth-dimensional cube, appearing like a series of slanted rectangles with pupilless eyes in the core. It's a struggle for Scalebane to process.

Dasco stands beside her, hands cupped behind his back. He taps his foot, eager to hear her thoughts.

She keeps examining the pieces. Mixed mediums make up a single row of canvases covered in reds and blacks. They come together to create mosaics of shapes and patterns, resulting in a sole dominant image. The major forms are symbolic religious icons: a crimson wolf, a hand, circles forming a sun. One work creates the infamous red landscape with scarlet rain and black clouds. It makes her eyelid twitch.

The further Scalebane explores, the more abstract the paintings are. They pay tribute to hieroglyphics and stone carvings of ancient times. Characterized versions of horned beings with forked tongues dance below beautiful, muscular humanoids made of light. Demons and gods. These fantastical entities together form a full collage of the planet Earth. His work is impressive, and Scalebane needs to decrypt it.

The art strikes an emotion in Scalebane. This isn't the usual hate fabricating her common state. It's fear. The canvases are windows into her childhood. They remind her of what she, her sister, and her mother went through.

Dasco rubs his hands together. "My Anima, those are much older ones. The muse shows me new things."

"The muse doesn't show you this red world anymore?" Scalebane asks. *What could be more than the horrors of Dreadweave Pass?* she thinks.

"No. It's different. The muse guides me anew with colours! I can't tell you how many times I've had to buy shades of red. I am so done with that hue." He laughs. "It is of little importance to you. It's refreshing to work in a fresh palette." He waves at Scalebane. "Come."

He takes her to the other side of the room, by his drafting table, where several of his works are in progress. A two-meter canvas rests on the surface, while four, in various stages of completion, rest on the floor. Beside them are a trio of finished paintings against the brick wall. These three showcase cosmic space and silhouette entities in blues, purples, and neon turquoise. Based on the vibrant tone and sheen, the soft skin uses oil paints.

"What is this, Dasco?" Scalebane asks, kneeling to inspect the first completed one. The monstrous canvases are four inches taller than her, and a head taller than Dasco.

"I am figuring that out." Dasco folds his arms and bites his fingers.

The art is a sharp turn from his usual works. It appears illustrative with intense details, minus a few interesting graphic compilations at the top and bottom. At the footer is a triangle with three burning flames at each point connected by red lines. Above is a skeleton laying sideways with a radiating light rising from its bones. Higher is a vast black ocean with a large pillar-like mountain in the centre of the painting. A wide plateau rests on the highest point, making the column resemble a nail. Above is a spiralling vortex with thunder and lightning. Ghastly faces and hands reach through the clouds. Further above is the base of a golden gate to the edge of the canvas. Partial circles cover the upper edges.

Her claw reaches for the triangle at the bottom edges. *Dega'Mostikas's Three Hells*, Scalebane thinks. She pauses at the far left flaming point, made of the deep red. "The muse is showing you a broader picture of the afterlife," she says, rising.

"It's their home," Dasco says.

Scalebane glares at the central rocky pillar and plateau. "What do you mean?"

"It chants in my mind through phrases, or single words. Then it blasts me with visuals, distorting my entire view. The ones of this, Dreadweave Pass you speak of, were horrific and violent. So much suffering. This is new. It's colder, neutral. The voice . . . it's doubled, like two beings talking. It keeps saying, The Midway, The Midway, the End."

"The End?" Scalebane says.

"Of us or it?"

Scalebane moves the first painting to view the next. The rings and golden gates continue at the footer, expanding up, creating seven circles and bright white clouds. Further are glass spheres with a gloss finish. Each dome contains landscapes that are one-of-a-kind, snow, grass, mountains, deserts, oceans, skyscraper-mushrooms, floating endlessly through the abyss. There are a hundred spheres floating, each with different sizes. Some are so small that they appear as a light dot.

With her afterlife upbringing, Scalebane can conclude that the muse is indeed showing the beyond. The works display Hell, the mortal realm, this Midway, Heaven, and realms afar. She flips to the final painting. A few more spheres are at the bottom. A radial spark, like an explosion, projects the colours of the rainbow into clouds, taking two-thirds of the canvas. Peeking through the blast are six-fingered hands made from extra thumbs, and the outline of a bald, grey humanoid head. The gas swirls shroud the details of the being. The one exception is the glimmers of tears running along the face, dripping past them and forming a river ending in a waterfall.

Underneath the rushing water is a naked, pale individual. His form is thin with defined muscles and jaw-length white hair. To a naïve human, this would look like a man. To Scalebane, this painted figure represents The First.

Mastema.

At the top of the painting is a dark spot. The splattered nature of the brush strokes says the addition is intentional. Its blackness sucks Scalebane in. No sheen reflects from this area, unlike the rest of the artwork. It's a special pigment absorbing light that contradicts the piece.

Scalebane blinks, pulling herself from the darkness. "These three are your newest?"

Dasco nods. "At the moment. I think the muse wants me to combine them and the one in progress. You can see I had a few smaller concepts, attempting to transcribe whatever it's been showing me." He grabs two incomplete foot-sized works representing the initial ideas of the final paintings.

"What have you been working on?" Scalebane walks to the drafting board. The blank canvas contains blazing blue and white ovals with midnight smoke around it.

"Its presence is far stronger with this painting," the other says.

"Describe it to me, Dasco."

"With this paining it keeps repeating the word, *look*, over and over. I witness these burning eyes while my vision turns to black. I take a step closer, and it pulls away before I can see any more. It's frustrating." He points to the completed canvases. "With these, it was like a drug, You know? Psychedelics have a way of transcending you beyond the limited view of the world and help you get a better sense of how the universe connects. The visions from the muse were similar to that, and painting these three was easy. My Anima, do you think this muse is from life after death?"

Scalebane folds her arms. "Without a doubt."

Dasco removes the final artwork from the trio, revealing the silhouette being. "This painting should be at the top of the other two. Then could this figure be . . ."

"God?"

He lowers himself to be eye view with the face, transfixed with the tears.

Scalebane continues, "That's the latest iteration of their name. Where I come from, they're named the Creator."

"The Creator?" Dasco's eyes widened. "So Creationism is true."

"To a degree. The Creator abandoned the universe a long time ago. What you see and feel is not from this . . . entity's will."

"What became of them?" Dasco asks.

"A mystery."

Scalebane walks from the paintings and to the series of red ones of Dreadweave Pass, finding the oldest row. The pile has collected dust, for no person has touched them since Scalebane came here years ago.

"What do you suppose it means, my Shadow?" Dasco asks from across the room, watching her damaged leg's wide arch as if convincing himself she exists. "Why would the muse want to show me these layers of the afterlife? Why does it want me to see it?"

"The muse has its own agenda," Scalebane says. She sifts through the piles of paintings until she finds a four-by-four-foot tall painting. It's a portrait of two humanoids in the familiar red landscape of Dasco's work.

Sister, Scalebane thinks while touching the paint. Her claws graze against the reptilian anthropomorphic being. The skin is white and grey, with black thick scales running throughout the muzzle, the back of the neck, and along the rims of the nostrils. The fiery eyes are identical to Namsruc's with a slow, hypnotic, deep orange. Raven feathers drape from the scalp, acting as hair, resting on the shoulders.

Scalebane growls, looking at the being next to her sister. Synarion. His distinguished purple irises and cauliflower ears are unlike anyone else's. His hair is a tattered mess and both of them wear rugged clothes covered in red dust and scorch marks.

Dasco stops a meter from Scalebane. "What does it mean? I fear meeting the muse, yet I'm enticed. With my dear husband gone, I don't have much else to live for. I need your help, Anima. This work compels my existence."

She doesn't lose focus on the portrait. "There's a reason to strive. Don't give up on yours. We're created to survive. If the muse wanted you dead, they would have done that a long time ago. Do not fear it. You've lived with this thing your whole life, and it is using you."

"Why now? Why reveal those eyes to me after years of fear and torture?"

"I wish I could answer that. As I wish you could answer to me why the muse doesn't show you visions of this." She lifts the portrait of her sister and Synarion.

Dasco shakes his head. "It has shown me many faces from this Dreadweave Pass, or Hell. I haven't painted a portrait twice. Perhaps it wanted to show me the suffering in the afterlife, or that they're alive, in some form."

Useless, Scalebane thinks. She grinds her teeth, body running hot. The veins pulse with energy, raising anger that she dismisses with one exhale. The burning sensation in her leg reminds her to remain grounded. She is mortal and can control herself while in the face of others.

The muse's agenda is not Dasco's fault. He's a pawn. Dasco is at its mercy, working day and night. His efforts are apparent from the countless stacks of paintings and his frail, putrid body.

It would have been better if Dasco didn't paint Namsruc and Synarion. The piece opens too many questions. She waited for Synarion to contact her, for they both had what the other wanted. Though, hers proved worthless thanks to the succubus's map. He's vanished off the face of the earth. The painting explains why—he's in Hell.

A flash of the exploding lava rocks blips in her mind. The demon's instructions to pierce into the afterlife were incorrect. Yet, if Dasco indeed paints representations of reality, then Namsruc and Synarion found another way into Dreadweave Pass. Why? for Synarion's own personal mission of finding love?

A sense of responsibility weighs on Scalebane for Namsruc reuniting with the fool who raised them. Synarion couldn't have known the demon's gate wouldn't work. He trusted the Hell creature. He doesn't trust Scalebane. The damn nymph broke their agreement and stole Namsruc. Namsruc is too pure to enter Hell. Scalebane is sure of it.

My dear sister, she thinks. Synarion adopted them and Namsruc was the empathetic twin. Scalebane was the rage. His teachings resonated with her sister and eluded her.

There's nothing for me here, Scalebane thinks. "You've done well." It's her own personal needs impeding a looming threat. This muse's greater visions appeared while Mastema's and King's plan forwards. That is the warning she must not ignore.

Dasco says, "I've prayed to anyone that you would return and guide me. Before you, I was so isolated. I didn't even tell Erol what I saw. This was my deep secret."

"You no longer have to be alone, Dasco. I'll return far sooner. These new visions the muse gives are intriguing, and concerning."

"Why is that, my Anima?" Dasco asks.

"Pieces are turning. The state of the world will not remain the same for long." She lowers the painting and sighs. "Keep your stamina up." Scalebane heads for the window.

"When? Tomorrow? A month? How long, shadowing Anima?" Dasco asks, following her.

"Have faith, Dasco Amoss. I must investigate details on my own. Sooner is what I can assure you."

She leaps through the window frame and onto the fire escape. She hops over the railing and lands on her three good limbs, claws splashing in a puddle. Staying on all fours, she pounces down the road as Dasco watches, biting his nails, as she amalgamates with the night.

CHAPTER 11
A MAN'S RESPONSIBILITY

The law's natural role in society is to play catch up while the crooks remain one step ahead. This is the classic cops and robbers. Iglesias and Archer are reliving this truth. They watch the news report of Lola Cabello and her miraculous escape from jail. The two detectives' jaws dangle. The reporter explains that the police found the blood of an Officer Clarkson in the shed beside his vehicle; he was to take Cabello to a new prison facility. With a limited federal budget, he performed this task alone. They mention Cabello's violent attack on a fellow prisoner, killing her.

Iglesias's mind swirls with countless questions. Did she have help in escaping? Were the Moths involved? She was silent for two years and then murders an inmate. Why? Back then, the military had intervened before he could interview the girl in cuffs. Iglesias flew too close to the sun. Clues pointed to unfathomable conspiracies of intelligent reptilians masterminding ash. It was ludicrous. Yet, none of the hard evidence found to date explains the Moths. They have plugs working within the law.

Do I tell her? Iglesias thinks. His hand grips his watered-down whiskey. He stared too long at the screen.

Lola Cabello made things more complicated. The wonderful Department of National Defence oversees this circus. Archer is the only one he can trust.

It's a liability.

He stays clear of danger and risking the lives of any other police officers since the fateful day they caught Cabello. Archer reached a level two detective. A couple of years into her new role means she is inexperienced.

What the hell.

They both go for a smoke, needing fresh air after the troublesome news. They stand to the side of the building against the black wood panelling near the bricks. The wind bites, blowing Archer's hair in front of her nose. She is his one comrade who understands, because she was there. Iglesias drops the truth bomb.

"Want to hear something crazier?" he says.

"Than that?" Archer asks.

"Between us."

Archer raises an eyebrow.

"Before the slaughterhouse, in 2016, I met Cabello."

"What?" Archer's eyes widen.

Iglesias takes a puff of his cigarette. "She called me, wanted to build a relationship of trust."

"You spoke with her?" She hugs her arms, dart in her mouth. Her face is stone cold, eyes moving side to side, reading his body language.

Iglesias exhales a puff and nods. "Outta the blue from the card that I gave Donnie Morris. She had to have had it since 2014. Claimed the Moths knew the Prime Minister, too."

"Bullshit," the other says.

"Nope. How do you think I found that phone at the art gallery? The evidence of Ashley Amber wasn't concrete. Cabello gave it to me, like the slaughterhouse. It wasn't my intel."

Archer's face hardens. "Fuck."

"I get it. I had to keep this close."

She takes her drag, and her arms relax. "I don't believe it."

"Believe it. She was in deep and I'm sure prison hasn't done her any good."

"You kept this from me and Beckman?" Archer shakes her head, taking an inhale.

"You would have done the same in my shoes," Iglesias says.

Archer exhales, looking at the bumper-to-bumper traffic across the parking lot that is the after-work rush hour. "Well . . ."

"Well exactly. Being in charge of a case slipping from your hands, with dirty cops infecting our department, you keep things close to your chest."

"But it was Beckman and I," Archer says.

"I didn't want to rope you two into it until it was solid."

Archer lunges forward with a coiled fist, stopping mid step. "I could hit you for this!"

Iglesias continues, "Yeah, yeah. Recall how the Moths took Chen from our cell? Cameras wiped. They have power. My methods weren't responsible, sure. It was dangerous, and that's why you'd have done the same."

She lowers her arm. "God damnit. Beckman know?"

"Nah, just you."

"Think she had helped to escape?"

"Most certainly." *She's taking it better than I thought,* he thinks. "We're not getting the full story."

"We never have and never will," Archer says.

"We were involved with the case for a while. I wouldn't have my doubts that they contact us for consulting." He tosses the butt of the cigarette into the parking lot.

"Time will tell," Archer says. "What was she like?"

"Cabello?" Iglesias asks.

"Yeah."

"Frantic. Ash-dasher at its finest. Underneath it, I don't think she is a bad person."

"They believe they aren't."

"Life throws them for a spin." Iglesias takes his keys. "Alright, that news put me off."

"You gotta tell me the whole thing, how Cabello found you, word for word, boss."

Iglesias chuckles. "How about another time?"

"Deal. Go be a dad." Archer waves goodbye, finishing her smoke, and heads inside while he walks back to his black SUV.

Unlike Iglesias, she has no one to take care of and be accountable for. She will be in turmoil because of whatever case she is working on, drinking until the wee hours at the bar, to no resolution. Living by oneself as an officer is not beneficial to the psyche. The bottle tempts you when you're weak and alone.

Iglesias is too familiar with these feelings, even being a single father. At least he has a place to go to when he is not out late with his friends. With any luck, José is home and safe. Iglesias remembers being young. José is a far better kid than he ever was. Iglesias mirrored the criminals that he busts. He obtained drugs, got into fights, threatened people, vandalized, you name it. It's what makes him such an effective detective. He can relate to the criminal world. He speaks the language, understands their motives, and sympathizes with them to a degree. Unlike them, he got out. Not without his wounds.

The drive from the bar doesn't take long, through some side streets, a major highway, and into the neighbourhood. He parks in front of the driveway. The lights are on. That's a promising sign that José is home.

He unlocks the wide white main door of the modern boxed, tall bungalow. This infill serves well for him and his son. It's not too large and is spacious. Inside, he takes off his dress shoes and passes the foyer living room combo to the island kitchen.

Iglesias calls, "I'm home."

It's a refreshing thing to say each day over the past couple of years. Before, while chasing ash, he worked too late. A teenage boy wouldn't criticize his father for working long hours. It was there, deep under that angst.

At the far end of the laminated wood hall is José, in the bright white kitchen, sitting at the island on the chrome stool, typing away on his phone. "Hey Dad," he says. His brown eyes don't leave the screen. Whatever is going on in that virtual world keeps him entranced.

Iglesias enters the dining room and snags the empty whisky glass from the marble counter and pours himself a straight one. He won't turn into his ex-wife. This is a unique occurrence. The news of Lola Cabello stings his psyche. "How did work go today?" Iglesias asks.

"Fine," José says. His tone is monotonous, tapping away at the text message app on the screen.

"In a couple months, it won't matter," Iglesias says, reading between the dullness of his son's voice. "Your head will be buried in those books." *College*, Iglesias thinks. It feels like yesterday his son was learning to walk.

"Yeah, it don't bug me," José says.

Iglesias smirks. That's the type of response you would expect. "Enjoy the time while you can. Trust me. School is way better than the work world."

José finishes typing and looks up. His son is a mirror of Iglesias at that age: a focused gaze, bushy eyebrows, and not enough facial stubble to pass for a man, despite a year off from being one. Iglesias even sees his ex-wife in those softer eyes and the wave of his hair. The boy adopted her brown hair and her jawline. Genetics are amusing, and Iglesias doesn't care how his son looks, for he is his boy.

José speaks. "I'm all for school. This job sucks. Getting sick of those pallets day in and day out."

"Manual labour is way easier at your age. I wouldn't dream of doing it today." Iglesias pats his stomach.

José smiles.

Iglesias slips his phone from his inner blazer pocket and checks the date. "What is it today? Wednesday? Do you have any plans tonight? We could order in, see what's on the tube. Streaming, or whatever it is."

"Dad, there's piss all on in the summer."

"Well, we could play a game."

"I'm hanging with Hailey. Gonna pick her up."

"Yeah, of course. You two have fun." Iglesias puts his phone away.

José's device buzzes, causing his leg to jump with excitement. His new red sneakers squeak against the stool's metal footrest. Iglesias gets a glimpse of the preview screen showcasing the text is from Tanner, the one friend who Iglesias detests. The brief text previews:

(Tanner: c   u   there 8:44pm)

Iglesias takes a sip of his drink. "What are you and Hailey up to?" He plays along, deciding to give his son the benefit of the doubt. Maybe José is brushing Tanner off. There's no proof of Iglesias's hunch. Tanner may not be involved with the Crystal Moths and his consistent white outfits are a coincidence. Get real. The Moths display fearlessness, ensuring their members are loud and proud. Iglesias has not mentioned this paranoia to José. It is obvious why he hounds him. A father's concern for his son's safety is normal. José wants to have fun, fool around with the girl, get into trouble with his friends, and live through some danger. Iglesias would, and did. He only worries that his son will slip into a world of darkness, and he won't get out of it. He fears that his son isn't as crafty as him.

José says, "She wanted to go to the mall."

"After that?" Iglesias asks.

"There's a show. Gonna check it out."

"Let me guess. Tanner will be there?" The name Tanner seeps resentment from Iglesias's words in a low, harsh tone. He cannot help it. The boy is a prick. This guy is the type of cocky piece of shit that Iglesias would have beaten at his son's age. He could put those pompous, inflated assholes in their place and remind them who's in charge of the streets through a boot to the face. It worries him that José looks up to Tanner and his insincere remarks.

"Probably, I dunno." José says. "It's a new set from DJ Flux Quantique. He doesn't come into town often. I'm stoked. Hailey too."

Must be a good of a show if he's playing on a Wednesday night, Iglesias thinks. Maybe he's a little old-fashioned and fails to comprehend the cool underground music like what his son is into. Iglesias likes proper instruments without a laptop. Musicians that can master the sonic spectrum. They're no different from Iglesias and his team, who each specialize in unique skills.

"You're driving, right?" Iglesias asks.

"To Hailey's. We are going to figure it out from there."

"Don't stay out too late." Iglesias takes another chug of his drink.

"Dad, I am eighteen."

"Yeah, not nineteen. No bars or booze. This show at an events venue?"

"I think. Hailey has the info. Trust me, I know what I'm doing."

Iglesias's face loses its smile. He looks at his whiskey and walks around the island and pats his son on the shoulder. "That you do." With that, he leaves his kid to obsess over his tiny screen once more.

As a father, and technically José's landlord, he could enforce rules against late nights. He could also say, "You can't be friends with people like Tanner when you're under my roof." Iglesias asks himself, *What would be the point?* José has to mature. Cocks are everywhere, and he ought to meet one while under Iglesias's watch.

José has maintained a consistent relationship with his girlfriend Hailey for two years. For high school, that has to be a decade. The University of Toronto accepted him, like Hailey. Other than his strange tastes in friends, he's a good kid. At some point, he must grow up and live his life. Parents struggle to let go of their child.

It's also paranoia. He's worked for the law for over two decades and has seen the Scum of the Earth. People lie, cheat, betray, and will resort to the most horrific acts to follow through with whatever strange sense of pride and justice they have in their pathetic systems. He would hate for his son to be tainted with such evil. People like Cabello lean into this profile.

A long period of dealing with criminals has contaminated Iglesias's mind. He wants José to have a better future. Iglesias wonders if he himself needs watching. He's handled himself well over the years. He has spoken to psychiatrists, taken time off to recover. Iglesias rebounds. Not with his desk job. Consultant bullshit, it's a demotion.

Iglesias retreats upstairs, heading for his office. There's no reason for him to go there. The hour is past nine at night. His job can wait until tomorrow, for his tasks are not pressing. The paperwork gets clogged. Any errors, whether by Iglesias or others, resolve in due time.

He boots his laptop and does an online search for Lola Cabello. With today's fast-moving technology, news is instant. He wonders if there is recent information available. The broadcasting companies keep a tight ship. Ever since Erol Terzi's death, CAMB news strives to stay relevant. They give updates as quick as their reporters on social media sites before gathering the facts.

Facts, he thinks.

Right, the gift that Lola Cabello handed over to him: a detail he didn't want to mention to Archer. He opens his drawer and takes a small black box. He pops open the lid and takes a broken horn. A normal person would see this and presume it to be a goat's. Spinning it around shows it comprises the usual type of material and shape with a rainbow metallic sheen. The difference is Cabello gave it to him. She wanted him to get this analyzed. She claimed the Prime Minister is involved with ash.

Bogus. Somehow, this relates to the Crystal Moths. He didn't have the courage to release this thing or have it tested. The wrong hands could get it. He'd have no cards. His son's safety is a concern too. The Moths are heartless pricks and strike low to those who get too close to their light.

The dress shirt he wore at the slaughterhouse wraps the horn. That day, he smeared a black liquid onto the white fabric to store its makeup. It splattered like blood, looked like blood, found with blood, and yet it is blacker than night. The spike and the dark stain on his fabric are the two pieces of evidence he has on the mysterious drug.

Lizard ash, Iglesias thinks. He chuckles to himself, like some crazy conspiracy nut job, as he types the following words in the search engine: *intelligent reptilians ash*.

"I can't believe I typed that," Iglesias mutters to himself. He takes a drink of his whiskey. His old intel believed in the nonsense. Chen did. His retired partner, Beckman, and even himself were teetering on the fence of lunacy. Now, he fears digging too far into the unknown for the safety of himself and his son, a conflict with his boredom as a desk monkey. Emotions are complicated.

The web findings disclose a diverse set of web pages. Video results reveal "evidence" of reptilian people hidden in drug commercials. The descriptions state a glimmer of an eye as proof. Some reference shapeshifters. There are websites with amusing names such as ancientworldknowledge.com and thesecretrealityofhumanity.xyz and warontruth.org among others. Some of them mention ash based on the preview text.

He clicks on a link that appears promising, lostconnections.net, which states: *reptilians were among us. Drugs, crime, and the elite.*

Before Iglesias skims the page, his phone vibrates in his pocket. He takes the device and sees that the caller ID is from an unknown number. A late-night call would be easy to avoid for a normal person. Detectives should investigate, even if it results in spam. Plus, what does Iglesias have to lose? He has an evening to himself browsing for intelligent reptilians online.

He answers. "Detective Iglesias."

"Hey detective," comes the silvery, smooth voice of a young woman.

Iglesias leans on his desk. He holds his breath, anticipation filling the air. A shiver runs along his spine, as if frozen fingers trace his skin.

Cabello.

CHAPTER 12
REBOOT

Jack retreated to his bedroom, giving Lola privacy in the living room. The last time she was here, she sat in a chair by the front entrance waiting to get tattooed. There's still the green cloth poster with white sacred geometry lines hanging on the wall with the text below it reading: peace.

Cigarette burn marks and mysterious brown stains cover the carpet. That's fine. The couch is what she needs. Jack provided her a pillow and a couple of blankets to stay warm. Being secluded, her cognition races, and her mind remains on high alert, making the rest futile.

At four-thirty in the morning and after walking under the relentless sun, it's not enough to calm her thinking. A car buzzes by outside, activating her drifting mind, ripe for combat. It could be the police, or Moths. The stolen cop gun hides under the pillowcase.

Fearful chatter runs rampant in the distressed psyche. *You will fail. They're coming for you. Family? Dead. You can't rest with Moths near.* Anxiety exhausts her brain, and at an unknown hour, she fades into the subconscious.

Jack wakes at dawn, clanging in the kitchen with the lingering smell of bold roasted beans brewing. Lola lifts the baseball cap from her head and gets up from the couch. Her short, greasy hair flies in random directions. She squints at the light that beams through the closed curtain cracks.

Her nose crunches and her wounds ache with fresh pain from the trio of injuries from Sierra, the self-inflicted, and Officer Clarkson. It will take a while to recover. She doesn't have mystical old world leaves like her former comrade, Synarion, had. It's traditional human medicine from here on out.

"Rise and shine," Jack calls from the small kitchen-to-living-room window. He's wearing his signature wife beater and sweats and may not own other types of clothing.

"Morning," she says.

"Sleep okay?" the other asks.

"Enough." Lola stands, feeling her body ache from head to toe.

"I left some fresh towels in the bathroom if you want to take a shower."

"Thanks." Lola rubs her arm, pushing the drowsiness aside. She leans against the doorway of the kitchen and says, "That coffee brewing?"

"You got it. Help yourself."

"I'll take that shower first. Hey, do you have anything that I could wear?" Lola stretches her tank top and sweats, showcasing the blood splatters and dirt on both sets of fabric. Chances are she has a nasty odour from these too, considering she's been sweating in them for a full day.

"I probably have some old clothes." Jack exits the kitchen. Ten seconds later he returns with a pair of jeans and a hole-covered black T-shirt. Looks like Jack has a diverse taste. "It's the best I have," he says.

"They're great. Thanks."

Lola takes the clothes and enters the bathroom, locking the door. Alone at last, she removes the filth-riddled fabrics. The faucet squeaks when turned and steam rises in the cool morning air. She steps in with her ice toes and rids herself of the chaos. She is careful not to irritate the wounds while scrubbing her thin body. Jail food doesn't promote muscle development. The shower head has low pressure, and the tub creaks with the steps she makes. It sure as hell beats the prison bathing areas where she was on her guard. Here, she is by herself.

After, Lola steals a swab of Jack's deodorant for each armpit. Ice Mountain Mint is her fresh smell. She slips into the clothes, wearing the same basic black underwear: a bralette with a broken elastic and a hole-covered hiphugger. She packs her cash from the sweatpants and pushes them into the jean pocket, and tucks the gun behind her back. Her hand grazes that precious ash bag. Giving it a squeeze, she stuffs it into her bralette. Baseball cap on, she leaves the room fresh.

Jack isn't in the kitchen. Rhythmic typing on a keyboard comes from further in the hall. A mug sits beside the fresh pot of coffee. She checks the cup to make sure it is empty and pours herself a cup of brew. A criminal can't be too careful about suspicious drugs. A second thought: it would be easier to poison the coffee itself. Jack wouldn't dare. Paranoia eats her mind.

Time to strategize. She needs her digital belongings and must decide how to proceed with the Crystal Moths. A lot has changed in a couple of years. Prison had the odd newspaper, and some inmates shared their TV with recorded news reports from CAMB. It gave her a small glimpse into the true world.

Getting more cash is her initial move. Her pocket stack won't last. She chugs the caffeine and pours herself another, waking up. Coffee has never tasted so good with its strong essence and a hint of sweetness that comes through in the aftertaste. It has a moderate acidity, with a pleasing bitterness that enlivens her taste buds. The roast's depth and aroma's complex nature enhances the flavour. She could get lost in it. The drink is a drug. So are reptile scales.

Lola walks through the hall and into the spare room, leaning against the doorway. Jack sits in an office chair beside a black desk with chips in it, showcasing the cheap particle board underneath. He's surfing on his laptop, slouched, cruising through a news website with Lola's name and mugshot featured.

"That didn't take long," Lola says.

Jack nods.

"I won't overstay."

"It's cool. There's no way they would come looking for you here."

"What makes you so sure?"

"Like I've said, I have no ties to the Crystal Moths. I help those that need it in the underground, staying low. Speaking of which, I have a client later this afternoon. You can chill in this room if you'd like. Use the computer to figure whatever the hell you need to do."

"Thanks," Lola says. "Look, from the world I've been in for the past while, support don't come from nowhere. People have agendas. What's your deal?"

Jack turns from the screen and sips on his coffee, looking at her. He says, "Like I said, I got a soft spot for girls in over their head."

"You're not expecting favours, are you?" Lola asks.

Jack laughs. "Like a fuck? Nah. I think you're a girl who got wrapped up in the wrong mix." He bites his lip and raises his open palms. "I mean, unless you're offering?"

She folds her arms. "Not a chance. Don't double cross me, got it? I'm not the same person you met that last time."

"Hey, I prefer not to burn bridges." Jack stands, taking his coffee and a printed design of some tattoo comprising three skulls. He stops by the doorway. "Consider this an act of goodwill. There are authentic people out there."

"Goodwill? Like last time?" Lola says.

Jack winks at her and heads to the kitchen, leaving Lola alone. She sighs, continuing to not believe him.

At the desk, she sips her coffee and cruises through the Winnipeg Sun website Jack opened. Beside Lola's mugshot is the headline: BREAKING NEWS CRIMINAL LOLA CABELLO ESCAPES PRISON.

Lola clicks the article link and skims the first few lines:

Law enforcement has issued a statement late last night that convicted criminal Lola Cabello has escaped during a transfer process from the Women's Correctional Centre outside of town. She is at large and the police consider her to be highly dangerous. Do not approach her, and share any information with the authorities.

She was to relocate prisons after a violent outbreak resulting in the death of a fellow inmate named Sierra Palacio. Palacio was a Crystal Moth drug dealer. Police believe that instigated the attack with Cabello, who has a history of assaulting anyone with relation to the gang.

Lola Cabello's last known location was along Saskatchewan Ave. Officer Clarkson was taking her to a temporary holding placement in Winnipeg downtown. Lola Cabello attacked Officer Clarkson during the drive and escaped. Police found his blood in a shed on a range road. The body is missing.

No other information is available.

Lola takes a drink and thinks, *Great.* She's best to stay low until she can find means of transportation. Guaranteed people witnessed her walking along the highway and in neighbourhoods. She prays to anyone listening that no one saw her after the sunset. A part of her ponders why the shapeshifter didn't pretend that Officer Clarkson was alive if they could morph into them. It would simplify things. The Moths aren't her allies. Too many useless thoughts. She must move onwards.

Time in prison doesn't offer the Internet and her eyes wander to the next news report. The headline catches her mid-sip of her coffee. It reads: ASH-DASHERS EXPERIENCE PERMANENT STERILIZATION.

She clicks the article to inspect the first lines, not wanting to get sidetracked.

Osteo-ashderm hit the Canadian streets in the summer of 2016 and branched out to the rest of North America. Its initial boom caught the world off guard because of the illicit substance users and the terrible recovery period. The government issued warnings regarding the dangerous drug. Addicts of the substance experienced a range of side effects, with the latest being the permanent sterilization of the reproductive organs. The impacts are more widespread in women than men with no known treatment.

Renowned bioengineering scientist Dr. Lang uncovered the unfortunate news with his research company, Manageficient Enterprises, after a comprehensive study of two years. They focus on biological modifications . . .

Lola stops reading, feeling a strange sinking sensation in the pit of her gut. She has no desire for kids. Her life cannot allow it. But Ash took the choice from her, dragging her into emptiness. Pregnancy should be her choice. No one forced her to keep taking the drug. That was Lola's doing.

Good job, idiot, Lola thinks. What other news has she missed? Should she mourn for the children she will never have? Her feelings tell her she should. Ash can numb those.

Priorities push aside nonsense with an elongated exhale, telling her to focus on other means: her website. It should have stood the test of time. Even without security maintenance and upkeep, she built it well. She types in the address and the page loads in its familiar black and grey background.

This is a minor victory, better than the sterilization. Raging hackers didn't crash the site. Thankfully, she paid well in advance to keep the hosting. Cloud mirror servers protect the source from clever web users wanting to inject malicious code through back entrances.

Her last update was from 2016, posting that she was gathering evidence on the Crystal Moths. This was before she fed Chen to the police, plummeted into the rabbit hole, became hooked on ash, met Synarion, learned of vazeleads, Mastema, and gave a succubus's horn to Detective Iglesias. So much has changed since and she has new proof to share.

Speaking of which, Lola loads a secondary browser, a Tor Browser, to access the dark web. It's no surprise Jack has the software. He's a clever boy. This program lets her navigate to her hidden intranet cloud storage containing her data. Lola can find her main email, and even the payment gateway she uses to collect donations on her site from generous users who believe in her.

First step: check if Jack has a VPN, virtual private network, to hide the IP address of the Internet connection. A search through the computer reveals the one installed titled *OmbraVPN* with a swirling black void for an icon. The same symbol with a green light above it rests in the bottom right toolbar. It's activated. Jack's brain contradicts his hick-like appearance.

Second: accessing her intranet. The data needs to be checked. She has the address, port, and encryption keys, yes plural, memorized by heart. The tattoo on her hip can access this if she had a smart device with a camera and the right application to decrypt it. She would have to disable the publishing and have a phone. Her recollection will have to do.

She types the intranet URL, configuring the settings to the correct port, and punches in each encrypted key in the pop-up windows to unlock the cloud storage. *INCORRECT USERNAME/PASSWORD.* She scratches her head. Her memory isn't as pristine as she thought. She retypes each character at a slower pace and hits enter.

The screen loads a file directory. Success. Muscle retention proves true. These files appearing on the monitor are from day one when she first uploaded that fateful video and article on her site in 2014. The interrogation audio of Chen in 2016 is there. It is why she went west to begin with. Notes, photos, and shaky videos make up the years in between, before she discovered the old world.

The videos from her time with Synarion are here as well. They're named:

201611200754.mp4
art_gallery.mp4
barknose_abigaile_01.mp4
barknose_abigaile_02.mp4

chen_recording.mp3

club.mp4

Documents

mul_condo.mp4

Notes

Photos

roadkill-interview.mp4

sewer_recording.mp3

toronto-alleyway.mp4

tweaky-trav.mp4

Unorganized

yegman_becky.mp4

That last file in the alphabetical list is the infamous event from Edmonton in 2014. The one Jack mentioned. She recorded the corrupt police working for the Moths and murdering her friends, Michael and Becky. She can't bear to witness the haunting sounds of the two souls fading away again. She has done it countless times. The fire inside reminds her.

The first file is new because Lola renames them once they're up. That means one thing: her last video before prison was uploaded. A brief flash of the police officer hitting her skull at the slaughterhouse raises a wide smile across her face.

She clicks on the footage to test if it's corrupted. The video buffers with a timer scrubber of an hour. She skims the clip, showing the violent events that occurred at the slaughterhouse with Synarion, the Crystal Moths, and the police. The recording captures gunshots, stabbings, cold rooms, hanging pigs, and even grenades. Bodies cover the concrete floor. The most important part of the recording are the shots with the two vazeleads who were there that day: Lereif Scalebane and Namsruc Scalebane. At the end, in the concrete control room, Lereif Scalebane breaks Lola's arm after she plummeted her knife into the vazelead's left thigh. Scalebane follows her attack with three vicious slashes across her face, giving her the obvious scars.

This is evidence of intelligent reptilians working with the Crystal Moths. The other videos are important too, such as the one with Bark Nose, the walking tree, and Mul, the succubus Scalebane decapitated. The vazelead's voice appears in the *mul_condo.mp4*. Same with her tail and boots. Lola's phone was in her jacket cuff. The mad theory of reptile people is one-hundred percent accurate, and she has it on camera, twice.

Her notes, documents, and photographs while tracking the Crystal Moths are here, too. She will review them later. At the moment, she basks in her findings.

The victor closes her hidden intranet and fires up the website ChickenFeed. It's a clever name for a payment gateway. She logs into her account and reaches for her coffee, pausing after seeing the total number of money she has: *EST. $14,998.05 CAD*. She cannot believe it and blinks thrice. The pixels don't lie.

"Fucking hell," Lola mutters. There is a God, and they favour Lola Cabello, even if she is sterile.

The payment gateway is a nifty solution for criminals, journalists, and the underground who wish to store their finances. These financial assets are far from traditional banking. Below the total summary, it provides sources of the exact monies. She has a mix of the Canadian dollar, the United States dollar, a few creditable crypto currencies, the British pound, and Euros. Further, the dashboard displays a list of timestamps. Ninety-five are from today and yesterday. The other twelve are from 2015-2016 before her arrest. Fans heard of her escape. The column beside the dates shows the donation source. Money came to her email address found on her website. Others are gifts sent to her numerous online accounts such as a vault for crypto, linked from her site.

Real people are out there and they long for the truth. The trickle of funds over two years and the sudden surge into her account since her escape is proof. These anonymous users understand that they are being deceived by the media and their governments. They want the facts. Lola gave the truth prior to prison, thanks to her secured data, polished and published on her site. She can deliver again.

It's time she gives them an update.

CHAPTER 13
STRONG-ARM

The range of currencies in Lola's ChickenFeed account ignites her with enthusiasm. The smile holds on her face, staring at the pixels. She has the means to regain control. She can pay for a fake ID, get a beater vehicle, smartphone, laptop recording devices, proper clothing, and disguises. With a phone, she possesses the power to reveal the evidence with a single scan. Lola will resurrect her investigative methods prior to Synarion. Jail gave Lola enough time to conclude that the balancer bastard used her for his own gain: keeping the old world hidden.

There's no point in dwelling on the fact that he's an idealistic prick. He looks at grand pictures and cares little of suffering individuals. She's not jaded, not at all. She can focus on dismantling the Crystal Moths, and if that includes the old world, so be it.

The first purchase: a brand-new laptop. The process of receiving physical money is more complicated. She can do it through transferring from one financial tech service to another that accepts the digital currencies, buy an extra computer, sell it, and the cash is hers. She will stay at Jack's longer for the shipments to arrive.

Before getting her equipment in order, she checks both of her email accounts. One is on the standard Internet. This address is available on her reporting website. There's a second email on the dark web where transactions and important communications occur.

On the Tor Browser, she loads the web app for the latter account. This is how she contacted Jack back in the day. It is how Synarion found her. In fact, there are so few messages in the past two years that Synarion's is in the top ten from November 2016. Some communications are compliments or notifications about her online wallet gaining extra money. The others are a range of underground service offers through mass spam emails. Filters don't catch each one, even on the dark web. No matter how hard you try to hide on the Internet, the hive will find you.

There's a single new email that catches her eye. It came in an hour ago. The name is one she hasn't thought of in years. The title reads: Eden's Forbidden Fruit.

<0000@wix3d3nbr34k3rkks.onion>

To: You

Break with the Serpent's Tongue.

Attachment: .zero

Eden Breaker, Lola thinks, recalling Synarion's mysterious hacker colleague. It is no coincidence they would contact her after she escaped prison. Is Synarion attempting to reconnect? She's unsure.

.zero isn't a common file type, if at all. After a malware scan, Lola runs the attachment in a text editor and skims the contents. It's gibberish. She surfs the web to locate a new tool for file identification. One download later, she places the .zero file into the detection software and it scans for several moments and states: ZIP.

She renames it to *zero.zip.*

A double click later and it prompts for a key encryption.

Of course, she thinks. The email contains no other information, though she tries the phrases "Eden's Forbidden Fruit" and "Break with the Serpent's Tongue" and "Eden Breaker." She even tests "Synarion" and a combination of the above. No luck.

There are ZIP file decryption tools she can look at. Later. She doesn't need old world nonsense after being free from it for two years. She deletes .zero from the local hard drive as a precaution.

Buzzing comes from the hall beyond the closed door. Jack's customer is here. They will occupy him for the next few hours.

She's bound to this room. That's fine. She can spend infinity online. She did as a kid, in college, and the skills are exceptional when remaining discreet.

Lola checks her public email account for the normies and crazies that use the Internet. This address floods with messages. There are warning signs of storage capacity being capped, meaning the mail stopped coming in six months ago.

Woops, Lola thinks. Not that it matters. She doesn't care to hear from anyone. This mailbox is as she remembers it: fans praising her for her supposed accomplishments. Some of the email titles are:

<albican@24hinbox.com: Viva la revolution!>

<zdmbiun490@fatamail.com: Eat the rich, you hero!>

<joehotguy@youmailnow.com: You've changed my entire life. I got my life together and moved out . . .>

There are the collections of hate mail that don't even skate Lola.

<xxx69.9987@wowmail.com: Rot in jail you whore. Hucker Dime called it.>

<m.k.smith@yopmail.com: Glad those gangsters fucked you up. Not as much as I would.>

<pattbru92@24hinbox.com: God will smite the wicked like you for killing Ashley Amber. I pray . . .>

<tetruppeufreppo-2887@youmailnow.com I'll skull fuck you so hard bitch. That piece of ass isn't gonna know . . .>

The list goes on, and on, and on, with prestige, intelligence and creativity. She has more important things to do than filter through the countless emails. She has optimism thanks to the cash fund.

Returning to business: emailing her brother and former friend Donnie Morris. It's why she wanted to log on to begin with. She has sent both of them hard evidence of the Crystal Moths. Donnie has replied to her. As for her family, she wonders if they even opened the mail, fearing for their own legal safety. Aaron prefers caution, and with sound reasoning. The shapeshifter threatened them. They must have seen the news.

Time to warn the people who matter. Donnie first, then her father and brother. If she ever escapes this mess, these are the three she wants to see. Lola starts a new email and types:

You

To: donnie.dube@youmailnow.com

Hey,

Hope you're safe. It's nuts out here and I fear things are going to get a lot worse.

Lola

Next, her family:

You

To: a.cabello@wowmail.com

Hey Dad, hey Bro.

I get it.You don't want to hear from me.We've been through that enough. I'm warning you to stay safe. I'm being threatened by your safety.

Lola

Writing these types of emails would have broken her heart before being arrested, before her addiction to ash. After killing multiple people, witnessing the most violent monstrosities and behaviours, she's numb. She doesn't even need a smoke, a drink, or ash to drown her emotions.

What am I becoming? Lola thinks, questioning if there will be anything left of her for her loved ones. "Fuck," Lola says through an exhale. *There's no going back.*

She curls her fingers and accesses her website. It's time for a message to the people. It's more than a thank you. This is a note to the Moths, to Synarion, Scalebane, Mastema, the old world, and each prick involved with this mass web of lies.

CAMB reported on Lola's escape, as expected. Her posting on her blog doesn't change a damn thing. Sharing an update exhibits strength. It will threaten these bastards with a bite.

She double-checks the VPN, making sure it's working as needed. Plus, the website lives offshore, being pinged to various mirroring servers in multiple regions. It helps distort the signal of her exact location and the website's true server.

Lola logs into the backend of the site, using the same credentials prior to prison. She starts a new blog post and types in the title and a sentence which are:

Snuff The Moth's Death Flame
Metamorphosis plugged in.

It is bound to cause quite the storm with the silly metaphors and guaranteed this information will appear on old Hucker Dime's report on CAMB. For fun, she checks the site's statistics. A massive influx of hits occurred over the past twenty-four hours. Curious bystanders, police, reporters, Moths, friend, and foe are swarming her website to see what she shall do next.

Their entertainer starts the dark web once more and browses through her email contacts to determine if she can find an identity forger. After, she will order a computer and some clothes.

A tap comes from the closed window in the room, reminding her she is in the living world. Lola pauses her search, then dismisses the sound. Two more taps against the glass makes her stand and grab the handle of her gun. She sneaks to the white curtains. A caw arises from outside, followed by another knock. It's a crow.

Or is it? Lola thinks.

The untrained mind would write off the animal as a nuisance. The attuned can read between the lines because the old world is living amongst them. Thus, she hides her firearm behind her back and pulls aside the drapes to see a black bird standing on the frame. It holds a darker box the size of a cantaloupe with a chrome handle in its beak. There's no visible latch or keyhole on the device.

Lola stands by the curtains, clear from view, and pops open the window, sliding the screen, and the crow hops in. It lands on the floor, dropping the package onto the carpet. The bones crack. Feathers fall off the creature. Chirps and groans erupt from the expanding throat. Muscles pulsate and the skeletal structure elongates as the featherless chicken wings morph into anthropomorphic arms with claws. The legs grow. Its transformation reveals a hairless, pale being in front of her with black eyes and the sharp smell of rotting crickets exuding from its skin.

Lola closes the curtains and faces the shapeshifter who snatches the box and kicks the feathers to the corner with their clawed feet. The tail sways, brushing the drapes.

"You can't get enough of me," Lola says.

"I bring you a gift," the shapeshifter says.

The buzzing from the kitchen stops. "Shush," Lola says. "I'm not exactly supposed to have guests. Especially Moths."

The hum rises.

The shapeshifter whispers, "Of course. My visit will be short. Do not fret."

"Are visits going to be this frequent?" Lola asks. "I just escaped, and the cops are after me. Then you appear."

"I understand, yes," the shapeshifter says. "Time is of the essence, and I need you to move."

"On my feet?" Lola says, tone oozing sarcasm. "Let me remind you, that dead cop handed me my ass."

"Motivation has a way of numbing trivial things."

Lola raises an eyebrow. "What could you possibly offer that would motivate me other than more threats?"

"I have a new target for you."

"Great, because I'm your personal assassin." She swings her hands up in defeat.

"Believe me, this is unlike anything else," the other says.

"What if I refuse? You'll threaten my family again?"

The shapeshifter smiles, showing their sharp fangs. "These are orders from another, more empathetic individual."

"A double agent?" Lola folds her arms. It's a further layer of complexity in the ever-ongoing descending hole that are the Moths. "Who do you want me to kill?"

"Not for me to know. I deliver. The network assures me this will entice you." They hand Lola the box.

Lola stares at the shapeshifter's black eyes, which don't flinch, and takes the container from them. "How does this work?" she asks, rotating the object. The glossy metal exterior has one circular glass component below the lid.

"A biometric fingerprint storage box, tech wiz."

Sarcasm even without the Oscar persona, Lola thinks, unsettled that they have her thumbprint. With the crooked law, faucets leak data, making it available for cunning individuals.

She presses her thumb on the pane. The top pops open, containing a fake ID stating she is Roxxy Navarro from Saskatoon, Saskatchewan. It has a clean portrait shot of her, that isn't her mugshot, suggesting it is a doctored photograph. The card includes her height, and the usual stats that come with an ID.

The next object is a set of keys. They belong to a Ford. Following that is a paper clip keeping a packet of documents together. She moves the three items aside to inspect the last one: a metal circular tube with a lid.

"What am I to do with this?" Lola asks.

"Did you see your brother bought a brand-new cradle? It's pink."

Lola clutches the box in a death squeeze, arms shaking.

"Aa---c-c-c-t f-aaaw-st," the shapeshifter caws.

Their spine twists with a snap; the body crumpling inwards, shrinking. The skin morphs white to grey as tiny spikes poke from the flesh with budding webs forming black feathers. Limbs break and readjust into wings and talons while the face extends. Teeth fall to the carpet. Her nose and muzzle stretch with the flesh peeling to create a beak, reverting into a crow. The animal caws and nods at the window.

Lola ponders kicking the bird. Instead, she opens the pane. The bird hops onto the frame and leaps into the air, flying to the skies. Lola closes the window, the curtains, and scoops the scattered feathers and teeth. She stuffs them into the black box. Jack doesn't need to ask questions. It leaves Lola wondering if the shapeshifter causes a mess each time it shifts into a crow. Evidence of her existence would be everywhere. People are too foolish to see what's right in front of them.

It's a meaningless observation. As it is pointless to have argued with the being. The old world loves to shroud themselves in secret and vague actions, sprinkled with threats.

A real thought: her brother. He's having a kid? Is he with the same girl? She can't distract herself. Time is ticking, and she needs to focus on the important details.

Lola sits, putting the box on the desk. She takes the metal cylinder, rotating it, and pops the latch. A beam of amber light flies in her face. She uses her hand to adjust her eyes to its richness and slides the contents into her palm. The item projects warmth onto her skin. There's no bulb or clear illumination source of the bullet-shaped thing. It's as if the brightness itself is solid, held between her fingers. Its heat remains the same as she rotates the object, observing the etchings. Glowing pierces through fragments, forming alien glyphs. The mysterious writings in crude shapes remind Lola of the Canadian painter Dasco Amoss's work. Though she cannot be certain. She's no gun expert and presumes this ammunition will function in her stolen Glock.

Old world nonsense, she thinks while putting the bullet back into its container.

Next, the documents: she unfolds the first paper. It's a postcard of a musical event happening in Toronto. The poster has huge bold lettering for DJ Flux Quantique and silhouettes of people's hands raised in the air with neon lights. There's an address, date, and ticket price. Fortuitous for her, the occasion is on August 24, 2018, a Wednesday night. Today is Tuesday the twenty-third. The flip side is white with printed text:

Dead Men Tell No Tales.
Yours Faithfully, Zero.

I got a new friend, Lola thinks recalling the strange email attachment .zero. Whoever Zero is, they're instructing the shapeshifter in discrete methods.

The next document is a ticket for the event and a piece of paper giving an address to a car lot in town. A confirmation number is on the receipt. Presuming that the automobile is present, she has to get to that parking spot, and drive an estimated twenty-three hours to Toronto. This is mania.

Below that are five one-hundred-dollar bills.

The final document is a complete standard page with a profile summary of her target. She squints, feeling her fingertips freeze. Fire burns from inside her palms. The fuzzy photo is of a pale man she doesn't recognize. The name beside it states: Mastema.

CHAPTER 14
CLUBBING

Lola used to relish as a scene girl in the dark underground clubs, and now she feels alienated at the thought of going to one. The last time she was in the night life eludes her, long before the days of being a fugitive. There was one visit with Synarion for intel. This latest mission is a similar scenario.

A part of Lola doesn't believe the document to be true. The circumstances raise her scarred brow in suspicion. Mastema does screen new members of the Crystal Moths one by one. Ever since Lola released that initial video in Edmonton, the gangsters are cautious regarding who they let into their organization.

To think, this is the man who orchestrates the Moths.

The photo implies a secret agent took the image, capturing the First, because of the top-down angle. The slight blurriness of the shot supports the theory. She didn't expect him to appear so pristine. His angled cheekbones mirror the sharp jawline. No signs of wrinkles are visible on his face. He wears a white suit, as higher-up Moths do. His slicked-back snow-white hair and golden rings make him one of a kind. His skin is as pale as his attire, fitting the description that she has learned from a Moth years ago: he looks like a vampire.

Previous online research states Mastema was a celestial being who appeared in the Book of Jubilees. He punishes for God and as the angel of disaster, flatterer of God, father of evil.

Why he chose a night club to interview people is a separate question. The nature of the light-bullet's engraved glyphs is another layer to the mystery. Lola takes the bullet out again and inspects the warm shell. Her hand should break through, yet the illumination consolidates, resisting her fingers. Squinting, she brings the radiant beam closer, following the etched curvatures of the inscriptions. It generates an intriguing keyword for her.

Lola starts a browser on Jack's computer and types in the search bar: *Dasco Amoss glyph language.*

The results populate with message boards asking the same question: what are the symbols found in Dasco Amoss's paintings? Professors, university students, and art historians discuss the Canadian artist's work in theoretical concepts. From the four forms she checks, no one has a verdict. The closest answer is Dasco is applying artistic flare by fusing various languages into a single, shared variation. She'd buy it if the bullet didn't contain the same glyphs.

How that applies to the real world is uncertain. The more Lola learns of the old world, she wonders if this is Mastema from the Scriptures himself. That would make him the First, the original creation, and is a fallen angel in the mortal realm.

The shapeshifter was right. This mission intrigues her. It was unnecessary to mention her brother's kid because the vengeful fire demands her to investigate. In the distant past, she would have presumed this was a trap fabricated by the Crystal Moths. Flash forward, and the shapeshifter freed her from jail. Double agent or not, this is worth her time. She mustn't squander it if she wants to reach Toronto from Winnipeg. It's a long drive.

She double-checks the documents again to ensure she has the information correct, then uses Jack's computer to outline the trip and jot the directions. Winnipeg to Toronto will require pit stops: gas, food, and caffeine. She also requires clubwear, make-up, and a wig. Online states that DJ Flux Quantique is playing at *Radiate Primate,* same as the postcard, in the heart of downtown. It's a mid-sized venue in a historical brick building that used to be a church based on the curved roof architecture in a search's photograph. With any luck, security won't be tight and she can slip the gun in with ease.

Lola finds a sheet of paper from Jack's printer and writes a note for him:

Hey, I got to bounce. Thanks. Hope to see you soon.

The last sentence is misleading. She has a gut feeling she won't return.

Lola grabs the black box, its belongings, slides the windowpane open, and hops outside. Goodbye, Jack. The hike to the car lot takes a couple of hours. She stays off the main roads, keeping her head low, baseball cap tight. The change in clothes helps shroud her face as cars drive by. She even walks by an old lady and a construction worker who do not bat an eye.

As she waits for the stoplight, a police cruiser stops at the red light. She turns the other way, pretending to gaze at the nearby street. The signal changes to green, and the unit drives off.

Thank God.

The car lot is a block over and is surrounded by a chain linked fence. The receipt serves as her ticket to get the supposed automobile. She approaches the man who stands at the red booth complete with yellow and black angled dividers, preventing cars from coming and going.

Lola arrives at the counter and hands the slip of paper to the gentleman. "Here," she says.

The wrinkled face brings the document inches from his eyes, adjusting his smudged glasses. He says, "One moment." The man opens a creaking wooden cabinet of keys. They jingle as he sifts through the hooks until he finds the right one. He slams the case and exits the booth, walking through the parking space. Lola looks around twice with sweat beading down her forehead thanks to the beaming sun. Nerves make her want to go.

A silver Ford Contour moves from the far left corner of the gravel lot towards the kiosk, kicking dust behind it. The man puts the car into park a meter away and steps out, leaving it running. "All yours, ma'am," he says while tucking in his light blue dress shirt

Lola hurries inside and slams the door shut. The man returns to the booth and presses a button, raising the divider. Lola shifts into drive and heads out.

Twenty-two hours is an enduring road trip. She can stand the test of time. She will make a few stops, the less the better for being spotted. Closer to Toronto, she'll need to locate a store for a wig, make-up, and even a burner phone for a new scheming plan simmering in her mind. Driving is a solid way to fabricate ideas.

First, she exits Winnipeg on Highway One, heading east for Toronto. The initial milestone is a small town called Prawda, an hour from Winnipeg. She stops at a corner store to get a ready-to-go turkey sandwich and a cup of coffee.

Mid-afternoon on a crowded expressway weekday is a different world from the weekend vacationers. Rows of semi-trucks, SUVs, and pickups going to and from work cruise by. An RCMP unit rolls down the opposite way. She passes a radar post, waiting to catch speeders. Lola is no fool, and drives with traffic, making sure she's not too slow or too fast.

The drive gives her time to ponder her mission, gripping the wheel tight with both hands. *What is the shapeshifter?* she thinks, wondering if they're watching her. If they are a double agent, then Mastema has betrayal from within. Lola can use this.

Her next milestone is another three hours, taking her from Manitoba and to Ontario's small town of Dryden. It's too minuscule to offer suitable disguises. Three hundred and fifty kilometres later leads to Thunder Bay. She gets more gas and has a brief break. Winnipeg is eight hours behind, far from the prison, and away from the immediate danger of the police hunting her. The media plasters her face across the country, leaving her ill at ease. A small bag tucked inside her bralette can help it.

No, she thinks and exhales through her nose. She can keep her nerves in check.

Her time window is limited to get to the Radiate Primate tomorrow. Eight hours puts her in the evening. The next town over is eleven hours, meaning she must drive through the night and into the early morning, watching the sunrise from the horizon. Her bones ache, her eyes are dry, and she could use a nap. Too bad for Lola. There are no breaks in the criminal world. In Sunbury, she fills the gas once more. Inside the convenience store attached to the station, she finds a prepaid burner phone. The device isn't required for the shapeshifter's mission, because who is she going to make a call to? It's for her own crafted plan she's schemed on the drive. Lola is not a pawn, performing assassination on demand. She has a few numbers memorized, such as a detective's who risked his life and career to work with her. Detective Iglesias. If he is in service, he will answer.

After a second brief rest, Lola is competent enough to drive for the remaining time to Toronto. Her handwritten directions are descriptive enough to guide her into downtown, where she can find the remaining items she needs. The total trip is twenty-four hours, including the stops and a nap. It's late Wednesday afternoon. If she's going clubbing, she must freshen up and select a disguise that blends in.

Lola spots the closest mall where she purchases a wig, a small purse, make-up, new leather boots, and suitable clubwear. Travel deodorant and mouthwash are a requirement. The cash between Officer Clarkson and the shapeshifter dwindles to a mere ninety bucks. She doesn't mind. It's not like she's planning on getting tanked at the club and she doesn't have time to extract her online currency into cold hard cash without a paper trail from banks to the cops.

Mastema is of the old world and, based on the light-bullet, an educated guess states Lola can't smash his face in with her fists. She needs to bring the gun into the club. Lola has been persuasive in the past. Reporting, and being a girl with common "attractive features," as she's been told, provides advantages in the world of scuzz. To be effective, she will need her energy to maintain a sharp, keen sense.

She parks the car in a supercenter parking lot and sets a timer on the burner phone before taking a well-deserved rest. Clubs don't start in the afternoon. The best shows happen far later in the evening. A few hours go by, and the buzzer hums several times. It's time to freshen up. Lola takes her bag of goods and heads into the megastore under the setting sun. She keeps her cap low while entering the store, heading for the back, often where washrooms are located. The store's after-work crowd of families and couples congest the aisles, forcing her to weave through the flesh sea.

A classic bathroom icon is above the shoe department and she takes a left turn, spotting the wide grey door. The knob's green label reads it's vacant, and she enters, locking the entrance. Next, Lola washes her face, puts on a fresh swab of deodorant, and swishes the mini bottle of mouthwash. No one should go to a club with turkey-coffee breath.

Dolling up resurrects a second nature muscle memory from a ritual of another life. Washing, dabbing on foundation, black and grey eyeshadow, and violet lipstick brings a strange pang of joy to her miserable existence. A swallow of saliva drowns her longing as she places the wig on her head, letting the strands drop to her jaw, complete with bangs matching the purple of her lips.

For the occasion, she treats herself to new lingerie, ridding herself of the sweat-dirt-blood-fused prison version. The ash bag rests on the bathroom counter as she undresses, inviting her. Jail made her street smart. She learned combat from Synarion prior and has gained more confidence since. Lola made it this far while being sober.

The drug's power pulls on her hand.

Her fingers tremble, running her hand over the matte material. She hasn't touched the drug in over two years. It's a steep slope, and she remembers the horrible comedown after a dose and the rising addiction day after day. It provided euphoria, expanding her mind and strengthening her physical capacities. She could sense others with intuition soberness cannot provide. That's its true power.

Lola wonders what ash could unlock for her, with her newfound experience. Time is of the essence, and she cannot be screwing around with drugs. She'll rely on her normal abilities.

She stuffs the ash and old clothes in the bag for future use. The club wear of choice: pleather leggings and a black tank top. Her outfit is modest and unadorned. The small purse is also violet to unify the look. The burner phone states it's past seven PM.

Game time, she thinks. Lola exits the supercenter and reaches the vehicle. She puts the bag in the trunk and stores the ash inside the cigarette compartment. With the key in the ignition and a twist, the engine hums to life. Sweat builds on her palms in anticipation.

The twenty-four-hour drive gave Lola a chance to scheme. She'll work with the shapeshifter while focusing on her prime agenda of revenge. The Moths will pay. If Mastema is indeed at this event, she cannot miss this opportune moment.

She parks the vehicle three blocks from the club beside a park to make an important call. She dials Detective Iglesias. Lola clears her throat, preparing to invoke confidence as the phone buzzes twice.

A grizzled voice picks up. "Detective Iglesias."

"Hey detective," Lola says in her fake silver-smooth tone. The persona helps intimidate people. She's unsure if it will work on Detective Iglesias.

A moment of silence passes. "I didn't think I'd hear from you."

"Yeah, I didn't think I would escape prison," Lola says.

"How did that happen?" the other asks.

"I'd love to play catch-up, but I'm not calling to see how you're doing."

"What is it?"

"Life took a turn. If my sources are right, I'll catch a key target tonight."

"Who is that?"

"The name Mastema ring a bell?" Lola says.

A breath of silence passes. "Somehow you think you found him?"

"We'll see. Either way, I need you to work your magic and get units to a club called *Radiate Primate* in Toronto. Some DJ Flux Quantique is playing and I have a hunch it will reek of Moths."

No answer comes in the other line.

Lola grips the phone tighter. "Look, I'd love to explain it to you. I'm sure you got in a ton of shit for what you did for me last time at the slaughterhouse. I need you to—"

Detective Iglesias cuts her off and says, "Yeah. Yeah, I got it." His voice is frantic, and he mumbles an inaudible sentence.

"It's tonight." Lola hangs up and removes the battery from her phone. She steps out of the car and chucks it into some bushes. Returning inside the vehicle, she takes the Glock's chamber and empties the bullets to reorder them. Lola opens the black box underneath the glove compartment. With a scan of her thumb print, it slides open, and she takes the light-bullet from its chrome container. Her hands shield the beam of light as she loads it into the gun's chamber with a click.

CHAPTER 15
ALL CARDS PLAYED

Fear for your child's protection is unmatched. Being powerless amplifies the emotion, twisting Iglesias's stomach into knots thanks to Cabello's words. His heart makes one irregular pump. Christ, it's amazing the tired organ isn't collapsing. His clammy hands squeezes the smartphone that presses against his warm ear, even after the girl hangs up on him. He doesn't want to trust what she told him. There is a chance whatever intel she has is incorrect.

She hasn't been mistaken yet.

José is going to a venue with rampant Crystal Moths. Tanner intends to be there. He saw the text message. They'll let the kid in without a doubt, thanks to the Moths. It's impossible to predict what type of dangers that will mean to his son. If Cabello is going to the same event as José, there is one undeniable truth: death trails behind her.

Iglesias puts his phone in his pocket. He springs from the chair and heads downstairs to the kitchen island where he last left José. He is not there.

"Son?" Iglesias calls out. "José? You here?"

Iglesias rushes to the garage. The car is gone. How long did he spend looking at intelligent reptilians on the internet?

"Dammit!" Iglesias shouts, hitting the door frame. His heart races as his cheeks turn hot in fear. He snags the phone and sits on the wooden step, tapping away on the screen, speed dialling his son.

One ring comes through.

Two rings.

Three.

"Hey, José here, please leave a message after—" Iglesias hangs up and dials again. He does so a couple more times to be met with the same auto response. Next, he sends several text messages that read:

> (you: Hey, don't go to the show.
> 7:40pm)
> (you: this is serious. Danger.
> 7:40pm)
> (you: SON, please pick up. Come home.
> 7:41pm)

He can't put faith in José answering. The fearful father must keep his angles open. He doesn't have the same strings he did years ago. Iglesias is a desk man and there's no way in hell the sergeant will let him make the tough call with no evidence. He could attempt, and would piss precious time away. Beckman, his former partner, is retired. Archer is the single person who can take action.

He speed dials her while heading upstairs and sits at his computer. He navigates onto his web browser from his laptop, typing in DJ Flux Quantique to see where he's playing. The phone rings. On the DJ's website, there's a large poster as the landing page showcasing the tour. The dates and addresses are below glowing lines and photos of hands stating New York, Montréal, and Toronto.

The call clicks and Archer answers in a dry voice. "You're calling late."

"Archer, it's urgent," he says. *There is no Ottawa date*, Iglesias thinks. There's Toronto. Cabello was right, and it's a four-and-a-half-hour drive from the city.

"Can't it wait till tumorrah?" Archer asks, with a slur. The background sound of a bar, people talking, and clanging glasses comes through.

"Can you go somewhere private?" Iglesias asks.

"Sure, gimme a sec, eh?" Archer says. Wonderful. She's been drinking away her sorrows. Iglesias used to do that with her job too. It's not for the faint of heart.

Iglesias can't sit idle. There's no chance in hell he will find a flight last minute. He must drive and chase his son. The clock shows fifteen minutes to eight. José had left while Iglesias was upstairs. An hour and forty-five minutes passed, if his estimation is correct. José picked Hailey up first, who lives a short distance away. He has to be over an hour and a half outside of Ottawa. José will get to the show closer to ten. Like any underground event, later the better for the scum of the earth who bring danger.

He can make it there in time by speeding, unlike a son. He closes the laptop and dashes downstairs. Iglesias didn't even change after work and has his gun, his badge, and keys. He reaches the main floor and rushes out the front, locking it.

"Alright, you got me. I'm all ears," Archer says. No background noise of the bar comes through the speaker.

Iglesias starts the SUV. "You won't believe who I heard from."

"Who?" Archer sounds monotone, oozing boredom as if she wants to forget her life.

Iglesias takes the phone from his ear, taps the speakerphone icon, and clips it into place on his dashboard. Iglesias shifts into reverse, slams the gas, flies out of the driveway, and changes into drive, flooring it. Tires screech and rubber burns.

He says, "Lola Cabello. She called me."

"Holy shit." Archer's voice makes a one-eighty. "What did she say?"

"She asked for another favour."

"Uh-huh. So she can cause a mess. How did she call you from? I mean, where did she call you from?" Archer asks. Liquor thrives in the bloodstream.

"It has to be in Toronto, where she told me to go. I didn't know the number. I don't know, I answered." *I was bored*, Iglesias thinks. "She informed me about a club where the Crystal Moths are going to be at."

"They don't miss a club, do they?" Archer asks.

"She claims Mastema will be there."

Archer laughs on an exhale. "For real? Where did she get this info from?"

"I have no clue. The same place she gets all her information. Do note that she was the one who gave me the phone after the art gallery, and the one who told us about the slaughterhouse."

Archer says, "Yeah, which led to the deaths of, what? Fifteen police officers? And she was responsible for murdering Ashley Amber at the art show. Don't forget the motel prior."

"Beckman, you, and I saw the evidence. It didn't line up."

"It was a bloodbath, like the abattoir plant where workers, Crystal Moths, and cops alike, died."

Iglesias presses his lips together.

"And we're still dealing with that investigation," the other says.

"She's a menace, intentional or not. She's working with us. Remember interrogating Chen? She gave us that recording." Iglesias says.

"Yes, yeah, I do." Archer sighs. "You got a phone call from an escaped convict. She's dangerous, boss."

"I'm still a damn detective. Criminals don't call people out of the blue. We have to act."

"I know, I know," Archer says.

"Where are you?" Iglesias asks.

"At Brierley's."

"Did you ever leave?" Iglesias asks. "It doesn't matter." *Alcoholic*, he thinks. "Look, it's on the way out of town. I'll come get you."

"Iglesias, I'm cut. I don't think—"

"Sober up on the drive, then we can call for support. It's not like you should drive home."

Archer doesn't reply. She would get behind the wheel. A few hours on the road will give her a chance to collect herself, chug water, and they can form a plan. Assuming she isn't drunk beyond repair.

"Okay," Archer says with a drawn-out breath.

"I'll be there in ten." Iglesias hangs up and flies through traffic.

He arrives at the bar and the SUV skids to a stop, taking several parking spots. Archer is outside, arms folded. She's holding a roof-mounted beacon, and marches to the passenger side. She places the magnetic lights on top of the vehicle, securing it, flicks it on and buckles in. The vehicle shifts into reverse, and they drive onto the road.

Archer speaks. "Okay, give me the rundown. She just called you? And where are we going?" The slur in her voice is gone and the sweet smell of alcohol is strong on her breath.

"Like I said, a call out of the blue. She is in Toronto. Some club called Radiate Primate, a DJ named Flux Quantique is playing."

Archer asks, "She there now?"

The dashboard clock states eight thirty. "Hard to say. Clubs run late, and, and . . . José is there."

"Fuck," Archer says.

"He left shortly after seven while I was upstairs. He's taking his girlfriend and meeting Tanner there."

"So the prick is part of the Crystal Moths." She presses her lips together in a tight squeeze.

"I think we were right."

"Cabello claims Mastema is there?"

Iglesias raises his one hand. "He's been her target from day one. She's been hunting him and working to dismantle the entire Moth empire. Her whole thing is revenge."

"And proving her innocence. Christ. She is clinging to this vigilante bullshit."

"But she is working with us," Iglesias says. "For some reason she trusts me. I don't want to exploit that yet."

"Okay. We need backup, right? People are going to die and there's gonna be a shit ton of Crystal Moths unless we do something."

"Is there any way you can pull some strings?" Iglesias asks.

Archer rubs her brows. "I mean, likely."

"Come on. You're in the position that I had."

"I don't have the years like you. The connections."

"It's Lola Cabello, she called *me*." Iglesias jabs his chest.

Archer sighs. "Okay. I'll get a hold of the Toronto police. The sergeant in drugs and crime will help. Likely. I mean, yeah."

She grabs her phone and makes the call. Archer is sobering up. At least her voice is convincing, and the sergeant doesn't have to smell her breath.

Iglesias focuses on the road, raging through intersections, weaving through traffic. People move clear, letting the red and blue flashing SUV roar through the streets and onto the four-o-one highway. Iglesias has a tight grip at midnight. He hopes he can make it in time.

Archer speaks. "Hey Sergeant MacDonald, look we got some big news . . . yep . . . Lola Cabello . . . she called Detective Iglesias . . . yep . . . that's right, Lola Cabello. Yeah. She called him . . . claims she has a tip that Mastema is going to be there . . . Mastema. Head of the Crystal Moths? . . . yeah." She recaps the story that Iglesias told her without mentioning his son. They don't need to be aware of Iglesias's personal investment; they may put him on the sidelines.

Archer continues, "Some club called Radiate Primate, heard of it? . . . yeah . . . trouble? . . . fitting for Crystal Moths, eh? . . . oh? . . . okay well, we're on the highway . . . okay . . . great . . . probably four hours . . . likewise." She hangs up and puts the phone in her windbreaker.

"And?" Iglesias asks.

"They are sending several units to monitor the venue. One for the back, a unit a few blocks away, and another a block from the front. They'll notify the club before the event starts that Lola Cabello is expected to be there."

Iglesias squints. "What does that mean? The club could be in bed with the Moths."

Archer says, "Well, they're going to be on standby, keeping an eye on the place."

"With three police units hanging around the club? Can we trust Sergeant MacDonald's officers? If what Cabello says is true, with cops there, there's no chance in hell Mastema is going to show."

"That's what Sergeant MacDonald says. He's clean."

"It's not him I'm worried about."

"We have to trust he can pull in the right officers. He's more interested in capturing Cabello than taking action based on whatever information she has. She's untrustworthy."

Iglesias wipes his face. If it gets José out of danger, he cannot argue with Archer. Cabello and Mastema take second place.

Archer continues, "It's early. Chances are it'll be quiet for hours. Cabello will be scoping the venue too. José is driving there. If Mastema does arrive, we have time."

That isn't the answer, nor strategy, Iglesias wants. He prefers to be discreet. Cop cars raise red flags. Paranoia leaches into Iglesias's rational thinking. Who is trustworthy? Sergeant MacDonald, his officers, Cabello? The Crystal Moths seep into the crevices of society. Iglesias needs to take a leap of faith.

His heart pumps against the bone. His eyes glue to the highway. This is adrenaline kicking in. It's a feeling he doesn't experience being fused to the desk. The workaholic is feeding his addiction, nurturing that unmatched rush being on the case, embracing the hum through his body.

Iglesias will get his son. He doesn't care what he has to do. José won't be in a bloodbath with Lola Cabello and the Crystal Moths. Work Iglesias and father Iglesias merge as one potent force.

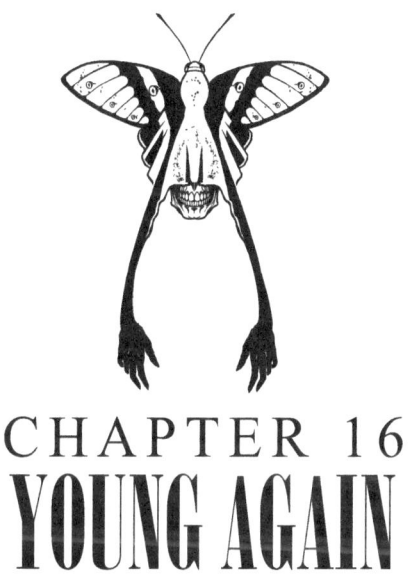

CHAPTER 16
YOUNG AGAIN

Her palms sweat with nervousness, thinking that Mastema could be at Radiate Primate. An army of Crystal Moths is possible. It's not new to her. A gnawing concern within her wonders if the shapeshifter is using her for a more devious plan. She must see this through if she wants a chance at Mastema. Faith rings true. Detective Iglesias is best to pull his weight.

She slides the gun into her purse's hidden zipper compartment, and double-checks her makeup before leaving the car. The ash-dasher couldn't leave that precious drug behind. It has too much power. So, she tucks it inside her bra, ready to grab if she needs it to end Mastema.

Scoping the venue before DJ Flux Quantique's show is crucial for a better understanding of the Crystal Moths' location. Lola scouts the rear of the venue first, walking along the sloped alleyway. The twisted street has pools of water filling the cracks. Several homeless people take shelter in the crevasses next to dumpsters, covering themselves with blankets even in the warm summer evening. Drugs fluctuate temperature. A block over is an incomplete tower in mid-construction, closing off the next street.

The club is smaller than the surrounding skyscrapers. There's a fenced area by a door. A smoking pit. Meaning, once you get inside, there's no return unless you wish to leave for good. It's a pain in the ass during a night of fun. It's even more when you're incognito. There are two fire exits on the sides. Windows on the second and third floor are another option.

She heads to the front, where five attendees are smoking. Two are staff, based on the rainbow tie-dye T-shirts with the grunge text *Radiate Primate* stamped on them. Their wrinkles and beards help judge their older age too.

One man catches Lola's eye, for he wears a black dress shirt with the white tie, and matching pants. It's either paranoia or a Crystal Moth. He stands beside a gal in a milky blouse and midnight skirt. A Moth? Lola will charm the group for intel.

The second girl, who appears to have left the house in lime green lingerie, eyes Lola head to toe in comparison. Both of the assumed Crystal Moths next to her also undress Lola in their perverted minds.

"Hey, any of you got a smoke?" Lola asks, raising her voice to a nasal tone.

"Yeah," says the man in the white tie. He grabs a dart from his pearl blazer, passing it to her.

"Thanks," Lola says with a wink. "Light it for a gal?" She takes a drag as he lights it for her. Lola breathes in, eyeing the group.

Captain Underwear Girl is yammering to a bouncer about a festival she went to with him. The other tie-dyed man glares at Lola. She is new blood, holding the silence for one more puff.

On an exhale, Lola speaks. "So, like, when does DJ Flux Quantique get on?"

The staff member says, "Closer to eleven."

"Hmmm, yeah, that's how these things go," Lola says. "It's been a while."

"Yeah?" asks the man in the white tie. He hasn't taken his eyes off her. They've been bouncing from her face and down to her push-up bra. "Well, you picked the right time to come back."

"That so?" Lola asks.

"First, DJ Flux Quantique is blowing up the underground music scene. We also have my homeboy DJ Flame who is opening. He goes on at nine. So, soon."

Lola smiles. "Wow, you're friends with the DJ, hey?"

He puffs his chest. "Yeah, I get around. What's your name?"

Lola sucks the cancer stick. "Roxxy. Yours?"

"Tobias. You're not from here, are you?" He cocks his head at her.

The remaining four in the group migrate. A staff member leans on the brick wall. Captain Underwear follows, keeping the bouncer's attention locked in. The girl in white gives Lola a once over. She and the second doorman go up the single step and past the wide wooden doors into the building. It's Lola and Tobias. Excellent, she is making a key connection. If she doesn't blow her cover, she can enter before clubbing chaos.

To answer his question, Lola says, "What gave it away?"

Tobias lights a smoke. "It's the way you walk. Also, you're here by yourself."

"You're good." She shifts her stance, rotating her left foot on the heel of her boot. "I'm from Saskatchewan. Not a lot there. Ever been?"

Tobias shakes his head no.

"I wouldn't recommend it. I attempted to get out once. It's too expensive anywhere else. If there's a show, I'm going to make it. DJ Flux Quantique is one of my all-time faves." The lies come too easy, because Alberta and Saskatchewan are similar in economic states.

Tobias smiles. "That's one hell of a journey from the prairies. You must dig his beats."

"Hey, it's probably the only show I'll get this year. Make it count." She finishes her drag by extinguishing it with a boot step. "What about you? Your girls didn't seem too pleased that you were talking to me."

"Sophie? Nah, we're not a thing." He rubs his neck, smirking. "She wants to. I think there are better catches out there." He hones into her hazelnut eyes with those last words.

Bingo. She's roped him in. Lola lowers her head, playing shy while putting on a wide smile. Guys believe they're in control when they are being led by clever, careful choices of physical and verbal action provided by the counter. Men are too bullheaded with pride to realize it.

Tobias speaks. "You? No friends? You flew from the prairies to see the show?"

Lola shrugs. "Guilty."

"That takes some serious balls. Respect." He finishes his drag and chucks it onto the street. "Listen, how about a drink? Pass the time before DJ Flame gets on?"

"That sounds great," Lola says.

Tobias puts his hand in his pocket and walks to the entrance. Lola follows. With a chivalrous gesture, he opens the door for her. One tie-dye staff member stands inside with folded arms. A narrow staircase to their right leads to the second level. The stairs become more crooked on the third floor. Past the bouncer is a large kiosk with wooden window covers open. That's where people show their ticket. After is a flight of steps, descending to the basement; pried black doors lead into neon blue lights.

The doorman's brows furrow as a frown sits inside his untrimmed ginger beard, reaching his chest. "Ticket," he says.

Tobias shakes his head no. "She's with me."

"It's fine," Lola says. She searches through her bag and retrieves the ticket. *Don't see it*, Lola thinks, keeping her handbag close to her. No man should rummage through a lady's purse, even if there is a gun.

She passes the bouncer the slip, and he reads it with a keen eye. He says, "Mandatory pat down."

Tobias steps forward. "Come on, man, ain't nobody here."

He sighs the words, "Standard process, Tobias."

"She looks like a threat?" Tobias says with the smudge of mockery.

Lola fiddles with her hair, tucking it behind her right ear for Tobias, keeping the scar hidden as much as possible. Simple gestures suck men in on a subconscious level.

The bouncer waves his arms around Lola and rips the ticket. "Pat done. Win, win." He puts the torn slip into a jar on a table beside him and grabs a green paper wristband from a pile on the surface. He peels the backing and Lola extends her hand, letting him place the band on her wrist. She's vetted in. A bit of flirting goes a long way.

"Don't tell Dave," the bouncer says.

Tobias raises his arms and squints. "Me? Why would I give a shit?"

"Later man."

Tobias heads downstairs, presuming Lola will follow. Having a date works wonders for her cover. His function is a pillar to return to while she scopes the venue. She catches up with him in the lower level. Washrooms are located on both sides before the main door. Noted.

"That was pretty smooth," Lola says.

Tobias says, "I come here often enough. I have my share of things that security would lose their shit on."

"Fun things?" Lola asks as she hugs her arms.

"Maybe you'll find out later," Tobias says in a smooth, controlled tone.

They walk through the entryway and into the blue lit room fifty feet in length. An empty club, other than a few other people is unusual, making Lola feel like they're in the spotlight. The raised stage is at the far end of the open space. A secondary mobile platform is on top of it with a pedestal where two staff sound engineers aid a man with frosted tips configuring DJ decks and mixers.

To the right is a set of stairs leading to a small lounge where fifteen people mingle in four green booths. The left contains the venue-long bar with a charcoal surface where three bartenders prep their station. Tobias gravitates towards the drinks where neon tape strips run along the bottom of the counters, shifting from pink to green to blue hues. This is a perfect place to shroud Lola's face.

A man, dressed in a white tank top and cargo pants, leans on the counter, sipping a highball. He's tapping away on his phone while scratching his bleached spiked hair.

Tobias walks to the individual, slapping him on the back. "Yo, Tanner my man. What's up?"

Crystal Moth, Lola thinks. Her hunch rings true. Tobias and that other girl must be. How many more are there?

Tanner locks his device, the screen's light showcasing his youthful complexion for a split second, and slides it into his pocket. He raises a drink to Tobias. "Getting ready for the big night."

"Ye, ye." He raises a couple of fingers at the bartender, signalling his order. "Should be busy. Clarisse is bringing in fresh blood, too."

Lola walks beside Tobias, opposite from Tanner. When Tobias is ready, he will introduce her. Once again, she lets Tobias think he is in control.

Tanner says, "I think the big man is going to be impressed. I got a couple of my friends from Ottawa."

Tobias raises an eyebrow. "No shit? I haven't recruited anyone for, like, six months."

"If you want a move up, man, that's the way you do it." He takes a swig of his drink. "Maybe you'll finally get to see him again."

Tobias snorts. "Please. He only sees new recruits and our bosses. We're dirt."

"Careful with what you say, man." Tanner leans over, eyeing Lola. She looks away, playing the shy girl. The quick glimpse of Tanner's smooth skin and patched facial hair says he has to be nineteen. That's a decade from Lola. These kids are clueless to the type of beast they poke.

Tanner speaks. "Don't get too distracted." He leaves the bar to the opposite end of the room, beside the stage. Two rum and cola high balls slide towards them on the counter. Tobias passes one to Lola and takes his own. He raises his drink.

"Sorry. Business," Tobias says in a flat tone.

Lola clangs his glass with hers. She says, "Are you guys . . .?"

"It's obvious with the white, ain't it?" Tobias says, flipping his tie. "Hopefully that doesn't scare you."

Lola takes a swig of her drink. The sweet burn swirls between the bubbling tingles of the soda along her tongue. It's been two years since she's had liquor, and she swallows it fast to prevent her face from making any strange twitches. "Why would it?" she asks as her voice goes up a notch.

A full bellied laugh escapes Tobias. "Girl of danger?"

"I came here on my own." Lola says in a calm manner, as if her words were silk.

"Well," Tobias pauses for a beat. "It doesn't look like you're going to the show alone anymore."

Lola giggles, looking away. Moths confirmed, and one of them is hers.

CHAPTER 17
MAN OF THE HOUR

Liquor, the mind's lubrication breaks the usual thought patterns shielding people from one another, and Lola is no different. She laughs, a genuine chuckle, thanks to Tobias sharing a tale of his days in high school. She is supposed to be undercover, keeping a keen eye on the circumstances of the club.

Tobias continues, "That's when my pal Carter came running through the hall to see what happened to Mr. Wilson. The entire school was watching him rip brown in his pants. I'm telling you, the rage in Mr. Wilson's red face, he didn't see that coming. We recorded it."

Smartphones didn't exist when Lola was in senior year. Flip phones with their high price and low-quality cameras didn't make it worth it. This reminds Lola of how young Tobias is. Excrement is amusing, no matter the age. Regardless, this is an enemy. She drinks, suppressing joy and shifts her focus on her mission. She plays her part and speaks. "Come on, was Mr. Wilson that bad?"

"Oh ya, I'm telling you. The guy was completely militant, controlling his classroom like we were child soldiers. He gave us shit, no pun intended, for being kids. Or us not paying attention in school, messing around on our phones. That's when Carter and I decided it was time to make him pay."

"Laxative coffee, that's a classic." She takes another drink, taking a quick survey of the club. Attendees trickle into the venue. The thick bassline intensifies with the resident DJ playing house tunes to ignite the crowd in the mood for the big night.

"How's Saskatchewan? Must be the Wild West there," Tobias asks.

"I mean, it isn't bad," Lola lies. "The parties are good when you find the right people. It's like anywhere. Avoid the normies, stay with your crew, and escape as soon as you can."

"What year did you graduate?" Tobias asks. He finishes the rest of his drink and orders two more.

Lola's drink is empty too. This will be their third one. *Take it slow.*

"2014," Lola says. It was 2010.

"Dope, same year. We could have been classmates if we were in the same city."

"Imagine that," Lola says.

"I would have asked you out."

He's convinced he has full control, wooing the girl, being a gangster. "You would have, would you?" she asks.

"Hell yeah. A girl named Roxxy? We would have owned that school."

"You're sweet. Which is why I have to ask. Why did you get involved with them?" She eyes his white tie, making her point clear.

The bartender returns with the two drinks, and Tobias is quick to take another chug. He adjusts his tie and looks around before taking a step closer. He's a good head taller. This close, they're brushing arms. The sweet aroma of his cinnamon cologne wafts towards her.

Tobias whispers, breath hot in her ear, "I didn't want none of this. Once you're in, you're in."

Lola leans back, squinting. "You don't say?" Sarcasm oozing from her words, for his statement reflects her own life. She's no Moth. They made her part of their game.

Tobias wraps one arm around Lola, resting it on her bare shoulder. The touch rattles anger across her body to push him away until he speaks. "We're being watched."

Tell me what I don't know. "What makes you say that?" She keeps her voice low.

"You ever go after a gangster before?" Tobias asks.

Lola looks into his deep chocolate eyes. "I've had my share of criminals." That is the first truth she's shared. She leans into his ear and whispers, "You didn't answer me. Why did you get into this?"

Tobias bites his lip. He says, "It's for my mom. She needs the cash to pay for medication. It was the fastest thing I could do. Now I'm roped into this mess."

Wonderful, he's a decent person in the wrong mix. Dealing with Crystal Moths was easier when thinking of them as faceless goons for the crooked rich and the old world. Seeing the human side of a Moth sprouts a speck of sympathy. It forces her to take a big drink to wash away the humanity. The rage must feed.

Tobias loosens his hold, freeing her from his body heat. He laughs in a stagnant exhale, showing unease. "Didn't mean to get that serious."

Keep him roped, Lola thinks. She touches his shoulder. "No, no. That's not what I meant. Sorry. It's just . . . I lost my mom." *What the fuck is wrong with you*? Ash would make her think clearer.

The bass rises, rippling Lola in the chest. She notes that the club is over two-thirds full. It's impossible to hear Tobias. How much time has gone by with them talking? Three drinks worth it seems.

He speaks. "Let's bounce."

"What?" Lola's brows flatten.

Tobias finishes the rest of his highball, slamming it on the bar. He puts Lola's on the counter and takes her hand. Her impulse is to pull away and throw a fist. Her rational mind tells her this is the advantage she's been looking for. Tobias is the key to finding Mastema.

He leads her through the growing crowd of people dressed in their most revealing clothes and sharpest fashion. Skirts, dresses, blazers, graphic t-shirts, and distressed jeans surround her. They also pass Tobias's Moth comrade in her white blouse from outside with another guy in a matching milky dress shirt. The Moths watch her.

Tobias takes her from the crowd and around the stage to the side where Tanner went. A Goliath man in a tie-dye shirt guards an ebony door. He moves aside as Tobias opens it. The base muffles once Lola and Tobias enter a red hallway with a narrow staircase leading to the higher level.

He lets go of her hand and says, "Easier to talk in the lounge."

"Lounge?" Lola asks.

"VIP only." He winks at her.

She trails behind him up the black wooden stairs that take a sharp turn right to the second floor where an additional buff guard, in a white suit, watches a red door. VIP lounge is verbiage for a Crystal Moth den.

Tobias squeezes past him without concern. Lola follows, keeping her head forward. Her date leads them into a neon green room with a haze from smokes filling the small atmosphere.

One more door is to the far right side. A curved bar at the opposite end has a bartender sporting a white dress shirt and a sable vest. Their long locks cover their ears. Violet eyes of the feminine masterpiece tell Lola that is a nymph. Greek gods sculpt their physique with a perfect complexion and balanced features. Looks like Synarion isn't the last. Another lie plastered onto his vagueness.

Suede burgundy couches with curved black wood frames line the purple walls where men and women dressed in white sit.

Three wide and narrow frosted windows adorn the top of each wall.

Tobias guides her through the space, passing circular tables with candles. Crystal Moths sit, talk, drink, and smoke on small stools. He reaches a vacant couch on the opposite side of the room, passing a few girls, like Lola, in their club wear. It's a three-seater. He settles on one edge, resting his hand on the armchair.

Lola sits on the other end, her movements stiff, clutching her purse. She feels the sweat building on her forehead as her jaw tightens. Nervousness bumps her heart in rapid palpitations. There's too much stimulation and details she needs to process. Who has guns? Knives? Are there more gangsters? Are these girls innocent, or in on the scheme? It's a safe bet each of these Moths has a firearm. Mastema isn't here. If he shows, there's no way she can assassinate him without putting her own life on the line.

Tobias waves at the bartender for more drinks, catching the purple-eyed model who winks at him. Lola wishes he didn't order more. Three rum and cokes hits far harder when having no liquor for a couple of years, not to mention driving across two provinces to get here. The booze controls her senses. Her vision: a slight sway. Hearing: numbing. Touch: wishing for security.

Keep it together, Lola thinks. A small bag she tucked in her bra would help. There's no privacy to take a bite. Her senses are keen and she must rely on them. She glances to the other corner of the room, parallel to the mysterious right door. On the ceiling is a small black sphere. A camera. Great. She's being recorded.

"Figured this would give us the chance to talk," Tobias says.

"Yeah, that's cool." She scoots closer, sitting in the middle of the couch.

The closed entrance to the far right swings open and Tanner storms in with a red-haired girl squeezing the hand of a boy with shaggy hair. They look fresh from high school with youthful wonder-gazes. Tanner takes the two to Lola and Tobias. The girl sits on the loveseat, her boy taking the arm seat, his one foot bouncing in its red sneaker. Tanner stands.

He says, "Ain't this a treatment?"

The boy and girl both force a laugh. She says, "You get this?"

"Damn straight," Tanner says.

The bartender comes by with Tobias's and Lola's drinks. Seeing her this close showcases the ears tied together, wrapping around the back of her skull. This nymph kept her cartilage.

Tobias leans in as they both take the glasses. "What were you saying? Your mom?"

Lola says, "My mother, she's not here anymore." She wants to drop their budding personal relation. Being in this room sends a warning sign to get the hell out. That's instinct talking. Her mission needs her here and to continue the fake interest with Tobias.

"That can't be easy," Tobias says.

"Family is everything, and when that's stripped away, what you have left?" Lola asks.

"Live life for them."

Lola nods. "Wise words."

Tobias shrugs. "It's what you can do. My dad left a long time ago. My mom had to deal with me and my sisters, and brother."

"They help you with your mom?" Lola asks.

"Some of them do. They're not rock stars. My bro is in jail. Another is dead. That leaves three of us capable. One of them is too poor, and the other believes Dad leaving is Mom's fault, so I'm paying for the costs."

What's he doing in this mess? Lola thinks.

Tanner speaks, making Lola's ear twitch. "He'll be here soon. Then we can get the show on the road. Trust me, man, he loves his tricks and showmanship. Once you're through the ringer, it's marvellous."

"I'm so stoked, bro," says the boy.

The girl scratches her septum piercing and whispers to him and the boy shrugs her off. "Hailey, relax. It's cool."

Mastema, Lola thinks. She shifts her angle to face Tobias and leans towards him, her bare arm brushing his blazer. The simple tactic entices him to glance at her cleavage.

She says, "Well, I think you're brave."

Tobias smiles as Tanner's obnoxious voice pierces through her seducing. He says, "Come on, Hailey, Mr. Iglesias is down his throat. Being important doesn't grant him authority over José's choices. I know this Iglesias. He calls the shots cuz he's my home boy!"

The guy, José, says, "Damn right."

Lola's spine tingles. If there ever was proof of a higher power, this is it. Detective Iglesias's reaction on the phone makes sense. How, of all circumstances, did Detective Iglesias's son end up involved with the Crystal Moths where Lola is? Perhaps people live in a deterministic universe and Lola is one piece playing her part with zero control.

"You cold?" Tobias asks. His arm slithers over her, wrapping around her waist with eager fingers.

Fuck, she thinks. Her stomach tightens. "Like I said, you're sweet."

Tobias checks his phone, showing that it's past ten-thirty at night. "Oh shit, DJ Flame is playing."

"I don't mind," Lola says, crossing her leg towards him.

"You sure? The show is why you came," Tobias says.

"I think I found something better." Lola takes a drink, washing away the forced flirting. It's bad, and it's working, because the naive Tobias leans into her. His gentle hand pushes her cup aside and grips her jaw, bringing her to his face.

Move away.

Too late.

Their lips press against each other and the taste of sweet rum teases her tongue. A door bangs open, freezing Lola's mouth. Tobias's grasp on her face loosens. The sound in the room silences. Tanner stiffens.

Three men step into the lounge. Two are in white suits, wearing shades, walking with confidence. One is bald with a jutting jaw. The other fashions spiked hair with an air of command on his smug grin underneath the sharp-angled nose. The protruding top lips suggest large canines.

In the middle of the new gangsters is the man of the hour. Golden rings glimmer under the neon lights as he adjusts his ghastly blazer and dress shirt. The sallow skin is whiter than the long bone hair tucked behind his ears.

Mastema is here, crime lord of the Crystal Moths, flatterer of God.

CHAPTER 18
BUTTERFLY VERSUS THE MOTH

Lola clutches her purse, transfixed by Mastema from the corner of her eye. The light-bullet is the first one loaded in her gun's clip. She could take the weapon from her handbag and shoot him. She might miss being forty feet away. It's too significant of a risk. She must get closer.

Mastema circles around the room, looking at each individual person he passes. The two shaded guards stay by the entrance, their hands cupped together, faces expressionless.

You're mine, she thinks. Shy of four years, she is face to face with the being responsible for her decline. Lola and Tobias both realize their frozen state, causing Lola to pull her lips away and sit straight, matching his posture, and wiping a smudge of saliva from her chin.

The crime lord speaks in an iced voice. "Good evening, my fellow Moths, my family. I have to say, I didn't expect to have such an audience for our newcomers. Isn't there some show going on?"

The room is silent.

Mastema continues, "It's always business. Don't worry; you won't feel the pressure after this." He touches his chest with both hands. "Unlike me. I take care of my Moths, recruiting each and every one of you. We're not a rugged gang looking to take over some street turf. Oh no. We have a greater ideology, bringing the Moths to the light. Many of you have been with me for years. That makes us family, building a grander vision."

A few of the Crystal Moths shift in their seating. Not a single person in the room averts their eyes from Mastema. His presence alone, although no taller than five-foot-nine, draws the viewers in. There's a power that radiates from his core that Lola senses dancing on her skin. His posture, hand gestures, and eye contact with the people channels energy.

Tanner whispers to the group, loud enough that she can hear. "This is him. Pass this, and you're in."

José gives Hailey's pale arm a tight squeeze and he exhales through his nose.

Mastema strolls around the circular tables in the centre with no direction in mind. He takes his time, examining each Moth, pausing his speech for dramatic effect. He fiddles with his rings on his fingers and nods to himself.

"Many of you are hard-working, lost in the darkness, longing for that missing light. Our organization is more than drug distributors, or organ sellers, or even commodities experts. We're looking to make society work for the people again. You're heroes, no longer wasting away the precious life you're given."

Mastema moves to the edges of the room, passing the door Lola and Tobias arrived from. He steps closer, ever approaching Lola. She could do it. Her prey is a mere four meters away.

He continues, "Life is a fleeting gift that the divine blessed us with for a short time. Religious or not, we are here. Many chose not to embrace their limited time pocket and waste it with what others struggle to keep. We can hone life, my Moths. I assure you I am the beacon you look for. My vision is crystal clear, shining the rays through to you as you fly to my warmth. Everyone wins."

He stops a couple of couches from Lola, staring at the Moth and two girls on the couch in front of him. The three don't move, faces expressionless. Mastema smiles at them, showcasing his bright teeth. He pivots to face the rest of the room.

"Aren't we having a fun night?" he asks.

A few Crystal Moths nod their heads, not daring to say a word.

He turns to the pair of girls sitting on the loveseat. He shifts to Tanner, then his two friends, Lola, and Tobias. Mastema says, "That's what I thought. Exciting. I see we have a few newcomers in this room. Doing the right thing can be lucrative. This, my dear Crystal Moths, is your power. You magnetize people with our ways. You are each a flare for those wishing to better themselves."

Mastema walks a couch away from Lola. He chuckles and says, "There, that's my esoteric grand-vision speech. Many of you are aware. The newcomers aren't familiar. This is a taste of where we're going. To be transparent, my family is fruitful. Each person has dreams of where we would like to go. Then reality kicks it in the ass."

He takes a deep breath, closing his eyes and exhaling. "When reality does damage us, it shatters our ego. It strips away our pride. That sin, that delicious sin, is so powerful. It leads to wrath, one of my favourites. I can taste it in this room. " He stops in front of Lola.

Lola chokes the handle of her purse. She could do it. He's close enough that it's a guaranteed shot. Tobias is a problem. His arm gropes her waist, constricting her movement to unzip her purse's compartment. There's the fact there are fifteen gangsters in the room. They would shred her to pieces. Not even her cryptographic tattoo would survive the goring. Her evidence would disappear.

When will she get another opportunity like this? The shapeshifter gave an explicit instruction and handed Lola's revenge on a silver platter. It's what she longs for. She's not afraid of dying. Her message is more important, and it's transcribed on her body. She needs to protect it.

Ash, Lola thinks. More than ever, she could use a hit.

Mastema continues his stride. "But, I digress. We have a business. We sell product. Yet, we're more than making money. We're forging powerful connections. Each of you plays an important role in leading us there. The white you wear symbolizes our cause. It scares the weak and attracts the strong who wish to learn of our methods."

A hum comes from one of the Crystal Moths sitting at a round table and he pulls out his phone. He taps on the device and looks at Mastema. The phone's screen eliminates his beard, encompassing the lower portion of his face. "Sir," he says.

"Yes?" Mastema asks. He stops in front of Tanner standing still as a tree.

"There's trouble outside," the Moth replies.

"Well? Deal with it." He laughs, looking at the room as if they're supposed to see the humour. "Isn't that why we have those fancy toys tucked into your belts at some youthful musical night? Certainly kids don't need that protection." He looks at Tanner's friends. "They're too innocent of that."

José swallows a thick accumulation of saliva, emphasizing his Adam's apple.

"Yes, sir," the Moth says while standing. "You don't want to stay here long. It's the police."

Iglesias, Lola thinks. She can't believe that he came through.

Mastema faces the Moth, squinting. "Didn't I make myself clear?"

"Yes, sir." The gangster waves at a few of the Moths in the room. The one on the couch, with his two gals, gets up. Four sitting at circular tables rise. From across the lounge, three more mobsters leave their seats, totalling nine goons.

The bearded Moth marches to the door beside Mastema's guards and pushes it open. Eight follow, one by one, through the lounge. The floor creaks with each step of their shoes until they're gone.

This leaves four Moths, plus the bartender, the two club girls, Tanner, Tobias, Mastema, and his guards with the shades. The initial shock of shooting Mastema will give her time to handle Tanner and Tobias. Spike and Baldy will be skilled. She can, to her distaste, use Tobias as a meat shield. Revenge kills empathy.

She has one chance. A judge of Mastema's mannerisms shows he's taking his sweet time going to each person in the room. He is close enough for a point-blank shot, guaranteeing no miss.

Mastema sighs and heads to the centre, ruining the opportune moment. Snagging a free chair, he drags it to the couches and spins it around, sitting backwards, forearms resting on the head as he leans forward in a teenage-attitude-dripping stance.

"Too much tension, eh?" He smiles, looking at Tanner, José, and Hailey, then Lola and Tobias as if expecting them to laugh. Tanner and Tobias chuckle in nervous breaths. The three newcomers press their lips into thin lines.

Mastema points at them with his ring-covered index finger. "I like to personally meet each individual involved with my family. You can't let strangers into the inner circle without understanding who they are. Isn't that why there are so many divorces?" He stares at Hailey, who strangles José's hand. "Sweetie, no need to be so nervous. You can free him. This is what we are working towards, freedom."

"Hailey," José whispers.

The girl follows the instruction, her hands trembling as they settle on her lap. She maintains unbroken eye contact with Mastema.

"You bring these two?" Mastema asks, nodding at Tanner.

"You betcha. Sir," Tanner says.

"Well done. Young and prime. I can feel the eagerness in them. It's that youthful blood that pumps in their hearts." Mastema points at the boy with the same finger. "What's your name?"

"José, sir." He crosses his leg, rubbing his red sneaker.

He gestures towards the girl. "Hailey?"

"Yeah." Her voice squeaks.

Mastema drags his finger to Lola and raises his eyebrows. Her heart stops, waiting for him to notice anything about her. His gaze holds. The crime lord doesn't recognize her face. His arrogance is either beyond human reach or her foundation and wig are pristine.

"Roxxy," Lola says. Her throat tenses and the heart pumps once more. A part of her is annoyed that he doesn't know who she is so he could see that Lola is the assassin as she pulls the trigger. Then again, they've never met and he must have had his goons, like Scalebane, handle Lola's threats.

Mastema says, "It's a pleasure to meet you, José, Hailey, and Roxxy. You must respect my decision to not let anyone into my business. Thus, I have to screen newcomers in a personal interview, followed by a skill-testing task. I'll analyze your willpower. We have gained too much attention in the past number of years. Although, considering where we're going, we will. Still, we like to operate in the shadows because we have recruited bad actors before. They've been drunk on the power that I was too gracious to give. Thus, tests are required."

Hailey raises her hand, wobbling.

"Yes, my dear," Mastema says.

"I'm here with my boyfriend. I don't want to be a Crystal Moth."

"No?" Mastema says. "It's a thrilling ride."

"No. I'm going to school."

"For what?" Mastema asks.

"I'm taking animal sciences, hoping to help our environmental crisis."

Mastema claps in a slow applause. "That's a respectable and humble career. The world is burning. It needs heroes like you. What of you, José? You're here to do this, and you bring your girlfriend?"

José nods. "We came for the show. I mean, yes, I'm interested. Tanner says so much about you guys. I . . . I don't like working dead-end jobs. I don't like what the cops have become, what they've done."

"Tell me about it," Mastema says.

José's leg bounces. "School doesn't offer much after you graduate. This whole country is crooked and can't do what is right. I don't make much money, the shifts are frustrating. I want the best of both worlds."

"Understandable. Tanner has been quite loyal. Haven't you?" Mastema asks.

Tanner's nods are quick and enthusiastic, mirroring the excitement of a puppy being showered with compliments.

"That is wonderful, José. You wish to be one of the great. We can work with that, interview you, and make sure you fit. Hailey, sweetie, you don't have to stay here."

They rope them in at any age, Lola thinks, remaining calm and unsuspecting.

Hailey grabs José's hand again, looking at him with wide eyes painting concern.

"It's okay," José says in a low tone. "We expected this."

Mastema turns around to his guards, then the two club girls who remain motionless, Tobias, Lola, and to the kids. "Didn't we establish there was a show downstairs? It's supposed to be fun. Fun brings happiness, and ultimately, what else is the point of life?"

Tanner nods. "Totally."

"Go on, sweet Hailey. Dance your heart away. José won't be long. I can taste he is promising. This is an initial interview. I wish to understand who he is as a person. My men will take care of the test. I'm a busy man and can't stay here." He waves at the pair of petrified girls. "You two, go have fun."

Hailey maintains her stare on José, giving him silent communication that only a couple would understand.

José says, "It's okay, babe. I won't be long."

A closed smile rises on Mastema's face. The crime lord's look lingers on Lola as the kids discuss their scenario. "And you, dear Roxxy? Do you wish to become a Crystal Moth, or has the charming young Tobias brought you here?"

Lola clears her throat and laughs. She believed it to be fake. Oh no, it's authentic with heavy-handed exhales. Fear grips her, causing her throat to tense. She coughs, then speaks. "I came for the show and found him. Tobias is nice."

"He is, isn't he? We got lucky with him years ago. Strong boy. Loves his mom." Mastema slaps his hands together, catching José's and Hailey's attention. "Well, there we have it. Hailey, you have three girlfriends to share the night with. You're blessed to witness me in person. Few do. It's a perk of being involved with Moths. This is the last time we will meet, unfortunately."

"See?" José says. "It's cool."

Hailey rises, defeated by pressure and reasoning. Her motion is robotic, not a fan of leaving José alone. Yet, she is a nice girlfriend and listens.

The prime moment to strike is now. No one would have believed Lola's claim to join the Moths. *Now or never,* she thinks. Iglesias's kid is at risk. There's Tobias to think of. He is a genuine human being.

She leans into his ear and whispers, "Keep your head low."

Lola squeezes his knee, and he gives a crooked smile, eyes running around her face, deciphering her cryptic message. She stands in sync with the two girls, feeling sweat trickle down to her ass crack. Hot blood runs through her veins. This is it. The gun is in reach.

Lola runs through her strategy: she can leap for the round tables, use it as a shelter from the other Moths, then shoot Tanner to immobilize him. Tobias, she hopes she doesn't have to. José will cower or run for Hailey. Lola will gun the remaining gangsters. There's the bartender. It's probable she has a gun under the counter.

"Enjoy the show, ladies," Mastema says, waving goodbye. "Your men won't be long, and you can enjoy him for the rest of the evening, my dear Hailey."

Lola strolls to the exit, closer to Mastema, unzipping her purse and clutching the handle in one causal motion. She eyes Spike's and Baldy's with stone faces. The other four sit, staring at the girls' scant outfits. Tobias squints. To her right is Tanner, standing with his arms folded. Hailey watches Lola for some sort of confirmation. There will be one.

Ten steps away from her target: Lola's heart hits her ribcage.

Eight steps away: time doubles with her stride.

Six steps away: a deep breath through her nose.

Four steps away: liberation for the Trinity of Souls.

Two steps away: an exhale. She lets go of the purse string, hand sliding into it.

Zero steps from behind Mastema, Lola yanks the handgun out point-blank from his skull. Her fingers squeeze the trigger, sparking a combustion. With a thunderous blast, the bullet erupts from the chamber. Beams of light explode, filling the room with a blinding brightness.

CHAPTER 19
EVENT HORIZON

A father's love transforms a regular man into the supernatural, who will stop at nothing until their son is safe. Iglesias is hellbent on getting José. He's speeding along the highway, soaring past civilian vehicles to Toronto; though desperate, he cannot let his emotions get the better of him. The father needs his training when they arrive at Radiate Primate.

The drive is enough for Archer to get sober. Water helps, too. She made her calls, keeping communication open with Sergeant MacDonald of Toronto regarding his officers at the club. During the ride, there's no new report from them after ten. Iglesias will be the judge of that.

In the city, the SUV buzzes through the downtown streets until they're eight blocks from the venue. They cannot go barging in, guns blazing. If the crime lord Mastema is there with Lola Cabello, they need stealth and must be discreet with their positioning. Iglesias has to keep his parental fear aside for José.

He brings the automobile into park and Archer takes the emergency siren lights off. Iglesias checks the time: it's nearing eleven PM. They shift into gear and drive to the club, meeting with a patrol unit parked nearby.

Iglesias exits the vehicle and jogs to the officers. He knocks on the driver's window, flashing his badge. The officer rolls down the glass and rests his elbow on the frame.

"Any word?" Iglesias asks.

"Not yet. You're . . .?" the man asks. His voice crackles. He can't be much older than José. *Stop it.*

"Detective Iglesias." He nods at Archer, who approaches with her hands on her golden buckle. "This is Detective Archer. We initiated the call with Sergeant MacDonald."

"Gotcha," the officer says. He shrugs. "We talked to the staff at the front. They said they're keeping an eye out for the suspects and we have been on standby since."

"What about the other units?" Iglesias asks. "The one in the alley and the third?"

"One of them left."

Archer folds her arms. "Excuse me?"

"That wasn't my call. We're staying at our post."

"Fucking MacDonald," Archer mumbles. She moves away and taps away at her phone, contacting the prick. Of course, he omitted that from their conversation.

Iglesias asks, "Are there any signs of Crystal Moths here? Cabello?"

"Negative," the second officer says. She is older than her partner, nearing thirty. "We've been here for two hours."

Iglesias puts his hands on his hip. "You understand that this is a high-profile suspect, right? And armed?"

"Yeah," the young officer replies. "We're at our post."

He's a kid, Iglesias thinks. It's not his fault. The issue lies in the chain of command. If these two saw nothing, he has to take their word for it. "You're doing well. Keep us posted if anything changes." He slaps the hood of the vehicle.

"Of course, sir." The officer rolls up his window as Iglesias walks away, wiping his moustache. The cruiser's window is a third of the way up when a static voice enters through the com. A law enforcement on the other line says, "Shots fired. Second floor, alley window. Over."

Iglesias stops mid step, hand on his upper lip.

For too long, the Trinity of Souls haunted Lola. A piercing bang takes the higher frequency. Whiteness covers the room from the supernatural light. The kick bass from the club below elongates as time comes to a halt. Sound stretches, becoming an unending drone of static. This blissful, extended moment is what liberation feels like.

The deliverance is short-lived. Adrenaline pumps into her system, accelerating time as the ray of sunshine fades into a blip shredding into the rear of Mastema's skull. It scorches his hair, ripping the skin, bone, and plummeting deep inside the flesh. Glowing amber pulses within the wound. The crime lord's body goes limp and slides to the side, toppling onto the ground with a thud. Revenge served.

The shock of the attack on their supreme leader provides milliseconds of space. She kicks the chair, launching it at Tanner. Lola makes a one-eighty, leaping to the closest round table and flipping it over. Candles topple to the floor as she lands on her shoulder. Behind her shield: two guards and four Moths.

She eyes Tobias from her peripheral view. He rolls off the couch and onto the ground. His frozen face watches Lola, speechless, as Tanner, Hailey, and José fumble with the chair.

A blast shatters the edge of her table.

Lola leans over the rim of the surface and fires at the four. Spike and Baldy haven't moved. One bullet, two bullets, three! She hits a Moth in the lungs, and he topples onto the ground. Another bullet whizzes past her. The remaining gangsters find shelter as she pulls the trigger two more times, aiming for the motionless guards. Her aim is true and the ammunition flies towards them.

Spike and Baldy phase from their location. The movement is rapid and jagged, appearing like a helicopter blade. Inhuman. The bullets slam into the wall. One Moth peeks his head out from his shelter and fires. The projectile grazes her thigh, hitting the hardwood floor. Particles fly into the air as Lola's gun speaks. She clenches her teeth as the bullet reaches Baldy's face.

His hand blips, snagging the round, holding it inches from his flesh. A grin rises on his visage, exposing two large fangs in place of where his canines should be. The guard tosses the ammunition and both guards brush their suits.

Iglesias turns to the police unit as the second officer presses her com to talk. "Where?"

The speaker says, "Inside the building. Likely second floor."

"Ten-four," she replies.

Show time. The driving policeman speaks into the intercom, notifying command of the gunshots, requesting for backup. Iglesias waves at Archer, who is on the call with Sergeant MacDonald.

"We're going in," Iglesias says.

"Now?" Archer asks, holding the phone away.

"Officers," Iglesias calls to the stationed two.

"We need backup," the driver says.

"My son—" Iglesias says. *Fuck it*, he thinks. "My son is in there. You can either join Detective Archer and I, or sit here and wait."

The speaker talks again. "More shots fired. Four more, correction, six."

Iglesias waves at Archer. They rush to the SUV while the police in front of him activate their sirens. Both automobiles speed to the club. They screech to a park in the middle of the road. The law enforcement officers burst out of their vehicles, guns drawn.

"What the fuck!" Tanner shouts. Even the three Moths stop firing, watching Spike and Baldy stride towards the group. Lola fires again. The bullets pass through their phasing blips as if they were walking through them.

Lola is in trouble. Correction, the humans in the room are in danger. She didn't think they would be old world Moths. Fangs and lightning speed. Vampires?

Tobias's gaze shifts from her to Spike and Baldy. Tanner and José freeze, feeling the weight of the chair resting on their laps. Hailey hasn't moved. At the bar, the bartender doesn't share the same shock as the others. Her hands rest on the marble counter with the crooked grin on her face. The purple eyes twinkling.

The guards' dress shoes click on the hardwood floor.

Lola mouths the word *go* to Tobias. Warning given, that's as good as it gets. Lola rises from the round table and fires at Spike and Baldy. Her aim is true. Their movements are unreal, blinking from danger.

Run, she thinks. *The back door.* She sprints, keeping her eyes on the guards. Her shoulder slams into a person's chest. She turns, gun pointed at Mastema, who now stands in front of her. No blood is on the floor. A gaping hole lives in his right eye socket. No blood or flesh is visible. Inside his skull is pure blackness.

Iglesias storms to the club. The DJ music blares at such a volume that it cuts through the closed doors, creating vibrations on the wooden planks. It would be impossible to hear a gunshot from here. The smokers in front chat and laugh, drunk and high, unaware of the police. A few stragglers watch the officers, along with the bouncer at the door. He marches to Detective Iglesias, who suffers from tunnel vision, needing to enter that damn club.

"What's going on?" the doorman asks, adjusting his black toque.

"Reported gunshots," Iglesias says.

"Where?" the other asks.

"Inside, second floor. How do we get there?"

"There's a staircase by the stage and one in the front lobby."

"Detective Iglesias," Archer calls out. "We need to set up a perimeter."

Iglesias points to the doorman. "We're going in. You make sure we evacuate everyone."

The other officers join Iglesias and Archer and the four barge into the main lobby, firearms aimed low. The bouncer talks on his earpiece, following Iglesias's command.

Iglesias speaks. "Archer and I will take the rear. You two secure these stair doors. We'll pin them in. Make sure the staff get the attendees out."

More gunshots come from above. Inside, the shots are subtle pops compared to the blaring club hits coming from the basement. Waves of people jump and dance as a single organism, oblivious to the horrors happening above.

"Go!" Iglesias says, taking lead down the stairs.

He pauses mid-step as the shadows on the ground twitch. He blinks. The jittering motion swirls clumps together to form pure black hands rising from the tiled steps. He blinks again. The darkness is dormant.

Lola pulls the trigger, sending a bullet blasting into Mastema's forehead. It collapses on impact, flattening to a coin that sticks to his skin. She rains hell, firing the last five bullets from her clip into his face.

Bang! Bang! Bang! Bang! Bang!

The rounds collect on his flesh, compressing into pancakes. A couple of them topple onto the ground, bouncing upon collision. Both Mastema and Lola watch the remaining pieces of pancake flat metal fall.

Lola fires once more. The gun clicks.

Tanner shouts again, "The fuck?"

Spike and Baldy stop halfway across the room. The three Moths stand from their shelters, watching the unthinkable.

Lola's face crunches into rage and she pistol whips the crime lord. He catches her wrist mid action. She tries to push. The sheer power he possesses makes her limbs quiver. She shouts and throws a fist. Her hand smashes into his gut, hitting what feels like concrete. He doesn't flinch. She ignores the pain and punches again. Mastema grabs that arm too.

The crime lord lowers her limbs with ease, crossing her arms as her mouth hangs open, dumbfounded as the rest of the humans. Yes, the light-bullet made an obvious hole in his right eye. The glowing amber is gone. The pitch black in the socket pulls her in. There's so much darkness. No illumination enters the space as Mastema's brow sinks, forming a scowl.

Nearby shadows dance, as if they were glitching on a computer game. The motion catches each human's attention, their faces squinting. They shift stances, showing more confusion than anything. Darkness doesn't move.

Mastema speaks in a low tone, mouth contorting into a frown. "That hurt, my dear."

Tanner and José fumble with the chair, kicking it to the ground with Hailey's help. Petrification overcomes Tobias. One girl tries to use her phone. The screen won't turn on. It's dead. She taps it several times to no luck.

With no other options, Lola lunges a knee. Her crossed arms in his grasp stop her from reaching his core. Lola gathers the saliva in her mouth and launches a spitball into Mastema's face. The bodily fluid splatters onto his cheek, drizzling down.

"Fuck you," she sneers. Lola strains her muscles to budge from her constraints. Limbs shake. A low, pained groan rumbles from her throat, echoing through the room.

The blackness inside Mastema's eye steams upward, swirling together. It spins around, turning from a gas into a solid, filling the space. The process continues until the matter recreates the bone, flesh, eyeball, and layered skin.

Mastema releases her hands and wipes the spit from his cheek. "Rude as well."

Lola punches again. It rebounds off his chest on impact, sparking the same pain in her knuckles as the previous attempt. She strikes with her other fist. She tries kneeing him in the groin: zero. Whether it was the shapeshifter's intentions or not, this mission failed.

She sprints, leaping over the chair and running past Mastema. The two club girls, José, Tanner, and Hailey run as well, attempting to make it for the closest door.

Lola's dash cuts short as a hand pulls the back of her tank top, ripping most of the fabrics and throwing her onto the ground with vigorous force. Her spine hits the floor, forcing her to look at Mastema upside down. Spike and Baldy phase to the exit before the humans can escape.

Mastema speaks, staring at her. "No regular mortal has knowledge of such ancient power. Somehow, you got your clever little fingers on a crafted ammunition designed to kill me. You're not able enough to make it, obviously. That means you made a powerful ally." Mastema walks around until he stands over her chest. He squats overtop of her.

Lola pants, unsure of what to do next. Her hands are free and are worthless. If she had a knife, any weapon to fight, she'd feel like she was defending herself.

She glances at Tobias, mouth hanging in shock, and at the group of kids. Horror paints their faces with wide gazes. She shifts to the supernatural guards who are cold as before. Her eyes lock on each of the three Moths. The same disbelief reflects in their expressions. The bartender wipes used cups on the bar, unphased, the sound of clinking glass filling the air. Lola is helpless.

"What's this?" Mastema says, looking at her hair. He pulls on the wig, freeing it from her sweaty scalp. "A cute disguise. You're not Roxxy, are you?" Mastema snags her face, squeezing her cheeks, turning her into a chipmunk. He says, "No. Not at all. This is not how I thought we would meet. My pride blinded me to your cheap outfit. You are an unexpected one, Lola Cabello."

Lola's teeth grind against each other while a guttural growl that resembles the sound of a wild beast escapes her throat. She snags onto Mastema's wrists, cupping the blazer and gold bracelets. She tries to pull him off her head with both hands. Her muscles burn to no verdict.

"The infamous vigilante from the Canadian prairies. A simple university student who stirred trouble in my operations." He frees her face and Lola lets go of him.

"I'm not done with you," Lola says. It's an empty threat. She is at his mercy.

"I'm sure you're not. As I'm not done with you. You worked as a beautiful scapegoat for my weakness in trusting others. You nearly exposed the great secrets of ash."

"Why don't you fucking kill me?" Lola says with hate oozing from her hissing words.

"Why? What a waste of talent. The mean Moths torture you, don't we? The poor girl who's lost her life. Her friend, her hero, her mother, and even worse, her living family detests her. Whatever allies you had have abandoned you. You are alone and we keep you around when we could have killed you countless times. Poor . . . poor little Lola."

"Go to hell," Lola says.

Mastema takes a deep inhale from his nose and exhales while smacking his lips. "The pride in your heart burns strong. It's got a hot kick to it. Mmm! Delicious. I've wanted to taste what keeps you going. You're not like the other humans, Lola Cabello. You're compelled. It's either your bloodline or your soul. You are driven. It has value. Yet, you've learned too much of the old world, and you are a problem."

Lola doesn't want to stick around for whatever sick game the crime lord has in mind. She scoots backwards, moving to Tobias. Inch by inch, she worms away until Mastema snags her ankles and drags her with one hand.

"We could have eradicated you long ago," Mastema says. "You're a fascinating specimen. A girl of the New World, so unassuming, and the more you grow, you come closer to the true you."

What the fuck is he saying? Lola thinks. She lifts her legs to break free from him. No luck.

"You're magnetized to the old world. An entity must have spoken to you on ash. How else would you unlock a power that my partners and I didn't anticipate. There's a force in your blood driving you far more than revenge. That, Lola Cabello, I think we need to find out."

Lola yanks on her leg. Mastema pulls her to him with a single tug, sliding her until they are eye-to-eye. He grins, hair dangling in front of his chin. "I think you and I are going to spend a lot of time together."

CHAPTER 20
A FATHER'S FEAR

Stress, Iglesias thinks and glances at Archer who fixates on the shadows. The two officers exchange looks while the bouncer looks around the room, his eyes shot open, mouth hanging. *Maybe not.*

"Come on," Iglesias says.

His heart thumps with each step, buzzing past the stairs and young kids laughing, unaware of the fast-moving officers. Iglesias prays his son is okay. José has to be in this mess somewhere. His gut screams at him to make the situation right.

The detectives move through the dancers, orbiters, and even people in the dark corners dressed in white. It is obvious who they are. One of them in a pearl blouse watches him. They glare, locked in a primal stare until Iglesias passes, keeping his gaze forward. More than ever, he would like to slam that goon against the wall and demand where José is. It's foolish and pointless.

He monitors each individual they pass, looking for potential threats. A knife, gun, brass knuckles, anything that can stop him from getting to those stairs. A vibrant and youthful aura radiates from their faces, assuring there is no danger.

They circle around the outside of the mass dancing form, passing the lounge. Even here, club attendees pack the place shoulder to shoulder, forcing them to push through. Iglesias spots the stage, and to the right, there's a door with security personnel standing with folded arms. His dread expands the dark basement five times its regular size.

This is Iglesias's nightmare—not making it in time. He fears his son is in that room with the Crystal Moths, thanks to Tanner and his own slacking. He keeps marching through the sea of stench and the oblivious who move in rhythm with the pounding bass music. The low frequencies hit his chest, knocking his burning heart.

Time crawls by as Iglesias pushes his way through moist shoulders with his elbows and shoulders, leading his partner to the other side. She's one helluva detective, trusting him on his instinct, going against what their training says to do.

The two break through the sweat masses to the rear of the club. He can't hear any more shots thanks to the wretched music. Is there a blood bath above? How many casualties? The bouncer waves them over, speaking into his earpiece. He shouts, "It's up there."

Bright lights beam onto the mumbling dancers with confusion painted on their squinting faces. Iglesias has a brief thought of scolding the bouncer by asking, *The fuck you standing here for?* He remembers that he's keeping civilians from this door.

Keep it together. "Make sure the attendees get out safe," Iglesias says.

The muffled bass from the music downstairs stops. A knock comes from the door behind the two guards. Spike opens it to talk to the Moth outside. The Goliath Moth from earlier mumbles to the old world guard.

The man steps in as Spike closes the entrance. He hisses, exposing his fangs. "The club is being shut down. Police have swarmed the area after her little stunt."

They either heard the gunshots or Detective Iglesias is here. At the moment, Lola prays for the latter. She has no other options other than prayer.

Mastema sighs. "Look at you, Lola. Once again rumbling chaos." He snags her by the neck and stands, dragging her. His grip is tight, cutting the airway from her esophagus, close enough to make her pass out. The room blurs, her head spins.

The crime lord says, "José, I'm sorry, truly."

The bouncer opens the entryway and the detectives step onto the first flight of steps. They creep around the corner, coming face-to-face with a red door at the highest level of the stairs. No firearm damage is in the wood. They back away to the corner's edge. It's the best shield they have in case the entrance bursts open. Iglesias and Archer are unprepared. They don't have bullet-proof vests. They lack communicators to organize with the other officers. That narrow hall to the top is a choke hold.

Iglesias whispers to Archer, "Fire low, use the stairs as a shield. I will open the door."

He must go first, for his son.

José looks at Tanner, then at Mastema as if he is supposed to speak. Hailey and the girls exchange looks, forming a silent pact that they're in this mess together.

Mastema continues, "We're keeping operations under a tight wrap these days. My business partners are sticklers for keeping old things buried. Again, I'm truly sorry." He snaps his fingers towards the bartender.

She raises her pristine eyebrow and hops over the bar. The remaining Moths wait for an order. Mastema heads for the opposite door, accompanied by the nymph. Their eyes meet in a silent exchange—the gangsters with each other, Tobias with a squint at Tanner, and José with wide-eyed fearfulness at Hailey. Spike and Baldy remain motionless.

Lola's boots drag against the wooden floor in a poor attempt to save her own skin. She lets out one last shout of agony until her face turns bright pink from the lack of air. Hatred, anger, and denial of the situation drown her mind and smother her heart. Her efforts are futile, and she kicks the tables and chairs, knocking them over and toppling candles and drinks onto the ground. The tiny flames extinguish with her hope.

As the door swings open, she catches one last glimpse of the two supernatural guards. Their mouths gape wider than the lengths of their skulls with the fangs extending, eyes rolling back. The entrance closes shut. As the distance grows, screams, gunshots, and the toppling of furniture becomes fainter and fainter. The Moth triumphs the vengeful butterfly.

The muffled sound of toppling furniture comes from above. A woman's grizzly shout booms through the closed entrance and into the detectives' ears. The crying fades. Footsteps fizzle out, followed by the clicking of another door. Either the Crystal Moths are gone, or they're being staged for an ambush.

"Okay," Archer says.

Snake hissing erupts from the next level. Gunshots. Thumping and tumbling follow with screams and cries for help.

Shit! Iglesias thinks.

Iglesias runs for the top floor, hugging the wall of the stairwell. The sounds stop. He snags the cold copper handle on an inhale. Gurgling comes from behind the wood. His grip on his gun tightens as he swings the door open. A young girl with hair as red as the blood splattering her body stands in front of him. The liquid spews from her mouth and oozes from two holes at the side of her neck.

"Hailey," Iglesias gasps.

He and Archer listen beyond her: a quiet room. The sounds were as short as it took him to get up the stairs. What? Three, five, seconds?

Iglesias lowers his gun and pulls the girl down the steps and around the corner. Archer keeps her firearm raised, shielding her partner, eyes on the open door. Hailey hacks and splutters in Iglesias's arms. Warm fluids stain his blazer and shirt as he holds her close.

"She's bleeding out," Iglesias says. "What's the situation?"

"Clear," Archer says.

"Shit," Iglesias lowers Hailey onto the step.

She wheezes and whispers. He leans in closer to hear her weak words through hot breath. "Vamp-vamp-eye . . . Vam . . . Vah—" Her eyes glaze over. No air leaves her lungs, turning his ear cold.

Detective Iglesias stands, concluding the worst. He signals Archer to cover him and the two go up the stairs. Each step they take reveals more of the second level. Bullet holes scatter the walls. Toppled chairs and tables disperse throughout the lounge by an empty bar. Blood stains smear the hardwood floor, with corpses littering the ground. There's a small window facing the alleyway with its vertical hinges open.

He leans into the room, checking the corners, and steps in, then spins to see behind the entryway. No one. To his right is another closed exit leading to the front lobby where the other officers are. No shouting. No gunshots. The muffled sound of distressed club attendees tickles his ear.

Iglesias lowers his weapon and examines the corpses. Most wear white, soiled with red. They have broken bones sticking out of their muscles and fabrics; two puncture holes rest on their neck, matching Hailey's. Scraps of flesh and chunks of meat splatter the walls and dangle from tables.

His heart pounds inside his chest, hoping that he will not find what his detective instincts say is true. Decades on the force have given him the expertise to comprehend the darkness of crime and their aftermaths. His critical eye leads him through the maze of bodies.

The gun almost slips from his hand when he spots red sneakered feet, his son's, resting in a pool of deep scarlet liquid, sticking out from a tipped over loveseat.

CHAPTER 21
THE SHADOW'S WARNING

Scalebane's unparalleled upbringing assists her in detecting the presence of danger. Her human companion, the painter oracle Dasco Amoss, is creating messages unlike anything she can fathom. It's a fusion of her past, locating her sister, and an unknown, unknown.

This muse is showing him the total story of Creationism by the absent Creator. Her concern is the subtle looming threat that would be too easy for unseasoned eyes to miss. Scalebane's experience with the afterlife ensures one thing: beyond the mortal realm, life is inhospitable. Yet, here she is with her people, aligning with the First. Safeguarding the vazeleads causes her to make strategic choices. Mastema isn't an issue today, unlike the muse's warning.

Her words to Dasco Amoss are true. She will return far sooner. In fact, Scalebane won't be resuming her duties with the Crystal Moths. She requires more time. Rithu Blacktooth and Jekos can handle the ash. If this muse's message is as terrible as she fears, it demands her undivided attention. Her leader needs the forewarning. He, like the planet, is unaware.

Her boot scrapes against the dust of the incomplete concrete flooring she stands on. *Click . . . Click, click . . . Click.* The nipping wind tugs at her cloak, threatening to carry it away as she remains on the edge of the skyscraper. Countless feet above, she watches the nighttime lights of downtown Toronto. Police vehicles flash outside of an old brick church, with humans evacuating it one block off. Dasco Amoss's studio loft is several streets from that.

Dega'Mostikas's Triangle. The Midway, the Creator. The First. Realms. Beyond the Cosmos. That shadow, Scalebane thinks, listing the key visual cues from the work. The last painting with the dark corner sends invisible icy pins dancing along her spine's scales.

A motion by a pillar catches her eye. She draws both sai, tail perked, facing the newcomer. They aren't there. She moves around the column. No one. The moonlight casts a dim shadow on the ground. It jerks as if being electrocuted. The action ceases and she sheaths her weapons.

Wind blows her cloak by. Several moments pass. *They are disturbed,* Scalebane thinks. This is evident proof that the lightless ones are aware of the events unravelling.

Scalebane unfastens the first few straps and pulls the zippers of her armour, the soft creaking of leather filling the quiet. She reaches inside to grab a pendant. This black matte stone attached to a chain proves the old world lives on through fragments.

With her somber glove off, she feels the coolness of the object against her palm, running her fingers over its intricate etchings. Ancient symbols of a lost language radiate orange from within the carvings with her caressing. Her eyes close as she moves the sphere around until it releases heat.

King . . . King.

Opening her eyes, the human civilization blows away from a sudden smoke-filled haze coming from thin air. The stars, the glass towers, and even the ground that she stands on morph into an underground cavern, with torches illuminating the space. A black throne sits dead centre, occupied by a figure clad in head-to-toe gunmetal armour.

The fog created by the stone encompasses her peripheral view, while she stares at the vision of King, her fearless leader. Even with the flames, the shine is dim. A gentle radiance from a sphere in his palm casts a subtle glow on the glimmers of his spiked plating. The silhouette envelops the rest of his body, leaving a hint of his presence.

"King, I have urgent news," Scalebane says. Her voice echoes as she speaks into the vision.

"Scalebane, you use your soulstone at unexpecting times. What is your urgency?" King speaks. His tone is deeper than what a soft skin can project, lower than a regular vazelead. The sound reverberates in the cave's open space with an added echo from the soulstone's power.

"Did you sense the shadows?"

"The shadows? What do you speak of?"

He missed it. "I fear we're in danger," Scalebane says.

"Our operations with ash are moving as intended, are they not?" King asks.

"It's not the ash," Scalebane says.

"Is Rithu well?" King asks.

"Do not fear for the safety of your son. I have assured his protection under my watchful eye."

"Do you summon me regarding my proposal?" King asks.

"King, I need you to reserve your questions and let me speak."

King's claws scrape against the armchair of the throne. A deep, resonant rumble emanates from his throat. He mentions the wretched proposition with each meeting. It's the main reason Rithu is with Scalebane, and it makes her tail squeeze her ankle to suppress her disgust for the frail boy.

Scalebane speaks. "I have a disturbing theory that we are being watched by powerful eyes."

"Theory?" King says. "You dare interrupt me for a theory?"

"This isn't one you want to dismiss, King."

"I will humour you so far," King says, "because you're invaluable. But don't think I won't lock you up for safekeeping."

"Imprison me, like the soft skins did to us?"

King's jaws clench, highlights of his nostrils flaring. "Don't you dare compare me to those monsters. Your freedom is proof of my difference."

His ridiculous attempts at hierarchy and power don't phase Scalebane. She plays by the rules, holding most of the cards since her sister vanished. Scalebane is the single female capable of procreation. King is not like the humans, reducing her to lock and chain, and needs her more than he will ever admit.

She says, "I fear that the ghouls of the Midway are watching us."

King straightens his posture. "What makes you say such words? They're neutral."

Scalebane could tell him her relationship with Dasco Amoss. He is too fragile and King will seize him, removing him from his natural environment. Scalebane respects the sacred space of his craft. "I need you to trust my forewarning."

King grips a fist, head tilting to the concrete walls behind her. He speaks. "Scalebane, what else have you been doing besides your duties? You should be with Rithu."

"Those are of little concern," Scalebane says.

"They linger in my mind," the other says.

"Your idle thoughts should not rest with me, whom I remind you hasn't strayed loyalty for hundreds of years. Your mind should be cautious of the ghouls and their Midway. They have eyes and ears everywhere."

"How would they know what we are doing, and why would it matter to them? In fact, they feed off of death. We're bringing them a feast."

"Their limbo realm and diet don't mean they're incapable of other interests. They're ancient and have access to immense powers."

"Power that can match The First?" King asks. "What horrors could you possibly be speaking of? Tell me, Scalebane, child of the afterlife."

"I have encountered ghouls in Dreadweave Pass. They relate to the lightless ones." *The dark spot,* she thinks, swallowing saliva as she recalls Dasco's painting with the black blotches.

"Lightless ones are a myth, fabrics of reality, like the air, the light, or the cold."

"Fabric frays, especially if Mastema does what he wishes."

"Scalebane, these are your own speculations from your past mixing in with paranoia of Mastema. You do not trust him and you want your sister protected."

"I warn you one final time: Mastema is unsympathetic to us and whatever he has planned will rattle the moral realm. Mark my words, it will awaken the lightless ones."

"Scalebane, your wisdom and insight into the afterlife are of immense value. You also steer into too many suspicion infused theories. Mastema is transparent."

"King, with all due respect, why do you think Mastema has not attempted to contact the ghouls or lightless ones? "

"Again, wanderings of an unsound mind. Mastema wishes to rid the humans that are the active danger of the Creator's work. They are destroying our home, their own, and given enough time their technologies will take them to the stars so they can infect each corner of the mortal realm. We can prevent that. The old world will rise again and the threat of man will be abolished. The First has no reason to destroy the beauty assembled by the Creator. It's a paradox of his existence. This is ancient history. It is why Mastema operates through actors and possession. A heavy hand of ghouls and suggested shadows could destroy the delicate work of the Creator."

"Beauty is in the eye of the beholder," Scalebane says.

"Hmm. Opinions aside, we have limited options, Scalebane. Throw your theories away and look at what is in front of you. We need powerful allies while we grow in numbers. Do I have to remind you of what the Nine are?"

"No, you do not. I'm versed in what they are, and what we do to them." Scalebane forces air out her nostrils. *Here we go.*

"Tell me." King sits back on his throne.

"Defective bloodlines, weaklings, children of street scum from the days of old. Their blood is corrupt and weak. They are our people."

"Exactly. I don't enjoy ripping their skin for ash. I would let them live the rest of the wretched lives if we had a better method of protecting our people and ensuring our longevity. Do you understand?"

"Yes, King." Scalebane bites her lip. This isn't going as planned.

"I don't think you do," King says. He rises from his throne, the gunmetal armour rattling with each movement of his limbs. He clutches his soulstone as he marches through the dark cavern. The torch lights graze his form, illuminating his true Herculean frame and facial features. Unlike the other vazeleads, a unique pattern of large and small charcoal scales, ash, give shape to his face, creating a gritty texture. His eyes match those of each vazelead, made of a smokeless flame, dancing in a slow motion. The short black scalp-feathers on his skull create a mohawk, bobbing with each step he takes through the halls. The flickering blaze of his sandstone irises pierces her soul. His eyebrows, formed by horns, slant into a scowl with his mouth hanging open, exposing several of the sharp teeth.

Invisible pins poke her foot and run up her left leg. She shifts her stance.

King slides a metal lock beyond Scalebane's view and reveals a stone door, entering a new room. The light from the hallway merges with the shadows as a groan and hisses come from the depths. He leans over and snags onto a limb, causing a shriek. Chains dangle as he lifts a bone-thin naked vazelead into sight. The flaming eyes dance in uncontrolled motions as if the rain were extinguishing them. Black oiled scabs run along their spines where the ash scales were plucked.

King squeezes their neck, lifting them high. The legs swing and the tail flaps in a feeble attempt at protecting itself. King says, "This is what we have to do to our own kind."

Scalebane pushes her tongue against the roof of her mouth. King wants to lecture her. It doesn't matter what she says next.

"The Nine here are doing their part, ensuring our people's survival. We despise their repulsive backgrounds and can respect their heroic actions. Each of us needs to be champions. Future generations will write our names in stone as our population grows with the assistance of you and my son."

Scalebane speaks on an exhale. "You've reminded me in the past that my mother was street scum. That makes me no different from the Nine. Feed one of them to be your son's perverted incubation machine." She would be best to tie her tongue.

King drops the frail vazelead and exits the room with the yowls of misery muffling once he closes the door. He returns to his throne. Once he sits, he replies. "Yes, and Hell swallowed your mother. She raised two beautiful hatchlings, found a way for them to escape Dega'Mostikas's Triangle and return to the living. Being a street scum was not in her bones. She evolved and embraced a warrior's way. You must become new too. You cannot be off chasing theories that hold no solid ground. Focus on Rithu, who you have dismissed since you began working with him."

"He's a boy and not ready to father. He barely can handle the difficult concepts of what we do."

"Elaborate," King says.

"He's inexperienced, naïve to the world, and I don't think he has what it takes to be as ruthless as we need if we are to continue work with the Moths. Rithu is better suited to match an empathetic mind, like my sister Namsruc."

"Namsruc who does not contact you and stays with the nymph? That Namsruc?"

"I will find her, I promise you." She squeezes her soulstone, claws shaking.

"Scalebane, I have to ask you. Are you loyal to our people?"

"Yes, of course."

"Your actions reflect that of a traitor."

"I—I—no, King. My concerns are for our future."

"Take responsibility and hatch my son's children. He is meeting Mastema in his home tomorrow. You'd best be there."

King releases his grasp on the soulstone. Their telepathic connection ends, leaving Scalebane at the top of the cool, incomplete skyscraper.

ACT

II

ACT II
LAWLESS ANTAGONISM

[Lola Cabello Documentary: CAMB Originals]

  [Take 1: Raw]

  [2018, October 08]

  [Hucker Dime: CAMB Reporter and Talk Host]

  [RECORDING:

  Look at me, huh, huh, on the other side of the microphone for once. This is good, good, yeah. I think you guys are covering important stuff. It doesn't get enough attention around the globe. Canadians are ABOOT hockey and igloos, such nice people. Mark my words, this series will get more views than the CAMB audience. Let's start. Sit here? Perfect.

. . .

I'm Hucker Dime and I've been reporting on Canadian news for over twenty years. Do I know Lola Cabello? Who doesn't? I was the first to report on her. CAMB News Now covers the facts regarding the latest news with stories that continue to evolve regarding you and your country. It's our duty to keep the people up to date. I've covered a wide range of murderous cases too, like the Drainer Cases, Snapper Cases, you name it. Of course, I like to pose a few interesting points people should consider. Facts can leave people in disarray and they don't ask the right questions. That's my specialization.

When Cabello first published her video on her blog, it changed things. I was intrigued. In the prairies, was a young girl striving to be a reporter. She survived a tragic incident. Her friend and her mentor, the infamous Michael Bradford, better known as YEGman, murdered in front of her. She was shot too, for Christ's sake.

Cabello's sly nature impressed me.

Who teams up with a claimed vigilante into a gunfight on a rescue mission, then decides to record the whole damn thing by stuffing her phone in her boot? Lola does, that's who. Of course, she was loose in the head to begin with. We need an edge to make it in this world, and Cabello's had a bite.

Yes, I watched the video, heard the murders and wanted to learn more. We ran the story when she uploaded the video to her blog. We continued it as a series after when she evaded the authorities from 2014 to 2016. I contacted her family here in Toronto. They had little to do with her at that point. Cabello kept us guessing. Lots of influencers had their thoughts online.

Other news outlets reported having seen her and skewed the evidence to sensationalize their coverage for the views. Not me, not at CAMB.

I think Cabello knew that. That's why she messaged me on social media, before the horrendous slaughter at the Allen Abattoir Plant. You boys going to cover that? . . . yeah? . . . want me to elaborate? . . . Sure, sure.

Cabello left a fake distressed voice message on my social media inbox. Again, cunning girl. She wanted the media there to broadcast the massacre she was going to unfold with the Crystal Moths. That notorious Canadian mob had some drug operation going on there. The plant had corrupt management right under corporate's noses. It fuelled Cabello to make it one terrible show. Civilians died. Police died. Gangsters. It was the same issue at the art gallery with Ashley Amber prior.

It doesn't matter if she's alive or dead; she's left a legacy.

Look, I've been covering this type of stuff for a long time. I've seen a ton of whackos, nut jobs, and sociopaths plunge into a world of crime. Folks love the attention. I'm not saying that Cabello suffers from Histrionic Personality Disorder, but she is delusional and loves attention. Look at her website. Look at her claims: the government and media are corrupt and part of a big conspiracy with the Moths. Use some critical thinking, and look at her actions. Lies and mass murder. She uses the skills of reporting she obtained in school to reinforce her confirmation bias. It's that simple.

The girl needed help. She began as a tragic story and mutated into a dangerous beast, inflicting real-world consequences on the innocent. This is what happens when mental health goes unchecked. It happened to Michael Bradford, the YEGman, and history repeated itself.

Where's funds for the wellbeing of our people? In the pocket of our Prime Minister.

It's sad. It's sad and just plain wrong.

END]

CHAPTER 22
FATHER LIKE SON

When Iglesias asks himself why his son lied, took his girlfriend to a DJ concert filled with gangsters, he understands. He cannot be mad at the ill-fated boy. Iglesias grew up in a different time and his rebellious nature was the same at that age. He shares this history.

"Ricardo Iglesias!" was a phrase that his mother used when he was in trouble. For example, in 1991, his father was watching the seventy-ninth Grey Cup on the tube. They couldn't afford tickets to see the game live in their hometown, Winnipeg. The Toronto Argonauts versus the Calgary

Stampeders was a big day for Canadians. The Grey Cup final made history as the coldest faceoff in NFL, with temperatures dropping to negative sixteen degrees Celsius.

His dad sat in his deep green recliner, drinking bottles of beer and paying little attention to his wife. It was easier to drink instead of intervene. Iglesias would watch games too. He'd even have his own bottle of beer if his father was in a good mood. Luck eluded him that night.

"Ricardo Iglesias," his mother said again, coming from upstairs. The steps creaked as she moved along the thick brown carpet. "You come here."

Iglesias glanced at his dad. The man took a sip of his drink, eyes glued to footballers in the snow. It was Iglesias against his mom. She walked to the living room where Iglesias sunk in the sofa, a failed attempt not to be seen.

"Would you explain this, young man?" his mother said, raising a can of soda. To an untrained observer, it appeared to be an empty can. Anyone who is aware of how to hide drugs understands that it's a simple tactic to keep the goods. His mom was no fool. She could sniff her son performing illegal activities.

"Nothing," Iglesias muttered.

"Nothing?" she said, looking at his father. "Guess what's in here."

His dad shrugged and scratched his bloated belly, watching the tube. She popped the lid of the fake can and pulled out a plastic bag filled with green and brown buds of weed. "This is the third time we have found this junk in your room. What is wrong with you?"

"I didn't put it there," Iglesias said. "You're making shit up."

"Hey!" shouted his father, sitting straight in his chair. "Don't you speak to your mother that way. You got it, boy?" There was a slur to his voice, dragging the end of each sentence. *B-o-o-ya.*

"It wasn't mine," Iglesias said.

"You're lying?" asked his mother.

"Get your act together, or I'm gonna make you." Iglesias's father rose, wobbling as he did. He slammed his bottle on the small table beside him. "You bring that weed in here, eh?"

"I said no," Iglesias said while standing. He was the same height as his mom. Being eye level with her stern glare and tight lips of rage made him feel far smaller. He stepped aside from both parents, who moved closer.

His father unbuckled his belt and gave it a snap with both hands. "Come here."

"No!" Iglesias shouted. "It's not a big deal."

"Big deal?" his mother said in a mocking laugh. "This can put you in jail. Forget that. What would the good Lord think?"

"Jesus Christ, don't give me that."

With a sudden motion, his father positioned himself in front of Iglesias's mom, brandishing the belt and aiming it at Iglesias's face. He swung in a sloppy arch, for the man was too drunk. Iglesias dodged it. With lightning speed, he snatched his shoes and retreated into the entranceway, evading his father's next blow.

"Get back here," Iglesias's father snarled.

"Fuck you, I don't need this," Iglesias said, grabbing his jacket.

"Where do you think you're going?" his mother asked. "It's cold out there, and quite frankly you have nowhere to go, no friends, and no relatives in the city."

"I can find my way."

"What? Dantrell? I bet you he's the one who gave you this dope and is tainting your mind. You need to come back to church."

"I'm not getting involved with any of your religious bullshit. Especially if I'm threatened by a drunk."

His mother gasped.

His father roared, charging at Iglesias as he approached the doorknob. He flung it open and stepped into the cold with his shoes crunching into the fresh snow. His dad reached for him and grabbed onto his collar. Iglesias swatted his hand as the belt flicked. It hit him on the right brow. He dashed down the stairs, covering his face, sliding on the second ice-coated step, and hurried across the street.

"Don't you come back, boy, unless you clean your ass up. You hear me? We don't tolerate that behaviour!" His father shouted, voice distancing as he ran past the block.

His mother was right. They didn't have family there. He didn't have friends. Dantrell was the one who Iglesias thought of once he made it several blocks away. He exuded an air of effortless cool, leaving Iglesias envious.

He hiked to the corner store, eight blocks from that church-going nonsense, and went to the payphone inside. Iglesias took some quarters from his jean's pockets. With no cellphones, one could vanish. Memorizing numbers became a common skill. Iglesias pushed the coins into the slots and dialled his friend's home line. Each metallic button gave a satisfying click. The receiver rang a couple times before his friend's smooth voice came through, with a slight distortion because of the reception quality.

"Hello?" Dantrell said.

"Yo, Dantrell, it's Ricardo. Your parents home?"

"Nah man. Sup?"

"I need a place to crash. Not going to my folks."

"What did you do?" His tone straightened with a lower pitch.

"They took the dope, man. I can't sell it."

Dantrell sighed. "Okay, okay. Can you sneak in through the window and get it?"

"What? No. My mom has it. That buzzkill will flush it by the time I get there."

"Jesus, man. Where are you?" Dantrell asked.

"I'm at the corner store," the other said.

"Fuck. The boss is gonna be pissed."

"Boss? You work for someone?" Iglesias said.

"Yeah, dumbass. I don't buy this shit outright. If I did, I wouldn't drive that rust bucket truck. Shit."

"Your boss cool or what?" Iglesias's face flushed, thinking the question was a stupid thing to say. The streets don't function that way. He is more sheltered than Dantrell. Spending time in church didn't help.

"I'll come get you. You can fix this with me."

Shit, Iglesias thought. "Word."

The phone clicked.

He put the receiver down and stuffed his hands in his pockets. His mind wandered while waiting inside the convenience store. He strolled through the aisles, attempting not to think about how he messed up. The usual cashier was working tonight. The zit-faced, four-eyed dork didn't bother him and read his magazine. Iglesias wasn't in the mood to talk. His mental state kept him occupied: what would he do? Would he sell drugs like Dantrell? Where would he live? He couldn't help wondering if he made a mistake. He should clean up his life.

The rumbling, broken muffler of a pickup truck outside silenced his reasoning. High beams blared through the windows as the vehicle parked out front. Iglesias exited the store and swung open the creaking passenger door.

"Boo-yah," Iglesias said.

Dantrell kept a tight grip at twelve o'clock on the wheel. He brought the vehicle into reverse and looked back, his curly black hair swaying. He slammed on the gas, unphased by the slick ice and snow like a true Canadian.

"So, yo, I figured how we're gonna fix this," Dantrell said. He spun the truck around and shifted into drive, leaving the neighbourhood. Goodbye parents, hello freedom.

"How much bread we owe?" Iglesias asked, hoping his friend wouldn't pass the blame on him.

They stopped at a red light. Dantrell pointed at a plaza at the next intersection where a liquor store was open beside a drugstore and a closed butcher shop. "It's not a lot. In fact, we can hit two birds with one stone, if you catch my drift."

"What you thinking?" Iglesias asked, playing stupid because he knew the answer.

"Make a quick stop. Check the back," Dantrell said. The light turned green, and he revved the gas, tires spinning for a second.

Iglesias looked over his shoulder at the bed of the pickup where a couple of baseball bats with nails pierced through them rested. Yes, indeed, Iglesias's thoughts were accurate. He spun around as Dantrell drove into the parking lot with one other car parked. Inside the liquor store, through the metal bars and glass window, a woman shopped for some booze. She wouldn't be a problem.

Dantrell turned off the engine and exited the truck. Iglesias took a deep breath in, closed his eyes, and told himself, *I can do this.* He had to. He refused to be a straight-laced Christian prude that couldn't have fun. Wicked Dantrell did. The way he was handling this situation was proof of it. His attitude and posture were strong. The guy made things happen. That's who Iglesias wished he was. He could learn from the best.

This is why he exited the vehicle and grabbed the bat from Dantrell. It's why he and his partner in crime placed the ski masks over their heads and snatched a couple of cloth bags.

Dantrell spun his weapon. "Let's bounce."

Iglesias nodded and his friend took the lead.

The two burst into the liquor store, the bell above the frame jingling. Dantrell swung his bat, smashing the first stack of liquor he saw. The ill-fated wine shattered with deep red and purple liquid pouring onto the white tiles and green shards bouncing.

Holy shit, Iglesias thought. He clasped his weapon with both hands and joined in on the fun. He struck at the mound of wine, shattering the remaining bottles.

"Don't do anything stupid!" Dantrell shouted, pointing the bat at the cashier. The middle-aged man raised his hands, keeping them clear from underneath the counter.

Iglesias locked gazes with the blue-eyed brunette, who didn't dare move. He lifted his bat high. "No funny business, you got it?" His arm wanted to shake with the rush of adrenaline. The energy buzzed inside, slowing time, giving him a sense of life he hadn't felt before.

The woman hoisted her hands up and closed her eyes.

Iglesias took one jolt forward. "Eyes open!"

"Yes! Yes!" she cried, a couple of tears glistened on her cheek, smearing her mascara. "Please. Don't hurt us. Please."

She was mid-thirties, twice his age. The cheap makeup flaked on her face. Her slanted plucked eyebrows were an iconic style of the era. Several beads ran through her streaked hair. Her bubblegum lips trembled. They were attractive, and a brief thought of his prick in her mouth excited him. Analyzing the scenario, it added a layer of shame to his psyche.

"Take whatever you want," said the cashier. He didn't blink, staring at the two.

Dantrell slammed the baseball bat against the counter. "Fill this!" he shouted while tossing the cloth sack. "Yo, homeboy, get some booze."

Iglesias went to work. Despite his confident words, he chose an aisle the woman wasn't in. His heart raced, for he hadn't robbed a store before. He snagged a bottle of whisky, some vodka, beer, and the bag was full. Thank God they wore masks. As cool as Dantrell was, Iglesias knew his face was pathetic, red, and scared. He glanced at the woman, who looked away.

The cashier stuffed the pack with the green from the register and slid it across the counter. Dantrell snatched the goods and tapped the surface twice with his bat. He eyed the brunette and spoke. "Later, tuts."

Dantrell nodded to the door and Iglesias followed him, thankful that the situation was over. Exciting? Yes. His heart pounded like a fist inside his chest and his hands hummed with an electric surge. Fear? Without a doubt. The mixture of the emotions left him in a state of bliss he couldn't describe while hopping into the truck.

The engine roared to life and Dantrell shifted gears and they got the hell out of there before the clerk and customer had a chance to call the cops.

Dantrell and Iglesias cheered, driving into the night. The two took off their masks and chucked the bats in the automobile bed through the small window slit behind their heads. Dantrell navigated them to a side street, where they parked away from the light of the main roads.

"Man, did you see the look on their bitch-ass faces?" Dantrell asked while shaking Iglesias's shoulder. Both of them smiled while exiting the vehicle. Iglesias held the bag of booze while Dantrell led them, lighting a smoke, towards Louise Bridge: the perfect place to bask in their success.

"You did well," Dantrell said while waving at him. Iglesias opened the sack and passed him the first thing he found. The whiskey popped open, and Dantrell downed a mouthful.

Iglesias was next, taking a sip. The liquid burned his throat. He had countless beers before, though hard liquor wasn't as common. He spoke, "Fuck, I've never done that before. That was insane."

"We got enough cash to cover the weed," Dantrell said.

"For real?" They hadn't even counted it yet.

"I'm pretty sure. There were a few hundreds in there."

"Damn right!" Iglesias took another drink.

The boys cheered each other and continued pounding the booze and sharing smokes. A slug of whisky here, some sips of vodka, then they'd wash it down with beer. Rinse and repeat. It's a triple whammy of liquor that seeped into their systems before they knew it. The eighteen beers were gone by the time they left the neighbourhood and wandered onto Louise Bridge. This late at night, there wasn't much traffic as they reached the middle of the platform.

Iglesias spoke. "Yo, my dad said this was the first overpass built in the city."

Dantrell chuckled. "The fuck do I care?" He chugged the rest of the whisky and smashed it against the metal railing. The glass trickled past the frame and onto the frozen river below.

Iglesias laughed, enjoying the recklessness of his friend's behaviour. It's what he needed to be. His parents' breathing down his neck made him scared. Away from them, he could be anyone he aspired to be.

Dantrell brushed his hair from his face. "I thought you weren't going back anyways? Who cares what your father said?"

"He is my dad," Iglesias defended, choking the vodka's neck. Yes, he was mad at them, though he loved his family at the core. He needed space.

"Don't be a bitch." Dantrell snagged the liquor from him and took a swig.

"Fuck you, man," Iglesias said while ripping the bottle from Dantrell and taking the drink of his own.

"Yo, chillax, at least you got some parents wanting to do good for you. They aren't playing hot potato so the other can smoke some crack or pork around."

"Yeah, well. I don't believe in that God bullshit and my father is a drunk. He is practically not even there." The words needed to be washed away. Iglesias swung the bottle back and took a large gulp. The liquor didn't burn anymore, and the cold was non-existent.

Those football players are pussies, his inebriated mind thought.

Dantrell wiped his chin. "I don't think you've seen shit. You froze at the liquor store."

"What?" Iglesias said. "That's not how it went. I stopped the customer."

"That slut? Please. You followed my lead. A millisecond can make an entire difference."

"Whatever. It was your idea." Iglesias scowled, feeling a rage burn inside of him.

"Of course it was. Like it was mine to save your ass."

"Hey, I did good."

"Sure, church boy." Dantrell looked into the river, lighting a cigarette.

The fire combusted, coursing through his veins. It's an anger that grew stronger that day onward. The nine bottles of beer, half a bottle of whiskey, and a fourth of vodka mastered his actions. Fury flushed his face. Disrespecting his drunken father was one thing. Pissing on Iglesias's ego was another.

"Fuck you," Iglesias said.

"Excuse me?" Dantrell asked, turning to face him. He exhaled smoke as a swift hand knocked Iglesias's shoulder. "Wud'cho say to me?" his voice slurred.

"I said fuck you." He pushed Dantrell's chest.

Dantrell chuckled. His eyes widened, a type of crazy look that only a true wild man could pull off. "You wanna go, church boy?" Dantrell put the dart in his mouth, grinning.

"I ain't no church boy!" Iglesias shouted. He charged at his friend, dropping the bottle of vodka. It landed in the snow, draining the goods while the two boys struggled for dominance. Dantrell snagged his wrist as he grabbed his other. He was a head taller, more skilled in fights, and knew how to manoeuvre in a wrestle. He jerked Iglesias's arm and towered over his form. He lifted his leg to trip him, failing to account for the ice which he stood on. His foot slid. Iglesias slammed his elbow into Dantrell's chest, knocking him back.

The force was too great, thumping him against the low railing. In combination with the sleek ground, he flipped over from the stomach. How that happened, Iglesias will not understand. Both were too drunk to have clarity. As Dantrell said, a millisecond makes the difference. Unlike the liquor store, this was life-and-death.

Iglesias bolted forward, grabbing Dantrell's ankle.

The weight of Dantrell's body was too immense, and his limb slid from Iglesias's cold fingers. Dantrell plummeted to the frozen surface below, crashing through the ice and into the subzero temperatures. He flailed his limbs, splashing in the biting waters, struggling to get up. His arms lost their traction on the delicate layer and glided below a moment after, vanishing into the darkness.

"Dantrell!" Iglesias shouted, gripping the frosted railings with the tightness of disbelief. "Dantrell!"

He bolted for a split second, then froze, realizing that running was pointless. They were halfway over the bridge. It would take him far too long to reach the bed of the river. If he did, he'd need the good Lord on his side to step across the thin ice and dive into the waters to save Dantrell from a frozen grave. God wasn't too fond of Iglesias that day.

A moment of genius struck the drunk. He could walk away. No one was aware that Iglesias was with Dantrell that evening. Sure, the two of them robbed the liquor store and Dantrell's truck was iconic with the muffler and rusted frame. Dantrell's boss? Never knew Iglesias. That dork at the corner store? Oblivious. His mother would theorize. Could the law prove it?

An effective detective like Iglesias in 2018 would have located each of Dantrell's friends. He would learn that a young boy had fought with his mom and father over weed that night. The evidence would lead to that kid meeting Dantrell at a corner store thanks to the signature truck's sound. A robbery happened ten blocks further at a liquor store after. A vehicle with the same description was at both stores minutes apart. Thankfully, there weren't detectives of that nature in 1991 Winnipeg.

Iglesias kicked the vodka bottle over the edge, letting it plummet into the grave with Dantrell. He left the scene. His hands stayed in his pockets and he kept marching. The boy stumbled upon a late-night café and got a cup of coffee to recover. Regret and excitement ran through his intoxicated veins.

Missing person posters for Dantrell scattered the town until they found the body in the summer. Not a single law enforcement suspected Iglesias. That was the end. It was his secret.

That night provided the first rush of many to follow. It sparked the adrenaline high Iglesias enjoyed while working on drug busts for Major Crimes. It's the same surge of energy that José would have had when entering Radiate Primate that fateful day.

Iglesias understands why his son did what he did. The rebellious spirit flows within their family. Unfortunately, the kid didn't make it through to the other side like his father.

This, of life's memories, runs through Iglesias's mind as tears glide in a series of pain on his scrunched-up face. The rain masks them. Yet, his bellowing cries silence the funeral as his knees smudge in the wet dirt, watching his son's black coffin lower into his final resting bed.

No parent should have to lay their child to rest. A father isn't supposed to pour their tears in front of their friends and colleagues watching the last of their family descend into the dirt. Iglesias's boy, the legacy, his friend, everything he had, is gone.

Outside of work, Iglesias didn't have relatives. As he recalls from his strange Winnipeg memory, those that remain are in

Spain, who his parents severed long ago. José's mother stands beside him as Iglesias rises, ignoring the mud on his trousers. The sweet smell of liquor radiates from her breath under the rain. She has some extended family here, like an aunt and an uncle. Closer to the road, a couple of news outlets interview Sergeant Bando. Detective Archer and his retired partner Beckman stay with the rest of the department.

"And he chose to stay with you," came a trembling sneer to Iglesias's right. Of course, she desired to start an argument at this moment.

"At least he lived his life the way he wanted," Iglesias says. *Stop it*.

"Father like son." She shakes her head, her lips pressed together in a tight squeeze. "Why couldn't you protect him?"

"Not now, Susana. There's no purpose."

"I know. I know." She reaches into her small purse and takes a chrome flask. The movement is so smooth that anyone not paying attention would have missed the action. Those that watched wouldn't think anything of it because of her casual confidence. The flask vanished into her bag. That is a clear sign of an alcoholic to Iglesias.

The mourning parents stand as the remaining guests leave, trickling into smaller groups and returning to their cars. At some point, Susana too steps away, and Iglesias remains. His body moves aside with his own closeted skeletons of a troubled youth. His heart stays. He will be there, next to his son's grave.

CHAPTER 23
FOR THE FUTURE

As the saying goes: there's the devil you know and the devil you don't. For Lola, she chased the former, longing to come face-to-face with them. She got what she wanted. Mastema, leader of the Crystal Moths, pierces through her eyes and into her soul.

Chained and gagged, Lola hangs from a steel bar bolted to the ceiling in the back of a tinted van. Mastema sits across from her, left leg crossed, watching with a closed smile. His one elbow rests on his knee while he fiddles with his ring-covered fingers pressing against his palm. His gaze strikes a burning pang that sinks into her heart.

The vehicle makes a few turns and goes over the odd bump. Lola's shoulders brush against the two Crystal Moths on either side of her. Spike's and Baldy's unnatural movements and fangs flicker in her memory. These goons could be any type of creature. A vampire is her first thought, considering what she has seen in the old world. The caked blood smeared on their lips, staining their white blazers, supports this theory.

Lola heard those screams at the Radiate Primate. These Moths killed a group of young adults. The Crystal Moth's strategy has changed since Lola's been in the game. The drug lords take additional care to remain discreet, unlike before where their reckless ways were getting into the public's eyes.

The blackness, Lola thinks, rewinding further to when she blew off Mastema's face. She cannot process what occurred. *Those shadows.* The old world's mystery lives.

Why they didn't capture her before remains a mystery. They fabricated a misleading narrative for years and Mastema ordered them to keep her alive when they could have finished her. He could have killed her in the lounge. The Moths silenced her when they could have broken her. At long last, they take her. It's another tier to this endless, disturbing rabbit hole.

Observations aside, she must escape. They've restrained her well. Beads of cool sweat glide along her spine, dripping from her scalp and underarms. The cuffs are too tight to squeeze her hands through. Even if she broke them, she doesn't have the strength to fight these three.

The van comes to a halt, and the door glides apart to showcase a closing garage. It's a spacious area, designed for multiple semi-trucks. There's a ramp to the left and shelving units line the back wall. Industrial. The vampire Moths unclip and slide her chains from the rod and take her from the vehicle. Her boots drag against the concrete ground as the group follows Mastema. His dress shoes click, echoing in the open space.

Fluorescent lights cast harsh shadows onto the two men in green they approach, whose eyes shroud in darkness from the flat caps they wear. These aren't the usual uniformed soldiers in buttoned work shirts, cargoes, black combat boots. In place of the Canadian flag patch on their left shoulders is a white *A* inside of a light blue shield. The top forms a maple leaf. These are mercenaries.

Keep it together, she thinks. Her sunken heart pumps with heavy thuds, reminding her of the fear humming through her system.

She examines her surroundings, gathering data on where she is. The van ride was not too long, twenty minutes tops, to the best of her judgment. They have to be in Toronto. The receiving point has several ports for large trucks. The exit by the ramp contains a stainless steel text logo mounted on the wall stating: Allen Sky Tower.

"Gentlemen," Mastema says, while extending his arms with a slight bow. "May you take us to Dr. Lang, please?"

"Of course, sir," one mercenary says. "Loading dock?"

"Let's take the front and see that new lobby."

"Yes, sir."

The group marches to and through the exit and into a long hall complete with bright white lights eradicating shadows. A turn here, an extended walk there, and they reach an elevator activated by the military's blue key fob. The small black box beeps, lights up green, and the chrome lift doors slide open. Six of them step inside and the second military man uses a red card, presses a button to level thirteen, taking them below the surface.

Not superstitious, Lola thinks. The observation served no purpose whatsoever other than a reminder of her apartment renting days. Many landlords refused to have floor thirteen because they consider it bad luck. The descending hoist is a greater concern. Towers kiss the skies, not dive thirteen levels below the ground.

The elevator stops, the doors glide open, and the group marches past the ten-foot ceiling lobby with a white, glossy round counter in the front. The polished pearl floors are a mirror reflection of the world. A blonde secretary types away on a computer, eyes lowered. Behind her, an eight-foot, backlit, stainless steel logo mounts the wall. The design contains gears forming a brain inside the silhouette of a human head with text below stating: Manageficient Enterprises. To the left and right of the structure are clear passages leading to the next area.

Mastema nods at the graphic with a smile, approving the artwork.

They take Lola beyond.

The new hall is wide enough for a two-lane road. People in lab coats, hazmat suits, and dress wear and additional mercenaries walk on concrete ground. Some carry boxes, notebooks, tablets, or move dollies. At the far end of the hall is an open foyer with glass railings overlooking lower levels. On each side of them are open windows showcasing small laboratories that the people enter and leave from. Scientists extract grey diamond-shaped objects into vials on white work counters.

Mine. Of all the thoughts desperate little Lola could have regarding the underground military science workshop, she thinks of ash. The scale held by the gloved hand of a scientist sucks her focus in. She has hers in her bra. *If only.*

"Ah, yes. Dr. Lang," Mastema says.

Spike and Baldy pass Lola to their mercenary companions. With an intense grip, each clamps onto her bicep, leaving no room for escape. The bloodsucker Moths didn't need to show any intimidation. These men, as far as Lola can tell, are human. She could take them, or so she believes. Her interest lies in the newcomer.

A five-foot-two feeble man with a comb over and thick-framed glasses takes a bow. He removes his wrinkled hands from his lab coat pocket and shakes Mastema's with a firm grip. His open smile raises the countless crows' feet along the edges of his eyes and exposes coffee-stained teeth.

"Mastema, my dear friend. I did not expect a visit so soon. I have meetings throughout the week, and no news on synthesizing."

Mastema holds Dr. Lang's hand with both of his, the gold-ring-covered fingers on top. "No, that's not why I am here. Did you not receive my text message?"

"I must have missed it. It's been quite busy here lately. The scales and the sha—" Dr. Lang shifts his gaze at Lola, blinking several times. The bewilderment on his face grows as he tries to make sense of why she is a tied, helpless animal.

Mastema's cold hands contact her shoulders, causing a sudden jolt of discomfort. A growl escapes her throat, ending in forced saliva slipping from the corner of her gag. It drizzles off her lip, resting on her chin.

"This is what I bring you," Mastema says. He pats Lola's upper arms twice. Her eyes wince each time.

Dr. Lang rests his hand on his mouth. There's no sympathy in those eyes. She's seen that gaze on Synarion, medical doctors, and on police officers. It's the look you're given when they're analyzing you to their own agenda. They don't see Lola as an equal, let alone a person. The doctor sees her as an object.

"Come," Dr. Lang says, waving at them.

Mastema releases Lola and joins Dr. Lang in the front. The military men and Lola take the middle with the Moths in the rear. She no longer walks with them, and returns to dragging her feet, forcing the mercenaries to put in a little extra effort.

"A strange turn of events," one mercenary whispers into her ear.

A glimmer of red swirls in the man's green eyes from her peripheral view. The damn shape shifting double agent. Discreet and ever-watching. With Mastema here and the security, it's unlikely they'll help her escape. The presence of the being adds to her continually burning inner flame; for all she knows, she was set up.

"This is the one you've been so infatuated with?" Dr. Lang asks.

Mastema speaks, "Infatuated? Intrigued is a better word. At first I dismissed her, and a tingle caught my attention. I thought it was the synthesizing. However, I'm no scientist. You're the expert and I am hoping you can shed light on the situation. No pun intended." Mastema chuckles, as if he made some kind of joke. It relates to Dr. Lang, because he expresses a closed smile.

It's evident the two don't care that she can listen to their scheming. This scenario gives off the same atmosphere as a spy novel. The hero at the villain's secret lab where the mastermind reveals their ultimate scheme. She can't deny the fact that her gut has shrivelled to a raisin. The flame has exhausted her energy. She prays to any entity listening: she won't learn their plan and will get the hell out of here.

Dr. Lang's hands cup behind his back as he talks. "You bring plenty of mysteries, my friend. You truly believe this girl can provide insight into such an ancient unknown that the brilliant minds I have cannot solve?"

Mastema shrugs. "We can try, can we not?"

"Yes. Both substances are intriguing, and you haven't shared the complete story with me, Mastema. Understanding the origins of the scale would drastically help us break the unknown chemicals found within the samples."

"In due time. My business partners would be quite upset if their sources were revealed. I simply provide the ash—a middleman, if you will."

Dr. Lang clears his throat and says, "If your partners decide to be more open, we can help them and you. Until that time, we're working in isolation with missing pieces of the puzzle. Our progress will remain stagnant."

"That is why I am finding a solution, so each of us is pleased. It is what I do. Believe me when I say this girl . . ." Mastema points at Lola with his index finger, keeping his rear to her, eyes on Dr. Lang, ". . . will be of significant interest."

"To synthesize Osteo-ashderm? Mastema, you make me wonder if ash fuses from humans."

Mastema shrugs. "That would be nonsense. See what she can offer. I think she has more value in our other project. Synthesization is a patch job to our grander focus." Mastema leans into the man's ear and whispers.

Dr. Lang shakes his head. "No. Not even my sister is aware. I am personally involved with it. Mr. Patterson isn't aware either."

Mastema raises an eyebrow. "What about Prime Minister Trudell?"

Dr. Lang shakes his head again.

"Good. The girl, take blood and whatever you need. I must keep hold of her. She is a Machiavellian."

Dr. Lang's eyes squint, showing his confusion, equal to Lola's about their situation. He stops, looks back at her, noticing the cheap smeared foundation revealing portions of her three scars. His focus shifts to the signature bullet scar beside her clavicle. "Oh, is this *the* Lola Cabello?"

"The one and only," Mastema says with a smile.

"I barely recognized her." He continues walking, reaching the end of the hall. They pass the clear railings, taking a right into a new corridor. They take the first staircase down. One after the other, they descend fifteen flights. The group follows. Transparent windows are on each side of them. These labs are barren, lights off, with large crystal cylinder pods filled with liquid. Silhouettes float inside, connected to tubes extending from the container to the ceiling.

"The fu—" Lola mumbles through the gag. There's more going on here than she can witness. The Moths have their wings cast wider than she once knew.

"Surprising, yes?" the shapeshifter whispers, breath tingling in her ear.

Dr. Lang continues, "Never thought I'd meet Cabello."

Mastema speaks, "Well, you have far more interesting things to do than follow the news. I mean, what does CRISPR technology scratch compared to what you're working on?"

CRISPR, Lola thinks. That's a term she missed while in prison.

Dr. Lang lets out a dry chuckle, taking a left turn. "Bioengineering is a much older science than CRISPR."

"What does it stand for again? Clustered . . . ?" Mastema asks, to Lola's convenience.

"Clustered Regularly Interspaced Short Palindromic Repeats."

Mastema snaps his finger. "That's it. Science loves its acronyms."

"Bioengineering goes further back," Dr. Lang says. "We've bioengineered cows and modern dogs. Docile creatures compared to the former."

They pass another lab, bathed in pure white light, illuminating the surrounding darkness. In the centre of the bare room, a three-foot tall pillar casts a distinct shadow. The chrome material of the object emits a pulsating glow, creating a three-dimensional effect by lifting the silhouette with each interval. The movement transforms the blackness into cloud-like blobs. A strange invisible force pushes against her body with each pulse. The act resembles the glitching shadows from when she shot Mastema.

Dr. Lang speaks, "I appreciate your confidence in me, Mastema. However, what I do is incredibly complex. Few people understand the process, myself included. You remove one of these key individuals and there is the vast chasm of knowledge lost. Each of them is as important as me. If the acquisition doesn't happen, we won't have the funds to stay afloat. I'll lose these good scientists."

"You'll get your money," Mastema says in a flat tone.

"On Mr. Patterson's terms. I can't say I am fond of having to work for a boss again."

"That's on paper. You can do whatever you want. I mean, you're in his tower."

"I suppose," Dr. Lang says with a sigh.

The group comes to a stop at the end of the hall next to a closed chrome door. He uses a key fob strapped to his belt on the black box beside it. The box beeps. Doors slide open, and they step inside to face an operating table dead centre with a spotlight beaming onto it. Hands and feet cuffs rest on the corners. Numerous surgical tools, needles, and other medical devices that Lola cannot recognize are on nearby rolling trays. As far as she is concerned, this is grave news.

Lola tries to jerk free from the men. Their grips are too tight. Animalistic fear has taken over, and she has to escape. Her thoughts spin: will they dissect her? What are they going to do with those needles? Does anyone know she is here?

"Stay still," the shapeshifter whispers.

She shakes her head several times while Dr. Lang and Mastema walk around the table. The mercenaries force Lola onto the surface. One holds her by the neck and the other straps each of her limbs in, with her hope diminishing with each buckle. The shapeshifter doesn't make eye contact with her while performing the task. Lola could call them out, expose them to the humans. What good would that do? These people wouldn't believe her.

Unless they're not a double agent? she thinks. It doesn't answer why the shapeshifter would give her intel to assassinate Mastema and help her escape.

A woman with a tight bun walks into the room. Her lab coat sways with each step. The mask conceals her true emotion. Her blue gloves reach for Lola's gag as she steps in front of the spotlight, and then she frees Lola's mouth. She, the doctor, and the First are unrecognizable with the beaming ray behind them. The three shadows have brief brushes of their features outlined on their forms. The military aren't in view.

Mastema's cold voice is clear as ever. "As long as you stay with me, you have free will to explore your dream."

Lola tugs on the tight cuffs around her wrists and ankles. Her muscles tense in futile resistance. The touch of a hand, adorned with a gold ring, against her greasy hair, compels her to move. His gentle contact distracts her from the slender tool approaching her skin. She clenches her teeth. Mastema removes his fingers, and the cold realization hits Lola that the assistant takes several vials' worth of fluid before removing the needle from her arm.

"Doctor, do you have any of the ash liquid variation?" Mastema asks Dr. Lang.

"Of course," the other says.

"Can you get it for me?"

"It's difficult to produce," the doctor says.

A grin rises on Mastema's face, shown in brief highlights of his lips and teeth due to the backlight against his face. "Scientists experiment, do they not?"

Dr. Lang squints and walks beyond Lola's view. The assistant is gone. It's her and the First.

"Who are you, Lola Cabello?" Mastema asks, leaning in. His face moves to the sliver of exposed skin at her hip. He lifts the fabric to showcase her heart-shaped QR code tattoo made of various black and white squares.

"What's this?" Mastema says. "Is this your famous kill switch?"

Lola bites her lip, exhaling heavy breaths through her nose. *Of course he knows.*

"You didn't think I was unaware of this, did you? I don't read minds. I have many ears. The police profiled you, silly girl." He shakes his head. "You truly believe that if you got enough evidence, you could distribute it across the Internet and somehow dismantle my entire operation?" His icy finger follows the shape of the heart, leaving a trail of goosebumps in its wake. Lola thrashes her legs, wishing she could push him away.

"What is your upbringing? Your family is obvious. Grandparents? Great-grandparents? Great-great-great-grandparents?"

"Fuck you," Lola says through her teeth.

"Concentrated light in the shape of a bullet, kill switch tattoos, obsession with ash, miraculously escaping prison, my, my. How did you escape prison? I was expecting you to be delivered here. Yet, Officer Clarkson is gone. Some blood and no corpse. How odd."

"Go to hell," Lola says.

"Who gave you that concentrated light? Did they assist in your escape?"

Dr. Lang and his assistant return with a vial of black liquid. The assistant pushes her glasses up her nose, looking at Lola with a gaze as dead as the doctor's. She steps away as Dr. Lang double-checks the measurement in the vial.

"Dr. Lang, can you do me a favour?" Mastema says.

"What is it?" he asks as he presses the needle against her other arm's vein.

"Remove this thing." Mastema points to the QR code tattooed. "Use it as a skin sample or whatever. Take it off. "

"Of course," Dr. Lang says.

He injects Lola with the black liquid.

Lola's body turns to concrete, her breath halting. She has seen vazelead blood: blacker than mould. Or is this concentrated ash? Synthesized? Endless questions flood Lola while the fluid channels into her bloodstream.

Dr. Lang removes the needle and passes it to his assistant. Lola's heart rate accelerates, feeling the weight of the two men leaning over her, their presence palpable. The sensation of warmth rises where the syringe was on her arm, spreading, radiating heat through her body. With each inhale, she takes in large gulps of air. Her breath shifts to quick and repetitive cycles. Sweat beads on her skin.

Dr. Lang says, "I haven't been able to break down the unknown four percent of Osteo-ashderm."

The room blooms, burning her eyes.

Mastema shrugs. "Not a problem. Categorize it, and name them accordingly."

Breathe. The silhouette forms blend in with the light.

"This is reptilian, the lacertilia suborder. It also contains bufotenin . . ."

You've had ash. Breathe in. Glowing orbs, photons, swirl around the space illuminating from the bulb.

". . . 5-HO-DMT . . ."

And out. Come on. She isn't in a normal place.

" . . . and somehow relates to the coca plant? You need to tell me what Osteo-ashderm is. It must be a biologic drug because the potency cannot be isolated. We need more of the creature."

Swallowing is difficult for Lola as her mouth dries with lingering, thick saliva. The laboratory lightbulb casts a halo of rainbow hues, painting the room in a vibrant and mesmerizing display. The walls expand and contrast. They're breathing. Her veins morph into hot rods, glowing purple below the skin. Yet, her fingers and toes are ice cold.

"I understand that, Mastema," Dr. Lang says. His voice echoes for several seconds.

I understand . . .

I understand . . . I understand.

Mastema. Mastema. Mastema.

Lola squints at Mastema, whose hair and clothes peel around to his back, bobbing as if he were underwater. No flesh or bone is underneath: a silhouette of a human. The flaps fuse into two glowing white eagle wings complete with black tips, dripping ink that dissipates into fog.

"What are you, Lola?" Mastema asks, voice distant. His lips don't move. In fact, the room has frozen in time. Dr. Lang's mouth is open, mid-sentence.

"Where did you get the bullet?" Mastema says.

Her body drops, or she rises, it doesn't matter; warmth envelopes her. The brightness of the lamps blossom. Whiteness devours the room, including the others. Mastema and Lola remain.

The First, comes a new, distant voice. It's not Lola's thought, and it's not Mastema's. There is another, feminine and gentle, calling to her. It's a welcoming one that she once heard before prison. Or perhaps it's the longing for her dead mother. In the end, the sound is bliss.

She's been on this road before. Lola was an ash-dasher. A span of two years has gone by and the effects are potent. She didn't have to escape, nor inflict violence. Terrible acts occur daily to no resolution. Lola needed this injection more than anything. Euphoria.

CHAPTER 24
FOUL EYES

The pure liquid injection dosage of vazelead scales is enough to render Lola useless. She phases in and out of consciousness. For two days? An hour? While lying on that operating table, they unlocked her shackles and took them. Her legs and arms flop in random motion, as if they were mutated into boneless flesh tubes. She is stuck as the watcher in her eyes, consumed by an excessive amount of the drug.

She swears a thousand stones tumble in her skull, rattling around, banging against the dome to fester an unbearable headache. At some point, her captors snag her and take flight because the transportation is too thunderous. Her consciousness fades again as her mind transcends higher than their aircraft and beyond the mortal realm.

Let go.

Return to us, Lola.

Familiar voices.

The End.

A singular voice, past the continual whispers that fuel her fire, merges with the world and is the same one she heard on previous ash trips. Its sound is a soothing warmth that captivates her. Once she trusted it. This time, she is unsure, swimming through a freezing ocean of blackness. The weight sinks her, though she is incapable of defining the above. Away she goes into obsidian.

Why?

The biting waters become an abyss of darkness, enveloping her in its chilling embrace. The force accelerates, pushing her through the currents, and her face smacks into jagged dry rocks. Dust engulfs her surroundings. A spotlight pierces through the ocean sky from whence she fell from and focuses on her. In front, a soft glow illuminates tree trunks, suggesting a dense forest. The sound of girlish laughter echoes through the woods.

Lola Love, comes a voice from the thicket. It bounces throughout the trees. No one calls Lola by that name except for her dear Becky. Becky Bubs. One third of the Trinity of Souls.

Lola Love!

"Becky!" Lola shouts. She scurries to her feet with the strength she failed to have in Mastema's grasp. She kicks up dust as she bolts into the dark forest. The trunks are thin and look like people with arms extending into branches as she dashes deeper into the darkness. The spotlight follows, casting sharp shadows against the trees.

Lola Love . . .

How is it possible? Then again, this is ash. It is Pandora's Box. She could be speaking to the dead. She's met beings of the afterlife in the past. Is it such a far leap to think it lets her contact souls from the other side?

"Becky!" Lola shouts, pushing branches aside. She's drenched in sweat, panting, and looks to a distant hill, spotting the outline of a girl with dreadlocks standing at the top. Lola rushes up the slope, dodging exposed roots and low shrubbery covered in thorns. Some of them scrape against her legs as she pushes past the last foliage to the summit. The girl is nowhere to be found.

At the bottom of the other side, a series of pillars with wide plateaus form platforms. On the initial terrace, by the edge of the forest, stands an individual in a grey hoodie with an extended frown.

"Michael?" Lola calls out. Yes, she is piecing the dreamscape together. Two of the Trinity of Souls are here.

The man turns and hops to the next platform, then the one after. Lola dashes down the hill and reaches the first plateau and takes a leap, landing on the new surface. She leaps onto the following. Michael is faster, and she falls behind. He vanishes in the endless blackness. The light from the sky-ocean follows her, bringing a mountain into view at the end of the plateaus.

"Lol-a-a-a!" comes an older woman's howl, crackling the last vowel. It's a familiar tone that pierces Lola's memory, yanking it to the surface of her consciousness. That sound calling her name is indeed her mother's. The Trinity of Souls is complete.

Through the force of death, and beyond the impossible, the three contact her. Lola needs to discover if it is the afterlife or a mirage. She leaps over the remaining platforms and to the mountain, climbing the steep, jagged rocks. Sweat runs down her face. The dry dust of the boulders cracks open her fingers. Her left leg shakes with effort. Her persistence pays off, and she reaches the top, pulling herself onto the surface with a groan.

At the summit, a zigzag path leads to the ultimate peak. A short woman stands at the top, watching her. The light reveals her features with each step Lola takes. Frizzy hair covers the woman's face, though she has the same thin frame as Lola's mother.

"Mom!" Lola smiles. A surge of heat emanates from her heart, creating a comforting sensation that spreads throughout her chest. That is pure joy; a feeling she hasn't experienced in years, thanks to seeing her mom once more.

The lady moves aside as Lola reaches the top. Lola steps forward, and her mom retreats. Even with the closing distance, there is too much hair to see the warm wrinkled face that Lola longs for.

"Mom?" Lola asks. She approaches closer again. The woman shifts away. They repeat this step dance until they reach the edge of the peak. "Mom," Lola says. She makes one more initiative forward and Lola's mother rushes towards her. She lifts her head and the frizzy hair jolts with electric energy.

The spotlight shines upon the lady, revealing the wrinkles of her mother with the matching Cupid's bow and nose. Erecting from her right is two-thirds of a man's face whose strong jawline and flat brows cast the infamous intimidation of Michael Bradford. To the left is Becky Murphy, with a crooked smirk melting into the being's central mouth. Becky's red dreadlocks dangle onto the shoulders.

The Trinity of Souls stare at her with their three eyes. A single one for Becky, Michael, and a large bloodshot one resting dead centre on her mother's face. Their mashed jaws form a snarl with rotting grey and yellow teeth.

"Why, Lola?" the being says, with the multiple voices speaking at once. "Why let us die?"

"I didn't mean to!" Lola shouts, stepping back.

The being's legs elongate into insect appendages, arcing over Lola. "Avenge us! Avenge us!" Their arms shoot for the ocean sky. The warmth that radiated from her heart snuffs out, leaving her innards colder than the mountaintop. Her loved ones wouldn't do this.

"I did it for you!" Overwhelmed by fear, Lola's limbs give way and she crumples to the ground, her body contorting into a shrimp. "I tried. I did," she whispers into the dirt. She can't comprehend what type of monster they've turned into because of her.

The Trinity of Souls shrouds the spotlight. "Avenge us! Die with us. Be one with us." Leaning closer, the being's jaw stretches outward, a menacing sight that signals Lola's imminent consumption in a single swift motion.

"No," Lola mutters, with reason entering her mind. Mom, Becky, and Michael wouldn't say such things. These aren't the people she adored. Ash lets Lola see the desires and worries of others. It's also a reflection in her consciousness. This abomination of the three is no vision of the afterlife. This is a demon she created.

The teeth elongate into fangs as a blazing putrid breath pushes her hair aside.

She needs revenge; she must to do right for her family and for those that have suffered. It's not for the ones that have died; it's for those that are alive.

Slime oozes past the dry, cracked lips, and onto Lola's shoulders.

There, beside her, a sharp rock fades into existence. This is her mind. She is in control and snags the weapon with a battle cry. Death's jaws close in. She rams the pointed rock into the central pupil, penetrating through the vitreous sphere and into the brain. A shriek erupts. Blood and translucent discharge splatters onto Lola as she pulls the rock free. She stabs the beast again. It twitches and cries, collapsing, with red splattering onto the ground. Hot steam sizzles on the stone and against Lola's face.

She ignores the acidic fluids eating her flesh, thrusting the sharp rock until the creature topples over. That's not enough. She steps over the Trinity of Souls, who raises their hands, begging for mercy. The boiling substances eat away at its own form, shrinking it to a human-sized body. Steam envelops Lola's view because of the chemical reaction, creating an acrid scent. Lola plummets the stone onto its face two more times for good measure. Her weapon bubbles, eroding, and she chucks it aside.

The steam clears, and the sight forces her to hold her breath. The being she killed wears her mother's clothes. Their face, it's new. The Cupid's bow and sharp-angled nose remain. The skin lacks wrinkles, hair thick and radiant, like her own. This is Lola. Her mouth hangs open with a forked tongue resting against her chin. The two yellow reptilian eyes stare at her.

CHAPTER 25
REPTILIAN OVERLORDS

Lola's eyes peel open with the sensation of hundreds of sharp diamonds scraping against her eyeballs. It's the dehydration of the eyelids moving. The lack of moisture glues her lips together and seals her tongue to the roof of her mouth. The sense of razor blades jabbing her throat emphasize the taste of dry blood along her gums and palate.

Water, Lola thinks.

The world is at a ninety-degree angle. Yes, Lola is lying down. It takes a moment for her to understand this as she uses her elbow to push herself off the ground. Her limbs wobble and she topples onto the concrete again. The action ignites a pain in her lower stomach, sharp with radiating heat. She's stripped of her clothes, left in her underwear. The ash bag tucked in her bra is gone. Bandages wrap her abdomen, hips, and thigh, covering where her heart-shaped tattoo should be. It's stained red.

Whah? Lola thinks. Her sluggish fingers struggle with the cloth that presses tight against her flesh. She manages to get a glimpse inside: a mucilaginous bloody mess of what appears to be grafted tissue. A slab of pink skin lays where her ink should be. There is no need to look at the thigh. It's clear they used surgical precision to slice off her kill switch, replaced by her upper leg.

"Fuck, fuck, Christ," Lola croaks. She blinks twice and rolls onto her back to examine her surroundings to see what other unfortunate news it has to bear.

One rectangular window, complete with metal bars, is at the top of the ceiling. Dirt covers the glass in front of the iron grating with a small sliver of daylight piercing through. What else? She rests beside a brick wall with chains draped onto the cement floor leading to a hook jammed into the ground. Two meters ahead is the jail cell door. The rods are thick and close together, bolted in place. Not a lone rock, pebble, stick, or object of use are inside the cell. Concrete. Outside of her cell, beyond the reach of the singular light source, is a hallway into blackness.

"The princess wakes," a smooth, cold voice echoes from the other side of the jail cell.

Mastema, she thinks. Lola makes a second attempt to sit. It's a success, and she rests against the rough brick wall.

"How was your ash? Sleepyhead." Mastema chuckles, voice reverberating against the space. "It awakens a force within you, doesn't it?" He steps from the darkness at the opposite corner of the hall. It prompts Lola to ponder how long he's been waiting in the dark. He stops in front of the cell. His hands rest on the bars with the rings clanging against the metal. "Am I what you expected? The big bad devil that ruined poor Lola's life?"

Lola tries to swallow saliva, except it's too thick and the glob sits in her throat. She doesn't want to reply. There is no point.

"Where'd you get it? The bullet?" Mastema asks, head tilting. The long bone-white hair grazes his sharp jawline.

Lola places her hands on her lap, making the chains scrape against the floor.

"Your demeanour and upbringing tell me you're incompetent to make such a weapon and to obtain the intel to assassinate me. You've found yourself powerful allies."

Don't talk to him.

A drawn-out breath escapes his lungs. "This is going to take some time, isn't it? That's okay. We have ample time since Dr. Lang extracted valuable data from you."

She bites her lip.

"You have so much value, my dear girl." Mastema takes a few steps to the side, letting the rings glide against the bars, echoing in the space. He continues, "When you walked into that lounge, I sensed a potent energy that I haven't felt in a long time. It's different from what you're projecting now. Which I must admit is quite tasty. Mmmm." He smacks his lips. "Your crushed ego has gusto. At the club, I detected a compelling sting that comes from an ancient time."

He stops at the other end of the cell and grips the bars, resting his forehead on the metal. "It took me down memory lane. At least until you blew my face off." His hands slide off the bar and he walks towards her. "This pivot may come as a surprise to you. Your goal was simple: get revenge. It's not your fault. You don't understand what you are or why Dr. Lang sampled you. You sort of fell into the rabbit hole."

"Where is my skin?" Lola says, her voice hoarse.

A loud clap booms from Mastema's palms. "She speaks. And so demanding at that. I tell you what, tell me who gave you the bullet, and I will give you your flesh. You can publish your convincing evidence online."

In Lola's foggy mind, her instinct is to say no. He had a doctor cut her tissue and take blood samples. This is Mastema, the drug lord and the First. Lola would be wise not to make deals with such a character.

"The silent treatment again." Mastema takes a key from his white pants pocket to unlock the jail cell. It swings open with a creak as he steps inside.

Lola scoots away, the jagged bricks scratching her shoulder blades. Mastema leans over and grabs the chains from the middle of the cell and in one tug, he brings her to him. On her back, she swings her foot in a slow arc, her heel missing him.

The weight of her body smothers her lungs, limiting her breath. Fear pins her dry eyes open.

Mastema flips his keyring, unphased by her petrified state, until he finds one and inserts it in the shackles surrounding her wrists. "I'm not sure why my men shackled you in the first place. What are you going to do?" Mastema smiles while standing. "Run? Look at you. Listen, I have to make the world move. Torturing is not my specialty. Quite frankly, I find it rather boring. What I care about is who gave you the concentrated light."

Lola sits as the First steps aside. She rubs her red and purple wrists, feeling the moisture that built on the skin.

"Think about my offer, Lola Cabello," Mastema says as footsteps rise from deeper in the hall, sealing their conversation.

He's unphased by the evidence I have. That bullet. The shaper. These three sentences are the first clear thoughts that enter her mind. She has more to bargain with, at the cost of betraying her mysterious ally.

A black limousine cruises on an S-shaped highway through the vast Canadian wilderness. Wide mountains surround the entire peripheral view with pine trees and shrubbery in the ditches. This is a familiar vehicle for Scalebane. She has taken this route in the past. It leads to Mastema's luxurious mansion.

The same soft skin chauffeur drives the automobile each time. She can detect his musty stench underneath his attempted usage of deodorant, aftershave, and showering. There's no scrubbing off the smell of an ape. It's in their glands.

This trip differs from her previous. King's son sits next to her on the polished black leather seats. The material squeaks when her leather armour brushes against it. Both keep their cloaks wrapped, hiding their vazelead features.

"*Take responsibility and hatch my son's children,*" comes King's voice in Scalebane's mind. Rithu's stench is as potent as the chauffeur's. Everywhere she goes, there's some unpleasant smell. It's part of life. However, there are boundaries for a reason. One example: bearing Rithu's hatchlings. That was Namsruc's choice, her dear sister, who is nowhere to be found.

Useless demon, Scalebane thinks, pondering how she will get into Hell, how Synarion and Namsruc did. *Useless painter.* Anger is getting the better of her.

"Why do you think Mastema wishes for us to join him?" Rithu asks.

"I couldn't tell you. Mastema is a fan of his theatricals." A part of Scalebane wonders if the fallen angel has communicated with King and is going to make some strange mating ritual for them. It wouldn't be beyond his realm of action.

"How did your mission go?" Rithu asks, leaning forward.

Too eager. "I'm sorry?" Scalebane asks.

"We haven't spoken since you left. Jekos and I kept the ash operation running."

She cups her gloves together. "Oh, yes. It went fine."

"I heard you spoke with my father."

Scalebane crosses her legs away from Rithu. "Is that so?"

"Yes, he said you're pleased with our working condition. Our—" Rithu clears his throat. "—bonding." He says the last word far quicker, as if embarrassed by it.

Scalebane nods. "He did, did he? And what do you suppose that bonding is?"

Before he can answer, the limousine decelerates to a curved bronze gate that splits midway. Brick columns rest on each side with one of them containing the electronics controlling it. The metal barriers slide away and the elegant car moves onto the private road.

Rithu leans back. "I didn't mean to interject, Scalebane. I respect you. I want you to trust me. You have my loyalty. And I . . . I think . . ."

By Dega'Mostikas, Scalebane thinks. "You're doing admirable work. King is right, I am pleased with you."

Rithu's chest expands with pride. He's a damn dog that needs constant reassurance from his owner. Pathetic.

Their ride reaches a U-shaped driveway with Roman style columns holding a roof, sheltering the limousine from that scorching sun. Scalebane exits first, keeping herself in the shadows to avoid the harmful rays. Rithu follows her actions. Even with her skin being sealed head to toe, she feels the boiling sensation of the light. Rithu can too. The rotting taste lingers in her mouth, as if her innards are decomposing. They reach the large red oak front doors as the panels push aside. Jekos, in his burgundy three-piece suit, steps out with a toothy grin. Beside him is a Moth with grease-coated dirty blond hair. His frail form says he hasn't eaten in weeks. A toothpick rests between his teeth.

A damp, must smell ending in a sharp sting reminds Scalebane of crickets. This stench projects from the Moth, who is no ordinary one. That distinctive scent belongs to the shaper. The same one Rithu employed to have Sierra assassinated.

The half-Imp takes a bow as the doors shut behind him. "Thank you for making time to come here, Scalebane and Rithu."

"What is this, Jekos?" Scalebane asks. "Shouldn't we be on the other side of the country?"

"Agreed," Rithu says. "We have the western ports neatly sealed with Allen Shipping Solutions. East leads to America's New York."

Jekos holds his one fist and balances on his heels. "I'm afraid that's not why Mastema brought you both here."

"Why the shaper?" Rithu asks.

The shaper shrugs.

"Mastema captured Lola Cabello." Jekos looks into Scalebane's goggles, piercing past the dark glass and into her fiery eyeballs. Jekos's prolonged, intense stare reveals his deep concern, despite his enthusiastic tone. It's a signal meant for her alone.

"That is good news, is it not?" Rithu says.

Jekos maintains his grin. "Of course it is. He thinks the three of you should be present for this. Well, specifically Rithu."

Rithu's tail sways.

Jekos waves them inside and the four enter. The large doors shut with a low, trembling click. Their footsteps echo on the white marble, amplified by the dome-shaped lobby of the mansion's entrance. The shaper walks ahead of them.

The half-imp continues, "An exercise that Mastema deems quite important. You see, Lola made an assassination attempt."

"How?" Rithu asks. He glances at Scalebane, then Jekos. "First she escapes from prison and then finds Mastema?"

Jekos shrugs. "She's a resourceful one. Look, Rithu, head to the basement where Mastema is waiting. I need to show Scalebane some numbers regarding the latest ash import since she's been vacant."

Rithu nods. "Any I should be aware of?"

"Same old we have been over," the other says.

Scalebane waves to the hallway completed with red oak running boards. "We'll be with you both in a moment."

Rithu nods his head with a quick jerk, so desperate to please. He hurries through the hall, passing original mounted paintings encompassed in golden frames to join the shaper.

Jekos and Scalebane follow them at a controlled stroll. This slow motion gives too much emphasis on the pins inside her muscles. She does her best to hide the pain. The half-imp is close enough that his signature firewood smell swirled with burning plastic seeps into her nostrils. His voice is low as he leans into Scalebane's hood.

"This wasn't a development that I had anticipated," he says.

Scalebane leans back. "Lola Cabello is a reckless soft skin. I'm not surprised she got herself captured." It's a bittersweet revenge. Prison wasn't enough of a punishment in Scalebane's mind. Cabello deserves pain for what she did to her.

His index finger taps her forearm, and he clears his throat, looking at the ceiling. There, above a mounted painting of lush forests, Zingalg, is a small black dome with a reflective sheen.

Cameras, Scalebane thinks. They're everywhere. She relaxes her spine, indulging her companion.

He speaks, "Have you thought about my proposal?"

The other replies, "No. I'm unsure if it concerns me."

"It certainly will when Mastema gets what he's looking for. I'm not talking about synthesising ash."

"Which is?" Scalebane asks.

"Full control. You struggle with it. It's why you avoid me. It's the source of tension between you and Rithu."

Scalebane stops, and Jekos steps in front of her, cupping his hands together. She raises her index claws and points at him. "That is between myself and King."

"You detest the boy. I can't blame you. He's so desperate to please you that he will do anything. It's pathetic."

"If only King heard you insult his son. Or Zoefani. Even Mastema would deal with the backlash."

"Yes, yes. I suppose you're right. You have good instincts, Scalebane. Yet, you're quite dense with what I offer." He raises his toxic green eyebrow.

"Why?"

"Rithu. Mastema."

"Why are you mentioning this? It's more frequent than before," Scalebane says.

Jekos checks behind and leans closer to Scalebane. The half-imp's eyes move back-and-forth, attempting to read her expressionless mask. "Lola Cabello accessed a rare bullet forged from concentrated light of the Heavenly Kingdoms, scripted with words of a long-forgotten book."

"Nonsense." Scalebane doesn't want to know what book. The soft skin couldn't have gotten such an item from beyond.

Scalebane cannot find a gateway into the afterlife. Another did. *Synarion*, she thinks.

The two continue walking, joining Rithu and the shaper. They've disappeared around the corner, an additional forty paces.

Jekos whispers, "Mastema is keeping information from us, including me. This bullet would end any angel."

"How would Lola get this concentrated light from the Heavens, let alone find the First?" Scalebane asks.

"Fair question. Mastema will want to extract intel from her. Afterlife material doesn't appear in the mortal realm. Those scriptures? Long forgotten."

"Why are you telling me this? I was to learn it."

Jekos rubs his hands together and a stuttering chuckle forces itself from his lungs. "If you're willing to accept my proposal, I may recall more than I currently remember."

"I'm sure you would."

"Weapons made of concentrated light should snuff out an angel. One scripted with the power to under Creationism will dissolve the First. Yet, Mastema lives," Jekos says.

"Then how does he live?" Scalebane asks.

"A concern indeed."

"No guesses?"

"Nothing concrete, you?"

Yes, she thinks, unwilling to share the news of the lightless ones. They're angered and Mastema was shot the night she witnessed the shadows twitch. He is toying with the beyond. It's her intel until she decides to join Jekos. "Not at the moment. You can't tell me how Cabello got into the Heavenly Kingdoms?"

Jekos scratches his head.

It is undeniable that Jekos played a role in the attempted murder of his master. Lola didn't reach the beyond. The cunning half-imp obtained concentrated light from the afterlife, the same place where Synarion and her sister reside. This could be her entrance into Hell. It's a stretch.

A dead demon's map is pointless. Dasco is proving of little use for finding Namsruc. The muse is taking him in a different direction. As she grapples with the enormity of this new path, her heart breaks into smaller pieces.

This is speculation. Scalebane is connecting dots that are far removed from one another. There are looming dangers coming from multiple angles. Mastema plays a key part in it, as does Dasco, and Lola Cabello. Jekos too, considering his shrouded order. Scalebane can't operate alone forever.

Lola scoots further from Mastema, whose hands remain in his pocket. He has that same analytical gaze that Dr. Lang had. She's a specimen. More than anything, she would love to rip his face off.

She pushes herself to her feet, arms shaking, using the brick wall for support. Standing, she winces as her grafted skin throbs with pain. Lola stumbles once, her knees grazing the ground, before she regains her footing, gasping for breath. The metaphoric stones in her skull rebound against the sides of her head and send several rattles down her skeleton.

Mastema shakes his head. Her physical weakness is apparent.

The steps grow louder. Two figures appear. One is a classic Moth in a white suit. The second is a lean, cloaked figure. The fabric drapes to the ground where leather boots glide on the concrete. Behind them, a charcoal tail sways with each step. It pauses Lola's breath. It can't be. Lola doesn't want to accept the reality of what is coming. Her heart races, signalling the truth's approach.

The Moth puts their hands in his pockets, standing off to the side. A swirl of red comes from one eye as he winks at Lola.

"Ah yes, Rithu Blacktooth," Mastema says. He strolls out of the cell to meet the newcomers.

This vazelead isn't Scalebane. He is taller, muscles more prominent and lean in proportion to his frame. The black cloak drapes over his skull and cascades onto his shoulders, adding an ominous touch to his leather armour. Like Scalebane, this Rithu Blacktooth dons a mask. Theirs is different: a sleek design with narrow goggles and a solid metal humanoid front.

Mastema extends his gold-ring hand and shakes Rithu's gloved claws. "I'm glad you joined me. I have a special task for you. One that your father has endorsed."

"Yes, my father mentioned this," Rithu says in a croaky, muffled voice, reminding Lola of Scalebane. Their people share the same dry cadence.

"You've gained so much experience working with my organization, alongside Scalebane. By the way, how are you two?" With a noticeable shift in tone, the First's voice becomes infused with an insatiable interest in their relationship.

"Well," Rithu says. "We have a good relationship."

"Wonderful to hear." Mastema's sound lowers an octave.

Lola detects the drama that she doesn't care to understand. The one she wants is in front of her, and she is powerless.

Mastema adds, "The task will involve this human, or as your comrade loves to say, soft skin."

Rithu's onyx goggles zero in on Lola, their lenses reflecting from the window's light. There's no way to determine the hidden expression. In an instant, a flash of Scalebane's face appeared in her mind. The image of the white scales with black rims around the nostrils and lips, glowing with fiery eyes, will remain etched in her memory forever.

"A soft skin?" Rithu asks.

"Yes," Mastema says while squinting at Lola. A crooked smirk comes across his face.

Rithu steps towards Lola. She focuses on his legs. They bend back like a bird. The angle is subtle, as was Scalebane's. His tail sways as he enters the cell. Lola slides backwards, raising her fists.

Additional footsteps resonate from the hall, followed by two distinct silhouettes. The first figure is slight, with a pencil-thin frame, standing shorter than Lola, while the second mirrors Rithu's appearance. The being sports a hood, cloak, and tail. Stepping into the light, Lola sees the menacing form adorned in leather armour, and the shine of dual sheathed sai. The mask contains bolted goggles and a metal muzzle with fangs, unique signatures of Scalebane.

Eat them, comes a voice in Lola's mind. With her wisdom, she can distinguish that it is the addiction talking, not her own thoughts.

Unlike the last time Lola saw the reptile, Scalebane has a limp in her left leg. It's the same limb she carved a knife into years ago. Seeing her in a crippled state gives Lola a strange sense of satisfaction. That vazelead bears responsibility for Lola's current circumstances.

Beside Scalebane is a man with vibrant lime irises and eyebrows to match. His suit is dark compared to his ivory skin. It's either the obscure details of his being or the wretched burning smell coming from him that tells Lola he is from the old world.

Mastema extends his arms while bowing. "Jekos, Scalebane, thank you for joining us. You've been busy and I hate having to pull you away from your operations."

Scalebane doesn't acknowledge Lola. *How?* she asks herself. Pompous piece of shit. The vazelead's dry voice projects from inside her mask. "Jekos shared the news with me. There's not a single scratch on you."

"It was close. Lola Cabello is a fascinating specimen who manages to beat the odds. She proved herself worthy enough that we're keeping her. We've spared her family, too." He nods at Lola, making her limbs twitch. "Even though she attempted to assassinate me. One that truly did sting."

The shapeshifter scratches their neck thrice.

Scalebane puts her hands on her sai. "Again, you walk unscathed from concentrated light."

"I got lucky," Mastema says. "Cabello couldn't have gotten it. She works with a spy, who I will personally shred to pieces over an eternity for attempting to orchestrate my assassination.

Scripted words from the Book of Consulo? Cabello knew my exact location and time. There's poison among our circle."

"What do you want with us?" Scalebane asks.

Mastema speaks, "Well, I had spoken with King. He wishes to give his son a unique task that pulls him away from the ash business. Though I think, Scalebane, you can help guide him from time to time."

"How is that?" the other asks.

Lola's laser concentration on Scalebane's imminent arrival rendered her oblivious to Rithu's approaching hand. Cluing in, impulse makes her form a fist. She shouts and her hand slams into his forearm, pushing his claws away. The attack captures the focus of the others and they watch Lola swing again. Rithu catches her wrist, pulling her.

"Don't you dare touch me," Lola sneers. She yanks her arm to no use.

Rithu lets go with a calm demeanour, his claws loosening their grip. As he tilts his head, his tail moves at a controlled pace side to side, revealing fascination rather than anger, a complete departure from Scalebane's nature.

"He needs guidance on torment," Mastema says. "Rithu has little experience with soft skins and the harshness of violence. He could use your insight."

Scalebane straightens her posture. "Torture? I don't partake in such horror."

"Why is that?" Mastema asks.

"She will pay for what she's done to me, to us. Not like this. I can't."

Mastema rubs his brows. "Can't, or won't?"

"Can't. Guidelines from my mother. Only inflict harm in self-defence or in one's suffering."

"I am suffering, Scalebane," Mastema says through his teeth. "My suffering is Cabello. Your people are suffering from the grasp of the soft skins. Protect your kind, your allies, and learn where Cabello got this bullet. She knew I was going to be at a club recruiting Moths. Only Crystal Moths have this information. She has a spy working for her from the inside. That is your self-defence, Scalebane."

A rattle comes from Scalebane's throat as Rithu pursues Lola. She can't keep fighting him. She's smothered against the wall. Her breath is fast as his pointed claws reach her grease-fused hair. He tucks the strands behind her ear. Her legs tremble, and if she wasn't so dehydrated, she'd piss herself.

"D-o-o-on't fucking touch me," she says, voice shaking. *God damn drug*, she thinks. The anger and anxiety emotional swings are familiar effects of a post-ash session.

She tries to push his hand. Her palm lands on his forearm, sending a jolt through her skin. It's not like when gawking at your crush, nor the feeling of success when completing a task, and it's not fear. This hum tingling beneath her flesh ignites her heart. It's a desire. Her hands grip his leather clad limb, the nails digging into the material, thinking she can peel it away.

Consume them, comes the same voice.

Rithu doesn't stop her fingers jabbing into his clothes. Lola moves closer, her hands moving past his arm and onto his breastplate. There has to be an opening, a buckle, an entry point, that will let her get the scales. The tail. It's floating bait, making Lola collapse to her knees, snagging it with both hands.

"What is this?" Rithu asks. He takes a step away, though too infatuated with the action to stop her.

"See?" Mastema says. "Rithu needs your help. He hasn't experienced a pathetic human, let alone an ash-dasher."

Lola's fingers slide against the smooth dark scales until she finds the charcoal ones lining the upper portion of the appendage. Yes, this is ash, fresh and wonderful, able to be plucked right from the source. Her hands dig into the edges of a dry one. Her other hand, choking the flesh, lets her pull it free from his skin.

Rithu hisses, yanking his tail away. Instinct forces him to whip her face, splitting Lola's right cheek open. It knocks her onto her ass while biting the ash. *Yes*, she thinks. The wonderful drug is hers. It will remove her from this horrific scenario. She chews on the drug, ripping off a third of the scale. It's so tender, filled with moisture compared to the brittle ones found on the streets.

Am I this weak? Lola thinks, swallowing. She took a small bite, enough to take the edge off and help her process her situation. It's what she's done before. It will suppress her headache. *Come on, Lola, think.* This is the worst mess she's been in, and she needs help to think her way out of here.

"Rather pathetic," Jekos says while putting his hands behind his back.

The shapeshifter nods in agreement.

Mastema speaks, "It's why this drug is so important and why the people want it. It takes you away and makes you better. You hear reports of college students taking it to boost their studies?"

Jekos squints. "How fascinating."

"It's amazing what humans will do," Mastema says.

"Won't Dr. Lang want her back?" Jekos says.

Mastema shrugs. "He wishes for more information on ash too. Little bits at a time. If we gave him too many toys, he'd run wild with them."

Rithu kneels to level with Lola as she swallows the chewed ash. His head arcs again, not saying a word. She needs the ash to kick in. It takes a moment. Finishing the drug will give her the courage to face her captor. She rises on her knees, closer to Rithu. Blood trickles along the side of her hot face.

A low grumble escapes Scalebane's throat and she stomps into the jail cell. "Don't let her have it."

Lola stuffs the remaining amount into her mouth. She winces as Scalebane's sharp claws snag her face, puncturing her skin. She grits her teeth and forces herself to swallow while Scalebane pries open her jaw.

Mine, Lola thinks.

Scalebane's fingers scrape her tongue, failing to grab the scale, then release her with a push, knocking her to the ground, head slamming into the concrete. The blow should have hurt more. Ash is working.

"What's so special about her?" Rithu asks. He hasn't moved, watching her.

"Nothing," Scalebane says. "Don't give her any more of your scales." She lunges forward, losing balance on her left leg for a split second, and snags Lola's scalp, lifting her with one hand. Lola's legs flail, kicking Scalebane's torso several times. The vazelead doesn't flinch, despite the weakened limb. The tough bastard raises her other set of claws to point at her. "Where did you get the bullet?"

"Out of your ass," Lola says with a chuckle. Yes, ash works indeed. There's a numbness fabricating boldness. It's lessening the obvious danger she is in, dangling in the air. The drug also makes her immune to her punctured skull and the burning pain from below the bandages on her stomach.

"Restrain yourself, Scalebane," Mastema says, his voice echoing.

That's not a natural echo. Another entity speaks. It's muffled. The scale is entering her system far faster than she is used to. Her body has no endurance to the drug.

She stares at Rithu's goggles. Though she cannot see his face, ash is wondrous. She sees him, beyond the flesh and bone. His soul communicates: curious, empathetic, spry, and desperate to please. He wants to understand her more than inflict misery. These traits are opposite to Scalebane.

An explosion of colours blooms from the window. An inexperienced ash-dasher would think it's lethal water flooding into the basement. Oranges, blues, purples, greens, and yellows wash away the dark grime found in this torture chamber.

Stay strong, come to me.

It's the neutral voice.

There's no time to ponder. Lola Cabello no longer relies on her one sense. Vision is limiting, with radiating wings made of light coming from beyond the jail cell. The feathers mutate like octopus tentacles, attached to a glowing silhouette of a human whose attributes are masked from the brightness. Beside them are three other luminous beings of lesser brightness. A fourth, even dimmer. Behind the five is the outline of a woman.

If Lola had cognitive abilities left in her, she would ask who the sixth was. There were only five in the basement. Thoughts and words cannot describe the unexplained. Experience is a must. Her core, the soul, tells her she is staring at the living Earth: Mother Nature.

CHAPTER 26
PUZZLE COMPLETE

Taking an inexperienced soul under one's wing requires a humble mindset, which Scalebane lacks. She didn't ask for Rithu or the obligation required of them to continue their people. Nor does she desire to show him the darker corners of the world, such as torturing a soft skin for information. We do not choose our duty. We can defy it.

Rithu's new task won't take his responsibilities away from the ash business. Funds are not a concern with the Moths, and Rithu is able to fly to and from Toronto. In the end, his parents are correct: Rithu needs experience to harden. Hell, he's no better than a soft skin.

A week passes, at an undisclosed location in Toronto. Scalebane and Rithu march over the metal bridge at their ash production warehouse. Below Moth workers take crates from delivery trucks. The humans pry the boxes open, taking ceramic statues of golden good luck cats standing on their hind legs, one paw raised. These labourers extract the hidden ash scales by breaking the maneki-neko open. Next, they remove them from their previous vacuum sealed bags and place them into new ones complete with humidity packs to prolong the scale. It's business as usual.

"I'm impressed," Scalebane says. She leans over the metal railings, looking at the painted yellow eyes of one cat statue as a hammer cracks it open. "You haven't dismantled our operations."

"You underestimate what I'm capable of," Rithu says. He places his leather gauntlets on the barrier.

Scalebane keeps her hands on her sai and watches as the workers who dare not look up at their dark foremen. "I'm sure Jekos had quite a bit to do with it."

Rithu rolls his shoulders. "On the contrary, Scalebane, he's been busy with other matters that he refuses to share with me. In the end, he is a Moth, and I don't trust him."

"Is that so?" Scalebane says, standing straight. Small razor pins pierce her calf, riding along her inner thigh. She catches herself on the railing.

"Scalebane," Rithu reaches for her.

She shrugs him off and shifts her stance. "Speak."

"Of course. Imps serve masters and his is Mastema. I can smell it in his foul blood. He is more stressed than usual."

"What master does his human half serve, Mastema or himself?"

"I am unsure. There was the attempted assassination on Mastema. Where is he? He got here a week before you and I and has failed to greet us as he does when we land."

Oh how blind you are, Scalebane thinks. At some point, she will have to bring Rithu in.

Juggling Dasco Amoss, managing Jekos, the looming threat of the muse, and monitoring the Crystal Moths is a burden she cannot manage without allies. The unfortunate realism is Jekos was right: she can't operate alone. In the absence of her dear Namsruc, she must introduce new partners.

Scalebane leans onto the railing again, tail swaying. "Tell me, son of King, the continuation of the Guardian bloodline, and the last born vazelead, need I say more? You can smell the blood of a half-imp who is nervous. What do your instincts tell you of Lola Cabello?"

Rithu turns to the ceiling, pondering the question before replying. "Well, she is strong-willed. The ash has effects on her that are prominent, far more than what I understood before. One week with her and she hasn't budged."

Scalebane's leans back. "And? Is that what your insight has told you?"

He clears his throat. "No. There's a power in her. How do I describe it? Alluring? I sense she isn't afraid of us. I can smell her hot blood. I want to understand why. Despite the methods you've shown me, she is resilient, no offence."

"None taken. Cabello is unique among the soft skins. I have been informed about her past that proves true."

"Such as?"

"She has ties to the old world," Scalebane says.

"Don't we all?" Rithu asks.

"According to the human theory of evolution, yes. Though I am referring to it living in her veins. Your mother's teachings would have told you of old world lineage."

"She taught me of the before times. Would Cabello's relatives also contain this connection?" Rithu says.

"This is the second time I've had the pleasure of seeing her, where violence wasn't our communication. She and I do not see eye to eye, and I want you to manage it."

"What do you mean?"

"To be frank, Rithu, I don't believe in torture. My mother's teachings run deep, which you would relate to." *There is my dear Dasco Amoss,* she thinks. It's a detail the boy doesn't need to know. The muse exists. It's not a conspiracy. Her calculations indicate that the torturing is going to persist. Jekos's concentrated light bullet shall remain a secret until Scalebane decides what to do with him.

Rithu scratches his throat. "Fair enough. I will do you well. You have my word."

"Good. Your initiative is proving you to be a valuable asset, one that I want to keep around." A toothy grin spreads across Scalebane's face under her mask. She doesn't buy her own words, not yet. Rithu, on the other hand, does. He straightens his posture, accepting his new task with boldness. She lacks trust in him. He's too naïve. He is usable at least.

"Keep your wits about you," Scalebane says. "Cabello is a trickster." She stands and marches on the path. "I'll return later tonight."

"Scalebane?" Rithu calls.

Footsteps power walk behind until Rithu dashes in front of her as she reaches for the door. "No," he says. His stance is wide, looking down at her.

"Rithu Blacktooth, this is an initiative that would please your father. You have to trust me, though. Stay true to your tasks and let me handle what I need to."

"Which is? We're supposed to be comrades. We are the same people, and we can't keep secrets."

"I will share with you my knowledge. Not today. It is important, and mark my words, I'll require your assistance in convincing King."

Rithu's posture slouches, his tail swaying side to side. "Why do you shy from me?"

"Because of a looming threat, beyond the Crystal Moths or Cabello. Let me gather concrete information rather than rumours of fear."

Rithu takes a slow step to the side, infatuated with her words, hoping she'll tease him with more. Scalebane swings the door open and grazes her tail against Rithu's chest as she storms by. She doesn't see his reaction and is confident it will excite him. He is loyal. She cannot deny her need of help and will integrate him little by little, allowing her to understand how trustworthy he is.

Before making sudden decisions, she will meet with Dasco. It's been over two weeks since their last gathering. A week of managing ash and a week of dealing with Cabello were far more than she preferred. The capture of the soft skin complicates her planning and King's disapproval means she must be more discreet until she brings Rithu into the fold.

Scalebane heads down the cracked concrete staircase. She bursts into the night alleyway. An open garage is to her right. A delivery truck is being unloaded by the Moths, with two standing in front. Both fashion cargo pants, white shirts, and hoodies with their hoods up. They don't dare look at Scalebane.

Behind the vehicle is the thin half-imp in his usual burgundy attire. He's discussing with a Moth sporting a silk pearl suit. An educated guess would say they're the replacement for Kai Pung to overlook the Ontario district. It's an operational detail that Scalebane should care for. Her absence and interest decline daily. Dasco is the keeper of her interests.

She walks along the gravel path, the crushing of rocks capturing Jeko's attention. "Scalebane! Scalebane!" he calls out, rushing to her.

Of course, Scalebane thinks. She stops to face the halfbreed who walks in front of her backwards. "You didn't greet us," she says.

He adjusts his vest and clears his throat before speaking. "Well, important matters. Similar to you vanishing at odd times, isn't it?"

"What is it? I must be going."

"As you do. We have no need to keep secrets."

"This again?" Scalebane says.

"Have you extracted anything from Cabello?" the other asks.

"She is strong-willed. Do not fear. I doubt Rithu will get her to speak."

"Is he aware?" Jekos's eyes scan Scalebane's face, desperate for an answer.

"You're fulfilling the mould of a cunning imp. Rithu is suspicious of you."

"Your people are." Jekos shifts his position to walk beside her.

"I plan on bringing him into the inner circle," Scalebane says.

"I see. Is this your acceptance?" A crooked smile exposes his thin teeth.

Scalebane shakes her head. "Not yet. There is a greater issue at stake that I need to understand. It involves you and your offer."

"Is that so?" Jekos asks. He folds his arms.

"You once said powers are moving. My own investigation is proving that correct."

"You will work with me?" Jekos's voice goes up a notch.

"In due time," Scalebane says as she grinds her teeth.

"I can wait, though the sooner you act, the better, for all of our sakes." Jekos extends a firm index finger towards her. His forwardness boils her with anger and if Scalebane didn't have her mask, she would have bitten the half-imp's finger. Jekos continues, "Make sure Cabello doesn't say a word. It would be disastrous."

"Is that a threat?" Scalebane raises her spiked brow.

"No." Jekos looks around and wipes his chin with the rough smear. "But by the gods, Scalebane. It's for your safety. Things will slip my hand if Mastema learns too much. Cabello mustn't mention the bullet, a crow, or a shaper."

Scalebane's tail perks. There's only one shaper within the Moths, and they have good ties with Mastema. "Is that so?"

"Listen, the synthesizing of ash is the beginning. You recall our meeting in Allen Sky Tower? The three men who came in as we exited were Dr. Lang, Prime Minister Stéphane Trudell, and Mr. Patterson. They are key players working with Mastema. Trust me, it's more than ash."

"How would you know this?" Scalebane asks.

"If you accept my offer, I'll share more with you. If you don't believe me, here's some information of value: those three men meet Mastema once a year to plan their strategy. Dr. Lang owns a company called Manageficient Enterprises. They specialize in bioengineering. Mr. Patterson is CEO of Allen Shipping solutions and their sister companies. The Prime Minister was an original founder of Allen Oil Site Solutions. He also holds a lot of weight in the legal realm. Next year is their annual meeting. These meetings don't involve King or your people. Hear their gathering. It will persuade you, my friend."

Scalebane winces. "You'll wait another year?"

Jekos lifts his arms in a shrug. "I've waited two, haven't I?"

"How did you get a concentrated light bullet? Such materials come from the Heavenly Kingdoms."

"Ah, you're wanting to find your sister I'm presuming?"

A rattle escapes her throat.

"Accept my offer and let our partnership flourish." Jekos bows and steps aside. "The tides are rising and you don't want to be on the side that washes away."

Words to ponder over as the half-imp returns to his ash duties. A painter awaits.

The travel to Dasco Amoss's loft takes no time when you can move on all fours, even with a weakened limb. The alleyways and shadows are advantageous for maneuvering through the streets, rooftops, and homeless tent encampments. She leaps onto the familiar emergency fire escape. His window is open, as she requested. The lights are on, suitable for Dasco's nocturnal self.

As with each visit, he sits in the far right corner, hunched over his easels, working on his most recent piece. Three new canvases lean against the brick walls since two weeks ago. The latest he's mastering uses black swirls, forming hands with bright green and blue fog at the edges of the canvas. Stars form the background with the lime and cobalt hues crafting the clouded cosmos. In the centre are his signature glyphs and circles, creating ritualistic lines with a radial burst.

Through the open window, a strong smell of a swamp intermingles with the artificial scent of plastic. That's the distinct aroma of smoked ash wafting through the air. The goddamned painter found himself unable to avoid the overwhelming influence of the potent substance. Dasco sways side to side. His movements are rhythmic and fluid. The sound of his brush swishing against the canvas fills the room as his arms move in wide, confident strokes. With a mesmerizing rhythm, his left hand wiggles, directing his right hand's brushstrokes with precision and grace as if the left was puppeteering his right. Dasco's head bobbles, tilted upwards, catching a glimpse of the unfinished ceiling. The soft skin is in a trance.

The muse, Scalebane thinks.

With a sudden halt, Dasco's body stiffens and his head slumps forward, a clear indication of surprise. Choking the brush, his muscles tighten with tension. His form jerks towards the window, his intense stare fixed on Scalebane. With a smile, he drops his tool in a jar of water, then jumps off the stool. With each stride, his open button shirt dances in the wind, revealing the sheen of sweat that coats his bony torso. A funk of strong cheese and must tells Scalebane he hasn't showered in days, if not weeks. Goddamn humans.

"My Anima!" Dasco calls, waving her in. "Fourteen days on and you return. The shadow stays true to their word."

Scalebane swings herself over and into the unit. "You seemed busy."

"Not for you. You're welcome here."

"Was that the muse working through to you?"

Dasco rubs his neck. "Yes, the muse was guiding me, continuing the cosmic story of our universe. It's broad, overlooking so many details, key events, and living creatures throughout space and time. I can barely wrap my head around what is being made."

"You took ash?" Scalebane asks.

"The substance prolongs my focus. With my dear partner Erol Terzi's passing, it's difficult to work. I don't take much ash. It's expensive, hard to find, and dangerous. Have faith in me. I've had my share of drugs. I need to ease the pain of Erol so I can understand what the muse is saying."

"Understood. If you require more, express your concern to me. Don't trust whoever is giving the substance to you. You're likely overpaying." Scalebane points with her claw to his canvases. "Show me what you've done."

"Yes, of course, my Anima."

Dasco guides Scalebane to his easel. The work in progress is too fresh to reveal its true intention. The presence of clouds and symbols suggests it is a crucial element of the collage. Ritualistic glyphs catch Scalebane's attention, reminding her of an ancient language from her childhood. Despite this, there are no distinguishing features or landmarks representing Dreadweave Pass, Synarion, or Namsruc. The muse has moved on and there are no more clues to their whereabouts in Dasco's work.

The disappointing news stabs her heart, spiking a hot pain. She needs a clue that will lead her to her sister. The unfortunate truth is Jekos is the single soul who can guide her to a gateway into the afterlife. It's a thought for later.

"Why did the muse change your direction?" Scalebane asks.

"I'm not sure. The visions are inconsistent. Sometimes they're blurry and unclear. They mutate their shapes. Other times, crystal. There's an urgency and spasmodic nature to the muse over the past week. It's pushing this information onto me as fast as possible, unlike prior where I could understand it."

One week, she thinks. A coincidence with Cabello's capture seven days ago? The latest development with the Crystal Moths is an example. Jekos's warning of Mastema and his three men: Dr. Lang, Prime Minister Stéphane Trudell, and Mr. Patterson complicate the situation. Mastema captured Cabello, extracted her DNA and is working with a doctor. There are too many coincidences aligning closer together.

"Impressive," Scalebane says. "How does the muse foresee these pieces working together?"

"Here," the other replies.

He sets the completed canvases and positions them on the hardwood floor. Next Dasco grabs the previous paintings Scalebane saw, assembling them. As one, they showcase the dead man with Dega'Mostikas's Triangle below. Above him is the spiralling vortex, then the Heavenly Kingdoms, followed by the Creator themself. Below them is the figure representing the First with the distant translucent spheres surrounding them, theorized to be dimensional realms. The three new paintings, of far darker tones, add onto the extending cosmos and bubbles. Dasco places them above the Creator, creating a congruent ceremonial sphere encircling the afterlife.

He falls to his knees and uses his index finger, following the paint strokes; he moves around the spiral and beyond, like a shooting star. His hand rises past the Heavenly Kingdoms and the Creator to the four new canvases, the darkest of the collection. Dasco taps the incomplete one with a black corner of swirls. "These beings have no light. It's like you."

Scalebane cannot help but chuckle. "Trust me, I am not the lightless ones."

"Lightless ones?" Dasco asks.

"The muse is warning you of them. Scalebane kneels beside him and points to the embedded language and shapes. "And these glyphs? These circles? A summoning spell for layman's terms."

"How do you know this?" Dasco asks, eyes squinting.

"A story for another time, my dear Dasco." Scalebane rises and reaches past her cloak to her tail. She plucks one of her thick black scales and reveals it to Dasco. "You've done well."

Dasco takes the ash, his mouth hanging open. She created ash from thin air! He spins the diamond between his index finger and thumb. It would indeed be the first time he's felt a scale so fresh, warm, and complete with a dab of black blood.

Scalebane speaks. "Keep working."

"Of course, my Anima," Dasco says, bowing his head.

Scalebane pats his knotted hair. "Stay focused."

"What is the muse's warning?"

"We'll learn that through your work with the completed summoning spell."

She leaves the painter to his studies, heading for his window and leaping into the night streets. There is no denying that this knowledge is worrisome. A ghoul of the afterlife aspires to be summoned here. Why? This muse curated the information, trickling it into Dasco's work for years. They could have chosen a clearer method of accessing the mortal realm. In fact, this Hell gate that Synarion and Namsruc used, or Jekos, would be a perfect example.

If the muse wishes to come here, she needs allies. Rithu can help persuade his father. Mastema is crafting devious plans that does not involve her people, according to Jekos. The half-imp offers an allegiance. He also accessed the afterlife to obtain rare material which clicks with her personal advantage. Scalebane will no longer function alone, for the sake of the world.

CHAPTER 27
WARM THE BLOOD

Lola's legs quiver as she hangs from shackles suspended from the ceiling. The sound of rattling chains echo in the room, anchoring her to the floor. Razor claws slice into her bare back with searing pain shooting through her body.

The slit of light from the window is the indicator of time, letting her estimate the vazelead, Rithu, comes in biweekly rotations. They feed her a little. There's next to no water. The torture has reduced her few clothes to scraps, hanging on by a thread. She hasn't showered in days. Lola has not broken.

This cycle continues. She endures. Time distorts and Lola cannot recall how many days or weeks it has been. Or has it been months? Years? It is pointless to look at the light from the window; the sun tells her that torture is near.

Her shit and piss pile in the room's corner until Rithu power washes the cell. He blasts her too, scorching her wounds and leaving her cold, shivering.

I'm sorry, Mom. Lola's heart sinks with guilt, acknowledging her role in her mother's death.

Where did you go? comes the faint memory of Lola's green eyed prison companion. Kendra, who she hasn't thought of since escaping. The girl was open-minded, kind, and didn't pry too much into Lola's life. She only requested for Lola to be with her. Hell, Lola cannot even recall why Kendra was locked away.

Thinking of Kendra causes Lola to question what she will do if she ever escapes from here. Fear of her family accepting her is a constant in her mind. They have the right to hate Lola. People like Kendra offered peace, and Lola dismissed it for her calling. She cannot even bear children if she wished it. At least she has a niece, according to the shaper. She won't see the kid grow. Will her brother even mention Lola existed?

Gentle scuffles come from within the room: a rodent wanting food. Seeing how the torturer is going, they'll nibble off her soon. The critter squeaks. Another scuffle, and a small brown creature wanders into the prison cell. Their petite pink paws rest on the ground. A red mist spins inside its beady black eyes. The spine snaps at a forty-degree angle. Yet another crack arises from inside. The fur falls and the pale flesh twists. Long limbs, lean torso, tail, and a bald head replace the mammal. It is none other than the shaper who got her into this nightmare.

"Cabello, you're in quite the situation, yes," says the shaper.

Lola grunts, shifting her position. It doesn't do much good. Her arms are numb, holding her body. She spits a blotch of saliva that tastes of blood. "No thanks to you. You set me up, you piece of shit," Lola says, grinding her teeth.

"I did, yes? The box was a mystery, doll. I delivered."

"That light-bullet went through his head and he rejuvenated within seconds. You can't hurt him."

The shaper paces to the other end of the cell, leaning against the bars. "Fascinating. Light bullet? As in concentrated light?"

"Give me a break. Concentrated light?"

"Photons work as a wave and particle. It would have taken great lengths to craft it to solidify the frequencies. Even greater to defy them."

"Don't offer a science course. I only did your task because you threatened my family again."

The shaper takes a step closer to Lola, standing to her side.

"Mmm, no threats. You wanted Mastema. Concentrated light, and he rejuvenated. His experiments with Dr. Lang must be further along."

"Meaning?" Lola says.

"Put it this way, concentrated light eradicates shadows, eroding the souls of the corrupt. Demons and angels aren't supposed to walk in the mortal realm. They need a host."

"That's not what I've seen," Lola says, thinking of the succubus, Mul, she met years ago.

The shaper continues, "No surprise, yes. The afterlife is dormant. Judgment weak. There are back doors and loopholes within its laws that the wicked bend to their will. Mastema is the real him."

"But your magic woo-woo bullet didn't do shit. The light and shadows? Everyone saw that."

"Yes," the other says.

Lola squints. "Who even are you?"

"Who am I? Well, yes, many names, over many years, doll. A name?" The shapeshifter grins a mouth full of teeth. "Nehom was one name long ago in a naive time. Shaper is the common of my kind. Though two-faced lives of a double agent changes my name with my form."

"Right, and who do you work for? Clearly you want to use me."

"I work for many. When we shed naivety, we become our true selves. Creatures of Mother Nature's garden have a prime goal of survival, yes? Endurance is key. Why bet on one side when you can master both?"

"You're a weasel. Got it. Mind doing me a favour? Get me out?" She shakes the chains with her arms which causes a spike of hot pain from the torture slashes along her back.

"Patience, Cabello. I can't stay long. Mastema's vampire guards can smell blood, even mine. If that bullet failed, Mastema is toying with shadows where light never touches."

"Even for your super light?" Lola asks.

"There's a darkness that none of us have witnessed. Lightless beings that don't take threats well. Mastema's immunity to the bullet tells me he is knocking on their door."

Lola shakes her cuffs, causing the chains to sway. "Your beautiful words aside, you going to undo these or not?"

"That's not my order to make." The shaper walks to the other side of the metal gate, examining Lola's bare back covered in long slashes.

"Why are you here? If you shapeshift, why don't you turn into a useful form instead of a rodent? Morph into me, unlock my chains, and we'll confuse them with the doppelgänger."

"Clever thinking. I wish I could, doll. You've performed well for me. Though, as you witnessed, I must consume the body before morphing into them," the shaper says. "I don't think you would enjoy that, yes?"

Lola says, "What do you want?"

"Do not mention the bullet, who I am, or how you escaped prison. Understood?"

"Oh, I was planning on sharing my secret ingredients with them. Switch sides," Lola says. Sarcasm is the one thing that keeps her sane in this cell. Hope is so far lost that she needs humour to process this wretched situation. She has pondered Mastema's offer. Reason tells her to stay clear of deals with the First.

"Funny. When I have a new order, I will return. Until then, hang tight." The shaper steps away and their body contorts, reversing into the small rodent. Fur sprouts from the skin, the bones contract, and muscles shrivel until they are a critter on the ground. They scurry into the shadows, leaving Lola alone. The wait won't be long. Poor Lola is popular.

Twenty-four hours later, footsteps of a newcomer resonate in the space. She doesn't look. Based on the stride and high click, it isn't Rithu. They're wearing dress shoes. From the shadow hall, the pristine white figure which is Mastema appears. He tucks his shining hair behind his ears while approaching the jail. Lola remains dangling from the chains, arms exhausted from her own weight. Her muscles are too weak to lift her head.

"Cabello, Cabello . . . Cabello," Mastema says, placing his hands on the bars. His rings scrape along the rods. "You're a tough one."

She looks to his white shoes, hoping he would leave. There is no will to fight him.

The crime lord squats, gazing up at her. "Where did you get the bullet?"

Go away, she thinks. Her soul is numb thanks to the continual pain. There's no need to lash out.

Mastema slams the bars with his palms, his hair flying in front of his face. "Are you this determined, or is Rithu so weak that I need to find a replacement?"

Don't look at him.

"Four months on and nothing. I've been patient."

Lola opens her jaw to speak, surprised by the amount of time that has passed. Her lips peel apart as her sandpaper tongue frees itself from the roof of her mouth. *Why bother,* she thinks and then she closes her lips.

Mastema's nostrils flare. "Who gave you the bullet?"

Another set of footsteps come from down the hall. These boots have a familiar stride; they belong to Rithu. A cloaked being reaches the jail cell and Mastema stands to face him.

"Rithu Blacktooth," Mastema says. "What are you doing?"

"I'm sorry?" Rithu asks. His tail coils around his leg.

"You've damaged her, look." Mastema points to Lola behind him.

"That is the point of torture."

"You don't want to kill them. By the Creator, she isn't this strong-willed. Get creative with your technique." He waves his index finger at the vazelead while walking by. "I don't have time to babysit your methods. Do better."

A rattle comes from Rithu's throat as the crime lord's dress shoes fade in the distance. Boots storm to the cell and keys jingle. The door unlocks with the hinges creaking in a prolonged swing of the turning metal. The reptilian steps in front of her. Lola doesn't raise her head. At some point, he'll start hitting her for information.

Her prediction rings true as a single claw slashes across Lola's chest. The chains dangle as she sways from the force. She pushes the pain away by clenching her teeth.

"Look at me," comes Rithu's croaky voice muffled by the metal mask.

Lola does not reply.

Rithu snags her jaw, forcing her to gaze at him. He squeezes her face, pushing her cheeks up to her dry, pink eyes. She used to wonder what was underneath. Lola wanted to see these cold-blooded humanoids. What's the point? It's unclear if she'll taste freedom.

"You will respect me," Rithu says.

"Why would I do that?" Lola asks, voice deadened from her crunched face.

"Because I am your saviour and your death," Rithu says. He digs into her throat, piercing past the clavicles. Lola grunts and wheezes; her body shakes with what little strength she has. He stops above her breasts. The already dampened bra soaks up the blood from the fresh wound.

Thank God, she thinks as a wave of relief rushes over her that he stopped. She won't break. Regardless, the pain is immense.

Rithu frees her and circles her in a slow stride. He whips his tail in the air, making a loud snap. Lola flinches. It's intimidation and a warning of what comes next. A hiss escapes his throat as his tail lashes against her spine. It splits open a new section of her skin from the shoulder blade to her lower back. Her mind is at its limit, and she cannot hold a complete idea as her thoughts fizzles from the burning exhaustion. She has no means to fight and the vazelead's determination won't waver. This is the end.

"You will tell me where you got the bullet," Rithu says. He walks around to face her and snags her skull, making her look at him, though her eyes angle to the side. Her vision is clouded, saturated, and she cannot focus.

Another rumble escapes Rithu's throat. He tilts his head and the force of his grip loosens. He moves her face side to side, up and down, as if he were inspecting her. His other claw pushes her sweat and blood covered hair from her face. He lifts her eyelids, gazing past the hazelnut eyes and into her soul. She doesn't look. She focuses on the ceiling's cracks. If she zones in on one section of the room, then this nightmare isn't real.

Let go.

Rithu frees her head. He removes his left glove. Unlike Scalebane's thin white and black scales, his hand encompasses thick charcoal scales, like ash. Lola's heart floods her body with a hum; fresh air whooshes into her nostrils, giving her newfound life. It's the last bit of adrenaline to feed her desire.

The rough, leathery fingers of her torturer glide against her wet forehead, running from her jaw to her cheek. He's intrigued by her. It's a skewer of ash teasing her, and she drops her head into his palm. Her face inches nearer to his fingertips. He lets her. She bites his skin, nipping into a dry scale. The odd behaviour makes Rithu jerk, taking the ash from her. He holds his hand with his right one.

"Please," Lola croaks. "Just a little." Lola can hear herself. It's pathetic. "I don't want to be in pain anymore." To her surprise, a small tear squeezes from her eye, trickling past her cheek and into a fresh wound, burning.

Rithu's stance lowers closer to her level. He's sympathizing with her, or feels shame. The situation is unclear. He plucks one of his scales from his knuckle and hands the nickel-sized skin to Lola. She leans forward and opens her mouth, thick saliva stringing between her lips. He places it on her tongue, claw grazing her bottom lip. She bites, chewing the ash into a paste. She closes her eyes and swallows.

Yes, she thinks and exhales through her nose. *There is a God.* Soon, the ash shall circulate through her system, and she will gain clarity and strength.

Several seconds go by in silence as the drug circulates through her body. Rithu breaks the silence. "Why are your people obsessed with our scales?"

"I'm unsure. Why do you despise us so much?"

"Centuries of systemic hate, long before your or even my time," Rithu says.

"We don't have to repeat the faults of our fathers." The ash-dasher is alive and well. The familiar buzzing hums from her core. The room is brighter. Her five senses tune in. Touch: deep bruising and stinging. Taste: metallic. Smell: putrid and rank. Hearing: breath. Sight: a confused boy. The sixth sense switches on with extrasensory perception.

Come to us, Lola, says the distant neutral voice. The spirit of the Earth is forever beyond reach.

Find the pai—, another entity speaks. It's darker, deeper, and snuffs out because of a closer sensation of the soul in front of her. Rithu: sadness. It pierces into Lola's heart. Underneath the anguish is fear. There's a lack of recognition, respect, and strength.

Rithu growls and equips his leather glove. "You're poisoning my thoughts."

"I sense pain," Lola says. She wonders if it's her own words or the ash projecting itself. She needs to think fast with precision. "A pain rooted in anxiety."

"Silence," Rithu says.

"Fear . . . acceptance from your father. You want to do him right?" Doubt is an emotion she can relate to, and she sees herself in him. Her family disowned her.

Rithu clutches her neck and bellows a demoralizing roar that rings in Lola's ears, louder than any underground concert she used to go to. "Enough!" he shouts.

Lola's voice squeaks from the lack of oxygen. "Scalebane. It's pressure, not from you. You've only done as you're told. You're supposed to . . . you're supposed to . . . It's complex."

"What is this?" Rithu squeezes tighter.

Lola gasps for air.

The walls, the jail cell, and even Rithu shatter into glass particles, spiralling inward to a black and blue vortex. The absence of oxygen, weakness, and ash transports her into the maelstrom of clouds mixed with elongated, eyeless faces moving towards the core. Their rotten flesh hands, covered in black holes, reach for her.

A reverberating voice, matching the one a moment ago, speaks. *The painter. Bring the End.*

Fingers release her neck and Lola takes a long breath. The spiral reverses, reforming the objects within the space as they were. She gasps with several coughs, her body shaking. Rithu takes a step closer as she exhales. Lola says, "Ash. It gives me insight."

"That is what Scalebane warned me of," Rithu says.

"You're unheard." She takes another deep breath to fill her burning lungs.

"Excuse me?" the other asks.

"No one listens to you, but I will." Lola swallows a buildup of saliva.

Rithu's tail moves back-and-forth.

This better work, Lola thinks. She has little tools to use and cannot rely on a vague shapeshifter spy, double agent or not, to help her. It's up to her to escape from this nightmare.

CHAPTER 28
DUAL SEERS

Patience is a virtue that few can master. Ageing made Scalebane lose her empathy and the strengths she had in relating to people. Her persistence with Dasco Amoss griefs her colleagues. It makes her wonder how Jekos stays in the shadows, despite hanging by the strength of a soft skin.

Time is fluid, and her brief visits to Dasco Amoss are a blip. To the rest of the world, she's given him regular appearances each month. Since Cabello's capture, she provides the painter a dab of ash to keep him focused on his task. Humans are fragile creatures, and the focus isn't getting him addicted.

Scalebane is in Toronto, under the night rain, four months after Mastema captured Cabello. Four months of pondering Jekos's offer. Nearing half a year of Rithu practising his torturing and no answers. Cabello is willed. Weakness consumes Rithu. It's as she predicted.

These are concerns for another day. Scalebane walks through the dark alleys, heading to Dasco's studio loft apartment. She lowers herself to leap, feeling the stiffness in her left leg, and adjusts her stance. With balance regained, she leaps onto the fire escape and heads to his open window. Even after nearing three years, she hasn't adjusted to her body's limits.

A powerful scent of swamp and plastic lingers in the studio. It's from smoking ash. This smell is far more prudent than the other times she has been here. Dasco must have gotten more of the drug, not from her.

Playful laughter comes from inside as Scalebane stops inches from the frame. Several voices are present. New smells tingle in her nostrils. It's not the usual sweat glands mixed with bacteria on Dasco's skin, creating a sharp sting with underlining shit-musk. These additional odors are of wood. There's flower, sweet, and tang. Another layer higher reveals perspiration with a fresh bite. Rhythmic slapping and a spank follow. A grunt and a feminine moan.

Scalebane turns the corner. Dasco isn't in his studio. On the second level, his low bed is a knotted mess of limbs, gripping hands, and thrusting hips. Dasco's curly hair bounces with each thrust, accompanied by two other men. They too are buck naked with Herculean sculpted bodies that would make the gods jealous. The three intermingle in a tangled, jumbled heap with a fourth, female. The glistening oil smothers their smooth skin, letting them slide around with ease, grabbing each other with lustful demand. God damn apes; fighting and fucking is all they do.

Scalebane leans over the window and steps onto the hardwood floor. The woman, on her knees with a leather strap buckled on her hips, turns to her, pushing her pearl blonde hair from her face. She stops thrusting into one man. He pauses mid suck, leaving Dasco's member in his mouth. The painter's tongue coils around the last man's. His gaze trails to Scalebane.

He moans with a mixture of surprise and joy. "Mmmmhmm!" Dasco pulls free from the group, fluids dripping from his chin and crotch. Wiping his jaw, Dasco hops off the bed and down the ladder to her, smiling. His pink eyes flicker as he opens his arms. "My Anima! I did not expect to see you."

"Oh my," comes the feathered smoker's voice of the pegged man. He plays with his moustache as his deep green, blushed gaze crawls up Scalebane with fantasies in his mind she'd prefer not to ponder.

"Dasco," says the woman. She exits her partner, making him groan, and snags a robe. She pushes hair from her face, revealing the pink in her sclera too. The silver silky garment drapes above her knees as she hugs her arms. At least she maintains her dignity by covering herself, unlike the intoxicated males.

Scalebane waves her hand at the three newcomers. "Remove your playthings. We have work to do."

Dasco rubs his eyes and looks for his boxers through the scattered clothes on the wooden floor. He shrugs and says, "Can we do this another time, when I am more coherent?"

"The point of the drug was to aid your connection with the muse, not have orgy parties with ash-dashers."

"This was a, uhm, uh, pleasurable side effect. I honestly didn't mean for the night to go this way. You must believe me." Dasco hurries to the woman as she steps down the ladder. He extends his hand. She takes it, reluctant to walk. His tug encourages her towards Scalebane. He wraps an arm around her, squeezing her shoulder. "This is Zea."

"Zea? Try me," Scalebane says.

Dasco clears his throat. "I've been painting long and hard nights until the sunrises and some time after. My Anima, it is killing me. The strain of working countless hours combined with ash. How much longer could I go? Progress is slow. You've seen it over the past year. I've taken the drug path. I respect it." He releases the girl and heads to his canvases until Scalebane's clawed hand snags his arm.

"Explain yourself," Scalebane says and releases him.

Dasco continues, "The lightless ones intrigued me. The muse is showing us the history of creation, then beyond. What lies before, and yet it keeps gravitating towards the lightless ones. Over and over, canvas after the next. Foggy beings as dark as night consume my art boards. Why? It was a wild idea, one I decided to explore. My dear Anima, I don't do research. The muse provides intuition. This is the first time I studied online. That's what other people do. I thought maybe it'd give me a breakthrough."

"And?" Scalebane asks.

"The internet is an amazing place, connecting people who once believed they were alone. I found Zea, an illustrator, similar to me. She was working in Montréal for a game company. Though beyond the point, she witnessed the lightless ones."

Scalebane raises a spiked brow, wondering if these are rambles of an inebriated man.

Zea squeezes her forearms. "I've drawn the shadows since I was a teenager."

"Go on," Scalebane says.

"At a young age I had sleep paralysis. It's common for people. Mine became alive. I spoke to an entity from another place, whether it was to a new dimension or galaxy. They called themselves the void watchers."

Dasco says, "It's a fascinating phenomenon that happened a number of years ago involving a cult named the Galactic Believers."

Zea speaks, "This void watcher spoke to me, similar to Dasco's muse. It told me of the great absorption of mankind from a being named the All-Being Entity, or ABE."

"This is where the Mandela Effect occurs. Are you familiar with it, Shadow?"

"No," Scalebane says.

Zea says, "It's when two people have conflicting memories of how an event occurred."

Dasco snaps his finger. "Correct. Many folks believed that the Galactic Believers' prophecy came true and ABE absorbed life on Earth, destroying the planet."

"Yet no one remembers?" Scalebane asks.

"Those that weren't absorbed remembered." Dasco's eyes widen.

Zea says, "I illustrated it, the void watcher, ABE, and these shadows. I let the void watcher channel through me, preparing for ABE's arrival. I informed humanity with videos online. I think that birthed the Galactic Believers. They called me the Oracle because I explained ABE would transcend us into a new dimension."

"Clearly ABE didn't succeed," Scalebane says, her tail coiling around her ankle.

Dasco heads to the kitchen, where a laptop rests on the counter. He takes the chrome object and taps away on the controls, returning to her. "Read this," he says, spinning the screen around.

Scalebane grabs the metal device, looking at the illuminating glass containing text on a grey background. She hasn't familiarize herself with human technology too often. It won't last long, like their reign of misery. In contrary, in moments like this, it would be useful if she did learn about their tools. "How does this work?" she asks.

Dasco stands beside her. He operates the machine by sliding his fingers on a rectangle on the flat surface of the object, controlling a small arrow on the screen. "Here," he says and points to the top. "I'll scroll for you."

Scalebane examines the text, seeing it is a story, or an eyewitness account of ABE and these Galactic Believers.

Title: Here's My Story

Posted By: mechanic_dude200, 2012.07.24

Hey, I didn't know where else to post this other than the thread. You are unaware of how long I've been searching to find folks like me who remember what happened. I can't tell my family or friends. They'll think I'm crazy. You hear how people argue over this event. Some say it happened and others don't. I've kept it locked inside and it's given me lots to reflect on. I apologize if I ramble a bit. It's a lot to get off my chest.

I understand that conspiracy theories are fun. People believe some of the wildest things, which makes it so easy for the rest of us to write those folks off as crack-monkeys. Conspiracists' evidence is contradictory or vague. Most of the time, no one finds the actual answer. Those conspiracy nuts sure try. Some are legitimate. If you want to get into politics, many beliefs are correct. Politicians tuck devious deeds under the table and life moves on. Conspiracies about the end of the world and extraterrestrial beings? Hard to hide or prove that it happened when the world is dandy. Maybe it isn't the government. Perhaps there is some underlying force that keeps us together. Call it God if you'd like. Call it the universe. I honestly don't care. A force binds us, some form of consciousness.

What is consciousness? That's an age-old discussion brought on by scientists and philosophers. Is it only humans that possess awareness, or do animals have it, too? How about a tree or a rock? I, for one, don't fret over it. What's the point? Nobody has ever proved it. If you dig too deep into a rabbit hole, you won't get out, like conspiracists. I lived my life. Well, I used to until that damn triangle arrived in the sky. ABE. The All-Being Entity. The cosmic . . . thing has an awareness that works in a two-dimensional giant shape. We're conscious, too. It is the underlying layer of our reality. Consciousness is in reality.

Before ABE, it was easy to avoid the Galactic Believers, his loyal followers. They came across as some wacky New-Age group, believing in what some chick going by the name of the Oracle had started. She foresaw humanity's bright future in the stars. The numbers grew, and ABE showed up. I guess she was right. He took so many people and destroyed so much of our planet, claiming Earth was to be absorbed into the bigger picture.

If you had asked me any of this before the event, I would think you were shooting smack. Today, I know we can sense consciousness in physical objects. Pansychism. ABE communicated with us for years, through the Galactic Believers and the Oracle. The whispers of millions of entities that he has absorbed, speaking only in fragments. I wonder if those individuals are alive, or if it is him manipulating us.

I remember watching with my own eyes as the giant glowing triangle dissolved civilization into small particles and sucked it in with a spiraling motion. People were too gullible. They couldn't resist ABE and his mindless followers. People find it so easy to give up on hope. Not all of us did. ABE's Galactica Array absorption is not the end-all-be-all he claims. He's persuasive, and his Galactic Believers are intimidating, yet ABE is vulnerable because he has an ego.

Still, ABE made Earth a mess. When he initiated the galactic absorption, he took his believers, and those who could not resist him, or those that were distracted. Part of the planet tore apart. I think that something about us resisting is what saved the

Earth. I was there when my wife ceased to exist. Much like the other survivors, the Galactic Believers confronted our family in our homes. Those black-suited fools. They disintegrated, like the rest, rising to the giant white triangle the size of the moon. Not me.

Blind luck. I am no university professor; I'm a mechanic. Odd jobs, you know? A bit of a science geek. Thankfully, common sense isn't bound to any sort of class or trade. That is why I believe I resisted ABE. That is why others did too. I wish I could say the same about my wife, absorbed in the Galactica Array. I wanted to give in, let ABE take each atom from my body so I could be with her again. Even after the absorption, I was positive I could hear her. For what I knew, it was ABE talking to me, wanting me to submit. Pondering this stuff can drive you crazy, like the concept of consciousness. So, I don't overthink it.

I hid for a couple of days. ABE remained in the sky during this time, his pure white form defied light and darkness, floating, never moving. The upward spiral of matter moved towards him. His essence, or power, crumbled dirt and flesh. I was frightened and didn't move. I even pissed my pants, I was so scared of making any sort of movement. What a coward. On the bright side, lying under a car for days is a great method to lose weight. That wasn't relevant, since ABE brought humanity into a new dark era.

I had grown weak. The lack of food and resting in my revolting filth was driving me insane. ABE's absorption stopped. Broken cars, buildings, animals, skeletons, dirt, and water remained frozen in the spiral. The change was unexpected, and I got up from under the vehicle. The higher up particles remained motionless in the air, as if suspended in time. I didn't believe what I was looking at. I don't think anyone did. In the midnight sky, the giant glowing white triangle froze too. Well, in front of North America. I wasn't sure what the other side of the world was observing.

Anyway, I saw other folks coming from under the rubble. I remember seeing one gal. Her eyes were puffy, likely from crying as much as I had. Hundreds of people appeared from under the remains of the city. We were unsure of what to say or what to do. ABE, the entity that was going to bring our doom, was motionless.

"Who dare prevent the absorption?" ABE's voice projected in my mind. By the look on everyone else's faces, I think that bastard was talking to them, too.

We watched in awe, waiting to see what happened next.

"This planet is mine," ABE spoke. "The atoms that are treasured here must be brought into the Galactica Array."

Some guy in front of me turned around. He pointed towards the giant triangle. "He cannot absorb us! We have resisted him."

"How?" shouted a woman.

"We must be special," the man said. "Our mind, or DNA."

"I prayed!" a man shouted, his voice trembling. "God answered me. He answered us!"

Before anyone else perked up, a pulsating wave erupted throughout the landscape. I felt it in my core, holding onto my chest as the force moved through me. I lost balance for a brief moment. Another surge pulsated, throwing me on my ass.

People screamed. I refrained from standing because the particles falling from the sky had my keen interest. ABE's spiralling absorption crumbled. The object shifted in reverse. Reality was rebuilding itself. I didn't believe it. Others didn't. I don't even think ABE did.

"Who defies me?" ABE shouted. This was the angriest I had ever heard the triangle talk. The prick was so well composed. About time something shook him.

Tingling ran throughout my body. I thought I was going to be absorbed, and I stood, feeling the ground hum. My eyes were wide, watching millions of colours vibrate from my hand, the road, the rocks, everything and anything. The entire world had a translucent layer buzzing and rising towards the triangle in the sky.

Next, the impossible occurred. Shadows, large and small, animated, morphed and grew, or shrunk, depending on their size, until they became a human form with arms and legs. No light touched them. They were pitch black, with millions of particles buzzing through them similar to a static TV. There wasn't a single darkness left; the world was bright with no shade as these lightless ones glided on the rising colours, like surfers, heading for ABE. Can you imagine what a world with no shadows looks like? None of us could, unless you were there.

ABE's glowing form shook in spasmodic motions. Parts of the triangle cracked like glass. Clouds blew away while the buzzing colours rose with the lightless ones. The sky itself distorted, rippling like water. I think. I can't describe this to you. It was as if there were an inverted ocean in the atmosphere, also covered with thousands of these lightless humanoids, filled with as many translucent colours as I could see outlining the ripples. Two worlds, one right side up, buzzing, and the other inverted, were merging. People ran; some stayed. I was the one to watch. If we were going to die, I at least wanted a show.

The sky-ocean extended downward as the dual tsunamis aimed for ABE, with the vibrant hues moving to him. The triangle fractured further, thrashing in a jittering speed that defied logic.

"This is mine to take. For I am the All-Being Entity!" ABE shouted.

The two heavenly tidal waves collided with ABE, the buzzing colours, and the lightless ones. Its impact caused the triangle to dissolve like ink in a bucket of water, taking the lightless ones with it. The forces rebounded and soared towards the surface of Earth.

I finally ran. A little late. I wasn't sure where. I was weak, hungry, and frightened. The massive force from above engulfed the entire sky. It surpassed previous observations in terms of speed. I could hear millions of voices talking at once, indistinguishable. The sky-ocean collided with me and sucked my body in.

I froze. Senses stopped. Black. Light. Reverse, like a VCR in rewind. My vision zoomed. Sensations were backwards. Explain how that feels, huh? Sucking in, pushed, pulled, invisible forces. I relived the moments of being under the car, ABE's arrival, the moment of me urinating myself, witnessing my wife dissolve (or reconstruct in this backward-time), and the sudden appearance of the first Galactic Believer. This continued until I returned to the point before any of this happened.

I dropped my wrench, shouting, catching the attention of my coworkers at the shop. It had to be a dream. No sweat drenched me. No piss-coated clothes. A strange sense of déjà vu rushed over my being. I had been through this before. I swear to God.

"You okay?" asked a coworker.

"Yeah," I said. "What day is it?"

"Thursday," he said.

I sighed, realizing I could answer the damn question myself. I reached into my pocket for my phone to check the clock. It matched my exact thoughts. It transported me years before any of this happened. The sky-ocean from those lightless ones had rewound time. No one possessed special DNA, mindsets, or divine power to resist ABE. What a foolish idea. Other entities caused it, greater than us, and greater than ABE. We couldn't see it. They took care of humanity and our planet.

It had brought me prior to the first Galactic Believer, so long ago. I had this knowledge and experience in my mind, yet it was a regular day of work. I left the shop and immediately called my wife. A tear left my eye as my heart burst. I cried. She was confused, lovely, as she is. I don't think she will ever understand why I was sobbing. I didn't tell her why. No way. I told her I missed her.

I took a stroll through the city, experiencing the buildings, listening to the sounds of the metropolis, and embracing the moment. There's some New-Age hokey shit, hey? When you go through an end-of-the-world experience, and life returns, you appreciate it a bit more. Maybe those free spirits were right in welcoming the present. Whatever those lightless ones were that shattered ABE were capable of abilities that scientists can't even fathom. I am unable to look at shadows the same way anymore—or anything, for that matter. The planet is alive. I saw those humming colours vibrate.

The years went by, and the Galactic Believers never arrived. ABE was a figment of my imagination. At least that is what sane people say. The classic Mandela Effect. I learned I was not alone. There were others online that shared the same memories that I do. We can discuss the destruction of Earth and the days leading to it in immense detail. We sound like conspiracists because there is no proof of it. It only exists as a collective narrative told by folks who haven't met. Another conspiracy theory that will drive you mad.

Thanks for listening to my story. It's good to see a solid community around this.

mechanic_dude200

Dasco takes the laptop from Scalebane. "That's one story of many."

She shakes her head, wanting to dismiss them. Though, the descriptions ring true to her studies. It resembles what she saw atop the tower while contacting King. "These are human ghost stories. Anyone can make them, especially with your technological devices." In her heart, she harbours doubt. Soft skins shouldn't have knowledge of lightless ones. They're a legend of the old world, unseen by modern eyes. The fact that there is a collective of humans discussing them throughout the globe churns her innards with a squeeze.

Zea scratches her head as Dasco places the laptop on the counter. She speaks, "Yes, and no. Although it started. Then . . . the lightless ones came."

Dasco talks. "There was a paranormal event a year ago at a club a few blocks from here. The people claimed shadows rose."

Yes, Scalebane thinks. She recalls seeing the animated shadow belonging to a concrete column.

Zea looks at Dasco before continuing. "These lightless ones that he is painting, they saved the planet. They stopped ABE from absorbing life, shattering him. They had the power to revert time and space."

"What of this ABE?" Scalebane asks.

"Gone? Shattered? The lightless ones ended them and we went onto a different timeline. It's hard to believe. So many people struggle with the truth."

Scalebane shifts her stance, providing mercy to her left leg. *"We are blind to what lies ahead of us and we could awaken forces greater than our control,"* Jekos told her a year ago when Kai Pung jumped off the tower. It's true; there are unknowns beyond the Creator.

She grips both sai as a low rumble seeps through her throat. This baked tale spews from whispers of digital texts and the rambles of two ash-dashers. Scalebane hasn't heard of this event. She's unaware of ABE or the recent Earth destruction and reversal. This is a waste of time.

Patience is key to cooperating with others. The muse's threat is too important for Scalebane to ignore. She releases her grip on her weapons with a deep exhale through her nose.

"What of them?" she asks, pointing at the two naked men. Their ash trip is alive and well as they laugh, whispering into each other's ears on the bed.

"Daniel and Craig? Oh." Dasco scratches his skull and smiles. "We were at an art opening earlier in the evening. One thing led to another."

"Get them out of here," Scalebane says. She scans Zea from the feet to the strap on poking between from her robe and into her round eyes. Despite the coral of the drug, her gaze holds depth. There's a familiar old world presence lingering in her soul, like she saw in Cabello's. "She can stay, only for today."

Zea and Dasco exchange looks, as if one should reject the order.

"No visitors here, Dasco. Our work is sensitive. Dress yourself and by the gods, bathe." She marches to the studio corner to see what he has worked on as Dasco sees to the task. His latest work in progress rests on the easel. It's a separate piece from the compilation of canvases he was labouring on. There are no ritual summoning circles, glyphs, or cosmos stars. It contains a vast open space with silhouette beings reaching outward from the canvas. They're escaping their two-dimensional plane.

A sudden pang hits her heart, staring at the painting, far more potent than her daily agony. Logic cannot repress emotions forever. As important as Dasco's work is, there's not even the slightest hint of Dreadweave Pass. No Namsruc. He hasn't painted a vazelead or a nymph since the one. She needs a resolution. That half-imp will get his wish.

She scans the rest of the work area, wanting to understand how the latest piece relates to the summoning circle. On the ground, beside the easel, are a series of seven torn sheets of paper. Scalebane grabs the charcoal illustrations comprised of quick strokes, each depicting a girl chained to the ceiling. Some have her behind bars. With each drawing, she gets thinner, with more scars accompanying the three across her face and one to the left side of her clavicle. The last illustration is the clearest, with her sitting on a hardwood floor surrounded by canvases, cross-legged.

Scalebane glances at the planks of wood on Dasco's studio floor. The dents and scuffs match the sketch. Without a doubt, the muse is channelling Cabello. The ethereal being wishes to have her as part of the summoning spell.

CHAPTER 29
PURPOSE LOST

Augugust 24, 2019, Iglesias's hollow body returns. Twelve months since José's death. His watering eyes stare at the foot-tall tombstone that reads: *José Iglesias. Rest in peace. 2000 to 2018.*

He tries to live for his boy and, despite his mind, he returns to his heart fused to this small grave. It plays memories of times that didn't come to pass: José going to college. Him graduating and getting a proper job. He'd start a family, find his own success and joy. Would have there been children who would have loved José when Iglesias was long gone? These wonders of a severed future mobilize into the tears escaping his eyes.

Too many unanswered questions remain, tearing his soul apart. That fateful night when José and his dear girlfriend went to Radiate Primate will haunt him. How did the cops in Toronto fail to find the Moths exiting the building? Did they not block off the roads? What of the bouncers? Law enforcement interviewed each of them and cleared them. Iglesias hates thinking the worst. The Moths, once again, package horrors in neat summary sheets for the law and media, while the true events are a mangled mess of confusion.

There's only one person who challenged that power: Lola Cabello. Iglesias admires her courage and boldness to battle against the impossible tide. It labelled her an unstable whack job who enjoys killing, like her predecessor Michael Bradford. The media leeched onto her. Hell, they're making that ill-tasted documentary about her.

Deep within Iglesias's heart, beyond the pain that weighs each day, there is a rage burning inside; and it's growing. It expresses itself in strange ticks. For example, he licks his inner lip, cleaning off the blood from biting too hard moments ago. Or he'll snap a pen as he did this morning. He tosses papers and groceries with excessive force onto the table.

CAMB calls the tragic event a gang shooting. It's complete nonsense, because Iglesias was there. Crooked players were involved with his son's death. He wants revenge. The internet brews conspiracies of animated shadows. Doctors comment: a mass hysteria. He saw the darkness move, bringing Lola Cabello into his mind.

Iglesias places a bouquet of roses against the tombstone, resting on the dirt between the patches of graveyard grass under the bright sun. José wouldn't have been fond of them. He would have preferred a cool graphic t-shirt or designer shoes. The flowers are for Iglesias.

One year on, 2019, and Iglesias's mind swirls with the same questions. His heart weighs on his existence, unable to escape the painful recollection of discovering his lifeless son, face buried in a pool of his own blood. It's not right. The world moved on. Susana wouldn't have. They both have no reason to talk.

He tries to tell himself he's seen countless victims over two decades on the force. Those families didn't have their day. Lost lives never avenged. It doesn't do him any good being on the other side, joining the sufferers who have to live each day with no justice. Iglesias has to learn to move on.

It isn't easy to let go of a person so dear. Building new habits, filling your time without those you care for is pointless. He has to keep his mind occupied to cope. Lifting his head and seeing the sun rise each morning is a brief reminder that life is vibrant. He has his former partner and Archer. The people living next to him are amicable. This is Iglesias' self-motivating mantra for getting out of bed. He's thankful this evening he is having dinner with Glenn Beckman and his wife. Iglesias needs a distraction.

The graveyard isn't so empty. Forty graves over stands another person wearing a black hoodie, trench coat, and cargos with their hood up. Their hands hide in their pockets. An innocent passerby would presume they're mourning the loss of a loved one. To Iglesias, they look too stiff. Who wears a long coat in this summer heat? Their presence is too perfect facing sideways, as if watching him from their peripheral view. It's enough to tell Iglesias he needs to leave. *Paranoia will eat you.*

Beckman's wife, Catherine, makes a mean casserole filled with cheese, pork, plenty of tomatoes, and chili oil to give it a kick. It's a type of spice that Iglesias prefers while Beckman stays on the lighter side. The thought of the food is what Iglesias pushes to the front of his mind during the drive to the small village of Wakefield outside of Ottawa. He's been effective at suppressing his feelings, thoughts, and fears for many years on the force. His effectiveness made him numb to his wife's divorce. It turned him into a rigid father. It helped shape José. He became his own man and took risks. His choices were fine, until he made one mistake.

Stop it, Iglesias thinks. Suppress. The pain is overwhelming, and his sinking face shows it.

He parks his SUV in the driveway of the deep forest green house. It has a new set of burgundy roof shingles since the last time Iglesias visited. He takes the paper bag containing two bottles of red wine and exits his vehicle, heads to the front door, and gives it a knock. Moments later it swings open. There stands the tall, thin Beckman.

"Detective Iglesias," Beckman says in a cartoonish formal tone.

"Detective Beckman," Iglesias says. He forces a closed smile while extending his arms for a hug.

They embrace with the tight squeeze and two slaps on the back, then step into the home. The smell of baking cheese bombards his nostrils, followed by the acidic tomatoes swirling in with the other hot spices in the meat. The chemical reaction channels through his nasal system, signalling his stomach to rumble loud enough for both men to hear it. He would love to eat away his sorrows and chug both bottles of wine for himself.

"So glad you could make it," Beckman says. "Love the beard, by the way."

"Thanks. Can't look at my old face anymore." Iglesias wipes the salt-and-pepper facial hair he sports. He rubs his upper lip. "Yours is gone."

"Yeah, eh? I lost mine after quitting. Hey, you're here on time too. Catherine is getting dinner out of the oven."

Iglesias takes his dress shoes off and Beckman leads him across the tortilla-coloured hardwood floor. On the pine wall to his right, there is a framed picture of the whole family. Beckman, Catherine, their son with shaggy hair, and the older daughter graduating from high school. Iglesias remembers that day. It would have been five years ago.

The two men walk into the kitchen where a short and stout woman has her hands in the oven with mitts, taking a bubbling golden casserole. "Evening, Iglesias!" Catherine calls.

"Thank you for having me," Iglesias says, stopping by the circular dark chocolate dining table. He rests the wine on the surface, gripping it as a pillar to keep his emotions in check.

"Of course, you're welcome here," Catherine says, placing the dish on the stovetop.

"I brought some wine," Iglesias says with a smile. He shakes the bag.

Beckman takes the bottles. Iglesias hesitates for a split second before surrendering it over. *Right*, he thinks. They're drinking that. He needs some. Beckman's locked gaze is one Iglesias once saw when they'd interviewed suspects. His former partner is aware he's a broken man and requires that drink.

Iglesias puts his hands in his pockets, unsure what to do with himself. He watches the retired husband and wife be busybodies. Catherine testing the main meal with a toothpick and Beckman pouring the wine.

"You're not bored yet?" Iglesias says, taking a glass.

"Me?" Beckman says. He slaps the cork onto the bottle and grabs his liquor. "Of course not. Moving to Wakefield has been the best thing for us."

Catherine takes a break to get the last cup and raises it to the men. "With both kids gone, Beckman and I retired, we can actually rediscover who we are. It sounds a little hokey, we focused on our children for the past two decades. Who are we?" She laughs and sips a drink, then spins around and gets to work.

"Makes sense," Iglesias says. "When you got the time."

"Different when you're a bachelor, I guess, eh?" Beckman says. "I don't think I can go hit the town with you. I'm getting too old."

Iglesias chuckles. "You and me both. That ship sailed long ago. In fact, it encouraged me to start a new hobby a couple of months ago."

"Come, come and eat," Catherine says while placing the main course in the centre of the table. It rests beside a basket of toasted buttered garlic bread glazed with crisp brown edges, a deep green and purple salad, and a bowl of asparagus. She fills each of their plates with a pile of food and sits. The two men follow her lead.

"What is that?" Beckman asks, taking his fork and cutting the meal on his plate.

"Gardening," Iglesias says while putting a mouthful of his casserole onto his tongue. The hot cheese smothered pasta, sprinkled with beef, floods his taste buds as he talks, despite the rudeness. It's an old habit of eating fast while on the job. "They're delicate things. You can do a lot of cultivating indoors these days with growing lights."

"That's fascinating," Catherine says. "We take care of our garden, too. Well, I do. It's not Beckman's thing."

"No way." Beckman shakes his head. "I lack the patience."

"They can teach you that," Iglesias says.

"You're not into plants." Beckman snorts.

"It keeps me busy. What about you? Watching your wife do the work?"

"Huh, huh, no. Actually, I decided to write a book." Beckman stuffs a fork of pasta into his mouth.

"That so?" Iglesias says. "I didn't know." Iglesias wouldn't. He hasn't been in touch with his old partner for shy of a year. Iglesias has shut most people out over the past twelve months. It makes him take another slug of his wine to flood the shame.

"It came to me during Christmas and I began typing some of our stories on the force. With a bit of a creative flare, they work great as detective thrillers."

"That's wonderful," Iglesias says.

"You okay if I use some of them? Change the names, even talk to you for consulting?" Beckman asks.

"No problem. We shared a lot of them in our youth when we were a little more spry."

Beckman chuckles. "Sure were."

"You two used to burn the midnight oil countless times," Catherine says, shaking her head. "That one poor man you guys would mock dashing on the street buck naked? I swear he was a victim of drug addiction and you boys kept imitating his walk for weeks. What's wrong with you?"

Beckman and Iglesias laugh, looking at each other. Both take a drink at the same time. She is right.

Iglesias looks to the ceiling, recalling the memory. "Marionette Mitch. Christ. You putting him in the book?"

"I have to be cautious of confidential information. At least, that's what my daughter tells me. Things are different and I'd like to get this story published."

"Fair enough," Iglesias says.

"How is Archer doing?" Catherine asks. "She's been such a lovely girl. I can't believe she hasn't found anyone."

"Well, that's not my business," Iglesias says. That is not the case. Archer and Iglesias have been close, along with Beckman, for years. At least, until 2018, with José's death. *Don't go there*, Iglesias thinks.

"You guys work in the same department and don't chat?" Beckman asks.

"I haven't been back since. I got no clue," Iglesias says.

"You have people who care about you," Catherine says.

Iglesias finishes the rest of his pasta, then empties the wine. He reaches for the bottle and pours a glass. He takes another drink and speaks. "Yeah, thanks."

"I'm glad you finally came for dinner," Beckman says. "I know you needed time. Don't push Archer out."

"Yeah."

"You call Susana?"

Iglesias shakes his head. "God no. I haven't seen her since the funeral, and before that, once or twice after I gained custody of José. She hasn't changed a goddamn bit."

"That's a shame," Catherine says while finishing her meal. She stands and takes her plates.

"You need help?" Beckman asks.

"Oh no, I have this," Catherine says, snagging the items on the table.

Catherine remains the same as she has been since he met her: a busy worm that can't sit and enjoy conversation. That lets Iglesias and Beckman retreat to his study, where he pours Iglesias and himself whisky. The two clang their glasses and Iglesias walks to the deep oak desk in front of a series of bookshelves. Beckman's closed laptop rests on the polished surface of the ordered table. Sticky notes, pens, and a notebook are in perfect alignment with the desk's rectangular shape. It doesn't resemble his old workstation at the office.

"So this is where the soon-to-be world-famous author crafts his words?" Iglesias asks as they both take a seat.

Beckman leans back in his chair, swinging in it. "Yeah, I got the idea in December, like I said, it was when I got a call from the documentary crew."

"Those guys," Iglesias says. He takes a sip of his whiskey, letting the smoky flavour ride in the middle of his tongue before swallowing. "They've bugged me countless times. You participating?"

"God no. They will fuck it up. Who are they anyway? Aren't they funded by Hucker Dime's company?"

"I haven't looked into it. They're making the damn thing with these interviews. It's been two years."

"That's because the story keeps evolving. They can turn it into a docuseries. That's the hype," Beckman says.

"Well, I think they don't have the full story. They need people like you, me, or Archer to talk about what went on. Otherwise, the thing is another CAMB spun tale."

"Yeah. Yeah . . . whatever happened to Cabello?" Beckman asks.

"Who knows? After that day, she vanished. Her body wasn't there in the lounge. Her DNA was on some drinks. They found a hair, blood. It's weird. She called me, of all people. Her plan went horribly wrong, like the slaughterhouse."

"The damn Moths, eh?" Beckman says.

"The fucking Moths. I think you did it right," Iglesias says. He leans over his chair, looking at the study. One corner has the small bar with a marble countertop complete with LED light strips outlining the shape. The other is the open window overlooking the backyard with Catherine's flowering garden. The deep purple carpet is a delicate touch. He takes a sip of whisky. "You got out."

"Hey, Donnie Morris spoke truth. Take the easy way out. Cabello should have listened to him. This thing is bigger than him, you, me, and her. What can a couple of detectives and some crazy vigilante do?"

"Write fiction books." Iglesias smiles.

Beckman chuckles. He bites his lip, pondering his next words. "It's good to see you, Iglesias. You're a brother to me, and it means the world to me you answered."

"I'm sorry, truly. I haven't been fair to you."

"Or Archer." He points at him with the index finger from his whisky-bearing hand. "Don't ignore her. You can ignore me. In fact, I don't blame you after dealing with my dismissive nature for nearly two decades."

Iglesias leans onto the desk, raising his glass. The men cheers and finish the liquor. Beckman nods to the bottle, asking if Iglesias would like another. He shakes his head no. "I have to drive."

"Fair enough. You doing fine, for real?"

"Yeah, I'm fine. I've gotta be fine." Iglesias shrugs the question off his shoulders. "I need to figure out what I have to do. The department wants me to return as a desk monkey, doing consulting work on a national level for drugs, ash, and whatever else. I'll get there. For now, I got the garden. Even then, what am I supposed to do, retire? Move into a small town? No offence, I'm single, alone, stuck in my own thoughts. They run through my head over and over. I don't understand why José would get into the Moths. He knows who they are." Iglesias puts his hands in his pockets. "Then again, shit, I did the same things after Winnipeg. Gangs, drugs, anything. José is— was like me. It angers me, Beckman. There are no answers. I'm mad at José, I'm mad at myself, mad at the system. It drives me crazy. That's why I gotta be fine. Otherwise, there's no end."

"You have friends, Iglesias. If you're not in the mood for a couple of retired old farts, there's Archer."

"Hey, I have a year on you," Iglesias says.

"Yeah, you've got heat. So does she. You know she looks up to you?"

"Yeah . . . " He wipes his beard, embarrassed that Archer admires him. Iglesias can't even look at his own reflection anymore.

"If anything, she can relate to you. You're two workaholics with a lack of social life."

Iglesias snorts and looks to the ground. It's a light jab of truth, for he and Archer both fail at having stable mental health. Archer likes her exercise and whatever else she does in her off time. Iglesias has his plants.

That reminds him to visit the store and get some soil and fertilizer for his budding lettuce. They're outgrowing their pots. There we go. Those are the thoughts that he must concentrate on. He needs to nurture new life, watch it flourish. The past mistakes will be there. He has to move on, beyond the realm of the living, and seize his heart. José would want him to.

CHAPTER 30
DEEP DIVE

Gardening requires patience, persistence, and effort. Effort is the trait Iglesias has. Patience, not so much. Persistence: he will attempt, standing in the aisles of a hardware store's indoor planting supplies.

He didn't think he'd get a hobby. Cultivation is far removed from his work interests. Watching plants grow is humbling, starting from a seed and sprouting through the dirt. It's the reason he picked this activity. He was obsessed with the ash cases for years. That damn drug contains an unusual mix of DNA, including traces of the cocoa plant. Chances are, those interests birthed it. Ash also links to the Moths, connecting

369

José. This new life is barren and unfamiliar, a reflection of the soil bags he stares at.

And pots, he reminds himself.

He reads each label, weight, and pricing for fertilizer and spots a figure at the corner of his eye. They stand at the end of the hall in a black hoodie, trench coat, and cargos. It's the person from the graveyard. He gazes at them. Under the hood, they keep their head lowered. No beard, smooth face. They move to the adjacent aisle.

Now I'm becoming a crazy plant man, Iglesias thinks to himself with a smirk. He snatches a bag of soil mixed with fertilizer and drops it in his cart with a clang. Next, he takes a couple of large clay pots and heads to the cashier.

The short old teller smiles at him while ringing his items through. She says, "Oh these pots are wonderful. I have them for my snake plant at home. They never stop growing."

"Isn't that the truth?" Iglesias says, waving his credit card. He wants to pay and go. He's learned people who love gardening talk too much for his taste.

"Total is forty, seventy-three."

Iglesias pays and takes the large bag of pots in a single hand and the soil in the other.

"Want your receipt?"

"No thanks," he waves with his fingers holding the dirt.

"Best of luck to you," the cashier says.

Iglesias exits the store and walks under the cloudless summer sky. On a concrete parking lot, the heat emphasizes, bouncing off the hard ground. One row over, a dark figure approaches him at an angle. He isn't the crazy plant man. His detective instincts are keen. He stops and faces the stalker, four meters away. The movement surprises the individual and they freeze on the spot.

"You're not good at this," Iglesias says.

The thin person lowers their hood, revealing the boyish face of a girl, or boy. The soft jaw leaves Iglesias unsure, as it conflicts with the broad nose. Their brows are thick and cheekbones pronounced with sharp angles. The androgynous complexion is too smooth to be male and not masculine enough to be female. Their buzzed head and baggy clothes don't assist the profile identification either.

They say, "Detective Iglesias?" The tone is not feminine and not harsh like a man. It's in the middle of the road. These traits help him identify the stalker.

"That's me." Iglesias widens his stance, squeezing his bag of soil.

"You were involved with the Lola Cabello case, right?"

"Yes, I was." Iglesias walks to his SUV, hoping that will end the interaction.

The newcomer hurries to catch up. "That means you had connections with Donnie Morse? The Crystal Moths? Ash?"

"Yes. If you did your research, you'd be aware that I shifted into a consultant after the abattoir plant slaughter." He pops open his trunk and drops his purchases into the vehicle.

"But you didn't. Did you? You went after Cabello again, last year."

"Excuse me?" Iglesias slams the rear compartment shut, facing them.

They retreat. "I don't mean to step on your personal life or anything, though, I kind of am. Sorry. I have to. You did go after Lola Cabello after she escaped prison."

"So?" Iglesias asks. "Get to your point."

"Listen," the newcomer takes a small notebook from their pocket, stuffed with papers and paperclips. They flip through the scribbled pages, pulling out a white business card. The matte finish highlights the glossy black moth icon on the back. They turn it over, showing the numbers: 1111.

"This," they say. "For ones represents going through a cycle. The Moths, that's exactly what they're doing. Moths go through four stages: egg, caterpillar, which is the larva, cocoon, which has the pupa, and the final is an adult where they spread their wings."

"I said get to the point, not give me a front seat to a National Geographic film."

"Okay," the newcomer gives a twitch smile. They wipe their face and speak. "I know who killed José."

"What did you say to me?" Iglesias steps forward, inches from them, towering a head and a half taller. Hearing those words makes Iglesias want to deck the prick. They have no right spitting such lies.

They move back. "Detective Iglesias, we need to talk." They extend their hand holding the business card. He takes it, examining the paper. This is new to him. It fits the characteristics of the Moths. "Not here, though, a secure place. My place, yours. Ideally mine. I can show you what is going on."

He passes the card. "What's your name?"

"The name is Disk."

Iglesias raises an eyebrow. "Disk? Like a floppy disk?"

"Yeah! It isn't a save icon. Cool. I use them sometimes, a little old and redundant when you consider how far we've come with digital storages. I mean, anyway, that's a sidenote. So are you going to join me?"

He should punch the weirdo. Considering they claim to have vital details on José and didn't go to the police, they'd be of value. The homicide department could grill them, discover how they got this information. Crooked law poisons the system. Gang shooting. Horse shit.

This wouldn't be the first time he goes rogue. Lola Cabello, despite her failures, was honest with him. This Disk could be another lunatic, such as his old intel, or lucrative like Cabello. He needs to take the chance.

"Where is your place?" Iglesias asks.

"I'm staying in a motel today. I live in Toronto and came here to find you."

"I must be important," Iglesias says.

"Oh, you are. I prefer online, and could have messaged you that way. I think we have to work together, in person. You need to see firsthand. Otherwise, you'll write it off as an Internet conspiracy."

"Okay." Iglesias raises an eyebrow. "You've intrigued me."

"Great!" Disk jumps.

Iglesias looks around the sparce parking lot to see his is one of seven cars. "You driving? I'll follow."

"I took the bus." Disk scratches their neck. "Can we use your SUV?"

Iglesias rubs his brow. "Sure." Disk might want to take him hostage, utilize him as a driver. The skittish nature and youthfulness of them makes it clear they are an online dork and won't do anything that stupid. "Get in."

Iglesias enters his vehicle and unlocks the passenger side. His new friend hops in, coat squeaking against the leather seat. They speak. "It's not far, downtown, near the Beechwood Funeral Cemetery."

"Right, where you were before yesterday, watching me," Iglesias says, starting the vehicle.

"I had to be sure it was you," Disk says.

"It's me. Talk while directing us." Iglesias shifts out of the parking stall and exits the lot.

"Okay, well . . . where do we start?" Disk fidgets with their fingers, as if waiting for Iglesias to take the lead.

"Tell me where we're going," Iglesias says.

"Much Less Motel," the other says.

"Gotcha." Iglesias presses his lips tight, pondering if this was a mistake.

Disk looks out the window, rolling their index fingers around each other as Iglesias takes the vehicle onto the street. He says, "Well? Keep talking."

"Oh. right. Usually, I have my notes on my computer with me. It would make more sense. I could show you it. Okay, but, uh, I can share some things with you. I've been following the Moths for quite some time."

"So have a lot of others," Iglesias says with annoyance seeping from his tone.

"Not in the way that I have. I'm part of a global network of people. We work anonymously or through code names."

"Like Disk?" Iglesias asks. He holds back a chuckle.

"That's correct." Disk says with seriousness.

"Okay, Floppy, what is this network?"

Disk looks to Iglesias' backseat, doublechecking if they are alone. They turn to look at him with a focused gaze. "We go by the name Eden Breaker."

Iglesias waves a hand in the air. "What does this Eden Breaker want with me?"

"Not so much you." Disk lowers their voice. "It's what happened to Lola Cabello. It is what the Moths are doing. The type of stuff that happened to your son. How the news happens to mention the Moths in passing? The law is careless that the gang is on the streets."

"Because society is sick of hearing about them. The media does this when there's too much of one thing. Bad for ratings."

Disk shrugs. "You know firsthand that tampered evidence has little to do with viewership. There are crooked cops and politicians. CEOs too are in bed with the Moths. This is the kind of stuff Lola Cabello was unravelling."

Iglesias shakes his head. "So what? You're a fan of Cabello? Got posters of her over your walls?"

Disk exhales, irritated by his constant jabbing. "I'll explain more we get to the motel. I'll tell you, though, that business card came from Donnie Morris in Edmonton. He received it from a local Crystal Moth named Alex G who wanted to recruit him. You know Donnie pretty well, don't you?"

"Yeah." Iglesias's voice lowers, realizing this kid may have some value after all. "My old partner and I grilled him a lot."

"Beckman?" Disk's eyes widen.

"You did your research. We knew Donnie Morris was a buddy of Cabello's. The two of them uploaded the video of Becky Murphy's and Michael Bradford's deaths at the hands of Crystal Moths. Lola withheld the evidence from the police and put it on her blog instead. She ran. Thus, her spiral began."

Disk nods, smiling, showing the gap between their front teeth. "Right. Her mother died when the law obtained the warrant and raided her home, thinking Cabello was there. Donnie Morris got death threats, like Cabello, and he took the easy way out. He contacted you. He wanted protection. You gave it, and he got out. Clean and simple."

"How did that card land in your hands?" Iglesias asks.

"We're Eden Breaker, we harvest the fruit," Disk says, smirking.

He wants to wipe that constant grin off their face. They fit the characteristics of a typical internet dweller, so smart with knowledge and so easy to snap. Iglesias needs more information first and presses his lips together.

Disk continues, "Anyway. Cabello didn't quit. Cabello went into the rabbit hole, fighting the Moths between 2014 and 2016, when you and your partner were assigned to the case. You guys followed her around while the Moths framed her for numerous murders across Canada. One death was the famous actress Ashley Amber on November 17, 2016."

"Yes, thanks for telling me about my life. I concluded that someone had tampered with the evidence on Ashley Amber's case. The amount of bullets didn't match the two bodies the Vancouver police found."

"Exactly. That is one example. After, Lola was at the abattoir plant. You said your intel told you the Moths had an ash lab there. Though I question if it was even your intel. That doesn't make sense. I bet it was Lola Cabello, wasn't it?"

This kid is swift, he thinks. His meeting with Cabello was in secret. Eden Breaker is a ridiculous name and Disk is a nerd, yet internet ragers have power. They dox people. They access confidential information, exploit credit cards. He chooses his next words with caution. "What makes you think my intel didn't give me the tip?"

"Because they're a lowlife drug dealer who didn't have any insight into the Moths and lives on the East Coast. The slaughterhouse is in Vancouver. Cabello was there. She had your card from Donnie Morris."

"How do you know this?" Iglesias asks.

"We are Eden Breaker. We infiltrate technology and obtain data, contacts, connections. Like I said, I'm more comfortable behind computers. This physical world, not my jam." Disk waves their hands in the air, dismissing it.

They pull into the parking lot of a two-levelled U-shaped Much Less Motel. Cracks run along the pink stucco building, matching the saturated red shingles. They exit the SUV. Disk takes lead to a unit marked *103*. They unlock it. Iglesias glances around the lot, ensuring there are no onlookers. The motel parking zone has several trucks and a couple of cars parked. The coast is clear and the other units have their curtains shut. He steps inside with Disk, then locks the door.

They march past him and ask, "You go on the documentary? The one they're making about Cabello?"

"No, I'm staying clear of that," Iglesias says, eyeing the scattered papers resting on the bed beside a laptop. "I don't need anyone twisting my words. Why?"

"That's exactly why, and there's more." Disk snags their onyx computer over and pulls on the back, sliding two additional foldout monitors, providing three screens. On the small table at the far end of the room are more papers and an open black briefcase with a corkboard pinned to the inside. It contains strings connecting photos and newspaper articles to a map of Canada.

"What does this have to do with my son's death?" Iglesias asks.

"We'll get there, trust me. The documentary is being created by an Ian Black, who happened to be at Dasco Amoss's art opening in 2016, where Cabello killed Ashley Amber, allegedly. Ian Black is good friends with Timothy Shepherd who was making the last movie Ashley Amber was in before he, too, was murdered at that show. Timothy Shepherd and Ian Black both got their funding from a holding company named Lang Enterprises."

Disk takes the papers from the bed, handing them to Iglesias. He inspects the printed emails between the two Hollywood directors and a Dr. Lang.

He skims it, seeing the three men talk about funds. An internet nerd can type a fake email. "I heard Hucker Dime was behind the documentary."

Disk points to the paper. "That says otherwise."

"How did you get this?"

Disk raises an eyebrow. "Eden Breaker harvests the fruit. Let me tell you, the Moths are far bigger than anyone thought. Lang Enterprises? Works alongside Allen Oil Site Solutions, the parent company of Allen Shipping Solutions. Lang Enterprises makes decorative statues. A couple are dragons and good luck cats." They reach for a black backpack on the ground and take out a six-inch statue of a dragon. "Remember these babies?"

Iglesias scratches his head. "It was a while ago."

"They held ash inside the hollow sculpture. Lang Enterprises manufactures the figures in Vietnam. Allen Shipping Solutions brought them over to Vancouver. Crystal Moths were at the art opening with these. A Dr. Lang discovers that ash sterilizes ash-dashers. Why did they push the drug so hard if they didn't know what it does? In three years, scientists haven't discovered where the scales come from and ash is still being pushed, no real concern by the authorities. It's the modern world's best kept secret."

Iglesias folds his arms and takes a leap of faith after connecting the strings in his mind. "Okay, you think the Moths are creating a population decline? That's quite an accusation to leap to." He can dance with a conspiracy nut.

Disk's face lights up with wide eyes and a full smile. "You're quick. There's more. Lang Enterprises funds Manageficient Enterprises, owned by the same doctor. You've seen Manageficient Enterprises on the news? Merging with Allen Oil Site Solutions? It's connected, Detective Iglesias. Don't you see?" Disk bolts across the bed and snags the briefcase with the corkboard pinned inside. They bring it to him. "The Crystal

Moths have been around for a long, long time. See this man at the top of the board?"

Iglesias notes the pixelated photo of a figure in a white suit, pale skin, and slicked back ivory hair.

Disk jabs the photo with their index finger. "That's Mastema. He took over the Moths long ago."

Iglesias squints. Cabello mentioned Mastema before, as did the ill-fated Chen.

Disk continues, "He has had these two working with him since. Notice their exposed canine teeth? Far larger than they need to be."

Below the photo, strings connect dual shots of higher quality. One contains a man with spiky frosted hair, and the other is bald. Both sport shades, white blazers, black button shirts and pants. The bulges Disk mentioned extend from their upper lips. People can doctor photos. Canines aren't that long.

Disk continues, "The three of them are what you think. They're ancient."

"I wasn't thinking that," Iglesias says. "How old are the Moths?"

"History stops recording them at a certain point."

"Who are these two working for Mastema?"

Disk laughs, the same nervous one before Iglesias almost decked them. "They're not human, like Mastema. Feeding off of energy or blood. We'll get there. I don't think you're ready."

Christ, Iglesias thinks. He walked right into a loony bin in a sliver of hope of finding answers regarding his son. Crazies have information. It takes patience and persistence to extract it from them. "Let me understand. You're talking about vampires?"

"Forget I said that. Seriously. Never happened. Let's reboot." Disk slaps their palms together. "Bam! Done. Look at the photos below Mastema and those men. That black and white one."

Below the trio is a photo with written text below stating 1905. Two males in three-piece ivory suits with prominent sharp fangs sit at a small round table. A third man in a pinstripe suit smokes a cigar, smiling.

Disk speaks, "That's over a hundred years ago with the Irish mob who infected Illinois and New York. Those canine teeth, coincidence? I don't think so. Same angled nose. Same jutting jaw."

Iglesias cannot deny they have the same facial features. He says, "Uh huh. A family birth defect. The Moths are old, no different from the Japanese Yachuza, dating back centuries. Ancient gangs exist. Explains why they have such influence."

"Further. Look at those photos."

To the right is a photograph of a marble sculpture of a pair of Herculean men gripping a naked woman. The hairless one sinks their teeth into her neck. The character, with cascading hair and a sharp nose, arcs their head, showcasing fangs. A written remark below the photo states: Rome 48 BC. A string connects to a painting where the same two males cower at the right of a cross held by a robed priest. Behind the religious leader, a skeleton wears the same clothes as the holy man. They're on their knees in front of a fourth with ivory hair in bone coloured armour. Smoke rises from the skeleton's mouth and into the outstretched hand of the figure in white. The note below reads: *1496, by Albrecht Dürer*. The last picture is a wall carving,

Egyptian, has a bald man and another with long hair standing beside a lady. The three have extended canines.

Disk says, "Energy vampires, blood vampires . . . satanic ritual blood drinking illuminati conspiracies are not far off."

"You realize this is beyond the deep end? It doesn't explain the Moth's power."

"Well, a hundred years ago, people talked of witches and demons. Several centuries ago, they talked about vampires. Vlad the Impaler? Today, the game is intelligent reptilians."

Disk lowers the briefcase and taps on their laptop, making a few clicks and opening a short video. "You can't tell me I'm the first person to have told you this stuff."

Iglesias folds his arms. Disk is right. His intel, cuffed Moths, and Cabello claimed the Moths were too large to take on alone. They've mentioned intelligent reptilians. Cabello handed him that strange fragment of the horn and he has the black blood.

Disk lifts the laptop and hits the space bar, starting a video in the middle window. "How do you explain things like this?"

Iglesias steps to the screen, arms dangling to his sides as his mouth hangs open in disbelief. It's security camera footage of an alleyway. The time stamp states November 17, 2016, the same night as Dasco Amoss's art opening, where Ashley Amber and Timothy Shepherd died.

The brief clip shows a silhouette of a cloaked being crashing into a dumpster in the alley and toppling onto the ground. A moment later, the being rises. A white scaled tail sways side to side, perking similar to a cat. The fabric of the cloak moves aside, revealing legs bending backwards like a bird. The being slides its tail around its leg and wraps the shroud over its body, concealing its form, and disappears off screen.

Disk pauses the recording. "I bet the cops didn't discover this video, hey?"

Iglesias wipes his beard. Indeed, they scrubbed the security footage from the art show and nearby towers and returned empty handed. The Moths cleared the important ones before the police found them.

"You've heard of intelligent reptilians. People talked about them before ash and even more because of it. You've sampled a scale to uncover its genetic makeup. You're closer to this than anyone."

Disk is correct. Iglesias is the closest to this case, other than Cabello. That horn and black blood enter his thoughts again. He hasn't gotten the DNA tested. With Jose gone, he doesn't fear the Moths taking his life if he deep dives into their crimes again.

"If you want answers about your son, work with me," Disk says.

It's as if Disk read his thoughts. Can he trust them? "You have information about my son?"

"Yeah, I have Eden Breaker tasked with it."

"You should have opened this conversation with that video." Iglesias's knuckle taps the laptop. "Look, I need to do some of my own investigating. Mind if I take a photo of these images you have on your art project?"

"What?" Disk blinks twice.

Iglesias points to the corkboard.

"Totally," Disk says.

Iglesias puts his hands on his hips. "I'll be in touch when I get some results. Want to aim for a week's time?"

Disk nods, sealing their deal.

"Perfect. Here's my card." Iglesias reaches into his wallet for his business cards.

Next, he takes his phone and snaps a photograph of Mastema and his ageless goons. He can use these with a reverse image search online to cross reference Disk's research. Iglesias will follow through with that horn Cabello gave him three years ago by calling in a favour from an old friend.

CHAPTER 31
PSYCHONAUT

The diamond-shaped scales flood Lola's system and dissolve her concerns as the days turn into weeks. Her torturer is her provider, replenishing the ever-growing hunger. When he is not with her throughout the week, she suffers muscle rot and aching bones. Her organs revert to raisins with a squeezing pain far worse than the physical beatings she experienced prior. Rithu returns two weeks on, giving her a taste of ash, saving her. She listens as she promised. The six senses hone into the young ambitious vazelead radiating coldness from his soul.

"It's okay," Lola says, looking at the steel humanoid mask. "Share your mind."

Rithu rubs his neck, keeping Lola on his thighs as if she were his lapdog. She matches the size ratio of one compared to him.

"My People's state is dire," he says.

"Extinction," Lola replies. Her arms reach for the ceiling at two light orbs dancing in the air. They swirl around the rainbow colours glistening the prison cell. Mother Nature. She is near, and so far beyond the window. Inspecting closer, these illuminations aren't the same. Fire? Eyes? Entities watch her.

Rithu continues, "Too many of us are sick and dying to breed. Lereif Scalebane and Namsruc Scalebane are the remaining females of our people that can lay eggs. By the Creator's luck, I was the last born vazelead. Do you understand the seriousness of that duty?"

You're endangered, scared, and threatened by man. It's unfair, is what Lola detects, though she says one word in her blissful state. The muscles are liquid, her voice gentle. "Yes." The ash dose was more potent than the previous visit, rendering her limbs useless. Besides, Rithu is not a monster. He needs an ear. She requires him to escape if she can gain his trust.

"Namsruc has gone. Lereif Scalebane sees me as a lesser. She has no respect for my abilities, and I have to win her over as a mate."

"Why?" Lola asks, grabbing onto Rithu's tail, playing with the tip, entranced by the glowing purple ash scales on the back of it.

"For the recognition of my father and my mother. To carry on the Blacktooth name. To continue our people's existence. We would be heroes for centuries to come. All Lereif Scalebane has to do is breed."

"It's a lot to ask of a woman of any kind."

"I never volunteered. We're forced into this. I also don't think I'm fond of Scalebane as an individual. I must prove myself, gain the respect. I understand the mutual benefit. How can she not?"

"No love in her," Lola says.

Rithu grumbles. "Nor in me. It's a practical engagement." He releases his tail from her. "I'm intrigued by the concept of love."

Lola's fingers shift to his mask's jawline. "Love is everywhere. It is the living Earth." *I sense it.*

"The romantic kind. I've studied history lessons, songs, and paintings from tales of old, when my people thrived, loved, and were free. My parents knew that time. Scalebane has her sister. Me? What do I have?"

Intuition guides Lola this day, and she sits on his crossed legs. Her hands slide underneath his hood to the back of his neck for a gentle hug. Her fingers run along feathers draping from his scalp. Creatures of Mother Nature enjoy affection. The moment holds and the coldness radiating from his heart lessens.

Rithu's heartfelt confession stood in stark contrast to the tumultuous moments that surrounded it. Her missing tattoo reminds her she lost her advantage. Weeks on and the shaper hasn't returned. Does anyone know she is alive? If they did, they didn't care.

Lola stops tracking days as she devours more scales. Time is a man-made construct that helps the concrete jungle prosper. Here, in the basement of life and death, ash matters.

The scraps of meat provided is enough to keep her heart pumping and her brain semi-active. The system demands drugs. She doesn't care about her living conditions of filth, funk, and grime.

To avoid their bond being discovered, Rithu must maintain his title. During the visits, he dangles her from the chains, pressing his metal mask against her forehead before beginning the torment, demanding answers. Her wails and cries tangle with Rithu's growls and shouts, booming through the vents and into the halls of the mansion. Music to the First's ears.

"It's okay," Rithu says, unshackling her shaking body. The pain is true, theatrical or not. She feels each blow. He carries her into his lap after each session, stroking her grime-coated hair. "I have you. I respect you. You're strong. You can resist." He takes a larger scale, places it on her tongue, and caresses her bloody face.

She chews. The ash will take her beyond suffering. Those twin white lights penetrate the fabric of reality, tearing away the prison cell, staring at her.

The End.

Pain and compassion. Bi-weekly, month after month.

What is time? It's an unclear answer, for each individual experiences it at different speeds. Age accelerates perception compared to a child. Isolation under a crime lord's mansion creates a sense of distortion. Ash sessions also fabricate uncertain times. The days without her drug are tiresome, and her internal organs burn greater than the withering determination to escape. She's accepted Rithu's infliction and company as her normal in return for ash.

Lola hasn't come to terms with new visitors. The shapeshifter fails to appear. Instead, another arrives at her cell in his crisp white suit and glimmering rings.

Mastema taps the bars with his jewellery. She doesn't have the strength to look at him and remains curled in the corner of the room. She's used the last of her scale for the week. Isn't Rithu supposed to be here today? Or is it tomorrow?

"Am I going to have to extract the information myself?" Mastema asks. "Or do I have to pass you to Dr. Lang again?"

Lola shakes her head no. Her heart stops a beat, making her limbs shiver. Christ, she cannot endure his torment without the drug.

"Then where did you get the bullet?" he asks.

Lola moves her head side to side once more.

Mastema points at her through the bars. "I'm patient and can outlive you. You're nothing compared to me. Do you understand?"

"You're the First," Lola says in a dry croak.

"You've done your research. Bravo, clever little girl. Then you are aware that I have all the time in the world. Seven months is a blink of an eye. If you want to play the long game, so be it. Rithu is going to gain so much from you and you shall suffer, as I have suffered. You will break before you know it." He takes a deep inhale while closing his eyes. "Yes, I can feel your pride withering. You have nothing, because you are nothing. That kick you had to your flavour is gone. I can wait, Cabello. I can wait."

He raises his hand and clenches his fist. It shakes. The sunlight from the sun radiating in the room flickers, catching Lola's eye. No, it's not the light. The shadows dance. She's witnessed this before at the club. It's Mastema, he controls the brightness and the darkness. Her mouth hangs open.

Mastema releases his grip, and the blackness returns to its rightful place. "I wait because I grow stronger." He grins and turns around, exiting the hall.

Lola buries her head in her arms. *Seven months*, she thinks. The duration down here and his harsh words must not get to her. She has Rithu, her caretaker, provider, and if the ash-dasher can keep her mind clear, her one chance at escape.

Five months later—one year later since her capture—a distant voice enters her mind as the ash fades. *Find him. Find the painter.*

"I will, I am," Lola mumbles. *Mother Nature*. She's curled in a fetal position at the corner of her cell, reaching for the ceiling, for an entity that isn't. The sound wasn't Mother Nature's; it was the other.

Her ash trip ends, and as per usual, her bones reduce to toothpicks. The muscles freeze. This year-long consumption, with scraps of meat for food, morphs her into a skeleton. She doesn't recognize her own arms in the air.

There was a purpose for taking ash. *Escape, yes.* It's not the euphoria. She needs to remind herself of that. Lola must use Rithu's softening spirit.

Footsteps come from the end of the basement hall in an unfamiliar stride. It isn't Rithu's usual walking motion. It has a high click in a fast-paced stride. She rolls onto her hands and knees, crawling. Standing requires too much effort. She reaches the gate, wrapping her cracked sandpaper fingers around the rusted bars.

A thin being in a burgundy suit walks to her, holding a chrome tray. Usually, Rithu brings her food on that dish. The lack of fat on the man's body is concerning, giving him a corpse-like appearance. His toxic green eyes match the eyebrows pairing with the burning plastic scent stinging her nose.

"Cabello, is it?" the man says.

"Yeah?" Lola says, voice croaking.

He rests on one knee, sliding the chrome platter under the jail door. "A sweet taste rides the Serpent's Tongue."

"What?" Lola squints.

The man stands. "Forbidden fruit never tasted so good." He winks and walks away.

"Hey," Lola calls out. He keeps moving, fading into darkness. "Hey!" Lola extends her arm between the bars.

Those words, Lola thinks. The torture and ash sessions scramble her mind and she doesn't recall where she heard them. The plate contains the usual scraps of chicken and rice along with a new item: an apple. There's a hole in the fruit. She grabs it and looks inside to see a small black earbud stuffed into the core.

With her index finger, she takes the speaker out and spins it. It's a regular wireless headphone. She brings it to her ear and listens with intent. Silence. Lola eats the food with her fingers, using her other hand, waiting.

Pointless, Lola thinks and puts the earpiece on the plate. *What was that phrase?* She hugs her purple and blue blotched legs, trying to recall. Ash fried her mind. Lola collapses her skull onto her knees.

A muffled sound projects in the room, and she looks up. There's a voice, subtle, inaudible. Another person talks. She gazes at the earbud. The Serpent speaks.

CHAPTER 32
HANDS IN EVERY POCKET

Making hard choices, such as allegiances, can make twelve months feel like a lifetime. Scalebane's people age slower than humans, though she feels the pressure of time, as sentient beings do.

If you accept my offer, I'll share more with you. If you don't believe me, here's some information of value: those three men meet Mastema once a year to plan their strategy . . . Next year is their annual meeting. These meetings don't involve King or your people. Hear their gathering.

It will persuade you, my friend. These were Jekos's words in 2018 when they captured Cabello and brought her to Mastema's mention. Twelve months on she joins Rithu to Mastema's mansion.

Continual pain cannot be easy on a soft skin. It's intriguing that Cabello has shared no information after the countless sessions with the son of King. The torturer and the torture share a strange form of respect. Each serves a purpose, testing the other's will. Scalebane's mother's words resonate: kill only in self-defence or to end suffering. Even now, flying over the Canadian Rockies in a helicopter, it raises a toothy grin on her face behind the metal muzzle. She would like to finish Cabello and obtain vengeance for her damaged leg.

It would protect Jekos's secret. It wouldn't explain Jekos's use of her. Is Rithu as pathetic of a torturer as Scalebane predicted, given Cabello's strength? Is she so determined that she is invincible? Or is another scheme afoot? Either reason works in Scalebane's favour.

Her thoughts keep her occupied as the flying transportation soars over the mountaintops. She wonders about her comrades' perspectives as she sits across from them. Jekos must be wondering why she hasn't accepted his offer. Rithu is uncomplicated and straightforward. He is on a never-ending quest to please Scalebane and his father.

The chopper lands on the helipad, surrounded by tall grass dancing in the wind. They hop off the helicopter as the blades slow to a halt below the clouding skies. Thank the Creator that the sun is gone.

The smell of a thousand corpses radiates in the open field as the two vampiric Crystal Moths greet them from the stone walkway. Scalebane didn't learn their names over the years. To her, they're leeches; like the soft skins, the Moths, and their leader. Unlike Jekos, who proves to be the most cunning of the group.

Dreadweave Pass, Scalebane thinks. Jekos has the answer to accessing the afterlife. After she hears the annual meeting, she'll decide to form allegiances. She has hope of finding Synarion and Namsruc. Her sister has been with their adoptive father for three years. It tightens Scalebane's stomach, thinking what toxic words that nymph has poisoned her sister's mind with.

The vampire Moths don't speak a word, taking a slight bow, as does Jekos. Rithu and Scalebane remain stiff. The five old world beings walk across the field and underneath the archways of vines, bushes, and trees. It's the same beauty that Synarion would appreciate as a balancer of Mother Nature. Namsruc, too, would see the wonder. To Scalebane, the ecosystem means little.

They turn a corner, reaching the front of the curved driveway with the sheltered roof. The bald vampire opens one of the two wide doors and steps into the foyer; Mastema stands in the centre below the dome entrance. As per usual, he wears a full white suit with his bone hair tucked behind his ears.

"The three of you?" Mastema asks, eyeing the vazeleads and Jekos. "Is ash that uninteresting? Or do we not have enough supplies, Scalebane?" This attitude is unusual from Mastema's calm and collected state. His one hand hugs his ribs, the other squeezes his palm, elbow resting on the other forearm.

Jekos cups his fingers together close to his chest. "Mastema, master, it's the yearly meeting with the three partners, is it not?"

"That's correct," Mastema says. Agitation comes from his tight voice.

"I was present last time?" Jekos asks.

"Right, you were. And you will be. I'm intrigued why Scalebane is here. I am also getting agitated why Cabello is in my basement for a year and yet no answer. I've expressed this time and time again."

Rithu says, "We're close. I feel her breaking."

Jekos says, "There's been no new assassination attempts. That's a plus." His eyebrows slant back.

Scalebane steps forward. "I'm here to review Rithu's progress. He must master inflicting pain on others. The bi-weekly visits give Cabello too much time to recover."

"The torturer experts," Mastema says, rolling his eyes. "Very well. I need to prep for the annual meeting. Jekos, once you're done with your colleagues, come find me in my office. We should expect Dr. Lang, Mr. Patterson, and Prime Minister Stéphane Trudell within the hour."

Jekos bows. "Of course, master."

"Oh, Scalebane," Mastema says. "The Prime Minister enjoys his fix of ash and we are in short supply in my mansion. Would you be so kind?"

A rattle runs up Scalebane's throat.

Mastema flicks his wrist. "A little pluck."

"We do not gift our scales, only the Nine do." That's a lie. She can hide her relation with Dasco from the energy leech.

"Yes, Lereif."

Don't test me, she thinks. Mastema is the single soul who calls her by her first name. It's a jab at her ego for him to feed.

"Be a dear?" Mastema asks, flicking his wrist again, puckering his lips. "A small one."

Scalebane's throat rumbles, ending in a deep growl from her bowels.

"Here," Rithu says. He wraps his tail around front and yanks a charcoal scale from his flesh, handing it to Mastema. The appendage contains several missing scales, replaced with minimal scabs. It takes another vazelead to notice the careful removal of scales. A mix of her disgust for Rithu's body and the oracle painters left her naïve to this detail. Rithu is removing his own skin. Why?

Mastema grins. "Excellent! Thank you, Rithu Blacktooth. You'd make your father proud." Mastema keeps his gaze on Scalebane as he takes the small scale. He waves his hands at the vampire Crystal Moths. "Meet the three men out front when they arrive."

The bald bloodsucker nods, leading spike-head outside.

Mastema speaks. "Amazing how those two endure the sun, isn't it?"

Jekos says, "Sunscreen can't last that long, can it?"

Mastema shrugs. "No, it doesn't. Human inventions do make life easier, though." He winks at Scalebane and heads up the circular staircase to his office overlooking the main entrance.

He waves at the group, not looking back, and vanishes behind the door.

Scalebane tilts her head to the hall, motioning at Rithu to move. "Give me a moment."

"Are you okay?" He reaches for her.

"Yes." She waves his hand, dismissing him.

"Right, of course." He lowers his hand and head.

Jekos clears his throat. "Rithu, can you do me a favour?"

"What?"

The half-imp reaches into his trouser pockets and pulls out a set of keys. "I left my meeting binder in my Mercedes. The pearl one on the side parking driveway by the helipad. Can you get it?"

Rithu looks at Scalebane, then Jekos. A rumble comes from his throat and he snatches the keys. Rithu storms through the hall and around the corner.

"Nervous?" Scalebane asks.

The half-imp says, "Not yet. Cabello won't break. Though I am eager to hear if you'll accept my offer."

"I'm here for the meeting, which you're sure will convince me, correct?"

"That's right," the other says.

"Will they let me into the meeting?"

"No, but you can listen." Jekos reaches into the front pocket of his vest, taking an earbud. "Of course, the design suits human ears. So, I think you could—"

Scalebane takes it. "I understand. You have a microphone on you?"

"You're learning human technology well." Jekos smiles, showcasing the disgusting black mouth.

Scalebane does her best to ignore his face and inspects the earbud. "I'll hear this conversation and make my verdict. I have many questions for you, Jekos."

"I have answers." Jekos pats her arm, causing Scalebane to let out a harsh hiss. Jekos exhales a nervous chuckle and heads to the second floor.

As for Scalebane, she should join Rithu. He is hiding a secret, not well. More pressing matters, such as this meeting, take precedence. She marches through the hall, passing the red oak wood door leading to the concrete basement. She reaches the back balcony and slides the glass door open, overlooking the beautiful Canadian Rockies. The snow-coated peaks cover the sun and cast long shadows over the dense pine forest. A sharp wind bites her while standing under the shade.

She met Mastema for the first time at this spot. Scalebane presses her palms against the mansion's stone wall. Using it as support, she lowers herself, left leg extending out, and sits clear from the glass door and windows. The balcony offers four chairs and a table, though she prefers to remain out of view.

She lifts a part of her mask to place the small black bud against her ear hole, holding it with her claws. She taps her right foot, excitement running through her veins, wondering what whispers the magic sound device will share.

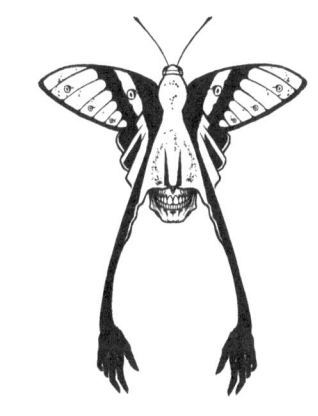

CHAPTER 33
THREE BRANCHES OF POWER

The subtle noise of footsteps fills the speaker. They stop, and Mastema's smooth voice booms to the point she moves the earbud away. "Jekos, it's quite an exciting meeting to have, is it not?"

"As with each year," Jekos says. "The helicopter is en route."

"Good. Tell me, you work closely with the vazeleads. Things are well with our ash distribution?"

"It's splendid. We're releasing the shipments in strategic manners to the top bidders. This country is first and we're trickling into the United States through a mix of currency and influence. Some batches made their way to the UK down the pipeline. Still, production is slow, to no surprise. The Nine can only create so many scales before collapsing from weakness."

Two taps follow, knocking on a table. Mastema speaks. "That will change with the synthesized ash." He chuckles. "Silly Scalebane, so protective over her own flesh. We wouldn't have to synthesize if she'd play ball and pumped out some hatchlings."

Scalebane coils her tail around her boot. It feeds paranoia in her mind, wondering if Mastema senses she is listening.

Lola bites her nails, unable to believe she is hearing this as the plastic-burning man's voice comes from the earbud. He gave her the food containing the speaker; now he is in a room with Mastema.

"That's a complicated situation," Jekos says.

The First continues, "No, it's natural: he's a male, she's a female. The Creator willed it so! Although, I do love when I mention it to her. That poor thing's shallow ego tastes so good."

"Mmmhmm," the other says. "Are you making progress with recreating ash?"

"Quite a bit. We won't need the vazelead distribution for long. That's the main agenda when the other three arrive. For you, my loyal imp, I'm asking of our two friends, Lereif and

Rithu. Scalebane is effective, though she has her own delusional goals. Emotions control her."

Scalebane's neck tenses.

Lola crawls to the corner of her cell, moving as far as she can out of view from the hall.

He continues, "Rithu, he's young, naïve, and impressionable. Why haven't they been able to get any information from Cabello? These reptile people run a slower clock than us. I mean, the modern human world has been here for a long time. By the Creator, vazeleads were enslaved by them. Their people's ways are extinct. Chop chop."

Jekos sighs, a subtle sound that his master doesn't hear, for it reeks of exhaustion. "Fair questions, Mastema. They are cautious of pushing Cabello to her limits. Humans are frail, wilful, yet frail."

"Hmm. They could snap her in a single twist of their wrist. Cabello is crafty. How did she get it? How did she find me at Radiate Primate? She either extracted information from a Moth or we have a plug."

Jekos speaks, "Your guess is as good as mine. Afterlife beings come and go through the mortal realm. Abridgement on each realm is lacklustre. It makes purgatory such a commonplace for the dead."

"One of many reasons we're changing it, Jekos. What we are creating is greater than the mortal realm, the Heavens, and the Hells. It is nonsense. The Creator didn't wish for such conflict."

Jekos says, "You would know."

"My dear imp, I was there before the Creator abandoned the Macrocosm. I witnessed their mighty hands craft this universe that holds life. I watched them forge the heavens, creating the gods and the numen to safe keep the mortal realm and defend them from Dega'Mostikas and his three Hells. The Creator wanted balance; they wished for life to coexist in a symphony of harmony."

"That didn't happen, did it?" Jekos asks.

"Violence, murder, passion, love. The seven sins and the seven virtues control our actions. I could go on. King understands to a point. It's why he aligns his people with us. Unification . . . his mortal mind can't understand. Who can?"

"Me?" Jekos asks.

"Not quite. That is the curse of being the First: perfection. I see the Creator's vision." Mastema sighs as a buzz erupts in Jekos's pocket. The noise is louder than their voices, stinging her ear.

Ruffling comes from Jekos's pockets and he speaks. "Oh, we are in luck. Our guests are here."

Jekos's footsteps move and moments later a door, the office's, opens, followed by more stepping. "Welcome, gentlemen. You're on time."

Hands cupping follows. Mastema speaks. "Prime Minister Stéphane Trudell, what a pleasure."

"Hello, friend," comes the thick French accent.

Mastema continues, "Mr. Patterson, thank you for your miracle working."

A hoarse laugh comes from the presumed Mr. Patterson.

"Of course, Dr. Lang. I haven't seen you in ages."

"Not true," Dr. Lang says, missing Mastema's joke.

Laughter of the others bombards her ear, and Scalebane moves the speaker.

Lola rests her palm on her jaw, intrigued by what is to unravel.

Mastema speaks while walking, "Let's get to it, shall we? Jekos will jot the notes. We'll keep this meeting as quick as we can. Please, take a seat, gentlemen."

The squeaking of chairs sliding and rumps on leather cushions consume the microphone as the soft skins settle in.

Mr. Patterson initiates discussion in his hollow voice. "I admire what you've done with this office."

Mastema says, "You have an eye for the finer things in life."

"More expensive things. Finer, I'm not sure."

Mastema says, "Oh, before we move on, Mr. Prime Minister . . . here you go!"

The Prime Minister says, "Ah, yes. Thank you, Mastema. I was hoping to get a purple firework for me. Your usual supply has been short."

Scalebane and Lola presume Mastema handed the man an ash scale. The Prime Minister likes his filling.

Clapping hands erupt. Mastema speaks. "Which brings us into the business at hand. The country. How are the people? The economics, and the details like the merger between these two corporations. Prime Minister, would you start us off?"

Prime Minister Stéphane Trudell clears his throat in a wet cough. "Of course. I am glad you brought this agenda first to the table. We are men of reason, seeing the same vision. The quicker we resolve the complexities of the merger of these two giants, we can ensure there will be jobs for Canadians. More jobs create a healthy economy, which is taxed accordingly, and we'll have the funds to support the civilians. They don't have to resort to crime. No offence, Mastema."

"None taken," Mastema replies.

The Prime Minister smacks his lips and continues, "Thus, we should start seeing a more lucrative economy. That is what we want as a whole. It is why the government is hands on with the merger of Manageficient Enterprises and Allen Oil Site Solutions. Dr. Lang and Mr. Patterson see eye to eye on their goals. We have to ensure Dr. Lang has his flexibility and Mr. Patterson has his fluent operations. That's why we're meeting today, to clarify and synchronize them. We must discuss the groundbreaking research Dr. Lang is conducting in his lab. This is part of Mr. Patterson's reasons to fund it, correct?"

Mr. Patterson's low tone comes through the speaker. "Correct. The acquisition of the other labs under your holding company. GeneChron, BetterLife, and Medi-First."

Prime Minister Stéphane Trudell says, "The bioengineering tech is far more advanced than any other part of the world. Dr. Lang's methods surpass the common CRISPR tech."

Mastema says, "Ah yes. Copy and pasting genetic code."

Dr. Lang speaks, "And an obsolete method of editing genes. My approach breaks down the DNA's two polynucleotide chains into basic sculpting clay. This surpasses the chain reaction risks of slicing."

Prime Minister Stéphane Trudell adds, "An example: we are capable of fixing the deformations of Jekos's condition."

"Wouldn't you like that, Jekos?" Mastema says.

Prime Minister Stéphane Trudell continues before Jekos can talk. "Though that level of bioengineering raises moral concern. People could be taller, stronger, smarter. Basic sculpting clay lets us even mirror other existing DNA."

Mastema snaps his fingers. "Emulation! The exciting part."

To synthesize ash, Scalebane thinks.

No way, Lola thinks.

The Prime Minister clears his throat. "Correct. That intrigues Mr. Patterson's personal goals. For the sake of Canada and humanity, it involves me keeping the regulations in check and eyes off of what is truly going on in Allen Sky Tower."

Mr. Patterson says, "Well, I want to make sure nothing comes back to bite me. I need Dr. Lang to accept my terms. He plays in his lab all day."

Dr. Lang speaks. "I would like to interject. Science takes time, cutting edge bioengineering needs experimentation. Regulations and operational restrictions, and secrets, hinder progress. It's why synthesizing Osteo-ashderm is hindered. That's the reason why I cannot, with confidence, clone your daughter."

Mr. Patterson's voice raises. "You said you could."

Prime Minister Stéphane Trudell says, "Gentlemen. Is synthesizing this recreation drug a top priority for the larger purpose of your technology?"

Dr. Lang says, "That's for Mastema to decide, who has left us in the dark as to what Osteo-ashderm is. It's a reptile. It branched off from the rest of evolution. I know—"

Mastema interrupts. "We'll get there."

Mr. Patterson makes a click with his tongue hitting the roof of his mouth. "Personal agendas aside, these uncertainties make the numbers wobbly. Dr. Lang's tech works in tests. So, it's a theory. Does it have practical applications? "

The Prime Minister continues, "Trust Mastema. I've worked with the gentleman for many years. He's introduced me to the finer things in his realm of business."

The words "finer things" remind Scalebane of the brief interaction she had with the demon she slayed, the same one with the useless Hell map. It reminds her of her true distrust of the Moths. " . . . *you connect with others, and next thing you know, you are in the Prime Minister's bed while his wife is on a book tour,*" the succubus had said. The country's leader is deeper involved than he is stating. Scalebane taps her claw as the men continue.

"But I digress," Prime Minister Stéphane Trudell says. "Mastema shares in due time. His areas of expertise come as a shock. We can't risk information leaking to the public. It's why our inner circle keeps knowledge segregated."

"The outer rim," Mr. Patterson says.

The Prime Minister sighs and continues, "There are bits I don't know. There are components that Mastema is unaware of that I handle because it is not his realm of experience. Dr. Lang, you know more about Subject Alpha than anyone. Patterson, we leveraged you as the foundation of moving the physical materials and funds across the world to this country. The point is, we have our specialties. There are no wedges in a well-oiled machine. We have to stick to our plan, sharing the same vision. You two work out the last details of how Manageficient Enterprises joins Allen Oil Site Solutions, personal deals or not, and I guarantee we'll have more progress. Dr. Lang wants freedom to experiment. Mr. Patterson doesn't need the lab exploding. He needs long-term profit. I trust both of you will resolve this in a reasonable time."

Dr. Lang says, "We're not fools, Mastema. Osteo-ashderm comes from somewhere different. These aren't rumours spread on the internet. The four of us are men of what I would consider greater intelligence. You don't even need that to understand that Osteo-ashderm, and Subject Alpha, come from . . . the otherworldly." Squeaking emerges from the leather cushion as he shifts in his chair. "It's a term I don't use lightly and an excellent segue into moving on from the merger and synthesized Osteo-ashderm. The girl. I want her again."

Mastema's dry chuckle echoes in the room. "Enticing, isn't she? Though not my taste."

Low laughs of perversion escape the men, except for the doctor who continues, "She is. She's unique. It is easy to extract her DNA and craft medicine."

Men, Lola thinks. She bites her lip, angered, yet not surprised. They took her damn QR code tattoo. They would use it to analyze her DNA. There is a power within that separates her from other ash-dashers.

"Designer drugs?" Mastema asks.

"Yes . . . you could. Subject Alpha's lineage is different. Her genetic makeup has unknowns, similar to Osteo-ashderm's situation."

Mr. Patterson adds, "In short, the pharmaceutical industry is cleaner than drugs. It would give you funds and get the people talking about another topic rather than ash. It'd take heat off the Crystal Moths. We can ensure population control."

"Go on," Mastema says.

"I've had my experts look into her family tree as far back as they could. Like each family tree, eventually the trail dissolves. Hers, though, enters folklore and myth."

"Myth?" Mastema asks.

Lola and Scalebane sit straight. Both suspected her origins, thanks to the dead demon's words.

Mr. Patterson continues, "We found practical evidence dating to a Spanish conquistador in the sixteenth century. Trace further past the Age of Discovery and things get muddled. My researchers went too far."

"Meaning?" the First asks.

"It's speculation," the other says.

"Humour me."

Mr. Patterson sighs, and his knuckle knocks into the armrest. He continues, "This conquistador kept journals and maps that were transcribed from older documents. He wrote the transcriptions were of writings from his family lineage."

"Which is? What's the common connection?" Mastema asks.

"They speak of a continent that never existed. Links to mythical titans."

Impossible, Lola thinks. Mul wasn't toying with her. Ash is leading her to her roots. Synarion once spoke of a lost continent.

She comes from Zingalg, Scalebane ponders.

Dr. Lang says, "It's pointless speculation of men wielding fire. Same last names, though surnames change because of translations and migrations. I'm a man of science. Her cells react differently from other humans'. Her body interacts with Osteo-ashderm with surprising endurance, as I've seen and as you've told me."

Mastema speaks. "She's unlike other ash-dashers that crumble into a chronic mess of addiction. Subject Alpha resists it, and uses it."

The Prime Minister coughs, gaining the attention of the men. "What of national security? Subject Alpha is a domestic terrorist."

Mastema says, "Subject Alpha is fine. As long as we keep her, our operations remain stable."

"I'd prefer to move her to Dr. Lang's lab. We have defence contractors there."

"Perhaps," Mastema says. "She's crafty. The laboratory has valuable information she could use. That skin we grafted from her? It contains a unique tattoo that functions as a cryptic key that unlocks her evidence to date. It's a kill switch that sends her data regarding the Moths, and anything else involved, public on the Internet. Separate her from the flesh and she cannot activate it."

Mr. Patterson asks, "We can't trace where she stores the files?"

"That's the curious part. It's isolated on a hidden port, otherwise we'd find it. My experts warn me from studying the tattoo key that it's a onetime use. You can't open the door to take the goods while keeping it. Though you can terminate the command, you cannot remove the data."

"Wonderful," Mr. Patterson says with a smudge of sarcasm coming from his high pitch. "What type of information does she have?"

"We cannot see without activating it. Which is why Subject Alpha is here, under my watch."

Prime Minister Stephan Trudel says, "On top of that, we have taken additional measures through the media to suppress Subject Alpha's efforts. CAMB is distributing a documentary with Lang Enterprises to expose the truth, our truth, not hers. I've also had the DND take over the Osteo-ashderm case with General Florence at the head in 2016."

"Yes, I recall that," Mastema says. "From a Detective Iglesias?"

"Correct. With General Florance in control, we had the DND seize evidence of ash. We can keep a balance of arresting

Moths for obvious crimes when they act out of line and push Osteo-ashderm into the dark until we are ready to go public with the wonder scale."

Mr. Patterson says, "We're at the end. Give us a couple of days. Between the shareholders and the fluctuating global markets, this made things uneasy for the stocks. Our teams are doing their best to ensure both Manageficient Enterprises and Allen Oil Site Solutions win from this deal."

Dr. Lang says, "My CFO is on top of this."

Mastema says, "I trust you people. As long as we get the income to keep funding Dr. Lang's research, then we are solid. I have a limited ash source, though crucial. Our partnerships are key to ensure the future of humanity."

Dr. Lang says, "And bioengineering is the only way we'll survive. With the climate crisis, nuclear threats, and our own limitations, we can correct our downfalls by editing our food and even our own genome. Ethically, of course, which would—"

Mr. Patterson cuts him off. "While we're dreaming of mutant reptile people, you'll resurrect my daughter from the dead, right? Can your bioengineering do that?"

Vazelead and soft skin, Scalebane and Lola think. A biting breeze sends icy touches dancing along each of their spines, causing their limbs to rattle. There is no wind.

Mastema speaks. "Sterilization is the focus, Mr. Patterson. Luxury drug or not, it trims the population. No need to make this personal."

Prime Minister Stéphane Trudell says, "Gentlemen, let's not get ahead of ourselves. We must keep our goals focused."

A knock comes from Mastema's table. The First speaks. "That's why humanity needs a shepherd to regulate its population."

The Prime Minister speaks. "We're playing in God's realm with this technology, gentlemen. It will take time to convince civilization. Education is a gentle process with micro-adjustments through decades and if not centuries. We'll get there."

Dr. Lang says, "We are the forefathers of a new era."

Mastema adds, "And the pioneers of transcending humanity."

Lola's hand drops onto her right lap, bringing the small speaker with it. Subject Alpha: herself who has old world ties.

Scalebane's throat closes, unable to accept genetic modification: vazelead and soft skins. King would not be fond of the news. Dasco's rough sketches of Cabello flicker in her mind. The Muse wants her and Mastema mustn't have his way.

Controlling the human population: as intended. Cloning and medicine will make natural ash obsolete in the plan. They're using Cabello and vazeleads to create a paradigm shift of the ages. This meeting doesn't mention the shadows or Mastema's resistance to concentrated light. The First has more secrets to unravel.

CHAPTER 34
UNSPOKEN WORDS

Footsteps come from the darkness. The sound makes Lola jump, and she knocks the headphone off her leg. She glances to the hallway. A cloaked figure approaches, matching her provider.

Shit, shit, shit, Lola thinks.

The black bud bounces on the concrete. She leaps for it. The object squeezes from her chicken-greased fingers and rolls to the central drain. It slips between the slits and vanishes.

Lola sighs and drags her arm away. *Be cool*, she thinks, and crawls to the bars as Rithu approaches. He stops in front of the jail cell door, claws sliding against the metal as he kneels.

Lola rests on her knees, eye level with him. Her arms dangle onto the horizontal bars of the prison, using it as support. Her head leans against the vertical ones, inches from the mask. The smell of swamp funk radiates from Rithu's scent. It's vazeleads and ash. They are the key.

To what? Lola thinks. She is unsure. Consuming scales is the most intuitive and potent magnetizing force she can think of. It is unlocking secrets inside her. *Those burning white eyes, the painter. The End.*

"Ash," Lola mumbles. Reasoning slips from her mind and her hand slips through the bars in a poor attempt to grab him. "Please. I need more. I can't do this without it." It's true. Lola suffers from dehydration. Each movement is tight and uncomfortable as if she is being rung out by invisible hands. Her ears ring and her skull swells inside. Caked blood rests along her nostrils whence red dripped from the night before.

Rithu's claw reaches around to his tail and with a single pluck, he takes a small scale, waving it in front of Lola. Her fingers graze against the warm drug as he pulls away.

"Please, please," she begs.

Rithu crushes the ash in his palm.

Lola's eyes scan his metal face, unable to sense his emotions. "What do you want? Please. I can listen to you. I need ash." She reaches for his fingers, and he recoils.

Rithu speaks, "A year has gone by. You are aware this?"

"Sort of." Lola's voice lowers in defeat.

He opens his hand and takes the crushed ash into his claws, waving it in front of her. She pushes her face against the bars, squeezing through to bite the scale. She's an animal. Deep in her mind, Lola is cognizant, aware of the meeting she observed, watching her pathetic state. This body acting is not Cabello. It's a weak ash-dasher, a shadow of what she was. She can fix that by getting a nibble. It will clear her head and let her craft a plan, reminding herself of why she has this addiction. *Just a little.*

Rithu fiddles with the crushed ash with both hands. "My people age longer, process life slower. It gives us an edge of longevity and wisdom. Your people move fast and burnout as you have on my scales."

"They're good," Lola chuckles, as if the answer is obvious. "I like them. Please. I can help you."

"My lack of progress angers Mastema. He reminds me of my failures." Rithu closes his fist. "He is asking questions. Scalebane is taking a newfound interest. Mastema is impatient, despite no new assassination attempts. They will take harsher methods if you don't tell them how you got the concentrated light. I can't protect you."

"I-I—"

Rithu's claw grasps her neck, cutting off her words. "Tell me. You've listened to me. I've poured my soul, sharing things I have not shared with any others. You listen, and I hold you dear for that. Now I need you to speak and I will listen. Help me with my situation by telling me where you got that bullet." He lets go of her throat, claws scraping against her flaking skin.

Lola coughs, shaking her head. Her hand slides through the bars, caressing Rithu's mask. "It doesn't matter. Nothing fucking matters anymore." *Am I caring for him?* she thinks. Her sober empathy and ash-infusing caring are mixing into one. Or, the drug let her see him for who he is, and she can't hate the boy.

Rithu grabs her wrist, pulling her arm. "You understand why I let you listen for the past year? Why I eased your pain to the torture?"

Lola swallows thick saliva. "Because I accept you? Fuck, Rithu, I'm some kind of pet, sounding board, toy." Lola squeezes the bars with her other hand, frustrated that he isn't giving what she needs.

"You're a lost soul, no different from myself. Unlike you, I have my loyalty."

"As do I. Why do you think I'm trying to stop the Moths?" *One bite.*

"Tried." He frees her wrist. "You can't."

Lola bangs her forehead against the metal. "Give me some."

"Tell me how you got the bullet," Rithu says.

Lola shakes her head. "I can't."

"Why won't you tell me? After the moments we've shared," Rithu asks. "Why is it such a safeguarded secret?"

"It's . . . it's . . . the only thing I have." Lola sits straight, hand resting on her exposed stomach above the grafted skin where her tattoo and bandages used to be. "They've taken my life away from me, Rithu. Everything. If I want to dismantle the Moths, information is my best weapon."

A rattle comes from his throat, tail swaying. "You're determined to succeed, despite hope being lost."

"That's what makes us different. It's why you're intrigued by me, isn't it?"

Rithu leans closer, exhaling hot swamp breath through the mask's human nose onto her skin.

Lola pushes her head against the bars. Each exhale builds condensation on his metal face. "If I tell you where the bullet comes from, what would happen to me?" Her legs shake, thinking of the end. It can't be over. Unless that was the ash trip's message.

"I fear our moments are over, Cabello," Rithu says.

Her stomach sinks, dragging her to the dirt. He can't be serious. "Hold them back. Please. I– I–I'm scared."

Rithu's hand reaches through and pets her head, running his claws against her greasy, matted hair. "I hear you."

Her eyes close, embracing his touch. "They'll kill me." She squeaks.

"I've kept you as long as I can. I wish it could be longer. If I don't get what I need from you, my father will see me as a child."

"Help me and I'll help you. Please. You're better than lineage demands." Lola extends her hands, grabbing onto Rithu's metal mask before he can pull away. "If you care about me, you would protect me."

A rumble projects from the depths of his throat and he reaches for the key ring clipped to his belt.

Lola's heart stops.

Before Rithu can take the key out, a new set of footsteps rise from the hall. They're in a swinging rhythm with aggressive steps. *Click . . . Click, click . . . Click.* Rithu turns to see a hooded figure moving towards them in a disjointed stride. With each movement, their tail sways in random motion, adding a spasm to their presence. The goggles and metal fanged muzzle glimmer from the slit of light in the window behind her.

No, no, no, Lola thinks with a wave of terror splashing against her rational thoughts. She releases Rithu and retreats, dragging her feet to the corner of a jail cell as he stands to face the newcomer.

Scalebane's signature rattle hums from the depths of her throat, ending in a hiss. "Rithu, what are you doing with her?"

"Extracting information," Rithu says.

"By levelling with her? Mastema is displeased."

"Cabello is resistant." Rithu curls his claws.

"Or you're incapable. Did her poison tongue weaken you?" Scalebane dashes inches from Rithu's face, sizing with him. He doesn't move, and she circles behind. "Are you as inept as I predicted? Proving your father wrong?"

"No," Rithu says in a gentle tone.

"What if Mastema saw you letting the soft skin touch you? What would King think?"

Rithu growls, tail perking.

"Betrayal," Scalebane hisses. "I see your tail, Rithu. You're prolonging your time with Cabello. Why?"

Don't say, Lola thinks, fingers scraping against the concrete.

Rithu whips his tail in the air, creating a loud snap echoing in the room. "Why do you distance yourself from me? Our duty to our people is greater than whatever agendas you're keeping. Those secrets from the Moths, from me, and from King are betrayal."

Scalebane stops in front of him. "Because your father remains deaf to my calls."

"Why don't you open up to me? I can reason with him," the other says.

"Key," Scalebane says. She extends her hand.

"Answer me," Rithu says.

"Key, and I will talk."

Rithu obeys, taking the key ring from his utility belt, pushing the silver item into her palm. She flips the ring and heads to Lola's cell. "I fear I cannot operate alone, Rithu. In an unlikely turn of events . . . " Scalebane unlocks the door and steps in.

"Back off," Lola exhales and scoots away. Her shoulders press against the rough brick wall. The reptile marches to her. There is nowhere to go. Her muscles tense, fearful of what is to come.

Scalebane snags the chains in the middle of the room, pulling Lola towards her in a single yank. The force drags Lola's scabbed bare back against the concrete ground. A tail slithers around her neck, squeezing tight. Lola doesn't have the strength to fight, staring into the soulless black goggles.

". . . we need to keep her silent."

Lola's stomach rises from its hopelessness, giving a sense of life and anticipation. Scalebane, once again, is a wildcard.

CHAPTER 35
FAVOUR

The meeting with Disk is on Iglesias's mind throughout the week. He searches online for Mastema and his two ageless goons. These inquiries are less fruitful. There is little information. Mastema's name only appears in the Book of Jubilees. No vampires.

The reverse image lookup from the photos reveals the older images. No surprise. He finds the photo from Illinois with the Irish mob. The results show the marble sculpture of the two herculean men gripping the nude female. The Egyptian carvings with the vampiric woman appear too. He also uncovers the 1496 holy painting by Albrecht Dürer.

He wipes his beard, seeing the similarities in the canines and basic features. This art is ancient, and coincidences are bound to manifest. Dragons are an example, appearing throughout unrelated civilizations. Another search shows vampires appeared in European folklore around the eighteenth century. China also has similar myths to them, as do the Greeks. Disk could have taken these photos and fabricated their information.

He is unsure what he was hoping to find. It's not difficult for a delusional person to connect false correlations from the internet, claiming it truth. Vampires are as far-fetched as Iglesias's theory of reptilian people. At least there is video evidence of reptiles, according to Disk. There's also the blood he sampled, if it strikes true. Hence, he called in a favour and sits, leaning against a green bar.

It's not the usual Good Fellows pub that he, Beckman, and Archer would meet at in another life. Instead, he chose a new location to avoid unwanted eyes. The law cannot see the information he will share.

I can't believe I'm doing this, he thinks. Hours ago, he was in some nerd's motel room, deep diving into a Crystal Moth conspiracy. Cabello went down the rabbit hole. Iglesias rode the edge three years prior. He was close to buying into intelligent reptilians and ancient gangsters puppeteering the nation; and Iglesias is here. A part of him believes.

He fiddles with the coaster while drinking a beer, far lighter than his usual choice of whisky. The man prefers a harder drink, though he understands he needs to remain level-headed. Liquor makes it too easy to suppress José's death. He watches the news from the mounted TV behind the bar. It plays CAMB with Prime Minister Stéphane Trudell discussing a business merger.

"So the ghost exists," comes a familiar spry voice, Archer's. She sits on the black plastic stool seat beside him and leans back to examine his beard, smiling with her signature crooked grin.

Iglesias turns and extends his arms. "In the flesh."

Archer gives him a one look over, raising an eyebrow. "Jesus. Who are you?"

A closed smile rises on his face. The beer, beard, denim jeans, and a t-shirt under his blazer. "I ain't got a clue."

"I mean, boss, I haven't seen you since the funeral," Archer says while waving at the bartender. "Whisky, straight." The grizzled pencil-thin man nods and snags a bottle.

"No ice?" Iglesias asks.

"Not anymore, waters it down." Archer rests her head on her one palm, elbow on the counter. "What happened?"

Iglesias takes a sip of his golden ale, the liquor brushing against his moustache. It tastes like water, and he needs a potent drink. When the bartender returns, Iglesias orders a whisky too, for old time's sake.

"I mean, I'm aware of what occurred. You shut people out. I didn't believe it when you texted me."

"You can thank Beckman for the encouragement," Iglesias says. *And a nerd who is throwing me into the vortex again*, Iglesias thinks while tossing the coaster onto the bar, turning to face Archer. "Beckman and Catherine had me over for dinner and we were talking. He's writing a book."

"You two have enough stories." Archer raises her whisky as the bartender brings Iglesias one. They clank their drinks and take a swig.

"It's last minute, thank you. I apologize. I needed time alone."

Archer shrugs. "I get it. That's me."

"What? Still?"

Archer scratches her head. "Sort of? I'm seeing this new girl."

"That so? How long?" Iglesias asks.

"It's been a few months." Archer sits straight. Now he notices a fresh glow radiating under her light tan skin, past the exhaustion. It brings a warmer energy to her usual bite.

"What's her name?" he asks.

"Amy. There is something there." She slaps the table. "Speaking of change. Why the new spot? This place doesn't give us the discount."

"I thought I would keep it fresh. How you doing, by the way?" Iglesias says. He wants to ease into the big question.

"I feel I should ask you that. The feds coughed up cash for the damage they've caused you and your mind, and what? Sitting at home alone, not talking to your friends?"

"Not so." Iglesias leans back. "I garden."

Archer chokes on her drink, clearing her throat. "Nope. Don't buy it. You're a doppelgänger for sure."

"Funny." Iglesias rolls his eyes.

"Jokes aside, things are okay. Major Crimes is the usual business. Chasing dealers and busting ops. Murder related to Moths happens here and there."

"The ash case?" Iglesias asks as he rests his arms on the bar.

"It mutated into the others. Inconsistent distribution from the Moths makes the evidence far and few between. When we find it, it is in the hands of some big cheese CEO or movie star. They have good lawyers. Like any of those heavy hitting drugs, it's on the street. They're often laced. When we need information, the dealer dies prior. Murder, overdose, accident, whatever. It feels I'm running around in circles. The DND is completely useless and they don't care for my help."

"I rarely hear from them either," Iglesias says. "Cabello?"

"Gone after that day." Archer waves her free hand in the air to emphasize the vanishing. "It's frustrating. Part of me wants to go on that documentary and talk about what goes on." Archer clenches her fists.

Iglesias shakes his head. "Don't bother. I looked at who is funding the whole thing, and it's done by Allen Shipping Solutions."

"What?" Archer squints.

He points to the TV. "Well, not yet, anyway. Manageficient Enterprises, owned by Lang Enterprises. It's a holding company. They also have a few studios they own to produce films."

Archer bites her lip and takes another drink. "Shit. I had no clue."

Nor did I, he thinks.

She continues, "Private funding, a CAMB original documentary. Old boys' club. I mean, how does Hucker Dime still have a show? Is he even relevant? He's no reporter. He bitches about what he doesn't like in the government and gives commentary."

Before Iglesias knows it, Archer finishes her whisky and orders another. He examines her face, seeing how the skin has sagged a sliver in one year, making her mouth sit in a natural frown. Despite the skin's glow of romance, there's not enough laughter in her life. The bags under her eyes as they gaze into her empty glass say more than words. The slight slouch as she rests both arms on the counter, watching the television, displays defeat. Her cheeks have a new puff, showing she drinks more than she used to. *Sort of* is right regarding her budding relationship.

"Don't let that job eat you," Iglesias says.

"Says you," the other says.

"Yes, says me. Because I went on that path and saw where it leads. Nowhere. If you think there's a future with this girl you're seeing, focus on it. Don't marry the career."

"Thanks, boss," Archer replies as the bartender returns with a fresh glass. "I'll take on gardening or whatever while I'm at it. We can share trade secrets."

Iglesias rubs neck. "I had to start a new chapter. I'm here, José is not. It's taken me a long time to realize that, and staying in the past reopens the wound."

"That's wise, and I'm happy for you, Iglesias." She presses her lips tight for a moment. "I can't imagine what you've been through. I have to admit, I've been a little pissed off at you." Archer laughs. "Fuck, you up and vanished."

"I'm going to make an effort," Iglesias says. He extends both hands to her. "Okay, look, there is a reason I wanted to meet you."

"Aha, a favour." Archer looks at the TV, her jaw tensing.

"I get it, you're annoyed. Beckman retired. I disappeared, leaving you on your own. It wasn't fair. If you aspire to be a good detective, find your own way. Yes, I need help and, well, it's going to sound crazy." Iglesias wipes his beard.

"Okay?" Archer says. Her eyes scan him, in the manner Beckman did, as an officer does to a suspect.

"You remember that guy you had that could jailbreak the phone? Three years ago?" Iglesias asks.

"Yeah, he's good stuff."

"You trusted him. Trust is a hard thing to come by." Iglesias licks his lips, not oblivious to the irony of tricking Archer into meeting him for his own personal agenda. "You have anyone in forensics? Private enterprise?"

"I think I do." Archer blinks twice. "They're solid. Don't you have one of your own?"

"Not me. I stuck to what we had federally. The things I have aren't normal objects. I need them analyzed."

"Like what?" Archer sits straight and brushes her hair back.

Iglesias looks around the bar and reaches into his blazer's inner pocket. He takes out two small plastic bags. The first contains the horn fragment Cabello gave him. The second has the cut square of his dress shirt stained with black. He slides them over to Archer for her to inspect.

"Take a look. I need to know what they are," Iglesias says in a hush.

Archer looks at the fabric, squinting as she brings it millimetres from her. "This is yours?"

"Yes."

Her eyes widen. "This stain, it's from the slaughterhouse, isn't it? When we found that blood-like substance?"

"Good guess," Iglesias says.

She spins the plastic bag around. "Well, we haven't seen it since the military took over."

Iglesias points at the second object. "That material there, I think it's a horn. Cabello gave it to me."

Archer lowers the cloth in a slow motion and grabs the fragment, flipping it. The light from the bar gives the material a soft rainbow sheen reflection within the onyx texture. "What are you doing, Iglesias?"

He scratches his beard. "She told me the Prime Minister was involved."

"Related to the horn?" Archer's voice goes up with a smidge of disbelief.

"I'm unsure. I need the DNA. That's it," Iglesias says. "I'd do it myself if I could. Understanding what these are will help. It will help—" He pauses, thinking about his wording. *It will confirm that Cabello was unravelling a big conspiracy. It will validate Disk's parallel research. It would confirm the past mad babbles scuzbags have told me. These two objects will ensure I'm sane.* "Nothing more."

Archer rubs her brow, placing the bag on the counter. "Look, we've been down this path, twice, chasing Cabello and whatever bat shit crazy plan she brews. People die. The first time was a fluke at the art gallery, then the abattoir plant. A third, at Radiate Primate? What will a fourth bring?"

Iglesias presses his lips together and looks away, feeling his throat tense. This is his need for answers. With a sliver of hope that Disk is right, he can get revenge, an emotion he hasn't accepted in himself. It's there. He feels the rage deep inside.

"You said you moved on," Archer says. She takes a large gulp and slams the drink down. "Cabello bore the brunt of the damage the first time. You took the aftermath, twice. What happened to her? She vanished. You say this job is eating me. It consumes you. Beckman was right to get out."

"I did too. For a year, Archer, I did. José was going to college. No more conspiracies of Moths, reptiles and ash. My son died. I tried again. This thing came back. It won't release me. Look, you don't have to go on this path with me, not like the other times. I'm not asking you that. It's dangerous. I need these analyzed. If you have somebody you trust, please."

Archer folds her arms and bites the nails on her left hand, staring at the bags. She ponders his request while Hucker Dime appears on the TV, filling the silence with rambles. She speaks. "He's in Toronto, my guy, works for a private lab GeneChron. He can take care of these. Tell me what the hell you're doing first. Has Cabello contacted you again?"

Iglesias shakes his head and finishes his whisky, letting the burn ease his tension. "This is new. Independent research. It eats away at me, Archer. The fact that there are no answers to what happened to José. There isn't a goddamned chance that it was a gang shootout. Not with Cabello there, claiming Mastema was at the club, the one that José was at with his prick of a friend."

"We went through this. The detective went through this—"

Iglesias interrupts, "That detective wna a lazy arse that wanted to close the case and likely pad his pockets under the table from the Moths. You remember the—" He pauses, recalling the twitching shadows. There's no point mentioning it. It was mass hysteria.

"Yeah, I get it," Archer says. She clears her throat. "Well, no. I don't. Amy and I are new. That's the closest thing I've had to caring for a person in a long time. Even then, it's not the same as you and José. It's always been me. Left the small town and those religious hicks and didn't look back. I can't understand what you're doing. But . . . but . . ." Archer snags Iglesias's now warm beer, taking a large gulp and pounding it onto the bar. "I cannot let you be a fucking idiot again on round four."

Iglesias raises his eyebrow. "What?"

"Yeah, if you want these analyzed, tell me what you're getting into. That's the deal."

Her sudden persistence forces a couple of, *huh, huh*'s on his exhale. "You're not naive to what they're capable of. They could ruin your life."

Archer shrugs. "They're not gonna win. If you have a lead, I want to know. You said it won't let you go. A year of gardening and suddenly you want these two objects inspected. I'd prefer to see if we can take action instead of having it chucked aside by the DND."

"What about Amy?" Iglesias says. "I'm telling you, you don't want to end up like me."

Archer shrugs. "That's the only way this is going to work. You let me into what you've got brewing, and I'll get these things to a lab."

Iglesias strokes his beard, pondering her offer. He doesn't wish to put her in danger. He told her to be a good detective.

She has to follow her gut, and it's what he would do in this situation. Archer and her stubbornness win.

The bartender returns, putting his hands on the table, eyeing both of them. He asks, "Another?"

Archer raises an eyebrow at Iglesias with that smug smirk under her pointed nose. The deal is over.

Iglesias shakes his head. "Yeah. This round on me."

The bartender heads off to fetch their drinks.

Archer scoots her stool closer, eager to learn his secrets.

"You'll get your hands dirty," Iglesias says.

"As if I haven't done that before." Archer points at herself with both sets of index fingers. "Look at me. You said so yourself, this job is eating me. The monotony of cat and mouse is not why I took this career path. What got you back into this?"

The bartender returns with their drinks. Iglesias laughs again, shaking his head. Archer is crazy enough to tag along. She is unaware of the depths that they are diving, thanks to some hacker kid named Disk. The two solidify their agreement with a cheer and take a swig. Iglesias shares the obscure information of his visit with Eden Breaker.

ACT III

ACT III
ORDERED BARGAINING

[Lola Cabello ~~Documentary~~ Docuseries: CAMB Originals]

[Take 1: Raw]

[2019, April 13]

[Donnie Morris: Friend]

[RECORDING:

I don't go on camera much. It's not my thing . . . Act natural? Hah. Yeah, I've been told that before. It doesn't make it easy. I think it takes practice, which I don't have. Being on stage? Radically different . . . Death metal. Yeah, my band was called Blood Bathers. I was the vocalist . . . yeah, I'm ready.

Lola Cabello? We met in Edmonton. She was going to Grant MacEwan University with her friend Becky. Becky Murphy. They were both scene kids. Becky was a raver; Lola was a goth. I'm a metalhead at heart, played in that band I mentioned . . . oh? For sure.

I'm a metalhead at heart, played in a band called Blood Bathers. Edmonton is a small city in comparison, so the scenes blended a ton. Naturally Lola and I met at shows, same musical interests, dark and grim stuff. We hit it off.

I followed her journalism site. She built the thing while in school, covering Edmonton serial killers. The years 2013 to 2016 saw a high occurrence of murders. Police funding was tight. She wanted to give people the actual news for safety and knowledge. You had the Snapper cases, the Drainer cases as a couple of examples. The Snapper in 2014 got Lola into trouble. Turned out the Moths made the whole thing up. The reason slips my mind. It's on the recording she uploaded.

Good transition, hey? Yeah. Heh. After Becky and Michael Bradford, YEGman, died, Lola came to me with that recording and asked for my help. She couldn't trust the cops and I know a few things about computers. I helped her upload it to her site, secure it, and protect her IP from doxing.

Boy, that went south. The band broke up because of what I did. The Moths threatened Lola and I. Cops breathed down our necks. Lola's mom died. I lost my job and moved in with my sister. I comforted Lola. She was so frustrated with her family and boyfriend at the time that she distanced herself from me. For three years, I went through a massive depression phase. I almost didn't make it out alive.

Why? Well, that video ruined my life. Lola's too. She kept chasing the Crystal Moths. I found a way out. Detective Iglesias made things easy from a legal standpoint as long as I worked with him. I stayed low; the Moths got off my tail. It took a long time to rebuild my life: lost a ton of weight thanks to a new fitness community I joined, tattoos, got a dog and a stable career, loving life for me.

She emailed me after she booked it. I can't imagine what Lola went through, living alone for years. I think that's what made her lose her mind. The system frustrated her. It fed a fire she couldn't let go.

Lola is loyal to those she cares for and didn't forget about me or her family. I think that's why she believes, or believed, she has to do this.

It took me years to acknowledge that I had a crush on her. My refusing to accept my emotions was part of my depressive phase, constant denial. I told myself we were friends when we met. She had that shitty boyfriend she fought with. It's hard when you click and love the same things. That type of connection doesn't happen often.

Okay, more than a crush. I was in love with her for years. I didn't have the balls to admit it to her, ever. Our lives spun out of control. I couldn't join her. I mean, you see the stuff on the news? Of course you guys have, that's why you're making this docuseries.

But yes, Lola emailed me a lot while on the run. She even sent me an email after escaping prison last year, 2018. She vanished. I have no clue if she is alive.

If she is, I'll hear from her again. I'm sure of it. She is loyal to the death. It makes it tough to forget her. Some connections are once in a lifetime. I have to move on, though, for my sanity.

END]

CHAPTER 36
ANIMAL REFLECTION

The vazelead's tail squeezes Lola's neck, forcing her to wince. "You worked with Synarion. You could find him," comes the vazelead's croaking voice. The constriction tightens, turning Lola's sickly skin purple. "But," Scalebane releases her throat, "time is of the essence."

She inspects the chains and shackles binding their captive, lifts them and pulls as if looking for a way to break them. Lola gasps for air, sitting, and watches, unsure what she should say, or if there is even a point. When Lola speaks, rage boils within Scalebane.

Rithu steps into the cell. "What are you proposing?"

Scalebane lets go of the bindings and grabs Rithu's head with both hands. She brings her forehead to his, the leather mask bumping against his. "Rithu Blacktooth, do you trust me?"

"Of course," Rithu says in reflex. "I've proven loyal."

"Good." Scalebane gives a light bump on his skull and returns to inspecting the chains. She squeezes the shackles to no luck. "Cabello needs to stay quiet. The only way to do that is aiding her escape."

Lola gets to her feet. This cannot be. It would be easier to accept Scalebane killing her. This shift in attitude leaves a raking itch that runs up Lola's body. Lola's impulse tells her that the vazelead is hiding her true agenda.

"Scalebane, what do you mean by keeping her silent?" Rithu asks.

Scalebane stands and spins around the room. "There's not much time. Mastema is in a key meeting and his vampires focus on guarding the Prime Minister. We need to get Cabello out."

Rithu says, "Through the other hall, there's an escape tunnel leading to a grate in a garage."

Scalebane points an index claw at him. "Wandering the halls instead of extracting information?"

"She has endured punishment to the point of death. Look at her."

"I must confess, Rithu, I didn't think you could get the intel from Cabello."

Rithu recoils, as if the words inflicted pain.

"Your inability or unwillingness to get the intel from the soft skin benefits us. You will tell me why. Not now. We need to remove these chains."

Rithu says, "I didn't receive the key. Only to the jail cell door."

Scalebane hisses. "Together we break this."

The vazeleads grab the links binding Lola's wrists. She doesn't dare flinch, having two powerful beings inches from her, ready to shred metal to bits. She can smell the distinct aroma from each of them. Rithu's is denser with thick moss. Scalebane has a hint of wood tickling her nose. More than ever, she wants to get a taste of their skin. It would give her the strength to take part in this wild escape plan.

Scalebane and Rithu yank on the chains. Both using their might. Limbs shake as the metal stretches, the oval shapes expand, bending, and snap in two. The cuffs remain. At least her hands are free to move. The vazeleads snag the shackles around her ankles and perform the same task: grabbing and pulling back. The alloy surrenders to their will, freeing Cabello. At long last, Lola can walk without the restraints and she attempts to stand, stumbling.

Rithu takes her arm and helps with a gentle lift. "She's weak."

Scalebane places her claws on both sai. "Evident. You've been feeding her too much ash."

Rithu coils his tail around the front, peeling a scale and putting it into Lola's mouth. She bites the fresh drug, feeling the brief hydration in the organic material and the speckle of metallic blood. She nibbles on the goods, squeezing out the moisture until Rithu pulls the scale away. With a single swallow, the paste moves through her oesophagus and into her gut where the power can seep into her system.

Finally, she thinks on an exhale.

"She cannot function without it," Rithu says. It's true, for Lola has experienced her need of ash in the past.

"You did a piss-poor job of hiding it," Scalebane says. "You're lucky I'm the only one you work with."

"Yet you didn't confront me? A year and you didn't mention a thing? You're full of secrets."

Scalebane folds her arms. "I've been occupied."

"Why do you want Cabello out? To kill her?" Rithu cocks his head. "You operate in such secrecy."

"We have a lot to discuss, son of King. I need to move a few parts before I can share what I know. You have to trust me for a little longer."

A hum runs through Lola. It's the ash. In contrast to a year ago with the liquid variant, her system is used to the effects. The small amount Rithu supplied acts as a cup of coffee. Unlike caffeine, this drug heightens her sixth sense.

More, comes a distant voice in Lola's mind.

Scalebane lifts a part of her mask, revealing porcelain scales. She takes a small earbud from her pocket and brings it to her ear. With no answer, she turns and storms from the cell, presuming the other two will follow.

Rithu urges Lola to walk, gripping her bare ribs and arm with his cold leather glove. She shakes on the first few steps and gains momentum.

"Where are you going?" Rithu asks.

Scalebane says, "You must go. The meeting is ending. Let me get the pieces in motion, Rithu, and I'll be in touch."

"Where are you going?" he repeats. "I couldn't find Jekos's binder!"

Scalebane disappears around the dark corner, turning left.

"Rithu," Lola whispers. "What is going on?"

"This way," Rithu says.

He guides her out of the jail cell and through the stone corridor. Cobwebs cover the corners of the ceiling and ground. Dust aplenty, with a few wooden crates scattered along the walls. Dangling bits of chains from Lola's feet scrape against the concrete floor, echoing. She prays that the guards upstairs don't hear it.

They reach the end of the hall. To the left is a staircase. The other side leads deeper into the basement. Snug against the wall is a table with torture tools: knives, whips, and electroshock sticks. There are two medieval contraptions she doesn't know the names of. They look painful and she's grateful Rithu didn't apply these. In a sadistic way, he cares for her. More like a pet than an equal. At the far corner of the surface are Lola's belongings coated with a fine layer of dust.

She frees herself from Rithu, using the wooden surface as support to grab her goods. After one year, her tank top, leggings, boots, gun, ID, purse, and cash were within reach. She scoops them towards her, hugging them. Rithu brings her under his arm again.

They walk to the opposite hall of Scalebane, through a maze of winding paths. Endless pathways to their left, right, and forward create an unsettling catacomb. The concrete ground morphs to dirt with each step. Rithu guides her to one last turn and they face a straight path of a hundred paces. Sunlight beams through. Heaven is calling.

If only, Lola thinks. Those are her emotions talking.

By this point, Lola has enough strength to walk on her own. They reach the end, facing a light coming from the hole in the ceiling that expands a foot higher. At the top are grills: the grate into the garage.

"Rithu, what is Scalebane planning?" Lola asks.

Rithu brushes her hair from her face, then uses his thumb to wipe a smudge of grime from her cheek. It could be dirt, blood, or a mixture of both. "I don't know."

"She let me live." *And has faith in my ability to escape,* she thinks. It makes Lola wonder if Scalebane will hunt her after. The vazelead needs her for some reason.

Rithu speaks, "I didn't want this. I hope you understand, Cabello."

Lola takes his claw, caressing it. Lola comprehends the reasons behind her torturer's actions, so words aren't necessary. The heightened state of ash links her mind to Rithu's perspective. He didn't want to torture anyone. The pressure of his father, obeying the Moths, and his duty to procreate weighs on his soul. If Rithu didn't torment Lola, his family would disown him, and another would have carried the task.

Rithu says, "I wish your people and my own could find peace."

"Wouldn't that make things easier?" Lola says.

"I am afraid that is long gone. Your people created a permanent scar."

That's history Lola isn't aware of. If only they could share another session together, he could explain. Instead, she reverts to her default mode with a soft smile. "At least you got to chain and beat one."

Rithu shows no sign of amusement. The metal mask doesn't help. He lifts his tail and pulls a scale. "Keep this. I'm sorry. I feel anguish for what we've endured."

Lola takes the scale and places her goods on the ground. She dresses herself as best she can, wobbling. The bindings on her ankles and wrists prove challenging. She gets the leggings on and two thirds of the boots. Next, she tucks the ash into her wallet, stuffing it in her purse.

Rithu speaks. "I wanted to kill you before we met. You knew too much. The past year I was supposed to torture you to build a stronger hate for your kind. Tasting your blood to remember what the soft skins had done. I feel only regret."

Lola puts the gun into her bag and swings it over her shoulder. She takes one step closer to Rithu and places her hands on his face, looking up at him. The vazelead is a metre taller. Pain, remorse, and sorrow project from under the metal. She hasn't seen his eyes. Actions are stronger than words. Intuition guides her and she lifts the mask, dragging the hood. For the first time, she comes face-to-face with a vazelead.

Unlike the initial glimpse she got of Scalebane, whose scales were white, Rithu's are charcoal. They're thicker, like ash, and cover his entire face. The small muzzle ends with a flat nose, giving him an anthropomorphic face. Spikes run along the bridge of the eye sockets, forming brows. Pitch black feathers rest on his skull, draping to his shoulders. They have enough weight that they function as hair. In fact, he's not that different from a human, except for the flaming reptilian pupils staring at her. As Synarion once said, their eyes burn with fire from the heat in their soul.

The smokeless flame flickers from Rithu's sockets. Thin pupils move left and right across Lola's face. Past them, she can see him as another living entity. There's no anger in there, not in Rithu. The generational hate seen in Scalebane is missing. He's a tortured spirit, haunted by a history that isn't his directly, being used as a chess piece. No different from Lola.

"You must go," Rithu says. His scaled lips move while projecting the words, showcasing an army of sharp teeth inside his mouth. A black forked tongue flickers.

"Right," Lola says. She shifts his mask into place. "Thank you."

Rithu leans, assisting Lola so she can climb onto his shoulders. Their combined heights let her reach the metal grate with ease. Her hands reach the cool, rough surface of the grate and she pushes it aside. Rithu makes one jump, propelling Lola up and her arms cling to the edge of the hole. Claws grip her boots and together they force her up onto the ground of the garage. She pants, rolling over to look into the tunnel. Rithu is already gone.

Lola drags the grating into its slot and stands. Several vehicles and a motorcycle under beige tarps house the space. She examines the walls, finding mechanical tools, a workbench, and a table with a corkboard containing various keys. The surface contains spray paint cans, a duffel bag, and to the right two cabinets.

Perfect, Lola thinks.

She pulls open the doors of the first storage. To her luck, they are unlocked and reveal a shotgun, ammunition, a few handguns, and a semiautomatic. Mastema must be cocky enough to feel he has no need to lock up these weapons. Lola fits the shotgun and ammo into the duffel bag, leaving the automatic behind. The second cabinet, also unlocked, has a small toolkit which she takes in case she needs to fix anything on the go. It also contains a motorcycle jacket and helmet.

Lola pulls the tarp off the motorcycle. It's a pristine crimson red Ducati Pannigale V4 S. Next, she skims through the series of keys on the wall behind the work table to find the correct ones. It takes several tries until she finds it. She hasn't ridden a motorcycle since she was a teen with her father. Plus, she's weak as hell. Lola checks the other vehicles and sees that they're historical collector's items: a black 1971 Lamborghini P4 hundred SV J, a silver 1936 Bugatti type LVII SE, 1957 Ferrari, and a 1939 Alfa Romeo 8C 2900B Lungo Spider. She didn't think random car facts from her father would return in her life. They scream for attention on the road. The Ducati is the least suspicious.

Mastema likes his rides, she thinks.

Lola heads to the front of the garage and presses the door's automatic open button. It makes a satisfying click of freedom. Sunlight pierces into the room. She shields her eyes, used to the dark basement. The whiff of fresh mountain air fills her lungs. Trees sway, rooted to the side of the gravel road. It's the true world. This isn't an illusion of the drug. She's free.

Considering the garage is electronic, it must send a notification to a Moth guard in the mansion. She can't stay and gaze in wonder. Lola slips on the jacket, grunting in the process thanks to her wounds. She straps the helmet on, throws her purse in the duffel bag and puts it over her shoulders. She hops onto the Ducati and turns the keys. The bike roars to life, and she rides out. It takes some adjusting to familiarize with its power. She's on top of an engine with two wheels. With gentle pressure, she applies acceleration, soaring along the path.

A flicker of twin flames dances in front of her and she blinks. They vanish, clearing the gravel trail. *Find me*, comes a voice in her mind. That's the last she hears while turning onto the main road, facing a bronze gate.

Shit. Her heart sinks into her gut.

It's weak, enters a new thought. This is her own, fuelled with determination. She revs the engine, and the automobile screams, rocketing towards the barrier. Lola lowers her head. The bike collides with the metal, bursting through to the other side. The gate dangles against the brick pillars with one hinge in place, sparks flying from the sockets. The butterfly flies free.

CHAPTER 37
PLASTIC GHOST

The Ducati roars on the highway at midday. If she was on vacation, the beautiful Canadian Rocky Mountains would be a wonderful cruise. Peaks engulf the sky on both sides of the road, with thick vegetation in the ditches. Tall pine trees attempt to match the summits, having variations of fifty to a hundred feet. The sun's rays caress the vegetation, plant life plentiful. It's summer. Lola is not on holiday. Her mind analyzes why Scalebane let her go.

In the underbelly of society, each player has their own agenda. The Moths' remain a mystery. Rithu wants acceptance. Scalebane's purpose is liquid, shifting for reasons Lola does not understand. Trusting her is not an option. She was concealing details from Rithu too, her own kind. More than ever, it makes Lola want to publish her information stored in her cloud. Without the tattoo, there's another way: her laptop. It will require publishing the evidence to each account and website she keeps in limbo. Unlike the QR code ink, which made it automatic. Unleashing the info is going to be worth it.

She left the computer in Synarion's home. The plastic hero's apartment is in Vancouver, on the west end of the country. Her last public location was Radiate Primate in Toronto, out east. Based on the mountains and the blue license plate of the Ducati, she's in British Columbia, the same province as Vancouver. She needs to find directions to the metropolis.

Time on the road allows for reflection. Uploading her evidence will expose the old world. Some people won't buy it, claiming its CGI, doctored. Others are going to believe, and it threatens the likes of Rithu, Scalebane, Synarion, and the other fantastic beings she has met. Should she care? The fire eats at her. She must do this.

Sympathetic thoughts are ineffective for her. She needs to get far from the Moths, in case they're on her tail. Lola keeps a close eye on the rear mirror for anything suspicious. She is alone most of the ride. Semi-trucks, logging trucks, vans, cars, and RVs cruise on both sides of the one-lane highway. She is careful not to drive too fast to raise suspicion. If an automobile, like an RV, is ten under the speed limit, she slingshots into oncoming traffic in order to advance a vehicle.

The bike soars past a green ditch sign stating: Highway One. A mental note of where Mastema's mansion is. Her journey takes her to the town of Hope. It's a crossroads where Highway One meets Highway Three, a good stopping point for truckers and people on the move. At this district municipality, a marker on Highway One points to Vancouver.

Lola fills the Ducati with gas and purchases water and a power bar. Quenching her thirst with refreshing cool mountain liquid feels reinvigorating. The experience mirrors her escape a year ago, when she shoved a cheap hotdog in her mouth. She eats the bar in incremental bites, not wanting to shock her stomach.

With an exhale, she watches the pink and orange sky with the sun hiding behind the mountains. This is an extended drive, and she needs energy. Lola takes a small nibble of the ash scale to keep herself upright and stuffs it into her jacket pocket. The comedown is unbearable, which she can worry about when she finds the nymph.

In three years, the balancer has made no attempt to find Lola. He didn't have to. She wishes he did. They shared something once. Not now, after he abandoned her.

Another two hours pass before Lola reaches the coastal city of Vancouver. High mountain elevations meet deep oceans with glass skyscrapers in between. The metropolis doesn't sleep. Day and night, vehicles buzz along, bumper to bumper. It's as Lola remembers while driving to the east side of the city to the familiar industrial park near the bay. Several brick and stucco three-level apartment complexes sit beside a series of warehouses and offices. A block over is a chicken refinery reeking with the foul stench of processed poultry.

A couple of avenues north is the major train line where shipments come from the docks. These tracks deliver goods from the West Coast to the rest of Canada. Lola bets it ships ash, too. Since 2016, a few more changes have occurred, and the city demolished the abandoned warehouse Lola used as a contact point with Detective Iglesias. They replaced it with new matte grey condo apartments. Gentrification is starting in Synarion's neighbourhood. With any luck, he hasn't moved.

Lola parks the Ducati a block away, keeping it discreet. She takes her duffel bag and hikes to Synarion's cracked stucco apartment. Her legs burn with each step. One turn right and the building stands before her, leaning at the same slanted angle. The structure's worn exterior, with chipped paint and unreplaced brown-stained windows, tells the story of years gone by.

A wind brushes against her skin, making her quiver. Memories flood her mind of a naïve time: a saviour, friend, and lover. Both souls fixated on the same goal of unravelling the Moths. Lola's method was direct, resulting in jail. The fool believed she could trust Synarion. He introduced her to the old world and aided in tracking the Moths' ash growery.

Three years on and that intel is useless. Lola's experience is beyond what the nymph can offer. She is here for her computer. That's it.

With a deep breath, Lola marches to the intercom beside the copper framed glass door. She punches in his unit number 307. It rings several times to no answer. She tries again. Zero. Looks like she will have to break in.

Lola walks around the premises, searching for an improvised way in. There are no balconies and the windows are wide, narrow, and made of thick glass coated in dirt and dust. The alleyway has an entrance beside the green dumpster. She pulls on it. Of course, locked. To her luck, it's a spring latch, being one of the horizontal doorknobs fitted for the cheap building. With a plastic card, you can engage the spring lock of these contraptions, flipping it open. Lola, the clever rogue reporter that she once was, is familiar with this tactic.

She glances for bystanders. There're two tents pitched along the alley with one man made of more filth than flesh, facing the wall. He holds a pipe, swaying, attempting to light the damn thing.

Clear enough, she thinks. Lola lifts the helmet's visor and places her duffel bag on the ground, unzipping it. She finds her ID in the purse and presses on the door with her body. It creates enough space between the frame and the door, allowing her to slide the card in. She wiggles the card deeper, locating the gap between the doorknob and the doorjamb being the lock mechanism. Levering the latch with the card, she disengages it and the door clicks open.

Bingo, Lola thinks. Breaking doors is a trick she learned long before meeting Synarion. She doesn't need him. Lola checks her ID. It's scraped and smeared thanks to this technique. She snags her bag and slips inside, stepping onto the burgundy carpet, going up the flight of stairs to the third floor. Her hand runs along the cracked concrete walls. This isn't a time for memory lane. The pungent smell of shredded chicken corpses pushes into the building, mixing with the hint of mould, dust, and curries of a passing home.

301 ... 302 ... 303, Lola counts the gold lettering on each unit. *307.* She stares at the splintered dark red door. It has the same scratched golden knob. She tries it; it's locked. She knocks several times. Silence.

Fine, she thinks. From her duffel bag, she retrieves her small toolkit. It has a thin screwdriver, perfect for this type of round lock. These doors vary from the former spring latch. They're often present in old buildings. She sticks the metal rod into the padlock, and with some wiggling, it clicks. The knob twists at her command and she steps into the apartment, sliding her bag with her.

The inside hasn't changed one bit. No surprise, considering Synarion wasn't much for change. He aged at a slow pace, like the vazeleads, and time didn't have the same perception for him. To her right is the kitchen with its unpainted cabinets. The sink contains no dishes. On the stove, the digital clock states quarter past eight at night. Next to it: the washroom with its door. Lights off. On the opposite end, a shelving unit houses plants, facing the open window beside a reading chair. The far left corner has his bed and closet. The final section to Lola's direct side has his tanned wooden table filled with tech junk and jars of botanical specimens. It's where she last left her laptop. It and the nymph are vacant.

She closes the door and locks it. The machine must be here. She storms to the desk and sees his computer is gone. She moves some cables, dead phones, and tools aside. Next, she slides the glass containers aside to look behind them. It's not here.

"Shit," Lola says. She looks under the surface, around it, and heads to the closet, flipping open the creaking doors and skims through his minimal sets of clothing. Synarion is living here. He must be out.

Thirty minutes of searching provides no resolution. Lola takes the helmet off and drags her belongings to the bed. She crashes onto the mattress, exhaling. There's time to look for that laptop. Synarion will return and she can't give a rat's ass what he will think. Knowing his nature, he won't be as aggressive as she.

Her eyes flicker as the ash dwindles in her system. The strain that her body has endured is catching up. The comedown of the drug is prominent, causing her limbs and bones to multiply their weight as she sinks into the bed. It's a strange mix of relief and pain. No one knows who she is or where she is.

Consciousness fades, and she drifts into a well-deserved rest. The slumber descends her awareness into a deep blackness. There's a sheen of light against two glowing white balls. They catch flame. The inferno engulfs them, morphing the objects into twin ovals. They're the eyes, watching her. *Painter . . .* the fire snaps, elongating into a creek.

That's not a dream.

It's the door.

Lola's eyes spring open and she rises from the bed, reaching around to grab her handgun. She points it at a newcomer fashioning a leather trucker jacket and black clothing. He raises his hands, perpendicular with his slicked blond hair, parallel to the iconic missing right index finger and cauliflower ears. The purple irises of the plastic ghost stare at her.

CHAPTER 38
LIFE THROUGH LOSS

Lola?" Synarion asks. Yes, Synarion embodies a natural charm in his concerned tone. It's identical to the first time they met years ago at a bar sharing the same tastes in whiskey.

"Don't fucking move," Lola says, hopping off the bed. Her feet hit the floor and her legs collapse against her will. Her knee slams into the hardwood. She drops the gun and tries to stand. Her arms shake as she grinds her teeth. Without ash, Lola is once again sober and useless.

Synarion lowers his hands and kicks the door closed. "I wondered when you would return." The nymph walks towards her. She reaches for the firearm. His boot contacts it first and slides it clear, and she lands on her palms.

"Stay the fuck back," Lola says. Her skull pounds from the force of a dozen hammers. The lack of ash sends a sensation of small needles piercing into her flesh. The muscles burn from exhaustion. Her bones might as well be rubber. She needs ash to control the situation. Where did she put it? She can't recall in this damaged, clouded state.

The nymph extends his hands to her. She swats them.

"I said back off," she says through her teeth.

"Let me help," the other says. "What happened?"

"Like you care?" Lola uses the bed as support, sliding herself up onto the mattress. Synarion tries to aid her again, and she waves him gone. Her efforts prove fruitful and she sits, panting.

Synarion scans her from head to toe, mouth hanging. He doesn't believe the scarred and scabbed skeleton is in front of him, complete with knotted greasy hair grazing against her signature scarred clavicles. Lola should feel an emotion. She would if it wasn't for the comedown of the drug. Her pain takes focus.

"Judge all you want," Lola says. "Taking the high ground."

Synarion bites his lip, looking at the floor. "It was a tough choice."

"No shit?" Lola brushes her greasy hair from her face. Her right leg bounces in a spasm thanks to her system's demand for ash. "You fucking left me to die and take the blame."

"That wasn't my plan," Synarion says.

"Yeah? What was it? Keep the old world hidden for your perfect balancing existence?"

"That didn't happen, did it?" Synarion folds his arms. "The Moths faded from public interest. Their actions are the normal, leaving people compliant."

"If you didn't betray me, maybe none of this would have happened."

"While you schemed behind my back? I'm no idiot, Lola. In some ways, yes. Not in this case. You were documenting the old world. I couldn't let you."

"That's why you did it." Lola attempts to get to her feet, reinforced with anger. She takes a step towards him, careful because of her weakened limbs. Each movement is stiff as if she were a marionette.

"No," Synarion says.

"Then why?" Lola tilts her head.

Synarion stands straight. "A fool's dream."

Lola's face contorts with hatred, and she launches a fist. Her attack lacks precision, causing her to waver and lose her footing. In a swift motion, he seizes her forearms, ensuring she doesn't take a tumble. With a sudden jolt, she pulls away and wraps her arms around herself for protection. Her body's weakened state won't let her inflict her will. Synarion deserves to have the living hell beaten out of him until he is black and blue, crying and begging for forgiveness. She yearns to scream at him and make him understand the horrors she has been through. She wants to cry and have the terrible things disappear with each tear. That won't happen. Time travel doesn't exist. There are no heroes.

The mixture of emotions makes her lips tremble, and she sits on the bed, defeated. A knot of saliva tries to worm its way down her tense throat. She swallows and speaks in a croaked voice. "You don't have any idea what I've been through."

Synarion remains where he is. "No, not specifically. I have a general idea."

"Do you? Do you have any clue? I was in prison for two years. Two goddamn years I kept my head low so I could escape that hellhole and return to what I need to do. I killed people, Synarion." After that statement, Lola realizes it wouldn't phase him. He has slain countless in his life and would have no empathy towards it. She continues, "I was tortured, for God knows how much time. Do you get that? Complete and utter misery because of you. It's because of you and what you did that day."

"I'm not to blame, Lola. I wasn't present these past three years. At the slaughterhouse, I had to do what I did."

Three years, she thinks. It's 2019. Rithu tormented her for twelve months. She clears her throat. "Yeah? And what is that? A fool's dream? What even the fuck is that?" Lola asks.

Synarion exhales, rubbing the back of his head. "It's a lot to explain, and I doubt you would understand."

She runs her index finger along her irises. "Kind of like you're freestyling those eyes. Doesn't keep the old world hidden, does it?" Her statement refers to his usual brown contacts she has seen him wear.

"I was meeting a colleague. Are you going to tell me why you are here? Other than to lecture me on the terrible things I've done in the name of Mother Nature?"

"You are a pompous prick," Lola says. "They made me need ash, Synarion."

"You were on that path already." Synarion holds his right wrist.

Lola licks her lips. "I was out. Prison cleaned me. The Moths threw me right back in." Lola unzips her biker jacket, dropping it to the ground. With one tug, she lifts the tank top, showing the scar where her tattoo once was.

Synarion stares at the spot, face still as a stone. He shifts to the shackles on her boots and wrists.

"If I don't have ash, I can . . . I . . . nothing w-o-orks." Her voice cracks.

"That's why you're here?" Synarion asks in a flat tone.

"No." Lola stands again. "I'm here for my laptop. Where is it?"

"I can't let you have that," Synarion says.

"Why?" Lola moves closer. "Because I'd expose your precious old world?"

"Yes."

Lola forms a fist and throws it at him. The blow brushes against his peck. Synarion doesn't flinch. He takes a step forward and places his hands on her cold, bare shoulders. She jerks, stepping aside, and continues walking to the other side by the kitchen. Her stiff legs are working again.

My pocket, Lola thinks, recalling where she put her drug stash. Her hand slides into the jacket's pocket on the ground and she tears off a small piece of the scale to chew on.

"Lola, you're not well." Synarion says. "You need rest. I can offer you hospitality. Get those cuffs off."

"Gee. You're so kind. Like before, and what? Throw me to the wolves again? You think I'm going to buy that, Synarion? Your life's choices have been to protect Mother Nature." Lola laughs, pointing at herself with a sinister grin. "She chose me, Synarion. Mother Nature chose me. Not you."

Synarion squints, his eyes moving from her head to her toe, analyzing her as if she were a sick animal.

"Mother Nature is speaking to me. I can hear her and see her twin flames. Her voice is angry, mad at people like you." Lola extends her arms, waving them around. "She's everywhere, within the living Earth. That's the connection that I have to your precious Mother Nature, one that you balancers wish you had. Each time I take ash she speaks to me."

"What happened to you, Lola?" Synarion asks.

His calm and controlled tone has the force of a brick and she hobbles to the bed, her face drooping with concern. The erratic mood changes are side effects of the drug. The scales take her to the outer limits with each hit, aiding her wisdom to see beyond the construct of human civilization. It provides her with a potent sixth sense, enabling her to understand empathy, compassion, and the interconnectedness of living creatures. Without ash, she is zero. Even if she got clean a second time, she is a fugitive, former reporter, and murderer.

"I feel a loss of my humanity," Lola says with an empty voice. She rubs her forehead as Synarion takes a slow step and sits on the other side of the bed. It's close enough to annoy her. She leans over and snatches her jacket off the ground. Boy, she would love to grab the shotgun and cap the bastard. There's no point. She needs him.

"Fine, I'll take the hospitality." Lola takes a deep exhale. Defeated.

Synarion nods. "It won't fix what I did. You are here and it would be rude if I didn't offer."

"Mmm." She wipes her face, wishing the ash would kick in. "I will get my laptop."

He smirks. "Don't be too sure that it still exists."

Lola raises an eyebrow, unsure if he is bluffing. If that's the case, she can still get her data from a new machine. "Like old times, eh?"

"I suppose so." Thoughts are becoming clearer. The minor hit of ash, her form of coffee, is making its rounds. Her addicted brain is playing tricks on her, too. Her limbs ache less. The hammers have stopped slamming into her skull. It makes her realize she reeks of sweat and blood. Her thin frame and battered body must shock Synarion. Her gut churns with embarrassment, causing her to avoid even glancing at her skeletal arms. She asks, "What happened, Synarion? Why did you leave me for the police?"

He wipes his chin. "This requires a drink."

"That's a luxury I haven't had in several years," Lola says.

"You sure you can handle one?"

"Give me the damn drink." Ash hasn't irradiated her of jadedness.

The nymph heads to the kitchen and pops open a cabinet, taking two glasses and a bottle of amber liquor. She watches him pour, ensuring he doesn't slip a mystery object into hers. Drugging isn't his style. He also has no reason to. Paranoia will eat the soul when living in the underworld of crime. Synarion returns, passing hers and raising his in the distant cheer. She takes a sip of the whiskey, embracing the strong bold flavours of cherry and bark, letting it rest on her tongue for a moment before swallowing. It burns on the way down, far stronger than she remembers, and is enough to make her clear her throat. It's a good sting, one that she missed.

Lola gives her legs a light slap. "You share yours and I share mine. Three years. Let's go."

Synarion strokes his neck, his eyes looking off to the corner of the room as if she opened a portal into his past. His lips purse, eyelid twitching, reliving what he saw. Lola hasn't seen him this way.

He speaks. "Three years for you, Lola. For me, it's been far longer."

* * *

I never meant to betray you, Lola. That fateful day, I faced a difficult dilemma at the abattoir plant. One that I don't expect you to understand. Yes, we aligned ourselves with Scalebane so we could save her sister, and that was the plan until Scalebane changed it. I was going to cover you in the control room when Scalebane gave me a choice that I couldn't refuse.

Again, a fool's dream.

She insisted that she alone knew the way to Hell. A hunch told me this was false. She hasn't been there since escaping its tormented grasps from her childhood and forgets the horrors it brings. Her sister, on the other hand, is more at peace.

Scalebane's tail constricted me. Combat was the sole means of countering her. Time was of the essence, and fighting wasn't getting us anywhere with both the police and Crystal Moths closing in. I needed bargaining power and agreed to her plan and proceeded to deal with the Moths in the slaughterhouse. To my luck, after, you and Scalebane were in conflict. I got Namsruc out. That's when the police arrived, and the rest occurred with Scalebane escaping and you in prison.

That's why I had to betray you. If I had fought Scalebane, we all would have been caught by the law. Then what good would I have been for balancing Mother Nature's garden? What would have the police done with a live vazelead?

Namsruc was feeble and fragile, and I aided her to health. Unlike her sister, she didn't hold a grudge. I explained to her why I returned them to their people. I wasn't a father, more of a foster home. They needed the culture and relations of their history. Of course, Scalebane doesn't see it that way. She won't forgive me. Namsruc understood, and she wished to help me. She wanted to understand what the right direction in life was. The Moths, the vazeleads, and the teachings I shared with the twins about the balance of Mother Nature created a moral dilemma for her.

I explained my deal with Scalebane and how I was hoping either of them would take me to King to reason with him. Sensing my conflict, Namsruc hesitated. She could see it in my eyes. My tone was not the same. She knew me to be the strong and energetic figure she once admired. A dark cloud hovers over this version of me.

Now, why did I want to go into Hell? My former companion slipped from my hand. The earth swallowed her in an unholy ritual's fiery flame, sending her to Dega'Mostikas's Triangle. It's a failed balancing tale of mine for another time.

Well, failed for me. The mission achieved equilibrium for Mother Nature. It scarred me. Valturus and I shared a long and deep history spanning thousands of years. Then she was gone. How am I able to be an efficient balancer if I am unable to maintain my own emotions? They took hold of me. I needed her and wouldn't accept defeat.

The afterlife is not what it used to be. Harsh judgments on a soul have vanished. You've seen it. Angels and demons walk this plane as if it is their own. Portals connecting this world to the next are unguarded, if you can find them. Powerful gatekeepers transcend the spirit for a short time to the beyond. As you know, Lereif Scalebane and Namsruc Scalebane were born in Hell and brought here. Mastema is the First, walking among us. You met Mul the succubus. She was helping me pinpoint Valturus before Scalebane ended her. Because of that, I knew there was a way to get Valturus without Scalebane.

Scalebane killed Mul, as you witnessed.

The portal Mul used stopped working long ago, hence she researched with me rather than directed me to a gate. I'm unsure what Scalebane thought she had, and I trusted my hunch.

Namsruc understood my need. She needed to confront her dilemmas, too. Time away from her people gave her a fresh perspective because the vazeleads are in a complex situation. Namsruc agreed to work with me. She had a colleague who could help get me to the other side.

Her contact is one I swore to secrecy for their own protection. We met with them, who guided us to Hell. Let me assure you, Lola, that place isn't anything you would expect. It comprises three realms within Dega'Mostikas's Triangle. Dega'Mostikas being the root of evil.

An unholy ritual of immense force creates a physical portal, taking you to and from Hell. It is how the Scalebane sisters made it to the mortal realm. It's the same type that took Valturus away. The one Mul used. These rituals require strength and power that few have today. This is why no more materialistic portals exist. Anyone that tries is bound to destroy the forsaken gateway sites.

There's another way into Hell: projection of the soul. It is dangerous, chaotic, and requires the most wilful might. Only a select few titled gatekeepers have the ability to control this form of dark energy. The old world documented this method. Doctors believed it was a disease, finding a black organism wrapped around the innards of the infected's brains. This was due to the touch of the infectious gatekeepers. The torment of the psyche gave it the infamous title of Mental Damnation.

Namsruc and I located the gatekeeper in the village of Murgo. Let me tell you, travelling to India from Canada with a vazelead isn't easy. Namsruc found us an in with Allen Shipping Solutions, who work with the Moths, and we snuck on one of their ships.

Murgo means Gateway of Hell in the Tibetic languages. Today, it contains a Buddhist monastery. Long ago was another story. Locals attribute its name to the harsh environment of blizzards, snowstorms, and gales at its fourteen-thousand-foot altitude. Its barren valley kills thousands of people and animals between the black mountains. According to Namsruc's contact, the name's hidden layer below references the home of a gatekeeper.

We climbed the elevation, battled the biting weather, and faced the harsh physical strains of cold and scarceness. We hiked high, far beyond the Buddhist temple, reaching a cavern that descended into darkness. In that dark hole, we found the being.

Mental Damnation takes its toll on the flesh. This creature couldn't walk, its bones were gone, and the muscles melded with the black substance. We had to convince the gatekeeper to infect us. They gave Namsruc and me a taste of Mental Damnation without the full dosage through precise control of their onyx tentacles. It pierces the mind, collapsing the world around you as your soul transcends into Hell.

We couldn't predict which Hell Valturus was in. I prayed to Mother Nature that she was in the one we found ourselves in. Dreadweave Pass.

Time distorts, moving non-linear compared to the mortal realm. We could be there for minutes, being months or years to your perception. What you see in this hellish landscape shifts through your own interpretation, making you think you witness things that aren't there. Your soul filters the objective truth of matter. A rock to Namsruc was Valturus's decapitated head under the black swirling clouds for me. I was losing my mind and Namsruc kept me grounded until she too would experience her own nightmares that did not exist: Scalebane, her duty to King. We couldn't find any clues to where Valturus was.

Parts of Dreadweave Pass were the same to both of us. Our minds both concurred that a tree was a tree, and a hill was walkable. It wasn't easy.

The gatekeeper agreed to keep Namsruc and me there for a short time, so the pressures of Hell didn't overbear us. Our first journey was a month long in Dreadweave Pass, and a day in the mortal realm. It shatters your sense of realism. We continued for a year and a half of your time, phasing in and out of Dega'Mostikas's Triangle. Again, time distorts and each visit in Dreadweave Pass varied. A day would go by, which was weeks in the mortal realm. Other times it reverted and a week in Hell was hours in reality.

The trials of Dreadweave Pass test your will. Visions surface each sin that you have committed through mirages and whispers in the sharp winds. The realm was endless. This was one Hell. There are two more in the triangle, and I cannot imagine what they must be like. I feared Valturus was in another, and I questioned if we had the fortitude to reach her. What are a couple of mortals compared to the infinite powers of the afterlife?

Our mission failed, though we gained new insight into ourselves. I understood my duty to Mother Nature's garden. Chasing personal dreams is not for me to bear. Namsruc had her own epiphany. She needed to return to her people and aid in their growth. The vazeleads are fragile, flirting with extinction.

I trust Namsruc will do the right thing. She believes I shall maintain my internal balance so I can best serve Mother Nature and protect this world. Moths aren't the sole threat to Earth.

Other bad actors exist. My purpose is to preserve equilibrium. I'm the last and cannot deny who I am.

I doubt if that's the closure you wanted regarding my betrayal at the abattoir plant. My past is mine. You're in your late twenties and I've been around for well over two thousand years, living many lives, as did Valturus. We watched the world live and die over and over. It leaves you numb. It warps your perspective, dismissing how each individual experiences a unique existence in Mother Nature's garden.

This is the conflict I deal with each day. Each waking moment of my life, I have to accept the conscious decisions I make to keep Mother Nature safe. Is an ecosystem more important than a dying race? Or will their death aid their surroundings? What about an individual? My judgements aren't perfect. You are an example of that.

I returned to Canada and my home, continuing where you and I left off before we met. Now, here we are.

* * *

Synarion blinks twice, his eyes darting towards the shelves of plants, averting his gaze from the haunting portal into his past. Desperate to escape his emotions, he gulps the rest of his whiskey, hoping to numb his pain.

Lola sits with both hands between her legs, spinning her empty glass. "It wasn't a complete waste of time. As you said, you found your own balance."

He squints. "At the cost of betrayal? Forgetting my duty?"

"You said I started that by scheming behind your back." She clears her throat. "That aside, Valturus, who is she?"

Synarion heads to the kitchen and snatches the bottle, deciding that they need another round. "Well, besides each other's fixation, she is the queen of vampires."

Lola shakes her head. "Of course vampires are real."

"Remember, myths and legends are born from somewhere, and are often more true than you'd think. Murgo is a perfect example. Storytelling is an ancient method of passing information to the next generation, ensuring that legacies, warnings, and truths live on." He walks to his dresser and takes a small chest, returning to Lola. He opens it and passes her a photo. "Remember this?"

She examines the Polaroid photograph with a date of 1969. It is an outdoor musical event with Synarion mid-motion dancing with a brunette. People in colourful bell bottom pants and beaded necklaces sit, stand, and dance on the grass. Lola recalls this image. He showed it to her when they first met. Synarion dyed his hair black. The pale woman's canines are far too long to be normal, similar to Spike and Baldy at Radiate Primate. Even in the saturated photo, her emerald eyes are striking.

"That's her?" Lola asks.

"We had our happy moments," Synarion says. He takes the photograph and puts it into the trunk.

Lola scratches her neck. "So let me understand, you had a love affair with the queen vampires, who is imprisoned in Hell, the same Hell that the Scalebane sisters grew up in?" The statement forces a smirk on her face because of the ridiculousness.

He raises his glass. "That is the truth. She found me when the old world collapsed. Valturus and I were the last of our kinds, to our knowledge. We bonded over it and had mutual respect for what we were."

Same reasons you liked me, Lola thinks. She takes another gulp of her drink, smothering the thought. Not in a million years would she say that. There was chemistry between them, and still is.

"Letting go is tough," Lola says. "Trust me. Side question, it's been bugging me with these Hell portals, the physical, and mental ones. Does a demon die when they're here, in the real world?"

"Ah, well, that depends. Heaven's judgements are non-existent. If it was the physical gate, their soul would be in Death's Vortex, the resting bed for all."

"If it was the mental damnation thing?"

"Is determined by their willpower."

"Huh." *That answers that*, she thinks, recalling her internal dilemma while in prison. "Thanks."

"Of course." Synarion bows his head.

"Namsruc and Scalebane aren't in contact?" Lola asks.

"I'm going to guess no." Synarion shifts to face her, one leg crossing the other.

"She was looking for you, Scalebane," she says.

"I'm not surprised. I took her sister. That means you've seen her recently?"

"Sort of," Lola says, voice flat.

"Wonderful segue into your tale, Lola Cabello. Tell me the torment of your time." A crooked smirk rises on his face.

The charm doesn't fail, even when she despises him. The ash mixed with the whiskey creates a complex blend that helps her forgive him, understanding the pain he experienced. She takes another gulp, leaving a single sip left. "My three years?" Lola asks.

"Yes. What happened to you?" Synarion raises his right eyebrow.

His question gives her time to reflect on the events: prisoner, forced assassin, failed murderer of Mastema, and tortured. A year of bonding with Rithu Blacktooth, the son of King, as a human therapy pet. Her rebound into ash, unlocking its power, trials, and the whispers that it brings. The branches of power whispering secrets, thanks to a mysterious green-eyed, burning-plastic-smelling man.

Of the horrific, fantastic, and outlandish things from the past three years, her biggest loss is herself. She is not the same journalism student from 2014, nor is she the determined vigilante that Synarion met in 2016. She's not the same as she was in 2018. Ash mutates her, giving a new purpose. Her soul is re-birthing.

CHAPTER 39
EDEN BREAKER

It takes courage to put aside the ego and accept outside aid. Scalebane is not one for help. She learned to rely on her abilities, to survive on her own; thanks to her mother's teaching. Even Synarion taught the sisters to defend themselves using their environment. Scalebane failed to realize that leveraging your surroundings includes accepting support.

Dasco Amoss's paintings are a looming threat. Synarion took her sister Namsruc, and Namsruc refuses to return. The painter sketches Lola Cabello. Meanwhile, Mastema is tampering with the unnatural. King is not concerned with the threats. Jekos offers a hand, as does Rithu. She needs to accept.

Releasing Cabello was urgent. In a perfect scenario, she would have taken the soft skin to Dasco Amoss to understand why the ghoul is channeling her. They couldn't both escape the mansion without going unnoticed. Scalebane hunted her once. She can do it again.

She waits for the three humans, Prime Minister Stéphane Trudell, Mr. Patterson, Dr. Lang, to leave the mansion prior to returning up the stairs. Jekos leads the men to the foyer, where the two vampire Moths take them to the helicopter. Once the doors close, Scalebane approaches Jekos.

She says, "We need to work together, if you tell me how to get into Hell."

Jekos squints. "That meeting changed your mind, didn't it?"

"Where's the entrance to Dega'Mostikas's Triangle?" Scalebane asks.

"Okay, I'll share with you. Do me a favour, will you?" He tilts his head.

"That was the deal."

"Call this number." He takes a business card from the pocket of his vest, followed by a marble pen, and writes on it. He places it into her palm and walks to the second level. The mysterious card's smooth matte finish is a thick cardstock. A printed phone contact in black gloss is above the blue ink handwritten message reading:

6044121134

Murgo. Through the False Gateway.

Fourth peak over the Buddhist monastery.

Destroy this card. I never gave this to you. Eden Breaker sent you.

Murgo, she thinks. If memory serves, that is on the other side of the world in India, far from Canada. An unsuspecting place in today's standards. Though history has legends of this location.

To fulfil her end of the bargain, after talking to Jekos, she takes a phone provided by a Moth guard in the lobby. She heads to Mastema's garden to be alone and calls the number on the card. Despite her distaste for human technology, Scalebane operates the device. The phone rings, and an automated synthetic voice speaks. To her, it sounds demonic. "Club Revelation, tonight, eleven. Find Eden Breaker and be set free. Club Revelation, tonight, eleven . . ." The message repeats once and the phone clicks, ending the connection. Then, she snaps the phone in two. What limited knowledge she does have of these devices tells her that smartphones can be tracked and recorded.

A helicopter ride later, Scalebane walks to the infamous establishment owned by Jekos in the metropolis of Vancouver. She has been here before, looking for Cabello, and detests its existence. Partying, dancing, and primal mating courtship let shadowed businesses operate undetected. It's far too noisy and rancid. Old world beings shouldn't mingle with soft skins.

The rain dampens her hood under the semi-clouded night sky. She keeps her cloak wrapped tight around her body, tail coiling her leg. Homeless individuals, ash-dashers, and other drug addicts fill the declining side streets. Each of them is in rough shape: infected arms whence dirty needles pierced, benders whose upper halves face the floor because of internal pain, skeletal bodies, possible corpses—or are they sleeping? Knife playing, bats, and random screaming are additional properties along the alleyway. It makes a black-cloaked figure with a mask not unusual. No civilian comments, no crook dares interject Scalebane walking through Blood Ally.

The neon red sign mounted on a brick building contains script text stating: Club Revelation. She knocks on the metal door several times and a tall, muscular man with no neck gives her the once over. They are the same height, twice as wide, and Scalebane could break his arm with one hand.

"ID?" the human asks in a thick Eastern European accent.

"Jekos sent me," Scalebane says, voice muffled from the mask.

The soft skin raises an eyebrow, focused on the metal fangs. "Is that so?"

"Indeed. I've been through this before. Either I could bring him here and he can have a word with you directly, or you let me through. He is a busy individual, and I don't think you want to get on his wrong side. Have you met his boss?"

"Ah," the man says, as if he recognizes her. "I was told you were coming." He glances at both sides of the alley and steps aside, letting Scalebane in. She storms past the red hall, containing a black wooden kiosk with a ticket seller. Her neon orange eyes watch Scalebane as she gives a toothy grin that matches Jekos's. Imps, disgusting.

Beyond the booth girl, Scalebane enters the principal attraction. From corner to corner, soft skins mix in with old world beings, chatting and dancing. The foulness of hundreds of bodies compressed close together, sweating from head to toe, floods her nostrils. Synthetic perfumes, deodorants, musk, peach, shit, funk, cheese, and swamp radiate from their pores. Pointy ears, sharp teeth, others far too hairy, some have rough bark-like texture. Scalebane questions which ones are human. Old world beings can look soft skins. Mastema is a perfect example. Vampires are another.

She walks towards the black bar that faces the DJ at the opposite end, with the dancers in between. Six brick pillars support the building and work as cornerstones for people to lean on and have more intimate talks. Further to Scalebane's right is the lounge section. Circular leather booths let larger groups have casual conversations. For Scalebane, she stands by the bar, watching, keeping her sai within her claw's reach.

A broad-shouldered man in an unbuttoned shirt, covered in sweat, approaches Scalebane. He pushes his spiky hair aside while dancing to the music. His eyes flutter: a sign of substance usage. His head bobs in sync with the hi-hat of the track as his torso is in unison with the rumbling base. "Sup?" he calls out.

Scalebane ignores him, looking off in the other direction.

The man circles to the bar, leaning on it. The scent of alcohol lingering in the air. He speaks with a clear, sober voice. "Eden of interest?"

Scalebane scans him, seeing his eyes no longer flutter. A gleam of red swirls around his blue irises and a wide grin rises, showing perfect white teeth.

"I'm looking for Eden Breaker," Scalebane says.

"This way," he says. He slaps the table and strolls towards the lounge area, his shoulders swinging in his strut. Scalebane follows. Clubbers step clear as the confident man passes the

OBSIDIAN'S COMMAND BY KONN LAVERY

booths to a backdoor where two security guards stand. They remain stiff as he swings the door open. Inside, the pair head down a narrow, creaking staircase. An amber light flickers above. They take a turn, passing a soft skin no taller than four feet, reading a magazine. The dance music muffles as the entrance slams shut behind them. In the basement, a wooden bar is to the right. Rows of thick red drapes hang in circular formations, creating private sections.

The man takes her into one, pushing the curtains aside. Scalebane enters, examining the couch on the floor with sawed off legs. Most of the stuffing is missing, leaving the cushions a bulbous mess. A crooked table contains numerous liquor bottles of various completion. Two pipes, several lighters, a straw, and a spoon accompany them. This is where heavy partying occurs.

"Eden Breaker is full of mystery," she says.

Being in the small room alone with the man, Scalebane takes another sniff of the air. The overwhelming smell of the club is far less pungent. This soft skin doesn't reek of mammal. His stench has a sharp sting to it, closer to an insect. It's a familiar scent.

The man's face contorts, his jaw spasms. As the bones twist and contort, a remarkable change occurs: the body shrinks in size, losing its muscles and adopting a feminine silhouette. With each strand of hair that falls to the ground, the skin grows paler, transforming into a ghostly, white hue. His eyes morph into black with a red sheen. Sharp teeth materialize in his gums. A tail pokes out from his pants. Once the transformation unfolds, the shaper is draped in oversized clothing. They remove the open shirt and slip from the trousers, leaving their pale form naked.

"I wasn't quite comfortable in that skin," the shaper says, raising their arms.

"A double agent," Scalebane says.

"Yet not obvious, yes? You see, you're not the only Moth that has multiple agendas. I come and go as I please, depending on the order, whether I execute Mastema's or another collection of like-minded beings."

"Being?" Scalebane's tail sways from side to side.

The shaper walks to Scalebane, their legs criss-crossing in a catlike motion. "Eden Breaker."

"You're Eden Breaker?" She raises a spiked brow that the other cannot see.

"Eden Breaker is a name for many. We're a single conscious effort of anonymous individuals that act as one with a strident goal of giving home to those that have none."

"Elaborate on this esoteric talk. I've heard variations of this nonsense over the years. None of which ever holds truth."

"Our founder kept it true. Long dead, yes. They saw a gap for the lost. They wanted to provide a safety net behind civilization. Whether for humans, or vazeleads, trolls, Root Walkers, it matters not. There are always outliers. We are their collectiveness. Though, anonymous as we are, that can't be, yes? There is a need for structure in a hive mind. Tiers create function. They keep us in line. Lower tiers act on tickets to build funds, as I am of four, the highest."

"Being the four rivers of Eden," Scalebane says.

"Educated in human religion?" Four asks with a focused gaze, not blinking.

"Humans were influential on my people." Spikes of pain roll up her injured leg and Scalebane shifts her stance. "Their religions, art, and language infected our ways."

"Wonderful. For simplicity, call me Four. For I am one of four."

"The other three?" Scalebane asks.

"All of me as I am them for I mutate as I please, filling the role of all four. Little of concern for you, as I am the highest tier."

"Who is above you? If your founder is dead?" Scalebane asks.

"We're a hive mind. We follow the path given to us by the founder and ensure the lost break free and relish in the forbidden fruits the world denies them of."

Scalebane taps the handle of her sai. She lifts her foot, realizing it rests on a sticky substance. "I asked to stop with the esoteric talk. A contact sent me here. What does this have to do with the Moths? Lola Cabello? Or what the humans are doing with synthesizing ash from our supply? Or, shadows?"

"I see. " Four cocks their head. "You possess a lot of knowledge. Many questions. Some I have answers to and some I do not. Mastema and the three men have plans for ash. Utopia of sterilization of the weak, elevating the pure. Transcending the souls of this world. What better way to ensure the Creator's vision? The same Creator who abandoned the mortal realm eons ago?"

"The First's Divine Plan contains more parts." Scalebane folds her arms. "You must be aware of the shadow anomaly a year past in Toronto."

"Yes, humans say it was mass hysteria," Four says.

"But it wasn't." Scalebane says quicker than she intended. "What else can you share of Mastema's plans?"

"You are clever, yes? Drowning in a personal mission, one you're willing to leave Rithu, your own kind, alone because of."

Scalebane's tail swings up and back down. "I will bring him in once I understand what this Eden Breaker is. Were you involved in aiding Cabello in Mastema's attempted assassination?"

"Quite the leap." The shaper tilts their head.

"But true." Scalebane puts her claws back on her sai as impatience squeezes her will.

"I asked my question initially." Four gives a toothy smile.

A rattle comes from Scalebane's throat. "I'm working with a soft skin. They're an oracle, speaking with a ghoul from the Midway, giving a warning. Are you familiar with the afterlife?"

"To a degree. The Creator made life, with the First being Mastema, then abandoned. I am sure he feels neglected, like a lost child."

Scalebane smirks, appreciating the slander towards the crime lord and his unbearable ego. "This oracle, a painter, works diligently to complete the ghoul's request of building a summoning circle. They want to be seen, showing the soft skin the history of Creationism. They've shown Cabello."

The shaper taps their chin. "Lola Cabello? Have they met?"

"No. That's the latest evolution of the oracle's visions."

"So you let Cabello go?" Four lowers their town.

OBSIDIAN'S COMMAND BY KONN LAVERY

Scalebane squeezes the handle of her sai. "Prior, the ghoul has made lightless ones prominent in the paintings, like a signature to each piece."

"I see, yes. Lightless ones. Shadows everywhere." Four points to a darkness underneath the table. "Forever dormant, watching, though not interfering with the cosmos unless angered."

"The shooting of Mastema disturbed them. Concentrated light didn't kill the angel, and the shadows expressed pain. Mastema must be harnessing them to resist the light. I warned my employer. He does not believe me. I've heard Mastema discuss with the three men. I ponder how informed my people's leader is. I fear he is as corrupt as them. This is not a path I agreed to. None of my people did, and I question if other old world Moths are mindful. The oracle paints a looming threat from ghouls who remain neutral. If they are interfering, will others celestial entities interfere? Mother Nature? The lightless ones? Therefore, you and I are talking. Mastema is vexing the slumbering."

"The First believes he must foresee the Creator's vision," Four says.

Scalebane hobbles around the table, eyeing its shadow below. "Where does this leave us, Four?"

"We work together," the other says. "Discover what this oracle and their ghoul wish. If they are showing lightless ones while Mastema inches closer into the forbidden, we must be cautious."

Scalebane stops circling, a third away from Four. "My question to you, Four, is why are the three men mingling with bioengineering, other than to transcend humanity? What do humanity's future, ash, and Mastema have to do with lightless ones?"

Four strokes their chin, pondering the question. "An acceptable query indeed. Eden Breaker has functions, people, around the world. I have been into the Manageficient labs. Fascinating experiments. Word is quick among Moths. They're aware that Lola Cabello escaped. Mastema wants her. Rithu's incapable nature angers him."

"Rithu is capable," Scalebane says. "Son of King is no buffoon, I assure you."

"Is that so?" Four asks, raising a hairless eyebrow.

"Should Mastema have her, comrade? The men referred to her as Subject Alpha."

"Perhaps not." Four looks to the ground. "Though, we're playing two roles, remember?" Their gaze meets Scalebane's again. "Work for the Moths, and concurrently working to dismantle them."

"What does that get you?" Scalebane presses her tongue against her lower front teeth.

"Progress for Eden Breaker," Four says.

"No, you, the individual. A double agent."

"I don't put my bet on one side of the coin." Four's nostrils flare for a moment.

"I see. Do we hunt Cabello for Mastema?" Her tail constricts around her ankle, hoping for the preferred response.

"Cabello is an intriguing specimen. Not of the new world with soft skins. Lineage of old. We have public cameras to find her. I question if bringing her to Mastema is correct. She has potential other uses we could leverage, like your painter. You should have kept her instead of setting her loose."

Scalebane wants to interject, explaining why she let Cabello go but decides to hold her impulsive reaction. She and Rithu helped Lola escape for a reason. Rithu knows enough to be dangerous, and it is time to rope him in.

Four takes a bow. "Our visit is short, mission clear, yes? I have other work to attend to. A double life as you have. We'll connect soon, Scalebane."

"Why did we meet here?" Scalebane says.

"Jekos's Club Revelation is a beautiful haven, sharing the same vision as Eden Breaker's safety net. He connects people. We are two-faced, you and I. He might be too. We will be in touch. Mastema and his three men taunt the ancient." Four claps their hands together. "Finish your personal agenda, quick, and we'll find Cabello."

Four's body twitches, the sound of bones cracking fills the air and the flesh contorts, transforming into a darker shade. The skull reshapes, causing the bones to stretch and lengthen. Hair grows on their scalp, framing their face in a soft, lustrous halo. They take on a conventional attractive female soft skin Scalebane has not seen. Four takes the baggy clothes, dressing, playing a new unknown role. Too many unknowns for Scalebane's preference.

CHAPTER 40
NUTS EVERYWHERE

Iglesias puffs on a cigarette outside of the same bar he met Archer at a week ago. She will arrive soon with the DNA samples. Iglesias was clever enough to keep a sliver of both materials for himself. When sampling at a lab, the element is destroyed during the extraction process.

If the results are to his liking, he'll present them to Disk. They have arranged a meeting at the same hotel after Archer's results. Iglesias presumes Disk went home after they met the first time. A week at a motel is expensive. This kid is dense and might have pissed their money away waiting for him. It doesn't matter. Disk agreed to meet.

Archer's silver Mustang pulls into the parking lot, the loud engine rumbling until the ignition turns off. Those wheels are new. Figures she enjoys a flashy vehicle. The girl is hotheaded, like he used to be, like José. His heart hollows a fraction more at the thought of the boy's stubbled face.

For José, he thinks, taking the last puff of his cigarette. He chucks it and steps on the butt to extinguish the flame. Archer exits the car with aviators on as he approaches. She chews gum, holding documents in a folder, waving them in the air, raising her brows in a sarcastic "lookie here" motion.

Archer speaks. "Teddy came through at the lab."

Iglesias takes off his own shades and puts them into his windbreaker pocket. "Thank you. This means a lot to me."

"Yeah, well. You owe me. They've been running a tight ship with the continual budget cuts from the federal government. It doesn't help the Department of National Defence wants to keep Major Crimes Drug Unit in check."

"Still, eh?" Iglesias asks.

"Things didn't change much after you went on hiatus. For three years these jokers maintain, failing to stop it. That's what they're interested in. There's no goal for finding the ash source, or the Moths."

"Figures. You got the DNA results?"

"Sure did. By the way, Sergeant Bando wants you to drop by and say hi," Archer says while passing him the documents.

"I'll keep that in mind." He has no interest in going to work. It's too close to his past, which will never be. It reminds him of neglecting José's time. He was chasing criminals for the greater good, that same good that ended with his son dead and Iglesias alone. Lawbreakers and delinquents are a constant and it doesn't matter how many of them are behind bars. Shifty lawyers and paid-out judges release the scuzz of society onto the streets.

A fool is what Iglesias was. He was blind to the fact that there is no change in the world and life is a fragile gift, taken away in a sudden swoop. Hindsight wisdom says he was better off spending time with those he loves rather than chasing madmen's dreams of a better tomorrow. Too late now. Corruption, money, and idealistic delusions move society forward.

"These are strange," Archer says. Her voice pulls Iglesias from his downward spiral. She steps to his side to view the documents as he flips them open. "I took a peek at them. You were right regarding the blotch being blood. Close to ash, actually. As for the horn. Shit. I don't have a clue."

"What do you mean?" Iglesias asks. He finds the horn sample document, skimming through the rows of data on the DNA test report.

"Look at it. It's completely unknown. Not a single percent found on earth, other than the damn thing is made of carbon and a few proteins."

"Like all life forms," Iglesias says. The paper sections off each row based on percentages of: Unknown A, Unknown B, Unknown C. It's ninety-nine percent unknown. Lola Cabello has taken him into uncharted territory.

He turns to the first sample of blood. Yes, it has the same elements as described in ash. It's missing the hallucinogenic properties. The drug is the closest thing to it.

The memory of Disk's security camera clip floods his mind. The grainy and pixelated recording was clear enough to show a humanoid reptilian tail swaying. They have video evidence, skin, and a blood sample. This information would be sufficient on its own to announce a missing person case. It's hard not to apply the same rules to accept reptile people.

"Yeah, strange." Archer folds her arms. "What's next?"

Right, Iglesias must bring Archer in. They had a deal, fair, and square. The excitement of the DNA samples and the thoughts of his son made him forget. His fixation on this is getting the better of him.

"Okay, you wanted to be a part of this?" Iglesias asks.

"That was the point." Archer shifts her stance. "You're providing consulting work. I'm on the clock."

"It's going to take some convincing." He puts his shades on and takes his cellphone, texting Disk:

> (you: hey, I'm on my way. Bringing in a colleague that can help.
>
> 1:45 PM)

"How so?" Archer asks.

"Well, I didn't believe it myself. The pieces keep aligning. I'll introduce you to an outsider I'm working with." Iglesias takes his keys. "Follow me."

The two hop into their vehicles with Iglesias in the lead. He grips his wheel at twelve o'clock, pondering the documents that rest on the shotgun seat beside him. It can't be true. Though that's the reason Cabello gave him the horn and why he collected that black liquid from the floor of the abattoir plant. It's a hunch and his instincts were right.

They drive to the same motel Disk stayed at. Both exit their automobiles with Iglesias holding the documents tight to his chest as they approach a new unit on the ground level. He knocks on the door with a loud thud.

He leans into Archer and whispers, "They're a bit twitchy."

"Gotcha," Archer says.

The locks rattle and swing open, with Disk standing in the same trench coat and hoodie they had before. They smile and make one jump to the side, waving them in. "Detective Iglesias, that's great!"

Iglesias and Archer step in. "This is Detective Archer."

Disk waves in a jerk motion. "Hi, I'm Disk."

"Hey," Archer says, taking off her shades.

Both officers inspect the room. It's the same as before. The laptop is on the bed. Two additional portable monitors attach to it. Papers cover the sheets, desk, and floor. The brief case with the cork board of Crystal Moths sits on the table. A new second panel of the same size rests beside it.

"You got a complete operation here, Iglesias," Archer says while strolling around the room. She leans over to examine some documents on the bed: newspaper reports, articles printed from online, photographs, sticky notes, and maps.

"It's a lot to take in and I'm digesting it," Iglesias says.

"Who are you, Disk?" Archer asks.

"One piece of a larger hive. We focus on helping those that fell through the cracks, those where the system has failed. We correct the mistakes done by the governing bodies whose corrupt authorities fail to complete their public servant duties."

Iglesias extends his hand to the kid. "They're a hacker."

"That's part of what I do," Disk says, folding their arms. "Can we trust her?"

Iglesias nods.

Archer removes her shades and smirks. "I've been vetted?"

"You betcha," Iglesias says. He points at Disk and Archer. "Give her the same pitch that you gave me. Start with the video, and work backwards."

Disk takes a deep breath with annoyance. "Okay." They take their laptop and rest it on their forearms. With a few clicks, they open the recording Iglesias saw before. Archer bites her knuckles, watching the short clip loop twice before Disk pauses it.

Archer's brows furrow and she points at it. "Play it again." Disk obeys, and the video loops three more times. "We spent countless hours scrubbing for security footage."

Iglesias says, "Hackers."

"Eden Breaker," Disk says. They put the laptop on the bed.

"Cute club names aside, who the hell you?" Archer asks.

"I'm a single function of an international organization, that's it. I'm in the first tier, we go by the name One. I had an online alias before Eden Breaker and prefer Disk. Still, I'm One. There's four tiers, complimenting the mythos of Eden as set by our founder."

"Who is?" Archer shakes her head in annoyance.

"Long dead, doesn't matter." Disk blinks twice.

"Okay, and what's your purpose, as tier one?" Archer asks.

"To find Iglesias. To keep tabs on Lola Cabello."

Archer puts her hands on her hips, glaring at him. He nods.

Disk continues, "Where has Cabello been for the past twelve months? Vanished. The exact same time as the Radiate Primate shootout. Oh, Iglesias, by the way, I have a request for the files. They're from a good source."

"What?" Iglesias asks.

"Sorry, the, uhm, the cameras. A source is getting them."

"From?" Iglesias leans forward.

Disk scratches their neck. "From Radiate Primate. I told you I knew what happened to your son?"

He leans back and folds his arms. "We've been through those. They were fakes in the lounge."

"Says the police force, part of the system, no offence. I'll show you when I have them. Anyways to the point—"

"Hold on, you're getting the footage from the club?" Iglesias says.

"Yeah, I said that."

Iglesias's throat tenses as Disk brings Archer up to speed. *Could it be?* he thinks. The kid claimed to have insight from the beginning. He prays it's true, watching Disk show Archer the corkboard with Mastema and the two Moths below it.

". . . And when you dig further, these henchmen don't age, like Mastema. Unlike him, they have these fangs when you analyze the photographs close enough. I'm researching for that. Ash appears in 2016 and their entire operation changes. Before they worked in the shadows, snuck into legitimate businesses, stayed low. It was as if they were in a slumber. With ash, they got aggressive, pushing the product out."

Iglesias walks to Disk and hands them the folder. "By the way, this will blow your mind. Look at it later. DNA samples."

Disk puts the documents on the bed with a toothy smile. "That's great, totally relevant. This goes deeper than the Moths being an ancient organization."

Archer speaks. "Is there any proof of this?"

"Yeah, here," Disk says while shuffling through some papers on the mattress and snags a printed news article of Dr. Lang's research into ash. "Check it out. That isn't my point. Disk walks around the hotel room and grabs the new corkboard with three sticky notes at the top. The first: Crystal Moths in pink. A second: Lang Enterprises in blue. Third: Allen Oil Site solutions in yellow. Pins and threads connect various components with portraits of CEOs and more Post-it notes with scribbles.

Disk continues, "Some of the stuff dates to the past century. Allen Oil Site solutions established in 1885, becoming a powerhouse in the Alberta prairies and expanding to a global distribution. From that point, they created sister companies, such as Allen Shipping Solutions to move their oil barrels. They expanded into importing and exporting international goods. They founded Allen Forestry Solutions to expand their energy interest. Before Prime Minister Stéphane Trudell rose to power, he was a shareholder for Allen Oil Site Solutions. Around the time of his campaign for office, Stéphane Trudell sold the shares. A silent investor, Mr. Patterson, became CEO, letting the former CEO Rick Pound retire."

Cabello mentioned the Prime Minister, Iglesias thinks. It's a fact he was involved with Allen Oil Site Solutions. Politicians are two-faced. Conspiring with gangs? Another story.

Disk chuckles and points to the blue sticky note of Lang Enterprises. "Meanwhile, Dr. Lang has those dragon statues made in Vietnam that I showed you earlier. He has an umbrella company for furnishing productions with a second organization, Lang Precision, that specializes in surgical equipment."

Iglesias says, "The Moths had affiliations in the red market."

"We didn't cover that in the drug unit," Archer says.

Disk continues, "No problem. Guess who ships goods from Lang Enterprises and Lang Precision? Allen Shipping Solutions. The working relationship between Allen Shipping Solutions and Dr. Lang's companies began in 2014. Ash came in dragon statues, packaged and ready to go. Need I remind you that in the province of New Brunswick, the first ash case occurred right here in Canada?"

Archer says, "Iglesias and I were there."

"Why Canada?" Iglesias asks. "There are plenty of other places."

Disk shrugs. "Testing ground? Easy entrance into the USA with our good relations? It gets more convoluted. Dr. Lang is a surgeon, researcher, that is public with his fascination in transhumanism and technology. He founded Manageficient Enterprises in 1994 because of it."

Archer says, "That's the bioengineering lab."

"Bingo. They explored ways they could enhance human genealogy. Reduce sickness, stop diseases, birth defects, you name it."

"They're pretty cutting edge," Iglesias says.

"They are. Why?" Disk points to the Crystal Moths sticky note. "Because Dr. Lang has connections to Mastema from the Crystal Moths, from Lang Enterprises in the red market to his bioengineering lab." They point to three additional sticky notes below. "GeneChron, BetterLife, and Medi-First. Mastema doesn't age. Neither do his two comrades. The Moths got a hold of ash in 2016 and Manageficient Enterprises develops groundbreaking bioengineering technology. His manufacturing company stores ash in dragon statues. He makes innovating research into ash. A little weird? They are finalizing a merge with Allen Oil Site Solutions. The Prime Minister is hands on with the deal. He and Mr. Patterson are behind Allen Oil Site Solutions. And don't even get me going about the news. CAMB? They're the government's little PR platform, if you ask me."

Archer looks at Iglesias, biting her lip. He raises his arms, following the points on the notes. "So they are in bed together, the Moths, orchestrating it. And?"

Archer points at the corkboard, "Based on this one line of research."

"Correct," Disk says. "Do your own investigating. This company hierarchy is public record. Use this as leverage. Either way, start looking into this Mastema character and see how far this goes. It's hard to avoid being recorded in history. I'm confident what you find will match my notes and this lab report you got."

"You did this in a week?" Iglesias asks.

"Sort of," Disk says, scratching their buzzed skull. "I don't sleep a lot."

Archer pulls a dart from her jacket pocket. "Smoke?"

"Yeah. We'll be right back." Iglesias takes his own drag and the two exit the motel unit.

Iglesias lights Archer's and his. They puff on their cancer sticks while watching the road. He is the first to break the silence. "Told you it is a lot."

"No shit." Archer takes a long inhale of her cigarette. "I think you've gone off the deep end, boss."

"It's Iglesias."

"Whatever. Who is this kid?" Archer says. "How did you find them?"

"They found me."

"But who?" Archer asks.

"To be honest, I don't have a real name. This is a new relationship, like my last intel."

"How can you determine any of this is credible? We worked our asses off to trace ash and learn who was helping the Crystal Moths. Disk claims these companies and the Prime Minister are involved? Mastema and ancient drug lords?"

"I didn't buy it at the first either. They showed me the video of that thing. You saw it."

She bites her lip.

"The tail?"

"I think you need help. You didn't talk to a therapist or psychologist about what happened to José."

"Disk has more than they are leading on. This kid has access to the Radiate Primate footage. I have to know who did this to José."

"Because they're a hacker part of some secret organization?" Archer's brows furrow. "You want this loser to be right, taking you on a righteous path to hell. Why can't you retire?" Her gaze holds on him as she takes an inhale of her drag.

A deep sigh escapes Iglesias's lungs, and he throws the butt end of his smoke onto the sidewalk. "You don't have to follow me. This is my life. Disk made connections far quicker than anything we have. They have shady methods online that we don't."

"You can't be certain," Archer says.

"No." Iglesias looks to the ground for a moment, then at her. "It's new intel that we didn't have. Internet dwellers are clever. I have to work on this."

"Fuck. I have to, too, bullshit or not." Archer finishes her smoke and flares her nostrils. Her eyes shift to the parking lot at a distant ghost in her mind. "I have to. I don't trust the DND. Things aren't getting any better. This umbrella company and merger Disk claims, I'll check if it's factual."

"We need to confirm it," Iglesias says.

Archer rubs her forehead. "Yeah, but this company stuff more so. That connection I have at the lab? According to Disk, is owned by Manageficient Enterprises."

"What?"

"GeneChron."

Iglesias wipes his face. *Right*, he thinks. How Archer was unaware beforehand would be a lecture he'd give if he were her boss. She's young and impulsive. Being within the law forces her to play by the rules. Iglesias, on the other hand, operates on the outskirts. He's far more cautious. He would have background checked this GeneChron prior. Iglesias is also paranoid, like Disk, and Cabello. Paranoia keeps you alive.

CHAPTER 41
FEED THE MONKEY

Three years on and she returns to where she was with Synarion. There is clear tension between the two, thanks to their opposing goals. The transparent nature of their relationship lets her heal. He removes her cuffs. She needs to eat proper portions, trim her hair, which grew too long, gain muscle mass; even then, ash calls to her.

A fresh shower stings her skin with each droplet of water drizzling against her wounds. The soap glides against the scabs, scars, and bruises, reminding her of the countless torture session she experienced. Toothpaste and floss lighten her teeth and leave them tingling.

One look in the mirror tells her she is a new person. Her father, brother, or Donnie wouldn't recognize her. Lola wouldn't either, if it wasn't for her own eyes that look at the blanched skeletal frame. Her niece would be unaware of the distinction. How old would she be? Ten months? It isn't important. She won't see the girl. If Lola can keep the Moths away from her family, she'll be at peace.

She stays the night at Synarion's. He offered her the bed, taking the floor. Once they shared the sheets together, and never again. She even questions her taste in males after her intimacy with Kendra. Men have been a prick in her life when all she wants is comfort. She must trust herself, which is following the ash. It's morphing her into a puppet, no longer in control of this addiction. An entity is speaking to her. Mother Nature? Once she spoke to her. These twin flames, they're novel. *The scales are the way*, is what the ash-dasher keeps telling herself.

Child of nature, comes the familiar voice, the mother's, as Lola lies on the ground, covered in sweat, staring at the ceiling. It is no longer an overhead. It's a black void with ripples of blue light. The entire room is gone. Metal, concrete, and the bed are replaced with rainbow-coloured energy swirling like a whirlpool above her. Lola's mind adjusts to focus on the undetectable to the five senses.

She ascends above, piercing through a vibrant array of moving colours, soaring through an everlasting fractal. With each twist, it spins further inward, revealing countless offshoots that lead to smaller fractals of light with endless possibilities beyond her reach.

The End, comes two deeper voices speaking at once.

Drawn in by the sound, she moves from a single captivating blue fractal to a muted grey one, then to a rich brown spiral, and to an eye-catching neon green swirl. In between these geometric circles, triangles and squares intertwine, creating a mesmerizing pattern of intersecting white lines.

Find the painter.

The colours and strokes of the fractal vanish. With the ash dissipating, her mind clears and she notices her body's presence once again. Devoid of the drug, sweat drenches her skin, muscles throbbing with increased pain.

Synarion sits cross-legged on the floor beside her, watching the trip. He rests one elbow on his knee with his chin is in his palm. She wonders what nonsense he saw while she was gone. Next to him is his laptop with CAMB's website's homepage. The headline article reads:

MERGER COMPLETE BETWEEN MAJOR TITAN COMPANIES.

Jobs promised for all.

Below is a photograph of Mr. Patterson and Dr. Lang shaking hands with wide smiles. The Prime Minister's signature tomato face covers the background, with his fingers cupped together.

Lola rubs her head, and with each motion, the room distorts, as if it were a painting coming to life. At the corner of her eyes, she catches fleeting glimpses of sacred patterns that vanish when she focuses on them. These reminders are a testament to the seamless integration of vibrations within the world that surrounds her.

"Was I gone long?" she asks.

Synarion shakes his head. "A few hours."

"The ash isn't enough." She looks at him. Mystical symbols radiate around his form, creating a glow around his head. It's a same bloom that each living creature has. Synarion's aura brings a strike of sadness. Like Lola, he is broken. She can't stay mad at him for the rest of her life. He betrayed her once. In a way, Lola's arrest happened because she didn't listen and broke their agreement. *It's the damn ash*, sober Lola reminds herself.

"You're walking a dangerous path," Synarion says.

"I won't do this forever. I heard Mother Nature calling."

"She speaks to few. Like the Creator, she doesn't see a point in contacting others." He heads to the kitchen and returns with a tray containing a black pot of tea and a small square cup. It's his magic remedy for rejuvenating the body. Though, he claims it isn't magic. Lola has witnessed its miracles of mending wounds.

"I heard another voice, deeper, cold," Lola says, taking an empty cup.

"That so?" Synarion asks.

"It kept saying, The End."

He raises an eyebrow.

"Find the painter, it said. The End."

"You're popular among the stars." Synarion pours tea into her cup from the pot. She sips on the maple flavour, despite the scolding temperature.

Lola squints. "Why me? Why not you, someone with more experience?"

"It's hard to say. The Grove failed Mother Nature, and balancers couldn't fulfil their duty. I'm a perfect example, as the last. The world is in chaos. You, on the other hand, catch the interest of Mastema. You intrigued me. The Moths didn't kill you. There's a fire in you acting as a beacon."

Lola rubs her head. "That shapeshifter I told you about? Used me as an assassin. Rithu kept me as a pet. Mastema didn't order my execution, not once. Dr. Lang and his experiments . . . What am I, Synarion?"

He closes the laptop. "You are sure Mother Nature is calling you?"

"No. I felt her before when I searched for Bark Nose in the forest, years before prison. She called me. Bark Nose confirmed it. I hear her now, though distant, and a new voice takes prominence." The Root Walker is an old world being Lola has not thought of in quite some time. It feels like another life whence she knew him, because it was.

Synarion rubs his chin. "This ash, it's destroying you."

"I don't think so. It's changing me," Lola says as she sits straight, then she takes another drink of tea.

"The withdrawals are worsening. The drug is killing you." He winces.

Lola runs her tongue along the roof of her mouth, thinking about his words. "Ash is guiding me to this painter. It's hard to say. I have to go further. It slips away before I can. I need more."

He folds his arms. "You're sounding like an ash-dasher."

"What about the Mother Nature balancer bullshit you do? Resembles a crackpot's manifesto if you ask me."

Synarion smirks. "At least it is a sober one."

"Mentally unhinged?" Lola says.

"If the shoe fits. The Moths, vazeleads, and other crooked minds are aware I exist. Yet they don't hunt me. They come for you. Hence this Dr. Lang has taken samples of your blood and skin."

"And what am I?" Lola squeezes her cup of tea, using it as a grounding object, to level her concern about what Synarion will say.

"Whatever it is, it made Scalebane fear their plan enough to aid your escape."

Lola eases the tension on her cup and places it on the ground. "Those men said my family roots mutate into myth. It has to be related to this entity calling me." She rises and grabs her jacket from the floor. She grunts, feeling a spike of pain run through what little thigh muscles she has.

"Where are you going?" Synarion asks.

"To get more ash."

Synarion stands. "Ash isn't readily available like it was three years ago. It's a luxury drug. You can't wander the streets and find it off of any Moth. If you do, it's a botched synthetic variant."

"Well, I need it. This is important, you understand?" Lola says.

"Yes, I do. This is why I'm humouring you on your ludicrous journey." Synarion scoops his laptop and places it on his desk.

He sits and fires it up again. "That's the reason why I'm going to help you feed your problem."

That's a relief, Lola thinks. From torture to escaping, she hadn't thought too far into how she would get connected online again, other than finding her laptop. Her next option would have been finding a public computer to access her ChickenFeed currency, and that's risking being tracked on insecure networks.

Lola takes a seat on the second chair beside him and watches as he loads a thor browser, gaining access the dark web's port. This is how he and Lola first came across each other, through the shadows of the internet. He starts up his email software. Sitting close to the nymph gives a whiff of his natural pine scent. Once she found it magnetizing, even now it teases. Sober wisdom finds it detesting.

"I'm getting in touch with Eden Breaker. Remember them?" he asks.

Lola does indeed. They provided a fake ID and credit card in another life. The mysterious individual also sent her a specific message a year ago. She was at Jack's place. Lola didn't learn what that zero.zip file contained.

She watches his computer screen, seeing he is using the same tacky email of oldworldshadow@wi7qkxyrdpvr.onion. His inbox is as bare as hers was the last time she checked her dark web account. Emails span from 2017 to 2019. He starts a new message while she examines the previous ones. A title, two dozen rows from the top, dated back to 2018, catches her eye, reading: Serpent's Tongue Breaks.

Wait, she thinks.

"Hey, Synarion." Lola scoots closer. "Can you open that?" She points to the email. "The Serpent's Tongue one."

"Why?" Synarion asks.

"I know that." *The plastic burning man.*

Synarion squints. "It's a key I got a year ago, though no file."

"Open it." She leans in, chin resting on her palm, fingers smearing her mouth.

Synarion obeys and double clicks it. A window appears with the email reading:

<0000@wix3d3nbr34k3rkks.onion>

To: You

Eden's Forbidden Fruit. Thank Zero. No questions.

Pf6pEwaV8qEuC8NmSfmvP2XpOtfFqWrbYGqnwkhh+kCvCKfydJ WBS79ydS76pj/F

"Holy shit," Lola mumbles between her fingers.

"You have the file?" Synarion says. A smart balancer, piecing this together.

"Yeah, I did. Sorry, do. Can you trust me?"

Synarion pushes his tongue against his gums.

"Trust me. Let me log into my email. Okay? Different thor browser tab, no funny business. I think, if I recall right, I got a file."

"Fine." Synarion rolls his chair aside, letting Lola take command of the keyboard.

She loads a new discreet tab, clear of Synarion's savings. It will erase her data after too. A few clicks and a username and password later, she logs into her dark web email. Lola homes in on the one from two years ago, ignoring the rest, opening the message: Eden's Forbidden Fruit.

"There it is," Lola says, leaning back.

<0000@wix3d3nbr34k3rkks.onion>

To: You

Break with the Serpent's Tongue.

Attachment: .zero

"May I?" Synarion asks.

"Yeah. It's a zip."

He takes control of the computer and downloads the attachment, scans for security, and renames it to zero.zip. With the encryption key from his email, Synarion pastes it into the zip's password gate field. The cursor switches to a loading wheel. A moment later, a new window appears, with four files inside:

- allen-tower-floorplans.pdf
- electromagnetic-flux-compression-safety-guide.pdf
- .forbidden-fruit
- banish-it-from-eden.txt

Synarion extracts them and opens the .txt file reading:

Disk <d3jdc6@kaa9cll.onion> beyond Eden.

He clicks on the .pdf floor plans, containing one page for each level. It starts with the basement belonging to Manageficient Enterprises.

"No fucking way," Lola says on an exhale, as if each word slides off the weight of the discovery.

"We've had this for a year." Synarion's voice goes up in disbelief.

"Yeah." Lola leans closer to the screen and points at the list of files. "What the hell is an electromagnetic flux-compression?"

"We'll find out." He scratches his neck. "I've been following Manageficient Enterprises's progress with the merger. Eden Breaker knew before us."

"Beyond Eden?" Lola says.

The two exchange looks, both concluding the same disturbing thought. Thanks to that text file, it's clear what Eden Breaker wants: contact Disk from beyond Eden.

"Thank Zero?" Lola asks.

"That's new to me, too." Synarion hugs his arms in a tight squeeze.

Lola rubs her head, moving her hair in random placements. "What of the dot forbidden-fruit?"

Synarion runs it through his security scanning software. The orange loading bar expands for several seconds, and a red exclamation mark fills the screen. Below the icon text reads: TROJAN, do not open. He raises an eyebrow.

Lola folds her arms. "Okay, yeah. We have a lot of work to do. This has sat here for a year, so it can sit a little longer. I need ash."

"Uh huh," Synarion says.

"How fast?" Lola asks.

"Ash? Eden Breaker is quick to respond. You must stay out of sight." Synarion types on his laptop in a new email message.

"I've been gone for a while. I doubt anyone other than the Moths are looking for me."

"I think you should read some of the news on you. It's not the Moths. Did you know they're making a documentary about you? Well, a docuseries, because the story keeps evolving."

"What?" Lola squints.

"It'll air on CAMB's network, too. Funded by Dr. Lang's umbrella company."

She rolls her eyes. "Great."

"Fascinating how fixated everyone is with you."

"It's not what I asked for. I want to do right," Lola says. She grabs her right forearm and digs her fingers into the skin.

"Instead, you keep burning everything in your path."

Lola's voice lowers to a whisper. "I can't stop, Synarion." Her tone is a beg for mercy.

He turns to face her, brows slanting. "There's no going back for you, is there?"

As she sits, she drives her nails deeper into her arm. Her leg bounces. The swirling drug and gripping fear create the spasm. It's true, Lola is incapable of stepping away. Revenge isn't the only thing on her mind. Her experience with Rithu, and ash, is giving her an additional purpose. The hunger for vengeance ignites her soul's fire. This new, unclear agenda merges with it. She needs more than dismantling the Moths and assassinating Mastema. The beyond calls to her. The twin flames illuminate the way, casting a soft glow in the darkness. She is unaware of what it involves. She's determined to find out, even if she has to consume a mountain of ash.

CHAPTER 42
FORK IN THE ROAD

Each time a person gets too close to the Crystal Moths, they slip off the edge, into a rabbit hole and beyond the conformity machine that keeps civilization safe. Compliant groupthink ensures that the herd survives. Stray too far, and it's over. Iglesias is near the Moths and is teetering the cliff, dragging his colleague with him. He lights another smoke, as does Archer, contemplating the news she shared.

"Teddy isn't a Moth. Once he is done, that test goes into a database," Archer says, lighting a drag. "You say Disk's research is good, then that's that. I figured it was fine, off the DND's radar. I didn't think I'd hand it to fucking Moths." She takes a big puff and exhales towards him.

Maybe it won't go anywhere, is what Iglesias wants to tell her. That isn't the case. They've seen what the Moths do. If this grand web of connections is true, it's too late and the Moths are aware of what Archer has done.

"I'll make something up," Archer says. "It's accurate. You're my consultant, had some research on the lead, and it's a dead end."

"What about Ted?"

"Teddy. He'll be good. They analyze weird samples. Ask anyone who works in a laboratory. Messing around with unknown substances is a pretty common. Detectives finding obscure objects related to the ash case without the DND being involved for national security is a whole other thing."

He lights a cigarette and inhales. On the exhale, he speaks. "I told you this is a dangerous path. You can walk out."

"Let you do it on your own? Please." Archer takes her phone, holding her smoke in her mouth while typing. "Hold on, telling Amy I'll be late for dinner plans."

Been there, Iglesias thinks. The girl is a disturbing parallel of his own past. He wishes Archer didn't join for her own sake. He's glad though. Disk doesn't have the guts to handle the physical world. They're an effective data head. Iglesias has street smarts and wisdom. Add Archer into the mix with her attitude, connections, and stubbornness, and they form a powerhouse.

"Okay," Iglesias says as he adjusts his weight onto his left foot. "Last chance, you're in the dirt. You like this Amy girl. You can apologize to the DND and let this blow over. You can live a happy life. You've seen Disk's video, the pitch, and the data. Or you have the option to come with me and the three of us can plan our next course of action."

Archer pauses typing. "Which is?"

"Well, I'd be interested to see this footage from Radiate Primate when Disk gets it. I want to cross-reference Disk's research into these companies."

Archer puts her phone away and flicks the butt of her cigarette. "Solid. I told you I'm in."

Iglesias smiles. It's a victorious one. That's an emotion that hasn't risen for a while. He's glad to have her aboard. They step into the motel to find Disk sitting cross-legged with their laptop on their lap, glued to the screen.

"Did you guys see?" Disk says as soon as they enter.

"What?" Iglesias asks.

"Manageficient Enterprises and Allen Oil Site Solutions finished the deal. They've merged."

"The evil masterminds," Archer says while walking to the briefcase on the desk. She points to the photo of Mastema. "You need to walk me through this again."

Disk hops off the bed and sighs, heading to the table. "Okay, we have a lot to go through."

"I'm not a beginner," Archer says. "Tell me where you got each piece of evidence."

"A range of sources. This is what Eden Breaker does. We work as a single entity, combining our skills and sharing information. When a member, or an outsider, submits a ticket, it funnels to tier one. If it's too big of a task, it runs up the flagpole to the experts. We communicate on a shared thread and vote. Simple."

Archer folds her arms. "How specifically did you get these photos and names?"

"I submitted internally to Eden Breaker. The ancient art you can find online."

Iglesias walks over to them in a slow stride, glancing at the three monitored computer. The right one has the CAMB website open with a photograph of Dr. Lang, Mr. Patterson, and the tomato Prime Minister. On the middle screen is a chat program. It resembles the old DOS interfaces he used in the eighties with the black background and white pixelated text. He takes a skim at the monitor, not leaning in.

The toolbar at the top reads: Snake's Tree. A left column contains a list of names and groups for communication threads. The far right is a ticket system. The title bar states: Operations. Each row has a number with either a red, green, or orange label with a plus button to see more. One expanded green entry reads:

NEW TICKET: oldworldshadow@wi7qkxyrdpvr.onion

TITLE: Old World Shadow Under the Moth's Wing

INTERNAL DESCRIPTION: Wishes to fly beneath the Moth's purple haze with Eve

STATUS: Cleared

ORIGINAL MESSAGE:

Eden Breaker,

It's your friend along the West Coast, with an odd, request. Don't think I've gone off the deep end, okay? My situation has mutated and once again, I am in need of multiple things.

First, do you have a connection to obtain a scale? Yes, that one. It must be a steady supply, as this will be re-occurring purchase. It's not for me. And as usual, payment upfront. I've sent it through the regular methods.

Second, it looks like I need a new ID with a new name. Remember the task you completed for me a few years ago with the credit card? Talia Marquis? You should have the photo of her. She's aged a little bit, you'll see from the attached mugshot. Those three scars are quite prominent.

As with each encounter, Eden Breaker, you are a Saint.

-S

=== INTERNAL CHAT ===

you: I'll take this one. Old world and I have done a lot together.

operator: And you can get the scale?

you: I have a few connections and have the photo of the gal on file.

operator: Task is yours. Submit when complete.

Talia Marquis, Iglesias thinks. There is an overflow of information on the display. For one, Disk is dealing ash. This is the inner working of a black-market trade system and the supposed Eden Breaker that Disk works for. The name Talia Marquis simmers in the depths of his mind. He's heard it before, yet cannot place where. An old case? He is stuck on the screen, forgetting to move to Archer and Disk. Archer's voice shoots him into the moment.

"Okay, and how did you learn they were vampires again?"

Disk points with both sets of hands at the corkboard. "The teeth! The same faces. I'm not the only one who sees this. Not only can you see it with your damn eyes, run this through any sort of facial recognition software and it'll give an identical match. These people do not age."

"Vampire elites, like in Hollywood?" Archer laughs, shaking her head. "You got to spend less time online."

Iglesias taps the monitor screen and says, " Talia Marquis. Archer, ring a bell?"

Disk's eyes widen. "Hey!"

Archer puts her hands on her hips. "Talia Marquis, Yeah. It does. Wasn't she on the guest list for Dasco Amoss's opening, where Ashely Amber died?"

"That's right." Iglesias steps closer, towering over Disk as their eyes widen. He speaks. "The one Lola Cabello was at. Disk, mind explaining why you're selling ash?"

Disk retreats to the bed backwards. They hit the frame, forcing them to sit. "It's nothing, I swear. Requests come in and Eden Breaker takes it. Look, we have to make cash to perform the feats that we do."

"Jesus Christ," Archer says, smiling. "You had that on your monitor?"

"Yea, I . . ." Disk cannot find words to express their foolishness.

"So excited to talk about vampire drug lords you left your secret hacker organization open for a couple of detectives to see."

"No! It's not like that." Disk's cheeks turn hot pink. "We're working together."

"You're wanting to hold the cards," Archer says.

Iglesias asks, "What else does Eden Breaker deal with?"

Disk's tenses in a frozen shrug. "You guys are asking a lot. My God, what do you want me to say? How'd you think I make money? I don't work at a convenience store."

"We should arrest this hoser," Archer says. She squints at Iglesias, tapping her foot. "Then again, we can't."

Disk's shoulders droop, looking back-and-forth at the two detectives.

Iglesias asks, "Who is Old World Shadow?"

"A regular client." They reach for the laptop and spin it so the group can view. "We developed a repertoire online. I've processed requests for a long time."

"Like fake IDs?" Iglesias says. A soundless laugh escapes his lips. "You did one three years ago for a Talia Marquis? This Old World Shadow requested it?"

"Yeah, and it's obvious it's Lola Cabello, isn't it?"

Disk clicks through their computer's folder structure and opens a photograph. Iglesias and Archer lean in, seeing a far younger mugshot of a girl in her twenties with a sharp angled nose bridge: Lola Cabello.

Disk speaks. "For real, I was gonna mention this, easing you into what I do."

"By starting with vampire drug lords," Iglesias says in a lowered tone of disapproval.

Archer speaks. "We have a direct contact with a colleague of Cabello."

Iglesias adds, "This Old World Shadow is getting her fix."

Archer's crooked smile rises. "She's alive. We have her."

Disk strokes their throat. "I mean, yeah. She's been missing for a year and out of nowhere, Old World Shadow returns and requests a new ID."

Iglesias walks beside Archer, folding his arms. He'd like to ring this little prick's neck for not opening with practical information. He says, "You didn't mention Old World Shadow before. You knew they were working with Cabello three years ago?"

"I said I was going to tell you." Irritation oozes from Disk's words. "I have a lot to share. Believe me."

"So why now?" Archer asks. "A little late to work with the cops, don't you think?"

"There's some funny business happening inside Eden Breaker. Like there is corruption in the law, the government. The Moths infect each thing they contact. I'm concerned with who I can trust. I background checked both of you. I know you're clear."

"Excuse me?" Archer asks, taking a step forward.

Iglesias extends his hand. "Easy."

"It wasn't much, I swear." Disk shakes their head several times. "I follow Cabello and you guys were involved." Disk rotates the laptop and starts typing. "Look, I didn't believe any of this stuff about vampires, ancient beings, or reptilian people until I dug into it. The proof is accessible if you understand how to navigate the web and talk to the right individuals. You detectives are familiar with that. It's why you're both here. You got damn close three years ago. The dots connect."

An exhausted sigh slips from Archer. "Since we're sharing with the class, did you know about GeneChron?"

Disk snags the lab result document beside them and lifts it. "Oh, yeah. As soon as you showed me this, I knew you guys fucked up."

"Thanks for the support." Archer says with a frown.

"Whatever." Disk rolls their eyes. "We make mistakes."

Iglesias says, "Back to this Old World Shadow, are you going to forge them an ID for Lola Cabello. Where does it get mailed to?"

"I'm sworn under oath," Disk says.

Archer chuckles. "Bullshit."

Iglesias says, "Come on, you said there is corruption within Eden Breaker."

"I trust Old World Shadow." Disk bites their lower lip, holding their tension.

"Think about it this way," Iglesias says. "If your Crystal Moth conspiracy is true, Cabello knew. That's what she was leading me to with that horn. It's why she called me. We should work with her and we should get in touch with her colleague."

"Let's think on it for a day?" Disk lifts their brows as their eyes dart from Iglesias to Archer. "This thing is deep, and it's why we have to be extra cautious. GeneChron? You messed up. We're moving fast and I slipped too with my monitor. We need to meet more frequently. Tomorrow? This was a lot to digest and you could proudly sleep on it."

Archer squints. "So you can book it?"

Disk says, "Why would I come here, stay for a week, and run away? It makes no sense. I want to work together."

Iglesias rubs his bearded chin. "I agree with Disk. Let's regroup. This isn't a normal case. Disk, text me your progress with Old World Shadow and I'll do some homework on my end. I'd like to double-check your research, if you don't mind."

"Yeah, totally," Disk says. "We have to build trust."

Iglesias adds, "Speaking of, the video?"

"Sorry?"

"Of Radiate Primate?" Iglesias asks.

"I'm getting it," Disk says with a flat tone.

Iglesias nods, staring at the kid. The moment holds. "Talk soon."

The two detectives leave the motel and head to their vehicles. Archer shoots him a raised eyebrow and smothered lips with a "what did we get ourselves into" face as she puts on her aviators and steps into the car. She is right. They're falling off the edge. Iglesias wants to make sure he's keeping his sanity in check. He is thankful that Archer can keep him grounded.

He drives home, remembering that he needs to water his plants. That stupid hobby of his is time intensive. As much as he would like to move on, nurturing new habits, he finds the task boring. It doesn't give him the rush that working with Disk and Archer provides.

He wants his previous life where he could check his son's room to see he is sleeping and safe from the evils of the world. He does this today and unlike the old times, José' isn't there. It's only him with a glass of whisky in his hand as his throat tenses.

The bedroom hasn't changed since that day. He takes a whiff of the air. His son's scent is fading with time. Not even the third drink can stop the sputtering from his lips due to the boy's fading essence as he slinks onto the carpet beside José's bed, sobbing.

CHAPTER 43
HELL AND BACK

Scalebane spins the business card between her claws containing the 6044121134 number that Jekos gave her. Murgo, what an odd location. With limited knowledge, she ponders why the gate to Hell is located there. She sits on a private jet flying to India. The Moths offer elite, bottomless cash. Perks with no questions asked at her level of authority. With one request, she can hop from Mastema's mansion to Vancouver, or to the other side of the world. It's astonishing, considering she has no actual money herself. Funds are a tool to the endgame.

The flight from Canada to India is long, taking anywhere from thirty-two to forty hours depending on how many stops. Private jets can cover half of the time and distance in one voyage before needing fuel. Scalebane stays in the cabinet during the pit stop. She doesn't need to be seen.

Downtime lets her prepare for returning to Hell. Meditation is key. Focusing on breathing pushes emotional-charged thoughts aside. She must harness her energy. This zen-like state serves as a time warp and she reaches India at the Kushok Bakula Rimpochee Airport in the northern east part of the country, south of Murgo.

The Moths are experts in smuggling. One gangster accompanies Scalebane on the journey, acting as the sole passenger. Within the cargo bay of the jet, she contorts into the small space within a wooden crate. The Moth brushes his white suit, waiting to close the lid. She squeezes into the tight box, sensing her left leg flare while her comrade nails the lid shut. He takes the luggage and drops it onto a vehicle. Scalebane senses rumbling as they drive from the airport. No questions asked.

The box cracks open miles away and Scalebane rises. She rolls her shoulders, bones cracking. Her body doesn't reduce to small spaces often.

"You're good to go, sir," says the Moth. The young man's light hair blows against his forehead. A smile of self-satisfaction paints his face.

"Well done," Scalebane says. She hops out of the box, boots slamming into the dirt. Steep tan mountains surround them. To the north, her destination, the peaks grow taller, coated in snow and ice.

Fourth peak over the Buddhist monastery, she thinks.

"When shall we come for you, sir?" the Moth asks.

"Rithu will contact you."

"Is that it? I could drive you to a town, Khardung. It's north, two hours—"

"No. Keep this quiet."

"Of course." The Moth takes a slight bow.

Scalebane pats his shoulder and snags her backpack from the crate. She doubts the man can hold the secret. Moths are loyal to Mastema. The soft skin is unaware of her exact location, other than the north. It will stay that way. He hops into the black jeep and makes a U-turn, driving to the airport, leaving Scalebane alone in the dust.

She's plotted the journey in Canada, and her canvas bag carries a map for reassurance. It's a two-day hike. Vazeleads move quick when on all fours to reduce the time. It eases the pressure on her left leg, utilizing the other three limbs. Boots laced and slung over her shoulders, she pounces off to the side of the main road, up a low gravel incline, vanishing from the highway and into the bleak grey and brown wilderness. It serves dual purposes. One: avert humans. Two: she can access the valley with a river. She can evade the cold until she passes Saser Kangri II with its steep snow sprinkled peaks which is the highest in the area.

Murgo is north of it, on the other side of the grassy canyon, following the stream. The temperature drops the further she travels. Winds bite, sending dust storms, and she understands why humans would call this the Gateway to Hell.

On the first night's rest, she takes comfort in a small cave, avoiding the freezing drop in temperature. A burning tingle in her limb reminds her that she shouldn't push her physical abilities. The constant pins that pierce her flesh leave her restless throughout the night. Anticipation keeps her blood running fast in her body. Sheltered from the nipping winds, she removes her mask and leather armour to breathe fresh air before closing her eyes.

The next morning, as the orange sun's rays pierces into the entrance of the cave, she wakes from a dreamless slumber. Scalebane covers her body with her armour, mask, gloves, and cloak to shield herself from the fireball's harmful rays. Even with the clothing on, she can feel her innards cooking from that poisonous sun. It doesn't suppress her will.

Her journey goes beyond the valley with great lengths that would leave a soft skin drenched in sweat. She finds the village of Murgo, complete with red, brown, and tan human structures on hills and the elevated white Buddhist monastery five hundred paces ahead. She stays clear of it, hiking higher, four peaks over. There is no path as she wanders up the steep incline of the mountain. With careful steps to avoid slipping, she presses on. After a hundred paces, her keen eyes spot a wide and short cavern.

She notes the stalactites covering the ceiling and jagged rocks that line the walls. She takes cautious steps into the entrance. The path narrows to a one-person passage. It descends deeper into the darkness until the light is gone. Scalebane is unfazed in the blackness, as her eyes adopt to such low, faint conditions. Generations of her people living underground have heightened their eyesight. She lifts her mask and ties it to her belt.

The path steepens into a sheer drop. The rest of the way down is a climb, using the uneven walls as leverage. This decline is thirty feet of careful maneuvering until her boots land on the ground, splashing into a puddle.

Droplets of condensation fall from the stalactites of the low ceiling. Water dripping echoes in the small space. The cavern's size is concerning. The gate Scalebane used as a child was enormous, intended for demonic armies. It would not fit in the structure she slouches in, inching further. Her mind says Jekos fooled her while her heart burns in desperation.

The trail zigzags, winding deeper, until she reaches the end. A twenty-foot dome encompasses the space with long needle stalactites. If she lifted her claws, they'd touch the lowest one. This open room has a moat with low fog above the water, reaching her ankles. Her path goes over a small stone bridge, taking her to the centre. Rocks illuminating green runes pierce through the mist. Jekos didn't fool her after all.

These crude symbols trigger a memory deep within the dark depths of Scalebane's mind. Her eyes widen as she freezes in place. The vision blasts her with the scent of metallic blood, dust, howling winds, and the sight of wretchedness.

Go my girls, I love you! her mother had shouted, turning to face a swarm of horrendous, stitched-together pink-and-red abominations. Scalebane held Namsruc's claws tight while they watched their mother's tail sway, daggers drawn, ready for battle. The atrocities hobbled towards their mother in marionette motions, as if they were commanded by some invisible, distant, force. Scalebane's heart had sunk into her stomach as a biting cold breeze scraped against her back. This was the same moment that a stranger's milky hand reached for hers and Namesruc's shoulders.

This being, resembled a man, but had pointed ears, looked down at them with concern in their purple eyes. He stood within a snowy landscape encompassed within a massive half circular stone frame, as if it were a painting. Glowing green runes were etched into each rock that made up the gate's outline. The fact was this stone entrance was a portal to escape from hell.

Scalebane's mother was a brave warrior, sacrificing herself for her children to return to the land of the living. The portal had closed that day once the purple-eyed stranger took the Scalebane sisters in. Those green runes around the frame fizzled out and its passageway rippled once and faded into the foggy air, leaving them atop a frozen mountain. If only Synarion kept his silent promise to their mother, the current situation would be different.

Scalebane shakes her head several times to shove the past aside and return to the present.

These illuminating crude and jagged glyphs mirror the gate of her childhood. Some of them match, others she doesn't recognize. Each are made of up various lines, dots, squares, triangles, and circles arranged, overlayed, and combined in different mosaics. None of them she can read. She swears she has seen these in Dasco Amoss's paintings too. They swirl into what appears to be a spiral matte ball with small spikes. The closer Scalebane walks to it, it is evident that the object is breathing. The surface is a smooth exoskeleton consisting of iridescent turgite plates, giving the points a rainbow gradient. It's a creature.

As she approaches, a high-pitched voice rumbles from its core, reverberating in the room. "Through the mind, one goes, understanding the depths they rose. Here I am, in the land of the damned."

Scalebane stops as the organism unfolds, exposing its soft pink underbelly form. This section contains indents and swirls of flesh. It's a brain with the tip of the organ housing a yellow reptilian eye. The black slit gazes at her. Insect legs run along the sides, underneath the lip of the back. It has no eyelids, making the creature's gaze constant.

She taps her claw on her sai. "What sort of being are you to engrave such ancient ruins?"

The high-pitched voice comes from a small horizontal beak below the large eyeball. As it speaks, muscles and tentacles vibrate, producing the pitches and vowels within the oesophagus. "Birthed against will. Instinctual survival dominant. Fight. Live. Die. Questions not answered, drives one mentally ill."

"Head games? Are we here for riddles?" It's fitting Jekos sent Scalebane here. Imps and demons love playing. Scalebane went to the last physical portal, based on that succubus's map, that resulted in fire and an explosion. There's another way into Dega'Mostikas's Triangle, one that requires a willful mind to pierce reality. The method shouldn't exist in today's world.

The creature continues, "How can one live in obscurity? When so much is forced behind the curtains of consciousness? Reality is masked in a dream with a false sense of purity. Mortals deemed never free. Beyond life, the soul lives at Heaven's hand. The judges. Sought unworthy. Here I am, in the land of the damned."

Land of the damned, she thinks, a phrase her mother used. "Beautiful," Scalebane says. She takes a step closer, two meters from the being. "This is no normal gate, is it?"

"I see, this world of beauty, and it is not for me. Visions of Hell ever prominent in the mind. Tainted and not divine."

"Mental Damnation," Scalebane says.

She's cunning enough to understand how she and her sister were born in Hell. Their mother shared what knowledge she could with them. At the time, they were too young to comprehend it. Their mother had a life before Dreadweave Pass and the brain disease. It's a side thought that catches her off guard. There's too much of her past here, making her clear her throat. None of it explains how Jekos got the concentrated light into the mortal realm or where Namsruc is.

The creature speaks. "A name familiar among mortals. In a time before the present, when things were common. Now forgotten. As am I, as are you. Prominent Hell is. I wonder of the obsession with portals."

"Obsession with portals? Were others here too?" Scalebane asks.

"Through the power of the mind, they transferred into the land of the damned."

"Land of the damned . . . Dreadweave Pass?" Scalebane asks.

The insectoid legs perk straight as if the creature is cheering. "A historian. I am humbled to be near such knowledge."

"I come from this land of the damned where the skies rained blood from mortal wounds. The place of purgatory for the judged to repent. The others, what were they? Another like me? A fair skinned purple-eyed one?"

"Words paint familiar in the mind. Yes, come here, they do, and travel through the psyche into Dreadweave Pass with what you call Mental Damnation."

"Impossible," Scalebane says. "Is there no physical portal into Hell?"

"Long done with the collapse."

"All gates should be gone. A spiritual one? That disease has been long lost after my mother's courageous actions. She ended the fallen God's power. Carriers of the disease included."

"Tales of heroism. Terrors of power are not needed to repeat. Such times have retired, and the power of the fallen God was potent in post time. Ripples of his will shall exist in this world and the next forever more."

Gatekeeper, Scalebane thinks. Her mother's teachings informed her of creatures like this being. They're carriers of Mental Damnation. Powerful entities capable of unnatural godlike power. "If you do indeed infect the willing with Mental Damnation, then this is not a literal portal. You are sending the soul of a person into Hell."

"Their spirit transfers to Hell and back when the mind is in slumber and most relaxed."

Synarion convinced Namsruc to take Mental Damnation. It's madness, and Scalebane is unsure she has the strength to follow. "You infect the willing?"

"With the fallen god gone, his control is no more. Though as the gatekeeper, my existence is this gift. A living being with mutations swift. It grew, I grew, as one we're anew." The creature's legs tap its soft belly. "The first gatekeeper, incomplete and deemed a bore. Chucked aside, left to rot, unaware that I plot. A physical neglect creates the strongest will. I embrace the organism within. Am I what I was? Is Mental Damnation it? Or are we new to adore?"

Black thick liquid oozes from the crevasses of the exoskeleton. The element defies gravity, rises into the air. Although Scalebane can't prove it, she feels this floating substance is watching her, waiting to strike.

"We do not give this powerful gift to the willing. Nor what I give is permanent, for I give and take. If I did, mortals would break!" The creature cackles, ending in a squeal and the black liquid swivels inside the cracks.

Scalebane says, "Meaning you control how long people have Mental Damnation? And for what? What could you wish from life with your master gone?"

"My will is mine to keep. Those that look at me flee. Though you have no reference to the former, I assure you the one half was more. The world evolves, on and on, as I remain here. This gift is what I am. Can I leave this cave? I won't and cannot. I have seen through the lives of others. It is unsafe for me. Unsafe for you. The vision of the willing lets me live as many times as I want. All I ask in return for giving the temporary gift is to watch, and live through the other's eyes."

Scalebane's tail sways side to side. "You can live through memories?"

The creature's legs tap its brain body.

Seeing as Namsruc and Synarion aren't here, Scalebane pieces together the probable scenario. This creature, the last gatekeeper, struck a deal with them. In exchange for memories, it infected them with Mental Damnation, letting them into Dreadweave Pass. Synarion looked for his dear Valturus. Their souls returned. Scalebane's cleverness sparks more ideas.

"Tell me, you have the memories of the people you gave Mental Damnation to?"

"Lives that I cherish, they consider nightmarish."

"Can you pass on these memories?" Scalebane asks. "I do not wish to go into Dreadweave Pass." That's a partial truth. Scalebane would love to discover what happened to her mother. She's not naïve enough to explore the endless wasteland of the suffering to find one soul from centuries ago, unlike the nymph. She continues, "I offer my memory to you, so you can share yours with me."

"Knowledgeable and cunning. A bold soul, I admire. A request I have not performed."

"Can you attempt it? Or tell me what happened to the other like me and the fair skinned one?" Scalebane asks and takes a step closer.

It curls with a squeak. "I cannot guarantee."

"Aren't you in control?"

"One must embrace the disease." The black liquid slimes from the creature's exoskeleton, rising a meter high, gazing at Scalebane. "Memories pass in between Mental Damnation, for I am a carrier, gatekeeper, while you . . . you are nix."

"I'm willing to attempt this if you are, in exchange for my memories," Scalebane says. "If that fails, you tell me what happened to them." She'd prefer to witness Namsruc's experience first-hand. Understanding her emotional state and thoughts would be far better than the riddles of this thing.

Scalebane gets on her knees and takes off her hood, letting her black and deep blue scalp feathers puff. "One attempt." Her flaming eyes flicker, pupils scanning the floating black ooze and the being's eye.

The creature groans and strokes its small beak with one pointed appendage. "Daring I admire. We will attempt your mission that illustrates dire. Stay still, you must, my child."

Scalebane places her claws on her knees. The creature's insectoid legs spread wide. Black liquid pushes out of its cracks, slithering towards her, separating into multiple currents. She keeps her gaze forward, ignoring the impending Mental Damnation. Her mind focuses on her breath. Meditation is key. The disease inches closer until the small streams reach her face. They slip into each nostril, ear hole, mouth, and even squeeze in between her eyelids, passing through the smokeless flame. The impact forces Scalebane's head back, prying her jaw open as the substance floods into her body and tunnels into her brain.

Sandpaper runs along her innards, scraping against the boulders that slam against her skull. Glass shards penetrate her mind, leaving her a thoughtless prisoner to the pain. Her ears burn with fire. Throat tenses, preventing air into her lungs. She smells her own metallic blood. The world around her fades into darkness, and her senses numb, helpless, and disconnected from her physical form.

Feelings rise from the depths of her heart, some that she once suppressed. Longing for her twin pulls at her soul. A brief flash of her mother's fast flaming eyes consumes her vision. The black and deep blue scalp feathers, mirroring Scalebane's, blow in the red dusty air. She gives a toothy grin below her grey sombre scales, the same loving smile she gave her children.

Before Scalebane can embrace her, it fades away. She is in the cave with her sister and mother. They caught a young naked human tied like a hog. He screams in agony as they skin him alive with crude bone tools. The sounds of the man's death bounce off the cavern walls and into the pouring blood rain splattering on the dirt.

Days of rainfall forced the Scalebane family into the cave, eating the raw flesh of the soft skin. It hurts Scalebane. They resorted to such animalistic behaviours, tanning the skin for clothing and consuming the flesh as sustenance. The disgusting act makes her psyche revolt meat.

Her body twitches. It's not the same as the one she is seeing. This sense comes from a memory sparking sadness. It's the first time Scalebane felt remorse in her life, understanding that they ended a living thing to save their own. Scalebane's heart skips a beat as her past blips again.

She's screaming with such power that her throat turns raw. A marionette flesh humanoid hobbles towards her in jerking motions. The limbs contain no skin, muscles stitched together with staples and thread. Its torso belongs to a muscular man, while the head is an accumulation of teeth. The eyes are gone, and the darkness within the eye sockets sucks Scalebane in. Her sister pulls on her arm.

Their childhood comprised of running from the monsters of Dreadweave Pass or being them. Days, weeks, months, and years of torture fly through Scalebane's mind as her scream elongates with the speed of time. She's flooded with each horrific encounter of these abominations. Skulls don't match the torsos. Multiple arms on a single body. Skinless mutants. Others with the upper portion of a humanoid while the lower is part cavalry, created from four human legs.

A wince escapes from her throat, her physical throat; not the one screaming at the top of her lungs.

Only the wilful stay, comes the creature's voice.

The rollercoaster of memories blasts Scalebane with a new vision. Bright red blood drenches her hands. She cannot stop her body, witnessing her claws dig into the open stomach of a youthful soft skin, no older than herself. Beside them, a wailing woman cries, tied, resting on the copper dirt. Next to Scalebane is her sister, who also eats the pink tubular innards.

Scalebane's claw punctures her physical knee, reminding her that these are visions.

No! the creature squeals.

Scalebane's eyes fling open as the black liquid rips from her face, retreating into the creature's exoskeleton. She collapses onto the floor, jaw hitting the stone first. As she curls her body, exhausted exhales escape through her nostrils, stirring dust, coating the blood caked onto her mouth, ears, eyes, and nose. She hugs her legs as her stomach rots. Her heart hollows out a smidge more. Losing her family, and the memories of such a dreadful place leaves her paralysed.

The creature's beak clicks several times, and it speaks. "A two-way channel, Mental Damnation is not, my dear. Though your life has experienced much suffering like the other . . . Namsruc. Yes, twin vazeleads."

Footsteps come from the cavern. Scalebane sits as her weak limbs shake. Her stomach squeezes as if she hasn't eaten in days.

Her skin is dry and her mind fuzzed. She reaches for her sai, standing.

The scent of the approaching individual is faint, and familiar. From the low entrance, another cloaked being approaches. Their tail moves from side to side as he lowers his hood. The flaming eyes are Rithu's. His mask strapped to his belt.

"Scalebane?" Rithu says, entering the dome. His long black scalp feathers swaying against his shoulders.

Scalebane takes one step and her leg gives out. She collapses onto the ground.

"Not so fast, soul traveller," the creature says. "You left this flesh cell for another in the after. Returning is an unfamiliar form."

Rithu hurries to help her sit. He looks at the being and asks, "What did you do to her?" A grumble rises from the depths of his throat.

"Upon her own will, she attempted to enter the land of the damned. Though time dissolves, she failed to penetrate her own memories. Interesting as they were, I could not share mine as agreed. The will is too weak."

Weak will, Scalebane thinks. *Synarion was right. No. Impossible.* She tries to stand, shrugging Rithu off, and falls. She grunts, curling into a fetal position. His claws wrap around her again. She speaks on an exhale. "Tell me . . . then tell me where did Namsruc and the nymph go?"

"They gave up," the creature says. "A fool's dream was his thoughts. Longing of love is impossible to wrangle. No amount of journeys through Hell can bring two souls together. Love is meaningless in Dega'Mostikas's Triangle."

"They l-e-f-f-t?" Scalebane asks. Her voice shakes as the sorrow in her overpowers the hate she once used day by day. Without anger, she is powerless.

"That is where my memory fades," the creature replies.

Scalebane surrenders into Rithu's arms. This is not the news she desired. She wanted to find her sister. It's unlikely because, for an obscure reason, Namsruc fails to return to her people.

Rithu lifts Scalebane, looking into her flaming eyes. "Scalebane, you were gone for weeks."

She blinks, dazed. "I what?"

"Two weeks and a couple days, to be exact."

"No. I left two days ago." Scalebane rubs her spiked brows.

A squeak comes from the gatekeeper. "Time distortion through Mental Damnation. You embraced the gift and the linear drifts. Flashes of the past create an aftermath, thus forever haunts you through its resurrection. Immortal memory lives. That is the true gift I give."

A wave of sadness washes over her, dragging her soul lower than her body. Her lip quivers with the desire to cry. Memories of her past loop in her mind, even in the midst of the mortal realm. Feeling the gentle strokes of Rithu's hand on her scalp feathers, she buries herself in his arms. His motion sparks the comforting memory of the purple-eyed father figure who once did the same when she was a hatchling.

The yearning to vanish and not be discovered again consumes her. The sheer magnitude of reliving her entire childhood is going to take time to process. She couldn't find her sister. Synarion won. Scalebane's defining characteristic is her lack of will.

CHAPTER 44
CYBER PALS

Throughout the summer week, Lola stays at Synarion's apartment. He lets her use the bed while she rests and sips tea to aid her recovery. With each passing day, her strength increases. His resources are hers as he gets more ash, except for his laptop. Of course, he takes it when he leaves. If he didn't, Lola would release her evidence. When the nymph is gone, she looks for her computer to no success. He may have destroyed it after all.

She can access her intranet from another machine and publish each video, document, and image herself. The process wouldn't be a one-shot like her QR-code tattoo. That requires the original design. She deleted it from her system long ago.

As much as she wants to release the intel, she needs Synarion's hospitality. His place functions as a base for the seasoned ash-dasher. Beyond the drug-induced visions, the practical information from Eden Breaker's Zero doesn't leave her mind. It infatuates the balancer too.

The two sit at his desk as they have before, with Synarion operating the machine. She slurps a bowl of chicken pho, embracing the salt and herbs against her tongue. This far surpasses the scraps of meat Rithu and the Moths threw at her.

Over the seven days between the ash sessions, they review the documents provided by Zero. The two research what an electromagnetic flux-compression, EMFC, does. These delicate instruments generate pulse magnet fields by compressing magnetic flux, measured in teslas.

Based on the Allen Sky Tower's floor plans with the basement belonging to Manageficient Enterprises, there's three of them in the lab. Each is in a self-contained space, connected to a row of capacitors, feeding into a single test space. The circular rooms are twenty feet in diameter. Their question is, why are they marked on the architectural diagrams?

The safety document contains technical information beyond the two of them. These devices generate high-power electromagnetic pulse energies, compressing a magnetic flux with large explosives. Key word: explosives.

It doesn't take a rocket scientist to understand what Zero and Eden Breaker are suggesting. Manageficient Enterprises is tampering with a dangerous edge of science. They partner with the sinister. Their lab must not exist. Lola's witnessed horrors are testament to the judgement.

Lola scratches her head. "Why do they have three of these things? What does it have to do with bioengineering?"

Synarion rubs his face with open palms. "Hard to say. Lots of uses for magnets. At those high levels, it can't be good. I did find info on gravitoelectromagnetism."

She pauses eating with rice noodles dangling from the chopsticks. "Grav-it-o-what now?"

"The relationship between electromagnetism and relative gravity. Gravity affects light and time, bending it. I'm not sure what for. That's what these things do, though."

"Bend time?" Lola asks.

Synarion hugs his chest. "No, they create a magnetic field and feed it into that one room on the plans."

The chrome pillar, Lola thinks, reflecting on being in the lab with Mastema and Dr. Lang. The shadow moved when it pulsed. She swears it did, like when she shot Mastema.

Synarion shifts windows on his laptop to a thor email software and loads a new message. "We've done our reading. Let's report it." He types in the email d3jdc6@kaa9cll.onion into the To field. It's the address stated in Zero's text file: *Disk <d3jdc6@kaa9cll.onion> beyond Eden.*

He folds his arms, knuckles pressed against his chin. "How do we want to word this?"

Lola swallows a chunk of chicken and clears her throat. "Uhm. Well. Is their name Disk? Or do they have a disk?"

"I vote name."

"Same," Lola says. "Mention Zero and Eden's Forbidden Fruit. The Serpent's Tongue has a gift. Something like that."

"Yeah," Synarion says. He leans onto the keyboard and types the email. The title reads: Disk, the Serpent's Tongue is Broken.

\<oldworldshadow@wi7qkxyrdpvr.onion\>

To: d3jdc6@kaa9cll.onion

Zero provided Eden's Forbidden Fruit for us to go beyond.

"Should we attach it?" Lola asks.

"Let's see where this goes," Synarion says.

They hit send and wait.

The following morning, a new message appears. Synarion sips his coffee at his desk as Lola exits the shower, drying her hair. Even after a week, showers are the gift of God. She marvels at each common world benefit as if experiencing it for the first time. The clothing she wears tingles. Fresh underwear has an unmatched completeness against her skin.

"The clothes fit well, thanks," Lola says as she squeezes her forearm. It bugs her he bought them. It's too intimate.

"Come here. Disk replied," Synarion says as he waves her over.

Lola drops the towel and hurries over, squatting on the chair. "What's it say?"

"I was waiting for you."

"Open it," Lola says.

A click of a button opens the email response.

\<d3jdc6@kaa9cll.onion\>

To: You

You mention the name of a dead man, right after making an ash request too? Cabello reading this with you?

Lola leans back.

"That's not the answer we were looking for, is it?" Synarion says. "Let's reply." He types at the keyboard with the following:

You

To: d3jdc6@kaa9cll.onion

Nice to formally meet. Thanks for the help over the years. You've maintained balance for Mother Nature. A dead man talks a lot for a cyber ghost. Take a look at this attached zip file.

Attachment: zero.zip

"Do we need that balancing bit?" Lola asks.

"It's important," Synarion says with sternness reinforcing each word.

"Uh huh. Keep me posted."

Another day passes. Synarion gets Lola more ash and groceries. She practices push-ups and lunges while he is gone. Without a computer, Lola is unsure of what to do with herself. That's how she spent her leisure time. In prison, she buried her head in books. Consuming media is what people do.

After three hours, the balancer returns with a couple of paper bags. He brings a magazine too, tossing it onto the bed. "Take a look at that," he says.

The cover has a picture of a man with a comb-over, moustache, and turtleneck folding his arms. The headline title states: Chasing Canada's Terror Ghost in the new CAMB Original Docuseries by director Ian Black. Below it are two additional articles within the *People's Reads* magazine. The titles are:

- Humanity's Shepherd into Bioengineering: An Interview with Dr. Lang

- Left in Ashes: Why the Term Ash-dashers Does More Harm Than Good

"Which one?" Lola asks, flipping the pages. She lands on the featured article showing the docuseries. It will air this Christmas season. *Great.*

"With Dr. Lang. Confirms what you heard in Mastema's cell," Synarion says. He puts the groceries on the counter and places his laptop on the desk. "Read it with a clear head."

"Yeah," Lola says. She flips to the interview. A photo of Dr. Lang forcing a smile is on the right side of the page. He wears the same lab coat he did when Lola met him. It sends a shiver along her arms, forcing her to rub them.

"Ash is on the table." He boots his computer, watching her twitching body.

He finds me repulsive, Lola thinks. She shouldn't think it. They have nothing and are nothing. Yet, she doesn't want him to perceive less of her. *Whatever.* He wouldn't understand what she must do.

The article is several pages. She skims it, sipping on Synarion's tea. Key paragraphs catch her attention, like the introduction:

Dr. Lang found his success in Vietnam, taking over his family's industrial factories. He moved to the United States of America, where he gained renowned recognition as a bioengineering scientist. His fascination with transhumanism drives his ambitions to provide a better future for humankind.

Another paragraph reads:

His company Manageficient Enterprise's newest laboratory is in Toronto, Canada, with the latest in technological advancements. The oil giant Allen Oil Site Solutions is funding their research in hopes of finding safer production options for their employees across the country. The federal government is looking to create more jobs for the Canadian people with these two corporate giants collaborating.

The key interest is the last paragraph:

Dr. Lang is proud of the lab's accomplishments. He says it has made leaps and bounds compared to his previous research and even beyond others in the field. He is vague on the details during the interview because they keep the data close. The doctor explains their information is in a closed network to prevent anything from leaking out. Allen Sky Tower's sheltered basement further reinforces their protection. He adds, "When the time comes, humanity will be informed. Key players, such as the Canadian government, are aware to ensure we stay within legal realms. I assure you, we aim to make announcements at the end of the year."

"Lola," Synarion says with flatness in his voice.

"Yeah?" Lola asks, taking another sip of her tea.

"Disk replied."

Lola chucks the magazine aside, snagging her drink, and joins Synarion to read the email.

<d3jdc6@kaa9cll.onion>

To: You

Nice fruit. Ripe for infection. Either you or an ally know too much about my hobbies. What do you want?

"Fair question," Synarion says. "What do we want?"

Lola puts the cup on his desk and sits cross-legged. "Eden Breaker sent the zip file in two halves, wanting us to work together. Yet, Disk isn't aware of it?"

Synarion speaks. "This may be a test. We're presuming this is Eden Breaker."

Lola extends a hand to the monitor. "It has to be. They know I am with you."

"If Zero is Eden Breaker too, then they aren't one person." He rubs his chin twice. "Okay, let's reply."

They type the following response:

You

To: d3jdc6@kaa9cll.onion

We were hoping you'd give us insight into your hobbies. If they are anything like ours, Allen Sky Tower is of interest. The Forbidden Fruit would do wonders in a closed network.

Synarion shrugs at Lola. She nods in confirmation, aware of the Dr. Lang interview and the .forbidden-fruit trojan virus in the zip file that they first scanned.

A Trojan in a closed off network is dangerous, she thinks. If anyone spends enough time on a computer, they are bound to have come across a virus. These malicious pieces of software are messy, and Eden Breaker has exceptional hacking skills, as they've witnessed. A Trojan virus appears as a gift and upon opening it, unleashes hell. The mystery of Zero is coming together.

The wait isn't long. Within two hours, another response arrives, and they huddle close to the monitor's pixels in anticipation of the words.

<d3jdc6@kaa9cll.onion>

To: You

You're both crazy. Not to be weird, but tell Cabello she rocks. Get yourselves a couple of USB sticks. One for mobile internet and a second to load that Forbidden Fruit. We're the Serpent for Eve.

"You've got a fan," Synarion says with a crooked smile.

"Apparently." Fandom isn't why she is doing it. There are countless cheerleaders on the sideline supporting her. This Disk character is new. Perhaps they can pull off this crazy plan with an anonymous hacker on their side.

A
C
T

IV

ACT IV

PERFORMING DESOLATION

[Lola Cabello ~~Documentary~~ Docuseries: CAMB Originals]

   [Take 1: Raw]

   [2019, November 05]

   [Kendra Green: Girlfriend]

   [RECORDING:

Thanks for having me. Yeah, prison, for eight months. Stabbed my ex. He deserved it. So this is about Cabello? Okay, I'm ready if you are . . . Go for it? Great.

I'm Kendra Green, I was in the Women's Correctional Centre outside of Winnipeg, Manitoba in 2018. I met Cabello there, and I liked her. She wasn't much of a sharer; her thoughts were elsewhere. I didn't mind. After my ex, I didn't want to expose myself to another man ever again. We had a physical connection, boy, that was obvious. Ask any of the other girls.

She felt the same about guys too, which let us be intimate, understanding without talking. I managed to extract some of her emotions. It was like prying open a splintered door. You get pricked along the way.

Lola wasn't interested in deep discussion. She enjoyed pillow talk and chit chat to pass the time. Anything with depth she'd ignore or change the subject. If I pushed, she'd walk away and dismiss me for a week as punishment.

I considered us in a relationship. She didn't. The other cellmates didn't mess with me because they knew I was with Lola. It made me feel special.

Something flipped in her. This new girl, Sierra, came into prison. She was a Moth and Lola couldn't stop herself. She picked a fight, killing Sierra. After two years of keeping her head low, she snapped, pissed her progress away. I was with her the night before. Lola was her usual silent self. I sensed she was gone, like she already committed the act, even with her arm wrapped around me. She had it planned out. Vanished for a year and to reappear on the news in Toronto with that tower . . . Wow. Next level batshit. I mean, I knew she had a background. Who didn't know of the infamous Canadian vigilante who blew Ashley Amber's face off? It was hot, in a messed-up way.

That was that. I haven't heard from her. I'm thankful.

I was more involved in our relationship than her. A part of me kept believing, hoping that she would come around if I showed a little more kindness. Come to think of it, my ex behaved that way too. You keep them hanging on by a thread, they'll keep climbing it. Reflecting on our time, it was foolish of me. Lola was in it for herself. The path of the dead she leaves behind is proof of it. It's not enough. Never. That's what consumed her.

END]

CHAPTER 45
INNER CIRCLE

Shame has left Scalebane hollow, smaller than her former self because her ego has shattered. This emotion floods her soul, poisoning her nature and rendering her self-conscious. *The will too weak*, the gatekeeper had said as she curled in fetal position, haunted by her past.

She couldn't break through the barrier of her mind. Rithu found her. Shame on her and her family name. Her eyes cannot meet Rithu's metal humanoid masked face as they return to Canada on a private jet.

Several Moths join them as part of the ash operation, typing on laptops or their cellphones. She and Rithu sit in the rear of the craft, using a fabric divider to give them privacy from the other suited members. It was by no chance Rithu found her on the other side of the world, in an ancient cavern.

"How?" Scalebane asks. She coils her tail around her hand, fingers playing with the appendage. Her right leg presses against her chest, curled in the seat. She extends her other leg for comfort.

"Jekos," Rithu says. "Mastema and King have been looking for you. We need to answer to my father."

I need proof of lightless ones, Scalebane thinks.

"He wants to understand why you're vacant. We have the entire flight to talk to him. Whenever you're ready."

"King won't want to wait." Scalebane unbuckles her leather armour's top three straps to grab her soulstone. Rithu does the same. After a year, she doesn't have concrete evidence of the lightless ones or her sister's location. She'll deal with her employer's scolding and handle damage control.

With a few strokes against the smooth matte surfaces, the objects project heat in each of their palms. The carved glyphs illuminate orange and they grasp their spheres. Light projects between both of their fingers.

The airplane vanishes from view. A new vision ripples in. Both see the familiar underground cavern that serves as the vazelead home. King sits on the stone throne in front of them. The plated layers of his gunmetal armour glisten from the torch lights on each side of him. His claws grip his soulstone glowing brighter than theirs. Unlike previous calls, King is channelling a three-way communication from his master stone.

"Father, I return to Canada with Scalebane," Rithu says.

A low grumble escapes King's throat, and he speaks in his iconic tone, far too demonic to be natural. "Vacant for two weeks and for what, Scalebane? A foolish attempt to locate your sister by willingly entering the afterlife, by the most unnatural means? I was present during the rise of Mental Damnation. It killed the other guardians."

"Yes, King," Scalebane says, monotone. She presumes Rithu informed him during their travel. Her mind wandered to self-pity during the trip.

"You understand that your mother's infection with Mental Damnation resulted in Namsruc and you hatching in Hell? Or that the brain disease was so potent, the fallen god came close to destroying our people and corrupting the heavens?"

"I'm familiar with the history of Mental Damnation, King," Scalebane says. This is the type of one-way conversation where she listens to the wrong she has done and agrees to do better.

King leans closer as he places one claw on his knee. "Why in the name of the Creator would you stoop to such measures to find Namsruc? She wouldn't have wanted you to do so."

"Because she and Synarion entered Dreadweave Pass. If she did it, I knew I could—"

"Except you couldn't, could you?" King asks.

Rithu shifts in his seat.

"No. I could not," Scalebane says. She swallows some saliva. That comment would have angered her before the journey. Her mental wounds lay exposed for the sinister to stab.

King sits back in his throne, making his armour jingle. "If it wasn't for Rithu, you'd be in that cavern, having that mind parasite feed off your memories. You should thank Rithu."

She's unsure if the gatekeeper would have. The creature was odd and reasonable. She wouldn't have cared. Scalebane hasn't thanked Rithu either. She won't even look at him. In her weak state, she accepted his embrace, being a scared child reliving her past.

Rithu speaks. "She was doing so for family. Blacktooths understand the importance of caring for our bloodline."

"I pray that you're wiser than that, my son. Mental Damnation is a long-forgotten evil with a rich history. It's one of the most taboo acts a soul can perform. As I said, it nearly destroyed our people. There're reasons the likes of Jekos would know it exists and where. Imps, treacherous things from the depths of Dega'Mostikas's Triangle." King puffs his chest, his claws digging into the armrest of his throne. "Through this, the unification of you and Rithu has failed. Why won't you look at my heir? Hmm? Tell him to his face after he saved your spirit, and I will bear witness."

Before Scalebane can defend her actions, another claw appears from the dark vision of King. This fist holds a glowing soulstone. Zoefani steps into view. Her silky midnight dress drapes against the floor. The long, elegant form stands beside her husband as the torch light dances against her silver scales. She shakes her head, causing the black scalp-feathers to sway, falling against her lower spine.

"Give the poor thing some time," Zoefani says.

Scalebane swallows a thick lump of shame-coated saliva. She deserves the punishment. She failed the trials of her will. *If I can't find my sister, what worth am I other than a Blacktooth egg dispensary?* A thought she'll keep to herself.

Zoefani continues, "Courtship takes effort, one that Rithu shall endure for a mate. Don't let his successes go unnoticed. He has grown much in the short time by overseeing ash while Scalebane chases ghosts. He works with Jekos, the Moths, and has aided Scalebane in her moment of need, on numerous occasions."

"He and Scalebane lost a prisoner, according to Mastema," King says.

Zoefani waves her hand. "Mistakes happen and minor damage done."

"Please," Rithu says. "Hear Scalebane's reason, Father, Mother. She has warned of a looming threat. Her actions are sound and I stand by them. The Crystal Moths are working towards a scheme that doesn't involve us."

King shifts in his throne as Zoefani places her claw on his breastplate.

Rithu says, "She acts in the best interest of the vazelead people. Why would this be different?"

"Because she is delusional of her sister's wellbeing. The nymph infected her mind prior to our teachings. It taints her soul," King says.

Scalebane sits straight, boot sliding to the ground. "Need I remind you, King, of the lightless ones?"

King shakes his head. "Not this again, Scalebane. I require eggs. Offspring from my son. Not chasing ancient evils that no eyes has witnessed, ever. They linger in mythos and sensed by the attuned. Ash and our survival are our priorities."

"Mastema isn't to be trusted." Scalebane squeezes her stone. "Why would I mention the lightless ones as a diversion while Mastema is close to synthesizing ash?"

"It is a challenging feat which we wouldn't have a concern of if we had hatchlings," King says.

"He sees beyond. I heard more, King. He's merging worlds that should not. Mastema seeks to edit our blood, mixed with humans."

"Blasphemy!" King hisses.

Zoefani tilts her head. "Why would you make such claims?"

"The same way I learned of the Moths' betrayal years ago with Namsruc. Their business partners are working towards a new era of transhumanism. Our future with the Moths isn't their interest, King. It's regarding merging our existences for peace."

"Let me speak with Mastema," King says. "It's obscure. The First is to protect the Creator's work, not reconstruct them."

"I should be there," Scalebane says.

"To make accusations against him? You'll flag yourself. I'll discuss with him and I will gauge the dangers of your warning. If Mastema is working behind us, I don't need you to take the blame, especially while working so close within their system."

"Of course, thank you King, for listening." *To a part of it*, Scalebane thinks. If she could get more proof of the lightless ones, she could handle both sides of the coin at once. Dasco's paintings aren't enough. Her instincts tell her they haven't got the full picture of what the First is planning. She needs to work with Eden Breaker to unravel the true secrets of the Crystal Moths and Manageficient Enterprises.

"We are well then? " Zoefani says. "Rithu has proven heroic and brought our dear Scalebane to us. This is a celebration, which King and I will toast to in your name with wine. I trust you two shall do the same."

"Of course, Mother," Rithu says.

King releases his grasp on his soulstone in motion with his wife and the vision of them fizzles out. The view of the grey divider inside the airplane returns. They put their soulstones away. Rithu glances at Scalebane. He shifts his gaze within the second. They won't celebrate with wine, as his mother hoped. There's no need to praise weakness. There is no bonding because of this moment. What is going to happen is, Scalebane will inform Rithu of her secrets because he is loyal, not because they are unifying.

"Did your sister find a way into Dreadweave Pass?" Rithu asks.

Scalebane nods. "Correct." She grips her wrist.

"Where is she, in Dega'Mostikas's Triangle?"

"No. She left the gatekeeper long ago. Rithu, I wasn't looking to go into Hell. You understand that, right?"

Rithu looks to the floor. "You explained the reasoning to me. You wished to witness your sister's thoughts, absorb her feelings, things that words cannot express. There's no need to be defensive with me, Scalebane. I am working with you. I said I trust you."

"Good." Scalebane looks through the window to the crisp blue sky and a blanket of white, fluffy clouds covering the ocean below. It's astonishing the heights they can soar with human technology. The view serves as a distraction from having to talk with Rithu more.

"You warned King of Mastema. Is it true? Is that why you let Cabello go?" Rithu asks.

Now is the time to bring Rithu into her inner circle. He has proven himself. "That's correct. Mastema's partner, Dr. Lang, is using her essence along with ours for experimentation. I didn't tell your father of Cabello's involvement. He needs to be let in little by little so he doesn't become angered and disagreeable. Look at how he reacted to my one accusation. Dr. Lang and Mastema spoke of elevating beyond humans. That cannot mean a promising future for us. Mixing soft skins and vazeleads? How much and how far? To paint the Creator's vision of a perfect universe? Sterilization of humans should be enough through ash."

Rithu ponders the question and taps his metal chin. "And Jekos? How did he know you would be in Murgo?"

"I asked him how to get into Hell. He knew," Scalebane says.

"You were aware she was in Hell?" the other asks.

Scalebane sighs. "I had a theory. There's a painter, an oracle. His works are beyond simple beauty. They're visions of the present, the future, and the past. They're cryptic and filled with more information than a codex. He painted Namsruc and Synarion in my childhood home. Thus, I tried."

"Of course, I would have too, despite my father's words today."

"You're as foolish as I am." A hint of a smile rises underneath her mask.

Rithu chuckles, fiddling with his claws. He asks, "Lightless ones? Aren't they a legend?"

"I fear not." Scalebane takes a deep breath. "The painter has foreseen their coming. He's progressing. I must visit him. I think it's related to what Mastema is scheming. Whatever is occurring in the lab is angering the lightless ones."

"What of Cabello? Or of ash? Mastema and King will need us to take care of these tasks," Rithu says. "I can't do it alone forever."

Scalebane crosses her leg towards Rithu and folds her arms. "What did Cabello do to you?"

"I'm sorry?' Rithu asks.

"She had a power over your mind. I am distracted. Not an idiot. You were aiding her over the past year, deflecting from extracting information from her."

"You let it slide," he says with a raised pitch of shock.

"Yes."

"So, you could work on this mystery? Why would it matter if we learned how Cabello got the concentrated light bullet?"

Scalebane shrugs, deciding not to tell him about Jekos. "Maybe related to what Mastema is doing. I'm uncertain. I don't think he should have knowledge of it. Answer me."

Rithu folds his arms and looks away, making Scalebane wonder what Cabello did to the son of King. He hasn't interacted so close to soft skin. Rithu's upbringing instilled in him a deep hatred for humans, as he was aware of the terrors they had inflicted upon the vazelead people.

Before he can answer Scalebane, a ringing comes from inside the inner pocket of his cloak. He reaches into the fabric pouch and pulls out a smooth rectangular shaped object made of carbon with a glass surface. A mechanical tune projects from the shape. This is a soft skin device. They call it the smartphone, the same type she used to call the number Jekos gave her.

He swipes the screen and answers, "Hello? . . . yes. I have her . . . you were right . . . uh huh. Here she is." Rithu takes the phone from his mask and passes it to Scalebane. "It's for you."

Scalebane holds the device by the edges as if it were a delicate instrument. It's not like the telephone in Mastema's mansion, which had a clear circular speaker and receiver.

"There's the speaker, and you speak into here," Rithu says, pointing at one end of the phone and the other.

Scalebane shoos his claws away. She brings the device to her ear hole underneath her hood and speaks. "Who is this?"

A high-pitched voice comes through the gadget with a natural crackle to the tone. "Scalebane!" *Jekos* . . . "I didn't think you would vanish for half a month after I told you how to get into Hell. The time distortion is a thing I forgot. Thankfully, Rithu came to the rescue."

"You didn't tell me it was Mental Damnation," Scalebane says.

"I didn't, did I? Well, I hadn't been to the location myself and knew that is how others got there. It makes sense it was a spiritual portal, hey? Come to think of it, I haven't seen a physical one in eons. Mul used the last gate to my knowledge. Remember her? You ripped her head off years ago when she owed me money! It's okay, plenty more where that came from."

Her portal was useless, Scalebane thinks, recalling the broken pillars and the map from the demon. "How did you—" Scalebane glances at Rithu who is polite and looks to the window. Scalebane pauses, deciding Rithu is too close to her, and rises. She heads to the far end of the executive section of the plane. "How did you get the concentrated light if the path to Hell wasn't physical?"

"Oh, I don't deal directly. I source it out. Eden Breaker comprises powerful connections to harvest the fruit," Jekos says. "Speaking of which, you met with my colleague?"

"Four, the shaper?" Scalebane asks.

"Yes, she's a charm. You didn't mention me, did you?"

"No," Scalebane says. She blinks once.

"Good. I operate best alone, like you," the other says.

"You're part of Eden Breaker?"

"I'm not in their tier system, I came before."

"Why trust me with this information and not your own?" Scalebane coils her tail around her ankle in anticipation.

"Time is of the essence, Scalebane." Jekos pauses, letting his words sink into her mind. "You and I see eye to eye. You care little for our common leader. Trust is a difficult thing to earn from you, so I needed to expedite our relations. Which reminds me, how did you enjoy the conversation with Mastema, Dr. Lang, Mr. Patterson, and the Prime Minister? Intriguing?"

"You take great risks with me, halfbreed," Scalebane says.

"They've paid off, haven't they?" Jekos asks.

". . . Yes." Scalebane doesn't want to admit it. Her discrimination towards halfbreeds, and imps, is a core part of her morale. Her ego has been so broken from her failures that admitting the truth to Jekos doesn't sound terrible. *Weak willed.*

Jekos says, "You didn't lose Cabello, did you?"

"No," Scalebane says through her teeth.

"As I thought. Can we trust Rithu? He was with you when you freed Cabello, right?"

"He was, and yes, Rithu is loyal." Scalebane sighs, admitting the words out loud solidifies the truth that she needs to accept Rithu's help.

"Alright, use him," Jekos says. "Don't bring him into Eden Breaker, not yet. Keep him at arm's reach. We'll need him to operate ash while you and I see to more important matters."

"Being?" Scalebane asks as she tightens her grip on the phone.

"I heard of your oracle painter and the importance of Cabello. We've pinpointed her location," Jekos says.

"As in the Moths?" She releases her tail from her ankle and it sways side to side.

"No. As in Eden Breaker. She has returned to Synarion, name ring a bell? And they're buying ash, for her, from us."

Synarion, Scalebane thinks. Her grasp on the phone causes it creak, then the glass cracks along the edge. If she meets the nymph, she can find Namsruc. The stars are aligning now that she clarified Synarion isn't in Hell any longer, thanks to the gatekeeper. "Let me deal with Synarion."

"Of course. I have no business with him. He's in Vancouver, go to him with Four and get Cabello. We'll keep her within our reach. We need to understand what she is doing with this ash. I assigned a project to her a year ago, and she finally accepted."

"Cabello?" Scalebane takes a step back as if his statement pushes her.

"Yes, one that you'll aid regarding Manageficient Enterprises and what they're building with gene editing. Their progress ceases at this moment. We have their building blueprints, and a plan hatched."

"To what? To the lab?" Scalebane asks.

"Listen, Four will meet you to find Cabello. They're unaware of the plan and will play along as Eden Breaker functions. Synarion ordered another batch of ash. This human gal could be a powerful ally. The group of you will share what each of you know to help Cabello's assignment."

Scalebane bites her forked tongue.

Several beats pass and Jekos breaks the silence. "Yes, you dislike her. Please remain civil."

"I have no feelings for the soft skin other than she is human," Scalebane says. The damn bitch crippled her leg. "Can we rely on her?"

"That's what you shall find out," Jekos says. "If what you say is true of the painter, then we should follow through with it."

"And what are you doing during this plan?" Scalebane asks.

"I need to meet with another member of Eden Breaker directly. A human within Major Crimes got a fragment of Mul's horn. A lab extracted her DNA. It's owned by Dr. Lang, which caught the attention of the Moths and the DND, reaching the Prime Minister and a hop over to Mastema."

"They have access to demon DNA," Scalebane says more to herself. She's piecing together the complex power of Manageficient Enterprises. DNA editing spearheaded by a doctor obsessed with transhumanism; backed by the First, who wishes to bring the Creator's manifestations into light. They have vazelead genetics, Cabello's old world blood, and a demon thrown into the mix for good measure. The seriousness of their situation is escalating far beyond what Scalebane predicted. They're knocking on the lightless ones' door.

CHAPTER 46
CONVINCING

The plants in Iglesias's home flop to one side with shrivelled leaves. They're not getting enough water or light which leaves them shrivelled, yellow, and dry. Each has unique requirements of heat and humidity which Iglesias finds himself incapable of offering. Not since he met Disk, who threw Iglesias in the same rabbit hole as Lola did several years ago. What happened to Cabello is a mystery. The prime objective is discovering what bastard killed his son. When will Disk have that damn video? They jump the gun too often.

He understands why Cabello did what she did. Family comes first. Vengeance is a toxic seed that has deep roots in one psyche. Iglesias can keep his job on hold. He's recovering. Revenge is a part of his recovery. This mess has caught the loyal Archer. It's in his favour. They have a rogue team.

The trio decide seven days was suitable downtime to process the information. They threw Archer into the deep end while she juggles her job. For Iglesias, he stews over the intel day after day, thinking about the Crystal Moths, their history, and these enterprises.

His research takes him online. Manageficient Enterprises is a good search topic. Public registry records show they own several labs: GeneChron, BetterLife, and Medi-First. Disk is correct. A local Toronto news outlet reports Manageficient Enterprises built a new lab every two years with rapid funding. He visits the company's website. Like each organization, they love a detailed history section to gloat their successes with milestones sliding onto the screen. The page reads:

The Story of Success

Since the inception of Manageficient Enterprises in 1994, the company holds its core values in the highest regard. Founder and CEO Dr. Lang's vision remains true to produce rapid technological solutions for gene editing and improve healthcare. His applications create tools for tangible and practical development.

- Manageficient Enterprises founded by Dr. Lang: 1994

- Lab One, Los Angeles, California in: 1995

- Lab Two, San Diego, California: 1997

- Lab Three, New York: 1999

- Lab Four, New York: 2001

- Lab One Expansion: 2003

- Lab Four Expansion: 2005

- GeneChron Acquisition,Washington,Virginia: 2006

- GeneChron Expansion: 2007

- Lab One Expansion #2: 2009

- BetterLife Acquisition, Los Angeles, California: 2011

- Medi-First Acquisition, New York: 2013

- Lab Five, Toronto, Ontario: 2015

Their latest addition catches his eye. The newest Manageficient Enterprises lab is in Toronto. It's their first international location. A search reveals it is in Allen Sky Tower. The same Allen as Allen Oil Site Solutions and the sister companies. Why would there be a laboratory in Allen Sky Tower? The history of Allen Sky Tower is clear: offices rented to other corporations, plus their headquarters. Iglesias writes his notes and scratches his beard.

He loads the city of Toronto's site to review issued building permits through their open data portal. Did Manageficient Enterprises get a permit to build a bioengineering facility in Allen Sky Tower? The official municipal website indeed states they did in 2014. A lab is an odd choice for a skyscraper. They have specific requirements in the infrastructure. Not to mention bio-waste. Each detail regarding these companies strikes strange.

Another search shows Allen Sky Tower began construction in 2012. The two enterprises were planning this laboratory from the beginning. Curiosity hits his nerve, and he accesses satellite imagery. One inquiry reveals an archival history website of global mapping dating to the creation of the skyscraper. He zooms into downtown Toronto to Allen Sky Tower seven years ago and jumps each month, observing the building process. The work starts with a deep foundation with intricate tubing and concrete, erecting past ground level and onward. It isn't uncommon for labs to be in the heart of a city. In the depths is unusual. Little by little, Disk's information rings true. Anticipation runs through his mind as the days crawl by.

One week passes, and the thought of Disk and their camera footage claws at his innards. A goddamn cocktease is what that kid is. He hopes they have good news as they, including Archer, hop on an internet conference call based on Disk's request. They texted Archer and Iglesias a web link to a site neither of them had seen before that processes video. According to Disk, it is more secure than the commoner's BoomChat app.

Iglesias loads the website on this phone. It shows himself at a bad angle. His beard can't hide the clear second chin. Shit. He moves the camera around, masking his shame.

"Hello?" Iglesias asks.

"Hey boss," Archer says in the distorted connection. Her face appears pixelated.

"So one week has gone by," says another voice. Its modulated sound creates a lower-pitched robotic tinge. The video shows a silhouette of a person in a hood. This is Disk, acting like a typical computer dweller. "You both in?"

"Yep," Archer says. "Thanks again. Weird at the office. The DND is making a stronger presence. They briefed our drug unit that they're tightening the ship, led by General Florence. It's got me paranoid because why now? Because I sent the fucking samples to the lab. Then General Florence booked a date with me."

"The General Florence?" Iglesias asks.

"Yeah, ring a bell? The guy is so busy, we're meeting in a couple weeks out, on a Monday. A big time general doesn't meet with level two detectives unless they want to silence them. Like you."

Indeed, the name triggers Iglesias's mind. He met General Florence once, when they lost the case. Correction: transferred the case to the military for the sake of national security. It was a demotion.

Disk says, "We'll make our meeting brief if they're hot on your tail. This encrypted communication keeps the data safe. There are physical eyes, though."

Iglesias says, "Agreed. We brought attention to ourselves. What of Cabello? Disk, you going to cough up Old World Shadow's address?"

"Not on call. I gave it some thought. We must work together. So yeah. Yeah, I will." They clear their throat, creating a strange glitched sound thanks to the vocorder.

Archer says, "The three rogue musketeers burning in a pit of fire."

Iglesias ignores her plea for help, masked as sarcasm, and speaks. "Disk, I can come to you in Toronto. Text me the address and we'll formulate our next steps."

"Wait a week. Let this cool," Disk says. "You'll get the address from a different number."

"What about me? I got to meet this General Florence," Archer says.

"Follow procedure," Iglesias says. "You and I won't talk. I'll take care of my plants. Disk will vanish. You have your cover story. A lead that went nowhere."

Disk speaks, "Don't chat with each other in the meantime. If you must, use this web link to communicate. Private browser each time. No traces, and the thread's history expires in twenty-four hours."

With that, the three leave the call. Online calls aren't his preference. He needs to look at people in the teeth and know what they're made of. He prefers smelling the sweat and blood. Besides, this tech gadget hacker stuff rubs him the wrong way. Who can say with confidence the law didn't wiretap them?

Iglesias is responsible for bringing Archer into this mess, despite her bullheaded nature. He sends her a message using the link Disk provided reading:

(you: Hang in there.
8:45 PM)

Archer replies within minutes.

(Archer: When you meet Disk, I'm coming with you.
I'm not getting left behind.
8:47 PM)

(you: Fair enough
8:47 PM)

His phone buzzes and a text from a new number comes in.

(613-228-9971: 806 70 Spadina Road
Apartments—Sterling Karamar
8:49 PM)

The following week, Iglesias picks up Archer and drives to Toronto to meet Disk at their small studio apartment. The two chat about the past seven days on the four-hour drive, discussing Disk, the lunacy of the situation, and the threat of the Canadian Military. It's a typical ride. It's like the old times. They'd brief each other on their knowledge and theories of what could happen next. The last time they drove to the metropolis, they were attempting to save José.

That video, Iglesias thinks. He asks Archer her thoughts. She has none. They need to see the clip.

Before the detectives realize it, the road trip is over and they reach downtown Toronto. They make a stop for coffee and a snack. Next, the apartment complex where Disk lives. It's metropolis living: street parking with paid meters; old school buzzer intercoms, flickering lights, cracked walls and chipped tiles in the hallways; shaking elevator, and a creaking eighth level leading to unit 806. Disk opens their door before either detective has a moment to knock.

They wave the two inside in a rush and close the door, locking it with several bolts after. The studio apartment fits the bill. A mattress rests on the floor with no frame. A hotplate sits on a small coffee table. There's one sink in the bathroom and an amazing computer setup containing six monitors, LED lights, and spinning fans. The familiar corkboards mount the walls beside it. This is where Disk spends their drug profits.

"Brought donuts and caffeine." *Not that you need any stimulants*, Iglesias thinks. He puts the tray of drinks and box on the table. He keeps the document folder close to his chest, containing the research he did on Allen Sky Tower and Manageficient Enterprise's new lab.

"Gluten-free?" Disk asks, sitting in their black and toxic green gamer chair. It looks like a space command station with the padding and the screens behind them.

"What? Goddamnit." Iglesias rubs his forehead. He's done this action before, once with José and Hailey. The boy's girlfriend was vegan. Disk can deal with it.

"Anything in the coffee?" Disk asks.

"Nope, black."

"Great," Disk says, rolling their chair over to the table. They snag a cup and pass it to Iglesias, then Archer.

Archer strolls around the small studio, examining the closed green curtains. She wanders to the six monitors, eliminating the singular light in the room. The glow emphasizes the bags grown under her eyes from sleepless nights. She says, "You got quite the setup."

Disk speaks, "I've been busy, so the place is a bit of a mess."

"Not judging." Archer walks to the bathroom sink full of dishes beside the overflowing garbage. It creates a sour funk they're forced to inhale.

Iglesias waves his cup to the monitor. "Drug dealing your main source of income?"

Disk shakes their head twice. "No. I'm Eden Breaker. Whatever they need me to do, odd jobs, selling, researching."

Archer says, "How did you get into this?"

"We going down memory lane here, or are we getting to work?" Disk asks.

Iglesias smirks. "Work." He squints at the monitors, noticing a video window with Hucker Dime at the top right. A layer behind has a clip of Donnie Morris. The kid has lost weight since Iglesias saw him. He still has his long black metal hair. "What are those?"

Disk points to the videos. "That? Oh. Nerding out."

"Are those interviews?" he asks.

"You betcha. Full, unedited clips of the Cabello docuseries."

Archer asks, "It's not out."

A wide grin rises on Disk's face, exposing a silver crown on their upper back tooth. "Eden Breaker harvests the fruit."

Iglesias sighs. "Piracy aside, you have Cabello's address. Super fan?"

"Old World Shadow's," Disk corrects, rubbing their neck. "Once I tell you that, we should switch to calls. It's risky that we're together. Especially with the military sniffing around Archer's business."

"I got it under control, mostly," Archer says. "I told Sergeant Bando it was from an old case. The week has been quiet."

"General Florance?" Iglesias asks.

"I have to meet with him. Monday."

Disk claps their hands. "Great, after we can go online again. I can't afford motels and I don't like sharing my address."

Iglesias scratches his head. "Yeah, those don't do it for me, kid. There's an energy to being in person, a type of magic you can't get from anything else."

Disk chuckles. "Magic? And I'm the crazy one."

"It's a figure of speech, Einstein."

Disk shrugs. "Sometimes I wonder if that's where this is leading to."

"What makes you say that?" Iglesias says.

Disk spins the chair to their desk and hammers on the keyboard, popping a new window on the bottom middle screen. Iglesias walks over to them. Disk nods at a small drummer stool beside a guitar tucked behind the workstation. He snags it, sitting next to them. The seat squeaks as he sits on it. *It's the grinding metal, not the weight.*

"So do you want to talk about Old World Shadow or magic?" Disk asks.

Archer stands between Disk and Iglesias. They exchange looks. Iglesias breaks the silence and says, "Show us the magic and we'll swing to Cabello and Old World Shadow."

Disk fires up a video on their computer and pauses it. From the paused preview, it's a security footage showcasing a nightclub lounge. The clip has a timestamp and date: 2018, August 24. This is it. The recording. Iglesias's heart stops and he scratches his beard.

"Yeah," Disk says. Iglesias's face must say what he thinks. "If you want magic, and vampires, and some answer to what happened to your son, only if you're ready."

Iglesias feels an icy hand land onto a shoulder. It makes him flinch. Archer gives him a squeeze and releases him. Physical contact isn't their custom. Under the circumstances, he doesn't mind. He has to see the secrets of the camera's lens. Who killed his son? His stomach sinks and his heart pounds with heavy thumps. He presses his lips together, nodding.

Disk hits play, and the clip runs.

White suited Moths occupy the lounge next to small round tables. Couches line the back where gangsters snug close to girls in short, tight clothing. A new Moth appears with a girl clutching her purse. The pixelation of the camera is tough to see the details. From what Iglesias can tell of the scars, it is Cabello. They sit on the couch. Tanner, José, and Hailey arrive. They settle beside the two, sharing the sofa.

The events that follow are unlike anything Iglesias or Archer could prepare for. Mastema enters, the same character from Disk's photo, with goons matching the kid's research. One is bald, with a long, protruding jaw. The other has spiked hair with an air of authority in his walk and a grin far too crooked with confidence. Big Jaw and Smug. Iglesias leans into the screen, as does Archer.

Mastema strides around the room and talks to the crowd. He spins a chair and sits, then continues to speak, directed to the Moths on the couch. Next, Hailey and the presumed Cabello stand with a couple of other girls. Cabello reaches into her purse while walking past Mastema and pulls a gun, firing it into Mastema's head.

The room freezes for a split second as the crime lord hits the floor. Moths at the far right corner wield firearms. Cabello and the gangsters position toppled over tables as cover. They exchange bullets. Wood splinters fly across the screen. José, Hailey, and Tanner cower on the ground. Big Jaw and Smug blink from their location. Iglesias thought it was him. He hasn't blinked. The vampires phase in and out as Cabello shoots at them. It's as if the camera was glitching, missing frames, except Cabello's moves are fluent. Smug and Big Jaw blip from one part of the lounge to the next. Mastema rises. Where a bullet hole should be is pure darkness. It swirls around, recreating his face. The shadows glitch: mass hysteria is false. He snags Cabello. She unloads her firearm into him and punches him to no use. The timestamp indicates it's when Archer and Iglesias arrived at Radiate Primate.

Mastema holds Cabello by the neck, dragging her. Despite his unmatched strength, she tries to resist. He speaks to the crowd, snapping his finger, and leaves with the bartender. The vampires step forward, their mouths open, extending twice as long as a human should. Large canines expand from their upper teeth.

José grabs Hailey while Tanner books it for the door. Smug blips to Tanner and snags his skull. The boy flings his arms in the air as he's lifted off the ground. Smug bends his neck and sinks his fangs into him. Hailey and José scream; though silent, Iglesias hears it loud and clear. Big Jaw strolls to them, unalarmed, raising their fingers, blade-like nails erecting from each hand.

Iglesias digs his fingers into his palm with such force it punctures the skin. Big Jaw corners José and Hailey with another girl. There's nowhere to run. The Moth phases forward, reappearing in an uppercut stance. The second girl flies to the ceiling as claws rip her stomach open, raining her intestine over them. Big Jaw snatches Hailey as the other gal splatters onto the floor. José punches the attacker as the vampire slices Hailey's neck and sinks their teeth into her. Iglesias's boy kicks, shouts, and hits Big Jaw to no use. The vampire tosses Hailey aside. He snags José by the arms and his jaws plummet into his throat. His face enters shock, confusion, and his eyes flutter, losing consciousness as if blood drains from his body within a heartbeat.

Smug and Big Jaw slaughter the remaining people in the room, civilians, and Moths alike. They blink from one corner to the next, ripping the souls to shreds, and phase off camera. The massacre took seconds, the time for Iglesias to run up the stairs. Hailey wanders off screen, in shock, with red oozing along her neck. That's when he and Archer found her.

Warm tears run past Iglesias's face, soaking into his beard, reminding him he is in a sour-smelling studio apartment. He blinks, failing to prevent the tears from escaping. The footage continues, showing himself and Archer entering the room, and Disk pauses it.

"How did you get this?" Archer asks. It's good that she broke the silence, because Iglesias can't speak. His throat will not open and his lungs burn thanks to the fire inside. His fingers are cold to the touch against his shaking knees, ears as hot as his cheeks. The fury tattooed onto his face is on full display to his colleagues.

Before Disk answers, a knock comes at the door. The surprising noise makes the three perk up, spinning to sound.

Iglesias stands. His emotions snuff out in a single breath. He reaches for his gun, then remembers that he doesn't have one because he is not a working detective.

"You expecting anyone?" he asks.

Disk shakes their head no.

CHAPTER 47
FAMILY REUNION

Whether the Creator made a direct interjection, or by pure chance, Scalebane and Synarion meet again. She stays in Vancouver when the private jet lands in North America while Rithu returns to Toronto. The young male indeed has proven his worth, as Zoefani would have put it. Scalebane can leverage that for the greater good of their people.

Off of the private Crystal Moth jet, Four meets her at the airport with a black SUV complete with tinted windows. The shaper does not appear the same as they did at Club Revelation, nor in their original form. They present themselves in new flesh: a young soft skin with a blond patchwork of a beard, pale, and a dangling Adam's apple. Their insect smell is still potent and clear in Scalebane's nose.

Scalebane steps in the vehicle as Four rolls the windows, chewing a toothpick. "You got the orders, yes? As do I."

"Yes, Eden Breaker contacted me," Scalebane says as she approaches the SUV, keeping Jekos in his preferred shadows. She gets into the passenger seat and slams the door with more force than intended.

"Excellent." Four says as they place one hand on the wheel. "We'll keep the jet here. Our visit shouldn't take long to get Cabello."

The two additional Moths on the flight exit the plane, on their phones, operating the ash business. Rithu ordered these goons to stay west and handle a new shipment. They aren't following Scalebane and Four, who drive off.

They leave the Vancouver airport and merge onto the highway. Four has a computer map on a screen as part of the dashboard of the vehicle. It's got an address marked, showing directions. An amazing engineering feat that impresses Scalebane. There's one good human invention.

"How did you learn Cabello's location?" Scalebane asks on the drive.

Four says, "Synarion is buying ash for her. Eden Breaker has worked with Synarion for quite some time."

"Who from Eden Breaker was in contact with him?" Scalebane leans back to take in Four's calm presence.

"A member of tier one," Four says, eyes on the road. "Not for me to know. Communication with Eden Breaker's system is transparent, letting us see tasks that come in. Tiers are anonymous names."

Scalebane looks to the window. "Is Synarion aware we're coming?"

"Not quite." Four licks their lips. "We will provide ash to him, and that is when you can make your introduction. A family reunion, yes?"

Of course, Four has Synarion's history with her. The Moths and Eden Breaker are exceptional in their background checking. She slithers her tail around her ankle. This gathering leaves her stomach in a twist, and sourness on her tongue.

Their drive takes them to the east side of Vancouver, closer inland, to an industrial park along the bay. The sun rides the horizon, casting long and wide shadows as the SUV parks by a concrete dock. In front is a silver vehicle with a man sitting in the driver's seat. The headrest is low, exposing cauliflower ears and slicked-back hair.

Synarion, Scalebane thinks. Her heart thumps against her chest. She goes to open the door and Four speaks.

"Wait," they say while reaching into their blazer, taking a vacuum sealed bag of ash. Four exits the automobile and walks between the two vehicles and pats the ash on their chest, clear for Synarion to see.

A couple of moments pass before Synarion exits. He keeps his fists in his pockets, eyeing the SUV, and Four. He stops by the rear of his automobile. "You're new. Where's the other guy?" he says. Voice muffled from the closed door.

Four shrugs. "Not here. You get me today. Got the cash?"

"Yeah," Synarion says. "Usually, they come to the car. What's your process?" He hasn't taken his hands from his pockets, and Scalebane has a hunch about what he is holding in there. It isn't money.

Four glances at the SUV and then Synarion. "Quite different, yes? We have business to conduct."

"I want ash. I pay. It's a simple transaction," Synarion says, stepping away.

Scalebane opens the door and steps out. The balancer freezes, his eyes squinting as the vazelead's cloak blows in the breeze, exposing the tail underneath. His gaze moves from her sai, landing on her masked face. He can't see her expression but understands her well enough to know it's a scowl.

"Synarion," Scalebane says, marching towards him. He takes his fists from his pockets, wielding a throwing star and a spiked knuckle. He gives her a once-over examination, mouth hanging open at the sight of her walking motion. The nymph hasn't seen her since before the damaged leg.

Four extends her hands. "Remain civil. We're allies here."

Scalebane stops behind Four, placing her claws on her sai, ready to draw if he makes a move that she disapproves. The flaring of her thigh runs heat inside her body, mixing with the fire of her rage. He keeps his battle stance wide, eyes bouncing between each target. Her claw taps the handle of her weapons. She wants him to take action. This damn balancer took Namsruc from her and at long last she has him. A pang strikes her. It causes her to blink several times. This is an emotional response.

Weak willed, comes the Gatekeeper's judgment ringing through her mind.

Four's voice pulls her from the spiral. "We didn't mean to ambush you. Eden Breaker is trustworthy, I can assure you."

"Did you hurt them?" Synarion asks.

"Eden Breaker? By no means we would. Eden Breaker takes many forms, faces, and trust me when I say we're here on good terms. I am Four, I am Eden Breaker."

"I must apologize because I'm not convinced," Synarion says as he squeezes his fists.

"You should be on your guard," the other says.

"Where's Namsruc?" Scalebane takes a step forward. Four extends their arm, landing on her chest.

The shaper speaks. "We need you to take us to Cabello. We understand you have her, yes? Scalebane, please elaborate the urgency."

Scalebane takes a deep breath, gaining composure. Her claw twitches. "Pieces are in motion beyond your control, Synarion. You as a lone balancer. The Moths are not in our favour."

"As I've strained. Let me speak with King." He lowers his arms while keeping both weapons in hand, ready to strike at a moment's notice.

"King aligns with Mastema. My methods here are rogue, and despite my reluctance, understand that I have to work with others to deal with an escalating situation."

"Being?" he asks.

"Cabello is taking ash, correct?" Scalebane tilts her head in a curious motion.

"Because you re-introduced it to her, tortured her for a year, and for what? To let her go? What is your angle?" Synarion's brows flatten, gaze fixated on Scalebane.

"You're familiar with the lightless ones, Synarion?"

Synarion's stance relaxes. "A myth, I am sure."

"On the contrary, quite real." Scalebane lets the seriousness of her words settle on his mind for a heartbeat. "There are outside forces at work that are interjecting into our world. The painter Dasco Amoss is channeling the messages of a ghoul. They wish to be summoned."

"What does this have to do with Lola?" Synarion asks.

"Dasco painted her as part of this ghoul's summoning request."

Synarion chuckles to dismiss her claims. He looks off into the ocean. "You're betting your entire plan on the works of a painter? A human one at that? Scalebane, I expected you to be more cautious."

Four adjusts their blazer's collar as a low hiss slips through Scalebane's teeth. Four says. "The Crystal Moths work with Manageficient Enterprises."

Scalebane adds, "They're synthesizing ash and using old world power to push humans into a new post-soft skin state."

"You didn't consider this when aligning with the Moths?" Synarion brings his eyes back to the two, searching their faces for a deeper answer.

Scalebane growls. "Focus, Synarion. Don't be a fool."

Four says, "They have Cabello's blood, a demon's DNA sequence, ash scales, and a fixation of editing genetics. Add that with human curiosity, and you can imagine where it leads."

Synarion squints, mouth opening a sliver.

Scalebane raises her claws up to emphasize her statement. "Dasco Amoss has completed portions of these forthcoming realities. They're visual works beyond anything I've seen before, showing the universe, the Creator, specific details I am unaware of. He even painted you and Namsruc in Dreadweave Pass. Your efforts rendered worthless, did it? Unable to find Valturus, queen of the vampires, in an endless plane of suffering?" She extends a claw, pointing at Synarion with a harsh jab. "Where is Namsruc?"

"Stay on topic," Four insists with dagger eyes on Scalebane.

"Dasco's ghoul is no mirage." Scalebane lowers her arm. "His visions are greater than his mind."

"You are sure it's a summoning circle?" Synarion asks.

"We know what portal glyphs look like. They are far too complex to make from memory, or by chance. Despite our friction, we have to work together." Scalebane bites her tongue, thankful that he cannot see her emotional response to her proposal.

Synarion presses his lips, glaring at the two.

Four says, "You can have this ash, on the house." The shaper grins, showing crooked yellow teeth. "Take us to Cabello."

Scalebane adds, "This is no ruse."

"Unlike the last time?" Synarion asks as he fixates on Scalebane's weapons.

"Times have changed," the other says.

"How did the humans get a demon horn?" Synarion says.

Four holds their left wrist and looks to the ground. "A detective turned it in. We got notified."

Synarion wipes his mouth. "A succubus?"

"I believe so." Four locks eyes with Synarion. "Details we can review once we're united."

He relaxes the grip on his weapons and looks into the sunset. He takes a deep breath and shakes his head. The fool has operated on his own for so long that he forgets how to form allegiances.

"You raised me, Synarion," Scalebane says, pushing the words from her mouth. "My focus is on my sister and my people's safety. I am telling you, it is not in Mastema's interest."

"We'll act as one? No hidden plan?" Synarion raises an eyebrow.

"Don't take Namsruc from me, and don't show weakness for Cabello like last time, and we'll work well together." Her nostrils flare up.

"What is your end goal here?" Synarion asks, looking at Four.

"Eden Breaker shares a common objective with Scalebane, and with you and Cabello," Four says without a hint of excitement. "I think I speak for them when I say we don't want the lightless ones to come here. Mastema's progress is angering them, and this painter is the key."

Scalebane says, "If we destroy the Moths along the way, so be it." She puffs her chest, now that she has completed her offer to him.

Synarion places his fists into his pocket, releasing his fingers from the weapons and returning empty-handed. "Scalebane, Namsruc went to Vietnam after we left Murgo. That was eighteen months ago. I thought you should know."

A low grumble comes from Scalebane's throat. She must maintain composure, squeezing the handles of her sai. He could be lying. If he isn't, what happened to Namsruc? Scalebane hasn't been in Vietnam, to her people, in years. Is she with King? He wouldn't dare keep that knowledge from her.

Synarion looks away and his voice softens. "Based on your response, I'm guessing she hasn't returned. I'm sorry, Scalebane. She'll come around when she is ready. She always does."

"If you had honoured our agreement, you would have Valturus," Scalebane sneers. Even scarred from the loss of her sister, she will still bite.

"Impossible," Synarion says, grinding his teeth.

"Mulier, your succubus whore, knew and she told me," Scalebane says. Even though the words are false, she knows it pricks him.

He takes a step forward, unscathed by her statement. "Lies. As you did claiming you knew how to get into Hell. You never did, and never could."

Four slaps the ash bag against her palm. "We're good? As one, yes?"

"No lies, Synarion," Scalebane says with a tightness in her chest that thins her words. *Weak willed.* "I can enter Hell."

"Deal with this later," Four says. "We're working together?"

"Together," Synarion says, looking at Scalebane.

A crooked grin grows on Four's face.

Scalebane clenches her claws in a single tight squeeze, then nods her head. She gave him a partial lie three years ago. Today, she intended these words to hurt him.

CHAPTER 48
PUPA

Synarion and Disk keep an open communication as the days continue. The balancer gets two USB sticks as requested. Lola and Synarion form their plan with Disk, reviewing the EMFC's safety manual and floor plans of Allen Sky Tower. Synarion and Cabello request disguises from Disk. Lab coats, IDs, and key fobs that will let them gain access to the mysterious basement.

He takes care of the cyber components of their scheme while Lola reviews the printed blueprints of the laboratory. Her mind trails to her ash sessions, asking: how far can one go and still be human? This question curses souls who push beyond their psyche. Mutations are required for growth, sprouting evolution, and change. Lola sure as hell has transformed since that fateful day in Edmonton in 2014. She's a killer and a cunning convict. If she didn't withhold the evidence five years ago, she wouldn't be here, an ash-dasher, riding the purple firework, believing she contacts Mother Nature. She is contacting her. Another entity is too. She feels it.

From an outsider's perspective, using normal senses, she sounds like a quack. It's a desperate cry for help. It took Lola a while to accept the true world. Hard evidence, ash, and rambles in her mind paved the way. Attempting revenge blurs, muddled in the mess of convoluted goals, agendas, and threats.

Through her past year of torture, there is one guiding light that has helped her get through the nonsense: Mother Nature. She has been leading Lola since she first took ash in Winnipeg with Jack in 2016. It required dozens of sessions for her to understand the vague communication Earth's spirit speaks. It's not in clear words, nor complete silence. There's intuition, twin fiery eyes. Her vowels dance in the wind, taking her to an unknown place, or thing. The vibrations channel on the hardwood floor she lies on within Synarion's loft.

To chase Mother Nature's message, the ash-dasher must transcend from her human self and jump into the extraordinary. Ancient cultures called it a spirit quest, modern humans call it a retreat, while Lola cares not of what the name is. She needs to follow Mother Nature by consuming more scales. Each one Synarion provides her, she tops off with the half of another. For this session, she takes two scales. It dissolves her ego, launching her far beyond.

Further . . . beyond, Child of Nature. . . comes the wind detected by her sixth sense. The voice is universal, neutral, and contains a mother's warmth directing her through the psychic barriers of her mind.

Ash aids this process. Her dosages increased over the past couple of weeks as she plummets deeper into the darkness. Here, she sees three dark figures in a black space, highlights of their forms are painted on by a distant ghostly glow. The middle silhouette is shorter than the rest. The sharp lighting angles to the side, licking the edges of their features. Frizzy hair springs above their scalp: her mother. The tall person to the right has silky, thick hair slicked back. Highlights of wrinkles are above the moustache: her father. The one to the left is her brother, standing wide and proud. His hand rests on a small child Lola hasn't seen before, also lacking details. Behind them are two more shadows, a girl with black-and-red dreadlocks: Becky, and a hooded broad-shouldered man: Michael. The Trinity of Souls.

Lola defeated these trials. She walks past them with ease. The dark figures puff into smoke, swirling in the wind. The fumes rocket upward, and she flies into a splash of rainbow colours. They morph in hues and tones from blue to purple, to red, orange, yellow, and then green. A face of a dozen children emerges in a circular shape above. Glowing white lines create shapes around them. The faces in the circle, together, form landmasses. This is Earth, with its creatures. The planet mutates into a muck of grey and red. It's burning. The Earth expands and a small seedling sprouts from soil, grows, then dies. Rain trickles onto the barren dirt, turning it to mud, rising. The water fills into an ocean, washing away the landscape and the entire globe.

This vast cosmos contains billions of twinkling stars surrounded by massive nebulas of rich pinks and blues. A naked, transparent woman stands on top of a cloud of this gas. Bark covers her knees, elbows, and portions of her pelvis and torso. The scalp comprises vines coiling around her shoulders and wrapping her limbs.

Below is a twin of her with charred skin and black spiked tendrils for hair. The two titans wave their arms together, moving around the fumes. Their actions mirror each other as they compress the stardust. The vapor becomes a semi-solid, getting hotter and brighter until it is a rock. Oceans form with clouds as both feminine beings close in on each other, curling into a ball. The scorched entity swipes a bark-clawed hand at the other, who deflects the attack. Vines protrude from her spine, snagging onto the attacker and flinging her off the world. The burned one drifts into the cosmos. With a single titan remaining, she encompasses the sphere in a loving embrace. Her body melts into mountains, rivers, and forests, sprouting over this new planet.

In the vast expanse, other gas clouds with massive beings create their own planets. Their humanoid forms of godlike muscles curl inwards, fusing with their worlds.

Lola soars from the world-forming titans, flying beyond the galaxies. She passes the stars, penetrating through an invisible wall. This new void showcases the celestial realm in full spherical view. It's a marble, one of countless marbles floating. Universe after universe.

Beside the sphere she exited is another without space dust. It contains a vast black ocean and a single large pillar in the centre. A wide plateau balances on top, forming the shape of a nail. A spiralling vortex consumes the sky, containing purple and blue clouds mixed with lightning and ghastly rotting faces.

Above the marbles is a series of seven halos behind a golden gate. Below the infinite galaxies is a burning red triangle. Expanding further, a large hand from a silhouetted figure encompasses Lola's view. An invisible force pulls her back to see more. The mysterious, gigantic being in front of her walks into blackness. No ground, no door. This being opens an invisible gate and leaves with a trail of tears dripping into the burning triangle.

Despite the absence of words, Lola's soul insists that this is the story of Creationism. They're fragments and incomplete moments. She understands the history of existence and how the Creator left the Macrocosm to its own devices.

Unity . . . threat, comes Mother Nature's wind.

This image of the universe gains texture, bumps and indents, compressing. She keeps moving away until the flattened picture's dints become clear. A canvas. Brush strokes add details into the work despite no paintbrush is in view. In the far top corner stands a naked man, pale with bone white hair. They've been in her life before. It matters not at the moment as the painting continues to expand. The darkest spot envelops the corners of Creationism. It grows larger.

No . . . comes the wind.

A pulse of energy grows from within her.

Summon me, erupts a new voice. It's not Mother Nature's. It's far different, reverberating with two beings speaking at once. The twin flames, they are conscious.

The First and the End . . . it says again.

The power hums inside of Lola as black brushstrokes splatter, one after the other, faster and faster. Obsidian inches closer to the bubble universes, threatening to devour it.

The pale naked man looks at the oncoming void. He runs on invisible ground in space, eyes slanted in fear. The obsidian engulfs him, taking her with it into a void.

Grow away! Mother Nature demands.

Alpha and Omega, the other says.

Lola's view pulls back and slingshots forward. Her light speed soars past the darkness, the golden gates, and into the marble containing the dark brushstrokes, vortex, and plateau. The acceleration is too fast to process the details of the environment as she flies into a black and blue floating figure's pure white eyes. Into the eyes, beyond the pure whiteness, a loft fades into view with brick walls and a hardwood floor. This isn't Synarion's home. Oh no. It's a painter's studio.

Sweat covers a man who wears boxers and an unbuttoned dress shirt. His head dangles upward, his gaze rolled back. His arm moves in wide strokes, gripping a brush. Paint hits a canvas illustrating a girl with three scars and short hair. Her eye sockets comprise marble universes. It's Lola.

A series of finished works rest on the ground to her left, forming a mosaic of what Lola witnessed. A connecting white line harmonizes the pieces, creating shapes with glyphs of an ancient language following the arcs. At the far end of the room, by an open window, stands a cloaked figure wearing a leather mask with goggles and a metal muzzle.

Scalebane, is the first true thought the ash-dasher has since the trip.

Back, Child of Nature . . . comes Mother Nature's whispering wind.

Summon me, complete the First with the End, the twin flames say.

A force of nausea surges from her stomach. The vision turns black. Her eyes fling open. She rolls over and uses her shaking arms as support, heaving. Her mouth dangles open. Drool seeps from her lips as she regurgitates whatever is left in her intestines in hot, thick, green bile. It splatters onto the wood in several plops. It slides close to a cardboard box containing white lab coats draping over the edge. She pushes it aside to avoid contamination and spits the remaining fluids out before rolling to the side. Her hand and elbow can't hold her weight.

Shivering, she gasps for breath, her body is unable to control its response. Ice gnaws at her limbs, leaving them tingling with a chilling sensation. Heat engulfs her torso, flaring with a hot stab. Dehydration takes its toll, stinging her eyes, scraping against the lids. Her head: split open by the drug demon.

Success, Lola thinks as she stares at the spinning ceiling. Her sober mind is returning as the room's bright colours wash away thanks to the saturation of the true world. Dull, mundane, and limited. It was worth it. She got a clear direction of where she needs to go and what she was told.

Lola witnessed the birth of the universe through god-like beings forming planets. Mother Nature created Earth with a twin sister. Beyond that lies many other universes. She saw the afterlife with the golden gates of Heaven and the burning triangle of Hell. Above, was the Creator and his first creation, Mastema.

The looming darkness: an unknown. The thought of it leaves Lola uncomfortable, and she hugs her arms, fighting the cold. This is what concerns Mother Nature. It's why the twin flames keep talking to her. She saw them for a moment, a black and blue floating entity.

Grow away? Lola thinks, recalling the conflicting words of her vision.

This being connected her to Dasco Amoss, the famous Canadian painter who took the world by storm with his revolutionary work. He is painting the universe through his own visions. Different from Lola's. He sees her as she sees him. The two are being brought together. Why is Mother Nature reluctant? Didn't she guide her to this moment? How this relates to the printed Manageficient Enterprises floor plans on Synarion's desk is an unclear like a dark, frigid vast ocean of possibilities.

Summon me, Lola thinks, reflecting on the words of the mysterious being. *The First and the End.*

The door unlocks and Synarion's head peeks into the dark space. It's night, and ash-dasher Lola neglected the lights. She uses her elbows as support to sit up, watching the nymph flick on the bulb. He stares at the ground, fixated on her vomit. It contains swirls of deep red mixed with the green and yellow. Ash is rotting her stomach.

"Lola," Synarion says with a sternness that sprouts from defensiveness, not concern.

"Yeah?" she asks in a croak. She expects him to scold her about the dangers of ash and why she should avoid it.

"Our situation has changed," he says.

"Yeah," Lola says. "I made a major breakthrough."

"Is that so? Likewise." Synarion swings the door open, letting the hinges squeak. He walks in, accompanied by an additional two sets of footsteps. A white blazer comes from behind. A long black cloak and scaled tail peeks from the doorway.

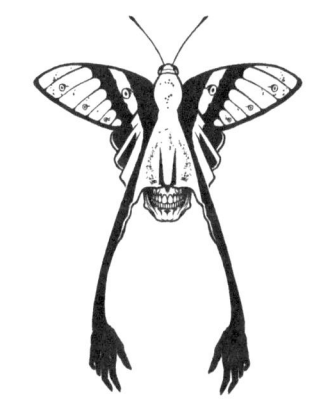

CHAPTER 49
BELOW THE BABBLE

I should have bought a firearm, Iglesias thinks, standing in Disk's studio apartment. The three wonder the same thing: who is knocking? It could be as simple as a neighbour needing help, a delivery, or the sinister. To their luck, Archer has her gun drawn. She nods at Disk to open the door.

"Why?" Disk whispers.

"Go," Iglesias replies.

Archer waves her weapon, ushering Disk as another series of knocks erupts. *Knock, knock, knock*. Disk creeps to the entrance as Archer places her back on the wall beside the frame. Iglesias stays at her side. He feels useless in the scenario.

Locks and chains jingle against the door, and Disk pulls it open a fourth of the way.

"Greetings, Disk, is it?" comes a high-pitched voice, sounding like a croak.

"Yeah?" Their face squints in a mix of disgust and confusion.

"Eden Breaker, I'm certain you're familiar with it, One," says the other.

"Eden Breaker? What's that?"

"How about you let me in and I tell you? Yaseen, that's your name, isn't it?"

Disk's cheeks turn pink. "No, it's not."

"Or I could finish your last name to aid the kind officers identifying you in your unit."

Disk glances at Archer and Iglesias and steps aside, swinging the door open. Archer raises her gun as a skeleton of a man comes into view, wearing a burgundy suit complete with a brown double-breasted vest and black dress shirt. The toxic green eyes match the eyebrows as the left one rises.

The newcomer speaks. "Do you wave that thing at everyone you meet? No wonder the people don't like you." The wide gaps between their teeth are more distracting than their obscure colouring. The man closes the door behind him and strolls into the room.

"Who the hell are you?" Iglesias asks.

"Hmm, yes, well, that is a pickle, isn't it? Eden Breaker, as Disk is. It is unfortunate that I happen to be here. Poor Disk can't even keep their identity hidden from us."

"Impossible," Disk says. "Eden Breaker doesn't have that info. My online profile is clean."

"You're not that good," the newcomer says with a wicked grin. "There is more than the internet when it comes to smoke and screens. You're a clever kid. Piece it together."

Archer keeps her firearm raised. Iglesias isn't concerned, walking from the wall to their guest. This individual will not harm them, despite their deformed body being enough to frighten the commoner. No mother could love a face so foul and skin so dry.

Disk rubs their chin, more fascinated than scared. "No, I'm invisible in person. Cash only. Unit under a different name. Online, untraceable. Though, I have some government documents that . . . that means—holy shit. No way."

The newcomer gives a slow nod. "Highest level of access."

Disk takes a bow, pressing their palms together. "It's an honour."

"Okay," Archer says. "Care to tell the nice officer with the gun what you two are babbling about?"

"I am Zero," the newcomer says.

Disk smiles and waves at Archer. "Put that thing away. This is Zero."

"Being?" Archer asks.

"The founder of Eden Breaker."

Iglesias folds his arms.

"It's the only explanation," Disk says.

Archer says, "You sure you they're not better at cyberwars than you?"

Zero speaks, "Trust Disk. They are a clever bean. Though, I have access to sources you cannot imagine. Which brings us to the topic at hand." Zero walks to the computer, seeing the video. They eye the folder Iglesias left on the stool and tap it. "Strange allegiances must forge to ensure the longevity of this world. I understand a General Florance is barking up your tree, Detective Archer?"

"Yes," Archer says, lowering her gun, keeping it held with both hands.

"He won't be kind to you. That man is spearheading the government's involvement with Manageficient Enterprises and their gene editing methods.

"He is involved with the ash investigation," Iglesias says.

Zero gives air quotations. "Yes, 'involved' as in running a tight ship of revenue. I'm not here to discuss ash. You're sore, Detective Iglesias. Put it aside. We have more pressing matters at hand."

"Being?" Iglesias takes a deep inhale, pushing aside the words, *you're sore.*

"The horn that Detective Archer sent to GeneChron. I must say, the improvisation you three have done is outstanding. Bravo." Zero makes several gentle claps with their palms. "Give yourselves a pat on the back."

None of them do so. Disk smiles as if they received a grade A report in school. Smooth complimenting words don't win Iglesias or Archer over. This is a stranger that has too much knowledge of their situation and it leaves both suspicious.

"Continue," Iglesias says.

"Eden Breaker has been working in the shadows for quite a while, as I'm sure Disk has mentioned. They've probably shared more of Eden Breaker than I'd prefer. What do you do? We're our own people and take our own actions. You're in this rabbit hole and you need to go deeper. I can verify your investigating. These pieces are accurate and moving."

"What investigating?" Archer asks, still holding her gun, stance stiff as a tree. "The legitimate, or the crazy kind with vampires and reptile humanoids?"

"All rings true, detective." Zero says with a stale calmness that silences the room for several heartbeats.

Iglesias folds his arms. "You're the puppeteer of Eden Breaker. A head honcho with master intel in a supposed structure of decentralized anonymous democracy. It's a contradiction, isn't it?"

Zero cups their hands together. "We need a kill switch if the fruit goes sour, and I am afraid things are."

"Hard to believe a stranger's words when there's little proof." Iglesias searches the newcomer's bright eyes, looking for anything that might provide a clue. "You talk a big game. This whole thing stinks of treachery and secrets since we first discovered ash in New Brunswick, 2016."

"Fair point, Detective," Zero says. They reach into their blazer's inner coat, causing Archer to lift her gun. He pauses. Iglesias nods at Archer and she lowers the weapon, letting Zero take out a USB stick. They hand it over to Disk. "Put it on a test computer if you don't trust me. These are schematics, floor plans, and a backdoor that you will enjoy." Zero looks at Disk while stating *backdoor*.

"Floor plans to?" Archer asks, dragging out the word *to*, emphasizing her question.

Zero points to Disk, who wastes no time sitting, digging inside their drawers and taking a small laptop. The group surrounds Disk as they boot the computer and plug in the USB stick, not concerned with the potential of malicious files.

Iglesias stands next to Zero, with Archer at his side. One whiff of the newcomer sends burning plastic and wood into his nostrils. Each characteristic of this stranger strikes odd.

The machine finishes loading, and Disk activates the file browser to cruise through the USB stick. They find:
- allen-tower-floorplans.pdf
- electromagnetic-flux-compression-safety-guide.pdf
- .the-mouth

Zero says, "Change that to an executable and—"

Disk interrupts from pure excitement. "And the backdoor becomes active. You require a receiving USB stick?"

Zero goes into his blazer again and takes two more drives, passing them to Iglesias. His fingers are hot to the touch. "I've fetched a plan, and I need you three to help execute it. Click the floor plans, go to the lab's layout."

"Hold up," Iglesias says. His eyes rest on the small USB sticks that have more weight on his mind than their physical properties. "We were doing well on our own and I can piece together what you're wanting us to do. Why?"

"You are in contact with an Old World Shadow, linking to Cabello, right?" Zero asks.

"You are Zero," Disk reiterates like a kid radiating excitement when meeting Santa. They click the floor plan document and cruise through the pages. "You sent Old World Shadow and Cabello the same intel, telling them to get in touch with me. How did I not see this?"

Secretive, Iglesias thinks. He's sick of Disk's incoherent way of sharing information. He fiddles with the two sticks. One is a standard black USB drive of three gigabytes. The other is a red mobile internet stick.

Zero speaks, "Your involvement must remain secret. I fear the fruit is rotten, though we have to play our roles to avoid attention. My colleagues are retrieving Cabello, bringing her to Toronto to follow the same plan as your group. You'll meet her and her team in Allen Sky Tower. I'll provide you with the access you need and the weapons required to get into Manageficient Enterprises's lab."

Archer speaks, "To install this backdoor into their computers?"

Disk scrolls back to the first page containing the lab's blueprints and Zero points to the top right of the plans, where a circular room is drawn. It's one of three equal sized rooms on the sheet. He says, "These are electromagnetic flux-compressions. Far too large for a simple experiment. Thrice, marked on floor plans. With that executable in the USB stick, you will have access to their controls and the lab files."

Disk's eyes widen. "We can download their data, wipe it, or turn off the power, crank the heat, disable gas tanks. Oh! Oh . . . with those big EMFCs, we could increase the teslas of—"

Zero cuts Disk off. "Of the electromagnetic flux-compressions."

"EMFCs electro, what?" Iglesias says.

Disk says, "Magnets."

"What do those do?" His voice goes up a notch, knotted with confusion.

"Not much," Disk says with a shrug. "Unless you're connected to capacitors generating megajoules of energy. Low levels are fine. It's when you raise the teslas produced, like megateslas, they contain excessive tons of force. See the size of those things? Twenty feet each? Crush those, and boom."

Iglesias and Archer exchange looks. Iglesias speaks. "Okay, science kid. Teslas the measurement?"

"Measuring magnetic flux density. Super cool stuff." A twitch of a smile rises on Disk's face that strikes Iglesias with a cold press of concern.

"It's more concerning your first thought goes to exploding the lab."

Zero raises their right index finger. "Ah. An implosion of the fields which will happen in under fifty microseconds. It's critical, Disk, that you increase the teslas at a gradual speed over ten minutes not to damage the equipment."

That same twitched smile rises on Disk's face, capturing the mischievousness swirling within their mind. "What should I raise it to?"

"Mmm. Fifteen hundred teslas should increase the liner speed at what we need. Aim for eighty percent, twelve hundred. Once our friends are out, crank it and raise hell!"

"Isn't the record twelve hundred?" Disk asks.

"Gradual speed." Zero repeats with a newfound sternness in their words. "These custom EMFCs have a manual override that needs to be disabled."

Disk opens a browser window on a software Iglesias doesn't recognize. "I gotta tell Old World Shadow and Cabello."

Zero says, "Keep this team out of the message."

"Why?" Disk winces, pausing their motion on the keyboard and mouse.

"The less shared, the less that can go wrong."

"Like how you operate in the dark? So cool." A glitter illuminates from Disk's eyes.

Archer brushes her hair aside, still refusing to let go of her gun with her other hand. "Why do they even have these things down there?"

Zero adds, "Well, my dear. That is getting into the area of metaphysics. A big question too. Let's just say magnets and gravity can react together. Gravity effects light. Mash those and you dabble in the realm of the gods, manipulating the fabric of reality."

Archer looks at Iglesias, both sharing a face of concern. This is moving too fast. It is what they were working towards: a truth to these conspiracies.

CHAPTER 50
MUTUALS

Fate is cruel, bringing people together who despise each other. Proof of it is the blond, white-suited Crystal Moth stepping into Synarion's apartment accompanied by the masked, cloaked figure. This iconic metal fanged muzzle and goggles combo is a signature look that drives needles of fear into Lola's heart. The swaying tail, arcing like a curious cat, leaves Lola petrified as the nymph closes the door.

She wants to kill Scalebane, run, fight, any option other than having to talk with her. From the moment they crossed paths in 2016, the reptile has been a source of harm.

Synarion extends his hand, open palm. He says, "Lola, I don't want you to do anything drastic."

Lola scoots away, locked on Scalebane, who stands beside the Crystal Moth patting a vacuum sealed bag against his chest. Although Lola hasn't seen Scalebane's full face, she senses judgement underneath that mask, and fair enough. There's a pile of blood and bile on the ground next to her. Lola's muscles are non-existent, emphasizing the bones beneath her skin. The bags under her eyes are far darker than the best smoky eyeshadow can offer. Her greasy hair is a knotted mess, and guaranteed she reeks from layers of sweat after the ash session.

Lola speaks as her heart pounds against her chest. "Synarion, wh-why-why is she here? Why, what? Why is she here, Synarion?" Her nails dig into the unpolished floor, scratching the surface. She scans Synarion's brown contact lenses and then darts to each of the guests.

"Things have changed," Synarion says.

"Yeah? Like how?" She gets to her feet and wipes some vomit from her chin and flicks her hand. The slime remains.

"By what madness has Dasco gotten us into?" Scalebane says in a low tone to herself.

Lola squints, connecting invisible pieces together from the ash trip moments ago. Yes, indeed, Mother Nature guided Lola away while another entity pushed her to Dasco Moss. Synarion might not be a loose screw as the situation unfolds. Scalebane did free Lola from torture. The question is, why?

"Lola," Synarion says, extending a hand to the Moth. "This is Eden Breaker. We've worked with them, or one of them."

"Clever nymph." The Crystal Moth waves at Lola with a toothy smile as their green irises mutate into a crimson red. That swirl, the same swirl her lawyer made when visiting her in prison. The same motion the mercenary and rodent had. It can't be, yet here stands the shaper.

"I go by Four with Eden Breaker. Long time no see, yes?" The shaper tosses the vacuum sealed bag at Lola. It hits the ground, sliding to her feet. "I brought you a present."

Lola ignores the bag. Her gaze is fixated on Four. "This is the same shaper who was my lawyer."

"I saved you when violence was imminent, correct?" Four says. "Memories fizzle from your ash-dasher brain, forgetting I live dual lives."

"Yeah?" Lola says. "Which one of those am I seeing?" Lola nods at the Scalebane. "She's been puppeteering us for years, Synarion. She twists your arm and has never, ever, had anyone's interest other than her own. Are you this stupid, Synarion? No wonder why your people were wiped out."

This isn't Lola. It's the ash comedown, hyping her emotional experiences. She understands and doesn't care. Faded auras surround these three. She has taken enough ash over the past couple of weeks that she doesn't feel normal without it. It's difficult to distinguish her sober life from intuition. Regardless, her feelings are getting the better of her. Lola is best to put on her big girl pants and listen.

"I'm not a huge fan of this either," Synarion says. "The circumstances are different."

Lola folds her arms. "You said Dasco, as in Dasco Amoss?"

"I did, soft skin," Scalebane says. "He needs you."

"Yeah." Lola leans over and grabs the ash, waving the bag. "Your scales like to talk."

A low rattle rises from Scalebane and Four places a hand on her forearm.

The shaper speaks. "Synarion here has been kind enough to offer us into his home, yes? Eden Breaker has been working with him for quite some time and has provided you with lucrative goods. An ID, credit card, ash. Scalebane set you free, Mastema wants you. Yet, we can't do that. The oracle painter requires your presence."

"Yeah, yeah, I get it." Lola waves her arms up high. "The whole grand picture. It's why you're here."

"It's not that, Cabello," Scalebane says. "It appears you have far more value."

"Really? That's why you had Rithu torture me for a year? That boy didn't desire to. He's caring."

"A year is little, soft skin," the other says with coldness seeping from their tone.

"Heartless prick." She bites her lip before speaking. "What does Dasco Amoss want with me?"

"You couldn't comprehend it." Scalebane shakes their head.

"Who is going to spit it out?" Lola's face etches with anger as she eyes all three of them. "I'm not joining otherwise."

Four says, "The oracle painter is ever close to summoning their muse, a ghoul. They demand your presence regarding a dark threat. We need to work with you."

Lola laughs, pointing at herself. "Me? Wow. Yeah, you love working with me. Going to threaten my family again, asshole?"

Four shakes their head. "Not this time."

Scalebane adds, "Manageficient Enterprises have made strident leaps in their development, thanks to your blood."

Synarion and Lola exchange glances. Both have been knee-deep in the allen-tower-floorplans.pdf and the electromagnetic-flux-compression-safety-guide.pdf. Zero's plan is coming together.

Scalebane continues, "The Crystal Moths work with them."

Lola says, "Yeah, we're up to date."

Scalebane raises her claws to add weight to her words. "In combination with your DNA, they have a demon's. A detective in Ottawa sent it into GeneChron, a lab owned by Manageficient Enterprises. They use a private military contractor named Advantis. Naturally, this unknown substance ran up the flagpole and is in the hands of Dr. Lang."

Lola says, "Dr. Lang being a fan of transhumanism."

"Supporting Mastema's divine plan."

Lola squeezes her arms. "Being?"

Four smiles. "Details that we are not certain of. It is mutating Mastema though. That concentrated light bullet I gave you should have done the trick."

Scalebane shifts her stance, looking at the shaper.

Four shrugs, holding their shoulders up. "But he regenerated. How? Well, he is full of surprises and a fan of Dr. Lang's experiments."

Lola rubs her forehead. "Yeah, I get it. Big bad stuff. I've been after the Moths for five years."

Four lowers their shoulders and walks around the room, noticing the desk with printed floor plans of Manageficient Enterprises, consisting of several pieces of letter paper. "I see you've done your research." Four squints, raising one piece of paper. A circle pens the south EMFC. "Exceptional research, in fact."

Synarion looks at Lola with intent. "This is why I brought them here. They understand that there is a greater issue. We need help with this."

"Until someone abandons them to the cops." Lola raises an eyebrow at Synarion. "Or strong arms their dad." Lola locks eyes with the vazelead's goggles.

Synarion swipes thin air with his right hand. "No scheming. This is bigger. We were looking at the lab, regardless."

"Now these clowns are here?" Lola asks.

"They have ins we don't. Look, I have to ask: how did this demon horn get into the position of a detective?"

Four places the paper on the counter and examines the box on the ground. It's open and they reach inside, taking a lab coat. The shaper says, "A detective Archer. Interestingly enough, used to work with Detective Iglesias, who was spearheading the ash case in the RCMP's Major Crimes unit. At least until the DND took over, which closed things nice and tight so we, the Moths, could continue operations. The general in charge of the ash case will take care of the detectives."

"That doesn't tell us where she got it," Synarion says. "The best of my knowledge, there were a handful of demons on Earth. In Canada, three?"

Mulier, Lola thinks, recalling Scalebane killed the succubus. In fact, it was the last time Synarion, Lola, and she had a civil conversation. Lola took a horn fragment without Synarion's knowledge and gave it to Iglesias. He finally made the practical choice with it and the Moths got their fangs on it. Her stomach rots with a tight bite, and it's not the ash comedown, it's the frustration that the Moths always find a way to deflect her attempts to expose them.

Four shrugs. "Tracking where old world beings are isn't my specialty. That's a balancer's, yes?"

Synarion scratches his chin. "That's what I am afraid of. I contacted Eden Breaker to remove the corpse of a succubus in Vancouver. Wondering if . . . " He glances at Lola before turning his focus onto Four. "Forget it. The point is, Manageficient Enterprises have the DNA sequence. Wouldn't this interest Mastema?"

"I'm sure it has," For says.

Lola adjusts her stance to brush off the thoughts of Iglesias, the horn, and Synarion's concern. "They have demon genetics, mine, and vazelead. It's catching the attention of the otherworldly which Dasco Amoss is seeing?"

Scalebane says, "Not quite working, communicating with. He's channelling the essence of a ghoul. It's his muse."

"Of a looming threat?" Lola's brows flatten.

Scalebane points at her with her index finger. "Dasco painted you."

"Do you trust him?"

Four snaps their fingers. "Shall we move on? Yes? We have a jet ready to go to Toronto."

Lola extends her hand. "Hold up, so what does a ghoul want with me and Dasco Amoss?"

"That is what we're going to find out, soft skin," Scalebane says.

Lola looks to Synarion. "Can we have a word? Outside?"

He nods. "You two, make yourself at home."

Four puts on a toothy grin. "So inviting."

Synarion shrugs. "I owe a lot to Eden Breaker."

Lola snags a pack of smokes from Synarion's table and they exit the unit, through the hall, and out the entrance. She lights a smoke, taking a deep inhale. The night scene of concrete industrial buildings and brick warehouses overlooks the bay, reminding her she is of this world. The scheming of reptiles, scientists, and the afterlife are another. On the opposite side of the water is North Vancouver with its glass towers illuminating in front of the mountains. It's Mother Nature's beauty mixing with human engineering, and so little of it matters when compared to the esoteric conspiracies they had been discussing.

Synarion leans against the stucco building, squinting at her cigarette. He never cared for those. "Are you good with this?" he asks.

Lola shakes her head. "I don't like it."

"Neither do I. What else did you have planned other than drowning in drugs?"

"I was following Mother Nature. She doesn't like this."

"Why is that?" he asks

"A feeling. She reaches for me and another entity interjects," Lola says.

Synarion wipes his chin. "You're sure it's Mother Nature?"

"Yes, Synarion. Christ, why do you belittle ash?"

"Use reason, with only you and I, do you think we could collapse the Moths who have the private sectors and an army behind them?"

I have me, Lola thinks. She would love to snap at him with that comment and remind him what he did. The statement wouldn't aid the situation. She takes another inhale. "I saw a glimpse of Dasco's work in a vision."

"Scalebane mentioned a ghoul."

"What the hell is that?" Lola sucks the cigarette, two thirds done.

"A magnificent spectral." Synarion folds his arms.

"You've seen one?" Lola asks.

Synarion shakes his head no. "I can't say that I have. Ghouls are complex beings that interject themselves into the affairs of the afterlife and the mortal realm as they see fit to best suit death's vortex."

"Being?" Lola blinks.

"The resting bed for all souls. They're neutral, and Mastema has caught their attention."

Lola looks to the grass, focusing on a single tall blade. "Why does Mother Nature want me to stay away?"

"We're in uncharted territory, Lola. I question what Mother Nature's alternative is."

Lola brings her gaze back to Synarion. "Let's wait."

"Do we have time?"

Lola finishes the drag. This is indeed far larger than her. It's greater than Scalebane, Synarion, or whatever that shaper is. They're pieces in some grand scheme of the supernatural. Souls exist. Lola's gut rots. It's not from the constant ash usage. Her instincts are telling her that this is dangerous. She doesn't like it, not one bit.

CHAPTER 51
IMAGO

Gut instincts are a solid method to keep yourself alive. Lola Cabello finds hers contradicts what she must do. Rising above her intuition sends her deeper into the endless spiral of reptilian drug lords, supernatural crime bosses, shapers, nymphs, and demons. The latest is seeking a painter oracle speaking to a being from another realm. In the depths of her mind, she senses some doors are best left closed.

The First and the End.

Her newfound allies have immense tools at their disposal, such as a private jet. It takes them to the east side of the country. The four-thousand-and-three-hundred-kilometre journey would be a forty-five-hour drive. They take Lola's duffel bag of weapons and ash with no questions. To no surprise, Scalebane passes the airport. These are also Moths, whose leader demands for Lola. The group's solution is straightforward: they embrace Lola as a fellow vazelead. She finds herself in a long black cloak, dark clothing, and a spare mask of Scalebane's. The stench of swamp reeks inside.

As for Synarion, he is unassuming. His bag containing throwing stars, communication devices, and the Manageficient Enterprises disguises which go unnoticed. The group stays in the divided executive section. The front is for the three ash-distributing Moths who mind their own business. They're on phones and laptops, working away. Four ordered an SUV to wait for them to arrive. It's too smooth for Lola's tastes. Based on her track record, going undercover doesn't work in her favour. There must be a catch. There's four hours of pondering for Lola to no resolution.

They land in Toronto and step into the vehicle under the early morning orange and pink sky. Four drives with Scalebane sitting in shotgun. Synarion and Lola take the back where she removes the ridiculous mask and cloak. The smell lingers in her nose and on her bare arms. She glances over her shoulder, seeing sealed boxes in the hatchback trunk. She shifts to the window, hugging her chest during the drive.

Synarion breaks the group's silence. He asks, "Has Dasco Amoss had this muse from birth?" and "What was his upbringing like?" along with "A ghoul? Legends say they speak with lightless ones."

Scalebane says yes to these questions. This is trouble. It's why Lola keeps her gun and duffel bag between her feet. They need to prepare for this ghoul. The same two questions swirl through each of their minds: what does this entity want with Lola? How does it tie into the lightless ones and Manageficient Enterprises?

On the highway, Scalebane unbuckles the top of her leather breastplate and takes a small stone. She rubs it between her claws while the sphere glows orange. More supernatural nonsense that Lola doesn't understand.

Scalebane speaks in a low tone, audible. "King, why do you summon me?"

Lola and Synarion exchanged glances. King is the one Synarion wished to talk to and de-escalate the Moths. Whatever Scalebane has must be a telephone of the old world.

Scalebane says, "Meeting? Of ash? My role? . . . of course. I will meet Rithu." She opens her palm and the glowing orange from the sphere fades. She stows it under her breastplate and buckles the armour.

"Everything alright?" Synarion asks.

"Mastema and the Moths are aware we used a private jet." Scalebane says with a flatness that presses down on her posture.

Four says, "It's theirs. Though the details are vague. Ash comes from the West Coast, yes? That's why those three Moths were on the ride."

Scalebane says, "We're in Toronto. Mastema is currently here. He and King wish to meet with me and the others responsible for overseeing ash, with Rithu."

"King is here?" Synarion asks, eyes latched onto Scalebane who shakes her head.

"No, he will communicate in with us."

"Business as usual to ask about your role?" Synarion cocks his head in suspicion.

"No, it's not." Scalebane's statement is filled with a concern Lola had never heard from her before.

Four speaks, "We best make haste."

"I won't miss this," Scalebane says with a low rattle. "I've worked too long with Dasco Amoss for this moment."

Synarion extends a hand. "If you need me when speaking with King, I can assist."

"Diplomacy is not your specialty, Synarion. " Scalebane says without looking him in the eyes. "You will not get to speak with King."

Lola looks at the nymph, whose eyelid twitches. No luck for the balancer.

They drive from the airport and into Toronto's downtown core, parking in an alleyway beside a historic brick building renovated for lofts. These condos are high end. The corner unit at the top has lights on and an open window. The group steps out with Lola taking her bag of belongings, as does Synarion. Scalebane leaps onto the emergency fire exit and climbs the ladder. On this first level, she leans over and says, "Unit S."

The three move to the building's front and wait in the lobby. The small white-and-green-tiled flooring covers the space. Wooden running boards and ivory walls lead to a copper-face clock above the locked door. It states 6:03 AM. Dasco must be burning the midnight oil.

Lola punches the letter S on the intercom and it rings for several moments. The front door buzzes and the group steps into the lobby and into a rustic black industrial elevator. She hasn't shaken the gut feeling that pulls her stomach down, clawing against her organ's walls. *Ignore it*, she thinks. *The First and the End. Summon Me*. The vision was clear: the darkness devoured Mastema. She must summon it.

The elevator makes it to the top level, ending with a clang. They exit and walk across the hardwood floor to the corner unit S with its door a smidge open. Inside, Scalebane stands by Dasco Amoss's rows of canvases arranged on the ground. The paintings create a larger image in a circular formation. To the left of the room is his workstation with a series of works lined up against the brick wall. Beside the easel is a finished piece of Lola with bubble universes for eyes. It's the one from her vision. A fire extinguisher sits on the floor to the right of it.

The painter pushes his messy hair aside. He wears the same unbuttoned blue dress shirt and boxers as in the ash session. A funk of paint and body odour with a tinge of swamp lingers in the room. He smokes ash and work countless hours. Lola isn't the only one who unlocked its usefulness.

"My God," Dasco says. "She exists." He walks towards Lola as if he's staring at a ghost, squinting. "This is as I envisioned her."

"Hey," Lola says with a wave. "I didn't think we would ever meet, not like this."

"You're familiar with me?" Dasco asks.

"Who isn't? I went to one of your shows." Dasco doesn't need to know that she and Synarion ruined his grand opening several years ago with Ashley Amber's death. It's a minor detail of little importance to the goal at hand.

Dasco smiles. "I am a fan of yours, ever since I saw visions of you. The muse wouldn't get you out of my head. It's safe to say you're briefed on this strange situation?"

Lola nods. "Strange shit."

A twitch of a grin rises on Dasco's face as he extends his hand to the open space. Something in his eyes tells Lola he is far more excited to see her than she is to see him. "I'm pleased to share with you, I've finished the ritual circle. I think we need you in the centre."

"Sorry?" Lola asks. "On the artwork?"

"Yes, I'm afraid so."

She squints at Synarion, then Four, and to Dasco. "Fuck, maybe take a girl out to eat first before getting messy."

Dasco scratches his scalp. "Forgive my manners. I don't talk to many people and am filled with excitement. It's not ideal to sit on paintings, I get it. There are better methods of executing the muse's vision. A larger canvas, possibly rolling paper. The amount of detail needed and textures couldn't absorb in a thinner pulp. Regardless, this is what we've concluded from the muse's visions." Dasco glances at Synarion, who squints. "I've painted you too."

Synarion folds his arms. "Have you?"

"Yes." Dasco extends his arm to Scalebane. "My Anima desired to find you. They said you were in Hell, though you are no demon?"

"It's not worth your trouble," Synarion says, curling his fingers. "I am here and I bring Cabello." He walks to the ritual circle, boots clicking on the wood flooring. He hugs his elbow, other hand resting on his chin, eyeing the golden glyphs speckled with black. The white lines also have the speckles. "I've seen these before."

Scalebane speaks. "It's the same ancient language that brought me and my sister to you so long ago."

"Effective for creating portals," Synarion says. "Or summoning. How do we activate it? Other than Lola being in the centre?"

"I'm resourceful," Dasco says. "The white lines cover the highest layer on the painting. The glyphs are a custom mixture that I've formed together with gold leaf and gunpowder, with a careful balance to avoid water."

"Interesting." Synarion's eyes follow the trail of ritual symbols. "We have to light it?"

Dasco nods and points to a fire extinguisher. "That's why this is here." He takes a bow and speaks. "The muse is eager. I'm eager. Shall we?"

Lola exhales stress and drops her bag with a thud. The practical side of her tells her to walk away. She eyes Synarion, contemplating what Mother Nature's vague signals meant. He nods at her with pressed lips. She says, "Let's get to it."

"This way." Dasco guides Lola to the circular group of canvases and points for her to step in the middle. "Sit there, that's what the muse commands."

"Then what?" Lola asks.

Scalebane's tail appears from underneath her cloak, ripping a small scale from the flesh. "Take this," she says, handing the drug to Dasco.

He passes it to Lola. It's warm in her icy hand. *Guide me*, she thinks. She spins the ash in her fingers and walks onto the paintings' wood backings. Dasco Amoss's works aligns the centre of the summoning circle to where four canvases meet. It lets Lola sit on the frames, cross-legged. Four, Scalebane, and Synarion gather in wonder. Dasco takes a lighter from his front pocket as he gets on his knees. The other three remain standing. Lola places the warm scale on her tongue and chews several times, swallowing, and closes her eyes. The ash will guide her, as it does with each session. This occasion is new, with a strange ritual ring and symbols of a lost world.

Dasco leans to the painting, pauses and looks at Scalebane. She nods, and he flicks the lighter, bringing the flame to the circle. It combusts with fire riding the white line, snagging nearby glyphs, and around small circles, never reaching Lola. It consumes the entire linework overlaying the canvases. The flicker rises a couple inches in height, tingling Lola's boots.

She keeps her eyes closed, feeling the element's heat. The smell of burning oil fills her nose. With deep breaths, through her nose and out of her mouth in common meditation, the hum of ash trickles through her system. Her mind feels as if it is being stretched apart, broadening with the sixth sense, detecting the five in the room. Though one is dimmer, she can't place why. An entity lingers beyond the vibrating frequencies of matter.

Child . . . comes Mother Nature's voice.

Despite her eyelids being shut, a mysterious shape pokes at the fabric of the black space. It's piercing through the barriers of her consciousness. The object, three claws, shred through the void and into her mind.

Stay back!

Her eyes fling open. The vibrant living world ash provides isn't here. Nor is the saturated normal reality. This view contains the same subjects, filtered in reverse black-and-white. Shadows illuminate the light while the brightest portions of the room, such as the lamp, are in total darkness. The other members of this séance remain frozen. Dasco's jaw hangs in pure amazement, showing a mouth full of white.

"The summoning is complete," says a voice. It's coming from her. She feels it in her throat. An entity is living within, creating a double sound, one lower pitched and another higher, accompanied by her own. They speak together. "Dasco, you have done well."

Dasco takes a bow. "My muse, is this you? I don't believe it."

"Belief is what we have, mortal." *What are you?* Lola attempts to talk. She has no control over her physical self, as if her body was turned to concrete, and the words project as thoughts. They bounce against the barriers of her psyche. *What are you . . . what are you . . . what are you.*

The muse speaks. "You are my vessel, mortal. I am the painter's muse and a ghoul from the Midway, as he predicted."

Lola tries to move, yet her body doesn't respond. She exists in her mind. The presence of Mother Nature is nowhere to be found, raking her heart with a frigid iciness.

Dasco's eyes widen with the night black sclera and light grey irises. His mouth moves as he speaks with the oral cavity projecting light within his throat. "I've listened to you my whole life. You guided me through schooling, helped springboard my career. I exist because of you. Why so long? Why?"

"Trivial achievements in the mortal realm. You required years of skill to develop an effective hand. These are not paintings, Dasco. I needed you to understand the universe, your realm, and the looming dangers that are coming from beyond to craft such a delicate ritual."

"Lightless ones?" Scalebane asks, who still stands still, claws on her sai.

"Correct. The End," Lola and the ghoul says.

"What is your name, ghoul?" Synarion takes one step closer.

"Introductions? If you prefer. Though, I assure you, this is the one time you will hear from me. Piercing into the mortal realm isn't what it was long ago, when physical portals existed. The mind is what remains."

"We're well aware," Synarion says as he taps his chest. "I'm Synarion, a balancer of Mother Nature. This is Scalebane, Four, Dasco, and Lola, who you're possessing."

"Lola, the psychonaught. Dasco, the visionary. Four, of many faces. Scalebane, the warrior from Hell whose mother is of legendary status. Synarion, a nymph, knowledgeable. We align the most to maintain order. My name is Malpherities. I represent the ghouls of the Midway on this matter."

Synarion squints as his eyes dart across Lola's face. She cannot tell what he sees, whether it is her or this thing that controls her body. She clenches, or tries to, to no success. Then she shoves, and her body doesn't react. This thing, ghoul, Malpherities, has locked her inside her own mind. A blast of cold helplessness washes over Lola, who can only observe.

Synarion speaks. "Why do ghouls care for the safety of the mortal realm? You're neutral."

Malpherities and Lola say, "If we don't control the looming end, it will shred apart the fabric of your universe."

Scalebane says, "You speak of the lightless ones and the divine plan?"

"Crafty one, aren't you?" Malpherities says. The ghoul forces Lola to lift her right brow. She feels as if invisible hands pull on her muscles to listen to the entity's expression. "Lightless ones existed before the Creator. They won't stop until they have protected this cosmos resembling a mould growing over a fruit."

Synarion speaks. "Protect? In the eyes that they see fit."

"They aren't concerned with the Creator's creatures or their design. Their focus is beyond the limitations of your linear time. It's why I relate with them."

Scalebane asks, "Can you stop them?"

"Stop them?" Malpherities tilts Lola's head against her will. "I am no ambassador of the lightless ones, mortal. They don't speak our words. I can navigate their intentions, even direct them."

"What is this divine plan?" Scalebane asks as her tail sways. "Manageficient Enterprises?"

"The lightless ones sense dangers and react."

Lola tries to control her body again by pushing, squeezing, pulling, to no success. The coldness that consumes her nerves coil around her sense of self, her soul. Invisible needles slip into her, pricking as she tries to scream. Her throat doesn't respond. She is trapped, listening to this thing command her flesh.

"When are they arriving?" Synarion asks.

"An interesting question, balancer. I struggle to answer, for the ghouls and lightless ones do not operate in mortal realm time. They are here, living in the essence of creationism. They're stable. If they weren't, your shadow would leave you. Considering we have linear time to spare, I am a gift bearer, providing a tool to stop this threat."

The group exchanges glances, lost by the ghoul's words which snuffed out all reason. Even Lola found her mind in a knotted mess trying to understand what Malpherities said.

"What?" Synarion asks, breaking the silence.

"You are witnessing it." Malpherities grins, forcing Lola to smile against her will. The sinister face even makes Dasco's smirk fade. Synarion's brows furrow.

What did you do to me? Lola thinks. She tries to command her body. It doesn't budge. *Mother Nature?*

Malpherities says, "Lola. Lola Cabello, correct? You have a fascinating history. Your haunted mind burns with fire and you are clueless of yourself. Intriguing how potent a soul can be and so dormant of its existence."

"Elaborate," Scalebane says with a tightness escaping her voice.

"Demanding, aren't you? I bring a gift, guiding the End to the First. Guides offer controlled interactions."

"Why me?" Dasco asks. His face remains painted with concern. "My muse, for my whole life. Why me, of all painters?"

"Ancient civilizations once knew the importance of artists, respecting their art. They were seers, piercing into the realms of the divine. This is long gone. Visual communication is fashionable, with trends vanishing before one can absorb what little depth they have. You listen. As have others. Lola and Scalebane have."

Synarion folds his arms. "None of this answers why your kind wants to intervene with the lightless ones eradicating the living. Sounds like a wonderful feast of the dead."

"Tides of balance are difficult to maintain. A balancer, such as yourself, should understand. This is not the first time we've intervened with the balance of realms to prevent them from shattering. The potency of this . . . Manageficient Enterprises . . . and the lightless ones will shred this universe to pieces. If you dissolve one reality, who's to say the mould won't spread? Hence, the gift."

The shadows, appearing as illuminating blobs of oil, dance in gentle pulses. Lola swears she sees hands rising from their two-dimensional plane. The flame, in pitch black, surrounding the ritual circle, has burnt most of the canvases. A heavy coldness drags Lola's sense of self down. Although she cannot place it into words, the feeling of something far darker, demoralizing and vast, hovers over her being. *No*, Lola thinks. *I don't want this gift.*

Malpherities forces Lola's face into a stern expression. "You have no choice, Cabello. This is a tool I offer for you've built a resistance through your desire for power that no other mortal can endure. This was my purpose for you, Dasco Amoss."

I don't want it! Lola says in her mind. She tries to control her body and scream as loud as she can. It doesn't flinch. No sound. She's a prisoner, witnessing more limbs rising from the shadows as the light-darkness things compress into physical, three-dimensional forms. Intense vibrations beat against her essence.

Malpherities speaks, "Witness the panpsychism that radiates throughout your world. It'll allow you to harvest the unthinkable."

I don't want it! A rotting sensation churns her sense of self with a nip of stinging regret that she had made a grave mistake.

The canvases reduce to shreds, leaving the frames in splinters. The fire shrinks to half an inch.

"What do you mean?" Dasco asks. He stumbles forward like a child about to be abandoned. "Will you communicate with me again? Share the history of the universe? The countless lost pieces of information that I failed to paint? Where do you go?"

Malpherities makes Lola's head bow. "You have done well, mortal."

A section of the flame dies, breaking the ritual circle. The remaining fire snuffs out in one blast. A wave of energy slams into Lola's face, knocking her back, skull rebounding against the ground. The body is hers again; the ghoul is gone, and the coldness that claws her skin remains.

Footsteps come to her and she smells Synarion's familiar pinecone sent through the smoke and blackness. Her eyes burn and they roll on their own behind her head. Her cornea feels as if someone has sliced them open, creating a sharp sting. Her eyelids flicker as Synarion holds her against his chest. His hand takes a gentle hold of her eyelids.

"Your eyes," Synarion says.

"Wh-a-at do you me-a-an?" Lola asks, voice shaking. She pats her face, blinking. The ghoul isn't here, and the pain remains. Her black-and-white reversed vision stays. The light-shadow hands leave their flat surfaces, rising along the walls to the ceiling with faceless heads gazing at her.

CHAPTER 52
ALIGNING VALUES

Scalebane wishes to stay in Dasco Amoss's apartment to better understand what gift the ghoul gave Lola. She could leverage it as proof for King. The group wouldn't let her drag the soft skin to the meeting with Mastema. It's also unwise giving her to the First. She'll deflect her employer, her people's leader, as she's done in the past. Working behind the Crystal Moths is tedious, and it baffles her that they haven't caught Jekos, unlike her.

A warm pulse comes from her chest—her soulstone. King is contacting her. "Time is of the essence," Scalebane says, eyeing Cabello on the ground, curled into a ball. Pathetic.

"Of course, go," Synarion says as he holds the human with such care, as he once did with Scalebane. The interaction twists Scalebane's gut with disgust.

"Anima, will you return?" Dasco takes a step towards her.

She ignores him, walks across the studio, and leaps out the window. Scalebane is swift through the streets on all fours. She weaves through the alleyways in the early morning. The homeless observe a darting shadow between blocks from their tarp tents. Mouths dangle open in disbelief. The sun rises one third past the horizon, leaving the glass cityscape in an orange hue. In no time, she arrives at Allen Sky Tower via the alley where Jekos and Rithu await. The halfbreed's hands rest in his pocket, his foot tapping.

"Why am I summoned?" Scalebane asks as she rises onto her feet. "You should have been present with Four."

Jekos raises his one brow to cast a firm face sprinkled with concern. "I'm moving certain pieces within Eden Breaker."

Scalebane glances at Rithu and then Jekos.

"You said we can trust him," Jekos says, nodding his head to Rithu.

Rithu takes a deep breath to puff up his size. "My father grows suspicious. After our last call with him, he wants to expedite our goals."

Jekos guides them towards the building through the loading dock. "That's the meeting's agenda. A bit of ash, a little mating, the merger, and specifically what we've been doing."

"Meaning?" Scalebane folds her arms as they reach the backdoor.

"Let me lead," Jekos says as he unlocks the entrance with a key fob. The door beeps. "We haven't been as productive as they would like. For one, you and Rithu aren't popping out eggs, even after your Mental Damnation stunt. That is not my interest. We have maintained ash, yet are not growing. That's because the Nine can't produce more, related to the breeding issue. We failed to keep Cabello and explain where she got concentrated light, or Mastema's schedule. I'm crafty, but, there isn't a lie in the world that could describe where Cabello got her resources from. This is what Mastema and King want us to answer."

Jekos takes them through the fluorescent lit hall, dress shoes clicking. "Were you able to find Cabello?"

"Yes, she is in Toronto with the painter." Scalebane whispers through her breath. Her eyes run along the halls, looking for any cameras. They appear safe.

"Excellent," Jekos says as they turn left to the chrome elevator.

Rithu says, "Is there anything I can do?"

"Follow my lead, and we will brief you on the details once we get through this excruciating meeting." Jekos presses the lift button and brushes his brown vest.

The doors slide open and they step in, silent on the ride, with soft jazz tunes playing. The shaft dings at the top floor and the three exit into the familiar circular space with the round bar in the centre. Like last time, the nymph bartender operates the counter. The group heads around the other side where Kai Pung made her fateful leap from the window a year ago. To no surprise, the glass has been replaced.

Mastema stands, facing the Toronto metropolis with a cocktail in hand. His white silk suit is pristine, with no wrinkles. He turns to them, tucking his hair being his ears. "Perfect, there are my three top family members."

Jekos takes a bow while walking and twirls his wrists in the air. "We live to serve you, master Mastema. Where are those vampire acquaintances? Surely they're your favourite?"

Mastema chuckles. "How bold of you, Jekos."

Jekos presses his hands together with a toothy grin.

Mastema points to his left. Bookshelves form walls, offering privacy within the office section of the circular loft. They encompass a black wooden desk and several chairs. The group follows the mob leader to the spot. Each takes a seat on the red velvet cushions. Jekos glides his hand against the dark polished armrests. Scalebane uses both claws to position herself on the fabric. Her leg acts as a plank of wood: stiff and numb. She pushed it too far today. Rithu sits straight, formal, and attentive to what will unravel. As for Mastema, he does not sit. He takes a sip of the cocktail, swirls it around his mouth, and spits it into a small metal garbage can at the side of the table. The desk itself houses a laptop, telephone, a couple of coasters, and a pile of papers held together by paperclips.

"Anyone want a drink?" Mastema asks.

The three shake their heads no and Mastema puts his glass on a black coaster beside the phone. "Let's get this meeting going, shall we? There are numerous topics. We'll start with the ash process. Not much has changed over the years, and we maintain a credible, consistent output through the Nine that King nurtures. The drug has gained a reputation throughout the streets, commoners, and with the upper class. It didn't take long for them to discover it sterilizes humans. If Dr. Lang wasn't first, another scientist would be. Will the weak stop using it because of that? No. Addiction relishes the gluttonous sin."

Jekos nods. "Not quite the same as pride, is it?"

Mastema smirks. "Yes. Or as fun. I must note, Lereif, you taste different today. It's potent as usual, with a newfound staleness. Why the shattered ego?"

Scalebane shifts in her seat. "We'll get to that, won't we?" Of course he calls Scalebane by Lereif. Pompous prick feeding off her ego. It strikes her enough that Mastema closes his eyes and takes a deep inhale, tasting her sin.

Jekos clears his throat. "Let's keep the meeting's agenda. Sterilization, part of phase one of the divine plan."

Mastema exhales and opens his eyes. "Correct. We want to expand faster. These two ash producers here can't figure that out, even after Rithu's heroic actions." Mastema extends a hand to Rithu and Scalebane.

And if you didn't capture my sister, we wouldn't be having this situation, Scalebane thinks. She would love to point fingers at him, as she has done countless times before. The Moths and the vazeleads have moved on. Scalebane has not.

Mastema says, "That's where the King will speak, isn't it, Rithu?"

Rithu says, "We discussed this on our flight with my father."

"So? I wasn't there."

"I'll call King." He takes the soulstone resting against his chest and rubs his palm.

"Excellent. Maybe one day he'll appear in person? Leave that cave and live a lavish life. Anyway, as Rithu does that, we know that the merger with Allen Oil Site Solutions and Manageficient Enterprises is a success. Dr. Lang is getting the funding and supplies he needs. The Prime Minister is interested in creating more jobs, growing the economy, increase taxes, and reduce crime and poverty. Mr. Patterson grows his company. The three want to expand science within this nation. Canada will become a global leader in the development of bioengineering. Of course, as Dr. Lang has spoken countless times on the media, exploring transhumanism."

"This is wonderful," Jekos says.

"Ash is playing a key part in the synthesizing project to help us escalate the usage of the drug in mainstream medical care now that it has credibility. Dr. Lang is a brilliant scientist and Manageficient Enterprises has made tremendous leaps in their research over the years. With this funding, they will skyrocket. Moths initiated the merger thanks to our family values. The Prime Minister is pleased and is opening new doors for me with Canada's southern neighbours, the United States of America. I'll meet the President, Vice President, and the Prime Minister next week."

Jekos says, "That's what we want."

Mastema knocks his knuckles on the table, creating a soft echo. "Which brings me to the principal topic of why I wanted to meet with the three of you, and King. There are countless moving parts. There have been a lot of hiccups along the way, such as our breeding issue, an attempted assassination, and Cabello's escape."

Jekos clears his throat. Rithu is motionless. His soulstone illuminates orange. Scalebane twines her tail around her ankle. The bashing begins.

Mastema circles the desk. "I fear there is betrayal within our organization. It is difficult to pinpoint considering there are many gears and few see the grand picture the way King and I do."

Rithu speaks, "King, we're here . . . Mastema is bringing us to the point of conversation, betrayal inside the Moths . . . King is listening and wishes you to continue."

Mastema stops at the front of his desk and sits on top of it. His legs cross as he puts his hands into his pocket. "I don't want to nitpick mistakes. However, Dr. Lang is making wonderful progress at Manageficient Enterprises, far more than I expected with samples of Cabello and ash scales."

Rithu whispers the responses through his soulstone to King. His voice is soft and muffled through the mask.

Mastema continues, "This betrayal within: Dr. Lang is the newest under our wing. He saw Cabello once. I pondered if he made the concentrated light bullet. He is playing with shadows and light. Although, concentrated light comes from the afterlife. The Prime Minister has informed me his general, Florence, learned that GeneChron, one of Manageficient Enterprises's labs, obtained an unusual sample of DNA from a Detective Archer. It's a demon horn from a succubus. In fact, Archer is the same detective who was working on ash in 2016. She partnered with Detective Iglesias, who spearheaded the case. If I'm connecting the pieces correctly, he was in touch with Lola Cabello." Mastema chuckles and kicks the marble floor. "I am no conspiracy nut, but I think you three understand what I'm leaning to."

Jekos looks at the other two and shrugs.

Mastema squeezes his fists. "Piece it together, you imbeciles." He releases his fingers and continues. "Cabello got her hands on a concentrated light bullet. Dr. Lang has demon DNA, Cabello's, and vazelead. He has far more than he should. Detectives who no longer work the ash case are sticking their noses where they don't belong. A bad actor is feeding resources and data to these individuals. It must be a person with special privilege, planting a rotten seed in our progress."

Jekos squints. "Dr. Lang?"

"No, foolish Jekos. He obtained the demon DNA. He's too new and, despite his frustrations with my secrecy, would rather work with me. Either way, I have the vampires going to the lab to erase this information. We can't give Dr. Lang too many toys to play with, can we? Cabello and ash are enough. Well, and the shadows." He sighs. "Imperfect gears in these moving parts. That's why the vampires will act as additional security. Now that you're briefed with my concerns, have you made progress in locating Cabello?"

Scalebane shakes her head no. "She slipped through our grasp."

"Hmm. I'm sure you understand this betrayer does not have the vazeleads', nor the Crystal Moths', interests at heart. Who else would try to assassinate me? Who would assist Cabello in escaping? Who would attempt to sabotage an entire lab in the basement of this tower?"

Jekos blinks. Rithu continues to transfer the words. Scalebane grips the armrests. This is tension they weren't expecting. How Mastema learned of their scheming is a mystery and best left for Jekos to deflect.

The half-imp unbuttons his vest and crosses his leg, spreading his arms wide on the chair arms. "Cabello is a resilient and crafty individual with ancient lineage. That can build resilience. She could have gotten the concentrated light and forged the bullet by a range of means. Don't forget, sir, there are other old world characters that are not fond of what we're doing."

"Shut up," Mastema says, nostrils flaring. "The balancer is not capable of such things, idiot. Who else is there? I'm far more knowledgeable than what most presume. I've placed my loyal Moths strategically. Of course, I can't know their inner workings; otherwise, they'd lose the discrete nature of their work."

A spy, Scalebane thinks.

Mastema continues, "That's the true strength of a leader, understanding when to trust, and when to not." He waves his ring-fingered hand at Jekos. "You're far too spineless, and stupid, stuck between two worlds. Others have unique insight and aren't fond of what I'm building." He leans forward, looking at the vazeleads.

Rithu raises his head. "King reaches the same conclusion. He protects his people and wants what is best for them. However, he fears Scalebane hasn't trusted the Moths, specifically Mastema. He . . ." Rithu looks at Jekos, and Scalebane. ". . . which he believes leaves her mind toxic, and she is unintentionally sabotaging the divine plan."

Scalebane's blood heats, tingling in her limb, running to her chest and into her skull. The feathers on her scalp puff, raising the hood an inch higher. She grinds her teeth. "What are you implying?"

Rithu says, "I speak on my own terms: Scalebane isn't involved in this. Father, Mastema, she has proven herself loyal from years of effort. She would nev— . . . yes . . . Father—" Rithu growls.

Mastema says, "We haven't seen eye to eye, Lereif."

Rithu says, "'King speaks. He's disappointed in me. He's disappointed in Scalebane, who cares little of anyone other than herself. She doesn't even care for her own sister anymore."

Scalebane stands, lashing her tail in the air with a loud snap. "I've proven loyal to our people! Where blindness thrives, I see through the façade. Moths aside, I warned of a looming threat beyond the visible. I've protected my sister while serving King. How dare you spit such false words."

Mastema shakes his head while Rithu finishes translating to his father.

Rithu speaks, "King says that Scalebane is driven by too much fire. She needs to fulfil her duty to their people, or we'll cast her with the Nine."

Scalebane swallows a cluster of saliva. She looks at Jekos to the right, then Rithu, then Mastema, who stares at her while cracking his knuckles, one arm tucked underneath his armpit.

Rithu continues, "King says that the synthesizing of ash is inevitable due to the lack of scales. They can provide more for the Moths by adapting their partnership, providing value. Seeing as Scalebane is unwilling to breed, her sister will."

Scalebane hisses. "She's nowhere to be found. I've looked for her."

Mastema walks around his desk and presses a button on the phone. He leans into the speaker and whispers, too low to hear.

Scalebane says, "Rithu, tell King that I would not harm the vazelead people. What I want is true to his hopes. The Moths are blind to a greater issue at hand. You must believe me. I have proof of the lightless ones. Let me get it for you." *I need Cabello*, she thinks.

Rithu transfers her message. "King is uninterested in your pleas. He says you have exploited your privileges, going rogue, chasing ghosts of your family and of the otherworldly. You've lost your mind, hoping to pinpoint the blame on Mastema when he has proven himself a powerful ally for the vazelead people . . . But Father, I tell you that Scalebane has done right. If you don't believe her, provide her one more opportunity to pro— . . . wait . . . Father . . ."

The elevator dings, slides open, and a cloaked figure steps out. Their long black fabric drapes to the ground, matching Rithu's and Scalebane's fashion. This is the signature look of a vazelead hiding amongst the new age of soft skins. Their custom wide boots stride on the polished floor. The clothing covers each inch of the body. A leather mask with rectangular goggles shields their face. The metal muzzle has sculpted fangs inside the smiling mouth. Even through Scalebane's metallic covering and the distance, she can smell the natural floral and smoke scent of the newcomer underneath the fabrics. It's a familiar blood. It is family. Namsruc.

CHAPTER 53
INTRUDERS

Lola hugs her arms, unable to comprehend the celestial event that occurred. The inverted reality lessens as the ash in her system dwindles. The contrast of vibrant and dark dampens while colours do not bloom, leaving her vision in a bleak grey. Light represents darkness while the shadows project lighter greys. The bright-shade hands and faces retreat to their two-dimensional planes. They pulse, vibrating with each motion of the living world.

"My eyes, my goddamn eyes," Lola says. Disbelief seeps between her teeth.

"What do you see?" Synarion asks.

"It's so dark, Synarion," Lola says through her defeated breath. "The shadows want to rise. They're watching. Anger."

He rubs her shoulders. "Stay together, Lola." He lifts her lids with his thumb and index finger. His mouth hangs, staring.

"What? What is it?" Lola asks.

"They're new," the other says.

"New? What the f-u-u-ck is th-i-is?" Lola asks, voice shaking. He looks to the window.

"Balancer," Four says. They take his backpack and unravel the printed sheets containing Manageficient Enterprises's floor plans onto the coffee table. Lola curls into a ball, wishing colours and proper contrast of the world would return.

"I'm needed," Synarion says.

Footsteps move around. She doesn't care. She wants this horror to disappear. *Mother Nature warned me,* she thinks. *I couldn't understand. I didn't want to.* Too late for Lola. She's along for the ride. The ravaging claws of defeat hack into her pride, leaving her a deflated mess on the floor. She longs to cry, to expunge her shattered heart. She chomps on her lower lip to suppress her pain.

"Time is of the essence," Scalebane says.

"Of course, go," Synarion says.

"Anima, will you return?" Dasco says.

"We're here for you." Synarion gives Lola a squeeze and stands, walking away.

More steps follow. Lola takes several deep breaths and opens her eyes. It's the same grey saturation. She shuts them again. *It's okay, keep your composure.* She stands, opening her sight. *Flipped, it's fucking inverted.* She stares at the once bright bulbs casting pitch black.

Think of the Becky-Mom-Michael super monster. I fought that beast and won. I battled my own mind. I got this.

Lola moves a couple of paces, catching Synarion's attention. "You okay?" He steps to her and Lola extends her hand.

"No, I'm good. Yeah." She takes another step, seeing how the shadows shift position, not natural to the light. They move around her, as if her body was an opposite magnet pushing them away. The greyness of the world leaves some objects, like the loveseat, matching the same tone as the bookshelf, rendering them invisible.

Four taps the coffee table. "Balancer, focus. Cabello is operational. Walk me through your plan."

Operational, Lola thinks. They don't care for Lola's wellbeing. Synarion does, in a warped way. She has to protect herself with this new mysterious gift. Her attention drifts to Dasco's paintings, walking to the easels resting against the wall on the opposite end of the studio. The small shadows between the slits bounce.

Don't freak out. You've been through worse. Within her, fear rattles across her chest, knowing her life will never be the same. Her throat closes a smidge at the haunting realization.

"I've been painting these things for years," Dasco says. He stands a metre from Lola, hands behind his back, fidgeting with his thumbs. He's nervous. As he should be, because Lola is no longer normal. Maybe she never was.

"I watched you paint me in a vision," Lola says. She points to the portrait of her with universe bubbles for eyes. The painting has notable contrast, making it visible in the grey world.

"As I saw you countless nights through the muse."

"What's this?" Lola asks, walking towards one finished artwork leaning against the wall. It comprises a being in a cylinder filled with liquid. Their skin is pale with reptilian eyes and hair of a human. Below it the tube splits into two directions, fusing to the dome of a reptile skull and human's.

"It's what the muse showed me." Dasco shrugs.

Hybrids, Lola thinks. She saw these beings in that lab a year ago. Dasco's work supports it. She stares at it, letting this entity draw her in. *What gift are you?* She blinks several times, moving away, hugging her arms, past the oracle to Synarion and Four. Practical discussions, like floor plans, will keep her sane.

Four speaks. "Accessing it through secrecy is the best approach."

"We're used to that," Synarion says. "We were looking to get in through the main floor's loading station."

"Clever. Lab coats," Four says with a flat tone.

"IDs too. Eden Break serves well," Synarion says on an exhale.

"We have weapons," Lola says. She puts her hands on the table and looks at the shaper.

"I have communication that we can use," Synarion says.

"Good," Four says.

Synarion taps the floor plan, pointing to a central server room. "The controls are here where we install the backdoor."

"Backdoor?' Lola asks. She curls her fingers and rests her palms along the edge of the surface for balance.

"Eden Breaker is working remotely with that Trojan file." Synarion's eyes run up and down Lola, analyzing her while speaking. "When we give them access, they'll delete the data stored there."

Lola says, "Yeah, they'd have cloud storage."

"Ah, not so. Recall Dr. Lang's interview? A closed network prevents remote access. That is why we must install a remote signal."

Four folds their arms. "Clever. Data destroyed. What of the lab itself?"

"Eden Breaker segregates their intel, I take it?" Synarion shifts his focus onto the shaper.

Four presses their lips together.

Synarion points to each of the three EMFC chambers. "There are overrides. Eden Breaker will shut down the central security doors, giving us access to manually turn off each one. We'll have ten minutes to get out, according to Eden Breaker."

Lola blinks several times, staring at the east circular EMFCs. The linework is too light. She swears it is invisible and leans into the paper as a hand rests on her shoulder.

"You sure you're okay?" Synarion asks.

Lola shakes her head, breaking the trance. "Yeah."

"You can do this?" His concerned tone shapes his words into a question.

"Yes, Synarion. I need some ash." She rubs her eyes, hoping that it will wipe away whatever nonsense is taking hold of her.

"And a smoke. Mind coming with me? It's a little hard to see." She extends her hand. He grabs it.

"We'll be back," Synarion says. "Familiarize with the plans."

He aids her out of Dasco's loft and outside on the main floor. They use a small plank of wood to pry the door open. She lights a drag. The lighter projects a black flame as she brings it to the tip of her cigarette.

"Why me?" Lola says.

Synarion looks to the night street, moving from her exhaled smoke.

She wants to lean into him, seeking physical solace. That's what Kendra was to Lola in prison, a tool to aid her emotional needs. Synarion can be that new comfort. He can tell her things will be okay. Her life will return to how it used to be when she was younger at university. That is untrue in the real world. You must protect yourself. Lola must remain strong. Her goals are apparent in her mind. The stakes of the game have changed, and the Moths are still the target.

"I learned I'm an aunt and I'll never see the kid," Lola says. *That was stupid,* she thinks, swallowing the regret.

Synarion draws in a deep breath.

"I didn't ask for any of this, Synarion," Lola says.

"Of course," he says. "None of us did. Yet here we are, working together. Because, despite our differences, we want the same thing."

"Being?"

"Peace."

"I suppose," Lola says and takes a big inhale. "You know what Mul, that demon, said to me, before Scalebane killed her?"

"Before you took her horn fragment and gave it to that detective?"

"Before that. She told me to find her, she'd show me what ash can really do."

Synarion scratches his neck. "That sounds like her. A tease."

"I didn't take ash willingly at first. The more I tried to do good, the more it changes me into something I don't recognize."

"You're still you, Lola," Synarion says.

She tosses the butt end of her cigarette onto the street and chuckles. "No, not anymore."

"I disagree. Your eyes have changed, yet I sense you and the persistence I admire."

Lola raises her eyebrow. "You don't need to lay it on thick. You've made it clear what your agenda is."

"I told you, Lola, I made a mistake and I wish—" he wipes his mouth. "Now is not the time for this."

"Yep." Lola squeezes her biceps and heads inside. She stumbles on the single step leading to the entrance. The reverted light isn't helping. It also wrecks the cool image she portrayed, shrugging him off. He is right. She is Lola: a goth dork reporter who likes the internet.

They enter Dasco's loft and gather around the coffee table. Synarion instructs Lola and Four regarding their exact path. They review the receiving elevator, one of two exits, that will bring them from the back of Allen Sky Tower and descend to the laboratory. They are going to take the long hallway into an open foyer. The linework contains numerous levels further below. They'll go to the lowest level, fifteen. Through a hall to the east is the main server room. It looks straightforward on paper. Execution is another story.

"Any questions?" Synarion asks.

Four says, "That data centre, there's two exits. Eden Breaker connecting will signal security. We'll be trapped."

"That's the point of the disguises. We'll have some weapons if needed. The plan isn't to get cornered and start a shootout. You can morph. Anything useful for this scenario?"

"I have a few." Four says with the playful eyes of a cat gleaming in their gaze.

Lola asks, "Is there enough time for people to escape?"

Four squints. "As in the workers?"

"Yeah. Ten minutes?"

Synarion says, "I presume so. There's the receiving lift and the main elevator."

"Fifteen floors, though, plus thirteen prior to the lab." Lola presses her lips together, with the weight of time and lives pressing on her back.

Synarion says, "This will surely trigger an alarm if these EMFCs produce dangerous levels of energy. It'll be a procedure for them to evacuate." He points to a small room drawn on the floor plans. "Worst case, they have a panic shelter designed to withstand tragic events."

We don't know, Lola thinks, clenching her teeth. She's with two old world beings. Why would they care about human life? They focus on the bigger picture, not considering a single person. Lola let lives perish in the name of revenge. She's not like the old world souls. They use people for their own gain. This will occur whether or not she likes it. She needs to take part and ensure it succeeds. *A temporary alliance.*

Synarion slaps the table. "We'd best go."

"Will you return?" Dasco's voice comes from behind Lola. "I have so many questions." He kneels by the burnt canvases, slouched with a frown on his face.

Synarion shrugs. "That I cannot confirm, friend. Your hospitality has been graceful and Mother Nature thanks you."

"Please, visit. I feel incomplete." He doesn't look at the group, gaze lost in his destroyed work.

Lola says, "You've done enough." She snags the duffel bag and heads for the door. Four rolls the plans and follows. Lola spots Synarion from the corner of her eye, he walks to Dasco, patting him on the arm, and then joins the group. The painter is on his own, left to wonder what happens next.

Outside, Four drives the SUV from Dasco's loft through the cracked downtown alleyways. The other two open the box in the back, finding lab coats, fake printed names with photos of them, and lanyards.

Lola buttons the white, or, according to her inverted view, charcoal coat, keeping her gaze on the ceiling. The shadows inside her sleeve morph, bulging with each pump of her heart. She swats her hand at it, and it goes over it, because it's a shadow. Beyond the window, the sun radiates a dark smoke. The world is too bleak. The reflection shows her scarred face and the fresh eyes. They're fogged over, lacking life, as if she were dead.

Keep it together. Eyes on the prize, she thinks and looks away, frowning. Her internal attempt at humour isn't working.

Synarion's hand bumps hers, holding a plastic case of contacts. "I usually bring spares."

"Thanks," Lola says. She assumes their colour is brown based on what he wears. With a careful finger, she pops them in, blinking twice. "How do I look?"

"Better. But keep your head low."

Both finish dressing with the lanyards over their necks. They equip face watches to monitor the time. Synarion's backpack contains communication devices. The small earpieces fit along the Helicis Crus, discreet. Lola takes the vacuum sealed bag of ash from her duffel bag and bites a sizeable chunk of the drug, stuffing the scale in the lab coat's inner pocket. The comms are both in Lola's and Synarion's ears. It's showtime.

Outside of Allen Sky Tower, in the alleyway, Four parks the SUV beside a white and red delivery van. The three exit. It doesn't take long for ash to give her the coffee buzz. With these gifted eyes, the contrast increases, giving a sense of distance. Her sixth sense mutates the saturated vision into striking distinctions of black and white; millions of shades of grey create a rich, upturned world. The light-shadows gain depth, peeking from their flat plane. They watch the group gather at the trunk of the vehicle. None of it tells Lola how this tool helps. At least the ash is doing its job. Without it, trauma would strike. She hasn't been in this building since Mastema brought her here a year ago.

Four takes the duffel bag and leads the two Manageficient Enterprises scientists into the loading bay. The shaper's key fob unlocks the door and they enter the hall.

The hallway is dark, thanks to the fluorescent lights. It keeps her on edge, watching for the few highlights of light-shadows in the corners. They pass the main lobby. The maze of pathways takes them to an elevator with steel doors complete with diagonal safety lines. This industrial lift requires a thumbprint and number sequence on the right-hand panel, with a light.

"One moment," Four says, glancing at the security camera in the far corner. They walk to a stairwell behind them and pass the door, closing it. A few moments later, an older man with frizzy hair exits holding the duffel bag in the same suit.

The clever shaper inputs a code on the panel and places their thumb on the scanner. The bulb above turns green. For Lola, it's the same grey. Synarion and she spent two weeks learning the floor plans and what EMFCs are, and they wouldn't have had the right fingerprint. Eden Breaker harvests the fruit.

The elevator door unlocks and they enter. Inside, Four presses a number sequence on the controls, descending them.

How many people has Four eaten to shapeshift? Lola thinks. "You've been here. I saw you a year ago."

"Eden Breaker plays multiple roles. They aided you to formulate this clever scheme we're a part of, yes?"

"I figured Eden Breaker would talk to each other." Lola keeps her focus on the elevator numbers along the top of the door's frame.

"Eden Breaker works as a collective master-slave mechanism, like computing. We operate our function as instructed, no more, no less. Step out of line and you're out."

"You don't ask questions?" Lola asks.

"No." The shaper reaches into the duffel bag and passes Synarion and Lola handguns. Lola grabs a knife from the bag, stuffing it into the coat's pocket. The other weapons are far too large to hide.

"Remember the plan?" Synarion says.

Four speaks, "I'll take the lead to the server room."

The elevator descends past floor five . . . ten . . . twelve . . . reaching level thirteen. The doors glide apart and they're presented with a large hallway with fluorescent lighting. Far too dark for Lola, and she stays close to Synarion while the shaper walks them through the hall.

After fifty paces, the corridor opens into the foyer as described in the floor plans. Glass railings run along the open area with levels below, as Lola recalls from a year ago. A pang hits her heart and soothes with a single beat. Ash is keeping her emotions in check like a good drug should.

Lab workers move up and down the space. A group of five to the left, holding notepads, talk to one another. To the right, several workers pass through a transparent door, entering a lab. Behind them are several more doors with lab workers entering. Men in military uniforms stand guard at the entrances. Their stern expressions focused forward. Their shoulders contain the shield-A patch she saw last time. Private contractors. They pass more lab coats, jumpsuits, and casual business wear employees.

Lola takes a deep inhale of the sterile cold air and exhales. They're wandering through a den of snakes, hoping not to be bitten with venom.

Four takes them to the left, away from the foyer, down another hallway. Windows on each side showcase stations.

These are closer to resembling the ones Lola used in high school and university. Counters contain varying sizes of vials and chemistry equipment. Scientists with goggles and gloves work in pairs. They hold mysterious liquids in glass containers on sample trays. The adjacent station has rows of microscopes with dishes of substances.

The group turns right, heading down a zig-zag staircase to the next floor. They pass four military men walking up. Their rifles held out, uninterested in them. Five lab workers with paperclips chat with each other on the stairs midway below. On the lower level, more glass windows peer into stations. These have ash scales on the counters with tools to dissect them. Scientists transfer the samples into stainless steel machines. On the other end is black liquid. This is the same concentrated ash that Dr. Lang pumped into Lola.

A different room shows three people strapped onto operating tables. Their muscles are non-existent, skin shrivelled into raisins. Their eyes flutter. Vials of black liquid are on a tray between them. These are ash-dashers, no different than Lola. Wires and patches run along their naked forms, plugging into a computer screen, showing pulses of brain and heart activity. One's head thrashes from side to side. Another reaches for the sky. The third is motionless.

The next turn, and thirteen staircases down, takes them to the lowest level, to the east pathway. On the right side are offices and meeting rooms with long boardroom tables covering the spaces with suited employees. Private army men walk past them. Lola holds her breath and eyes their attire.

Their uniforms contain additional tiered arrow patches, showing rankings.

She gazes to the left side which has one lab positioned fifteen feet lower than the ground. Giant glass cylinders, filled with liquid, are in rows of six, four columns. Inside the bubbling foggy water are unformed hands and bobbing heads. It's too clouded to see more. Tubes and wires connect to the pods. It is an odd reflection of what Dasco painted earlier.

Underneath the tanks are the light-shadows. No amount of fluorescent bulbs can remove darkness from a room. They vibrate far faster the closer they are to these test tubes. Synarion grips Lola's arm, helping her move. She didn't notice her slacking pace. New life exists in those pods, and a hollowness inside her gut is unsure if she wants to find out what they are.

"They're moving," Lola whispers to Synarion.

"What?"

"The shadows, the lightless ones, whatever they are. They're pissed."

One turn left and they pass the last lab that is near pitch black to Lola's eyes. This means it's a blinding light. There's a small three-foot sized chrome pillar in the centre of the room, casting a single sharp light-shadow. This pillar's material glows in pulses, elevating the darkness into three dimensions on each interval. She's seen that before, when Mastema brought her here.

The vibration causes Synarion to slow his pace as a head rises from the light-shadow, defying logic and physics. Lola squeezes his arm, keeping up with Four.

The relationship between electromagnetism and relative gravity. Gravity affects light and time. Synarion's past words rise in her mind. This is science fiction mixing with the supernatural old world nonsense as far as Lola is concerned. Is it related to the Moths? Yes. It's going to burn.

The group makes their last turn to a hallway with a single door at the end. This checks out based on the floor plan. Four slows their pace halfway. There are no labs or offices, or boardrooms. These closed doors have no glass walls. Four stops and drops the duffel bag.

"Four?" Synarion asks.

Footsteps rise from the hall, multiple in synchronization.

A siren booms throughout the space. The tone shifts brighter for Lola: emergency lights. Four squints, staring at the flashing bulbs mounted at the corners of each fluorescent frame. Soldiers rush behind them before the turn, passing the group, unaware of their existence. Something else has their attention.

CHAPTER 54
HIGH STAKES

The plan is simple: sneak into a private military guarded tower containing a bioengineering lab, wipe the data, and implode the building with super magnets. This isn't a scheme that Iglesias would have brewed, nor would have Archer. Not even their latest sidekick, Disk, would have. This comes from the bold and cunning mind of their green-browed guest.

This mysterious member of Eden Breaker has the floor plans for Allen Sky Tower, drilling Archer and Iglesias on the mission. Disk listens to their important role with eager eyes. The plan goes as follows:

Step One: equip Zero's disguises as couriers delivering toxic equipment. Zero has the shipment details prepared.

Step Two: drive the delivery van to Allen Sky Tower containing the package, a fake supply, housing weapons.

Step Three: take the loading elevator to the Manageficient Enterprises laboratory. Place the decoy bomb in a location away from the data centre as a distraction. It will ensure workers have more time to escape.

Step Four: reach the server room on the fifteenth level.

Step Five: install the USB stick to the operating machine. Disk will wipe the data, turn off the security, letting the team increase the teslas of the three EMFCs.

Step Six: the elevators shift into an emergency mode with no security, ensuring the workers can escape. In ten minutes, it collapses. No more unethical experimental sciences fusing humans and the beyond.

Zero loaded them with communication devices to speak with Disk. They'll work at the deep underground levels. The outfits are a perfect match to the delivery courier company Canada FastDirect with the crimson red and white striped polos and black pants. The quote, "Eden Breaker harvests the fruit," blankets how Zero obtained the plans and the items.

It raises red flags for the detectives as they button their fresh shirts. The group stands outside of Disk's apartment, in the alleyway, beside the matching Canada FastDirect delivery van.

Iglesias asks, "How did you get this?"

Zero says, "I work in the shadows, far beyond the reach of whispering words and data points. Take comfort in me being an ally for now."

Iglesias raises an eyebrow. "For now? Is this even a real order of theirs?"

"Oh yes, they placed it last week." Zero pats the fake shipping polystyrene foam rectangular boxes in the back of the open delivery vehicle. Both of them have radiation stickers on them and warning labels with detailed print. "Use these items, as we discussed. There's a handy weapon you'll find in here, Detective Iglesias. The Moths infect the tower, including the two vampiric goons you seek. Do not hesitate."

A deep exhale escapes Iglesias's lungs. "Right." Those are the words he wants to hear. He thought they'd ignite him with anger. It leaves him concerned. He and Archer are pieces of a game of chess. The Moths master it. The media, government, and law are pawns. Eden Breaker is a new player. They haven't steered them wrong, and if it gets him closer to these pricks who killed his son, he has to play.

Detective Archer asks, "You're certain? And you're sure about what we're doing? It risks civilian lives."

Disk sits on the bumper of the van. "Zero is telling the truth. This is stuff I've been looking into forever. You saw my research. Zero confirms it. If we don't act, I think a lot worse is at stake here."

Archer folds her arms.

"We'll make sure the workers get out. Eden Breaker isn't for murder."

Iglesias wipes his beard. "It's more than a blind father seeking revenge for a son. We knew the Moths had their hands in the government and private sectors."

Zero cups their fingers. "Cabello will be there, thus you must move. You both have the same instructions to head for the server room."

Archer waves at Iglesias. "Come here for a sec."

The two detectives step to the side of the van. Archer whispers, "It feels rushed."

"Agreed," Iglesias says.

"I should call this in. That's the training. We can get the proper proof of illegal activity, pin it on these CEOs and the Prime Minister."

"Look how well the rules worked for us last time."

"My gut says no," Archer pushes the words through her clenched teeth.

"It's a double-edged sword of being good at your job." Iglesias extends a hand. "Besides, if Cabello is going, we either act now or be too late."

"Uh huh, I get why you kept Cabello a secret. I don't like working in the shadows."

Iglesias adjusts his postal hat. "With these disguises? We're discreet. Those magnets are going to incinerate the lab. No evidence."

"People will die." Archer raises her voice louder than intended. She steps closer and speaks on a whisper. "Cabello is involved."

"Which is the point of the decoy," Iglesias says at the same lowered tone. "They'll have around twenty minutes. The lab isn't that big."

"Fifteen floors."

"They're not long halls. Look, I'm giving this a go. I'm in deep. You can back off. Call this in if you think that's right. I won't stop you."

"Like I'd make it in time?" Archer pauses for a beat. "Besides, with our two new friends, they'd be hot on my trail before I could do anything. Zero knew Disk's birth name, found us. They have long tendrils." She reaches into her pocket, taking a cellphone. "This? A decoy bomb? Crazy. We've evacuated people before. It's a mess." She puts the phone away. "No. I said I was with you."

Iglesias places his hand on her shoulder. "Together."

They step around the vehicle. Zero rolls his shoulders back and asks, "Detectives?"

"We're good," Archer says.

"Okay. You got your part. Disk has theirs. I must go. Smoke and screens keep this whole thing going. Best of luck." Zero takes a bow and walks past the van, heading for a parked pearl Mercedes.

A Moth, Iglesias thinks. Paranoia. *They don't own white.*

"Let's do this, hey?" Disk says as they hop off the van bumper. "I got you guys. Your stuff is safe with me. Just get back in time."

"Thanks," Iglesias says, and he slams the back doors shut.

Step One is complete. Disk returns to their apartment. The detectives drive off. Both light smokes, thinking about the mission. This mirrors a spy movie by infiltrating the villains and going out with a bang. They could drop the whole thing and return to their mundane lives. Detective Archer can chase petty street dealers day in and day out, passing information to the military. Iglesias can focus on his plants. Both used these methods. Neither of them wants it. They desire what the law cannot provide with crooked minds involved: justice.

"You're going to be okay?" Archer asks.

"Never better," Iglesias says. He chucks his cigarette out the window. "I know the plan. Simple for us. In and out."

"If you see those, uh, two men?" Archer asks.

"Men? Christ, I'm no supernatural nut. Those were damn vampires. I'll shoot them before they can blip."

"Fuck, we need holy water, a stake, or throw garlic at them. Does that even work?"

Iglesias shakes his head. "That's what the gun is for."

They park at the shipping and receiving garage of Allen Sky Tower in the alleyway. The van reverses into the dock, where a couple of men in white suits meet them. A third individual in a military uniform stands behind them. The patch on their shoulder confirms they're not Canada's soldier. He is a mercenary. Allen Oil Site Solutions and Manageficient Enterprises climbed the ranks with the Moths.

"We have a delivery order," Archer says. She exits the van, opens the back, and slides a ramp out, lowering it to the concrete. She grabs the dolly containing both radioactive boxes from the vehicle, rolling it onto the dock.

Iglesias steps out of the vehicle and flips a clipboard that carries a form of the supposed elements they're bringing. "We gotta take it to the lab. Sign here."

The man in the military uniform steps between the two Moths, taking the document. He is young, José's age, if he were alive. This kid doesn't know what the hell he is involved in. The boy scans through the paper. "Chemicals, more chemicals. That checks out. A server rack?"

"Hey, we deliver. The labels match what you're expecting?" Iglesias extends a hand to the boxes. Archer holds the dolly, ready to go.

"Let me check." The boy reaches for his comm on his belt and speaks into it. "Hey Serg, we expecting a server rack? . . . the order number?"

Iglesias points to the order number at the top of the sheet. Zero better have given them a real order number.

"B6010353 . . . perfect. Thanks, sir." He releases the comm. "We're good." He takes a pen and signs it, giving them a nod. "This way, please."

Iglesias gives him a closed smile and a nod. *Thank God.*

Step Two complete.

The spies follow the mercenary to the loading door, who uses their key fob to open it. Their Moth friends stay behind. Through the bright hall, they pass the main lobby and reach an elevator with yellow and black diagonal safety lines. The soldier presses their thumb on the scanner and the entrance opens. In the industrial lift, their escort punches in a few numbers on the command controls. The shaft hums to life and they descend deep below ground.

Their silent ride ends with a ding and the doors slide aside. The soldier directs them into the long bright corridor, leading to a multilevel foyer with glass railings. People in white coats, suits, and military uniforms buzz in and out of transparent doors.

"You in?" comes Disk's voice through the small earbud.

Archer, behind Iglesias and the kid, whispers, "Yeah."

Iglesias's heart pounds against his chest as he keeps his gaze locked on the mercenary leading them.

They're guided past the open space, passing the railings and into a hall to their left. Glass windows on each side peek into labs; scientists work with chemistry beyond the detectives' knowledge. The soldier stops beside another elevator, next to the first set of glass windows. He presses a control button beside a staircase leading further down. The shaft dings, the doors slide open, and the group steps into the lift. Several researchers join them for half of the ride. Time ticks in Iglesias's heart. The levels pass by. Another floor down and they make it to the bottom, level fifteen, and are the last to leave the lift.

Archer slips the phone from her pocket. One press of the side button and a red light pulses in increments of two. It's activated. She slides it to the ground as they exit. She nor Iglesias glance at the ever-present video camera in the elevator.

Step Three complete.

To the right of this hall are offices. The left contains the impossible. Iglesias and Archer swear their eyes deceive them. Incubating chambers filled with frosted liquid rest fifteen feet lower. Bobbing heads peek from inside.

A turn left and there's one more lab with a bright white room containing a chrome pillar casting a shadow. It projects a powerful pulse felt beyond the glass. Gravity. Whatever's going on here isn't in the public's knowledge. That crazy kid Disk was right. Iglesias's hunch too. Except no intelligent reptilians.

"Those chemicals are okay for a few minutes, right?" the soldier asks, looking at Iglesias.

"Yeah, why?" he asks.

The mercenary points to an upcoming door at the end. "The server room is first. Want to drop those off?"

"You're the boss," Iglesias says.

Archer whispers, "Server room."

Disk speaks into Iglesias's ear. "When you're in there, Iglesias, put the USB stick in the command station before you do anything else."

"Short and sweet," Archer says.

The soldier guides them to the far end and opens the entrance. He takes them through a row of eight-foot black metal server racks with green and blue buttons with dim lighting. Ten rows, sixty feet long, encompass these computer columns. Ethernet cables in yellow, blue, green, and red run from the rear of the machines in neat linear lines.

Step Four complete.

Voices rise in the silent room. The soldier picks up his pace. Iglesias and Archer turn a corner with him, coming face-to-face with a short man with thick-framed glasses and a lab coat. Dr. Lang, as shown in Disk's research. He is arguing with a server technician beside three men. One wears an ivory shirt and pants with a bushy beard. The other two have white blazers, black shirts, and shades. The first fashions spiked hair; the other is bald. Smug and Big Jaw.

Iglesias's heart stops, feeling his throat plummet into his stomach. It's them. *Can they smell fear?* he thinks. That's a strange thought, though instinctual. These aren't men. They're monsters.

"You do not have permission to be here!" Dr. Lang shouts.

Sharp canines peek from under the top lip as the bald vampire speaks. "We will get what we want." His voice is crisp, dry, and unassuming from the video Iglesias witnessed.

The technician on the computer keeps typing away. "Downloading the data."

"I forbid you," Dr. Lang says. "You're fired!"

Big Jaw says, "He's getting a promotion."

Iglesias takes a few steps away, beside Archer. The two detectives must collaborate if things go wrong. Unforeseen schemes are happening. There are too many players in the server room.

"Anything I should be aware of?" asks the soldier.

Dr. Lang points at the three twice in frantic jabs. "They are deleting the data from the servers that we have collected from our samples. It's a breach of agreement with the merger."

Smug puts his hands in his pocket. "There is no contract under the Moth's wing. Only the divine word."

The human Moth watches during the interaction, acting as an extra arm if needed.

Big Jaw takes a few sniffs, nostrils opening, with obnoxious inhales. It's enough to catch the humans off guard and the technician stops typing. The vampire shifts his stance, facing the three newcomers. He steps forward. Even though he is wearing shades, Iglesias fears he is looking at him. He stops a meter away, too close for Iglesias's liking. His heart thumps with forceful beats.

"I know your blood." Big Jaw exposes his far too long canine teeth that grow past his lower set. "It smells familiar. Both of yours . . . runs so hot."

The lights turn red, sirens boom. Thank God. That little fake phone triggered security. The entire group stares at the ceiling, providing Iglesias an opportune moment.

Fuck this, Iglesias thinks. Archer shares the thought, both reaching for the polystyrene foam boxes. One flip and the clasps fly open, springing the lids. They grab the goods inside: Archer takes a handgun; Iglesias snags the weapon Zero mentioned. The metal contraption resembles a crossbow combined with modern technology. This object is compact, containing a foot-long wooden spike, ending in a silver tip. It's in the chamber with a belt of additional stakes dangling from the semiautomatic stake gun.

Weapons raised, Iglesias pulls the trigger. The firearm releases the stake, slinging it through the barrel, soaring through the air. Big Jaw bolts an inch before it pierces the middle of his torso. The wood shatters his left ribcage with a crack and plummets into his organs, shreds through blood and flesh, and lands into the heart.

A howling screech rises above the sirens. His body seizes, hands extended wide. Fire combusts from the wound, devouring his clothes and flesh. A blast of heat radiates from the soul. His skin cooks into flakes of ash while his body moves in uncontrolled spasms. He reaches for the stake and collapses to the floor, legs disintegrating to dust.

Smug hisses, the bottom jaw snapping and extending to his clavicle. Dr. Lang screams, stumbling back, as Archer points her firearm at the soldier.

"On the ground!" she shouts.

Iglesias aims at Smug and fires. The vampire phases, like in the security camera footage. The human Moth whips out a gun, as does the mercenary, and hell breaks loose.

Bullets fire from both sides. Iglesias takes a handgun from the supply, dual wielding. The detectives take cover behind the corner of the servers while their opponents do the same. Dr. Lang snags the control of the computer in between the crossfire. The IT technician bolts it, dashing past the soldier.

"What's going on?" comes Disk's voice.

"Things went south," Iglesias says.

More bullets speak from the soldier and human Moth, bouncing off the metal servers. Iglesias peeks around the corner and opens fire. Dr. Lang ducks, then yanks a drive from the computer's open side. He takes a leap of faith, dashing from the combat, passing the mercenary who speaks into his comm as the Moth shoots.

A hiss comes from above, louder than the alarms. It's too close. Archer looks up, facing Smug pouncing from the top of the tower. She opens fire. The bullets sink into his body. He doesn't stop. Iglesias spins, unleashing his stake gun. It strikes Smug in the arm, knocking him back for a split second. He fires again. Archer empties her clip. Smug jumps onto them, fangs open. A piercing sting. Slash! Iglesias slams against the server. Archer hits the floor. The creature blips away.

Warm liquid pumps onto his neck.

CHAPTER 55
BLOOD DIVIDED

Scalebane sought her sister for years and cannot fathom that she walks towards her. The smell is reminiscent of her childhood. Her stride, height, face covering, and clothing match. Scalebane is star-struck and dumbfounded they're meeting in Allen Sky Tower. She ventured into Hell to locate her, and Mastema calls her with one button.

Namsruc drops her hood and unbuckles the mask. Her raven scalp feathers drape to her shoulders, combed back from the top of her skull. The flaming eyes are slow-moving with a deep red, different from Scalebane's or their mother's, which dances fast. Namsruc's spiked brows slant back, expressing concern.

The smile behind the black scaled lips shows joy. Unlike the last time Scalebane saw her sister, she is healthy with the right amount of meat on her bones and is capable of manoeuvring on her own.

"Scalebane," Namsruc says, opening her arms.

Scalebane's tail perks and she bolts to her sister, ignoring her limb's constant nagging. The two vazeleads hug one another, wrapped tight around their sibling. Their tails coil together in a loving embrace. Each breathes in a whiff of the other, enjoying the familiar bog scent of their bloodline. This feels like a dream. The past few years have been the longest in Scalebane's life. Namsruc is here, at long last.

She takes another big inhale of her sister and squeezes her. "Namsruc. How, when? I mi-i-issed you so mu-u-ch." Her whisper ends in a tremble.

Namsruc leans back and reaches for Scalebane's mask. "Sister, my dear sister. I need to see you."

Scalebane grabs her hand. "Not with them here."

"We're friends here," Namsruc says.

Scalebane glances to Jekos, Rithu, and Mastema, who watch. She faces her and undoes her covering enough for her to gaze into her eyes. Namsruc takes off her leather glove and places her bare scales on Scalebane's spiked jawline. The simple touch floods her body with warmth. Yes, it's her.

"I've been looking for you for so long," Scalebane says. "Where did you go?"

"I'm so sorry, my dear sister. I didn't mean to cause you harm, or worry."

"Tell me, why?"

"I needed time," the other says.

Scalebane lowers her mask and buckles it. "I looked for you, high and low, for three years. I found the gateway into Dega'Mostikas's Triangle. I tried." *Weak willed.*

Namsruc caresses her sister's shoulder. "My Scalebane, I'm sorry. That is what I can say."

"How did you get into Hell? Your soul pierced through. I don't understand."

"Synarion reminded me of his teachings, sister. Meditation, clarity, clearing my emotions. These are things he taught us. I did not wish for you to find me in there. My dear, I cannot imagine the nightmare you saw. We do not belong in Dreadweave Pass. My actions were my own. I didn't mean to drag you into it."

"I needed you. We have to stay together." Scalebane takes her sister's hands. "Did Synarion hurt you?"

A light chuckle comes from Namsruc. "Of course not. Why would he do that to his children?"

"We're not his children," Scalebane says through her teeth.

"He raised you and me for a century and brought us to our people." Namsruc's voice goes up a notch.

"He abandoned us." Scalebane counters with a hiss.

"We needed to learn of our culture to keep it alive," Namsruc says.

"You've returned?" Scalebane's spiked brows furrow. "After what the Moths have done to you? Why here?"

Namesruc looks to the ground and rubs Scalebane's knuckles before speaking. "A lot has occurred in the past three years.

Synarion explained what the Moths were doing, what you offered him as a deal, and what happened to Valturus."

A low grumble comes from Scalebane's throat. "That awful vampire."

"He's blinded by love." She shrugs. "We can't fault him for that. Whatever spell she put on him centuries ago remains true. It's why he does not believe in King's or Mastema's ways."

Scalebane releases her sister's hands and tail. Her heart closes an inch. Her guard must be up. The meeting is too peculiar not to raise concerns. "The Moths tortured you, like an animal," Scalebane whispers.

"Animal, yes. It wasn't torture. They needed the scales, can't you see?" Namsruc asks.

"See what?" Scalebane squints.

Namsruc extends her claws to Mastema. "Our greater purpose, what King has been sharing. My time away let me realize this. It's why I'm here, Scalebane. Synarion's old teachings hold true of balance. He doesn't follow them. I do. I remember the lessons, my dear sister. I cannot keep grudges against such simple humans who were misguided and put me in a cage. I cannot hate King for finding logic in aligning with the Moths. I understand why he needs us both to hatch children with his son. Mastema is not our enemy. His rise and our allegiance are part of the natural order."

Scalebane takes a step closer, leaning into her ear. "I assure you, what Mastema does is not in anyone's favour. King is blind."

"Please, Scalebane. Listen to what King has to say." Namsruc takes Scalebane's hand and guides her to the rest of the group.

She pulls away. "The lightless ones, my sister."

Namsruc tugs again and Scalebane obeys, humouring her because she is blood. Scalebane sits beside Jekos, gripping the chair for support, careful not to lose balance. Namsruc squats in front of her, tucked between the extended left leg and her folded right. Scalebane's claws dig into the armrest of her chair as Mastema walks around his desk and sits.

An object pokes Scalebane's arm, and she glances to see Jekos extending his hand with a key card behind Namsruc's head. Mastema is turning the corner. Scalebane grabs it and slides it under her belt as the fallen angel turns and sits. Jekos must sense Scalebane's desire to escape. The meeting isn't going in her favour.

Rithu squeezes his soulstone, channelling King's voice. "Namsruc returned to her people understanding the greater purpose. She comprehends the pointlessness of defending the soft skins and is determined not to run from her duty. She'll produce offspring with Rithu. Which you will do, because you must. We're at a paradigm shift."

Mastema leans forward, putting both forearms on the desk. "The New World Order is beginning."

"How?" Scalebane asks. "Why is this crucial to the breeding?"

Mastema claps his hands together. "That's one piece of it. It's important to King and the future of your kind. But the main purpose of this meeting is dealing with a spy in our midst. King and I have spoken enough, and we understand your anger. It's why you let Cabello go. That's why you attempt to help her with the lab's destruction. We do not hold it against you. Though we do have to adjust your duties."

They figured it out, Scalebane thinks. Her mind spins around several times trying to comprehend how Mastema discovered their actions.

Namsruc scoots to face Scalebane and takes her hand. "Please, they're not attempting to hurt you. They're upset, not mad. Mastema and King are not Erol Terzi or the horrific abominations of our childhood. They want us to grow together."

"They're upset?" Scalebane raises her voice to expel her fire. "What of my rage? I have maintained loyalty, and this is what I receive?"

Namsruc strokes her knuckles. "We understand."

"I do not wish to become a breeding machine so King and Mastema can strip the scales from my offspring. I don't wish for the burden of raising children in this unforgiving world."

Rithu, as King, says, "These are where our concerns lie, Scalebane. You have proven yourself loyal and worthy in the past. Time erodes the willful. You have infected your mind, shifting the enemy's attention from the soft skins to us."

"I assure you, that is not the case." Scalebane pulls her hand away from her sister and stands. "I warned you, King, of the lightless ones. They are coming."

"Because some soft skin painter saw it in one of his intoxicated visions?"

"That matters not. Each of his paintings comes true. He painted the entire history of the Creator, including the First being born. The human drew Cabello. Tell me that is an inebriated fluke? I have proof."

Mastema adjusts his seat.

Scalebane continues, "Mastema has no interest in us. He wants scales to synthesize it. It is why he seduced the Prime Minister of this country to expedite the merger of two megalith organizations. They will streamline ash for his own gain. He doesn't care for his Moths. The concept of family is a mirage so he can manipulate our lives for his divine plan. They're fusing vazeleads and humans into a new species. Hybrids! How do you not see this? He is the First, the flatterer of God, and destined to continue on the Creator's vision."

Rithu says, "The First is the Creator's finest. He acts as a gardener, letting life flourish. Scriptures throughout the years mutate truth, turning him into a villain. Mastema hasn't harmed us. Your painter should show you if he were not malicious. You forget the history you studied, Scalebane."

Scalebane lets out a hiss and speaks, "The First, yes, and an angel. How is it that an angel becomes fallen? He feeds off of ego, an energy vampyre. Even as we speak."

Mastema waves his hand. "Fallen, not fallen. Vampyre with the *y* and not the *i*. Good and evil. Scalebane, these are abstract concepts. They're vague and pointless when looking to complete a vision. Have you ever considered it was intentional to shed myself from the light and embrace the darker sides within the Creator's realm? History has shown that Heaven and Hell cannot get along. Their well-documented wars leave the judgement of the afterlife laughable. The Heavenly Kingdoms are dormant. Dega'Mostikas cares little to control his three

Hells. Force does not work, Scalebane. Therefore, we operate behind the scenes, changing the mortal realm from the inside, balance of dark and light. It's why I am who I am, for the Creator."

Scalebane retreats several steps. "Working in shadows because other forces threaten you if you go too far. Your divine plan angers ancient entities older than the Creator themselves. King, let me bring the proof to you."

Namsruc rises.

Mastema continues, "I assure you, the plan is to remove the humans and balance this planet."

"What of the others?" Scalebane asks. "The entire mortal realm?"

"One thing at a time, Scalebane." Mastema points his left index finger at her. "You fail to see that. Why your balancer father or whatever he is couldn't, I don't know. This is the truest form of equilibrium, according to the Creator's eyes. You sabotaging us is rooted in fear. Fear is a natural response to the unknown. We aren't going to punish you."

"Scalebane," Namsruc says, extending her open palms. "Please." A frown rests on her face.

Scalebane looks at Mastema, her sister, then Rithu. The three watch her. She moves to Jekos, who stares at the floor. Somehow, Mastema knew about the plan, and they pinpointed it on Scalebane. An ally betrayed them. Jekos wouldn't have brought it this far to backstab her. Rithu? It is unlikely after challenging his father and mother. Cabello and Synarion make no sense nor have the contacts. That leaves one ally that's been in the dark with them.

Four, she thinks.

"Scalebane," Rithu says. "We can work through this." He flinches. "King says that there is no need for punishment."

"If I resist?" Scalebane asks, taking two more steps away.

"I make myself clear, Scalebane," Rithu says, speaking as King. "I will treat you as the Nine and you'll breed with my son." Rithu's tail coils around his ankle. "But Father, I—" He doesn't finish his sentence. Scalebane keeps walking.

Namsruc follows. "Sister, how can you not see? The pain and torture our people have endured for centuries shall end. This is what we wanted."

"I want freedom, Namsruc." Scalebane sneers. "We didn't trade one master for another."

"We'll make her understand," Rithu says. "Seize her and report back." The orange in Rithu's soulstone fizzles out and he looks at Scalebane as Namsruc turns to him. She doesn't believe the order either. Mastema reclines in his chair.

Rithu rises from his set. Namsruc faces Scalebane and takes another step. "Please sister, come with us. Give it time."

Scalebane hisses, backing towards the glass window in a slow stride. The elevator dings and slides open. Five men in white suits march in her direction. She takes a glance at the pane. Namsruc and Rithu dash, hoping to reach her before the Moths. They are doing what they must to serve King and their people. Scalebane understands the greater picture. She will help them, even if she has to betray her sister.

"I'm sorry, my dear sister," Scalebane says. Her throat tenses.

Sirens blare, causing the approaching Moths to freeze. Mastema looks up, as does the nymph bartender, Jekos, Rithu, and Namsruc.

Opportunity strikes, and Scalebane spins, dashing for the window.

"Scalebane!" Namsruc shouts.

The wide arc of her left leg slows her momentum. Namsruc and Rithu close the distance as she coils a fist. Leather slams it into the glass, shattering on impact as she skids to the edge, sliding to her hands and feet. She slips over the brink and plummets to the surface of the earth. Her claws hack into the window of the floor below with enough force it leaves a deep jagged scar and brings her fall to a halt. With her free hand, she punches the glass. It breaks. Her body frees and she descends for a moment before snagging onto the frame and pulls herself into the tower.

On her feet, she scans the space. It's an executive office complete with expensive wooden furnishing and golden frames containing abstract artwork. She marches out the door, grinding her teeth to fight the internal needles, reminding her to slow down. Rithu and Namsruc don't follow. That security warning has them occupied.

An elevator is at the far end of the room, past ten rows of open workspace cubicles. She takes Jekos's key card and heads for the lift. There's a spy to catch.

CHAPTER 56
CROSSFIRE

Red lights pulse throughout the hallways. Mercenaries march in synchronized steps. They pass the corridor containing Lola, Synarion, and Four. A mysterious source triggered the lab's security that didn't involve their plan. Chaos isn't new to Lola. With ash streaming in her system, she's prepared.

"Let's get going," she says, heading for the server room at the end of the path. Four nods and takes the duffel bag.

Synarion and Four join her in the data centre. Gunshots speak from the rows of black towers. Lola takes her firearm as Synarion wields his throwing stars. The shaper follows, handgun drawn. A flame flickers ahead. Around the corner, a dolly containing boxes rests at the corner against a server rack. Two delivery workers sit on the floor beside a collapsed burning Moth with a stake in their arm and their stomach. Fire dances from the gangster's wounds, burning their clothes. On the other end of the aisle, a soldier and a Moth hide behind a tower. A pile of ashes and burnt fabric divides the opposing sides. The Moth fires at the newcomers.

Lola tugs Synarion to the metal barrier. It misses him by a hairline. Synarion steps out, flinging his star at the Crystal Moth. The blade soars past the servers and strikes the man in the side of his skull. He topples over. His head thumps against the panel, catching the soldier's attention. He drops his firearm, hands raised.

"Away from the gun!" Lola shouts. She leans from their cover. Four releases the duffel bag and approaches the mercenary. Synarion stoops to the pile of ashes and sifts through the remains with his boot.

The two delivery workers: a woman not much older than Lola, and a middle-aged man. Even with the beard and added weight, Lola has seen him. It's been a long time. He's clutching his neck. Blood seeps between the cracks of his fingers. She recognizes that Moth with a stake in their arm and gut. The spiked hair, sharp-angled nose, and canines are indistinguishable. This is the dubbed Spike vampire at Radiate Primate.

"Iglesias!" the delivery woman shouts, standing. "Shit, shit, fuck, Christ. We need a doctor."

"Archer, the stake gun," Iglesias says.

Archer snags an obscure crossbow from the ground and aims it at the burning Moth. The firearm unloads a silver-tipped wooden bolt into the Moth's chest, missing the heart. The wound bursts into flames as the vampire hisses, looking to the ceiling. Their skin underneath the scorching suit bubbles, the flesh darkening. The fire reaches his hair, scathing it.

"What the fuck?" the mercenary says. Four drags him over to the group.

Archer fires again, hitting him in the clavicle as Synarion lifts a necklace from the ashes. He calls out. "Wait a moment."

She doesn't lower the weapon. "Not wise, buddy."

"Yes, bloodsuckers. He's immobilized." Synarion leans over the vampire and dangles the pendant in front of him. It contains a bat emblem, the wings creating the circumference of a circle. Daggers replace the fangs. "This is a symbol of loyalty to a master."

Spike pants in heavy exhales, squinting, as the fire runs rampant over his form.

"Meaning that dead vampire was once a human familiar. What of you?"

The vampire hisses.

"Were you human, or the master?"

The vampire's clothes reduce to ash, leaving his boiling skin exposed. Spike's tight laugh mixes pain and amusement in each exhale. "You . . . Valturus. So long ago. Her plaything, if I recall."

Lola walks to Synarion, leans, and whispers into his ear. "Don't do anything fucking stupid, got it?"

Synarion says, "Some skeletons you can't dispose of. We need to move."

Iglesias steps from the tower and snags the crossbow from Archer. "He's mine." He holds onto his neck with one hand, the other aiming at Spike.

"My strike is true," Spike sneers.

The vampire roars, fangs peeking beyond the flames. The left tooth cracks because of the heat. Iglesias pulls the trigger, unloading the stake gun into Spike. The bolt pierces into his throat, and a second shot into his heart. His entire form combusts into an inferno, forcing Synarion to move. Screeches of horror at an unbearable pitch pierce into the observers' ears as his arms flail. Slabs of meat fall, reducing to powder, leaving a charcoal skeleton under the blaze. Spike's hand reaches for the heavens as the scorching temperature devours the remaining bones. His fingers are the last to go, lessening to a pile of grey dust and a matching bat pendant on top.

The soldier scoots away, bumping into Four's leg, unable to comprehend the scenario.

Archer holds Iglesias as he lowers the gun. "We need to get him out of here."

Iglesias shrugs her off. "I'm fine. The USB stick, hurry."

"You're far from that," Archer says in a tight voice.

"Do your job, detective." Iglesias reaches into his pocket and takes two drives, matching the ones Synarion has, and passes it to her. The shaper squints, watching them interact.

"Okay, okay. We're getting you out of here," Archer says.

"Go." Iglesias waves the crossbow in the air. His eyes wince and his breath is heavy.

Archer rushes past Lola, heading for an open server panel with a tray for a keyboard and monitor.

"Detective Iglesias?" Lola asks.

He gazes at her with dark bags under his eyes. "Long time no see, kid. Help Archer, will you? You're a techy."

"How did you two get here?" Lola asks. She blinks, trying not to look at his fatal wound.

"Go help her. She'll explain."

Lola tucks her gun behind her back and reaches Archer, passing Four. The detective glances at her and raises the stick. "You get what we're supposed to do with this?" she asks.

"Sort of, here." Lola takes the USB sticks and steps in front of the computer. The front casing contains a couple of ports, letting her inject the devices. One provides mobile internet access, and the second activates a folder in the Explorer of the OS. The drive has one file titled: .forbidden-fruit.

"We gotta rename it," Archer says. "To an executable?"

"Yep. A Trojan Horse." She taps on the file and renames it to forbidden-fruit.exe. She double clicks on it and a new black window opens, enabling the malware. An apple made of text-art is in the centre of the screen with a three-frame animation of a snake peeking behind it. Below it reads: YOU ATE THE FRUIT. DELICIOUS.

"It's activated," Lola says.

Archer taps on her ear and speaks. "Disk, we're in . . . you got it? Perfect." She storms past Lola, Four, and their captive to Iglesias. "He's not going to make it if we keep pissing around."

"What of this one?" Four says, tapping the tip of their gun on the soldier's head.

The man says, "Look, I can't offer terrorists anything."

"We're not here for you," Lola says with bitterness in each word.

"You call for help?" Iglesias asks with a tired softness to his question. He leans against the tower, using Archer as support.

The doors to the data centre burst open from where Lola, Synarion, and Four came from. A second entrance opens from the other end. Footsteps fill the space between the blaring sirens. They've got company, cornered, as Four predicted.

"Keep watch on him," Lola says to Archer and Iglesias.

Synarion takes his throwing stars. "I'll take the other door. You and Four handle this end."

The shaper and Lola take their positions against the server racks. Around the corner, twelve mercenaries position themselves behind the rows of servers. They open fire, bullets propelling off of the metal casings of their cover, creating sparks.

Lola's gun unloads rounds their way. The ammo misses as they receive more arsenal. Gunshots come from behind Lola and Four. The soldiers advance one server tower at a time. A mercenary shoots, letting another zigzag through the rows. They implement a simple strategy: compress the enemy, cornering them until they are forced to surrender. Lola leans over and fires again. A bullet grazes by her face as she retreats.

"Careful, yes?" Four says as their eyes swirl red.

"Shit," Lola says, feeling the heat on her cheek. *More.* She reaches into her pocket, taking a strip of ash. At the corner of her eye, Four's jaw splits vertically as a bone snaps.

A howling scream comes from the other side of the data centre. Four's eyes return to normal and the gap seals. They raise their gun.

The wall of bullets diminishes. Several more cries follow. Lola leans over the tower: the front row of soldiers aim at her, shielded by their shelter. The mercenaries behind them face the other way. Numerous toppled bodies appear on the ground, one after the other.

One soldier opens fire, as does Lola. Hers hits him in the chest. He falls. Four's firearm sends a bullet, hitting another mercenary. A cloaked figure leaps on top of the server racks and to the next row, getting closer to Lola and Four. The bright inverted room, through Lola's eyes, makes Scalebane clear as day.

The vazelead twirls her signature sai and jumps down, stabbing a soldier in the face. Her tail whips in an uncontrolled chaotic motion, causing the military men to disperse. Five left, Lola fires and hits one in the leg and the second bullet in his torso. Four's ammunition penetrates one's skull, scattering bone fragments onto a tower. Three left. Scalebane swings wide and a man lunges his fist into her chest. She hobbles back, lashing her tail at him. The tip splits open his nose, and she springs forward. The sai jabs the mercenary through the jaw and into the brain, lifting them off the ground. Two left. Lola shoots the same target, hitting the neck. The last opponent falls victim to Scalebane's tail coiling around his gun-wielding hand. She directs it to the floor and pulls him towards her. Her sai plummets into his body armour: once, twice, thrice! Her strength breaks through the vest and the blade pierces his lungs.

Lola dashes to help their comrades as golden shells continue dropping. Iglesias holds his own, keeping his stake gun pointed at their prisoner. The kid keeps his hands raised, not diverting his gaze from the detective. Archer and Synarion maintain their spot on the other end. Sparks appear as bullets ping off of server towers.

Another scream—their reptilian ally—comes as Lola joins Archer and Synarion. The three fire at the remaining soldiers. Scalebane appears from behind them, four rows over. Within minutes, Lola, Archer, Scalebane, and Synarion eliminate the smaller squad.

"Your daughter is here," Lola says to Synarion.

"Scalebane?" he asks while putting away his throwing stars and equipping his spiked knuckles.

From the far end of the hall, their cloaked ally storms to them, keeping their sai drawing. The chrome tips drip red onto the ground. Her tail stays perked. She hisses, storming past Archer, Synarion, and Lola.

"Holy fuck," Archer mutters under her breath.

"Mastema is on the top floor," Scalebane says. "Along with my sister. They uncovered what we were doing, because there's a spy amongst us." She keeps walking towards Four.

"A spy?" Four asks, raising an eyebrow.

"Don't play coy with me!" Scalebane roars, projecting the sharp sound of a jaguar as she leaps at the shaper.

"Scalebane!" Synarion shouts.

The shaper steps to the side, dodging an oncoming attack. "Stop this nonsense!"

"Four is Mastema's eyes and ears. We've been set up from the beginning." Scalebane swings again. Four dodges.

A triple agent, Lola thinks. If she could have pierced the shaper's mind and sense them with ash, they'd be in the clear. Her visions distracted her too much to care about Four and their words a year ago, "*Why bet on one side when you can master both?*" Goddamn slime.

Four jumps clear of Scalebane's flailing tail. Their body cracks, muscles mutating, as the skin morphs colour. The hair falls off as spikes poke through the flesh and blossom into black feathers. Scalebane pounces towards them. The shaper's anatomy shrinks: the skull elongates and the arms expand into wings. Scalebane plummets onto the pile of clothes as a crow soars from underneath, swooping to the ventilations. She lands on her knee in a loud thud, grunting.

Lola aims and fires twice at the bird. Her bullet pings off the ceiling. Synarion pulls out a throwing star and flings it as the dark creature reaches a gate, their claws digging into the metal slits. The throwing star soars towards Four as they morph again, losing wings and gaining brown fur. It's the familiar rodent. It squeaks and squeezes in between the slits as the blade slams into the metal, stuck in place.

Scalebane, stands, limping. "I should have sensed it."

"You caught it now," Synarion says.

"There's not a moment to spare. This plan, we need to execute it and get out."

Archer presses her ear and speaks. "Okay, Disk says that they have access to the server system."

Iglesias pants. "A guy . . . named Zero . . Eden Breaker . . . helped us." His skin is faint. He's losing too much blood.

A second team, Lola thinks.

Synarion kicks the soldier prisoner, knocking him to the ground. "Get out of here!" he shouts. "Come on, go!"

The mercenary rises, keeping his hands in the air, and steps backwards, eyeing the group. The last thing they need is to have a soldier hear the plan.

"Go," Iglesias says. He lowers the stake gun. It's far too heavy. The boy turns and fast walks away, hands raised, until he leaves the data centre.

Archer says, "Okay, I'm not sure how much Zero told you. This Eden Breaker stuff is shady."

Lola says, "We're aware. That crow was part of Eden Breaker, we thought."

"Great," Archer says.

Synarion says, "Scalebane? You know the plan."

"Fragments," Scalebane says while sheathing her sai.

Archer helps Iglesias walk to the group. He says, "There's three magnets, EMFCs . . . we have to shut down. The south, west, and east . . . Disk has access to the computer, from a remote location, and will . . . will unlock the doors so we can manually disarm these chambers. There's a central switch, it needs two people to pull . . . security."

Lola says, "We disable it. Disk increases teslas. It implodes.

"Bingo," Iglesias says.

Synarion speaks. "Based on the floor plans, they are of equal distance at this basement level. The hall we took will take you to the south and west. It's a stretch with intersections. Keep heading straight. The east is through the second entrance. I can handle one on my own, taking the south. The rooms are evident, being at the end of the halls."

Scalebane says, "Synarion, Namsruc is here."

Synarion raises an eyebrow.

"We can't demolish the tower."

"She'll get out," he says.

"We can't be sure."

"Scalebane, we have to believe in her."

Scalebane growls.

"If she is with Mastema, he will ensure they escape. He needs her."

Scalebane shakes her head, then speaks. "I'll take west."

"We'll meet at the top floor by the receiving lift," Synarion says.

"The three of us can take the east," Archer says, volunteering Iglesias and Lola. She presses her lips tight, trying to mask the fear in her eyes.

Iglesias lets go of her and walks to the computer, squeezing his neck. "I don't know about that."

"Excuse me?" Archer says. She storms towards him. Lola curls her fingers, knowing the hollowing truth he speaks.

"I'm not doing so well, kid," Iglesias says as his eyes close halfway.

"You haven't lost that much blood. It's poison."

Synarion asks, "Did the last vampire bite him?"

"Yes? I think," Archer says. "He jumped Iglesias and I."

Scalebane says, "We have to move."

"Fuck!" Archer shouts.

Iglesias says, "Okay, Disk said we have ten minutes . . . to escape once those magnets activate. Look, the . . . uh . . . plan took a dive. We didn't expect others to be in the server room. That soldier will call for backup. And . . . and that's going to be the first wave. If they send a second group here, they'll yank this internet stick and disable Disk's access. This whole plan is ruined."

Archer's eyes water, and she shakes her head while grabbing hold of Iglesias's stained shirt. "Don't y-o-ou fucki-i-i-ng say it."

Iglesias tries to shrug off. She will not go. "I'll hold base here."

"Fuck," Archer says under her breath while stepping away. She rubs her forehead several times. The man is right. Lola's throat tenses. She never wished this for Iglesias who has helped her over the years.

"I don't get this supernatural bullshit." Iglesias looks to the ground. "Shapeshifters . . . reptile people, and vampires. Whatever is happening to me, I feel it, I don't like it . . . I don't want it."

Synarion reaches into the inside of his shirt and takes a gold ring. It's a circlet Lola has seen before, complete with vines and fangs holding in a red gem, similar to the emblem he took from one of the dead vampires. He says, "If an original master vampire infected you, there is no saving you other than providing peace in your eradication. Their bite will convert you within the time this plan executes."

A weak chuckle leaves Iglesias as he extends his hand to Synarion. "There you have it."

"Goddamnit!" Archer cries, punching a tower's panel.

"We must go, now," Scalebane says.

Archer grabs onto Iglesias's shirt again and wraps her arms around him in one last squeeze. "You bastard. You grisly old b-a-astard."

Synarion and Scalebane are the first to exit, leaving whence Lola arrived. As for her, she puts her arm on Archer as Iglesias leans against the server. "We have to go," she says.

Archer wipes some tears and nods.

"I got you," Iglesias says. "Get out of here . . . in one piece and we'll . . . blow this place to smithereens." He forces a smile as his eyelids flutter. His skin, even though it is deathly white, has a strange toxic hue undertone to it. Lola can only imagine what tone it is. His gaze shifts to Lola and he speaks. "You're a tough son-of-a-bitch."

Lola smiles. "I wish we got to talk more."

He nods at Archer. "Have this one share some stories about me. Go," Iglesias orders.

Scalebane and Synarion reach the end of the red, flashing hall. A part of her wants to stop and say something to the nymph. What? Her shattered ego leaves a hole in her heart that serves no purpose. She turns to head west. Synarion says, "Scalebane."

She pauses mid step.

"Be careful." He clenches his ring-wearing fist and his hand distorts, vanishing before her eyes. His arm follows with the rest of his body, making him invisible. Even his natural pinewood scent is gone.

Magic, Scalebane thinks. She continues through the hall, thinking she should have replied with a *you too*. The words trouble her. She's had years of hate for him. It's the last thought she should have. *Weak willed.*

Her mind homes in on the mission: the west EMFC. She storms past scientists who cower to the wall at the sight of her. She reverts to her fours, dashing through an intersection. Bullets plummet into the walls, missing her. Mercenaries and gangsters alike pursue the dashing hunter. Though she is quicker, sprinting along the long hall. At the far end she can see the metal doors, a small spec. It's a stretch. She'll make it.

A lab to her right catches her eye, and she pauses for a heartbeat. Scientists in white coats, and jumpsuits, disassemble the room containing human-sized tubes of foggy liquid. Bobbing blanched heads of undeveloped beings float within. Two mercenaries watch the workers. This is the unholy fusion of bioengineering Dr. Lang is obsessed with.

A soldier inside spots her and takes a radio from their belt, speaking into it. Scalebane bolts down the hall at lightning speed. She passes two lab coats. One dashes clear from her. Fear freezes the other person. Her shoulder knocks into their leg, throwing them to the floor. Her sprint takes her to the titanium entrance, a couple of meters wide, with circular windows on each side. To the right is a panel with a touchscreen and a flashing red light.

Scalebane stands and slides her claws in between the slit of the doors and pushes it aside. Eden Breaker did their job and Scalebane steps into the cylinder shape room. A small staircase leads her to the main controls in front of a large chrome pillar.

A series of smaller tubes run parallel with them. It's the electromagnetic flux-compression, with several monitors bolted four meters from it with more cables and metal tubing. Switches and valves accompany the dashboard. Orange and amber lights flash on the panel. A central switch made of the thick steel is dead centre surrounded by black-and-yellow diagonal lines. The resistance of the control would require two soft skins to shift. For Scalebane, her claws wrap around it, standing firm, and she pulls.

The lever slides with her, releasing a hydraulic hiss. Another siren beeps at opposite intervals from the continual warning throughout the lab. Its loudness slams into her ears, making her growl. She takes a step from the EMFC. Various circular valves on the system rotate to the right where red lines indicate the readings are too high. Job complete.

In the hall, a squad of four mercenaries and three Moths rush to her. Scalebane takes her sai out, squeezing them with her leather gloves. Soft skins do not strike concern in the hunter's mind. She exits the EMFC room. With one spin of her weapons, she engages, unleashing the hell from whence she was born.

What's wrong with me? Iglesias thinks. With each passing moment, his strength diminishes, causing him to rely on the tower for support. He needs to maintain his focus and not let his mind wander. As he takes a deep breath, he closes his eyes, feeling the tension melt away, until the sound of a distorted voice breaks the silence.

"One of EMFCs powered up," Disk says. "I'm increasing the magnetic field strength. Two to go."

Iglesias opens his eyes, and the world appears saturated. Although, he swears his sense of smell is heightening. The servers have a distinct hot rubber sensation. Higher, there's a metallic tinge. He looks at the corpse of the slain Moth. That's the tingle of blood, once repulsive. Its essence has a newfound gravitational pull, like a nicotine, calling to him.

"Good job, kid," Iglesias says into the com. He stumbles towards the lifeless body, sinking to his knees as he feels the sticky, crimson fluid seep beneath it. He speaks into his mic. "How's my situation?"

"One second," Disk says. "Cameras show you got three soldiers coming in. I think."

"Gotcha," Iglesias says.

"South entrance, the one Cabello and Archer took. Stay on guard."

"Uh, huh."

"Woah, another EMFC's manual safety disabled. That leaves Cabello and Archer's."

Iglesias doesn't respond. He gets onto his hand, using the other to scoop the blood. This is not normal. This supernatural bullshit is a bad dream. One day he went from operating his life as a detective, desk monkey consultant, to being a mourning father. A conspiracy took hold, resulting in his forthcoming death because he needed revenge. He has exhausted his purpose in life and goddamnit, they weren't getting away with murdering his son. At what cost? This is the question he ponders as he lifts his red-coated fingers and licks them.

Lola and Archer rush through the hall. The detective pauses at an intersection. With a quick motion, she grabs Lola's arm, preventing her from venturing further. Two soldiers stand across the corner by a set of stairs, their arms waving, beckoning the scientists and workers to ascend.

"Keep it together," Archer says.

Shit, Lola thinks. Her vision is grey, limbs weakening. The ash is wearing out. She reaches into her pocket and takes a strip, chewing on it. *What the fuck is this gift supposed to do?*

She leans to see the mercenaries. "We can take them."

Archer shakes her head no. "Let's not make accidental shots at civilians. There was another way, according to the floor plans. Come on."

They pass empty labs with missing computers, documents, and samples. The workers are gone. The contrast of the world resumes for Lola, giving the pulsing hall more depth. Turning the corner, they face several Moths leaving a lab's entrance. Both groups raise their guns. Bullets fly, vanishing into the walls. Lola takes shelter against the wall, leans over and fires.

One of the white suits gets bold, stepping out from their sheltered doorway as the ash floods Lola's system. She senses the blood boiling under his skin as his heart pumps fast. Sweat drizzles along his skull. She leans around the corner and shoots, hitting the man point-blank in the forehead. He tumbles with red splattering against his two comrades.

Archer's gun speaks as Lola hides. The other Moths peek from the doorframe and fire. A projectile grazes Archer's shoulder, and she slams against the wall.

Now, comes the familiar voice of the other. Lola steps out and fires; one bullet soars into a Moth's lungs. The second blasts the man's jaw, exposing splintered bone and leaving the ash-dasher victorious.

"You hit?" Lola asks.

"I'm good. Keep moving," Archer says through an exhale.

They head down the hall, taking a couple of turns to circle around the other intersection. Lab workers run past them in fear. These are people, normal civilians trying to get by. They also are fools if they don't realize the type of terrors they were creating. Cabello feels sympathy for their poor actions. These individuals are bugs on the beast's back. Lola must remind herself of revenge. Compassion gets you killed. Synarion took advantage of her. As did Scalebane. Lola needs to keep her goal clear. These are the enemy.

One last turn and they move to the fifty-foot-long hall leading to the two titanium sliding doors. That's the EMFC, as memory serves for the floor plans. At the end of the corridor, each of them takes a panel, gripping the edges. Lola and Archer pull, opening the doorway. They step into the circular room, which produces a steady hum complete with the chrome cylinder in the centre. An invisible force dances along Lola's skin, which radiates stronger the closer they walk to the chrome pillar. This is the potent gravity humming against her chest. The main controls, including the large switch, are along the dashboard in the front.

"Here," Archer says, stepping down the stairs.

"Lola?" comes a familiar gruff voice from the other side of the chamber. This tone rises from her memory, buried from her long distant past. It must be from the ash.

"Hands up!" Archer shouts.

Or perhaps not.

A man emerges from the opposite end of the EMFC pillar with his arms raised. The short hair and a broad jawline create a strong masculine look. He wears a military shirt and cargo pants with boots. The sky-blue eyes lock onto her, striking Lola's memory.

"Michael?" Lola asks, raising her gun. He can't be alive, for the Trinity of Souls, Michael, Becky, and Mom, have haunted her for so long. It's why she went down this spiral. It can't be him. He lacks an aura, which she has encountered before and dismissed. His presence hits her with a potent pulse more forceful than the towering EMFC.

"What the hell is going on?" Michael says.

"Bullshit." Lola's nostrils flare. She steps forward, coiling both sets of fingers on her weapon. Her sixth sense can't detect him. It's blank. She's no fool and can see through the deceiving lies. The better question is, how did the shaper get a hold of Michael Bradford's DNA?

Archer says, "Don't fire. We have no idea what this shit is about." She glances at the door. Three Moths approach. "Lola, we don't have time for this."

Lola puts her gun away and unsheathes her knife. "You sick fuck," Lola whispers, recalling the shaper devouring bodies to take form. The Moths would have had to give Four access to corpses via the crooked law. This realization surges her with newfound energy. The flickering flame within her combusts and she lunges at the man. He steps aside, deflecting the attack, and she slices again. Her comrade heads for the door's entrance and fires at the oncoming enemy.

"Lola! I have no idea what is going on," Michael says.

"A triple agent? Kind of shitty one if you didn't know you'd hand me Mastema on a plate."

"What?" Michael says, squinting.

Lola lets out a battle cry, shoving the knife at him, slicing his shoulder. He grunts and launches a fist. Lola ducks as he sends a roundhouse kick. She leaps backwards.

Michael says, "It's this laboratory. I woke up in the cell. I remember dying, Lola. I remember how it felt."

Silence, comes a voice. Lola shouts and hacks down. He steps aside and Lola swings again. He snags her wrist. Lola throws a punch; Michael grabs it. His arms shake as do Lola's. Both struggle for control.

"Will you listen to me?" Michael shouts through his clenched teeth.

She grunts and lunges her knee, hitting him in the gut. Both step away. Gunshots pierce through the sirens. Several projectiles ping off the metal EMFC encasing.

"If you're fucking Michael, how did we meet?" Lola asks.

Michael grips his wounded shoulder, panting.

More bullets exchange by the door.

"How did we fucking meet?"

Michael shakes his head. "Lola, we don't have time for this. I think they cloned me or brought me back to life. I got up minutes ago."

Another bullet bounces against the encasement.

"In here?" Lola asks. "I watched you die. You're scared shitless of Mastema, aren't you?"

"Will you listen to me?" Michael raises his voice, piercing eyes latched onto her.

"Lola!" Archer shouts.

Lola turns around to see Archer has taken care of the Moths. She heads for the large switch. Michael moves around the pillar.

Don't give in, a thought enters her mind. She is unsure if she is thinking it, if it is the ash, or Mother Nature, or the other. It holds more truth than the mirage of her past can show. She must stay true to herself. She's experienced the trials of fire, faced the Trinity of Souls, and won't fall for it in flesh and blood.

She bites her lip, takes one inhale, and steps around the column. Michael is gone. A girl, Lola's height, with brunette hair, stands in his place. The military uniform drapes on her thin, pale form.

"Lola Love," she says.

"Don't you fucking dare," Lola says, grinding her teeth. Even without the black and red dreadlocks, she recognizes her Becky Bubs's elegant cadence.

"Cabello!" Archer shouts. "I can't move it."

Becky tilts her head, smiling. It's the same smile Lola longs for. It immobilizes her for a split second. A white appendage ending in a spike springs from behind the girl towards Lola. It pierces her shoulder, pulling her into the girl's splitting face. A vertical array of teeth expands from her top jaw down to the pelvis, shredding through the shirt.

Claws snag onto her shoulders as she reaches for her firearm. The fangs slice against her skin as she raises her gun. Teeth pierce into her forearms, poking through the other side. She fires. One, two, three! Bullets splatter against the hard palate of the oral cavity. Blood and flesh spray her as the deathly grasp on her body releases. Lola groans, pushing herself out of the shaper's moist mouth in a coating of saliva and blood. Her hand coils around the tail and she rips it from her shoulder. Her eyes wince to absorb the pain. With a kick, she sends Four to the ground in a bloody mess of human and old world gore.

Lola screams a throat full of anger and curses under her breath. Any agony she felt is snuffed out thanks to her rage. This isn't the time to have remorse or question her actions. It wasn't Michael, nor Becky. Her memory of them is clear. She watched them die years ago. This is a typical Moth trickery from the dead shaper.

Lola sheaths her knife and puts her gun away. One look at her ripped forearms tells her death was too close. She turns to see Archer behind her, jaw hanging, looking at the torso-wide mouth of the corpse.

"We're good," Lola says.

The two rush to the main controls and take hold of the switch. Each of them pulls, sliding the control. Lola grunts, pushing the agony aside, arms dripping in body fluids. The gravitational pull of the pillar pulsates with a heavy shockwave against Lola's tender wounds like a hot wind. Both hers and Archer's hairs lift an inch with each pulse before falling. The chamber projects a loud siren, indicating their job complete.

"You got company," Disk's voice comes through Iglesias's com. It's muffled because the metal tinge in his mouth overwhelms his senses more than a lake of water ever could.

It tastes . . . it tastes . . .

The south entrance door slams open and footsteps storm into the room.

What am I doing? he thinks, standing, not finishing the previous thought. Iglesias takes a handgun from the polystyrene foam box. He raises the weapon, using the racks as support.

A bullet whizzes past him, hitting the top of a tower. A soldier peeks from his crouched position, firing a couple more times. Iglesias leans over, squeezing in between two sets of servers, and fires. He doesn't have the strength. What the hell can he do?

The red lights flash faster, in a consistent pulse, a second apart. The sirens blare at a constant stream.

"Third EMFC down," Disk says. "Holy shit, they did it."

They got ten minutes, he thinks. The lab implodes soon, taking him with it before he turns inhuman.

Soldiers shout at each other, inaudible through the warning signals of the speaker. The mercenary stands from his crouched position. Iglesias sees the foot at the end of his handgun. He vanishes from the hall and that leaves Iglesias alone.

They're no fools. This is over. Those mercenaries have lives, unlike Iglesias, who lost his boy. He's going to lose more if this mutation finishes.

"They're gone," Iglesias says into his com.

"You got time," Disk says. "Everyone is getting out. Can you walk?"

Archer's voice comes through the speaker. "Iglesias, I'm coming for you."

"Don't. You won't make it," Iglesias says.

Disk says, "For your own sake, Archer, don't. The distance from the server room from the south EMFC, then to the main elevator, isn't plausible."

"Listen to the brains," Iglesias says.

Archer says, "Goddamnit. Iglesias, you can walk, right?"

"Fuck," Iglesias mutters. He puts his gun away and reaches for the smokes in his pocket. He could get out. Maybe. It's difficult to tell as his body slouches over the controls.

"Vampires," Iglesias says to himself while lighting a drag.

"Iglesias?" Archer says. "You fucking dumb shit."

"Iglesias?" Disk says. "Can you hear me?"

"Iglesias?"

He puffs on the smoke, looking to the ceiling. This is the end. Or so he hopes. Is it possible to implode vampires? How long does it require to mutate—ten minutes? The group should have rammed a bolt into his heart. A counter thought: why couldn't his son, José, have been bitten by Smug and not Big Jaw? If what the cauliflower-eared guy said was true about an original vampire, then Iglesias's son would have turned too. They could have lived forever. It's a foolish idea. Life is grey. There is no good, nor evil. Only randomness.

Iglesias takes another puff and looks over at the stake gun on the ground, wondering if he has the strength and will to take his own life.

Lola and Archer bolt from the EMFC room and through the hall. Workers and mercenaries alike are long gone in this section. The detective talks into the com in her ear, to Iglesias. Lola catches the tail end of the conversation as her voice trembles. Iglesias isn't making it out.

"Fuck!" Archer shouts. Her eyes glisten. Lola checks her watch to see that they have nine minutes left as they head for the staircases. Elevators are too risky and slow considering others are evacuating. There's no point in fighting the intruders because this lab is going to hell. They sprint up the flights of stairs, heading for the top. Fifteen floors are a hike, shredding three minutes of their time.

On the main floor, they reach Synarion and Scalebane, who meet at the rendezvous. They are standing at the edge of the corridor leading to the receiving elevator. Sixteen mercenaries evacuate employees into the industrial shaft.

"We can take them," Scalebane says.

"Wait a moment. This is their last load," Synarion says, watching the soldiers enter the lift, leaving the hall clear.

"We shouldn't piss around," Archer says. Her voice is tight, choking. "Iglesias did his job. We got what, six minutes?"

Lola stands behind the three, her body tingling with unease. It isn't her wounded arms. The ash's sixth sense is urging her to leave, sensing danger. Another feeling simmers underneath, one that is her own.

"The last of them have left," Scalebane says.

This sensation mutates into a thought, trumping the drug.

Synarion says, "The elevator takes what? Several minutes to go up and several down?"

The impression fabricates into coherent words that surprise her . . .

"It's fucking tight," Archer says.

. . . I don't need them. A coldness claws Lola's back as she considers the words. The detective is innocent. The idea is regarding the two old world beings. They've schemed behind her back and have direct relation to the Moths. Like Lola, they're drowned in personal agendas. Their goals do not involve her. Lola does not need them as they do not need her. Scalebane is a key asset to these problems. From the reptile's words: Mastema is in the building with her sister. There's a high chance they got out, along with other players.

This icy realization flows down her arms and tingles her fingers.

What is Scalebane to Lola? Does Synarion matter? They've used her, and she has extracted the information she needs from them. She has done fine on her own.

The group rushes from the corner and down the corridor. Lola stays behind the three, pulling out her gun.

I don't need them, she reminds herself.

Peace. . . A force pushes against her. It's a warm tone. Mother Nature.

Lola swallows a thick glob of saliva, blinking, suppressing the invader. Yes, this spontaneous new thought has legs. She can trim out these wildcards that have taken advantage of her, used her, and abused her. This narrow moment of opportunity shines bright and pulls her in. Not ash, nor Mother Nature, not even the damn useless tool can control her. Lola is her own master.

I am the End. She raises the weapon and pulls the trigger. Several bullets soar into Scalebane's back. They shred through the cloak and past her leather armour, sinking into her organs. She yelps, tail flipping in uncontrolled motion.

Synarion spins, wielding throwing stars as Archer raises her handgun.

Lola fires again, hitting Synarion in the kneecap. He falls and throws his weapon. Lola steps to the side as the spinning blade zooms by her.

Click—click, click—click. Scalebane bolts towards her in an unstable dash. Lola shoots. It misses. Chrome sai sheen under the saturated light. The gun speaks. Dual metal tips plummet onto Lola's hand, throwing her damaged arm to the ground as she pulls the firearm's trigger. Stunned.

Scalebane twirls both sai.

The corridor flickers; light-shadows jump into view. A commanding force pushes Lola from her psyche, dropping her into the passenger seat. Humming energy runs through her body, rippling to the ground.

Vibrations control her actions, mutating her into a puppet as the darkness creeps into her form, seizing control of her limbs. Humanoid shapes rise from their flat shadow plane below Lola's feet.

Scalebane's blade tips swing towards Lola's ear holes. A throwing star glimmers behind her.

Darkness rises from Lola's boots, enveloping her body. Scalebane's sai and Synarion's star collide with the blackness to be met with an invisible force. All three blades freeze, countered with immense resistance. Lola's vision phases a foot away, as if she teleported. Scalebane's weapons push through the force, swinging thin air, arms crossing. The star pivots into a glass wall.

The sense of cold nipping hands controlling Lola's body slither away, like snakes retreating. Lola's body returns to her. She raises her gun and pulls the trigger. The bullet pierces Scalebane dead in the heart. She spins once as Lola steps forward and kicks her. The vazelead falls to the ground in a splatter of black blood in front of Synarion.

Archer's firearm wielding hands shake.

The light-shadow whence Lola stood deflates, returning to their two-dimensional space.

Embrace it, Lola thinks, aiming at Synarion. "This isn't about you, Archer."

"Lola," Synarion says, grinding his teeth.

Scalebane attempts to stand and falls, barking.

"Shit," Archer says, lowering her gun. She takes several steps away and heads for the elevator.

Synarion lifts his hands. "Have you gone mad?"

Don't fall for it, Lola thinks, walking to him.

Stop! comes another voice. The supernatural creatures that haunt Lola's mind, whether true or fictional, have tormented her for too long. She has built strength to resist them. The Trinity of Souls: defeated. Ash: hers to command. She witnessed the universe and has come face-to-face with the literal darkness of existence. She has not fallen. Whatever warning this is, Lola will not listen. This is for her.

Her eyelid twitches as the shadows shift around her feet, swirling with her motion.

Synarion's face crunches as he bites his lip. He makes a quick motion, faster than a man, into his utility belt. He flings another throwing star. Lola pulls the trigger. The blade plummets to Lola's face. Her shadow springs up like a cobra in front of her eyes, bending the attack at a one-eighty-degree angle. The projectile lands into Lola's gun-wielding hand, shredding the flesh, wedged into her bone. The bullet slams into his gut, flying out the other side. Her silhouette descends to its rightful place. She fires again, the weapon clicks. It's empty.

The balancer grips his stomach, wincing in pain. Lola drops the firearm and dashes, passing Synarion and Scalebane. She doesn't look back, for she isn't out of the woods yet. Archer is at the lift at the far end of the hall. The control panel to the right of the elevator is lit, showing she has activated it. She glances at Lola grasping her bleeding hand. The throwing star is stuck in it. The detective puts her gun away as the doors glide open.

CHAPTER 57
FOR FAMILY

Her life cannot end this way. Scalebane has come too far. The black blood says otherwise, sputtering from her open chest wound after each heartbeat. She tastes her own metallic flavour on her tongue. Her lung has a lodged bullet. It's difficult to breathe with fluid filling the organ, causing her to cough.

Weak will, she thinks and tries to push herself. Her body collapses and she yelps. She doesn't have the strength and Cabello has a far better shot than she did years ago.

One grunt comes from behind. Synarion rolls her over, taking her into his red-coated arm. Scalebane attempts to breathe, coughing as her form convulses on his lap. He unbuckles her mask to see her face. The air is cold, so cold. Blood drips from her scaled lips. He pops out his contacts, letting his true eyes stare into the flame of hers.

A flood of emotions runs through her she cannot control. It tingles with the warmth far greater than the pain running through her body. Those purple irises, those are the ones that brought hope to her and her sister. He raised them as his own, cooked for them, taught them how to fight and learn newfound values. The nymph gave love, warming their lives, as he does now, caressing her scalp-feathers as he did when she was a hatchling. Each stroke sends a calm pulse of energy over her system.

She wonders if Namsruc made it out. They were on the top floor, and there's not a chance in hell Mastema would let such a valuable asset go. Despite the manipulation, she feels her sister lives on. That's what is important. Unlike herself and Synarion, deep underneath the earth.

Her heart pumps in uncontrolled pulses as her trembling hand reaches for Synarion's chest, pawing him. She swallows some blood mixed with saliva. "I'm s-s-ca-ared," she says. Shot and broken, she cannot control her emotions anymore. "I don't want to die."

"It's okay," Synarion says. "It's okay." His face winces. He's in discomfort, though remains strong for her.

Synarion strokes her jaw. He, too, is aware this is their demise, and they are going to be okay. Her sister was correct from the beginning: Synarion didn't intend to hurt them. Scalebane felt anger for centuries, believing he betrayed them. Now, she wants comfort as the impending death awaits.

"Put her on here!" a voice shouts from behind.

Scalebane doesn't have the strength to see as Synarion turns. A short man in a white coat appears. It's Dr. Lang. He is with two mercenaries and a woman with a tight bun, his lab assistant. The soldiers rush to Scalebane and lift her. The lady pushes boxes off a four-wheeled metal dolly for the men to place her on. Synarion grunts in pain, standing.

"Can you walk?" Dr. Lang asks.

"Manageable," Synarion says. "They've taken the elevator."

"This way. Go! Go!" Dr. Lang shouts.

The group rushes from the main corridor. The oxygen gnaws at her muzzle, the air failing to enter her lungs. It burns her innards. They're taking her somewhere else. Scalebane cannot tell. The two mercenaries roll her on their dolly, jogging behind Dr. Lang, Synarion, and the lab assistant. She watches the tiles of the ground until they reach a circular door. It pulls open. The men bring the dolly into a fluorescent lit room. A loud clang of a metal slamming follows. Hydraulics hiss while locks and bolts click.

Outside sounds are gone.

She can't feel her face anymore.

Synarion leans beside her, taking her hand and wrapping her in his arm. Her tail slithers, coiling around his wrist. Her eyes flutter and close as a rumble comes from beyond, shaking the room.

"Father," she whispers and takes one concluding inhale of his pine and bark scent. It floods her with a warmth she's lacked for centuries. The pain is gone. He is the forest, keeping her sheltered under his branches. Hate does not exist. Her heart makes a final pump before letting go. At long last, peace.

CHAPTER 58
BOUND BY JUSTICE

Don't enter that elevator, Lola thinks, running at full speed to the detective. Archer doesn't move. The distance closes and Lola reaches her, skidding to a stop. Her bleeding hand drips blood onto the ground, painless thanks to the wonders of ash.

Archer bites her lip, brows furrowed.

"Long story," Lola says, panting.

They get in and Archer presses the controls, sending the shaft up. Lola checks her watch. They have three minutes. The lift closes, leaving behind the madman's laboratory and the ghosts of Lola's past.

The elevator soars with one minute remaining. It dings at ground level and the doors glide open. Seconds tick to their death as they rush through the halls, heading for a side emergency exit—being the closest. A low rumble comes from below, shaking the ground. The building creaks, walls splitting. They push the door's release and dash onto the road.

They emerge from the alleyway to see police cars, ambulances, and firetrucks have sectioned off the area for several blocks. A sizeable crowd gathers behind it, whispering to each other and recording as the tower rattles. Lola and Archer head for another side street as the windows shatter. The earth shakes with gravel and pebbles vibrating. Concrete cracks and a nearby fire hydrant explodes, dispersing water. The tower's ground level combusts with flame, the glass doors turning to shards. With the main floor reduced to an inferno, the upper levels fall, crumbling in on itself. Dust and flames erupt as one level after the other crushes the lower.

Lola and Archer take a turn to the next block. They move behind a brick building as a gush of heat, wind, and debris blows past them. The two hide between a rusted dumpster and the wall, letting the tide of chaos soar by. It takes several minutes before it ends. They cough in sputtered exhales, forced to breathe in the aftermath of particles, even using their shirts as a filter. Both stand and walk through a zigzag side street and towards clear air. They slow their pace after a block. Lola checks her wounded arms. Dust coats her exposed blood and Synarion's blade.

Archer raises her gun. Lola pauses, looking at the detective.

"What the fuck was that?" Archer asks. "Back there, huh?"

Lola lifts her arms, letting the red liquid drip down her chalk coated skin. "They were bad news."

"They were people," Archer says.

"They only care about keeping the old world hidden. It wasn't worth your trouble." *Neither is this,* she thinks, questioning if she could leap clear of danger before the detective pulls the trigger.

"That's two dead. Iglesias? Another. Those mercenaries, the Moths, and who knows if the workers got out."

Lola needs to choose her words with caution; otherwise, she won't make it out. "We hit the Moths where it would hurt them. That was the whole point of this, wasn't it? The lab is gone, data destroyed. Now what? You gonna cuff me and bring me in? You have that general who wants to talk to you. You're not out of the woods yet."

Archer's nostrils flare, unsure how Lola knew.

"Listen. We can work together. It's what Eden Breaker set us up for."

"So you can shoot me too?" Archer's face tightens.

"No. Why do you think Iglesias worked with me?"

"Don't fucking mention his name." Each word Archer speaks expels the heat of flame.

Lola bites her lip. She continues, "I'm not going to cause you harm, okay?"

"You let them die," Archer says.

"As they did to me years ago." Lola speaks each word slowly, with careful consideration. "If you bring me in, what is that going to do? You'll risk losing the only one who can help you with the Moths."

Archer's lower eyelid twitches.

Lola's breath escapes through her nose. *Come on.*

"Fuck," Archer says while lowering her gun. She jerks her head to the road. "Get out."

Lola lowers her hands and takes a few steps away. "I'm sorry. He was a good man."

Archer wipes her face with her arm. It's a signal for Lola to leave. Archer can return to the law, massage the details, and Lola needs to vanish before anyone spots her.

She heads down the neighboring avenue, staying in the alleyways to remain hidden where the sun doesn't shine. An engine's hum comes from down the road whence she came. The sound projects louder with each passing moment until a white van makes a sharp turn into the side street, winding in between the dumpster bins. The aggressive nature of the driver combined with a paint job jolts a memory in Lola's mind: the identical automobile one year ago. It took her to Allen Sky Tower with Mastema in the back.

The engine screams as the motorist presses on the gas. Lola moves to the middle of the road. It must be the First. She can sense it lingering in front of her chest, wanting to burst out and jump into the van.

Lola takes a deep breath in.

The vehicle closes their distance.

Focus.

The consuming shadows in the alleyway suck to her feet as the chrome bumper blasts through where she once stood. In the air, the light-shadows teleport her and she lands on top of the van.

Tires make drastic shifts left to right, screeching, dodging dumpsters and attempting to shake her off, to no luck. Taking her knife, she thrusts it into the roof, piercing through and pinning herself to the metal. They aren't getting rid of her.

With a handgun, a man crawls halfway up through the sliding side door and uses the roof as support. He fires, missing. She frees the blade and slides to him, kicking his wrist before he can pull the trigger. She plunges her blade into his tendons, forcing him to release his firearm. It rests on the roof. Another sharp turn from the driver launches the Moth from the automobile. The gun slides. His spine collides with the edge of a dumpster, taking her knife with it, ending with a loud bang. She seizes the gun before it, too, flings from the roof.

They make a sharp maneuver onto a main road with traffic honking, skidding clear of the reckless driving. The van accelerates. Lola glides to the side door as it attempts to close. She snags the edge with one hand, gun in the other, and swings down. Her boots kick the first person she collides with inside—a human Moth. His nose crunches. The collision slams his skull into the metal wall dividing them and the driver.

She lands on her feet as the door slides shut. Firearm raised, she scans the small interior: one Moth knocked out. A green-browed man stands beside him, along with two cloaked and masked beings. Mastema himself closed the van on the far left.

Hisses erupt from the dark figures. Vazeleads. One is taller, who she recognizes: Rithu. The other is new. The green man smells of plastic, reminding her of their jail cell interaction.

This close distance between her and Mastema is magnetizing, shifting her stance to him. That strange tingling she felt in the front of her core is pounding against her chest, making her bones and flesh dance with an intense energy she has never encountered, even on ash. It's the gravity of his existence calling to her.

Clapping erupts from Mastema, followed by a rising chuckle. "Well done, Cabello. You pulled off your little stunt, killed my spy, my immediate plans, and destroyed my toy tower. Do you feel like a big girl, taking down the evil boss?" He waves his hand at her gun, which points at him. "Put that away. You've tried that before. The only one who is going to end up hurt here is you."

Through Lola's inverted view, the bright illuminated van contains the light-shadows devouring the confined space. They extend hands to every soul. A few eyeless faces peek out, observing. They're here for Lola. She can work with them and obeys the First, lowering her weapon.

"Good," Mastema says. "Something is different about you. Leaping onto vehicles isn't your addiction to ash. No. Your soul's taste still has that kick, though it has a depth."

More light-shadow hands appear from their two-dimensional space. They're ready. The humming in her core commands her, and if she is being truthful, she is tired of Mastema's long-winded blabbering.

Mastema continues as Lola walks towards him. "You've made it so far just to act naïve—"

He stops talking because she lifts her free hand and reaches for his face. Rithu and the second vazelead step closer. The burning plastic man doesn't. Mastema takes hold of her wrist to move it out of the way. Their skin contacts. The shadows in the space swirl towards his grip, slipping between the cracks of their flesh and removing all darkness, or light in Lola's case. The others stop moving. A potent cold bite blooms from the touch. Mastema jerks his arm away.

The lightless hands reach out for him as they fly back to their original locations. Lola snags his throat. She wraps her other forearm around his head, locking him in, and the light-blackness streams towards them.

Gasps and mumbling come from behind.

Icy bites return, running up Lola's arms. They slink onto the First too. His face winces, mouth gaping open. He tries to push free, cornered in the back of the van, with Lola smothering him against the siding.

A tight groan escapes his throat. His hands shake as his fingers slide against her, trying to move her aside. Each time he touches her, an icy sting nips both Lola and Mastema. Lola is used to pain with years of suffering because of him. As for the First, this is new.

Mastema's motions mutate into flailing and his whining grows into an agonizing cry as their bitter, frozen embrace sharpens in frigidness. Her own skin whence the shades reached turns numb, shifting into deeper tones. Black smoke—white for Lola— seeps from the First's eye sockets as his skin peels around his face.

"St-o-o-p," Mastema stutters.

A whip erupts in the space and a scaled appendage coils around Lola's arm, yanking her from the First. It knocks her onto her back. Shadows spew from the broken contact, returning to their rightful place. The First slinks to the corner of the van, hugging his damaged face.

Rithu storms over and reaches for Lola as she rolls clear of his claws and springs to her feet. Firearm raised, she points it at him. He pauses. She cannot see his eyes, yet, the ash humming through her allows her to perceive his soul. Words are unnecessary. The kindness is still there. That boy shares the same feelings for her, unintentional though they may be. They're two beings wrapped in a game they didn't ask for. Their warped connection has built a sense of care, locking them in their stances. Neither one of them wishes to strike.

A second tail emerges from behind him and splits Lola's gun-wielding hand, knocking her arm to the side. She pulls the trigger; the bullet shreds into the wall of the vehicle. The vazelead lunges at Lola and slams her against the side door, forcing her to drop the firearm.

The sound of a latch opening comes from her left. Traffic erupts as both rear doors swing open. Cars of the downtown metropolis fill the visual spectrum with a yellow cab right behind them. The hint of floral and smoke arises from the swamp-breathed vazelead in front of her as she bends Lola's arms to her will, bringing them down.

"O-o-u-u-t," Mastema moans. "Out, Namsruc, out!"

Lola grunts as the vazelead's tail coils around Lola's right leg, limiting her movement. She grinds her teeth, defeated. Her cloaked captor, Namsruc, restrains Lola and drags her to the open back door. Despite being overpowered with brute force, Lola doesn't feel anger. She has learned much from this encounter and closes her eyes, clears her mind, and embraces the light-shadows. They guide her now; not Mother Nature, nor anyone else.

"Rithu," comes the croaky voice of Namsruc.

He remains still, conflicted.

"End her!" Mastema shouts, his face scrunching into a prune.

A rattle rises from Namsruc's throat and she slams her metal mask onto Lola's nose, dazing her. The tail slides up and coils around her neck, constricting her breath.

Come on, Lola thinks, hoping to control the shadows again. The hum of the lightless ones fails to reach her.

A second set of claws pushes Namsruc aside and snags her tail, yanking it from Lola's neck. Rithu snags her with both arms, lifting her. With no words, he tosses her out of the vehicle as air enters her lungs once more.

Midair, Lola opens her eyes as the cab closes distance. She reaches for the closest shadow-hands she can find—under the van. They lock forearms and she directs herself from the physical world to them. Below the automobile, she snags onto the next group of lightless wrists, followed by another, taking her clear from traffic. She springs from their grasp, body slamming against a brick building's corner leading to an alleyway, shielded by the sun.

Yes, the inner fire rises, scathing her pride because she couldn't put an end to Mastema right then and there. Maturity tells her she won. The First's perfect empire has holes: the burning plastic man and Rithu failed to intervene. Wrath dances with joy, pleasured by the clear fact that Lola can hurt him.

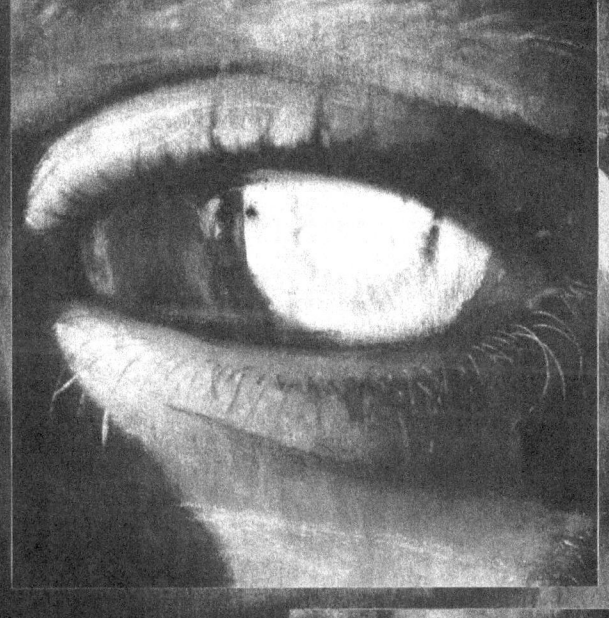

A
C
T

V

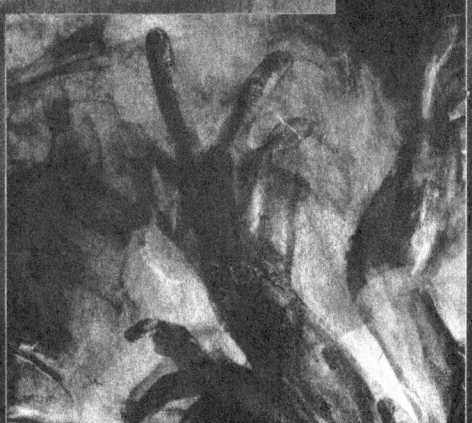

.

ACT V
SUSPENDED ACCEPTANCE

[Lola Cabello ~~Documentary~~ Docuseries: CAMB Originals]

  [Take 1: Raw]

  [2019, November 29]

  [Bridgette Archer: Detective on Cabello Case in 2016]

  [RECORDING:

  Hi, Ian? Hi, Jordyn? . . . yeah. You guys have been persistent over the years. Well . . . cash isn't why I'm here. So how does this work, like an interview? . . . Sure.

Okay, so talk? Yep . . . got it.

I'm Detective Archer. Bridgette Archer. I was on the ash-Cabello case in Major Crimes as an L1 in 2016. She was filed as part of the drug unit's responsibility because she had evidence of the Moths. At the time, she hadn't killed anyone. Detectives Iglesias and Beckman were in charge, and I worked with them until Beckman retired. The DND took over with the military after the slaughterhouse.

There's not much to tell about Cabello. I never knew her. Selfish, focused, tunnel visioned. She went to prison, reappeared in 2018. Iglesias had a connection with her. She trusted him. He was the real deal and wanted what was right. It meant he broke the procedures sometimes to take shortcuts. But hey, he got shit done.

After Iglesias got the call, he contacted me, and we were off to Radiate Primate. You know what a mess that was. They didn't get answers to who killed his son, did they? I wasn't on the case. Federal drug unit, remember?

Cabello vanished for a year, only to reappear at the Allen Sky Tower bombing. It's crazy how they found footage of her. Being on the street doesn't mean she caused the bombing. The DND found some other loosely connected evidence of her stepping out of an SUV in the alleyway of the tower. I'm not convinced. I was there. Why wasn't there footage of me on the streets?

Since then, I work with the DND as an expert consultant. Got some inside info on ash. It's more of a high-level position and less on the streets. Still on Major Crimes, L2.

. . .

I don't know what you want from this interview. A story? Feelings? Facts? A witness's testimony goes a long way in court. On these types of films, you people enjoy clipping the statements for sensational views. I'd say let the full interviews run, let the people decide.

. . . Iglesias? Yeah, vanished around the same time. He's filed as a missing person.

. . . I don't know.

. . . I wish I knew.

. . . Hah! Now that's a conspiracy. Yes, he worked with Cabello twice in the past. Because he vanished at the time of the Allen Sky Tower bombing, as Cabello happened to be nearby, you're making a distant correlation between two parallel events deeming them domestic terrorists. Stop spending so much time online, you'll rot your reasoning skills.

Did she make out alive? We can't be certain. That collapsing tower brings a lot of heat and concrete with it. Maybe it ate her up.

It's odd, after they dug through that rubble, they only found bones and teeth? Later identified as a few Moths with files on them. I think a few private army men too. No lab workers or office workers. Cabello makes a mess wherever she goes. There's a correlation for your film.

Remember, I said it wasn't for the cash? I wanted to set the record straight. Detective Iglesias was not going to come on your documentary. He didn't trust you. Look at who is funding this shit. I came here to tell you to your face that Iglesias was a good man.

. . . We're done? Right.

Clip this video however you want, hipster. Mark my words: this entire interview will be online before you know it. People harvest the fruit.

END]

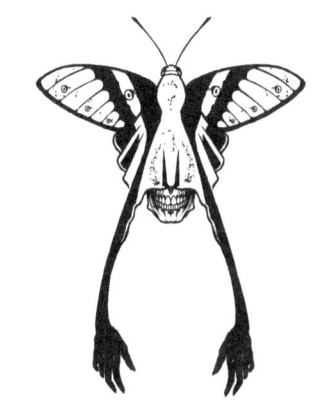

CHAPTER 59
THE DEVIL YOU KNOW

How much pain should one feel when life fades away? It's a question Synarion asks himself each time he encounters death. A human's lifetime experiences a small fraction of demise in their century, if they're fortunate to live that long. Multiply that by twenty-four, two thousand and four hundred years offers a great deal of passing. It builds layers of resistance over the heart, even when staring at a child you raised.

Although brief, the hundred-year time period played a crucial role in the growth of the Scalebane twins. Youth don't forget their first interactions. Synarion cast a permanent imprint on their psyche, their way of life, for better or worse.

A century means little to Synarion, though he cherished their moments together. Gripping her soft black and blue scalp-feathers triggers blips of memories. Their tails would coil around his fingers as light purring came from their throats. He'd feed them lentils, stroke their feathers, and teach them the importance of nature.

Scalebane's tail wrapping around his wrist loosens and falls to the ground beside him. The fire once surrounding her eyes extinguishes, leaving glass yellow-tinted balls. His fixation on the corpse in his lap makes him blind to the rumbling beyond the walls. It doesn't last long. What are seconds compared to a century?

"Sir, you're hurt," comes a woman's voice.

Synarion fails to respond. With his one hand, he closes her eyelids. *Rest,* he thinks.

"Sir," says the woman. "Dr. Lang, can you come here? He needs help. I think he's in shock."

The short older gentleman approaches Synarion's side. He pushes his glasses up, leaning down to examine his wounds. "Come with me. There's a med kit here." He waves at the two mercenaries. "Excuse me, men, can you aid him?"

The soldiers obey, marching to him, snagging his arms. He grunts as the scalp-feathers slip from his grasp. There is no need to resist. It is pointless to express anger. He wants to feel sad, burst into tears, wail in sorrow, though he is numb.

These kind humans take care of his wounds. Unlike Scalebane, his blood is red, making him blend into the human society. Their lack of medical equipment gives the doctor little to analyze his body with. Lola's bullets went through him. They clean, stitch, and wrap the injuries. The fluids match. Organs? No. Dr. Lang eyes him once over. His mouth flattens into an analytical mode while the hand runs along Synarion's leg, stopping on an upper thigh muscle that doesn't exist on a human. He blinks, stands, and pats Synarion's shoulder, telling him to get lots of rest.

Dr. Lang orders the mercenaries to guard Scalebane's body. It is pointless, considering they're trapped underneath tons of rubble below the earth. Synarion sticks to himself. He's a lab worker. Scalebane is going to decompose. At least they have the decency to cover her with a white blanket. Black stains bleed through the material like the holes in Synarion's heart for each loved one he has lost.

They have food, supplies, and blankets. The generator is sufficient, despite the flickering light. An air vent aids in diluting the rotting stench from the corpse. Their space is compact, no more than four hundred square feet. Each of them asks themselves: who will rescue them?

Their downtime gives the humans time to talk and reflect on what happened. They question if it was an accident with the EMFCs, a terrorist attack, or a computer malfunction. The people discuss Scalebane. "Is that ash?" and "Intelligent reptilians?" along with "Are they aliens?" Synarion doesn't speak, letting their imaginations run wild. They don't bother him, even with his purple eyes. He's a rare bird, as Lola once said to him. The bloody lab coat keeps him discreet, except for the doctor's prolonged stares. His mind ponders Lola Cabello's actions. He understands her choice despite not agreeing. Fire consumes her and he comprehends if that flame will ever calm.

Dr. Lang makes one statement that causes Synarion's ear to twitch. "Even if we don't survive. The data we got from the samples will be on my dying corpse."

"Ash and Subject Alpha's?" the assistant asks.

"And the horn."

Horn . . . Lola, Synarion thinks. He can't sabotage Dr. Lang's portable hard drive without being noticed. Damn Cabello, too hotheaded to understand the dangerous knowledge she's given her people.

Time is in the beholder's eye. What feels like an eon to the humans is a day for Synarion. They've been under the earth for ten. The funk of Scalebane's corpse lingers in the room, even with the recycled air's cleaning system. Synarion's wounds heal in little increments. He's not used to the gradual process. Mother Nature spoiled him with the diefym leaves for rapid rejuvenation.

He hobbles around the small space in between long rest sessions to keep active. During downtime, he fiddles with his gold ring sculpted with vampire fangs. It's his one reminder of Valturus. She's no longer here. Scalebane claimed she knew where she was in Dreadweave Pass. It doesn't matter. She is gone too. Each soul he meets ends in Death's Vortex. Synarion remains, contemplating his next move for Mother Nature. This is the cruel joke of his life. He has to continue for Earth. Beneath the layers of resistance, his heart feels putrid because of his lack of empathy. He wishes he felt more for the lost. Perhaps there have been too many holes in his heart to even have the organ be considered one. A fool's dream cannot derail duty.

The muffled sound of rubble, scraping, and machinery lifts the humans' spirits and postures. On the eleventh day, sawing and sparks come from the reinforced door. The meter-thick metal slab bends aside and falls, colliding with the concrete ground, raising dust.

Bright light beams into the dim space from worksite tripods, casting sharp shadows. The group shields their eyes, each standing. Synarion remains seated on his blankets. It's difficult to see the newcomers through the dust as they hop onto the fallen door. Highlights of three beings in hard hats catch his eye. Two of them hold cutting power tools. A couple more silhouettes appear in the entrance. These two climb onto the slab of metal and step in front of the construction workers.

One is a thin man in a burgundy suit, also wearing a hardhat. His skeletal fingers cup together, palms pressed against his chest. A strange toxic sting radiating from his form and into Synarion's nose. The appearance and scent match the description Lola gave of a plastic burning man who visited her in Mastema's mansion.

The other newcomer is taller, dressed in a full white suit whose porcelain hair tucks behind his ears. His thin and wide-shouldered presence fills more space than the others, stepping in front of his group. The pompous gravitas of his being compliments his lack of a safety hat. He pulls Synarion in with a potent invisible vortex. It has a vampiric quality, weighing on his pride.

The thin man turns to the construction workers. "Will you three be so kind and prep the firefighters and paramedics as we bring these fine folks up?"

"Mastema!" Dr. Lang shouts, stepping towards the man in white. "Thank you! You've saved us." He raises his hands up high to the man, as if he were some sort of god.

Mastema, Synarion thinks. That's a name Lola Cabello shared in the past. This is the First, leader of the Crystal Moths, and a fallen angel of pride. It explains the continual sucking of his ego.

Mastema's dress shoes click as he walks across the metal door. He hops down and steps into the room, passing Dr. Lang. "I'm pleased you survived, Doctor. This lab was crucial to us." He stops by the white sheet and lifts it, seeing Scalebane's corpse. He drops it. "Jekos, take care of this."

"I want her," Dr. Lang says, hands forming fists. "That is ash. That humanoid reptilian answers one of the biggest questions for humankind. We are not alone."

Mastema presses his index finger and thumb between his brows. He sighs. "Fine, you can have a new toy. I suppose you're a smart cookie, anyway."

Dr. Lang bows. "We will make good use of her, I assure you."

"Yes, I'm sure you'll clone, bio-this, and engineer-that." Mastema walks past the mercenaries, giving them a slight bow, passes the assistant with a wink, and stops in front of Synarion.

The balancer stares at the white dress shoes. They're polished well. He swears the shadow below the soles twitch.

"You have an interesting flavour," Mastema says.

Synarion looks up at him. "I was shot."

"No, no, it's something else. It's . . . " He trails off, looking to the flickering ceiling light.

It was worth an attempt. Synarion will not fool a fallen angel leeching off of pride. The First is too experienced to be blinded by a lab coat.

Mastema raises his fist, pressing his fingers deep into his palms. His arm shakes, creating a rumble throughout the space. The humans look around, whispering if it is an earthquake.

The sharp shadows in the bunker pull to Mastema, like a vacuum inhaling fabric. Dr. Lang gasps as his assistant screams. The soldiers point their guns at the ground. Dozens of silhouette hands escape the blackness, reaching into three-dimensional space. Heads and limbs rise in a black current as the darkness in the room sucks below Mastema's feet, riding up his leg, past his torso, and compresses into his fist. The lack of shadows gives the environment a surreal visual, as if they don't belong.

Synarion stands, a half inch taller than the First, who opens his palm. He holds a floating orb of pure blackness. Small limbs reach out, attempting to escape, swirling around the sphere.

By the Creator, Synarion thinks, understanding this is beyond that.

"We did it," Dr. Lang says. As the doctor blinks twice, he realizes the collective horror: wide eyes, and open jaws that settle over the rest of the frozen humans.

". . . it's shame," Mastema says, finishing the trailed statement. A long grin rises on his face. He folds his hand onto his palm, snuffing out the dark orb. Shadows run down his form and to the ground in their rightful place. "This is the famous balancer I've learned of. Balancers of the Grove believe in protecting Mother Nature, correct?"

Synarion winces.

"You and I have a lot more in common than you think."

This turn of events doesn't surprise Synarion in the least. The First does not care about organized crime or working in the darkness. Mastema's goals are far more complex. He ropes people into his circle to do their bidding. The fallen angel did this with the vazeleads. He's done it with the government, law, and the private sector. The question is, what will he offer Synarion?

CHAPTER 60
ASH BORN

Being charged for murder, drug possession, and withholding evidence from the law will result in jail time. Domestic terrorism skyrockets it to a whole new level. Orchestrating the bombing on civilian property with hundreds of civilians at risk is bound to make you the most wanted criminal across the country. It's not terrible, as long as you don't get caught.

Her actions activated the Department of National Defence. Major Crimes is on the hunt. The media relishes in the low-hanging fruit. Even the military stick their noses in. Therefore, it's critical to be outside of the law, remain hidden, mirroring the lives of a forgotten time.

The old world's dangers persist. People are blind to the genuine threats surrounding them. It's not the domestic terrorist. She's on their side, the human side. Danger comes from the buried past.

This attack on Allen Sky Tower sends havoc into the hearts of naive Canadians. It strikes the Moths where it hurts. Mastema is out there. Lola guarantees that. Whatever unholy research he proceeded with in that lab is gone. This is certain to leave a scar on his plan.

For Lola, she stays low, making sure that her location and identity are discreet. She has newfound allies. They aren't the sinister or deceiving kind of the old world. Genuine people support her in improving the planet. The rest of her kind will understand her actions in due time.

Disk, Dasco Amoss, and Archer will hear from her. Archer is interested in justice, like Cabello, and how Iglesias was. Dasco's insight is fruitful. Disk is versed in the power of the cyberworld. Balancing, ecosystems, or old world nonsense do not exist. The afterlife isn't tangible. These are authentic people, understanding the true consequences of the dangers that others create.

Until they meet, Lola returns to the west side of the country via train hopping, squeezing between freights. Her wounds are brutal, and she needs rest at the ill-fated nymph's apartment. His magical leaves will help in rapid healing. Chances are Synarion did destroy her laptop. That's not a concern. She can use careful extraction of her ChickenFeed currency to avoid being tracked and get a new computer. Mastema's mansion is in

British Columbia; she will find him. The mission continues, and she brings the End with her.

Hiding in a locomotive cart gives her time to reflect. She spent countless hours pondering the events that brought her here. Kendra, her prison partner, could attest to that. Unwanted thoughts creep into her consciousness when while she is alone. It's like the shadows that watch her from the corners, ever present.

The shaper used her as an agent, double, and triple, and played their cards too close. Rithu, as authentic as his compassion was, saw her as a mere pet. He aided her in their final conflict. The ghoul who controlled her took advantage of the moment and gave this mysterious gift. Mother Nature cries for her to be civil.

There's her family who would not recognize their own kin. Her genetics will live through her niece. As much as Lola wants to meet her, she cannot put them in danger. The Moths are too close. Donnie was wise to get out.

Pain bites her heart, neglecting the empathy that makes her human. She should care that she murdered Scalebane and Synarion, both of a dying kind. Ash once helped her tune into those emotions. Her power grows, and she can control the drug. There's no need to mourn those who wronged her. It makes her question: how much of her own humanity must she lose to save it?

The slumber doesn't last. Her own shadow haunts her. It watches, dancing in jerking motions within the current of her silhouette. She needs the ash to keep her eyesight from saturating too far into bleakness. Her supply is low. This is where her comrades come in. Allies, like Disk of Eden Breaker, can provide her need.

The Trinity of Souls is no longer in control. She has conquered the dark depths of her spirit and battled the three-headed demon within. She has never been more certain of her task.

Cabello is in charge of her future, or so she likes to tell herself. She sits in Synarion's old apartment, chewing on her last bit of ash. Her white irises shift to the light-shadows in the corners. Their bright heads bob from two dimensions to three, floating in dimensional water. The ever-present faceless gazes smother Mother Nature's once prominent presence.

Lola is not in federal prison and is away from Mastema's torture chamber. She's bound to a new type of shackle: the loss of her former self. It latches into her psyche, weighing her soul. That is what makes being a convict terrible.

These bindings fuel the ever-growing wrathful fire that melted her innocence, forging her into a heartless killer. Her fundamental denial kept her going when the Moths took her life away. Lawless antagonism of the corrupt law worsened it. Through ordered bargaining of ash, she was reborn. The innocent and guilty witnessed her performing desolation in the name of relentless revenge. She has suspended acceptance of never going back.

She will not taste of freedom. Obsidian ensures it.

CHAPTER 60: ASH BORN

ALL WORK

Ash Born Series

- Crystal Moth Conspiracy: Ash Born Book One
- Obsidian's Command: Ash Born Book Two
- World Mother Ascension: An Ash Born Novel

Mental Damnation Series

- Reality: Part 1 of Mental Damnation
- Dream: Part 2 of Mental Damnation
- Purity: Part 3 of Mental Damnation
- Mortal: Part 4 of Mental Damnation

Terrors of the Macrocosm

- Rave
- Cultivate: Seed Me Relapse Edition
- YEGman

Short Stories of the Macrocosm

- Into the Macrocosm: Short Stories of the Dark Cosmic, Bizarre, and the Fantastic
- Beyond the Macrocosm: Interactive Short Stories of Dread and Wonder

Rutherford Manor Series

- The White Hand: A Rutherford Manor Novel
- Fire, Pain, & Ruin A Rutherford Manor Novel

Audiobooks

- Cultivate: Seed Me Relapse Edition Audiobook
- Into the Macrocosm Audiobook
- Rave Audiobook
- Fire, Pain, & Ruin A Rutherford Manor Audiobook

Novel Scores

- Frequencies of the Macrocosm Score
- Missing Head Highway Rave Novel Score
- World Mother: Seed Me Novel Score
- Sounds of Society: YEGman Novel Soundtrack

All publications, including short stories, are listed on konnlavery.com/publications

ABOUT
THE AUTHOR

Konn Lavery is a Canadian author whose award-winning fiction has reached the bestselling charts on Amazon and in his hometown, Edmonton. His work has been described as uncanny and immersive and frequently falls under the Dark Fantasy and Horror genres. Each of his stories are housed within the expanding universe known as the Macrocosm spanning across time and space.

He has been recognized by reviewers such as Reader Views, Readers' Favorite, Literary Titan, and by award programs such as indieBRAG, The Wishing Shelf Book Awards, eLit Awards, and Dan Poynter's Global Ebook Awards. His work has also been curated into the Edmonton Public Library's Capital Press collection.

Konn started writing stories at a young age while being a homeschooled vegetarian, enthralled with storytelling. After graduating college, he began professionally pursuing his writing with his first release, Reality, in 2012 while balancing his graphic design business. Konn's visual communication skills have been transcribed into the formatting and artwork found within his publications, supporting his fascination with transmedia storytelling.